THE DRAGON GATE OMNIBUS

VOLUMES 1-3 OF

THE DRAGON GATE SERIES

RANDY ELLEFSON

Evermore Press
GAITHERSBURG, MARYLAND

Evermore Press, LLC
Gaithersburg, Maryland
www.evermorepress.org

The Dragon Gate Omnibus Vol 1-3 / Randy Ellefson. -- 1st ed.
ISBN 978-1-946995-81-0 (paperback)
ISBN 978-1-946995-82-7 (hardcover)

This page intentionally left blank.

CONTENTS

ACKNOWLEDGEMENTS

Special thanks to Kristi-Lee Landrey, Sandra Chiwike, Erica Thajeb, Daniela Zorilla, and Annika Powers.

Edited by JJ Henke

Maps by Randy Ellefson

Cover designs by Miblart

Series Introduction

The Dragon Gate epic fantasy series follows four friends from Earth when they are mistaken for the Ellorian Champions and magically kidnapped to complete quests in their place. This book includes the first three volumes. More books are available at http://store.randyellefson.com.

The Dragon Gate (Volume One)

He swore an oath to protect all life. Now he must kill to survive.

Being a knight at the Renaissance Festival is easy, but when Ryan is magically kidnapped to another world, the quest he must do might leave him dead. Mistaken for a dragon-slaying knight, he must kill the dragon queen to be sent home.

At least he is not alone. Three of his friends are kidnapped beside him, all of them mistaken for the Ellorian Champions. The real heroes have been missing for years, but they may hold the key to keeping everyone alive.

THE LIGHT BRINGER (VOLUME TWO)

The power to heal only comes when she believes.

On her quests to other worlds where elves, dragons, and magic are real, Anna is thrilled she can save the dying – and destroy the undead. But on an Earth where magic has awoken after a thousand-year sleep, she is frustrated that the gods do not answer her.

And jealous, too – other people are casting spells and healing the wounded, dealing death and bringing life. Some threats have come from other worlds, and now she feels that nowhere is safe.

No one understands why it's all happening – or that Anna and her three friends mistakenly triggered the awakening. To save everything that she loves, Anna must overcome her shaken faith and face her destiny as The Light Bringer, or the new reality they unleashed may destroy all life.

THE SILVER-TONGUED ROGUE (VOLUME THREE)

Will impersonating a legend cost him his life?

While being mistaken for one of the missing Ellorian Champions has made Eric afraid for his life, playing along during quests has also saved him from death. He just wants to be free of the danger, but now the real champions' families have captured him and his three friends, stripped them of power, and put them in chains.

If his quest to recover a dragon egg from the trolls who stole it is thwarted, his fear of never getting home to Earth may come true. Can Eric live up to the reputation of Andier, the Silver-Tongued Rogue, and persuade his captors he had nothing to do with the real Champions' disappearance? Or must he and his friends try to fight their way to freedom?

FREE BOOK

Join my newsletter to get a free eBook, a chance to join my ARC Team, see bonuses, get early looks at covers, learn about live events, and more: http://www.fiction.randyellefson.com/newsletter

Volume 1

The Dragon Gate

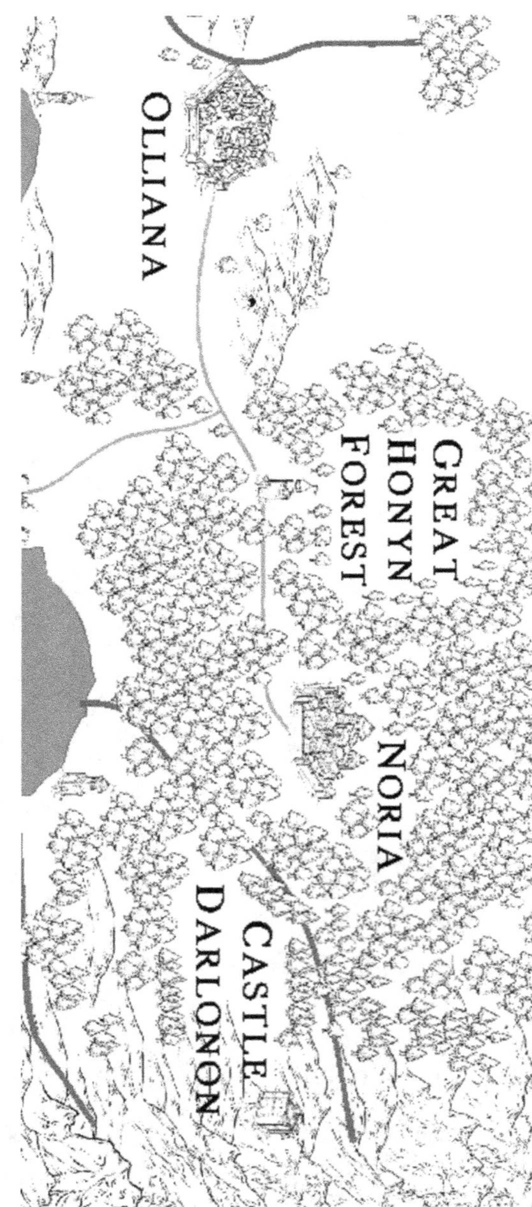

Partial Map of the Kingdom of Alunia, on Honyn

View a larger, full color map online at
http://fiction.randyellefson.com/dragon-gate-series/the-dragon-gate/

THE LONE SURVIVOR

Lucion stared unseeing into the campfire. His ears strained to hear past the rustling treetops and creaking boles of the dark forest. Gusts of wind tore through the woods as if searching for him, the noise drowning out the chatter of his four companions. If anything else was moving out there, his group would never know it. The coming storm didn't concern him, but the ogre footprints did. They looked a week old and likely meant no trouble, and he was certain enough of this to have lit the fire and slapped deer meat over it, but the value of alertness wasn't lost on him. His own prey lay chopped in pieces before him.

The hunter's gaze shifted to the ruins of Castle Darlonon perched among the looming mountain peaks overhead. For a moment, he thought lights twinkled in some of the windows. A cautious glance at Rogin showed his brother hadn't noticed the lights, which was just as well. Rogin had told enough stories about people going up there and never coming back that no one believed much of anything he said anymore. Just minutes earlier he'd sworn a dragon had appeared in the night sky, but of course that was impossible. As Lucion turned the deer haunch over, Rogin walked off into the woods to relieve himself and the darkness swallowed him. As if to celebrate, the woods groaned loudly, and the wind howled through the treetops. Lucion shivered.

"It smells so good here," said a woman's voice, and the men turned in surprise, seeing an elegant woman breathing in deeply through a pert nose, her full bosom straining against the red silk of an evening gown. Golden hair framed a heart-shaped face and tumbled past her petite waist. She stood at the clearing's edge, her radiance making the shadowy woods seem all the more dark. Her green eyes boldly danced from one man to the next, appraising them. Captivated by her allure, they hardly noticed she could not have been more out of place so many miles from any settlement.

"I haven't smelled such fine meat in so many years," she purred, eyeing Lucion. He could've been the most handsome man alive for the way she gazed at him.

Mesmerized by her attention, he pleasantly replied, "It is only fresh deer, my lady, not even seasoned, but you're welcome to your share of it and all that we have."

Her bright eyes locked onto his as if the others didn't exist. He wished that were so, for he wanted her all to himself and trembled as she came nearer. Fine words had never been his to command and he stood at a loss, adoring eyes saying more than words ever could. As she stopped before him, her feminine scent washed over him. He smiled like a schoolboy.

In the silence, she kindly asked, "Why so quiet? Dragon got your tongue?"

Not noticing the subject had come up again, he stammered, "Uh, n-no, my lady. Dragons, well, they uh, they don't show themselves around here no more."

Eyebrows arched in surprise, she asked, "Is that so?"

"Yes, my lady. They were banished by the Ellorian Champions some years ago, to another world. The Dragon Gate up there in the castle keeps them away. You'll be safe here, that I can promise you." And he meant every word, for his heart would burst if anything happened to her. He didn't mention that the champions had disappeared without a trace some years ago and that if the dragons ever got loose, no one would be able to send them back. The planet would be destroyed. There was no sense in worrying her.

Seeming amused by his assurance, she asked, "So then you haven't seen a dragon recently? Tonight, for example?"

Startled, he wondered how she could have known and replied, "Oh no, nothing like that. Uh, Rogin here did think he saw something in the sky earlier, but it was nothing." He couldn't tear his eyes away long enough to look for his brother. It was good that this was so, for he might have noticed Rogin was still missing and alerted her to this.

"What did he think he saw?" The seductress slowly ran a finger down his chest. The long, bright red nail was sharp enough to cut through his shirt and draw blood he didn't notice.

Lucion hesitated for fear of causing concern, but then she leaned closer and breathed him in long and deep, clearly enjoying his scent. Aroused, he confessed helpfully, "A dragon."

As if expecting that, she smiled in satisfaction, her green eyes finally leaving his to look over the others. They stood as mesmerized as Lucion, who felt as though a pleasant heat had ceased bathing his face. The sudden coldness startled him. His devotion faded long enough that he wondered aloud, "Who are you?"

Her gaze returned to his playfully. "Someone who doesn't like witnesses," she purred.

Before he had a chance to understand what she meant, his head flew from his neck, a bemused smile still on his face. It was still rolling across the ground when she went for the nearest man, who stared stupidly at the long, gleaming nails dripping with Lucion's blood. She raked open his belly, shoving a hand inside to pull out organs that she bit into with delight, dark blood spurting across her face. As he collapsed beside the fire, the others fumbled for weapons and the woman spoke a strange word.

Her appearance morphed and grew as they watched in awe, golden scales reflecting the firelight as two enormous, leathery wings blotted out the dark sky. A sinuous neck lifted her giant head into the night, two baleful eyes glaring down on them with lust. Four thick legs and feet ending in talons supported a huge golden body that no normal weapon could pierce. She took her time, snapping up the next man in her fanged mouth and cracking him in half. She hadn't tasted such warm blood in years and relished it like wine. The last man turned for the woods, but her barbed tail snaked out to impale him where he stood, holding him aloft. The dragon chewed slowly as if savoring every morsel, her forked tongue licking her lips as she gulped them down.

Her jaws weren't the only ones agape, for out in the bushes knelt a staring Rogin, horror riveting him to the spot. As he watched, the golden dragon lifted into the night air with a powerful leap and thrusts of leathery wings, scattering embers across the clearing. Then she sucked in a great breath and blasted fire down on the evidence, setting the forest ablaze so that Rogin crept away on his hands and knees, his back awash in heat. With a snap of her wings, the dragon turned and soared away to Castle Darlonon, where she rose into the sky and then plunged down inside to disappear.

And Rogin ran. He ran as far down the road toward Olliana as his legs would carry him, finally collapsing before a startled farmer, tales of dragons, fire, and death pouring from his mouth. At first no one believed him, but soon lights appeared in the ruined castle at night and ogres trolled the woods, chased from the peaks by mercenaries at Darlonon. Just the one dragon had been seen, but the others couldn't be far behind now that the

Dragon Gate stood open. Someone had to close it, but only the long-missing champions could.

CHAPTER ONE

RENFEST

With thundering hooves, the golden knight's steed charged, lance aimed left toward the tilt separating him from his quarry. A dummy on a pole held forth a small metal ring for him to pluck free, and with a clink it slid down the shaft as the crowd politely cheered. He lifted the prize aloft, cantering around the stadium to a smattering of clapping. He wasn't what they really wanted and he knew it, cheers turning to jeers in his mind. As more knights thundered in and the crowd roared for the main event, he left the small arena, unable to watch the other knights charge each other. But he heard the battle screams, the cracks of lances shattering on plate armor, the clatter of plate armor as men crashed to the ground.

Sighing, he dismounted and pulled off the blue-plumed helmet, his feathered blond hair hiding the ear buds that were wirelessly tethered to the smartphone tucked inside his armor. Any signs of modern technology were strictly forbidden at the Maryland Renaissance Festival, or "RenFest," as the locals called it. It ruined the illusion of the time period. Like all performers, he was supposed to show bewilderment when guests pulled out a camera. It was as if the whole faire, population included, had been transplanted from Medieval times and was unaware it wasn't somewhere in England around the 1500s.

Ryan led the white gelding to the stables, feigning smiles at young, busty women trying to get his attention, their pushed-up bosoms tempting his blue eyes. Being tall, handsome, and muscular readily attracted women, even without the costume, and pretending to be a hero got him more attention. If they knew the truth about him, they'd look the other way.

As he pulled the saddle off, a familiar figure arrived beside him. Eric Foster stood dressed for his role as a jester at RenFest, wearing a parti-colored jumpsuit of red and blue, a matching three-pronged hat, and pointed shoes, all with bells. He looked ridiculous and had to be almost as uncomfortable as Ryan in the brutal August heat.

"How'd the joust go?" Eric asked, taking off the hat to wipe sweat from soaked, black hair. "When are you gonna move on to the real thing?"

"When I'm ready."

"Why aren't you ready now? You're better than the others at that ring thing you just did. I'd think that makes it easier to hit bigger targets like them."

"Can't argue that."

After an awkward pause, Eric asked, "Worried about getting hurt?"

Ryan opened his mouth to say no but realized it was close enough to the truth. "Sort of. People getting hurt comes with the territory."

Taking a sip of water, Eric observed, "You always seem to avoid contact sports. I'm still surprised you weren't on the football team in school. It's not that big a deal, you know. I get hit every day. You get used to it."

"It's not me I'm really worried about," the big man confessed, wincing as someone un-horsed a knight in the stadium. He realized his answer wasn't entirely true. He'd seen his brother paralyzed for life and the idea chilled him. To be dependent on others for so much was a helplessness he couldn't imagine. It gnawed at him every time he tended to his brother since the day of the accident so long ago.

"I guess that's better than being a wimp," Eric remarked lightly, "but if you really want to do something, you shouldn't let that hold you back. Accidents happen."

Ryan frowned. "Yeah, but we don't have to invite them. I should just forget it and accept I'm never gonna do it."

"How's that going to make you feel better?"

"It's not, but it's better than the alternative."

"Which is?"

"Let's go."

Ryan led the horse into a stall and latched the door. As they exited the stables for the faire grounds, he realized that Eric would never understand, not when he did martial arts every day as an instructor. Ryan didn't know how he could stand it, but Eric proudly admitted getting beat up all the time as a kid until learning karate. Ryan had little experience with violence, but all of it was bad. He'd never been struck by anyone except the one time he stupidly wondered aloud what a real punch felt like only to have Eric show him. He smirked at the memory.

As they strolled along, Eric deftly picked the pocket of a father of two, then returned the wallet to the surprised man as people chuckled nervously.

Ryan watched with mixed feelings. His friend had never given him a reason to distrust him, but Eric had spent years on the streets after his parents abandoned him. Eric's last foster parents had turned him around, but it was a hard life for a rich kid like Ryan to imagine, sneaking into places, stealing things, and spending time in jail.

They stopped at the knife throwing contest, where Eric mocked a teenage boy's inaccuracy until the booth worker took his cue and reacted.

"Think you can do better, Fool?" the man asked, handing Eric the knives. Ryan stood back, having seen the pair reenact this every weekend for a month. He knew what was coming and tried to play his role, feigning surprise by the skill the jester was about to demonstrate.

Eric said, "I have more experience dodging these than throwing them!" He casually tossed one at the tree stump target and hit the bull's eye. Acting startled, he did it again, then switched hands with the same result as people applauded. Again and again he struck the target, even tossing knives over one shoulder, under a raised leg, and blindfolded, though his accuracy dropped.

Finally, Eric turned on the booth worker amidst the cheering. "Is this some kind of trick? They all hit the target. I want my money back."

"You never paid."

"Oh. Right. Well then, I, uh, guess I had better be going." He turned.

"Hey! Get back here!" The booth worker called as Eric ran away. Turning to Ryan, he demanded, "Sir knight! Do something!"

Unsheathing his sword with a grand gesture, Ryan turned and called after Eric, pretending to give chase. He pushed his way through the crowd, watching Eric disappear but knowing where he was probably going.

Eric heard Ryan's voice fading and stopped running. The big guy would find him soon enough. He walked by the Market Stage, the Boar's Head Tavern, and the strong man pole where Ryan sometimes slammed the mallet down so hard that the bell at the top not only rang but practically flew off. He ignored the shops selling trinkets, his eyes fixed on a fortune teller to one side. She had long blonde hair and hazel eyes in a face that turned heads, and his pulse raced on making eye contact and seeing Anna Lynn Sumner grin at him. He stood in line for his turn with her, and when the last kid was gone, Eric flopped down across the scarf covered table from her, bells jingling.

"You know I have to read your palm while you're here," she said in greeting.

"Of course," he said, handing it over. "So, what can you see?"

"A bunch of bruises," she replied matter-of-factly. "You need to take better care of them."

"It's kind of hard in my line of work," he replied, "but that's not what I mean. Tell me my future, oh Mistress of the Heavens."

Chuckling, she said, "You know I don't believe in that sort of thing."

"Then why are you giving palm readings all day?"

"Because the kids believe it and it's fun to see them dream."

Feigning exaggerated sadness, he asked, "Don't you dream anymore, poor Anna?"

"Of the supernatural that doesn't exist? Hardly. I outgrew that sort of thing."

"Don't let Ryan hear you say that, or he'll call you a 'godless one' again."

She laughed. "Yes, I know. He's funny with that. Religious people and their desire to save the world. How can we stand to live among them?"

He smiled, for they'd talked about their mutual atheism before and tried not to bring it up before Ryan too much. The big guy was reasonable unless someone questioned the existence of God, but at least he didn't go around quoting Scriptures. Few people could stomach that, least of all Anna. They knew she saw plenty of fallout from religious beliefs at the hospital where she worked as a medical resident. She sometimes complained that some people avoided real care in favor of some superstitious belief or other nonsense. Either that or they took matters into their own hands with some harmful treatment and made it worse. That reminded him of something.

"Are you ready for tonight?" Eric asked, turning a little more serious.

She pursed her lips. "I guess. If convincing him doesn't work, then we'll all just go without him."

Between her gaze going over his shoulder and the clinking of plate armor getting louder, he knew that the man they spoke of was approaching. "Still meeting at your place about it?"

"Yeah. Remind Matt. He's the key to it."

Eric grinned. "Don't sell yourself short. You could convince *me* to do anything."

Anna rolled her eyes. "You're an impossible flirt."

Deciding to quit while he was ahead, Eric rose, bowed, and added, "Your faithful servant," before stepping away as Ryan joined him, sword sheathed again. The knight nodded at her.

As they stepped away, Eric cried a loud protest to those in line, "She said I have no future, that I'll be imprisoned this very night!"

"No surprise there," remarked a passerby.

They went in search of Matt Sorenson, whom they found beside the nearby Lyric Stage, ready to assist another performer doing magic tricks for kids. Eric had taught him some sleight of hand that he still struggled with, but

Eric knew that this wasn't the reason Matt looked nervous. He had stage fright and had joked that if he could do magic for real, the first spell he'd cast would be something to cure him of this condition.

Eric saw Matt's green eyes spot him and Ryan. Matt made a sign with his hand. *Hi,* the fingers said.

Eric made his own gesture. *Hey. You'll be fine. Picture them naked.*

No thanks.

Suit yourself. There's a hot redhead at your one o'clock. Eric saw Matt look that way and waited for the reaction.

Dick.

Made you look. Remember, tonight at Anna's.

Ok.

See ya.

Right.

Matt watched them turn away in search of bored people to entertain, wishing he could do the same. Just then the other illusionist called to him for help, and he steeled his nerves to step on stage. A sea of faces and applause greeted him. Everywhere he looked eyes met his. They were inescapable. His heart fluttered and suddenly his stomach churned, and he fell to his knees, vomiting all over the floor. Thinking it was part of the act, the kids cheered while shame over-came him and he retched again and again. Kneeling over the mess he'd made, he realized making his lunch reappear was the closest to a magic trick he'd done before an audience.

CHAPTER TWO

THE PENDANT

Ryan plowed down River Road in the wealthy suburb of Potomac, Maryland at twenty over the limit, the radar detector silently watching for cops. He'd gotten enough speeding tickets to earn a suspended license before, but now instead of slowing down, he just drove prepared. As he made an illegal pass around a Sunday driver, the Dodge Charger roared like his pulse, but the questioning look Anna shot him made them go quiet again.

"What?" he asked defensively, feeling guilty. He knew he shouldn't do it with her in the car, at least, but he couldn't help it. "I did it safely. No one was coming." When she didn't say anything, he added lamely, "C'mon, I made that pass in two seconds, and there wasn't even another car in sight."

"Yeah, I know," she admitted, playing with a pendant around her neck. He'd never seen her without it; it was some sort of family heirloom, a square-cut diamond surrounded by a rectangular silver frame. "I'm just surprised you keep doing it. You're always so careful about everything else, but then you drive like a maniac. It doesn't make any sense. I thought you were afraid to get hurt."

He stifled a frown. It was his own fault people believed that, since he let them, but it frustrated him anyway.

"What's the rush?" Anna asked.

He shrugged. "I need to get home to Daniel."

She sighed. "Didn't you just talk to him? Your brother will be fine until you get there. You don't have to get us killed on the way."

He looked sideways at her and eased up, so they were going all of two miles per hour slower. It was a gesture of conciliation without really ceding the point and he sensed more than saw her wry look. They finally turned off the road, having passed many mansions that paled in comparison to the LaRue estate. He noticed Anna gawking like she'd never seen it before, especially when they pulled up by the six car garage, where a red '77 Lamborghini Countach, a silver 2020 Aston Martin convertible, and a yellow '79 Ferrari 308 GTS were just some of the mint condition cars sitting idle. Ryan ignored them as he thrust open the car door and put a foot out before the Charger even stopped.

"C'mon," he said, exiting agilely despite his height and physique.

As she struggled to keep up, Anna looked back at the black car with the huge dent in the driver's side door. "Why don't you drive one of these other cars?"

"Because I don't deserve them," he muttered.

"What? Why?"

He opened his mouth to explain but realized it might lead to a subject he didn't want to discuss. "Long story."

"You could be driving one of these and yet you bought that car with a dent already in it. And you won't fix it. C'mon. Level with me." When he didn't respond, she added, "You're a strange one, Charlie Brown."

He nodded to himself. Maybe it was true. That was the problem with secrets. They made you do things but not explain them, leaving people to invent a new truth and a new you along with it. It made him keeps friends like Anna at arm's length. He suddenly felt lonely as the mansion's shadow swallowed him.

The main house had two wings where Ryan's rich parents entertained senators, foreign dignitaries, and "old money" like the LaRues or business owners who sought their favors. Those who hadn't been here were seldom aware of his family's wealth. Part of him resented the money and he knew perfectly well why – all the money in the world wasn't saving his brother.

The three-story foyer had a massive chandelier and polished, decorative tiles like a public government building or fancy hotel. Crystal figurines and marble busts stood on elegant cherry furniture in the halls, and Ryan tried to ignore them as he strode by. He always felt like he wasn't supposed to touch anything, which was one reason he liked the dented car; it was already screwed up. On some level he knew he and it were the same and had felt drawn to it the moment he saw it, the same way this house repulsed him the second he turned into the driveway. Urgency brought him here at a clip, but something deep inside him made him want to get away just as soon as he arrived.

They found Ryan's brother in the large, gourmet kitchen, where he sat tilted way back in his custom, powered wheelchair so that he faced the ceiling. It let him take the pressure off his legs and butt to avoid sores, though Ryan knew that wasn't why he liked it. His long black hair was pulled back to reveal two pierced ears. On his left forearm lay a tattoo of a snake coiled around a knife. Such displays went against their un-cool parents, but they'd always let Daniel get away with certain things due to his injury, a fact his brother took advantage of and resented at the same time. Ryan did, too, because he saw them as signs of his brother's unhappiness and wanted Daniel to be at peace.

Daniel flashed a grin at Anna while flicking a raisin at Ryan's head and joked, "I knew it was you from the screeching tires. You should be careful. You don't want to end up like me."

Ryan got down on one knee beside him and squeezed a hand. "If I could trade places with you, I would."

Daniel rolled his eyes. "I know. I should know better than to joke with you about it. How'd RenFest go?"

"Where's Susan?" Ryan asked, looking around for the live-in nurse and ignoring the attempt at changing the subject.

His brother nodded to another room where a TV could be heard. "Watching the tube."

"Susan!" Ryan called, rising. "Come in here!"

Daniel shot him a look of annoyance. "She doesn't have to be with me every second, you know. I told you to stop that. I don't even need her. Or at least not for that anyway," he added suggestively.

Ryan squeezed his shoulder. "Don't get so worked up. I just wanted to talk to her about how you're doing."

"Yeah right," muttered Daniel, using the joystick to reposition the chair upright. While he was a quadriplegic, he had full use of his right arm and hand, but his grip with the left was too weak to do much with. He still had control over his bladder and related areas, but he'd never walk again and really had no need for the 24/7 nurse Ryan had insisted on hiring. He was in no danger of respiratory failure or similar life threatening complications, but Ryan was deaf to guidance on these matters, even from world renowned doctors, for once he'd gotten it into his head that some quadriplegics could die suddenly, he'd never forgotten it. Not all quads were the same, but telling that to Ryan was pointless.

Anna leaned over to kiss Daniel. "Hello. How have you been?"

"As heartbroken as always that you won't kiss more than my cheek."

She shot back, "Isn't that why Ryan got you the nurse?"

While Ryan cocked an eyebrow, Daniel said, "I wish," and rolled out of the room as the nurse arrived.

Patting Ryan's arm, Anna said, "I'll watch him," and hurried after Daniel, who she found doing donuts in his wheelchair on the hardwood floor. "Don't run me over, please," she said.

He stopped and sighed. "Only if you were Ryan."

"He drives you crazy, doesn't he? Would you like a long break from him?"

He looked surprised. "Are you kidding? I'd *love* that. Planning to kidnap him? It's the only way."

She laughed but not without concern at the truth of it. She knew Ryan frequently called or texted to check on him and that the well-meaning attention caused tension and arguments. "Me, Matt, and Eric are going on that trip to England that we've been planning for forever. Ryan's been planning, too, but never committing to it."

"On account of me."

"Yeah. He doesn't want to leave you despite all of this." She gestured at the luxury around them. "Has he ever gone on a trip without you?"

"No. I haven't gone more than eight hours without seeing him since I was a little kid, so I don't know how you'll pull that off."

She played with the pendant around her neck. "We have an idea, but you might find it intrusive."

He laughed. "Not more than his hovering. Let's hear it."

"We thought to install web cams here in the house. Matt's a techie and good with that sort of thing. If Ryan can see you in the cameras when he wants, maybe he won't bug you so much when he's away. And he might just agree to come with us."

"That's actually not a bad idea. He can check on me without me knowing it. And I can randomly give the cameras the finger when I feel like it, just in case he's watching. And it sorta fits this whole thing."

Failing to hide a smile, she asked, "How do you mean?"

"It's a nanny cam, basically, like I'm a frigging baby." He seemed amused, at least. "That's how he treats me."

"We don't mean it that way, of course."

He waved that off. "But Ryan would. I'm all for it. Shit, you should've done it sooner."

"No objections from your parents?"

"Nah. I know Matt's good with security."

"Do you think Ryan will go for it?"

"Oh, I'm sure he'd love it, too. But as for him going to England with you because of it, I don't know."

"Me either.

"Seriously though. It would do him more good than me to find out I'll be fine without him."

Anna nodded. "Wish me luck."

"You're gonna need it."

A fortnight later, Ryan, Anna, Matt, and Eric stood in the English countryside, the giant stone monoliths of Stonehenge looming nearby in the dark. The place was deserted. It had closed hours earlier when they'd been here for a private tour that allowed them to walk among the stones, and Anna had lost her pendant in the grass during this tour, or so they surmised. They hadn't been anywhere else but the big SUV Ryan had rented, and a search of that had turned up nothing.

Ryan sighed, staring at the little glowing screen of his iPhone in the dark. He still had no connection to check on Daniel. It had taken a week of enjoying the web cams back in the U.S. before Ryan had finally, and very reluctantly, agreed to make the trip. So far it had worked, and he was just starting to relax a bit, but out in the middle of nowhere, a flaw became apparent.

Suddenly a hand closed over the screen and he looked up, startled. Matt was frowning at him. "C'mon," Matt whispered. "Put it away. You can check on him later. Anna needs our help. At least make a show of looking even if you don't really care."

"Of course I care," Ryan muttered, putting the iPhone into a pocket with an effort. He knew the pendant was more precious to Anna than even his golden cross was to him. It was a family heirloom that her aunt had given her, and she'd confided that inside the diamond were strange letters that only a jeweler's glass let you see, but no one could read them. Losing it had been bound to happen sooner or later, as she was always pulling the pendant back and forth on the chain, stressing the fragile lock. His eyes went over to where Eric was leading her by the hand toward the monument, a large flashlight he'd found in the car sweeping back and forth.

Matt turned toward them. "Then let's go."

"Right." Ryan fell in beside him as they marched up the gravel path, passing the circular earthen bank and ditch and a ring of holes in the ground to enter Stonehenge. Few of the center stones remained and most of the larger sarsen stones that he recognized from pictures were gone, too. "So what did they say this place was for?"

"Solstice rituals or something."

"It's a lot of trouble to go through just for a ritual, isn't it?" Ryan asked, laying a palm on a cold stone. It was huge, ponderous, and formidable. Someone had put a lot of work into this. "They must weigh a ton."

"Twenty-five tons, to be exact," corrected Matt. "The big ones came from twenty miles away. It makes you wonder what they really did here. It does seem like a lot of work for just a ritual."

"How long ago was this built?" the big guy asked.

Matt smirked. "You weren't listening at all earlier, were you? Something like 3000 to 1600 BC."

Ryan glanced around at the open countryside, wondering if a passing cop car would see Eric's flashlight and show up to arrest them for trespassing. Then he noticed something and went off to investigate, stepping around a toppled stone to discover that the air beyond it tingled strangely, like he'd walked into an electrical field. A faint light shone near a pair of giant stones with a third stone lying across the top. On the trilithon's surface, a few feet above the ground, three oddly shaped lights were glowing blue. Had the moon shone brighter he might never have noticed. When he stopped beside them, he found Anna's pendant lying there in the grass, reflecting the glow on its silver parts. He picked it up absently, staring at the trilithon.

After a moment, he realized they'd stopped here earlier to see an ancient carving of a dagger and axe on the stone. The glowing symbols were beneath these and seemed vaguely familiar, though they hadn't been here before. He'd seen such symbols in fantasy role playing games.

"Norse runes," he said to himself, trying to remember how to read them. They were a form of alphabet used for communication, divination, and magic. With every moment, more lines of text appeared on the once dark and silent stone surface, letters swirling around the monolith to cover all sides.

"Guys!" he called in amazement. They turned to see words of blue fire igniting their way up the stone surface, covering the lintel stone on top.

Eric called, "Get away from there, Ryan!"

He blinked at the suggestion and then realized Eric's instincts about danger were infinitely better than anyone he knew. He backed away, but on seeing looks of fear on their faces, jogged toward them, meeting at the center of Stonehenge.

"What the hell is going on?" Matt asked.

"I think we should get out of here," Anna said, taking the pendant from his hand.

Moments later, every monolith burst into blue flames. An arc of fire spread between them and to places where missing or fallen stones now reappeared like ghostly apparitions from the past. The outer ring of sarsen stones encircled them as flames raced around the lintel stones on top, starting at the original entrance to the site and coming around again. They were the first ones in ages to see the full shape of Stonehenge as it was meant to be, but they didn't have long to admire it. As the flame wave circled to where it started, everything disappeared in a blinding flash.

Ryan could hardly see for all the swirling and flashing lights surrounding them, a vortex of air drowning everything out. It looked like Anna was screaming. He tried to step toward her but couldn't move his feet. He looked down and saw only blackness below him. The earth was gone, as were the huge stones and the sky.

While he watched, Matt's jeans and shirt changed to a long, dark robe, a staff appearing in one hand. Startled, Ryan looked at Eric, who now wore leather from neck to toe, a bandoleer of knives across his chest and a short sword at one hip. Then this disappeared and for a moment he was naked before his Earth clothes returned. Ryan's eyes went to Anna just as she switched from bare to her normal clothes, and a moment later she wore a long white robe. He glanced down at himself and saw a suit of golden armor, a big sword strapped to his waist and a golden lance in one hand. Then the noise, wind, and darkness abruptly stopped.

Squinting and shielding his eyes in the bright sunlight, Ryan tried to make out his surroundings. The air tingled and he felt invigorated and refreshed, as if awakening from a deep sleep. Words of blue fire were fading from the stone pillars around them, but it wasn't Stonehenge. These were a foot in diameter and well kept. The tallest were at the back and they decreased in size to an inch high in the front. A raised dais lay underfoot, where more decorative markings faded from view. Above them in a towering hall of grey limestone, sunlight poured in from huge stained-glass windows depicting dragons, elves, knights, and other fantastic sights.

And there were people, standing at the far end of the room, staring in amazement. Dressed in finery befitting a royal medieval court, scores of them stood against the tapestry-covered walls, fur-lined or silken tunics and leggings as well-kept as their brushed hairs and trimmed beards on the men. In the room's center stood a tall, robed figure, white hair and a matching beard flowing past his belted waist. A large book lay open on a podium before him. He lowered a staff similar to the one in Matt's hand to the floor and looked every bit the wizard. Behind him stood a pair of thrones, one empty, the other bearing a regal woman in an elaborate gown, a golden crown upon her head. Nearby stood people that looked like they might be her advisors, one of whom rose and came toward them with an outstretched hand.

"The gods be praised! They have come!"

The crowd murmured and the queen rose slowly, eyes moving from one arrival to the next, studying their faces. Ryan didn't know what to say or do and sensed that little of either was probably best. At last the queen raised her chin regally.

"Welcome," she began in a clear voice, a smile growing. "Welcome to Olliana, capitol of the Kingdom of Alunia, on the world of Honyn. I am Queen Lorella, ruler of this land, and I have summoned you for a noble quest, to free our land of dragons as before, and return peace to our world."

While a round of cheers greeted this announcement, Matt leaned over to Ryan and quietly repeated, "Quest?"

"Did she say 'dragons'?" Anna whispered, wide-eyed.

"Yes," replied Ryan in amazement, wondering if they were sharing a delusion. He was dreaming. That was it. He was back at their hotel room having a cool dream. He relaxed.

"We are most excited by your return to Honyn," the queen continued, "and word will go forth at once that the Ellorian Champions have answered our call, for so many worlds depend upon your aid that all will rejoice at your return after these many years." She paused expectantly and Ryan realized all the important-looking people were staring at him. The queen clearly thought they were someone else but now was probably not the time to ask who. He cleared his throat.

"Thank you for this reception, Your Majesty," he replied, voice booming off the tall walls as he played a part just like at RenFest. Improvising this sort of thing now came naturally. Why couldn't all of his dreams be this awesome? "What is the nature of this quest?"

Queen Lorella announced, "You must fight your way to the Dragon Gate, defeat the dragon guarding it, and reseal it. If you fail, every life on Honyn shall perish, as shall each of you."

Under his golden armor, a sheen of sweat soaked Ryan's clothes. Kill or be killed? Dream or not, that struck a nerve and brought up old, painful memories. Distracted, he slowly became aware that Anna was urgently whispering his name and that everyone was waiting for his response. He cleared his throat. "We're honored to answer your call," he said, projecting confidence, "and look forward to fulfilling your quest."

That brought happy murmurs from the crowd but not Eric, who whispered, "Ryan, don't promise anything like that."

Fingering the lance, the supposed knight murmured, "Well I had to say something, didn't I? Besides, this isn't real."

"Well, maybe not," Eric began, seeming less confident than usual, "but watch what you say."

"You are most welcome, Lord Korrin of Andor," Queen Lorella replied to Ryan. "Please accept our invitation to a great banquet in your honor tonight. While your suite is prepared, my Prime Minister and the Arch Wizard of Olliana, Sonneri, will explain what lies before you. The quest will begin to-morrow." She regally turned to leave, an escort of pages following.

"Great, this dream will probably end without anything cool happening," observed Ryan. He pinched himself, surprised that it hurt. It felt real.

As the queen disappeared, a tidal wave of chattering sycophants plunged toward them until guards intervened, cleaving a path for Sonneri and the queen's Prime Minister. The latter wore golden trousers and a sash over his embroidered tunic – a rectangular piece of cloth slipped over the head and belted at the waist. Sonneri's pine staff thumped on the floor as he approached, one hand on his prodigious belly, grandfatherly eyes bright. He pulled a pipe from his blue robe and lit it with a snap of his fingers. He looked pleased as he bowed.

"Greetings," said the wizard in a gravelly voice. "We are most surprised to see you here."

"So are we," Matt wryly observed.

"If you, uh, summoned us," began Anna, coming forward, "why are you surprised to see us. Were you expecting someone else?"

He bowed even lower to her. "My lady Eriana, no one could possibly come in your stead, but you have not graced a world with your presence in many years, and so we did not expect you to come."

"I see," she said. Her eyes lingered on a slender figure observing them from beside the empty thrones. As if noticing this, the man turned away, the cloak on his back swirling to reveal an embroidered tree. Fluid, graceful steps carried him away.

Sonneri continued. "If you'll come with us, the Prime Minister and I will answer your questions about the quest."

Ryan gestured for the others to precede him as they stepped off the dais. Dreams always centered around him and yet the others seemed focused on everything *but* him. And he had to admit that this felt real. He felt the heat of the sun each time he stepped into it. The voices around him had an accent he couldn't have imagined if he'd tried. He took a deep breath through his nose and caught a subtle but acrid smell of sweat, as if those nearby didn't bathe often. If this was a dream, his senses were far more alive than usual. A nag-ging feeling told him something was wrong and he began to frown.

"After this meeting," he started, addressing Sonneri, "we could use some time alone to discuss matters, if that wouldn't be too much trouble."

"Certainly," agreed the wizard.

Ryan brought up the rear, noticing that his finely carved, golden plate armor fit perfectly and was well adjusted despite the number of straps holding it together. Even the underlying chain mail was the right size. A golden sword sheath hung from one hip, where a helmet held fast to his waist, tightly tied to keep it from bouncing. That's when he noticed how quiet the armor was. His RenFest made all sorts of noise, chain mail clinking and straps squeaking, but not this one. It seemed designed for stealth and actual usage.

As the throne room disappeared behind them, he cast a glance back, wondering if stepping onto the Stonehenge-like dais would send them home. That's when the similarity between it and the monument struck him along with a suspicion as to the real nature of England's most famous archeological site. Maybe they'd learned what it was really for after all.

CHAPTER THREE

THE QUEST

Eric entered the War Room behind the wizard Sonneri and Prime Minister, the others trailing him. He had already noticed that his comfortable black leathers were supple and well worn. Metal studs designed to deflect swords dotted both the tunic and the arm bands that covered his black linen shirt. His fingers discreetly picked his own pockets, discovering coins, an unworn ring, some small tools he guessed were lock-picking aids, and a hidden knife. Other blades were scattered about his person, some in view like the dagger and sword on opposite hips and the bandoleer of throwing knives across his chest, but smaller ones lay along his forearms, thighs, and even the back of his neck. He suspected more knives were in places he couldn't reach now, like the soundless black boots that fit better than any he'd ever worn. A pouch at one hip held a white powder that reminded him of the chalk he used when rock climbing.

As he moved to a large table, he was caught between wanting to study every last item he saw, playing a part that he sensed required more nonchalance and confidence than he felt, and blurting out questions to his friends about their opinion of what was happening. He knew this was no dream, and yet how could it be real? Now appeared to be a chance to get answers from those who'd brought them here, so he focused on that. Getting reactions from his friends would have to wait. In fact, he hoped their own sense of decorum kept them from saying the wrong thing. Ryan in particular looked like he wasn't taking this very seriously up until now, when Eric saw him frown and look concerned. He fixed each of them with a stern gaze, wishing that more than he and Matt understood sign language. He took the opportunity to sign a few comments to his supposed wizard friend.

He signed, *I don't know what's going on but take this seriously until we're alone, okay?*

Yeah, no problem.

Try to influence the others with demeanor, etc.

Especially Ryan.

Exactly.

Eric saw Anna watching him intently, a question in her serious eyes, and he sensed she was on board.

They stopped around a large hexagonal table where Prime Minister Diam spread several maps of Olliana, in Kingdom Alunia, and nearby kingdoms. Along the walls hung swords, lances, other weapons, and tapestries of battle scenes. The standing suits of armor showed signs of use and suggested historical significance. Glass cases lined the room and presented peace treaties and other scrolls. Ryan leaned his lance against one wall, gazing up at the banner tied to the end. Eric wondered what was on it.

"It's been some time since your last visit," began the Prime Minister.

Eric tried to hide his surprise. If they were thought to have been here before, didn't anyone recognize this wasn't true? Did the four from Earth look enough like whoever had been expected that no one could tell the difference? That was a question he couldn't ask.

"Yes, it has," Eric said. "Can you remind us of the situation then and since?"

"Certainly," the Prime Minister replied. "While both good and evil dragons exist on some worlds, only the latter existed here on Honyn. They long terrorized villages and towns in all kingdoms, but they generally acted alone, so the threat was manageable if not entirely satisfactory. Trouble arose years ago when a strong leader coerced coordination from the others. A female named Nir'lion rose to power and was the most aggressive we've ever seen. The resulting campaign of terror was so fearsome that when we last summoned you, you determined they had earned a banishment from Honyn."

Eric saw his friends look surprised. They needed to control their expressions better. He tried to divert attention to himself by asking, "And is that what we did? Banish them? To...another world? It's been a while. Please refresh our memory, almost as if we've never been here before. We won't be offended if you tell us something we remember."

"Yes, Andier."

The martial artist cocked his head. "How did you say that name?" he asked as if it wasn't pronounced correctly.

The Prime Minister looked concerned. "Did I not say it right? I beg your pardon."

"Well, let me hear it again and I'll tell you."

"Andier of Roir, the Silver-Tongued Rogue."

Great title, Eric thought. "And do you have my companions' names learned so well, too?"

Matt discreetly made signs with his fingers at him. *Nicely done.*

"I would certainly hope so," the Prime Minister replied. "The knight is Lord Korrin of Andor, the Golden Knight, whose charming smile dazzles the ladies more than his gleaming armor. The Dragon Slayer, the Lord of Hearts, the Pride of Andor. A man whom women want, and whom men want to be."

On hearing this, Ryan raised an eyebrow and began to grin until catching Eric's eye and receiving a subtle but stern shake of the head. The supposed knight pursed his lips in amusement.

The Prime Minister turned to Matt. "Soliander of Aranor, the Majestic Magus, the Flaming Hand, the Lord of Power, a wizard so potent that whole armies have been known to balk at your name. Few have dared challenge you, and none have been the victor." Matt nodded as if unimpressed.

With a nod at Anna, the Prime Minister said, "The lovely Eriana of Coreth, a golden-haired beauty whose healing touch brings life to the dying and hope to the lonely. Said to be favored of the gods, perhaps even a lover, for the strength that flows through the Blessed One is unmatched among mortals. The Lady Hope, you've left many a warrior smitten by your healing hand." He bowed and then turned back to Eric, who tried not to grin at the atheist Anna, who wore an expression of muted annoyance.

"And finally, Andier of Roir, the Silver-Tongued Rogue. With a mind full of tricks, an ear for the unsaid, and a knack for entering places uninvited, the Slippery Serpent can learn more about you than your own mother."

"Very good," replied Eric, thinking they were in an awful lot of trouble. "And you refer us as the champions, not by any other name? Some places give us nicknames."

"Not here, Andier. You are, of course, the Ellorian Champions, from the world Elloria, though most simply call you the champions. With your permission, we may continue?" The Prime Minister pointed at the map. "You recall there is an old castle, Castle Darlonon, nearby in the mountains. It's a ruin and therefore largely forgotten, and so it was here that you created a device with a dual purpose."

Sonneri interjected, "As you no doubt remember, this device, the Dragon Gate, would not only remove the dragons from Honyn but prevent them from returning. The details of how to operate it were not revealed to us, and only Soliander knows how it works." He looked at Matt, who looked uncomfortable with the revelation.

"Or so we believed," added the Prime Minister. "Two weeks ago, a dragon was seen flying over the peaks east of here. Investigation revealed there is great activity at Castle Darlonon when there should be none, and that the gate stands open. We believe the escaped dragon is Nir'lion, and it's a certainty that she intends to release the remaining dragons, which must be prevented."

"Only one came through?" Ryan asked.

"We think so," admitted Sonneri. "We suspect that whoever released her has a plan that requires only Nir'lion for now and that the others continue to remain behind, but that is conjecture. Suffice it to say that if the rest had come through, we'd be battling for our lives."

"You don't know who released her?" Anna asked. The men shook their heads.

"What about the Dragon Gate?" Matt asked. "What condition is it in?"

Sonneri replied, "We believe it's intact."

"You haven't seen it, then?" Eric confirmed.

"Not directly, no, nor has anyone else. The castle is guarded by members of the Dragon Cult and mercenaries they've hired. No one has been able to get inside except a magical spy I sent."

"Who is this cult?" Ryan asked with distaste. Eric knew he didn't care for them because the ones on Earth often perverted God's word, according to his friend. He couldn't disagree. They were typically nut jobs.

Sonneri sighed. "They are fanatical dragon worshipers who believe this world rightfully belongs under the rule of dragons. The banishment outraged them and they vowed to release the dragons and seek revenge on not only you four, but Olliana, as well."

"Perfect," said Eric wryly.

"So do you think they're the ones who freed the dragons?" Anna asked.

"Doubtful," replied Sonneri, puffing his pipe. "They have some wizards among them, but none powerful enough to unweave the spells Soliander wrought."

"Then who?"

The wizard Matt answered, "We're hoping you'll discover this."

How are we supposed to that? Eric wondered. Unless whoever did it was standing there at this Dragon Gate when they arrived, how would they know? It wasn't like they even knew anyone here to begin pointing fingers.

"At this time," the Prime Minister began, "we believe Nir'lion doesn't know we're aware of her return, and we intend to keep it that way."

"Probably wise," Eric interjected.

"She seems intent on staying out of sight," the Prime Minister continued, "and if she's openly discovered, she may hasten the release of the others. We also have an advantage if she doesn't know we're prepared. However, a secret of this magnitude is hard to keep, and word has spread across Honyn. Some foolish men have tried to reach Castle Darlonon in a reckless attempt to kill her, but we've stopped everyone who's tried with a force of men guarding the castle road. Doing so is precarious due to the danger of being detected, however, so time is of the essence. Another factor is that other kingdoms have concluded that we're responsible for her release and are in collusion with the dragons to attack their lands."

Eric frowned. Another kingdom getting involved only worsened things. "Why would they believe that?"

"Because they are fools," muttered Sonneri, glaring at the map.

The Prime Minister sighed. "When Olliana last summoned you and you completed the quest on our behalf, great attention and praise were heaped upon us. The stature of Kingdom Alunia rose considerably and we became a more powerful and influential kingdom. This was not viewed favorably by all."

Sonneri interjected, "In short, they became jealous and have assumed that Alunia is power mad, and madness it would be if they were correct. They believe a wizard of Olliana freed the dragons at the request of Queen Lorella, who subsequently made a deal with Nir'lion that Alunia is not to be attacked. Instead, we will wage war with the dragons upon the rest of Honyn."

Looking confused, Anna observed, "But that doesn't make sense. Why would you have summoned the, uh, four of us before to banish the dragons if this is what you wanted?"

Sonneri replied, "Banishment was your decision, not our request. If you remember, the previous quest's requirement was to control the dragons so they could not work together against our world, and to nullify them permanently."

Tall order, thought Eric. *The four we're impersonating must be really powerful.*

"Also," continued the wizard, "the assumption is that Alunia became power mad after that quest and only now made a deal with the dragons."

"I see," said Anna, looking concerned.

The Prime Minister pointed at a region on a map. "Most recently, a neighboring kingdom, Rokune, has threatened action against Olliana and this hastened our attempt to summon you. They are not the only kingdom preparing for war, but they are the nearest. Since you have not answered a summons in many years, our announcement that we would try was considered a shallow, empty gesture. However, now that you've arrived, the queen's messengers are quickly sending out the news."

Perfect, thought Eric, wondering if now was a good time to confess. Being sent back probably required Sonneri's cooperation, so they had to stay on his good side.

"Since this began," the Prime Minister continued, "tensions are high and the queen hasn't quite been herself. I must beseech you to resolve matters quickly." He looked expectantly at Ryan. On seeing this, Eric realized the big guy was the apparent leader of these champions. He wasn't known for decisiveness.

Matt asked, "Is there an historical record of what we did here before? It could refresh our memory." Eric looked at him in approval, thinking it was a fantastic idea.

"Yes," answered Sonneri, looking apologetic, "though I must confess we made a copy of the scroll you provided before locking away the original, which was regrettably stolen years ago so that its secrets are likely known. I will have the copy delivered to your suite along with a scroll describing our gods and religions for Eriana to re-familiarize herself with, as is customary, of course."

Anna exchanged a look with Eric, who knew what she was thinking – there was no master plan, destiny, afterlife, ghosts, or any of that other baloney. He'd let her vent to him later. Now was not the time and she seemed to know it. Sonneri's words also suggested that Eriana, and now Anna, had to learn the gods of each world she visited and commune with one, getting familiar, before being able to have one heal through her. Being able to ask someone about such concerns would've been nice, but everyone thought they were the real Ellorian Champions, who would know such things.

As they exited the War Room, a court page advised them that Queen Lorella had arranged for a castle tour. It could have been an innocent excursion were it not for the noblemen and women who were let loose upon them. They spent an hour fending off questions about past exploits, where they'd been, what it was like to be so revered, what they thought had happened to let the dragons loose upon Honyn again, and more importantly, what they were going to do about it. After Ryan tried to be helpful and answer these questions despite being clueless, Eric took over to deflect the inquiries, claiming they needed to keep certain things to themselves. People kept asking anyway, and it was with some relief that the tour finally ended.

Along the way they'd seen much of Castle Olliana, a living home full of royalty, dignitaries, pages, scribes, and people on court business, including knights and wizards who asked questions they deflected. White towers swirled gracefully into the sky, spiraling up to blue domes topped with silver points. The four large, corner towers served the royalty, the knights and their squires, priests and clerics, and finally the kingdom's arch wizard and followers. But they saw signs of the dragon rampage in that some buildings were destroyed and others seemingly permanently burned by dragon fire. Their suite lay in the royal wing a few halls away from the queen's, a prestigious location. A steward advised them of various housekeeping matters before leaving and closing the doors, which Eric crept up to, listening to the footsteps fading away.

"Okay," he said at last, turning back, "we're alone."

FRESH WOUNDS

Anna had seldom if ever seen Eric look serious, as he was so often quick to joke, but she knew of his troubled past and that there had to be more to him than one-liners and sarcasm. His demeanor since they'd disappeared from Stonehenge had made more of an impression than Ryan's casualness, though that had since vanished. The strain of pretending to be fine over the past hour, with all those people asking questions and looking to them for help, while a growing dread had been filling her had made her relieved to be alone with her friends. But she excused herself, looking for a bathroom and heading through an adjacent doorway, where she found only four bedrooms, none with toilets or a sink. Each had a tub, washbowl, and chamber pot, to her dismay. With a frown, she closed an ornate door behind her.

As she walked, she caught her reflection in a mirror and stopped a moment. While she'd noticed elements of her outfit, the full picture only now became apparent. Golden patterns and symbols she didn't recognize covered the bottom edge, cuffs, neck, and hood of her white robe. Her long blonde hair was now in a French braid, a golden pin through it. She wasn't wearing much else except a few rings, a bracelet, and an amulet that depicted one figure kneeling beside another that was rising from a supine position. No sign of her pendant. Seldom one for much makeup, she noted that all of what she'd been wearing on Earth was gone.

She had already sensed she wasn't wearing much beneath the robe, including a bra. The undergarments proved to be just a thin, long shift, skirt, and white leather boots. What had happened to her Earth clothes? The thought made a rush of questions and anxiety seize her and she desperately wanted to talk to the boys, so she rinsed her hands in a bowl, not finding soap, and headed back. She returned to where she'd left them, finding them talking quietly together. They turned as one and she saw only serious expressions.

Letting out a sigh, she sat on a couch that looked like the expensive furniture at the LaRue estate, albeit in medieval style. Out the window behind her waited a balcony that she wanted to check. It might be nice to view their setting without onlookers asking questions she had to dodge.

She asked, "What did I miss?"

Eric pursed his lips. "Well, we've agreed we're not dreaming or having a shared delusion of some kind."

Ryan added, "At first, I thought it was and didn't take it at all serious. I wish I had. Now I promised that queen we'd do something."

"Yeah," said Matt. "I kind of wished you hadn't."

"How was I supposed to know?"

Matt joined Anna on the couch and pulled what looked like a spell book from a bag he'd arrived with. As he flipped through it, she thought that any artist could have drawn the fantastic pictures, but the pages had the look of frequent traffic. There were spills and stains, bent corners, and torn pages. Someone appeared to have *used* this thing. Extensively.

Anna remarked, "Something tells me this isn't even Earth."

Eric pulled out the short sword he'd arrived with and examined it while saying, "This…wizard, Sonneri, can probably tell us how this summoning thing works, to send us back, though I doubt we'll understand it. It appears to be magic."

"Or science that they think is magic," observed Matt, not sounding like he believed it.

"If it's just science," Ryan began, pulling out his own sword, "there'd be more of it, right?"

Anna nodded. "Right. I saw no electricity, air conditioning, even plumbing. No planes or cars. Out the windows I only heard wagons and horses' hooves on stone, and I saw people buying things with gold, silver, and bronze coins, not credit cards or even paper money. There's certainly no internet, TV, or smart phones. If we're still on Earth, we've gone back in time, which is just as implausible."

At her own mention of smart phones, she cast a look at Ryan, but he hadn't reacted. They didn't need him realizing he couldn't check on Daniel right now. Seeing his scrutiny of the sword, she looked and bluish-silver steel, with elegant, golden script flowing down the blade. Similar script curled around the shaft of Matt's staff and graced the pages of the book he continued flipping through.

Eric interrupted her thoughts. "This sword is perfectly balanced."

"This one, too," said Ryan. "Really light, too. It's surprising. It doesn't seem like any metal I've ever seen."

"I hope you don't need them," Anna remarked.

"Hard to argue with that," admitted Eric, putting it away and feeling around his outfit for something, which she realized was throwing knives when he pulled several out, testing their balance in his hands. His belt had a rope tied around it. "Whatever happened at Stonehenge could've been technology we just don't know about. You know, something like motion sensing lights could seem like magic to the ignorant. Even Sonneri appearing to light his pipe by snapping his fingers could just be technology that reacts to sound."

Anna knew they might have indeed traveled by science regardless of what anyone on Honyn thought, and maybe it was better for people here to think that whatever the truth might be. After all, performing magic took skill, talent, knowledge and discipline, which were all reasons Matt was no Soliander. But science required none of these things. Once someone smart enough to build a device had done so, anyone could use it. People with automatic guns didn't need skill to kill a highly trained Samurai. It was how the weak could defeat the strong and upset what some considered the natural order of things. Then again, magic items allowed unskilled people to cast spells, too, but within limits. If Soliander's staff, which they apparently had, possessed some power to facilitate this Dragon Gate closing, maybe they stood a chance of doing that, but it was an unknown and far too risky.

"So what do we do?" Anna asked. "We can't really do this quest."

Eric nodded. "If this is for real, and we just decided it is, then there's a real dragon out there, too, and it sounds like she wouldn't hesitate to kill us for trying to screw up her plans."

Ryan said, "True, but this world is in serious trouble, and they think they can't protect themselves and we can, so we'd be turning our backs on them."

"Not really, because we're not who they want," Matt observed, "and they don't even know that. They've got to send us back and try to summon these four people again. Maybe it will work this time."

Anna nodded, thinking she'd almost like to stick around and watch the result. "Yeah, it's the only responsible thing to do."

"Yeah, you're right," Ryan agreed. "So when do we tell them?"

"Before this banquet tonight," suggested Anna, feeling guilty. "We've got to do it before everyone gets too excited."

"I think it's a little late for that," Eric remarked ruefully, rising. He cocked his head and Anna had the impression he'd heard something from another room. That impression grew when he started moving in that direction.

"Sonneri's probably the one to send us back," Matt observed, "so we should approach him in private, I think."

"Good idea," said Anna. "Maybe he can even help us figure out how we got substituted for these people when we tell him."

While Ryan carefully swung his sword, Anna's eyes followed Eric as he reached the doorway of a bedroom. He suddenly leaned back sharply and she thought something had narrowly missed hitting his face. Then his arm rose swiftly, meeting and blocking the arm of someone swinging a dagger at him from inside the bedroom.

"Eric!" Anna yelled in panic, rising.

The martial artist retreated and a figure in black followed, lunging from the doorway. Eric grabbed the man's forearms and fell back, pulling the intruder onto his upraised foot and throwing him headfirst behind him. A table shattered under the assassin as Eric rose to go after him, with a quick glance into the bedroom.

"Ryan! Another guy coming in through the window!"

The big man stepped into the doorway, a knife meant for Eric's back bouncing off his golden armor. Startled, he backed away and yelped, "What do I do?"

Rushing the first guy, Eric replied, "Stick him with the sword!" With that he kicked the first assassin in the face and the intruder flew backwards, dropping another dagger.

Anna backed away from the fight, caught between wanting to help and running. Matt had risen and come to stand near her. Together they moved behind the couch toward the balcony.

Also wearing black, Ryan's foe drew a sword, prompting the knight to raise his own without the confidence Anna had seen him use at RenFest. Those were staged combats where he knew every last move his opponent would make beforehand, having practiced it together for hours. How would he fare when someone meant to kill him? The intruder's blade sliced at him much faster than Anna expected and he barely blocked it, backing away. "There's another one coming in!" he called.

"Oh my God," said Anna.

Ryan's attacker glanced behind before resuming almost recklessly, forcing Ryan back. He leapt away from the knight and turned just as the third man entered. This one wore brown and green leathers and hardly spared Ryan a glance as he leapt after Ryan's attacker. Their blades met with a loud ring.

"Is he helping us?" Matt asked.

"Think so!" Anna answered in relief. Her eyes lingered on realizing this man had slanted eyes, a delicate heart-shaped face, and otherworldly gracefulness. She could've sworn a pointed ear sometimes peeked out from under the blond hair. The word "elf" popped into her head.

Ryan exchanged a startled look with them before moving around the room to guard them. "Stay behind me."

"You don't have to tell me twice," remarked Anna, clinging to Matt. She pulled her eyes off the apparent elf to Eric, whom she'd never seen fight for real. A round of flying fists happened so fast that she couldn't follow it, but then the assassin drew a sword and so did Eric. Did he know how to use it? Eric blocked a swing, the blow jarring the blade from his hand to the floor. Anna gasped, but he kicked the man's wrist and that sword fell, too. His attacker punched him in the jaw with the other hand, knocking him back, then threw a knife that struck his chest, bouncing off the studded leather.

"Son of a bitch!" Eric looked a little disbelieving, then angry. He grabbed his own throwing knife but hesitated to throw it. His attacker drew another, raising one arm, and Eric flicked his wrist. The knife stuck in the man's stomach. Another followed into his upraised arm. Then Eric leapt forward and up, spinning in the air, his foot slamming into the man's face and hurling him backward into the wall before ricocheting him forward to the floor face first, where he lay unmoving.

Anna just stared at the aftermath until Eric turned to the other fight unfolding. The second assassin's back was to them, which apparently gave Ryan an idea for the way he quietly approached them, raising his sword high. He brought the pommel crashing down on the assassin's head. The blow thrust the man forward and right onto the elf's sword, which impaled him through the chest. The assassin fell back, almost striking Ryan, sightless eyes staring at the ceiling.

"Oh my God," the knight said. "That's not what I wanted!" His eyes danced about the room, from the dead man's eyes, to the blood pooling on the floor, to the pity in the eyes of those looking at him, and finally to the sword that had done this. He dropped it with a clatter and clamped his eyes shut, one hand over them.

Anna saw crimson spreading out beneath the man Eric had fought. Despite being afraid to go near, the medical student in her took over and she went to check his pulse, not finding one. Eric helped turn the man over. He'd fallen on the knife in his abdomen. He was dead. Anna exchanged a stunned look with Eric before they rose. Matt had gone pale, holding onto the couch to steady himself. The elf knelt to wipe his sword on the other victim's clothes and an awkward silence filled the room, broken only by Ryan's distressed breathing.

"Thank you," Anna started, struck by his piercing green eyes, delicate nose, and graceful, efficient movements suggestive of strength beyond his lithe, tall frame. Long blond hair fell behind his pointed ears, some of it braided.

"Who are you?" Eric asked, another knife ready. "What are you doing in here?"

"I observed them climbing the walls and followed," the man replied in soft, musical voice. "Their intentions were clearly ill."

Suspiciously, Eric asked, "How'd you come to see them?"

Anna thought he should be more polite, given that the elf had saved their lives, but she wanted to know, too. Was he spying on them? Paranoia seemed appropriate.

"My suite is across the courtyard from yours," the man answered, gesturing out the balcony.

Anna looked and saw a dimly lit window with a terrace, from which hung a long tapestry that had partially torn away during the man's descent on it. She came forward. "You were in the courtroom before," she observed, remembering the man with the tree-embossed cloak.

"Yes."

"I'm..." she hesitated, trying to remember her supposed name, "I'm Eriana."

He looked her in the eye and frowned. "No, you are not."

She hesitated, unsure what to say.

"I appear to be the only one not fooled by your charade," the man continued, looking from one to another, "presumably on account of the length of time those you impersonate have been absent."

They exchanged a nervous look.

"Why does that matter?" Matt asked faintly. If he didn't look at the bodies or all that blood, maybe he wouldn't pass out.

"Four years is a long time to humans and your memories fade."

"So..." Eric started, "four years is not a long time to you?"

"Correct."

"Because... you're an elf?"

"Of course."

Ryan pulled his hand down and opened his eyes. "An elf?" He scrutinized the man and finally said. "Are these supposed to be real, too?"

"Do you think I'm an illusion of some sort?"

"No," replied Ryan quietly, "I just don't think you're for real."

"I am of the flesh."

Eric interrupted. "We can discuss this later. The important thing is these men just attacked us, and everyone thinks we're Andier, Eriana, Korrin, and Soliander, but you don't. Why don't you tell us what's going on?"

The elf cocked an eyebrow. "I was hoping you would tell me. I am Lorian of the House of Arundell in the elven city of Noria, in the Great Honyn Forest. I have known the champions on several occasions and know you are not them. However, it may be best to continue your charade with others until we can speak further."

Eric nodded, suggesting, "We need to get some guards in here in case there are more of these guys." He looked at the bodies in consternation and Anna knew he had to be upset about having killed someone, maybe less so than Ryan, but still. Any curiosity about this champion stuff had abruptly ended.

Lorian put away his sword, bending over a corpse. "We must inform only the Queen's elite guard. Few others can be trusted."

Surprised by that, Anna asked, "Do you think someone here sent these men?"

"Possibly," replied Lorian, turning down the collar of one to reveal a tattoo of a dragon silhouette. "These are Dragon Cult members. It is interesting only two were sent. For such a formidable group as the champions, this is absurd. Professionals would not have been so easily dispatched, either."

"That was easy?" Ryan asked quietly.

Matt asked, "Does that suggest these men knew we aren't the champions and could be more easily killed with just two assassins?"

Lorian turned appraising eyes on him. "Excellent question. I do not know."

Eric observed, "Either way, this means the cult knows we're here, and they're likely to tell the dragon we're coming if they're in contact with her. The element of surprise is gone."

"That was unavoidable from the start," Lorian remarked matter-of-factly. "With the queen's announcement of your arrival, they'd have known long before you reached the castle. They'll be expecting you."

Anna hadn't thought of that, but it wouldn't matter with them going home soon.

Eric lent a hand as the elf dragged one body to the other. As Lorian picked up the dead man's sword, Anna noticed it was badly nicked from contact with either Ryan's sword or the elf's, but Korrin's was unscathed.

"Now might be a good time to decline the quest and be sent home," suggested Anna, worried about Ryan but unsure what to say.

The elf cocked an eyebrow. "That is not possible."

"Why?" Anna asked.

Lorian looked confused. "You cannot refuse a quest. It is woven into the spell that summons you and requires completion before the counter spell, that which sends you back, will work. If you refuse the quest or fail in it, you will remain here until your death."

Ryan went pale and a stunned silence followed. Anna's eyes fell on the dead.

"And if we accept," she said, "we'll all get killed."

CHAPTER FIVE

A Conscience Riddled

After the attack, the elf Lorian had fetched the Prime Minister and a few elves to discreetly remove the bodies and blood-soaked rugs. They'd been given a new suite to the relief of both Matt and Ryan, one for being squeamish about blood and the other to escape the reminder, though it didn't help. Death had left no room to think this wasn't real.

Lorian had convinced Queen Lorella to let him lead the quest through the elven woods to save time, help them approach Castle Darlonon unseen, and to let Lorian gather elves to assist. They didn't mention wanting to speak more in private and Ryan wondered if the queen had suspected something from the long look she gave before agreeing. Perhaps politics were at play, yet another thing about which they knew nothing here. Maybe they shouldn't tell the truth about anything except to Lorian.

Now they nervously waited for the banquet, unsure what was expected of them. Each wore new finery courtesy of the queen, Ryan and Eric in tunics and tights, Anna in a lovely gown that had required a maid's assistance to get into, and Matt switching his somber, black robe for a more pleasant white.

"You know," started Matt, "we should all be really tired by now, since it was night when we left Earth and we've been here for half a day it seems, but I don't feel that way."

"I noticed that, too," Eric said. "It's probably four in the morning on Earth."

Matt suggested, "Do you think the summoning spell rejuvenated us in some way?"

"Possibly. It did change our clothes."

"And trapped us here," Ryan interjected sourly, breaking his silence. He hadn't spoken much since the attack. Anna had privately consoled him for a few minutes, but it hadn't helped, partly because he didn't let it.

Matt asked, "Do you think we can we trust this Lorian guy?"

Anna shrugged. "He's an elf."

Ryan shook his head. "How do we know he's not human with prosthetics taped to his ears?"

"Oh, come on," Anna chided. "Didn't you take a good look at him? There's no way he's human."

No, Ryan thought, *I was too busy looking at the man I just killed.*

Matt fingered his staff. "It wasn't just the ears or the eyes, either, but the way he moved, and something I can't put my finger on."

Ryan said, "Even if that's true and we accept that elves are generally good people, that still doesn't mean he doesn't have his own plans or agenda. We can't just trust someone because he's an elf."

Anna nodded. "True, but saving our lives goes a long way." At the mention of saved lives, Ryan frowned.

As someone knocked on the door, Eric said, "I think tonight we should all sleep in the same room, with one of us on watch."

"Good idea." Matt went for the door, adding, "Let's stay together at this dinner, too."

Eric nodded. "Or for that matter, until we're back on Earth."

They followed an escort down halls and an ornate, grand staircase, celebratory music growing louder until they reached the banquet, when the music stopped and all eyes turned to them, applause and cheers erupting. The Great Hall stood seventy feet high, with large tapestries of hunting scenes covering the limestone walls. The musicians sat on a balcony at one end opposite an enormous fireplace. In between stood six tables long enough to sit fifty people each, every seat filled but theirs.

They soon sat at a prominent place near the queen, Prime Minister, and the wizard. Ryan as Lord Korrin and the Anna as Lady Eriana sat on one side, Matt as the Majestic Majus Soliander and Eric as the Silver-Tongued Rogue Andier on the other. Lorian and two elves looked on nearby. Queen Lorella made some suitable comments regarding the occasion, during which Ryan noted the food looked familiar – turkey legs and breasts, hot breads and buns, chopped and whole vegetables like carrots, radishes, and ears of corn, stuffing, roasted boar, some kind of fish with the head still on, a pasta dish in red sauce, and wines and meads. While dining, Ryan first evaded questions with mouthfuls of food as an excuse, but soon he deflected people with his own questions, particularly those of several knights asking about his equipment or battle strategies. They seemed pleased at his inquiries and eager to brag, so he let them, but their related exploits ground everything in stark reality, reminding him he was an abject novice and imposter.

After dinner, when servants cleared the floor for dancing, Korrin became the object of many a woman's – and in truth, a few men's – fancy. Ryan's upbringing had included lessons in this kind of ballroom dancing, and though he didn't know the steps, he learned more quickly than Anna and Eric. He wasn't in the mood for it, and while some of the small talk with strangers distracted him, others kept asking about Korrin's exploits, reminding him of death.

During dinner, Eric had sipped wine while discreetly observing the attendees, from wait staff to guards, nobles, elves, and even the queen, whose eyes weren't the only ones on them. Glances came from all corners, but one group had felt out of place to him, their manners less refined, their glances too obvious. They seemed less like courtly fops and more like those living by their wits and sword. A rather dashing man among them had caught his eye and exchanged nods. Eric knew when someone was keeping an eye on them and hadn't liked it.

He hadn't failed to notice Ryan's preoccupation since the attack. Their talk at RenFest about Ryan not wanting to hurt anyone stayed fresh in his mind. Perhaps the big guy really meant it, though he didn't know why that was such a big deal to him. You had to draw the line at people trying to kill you. If the attacker ended up dead as a result, it was their own fault; they should've thought of that before attempting murder. Ryan had been right to do what he'd attempted, and while being remorseful was one thing, beating yourself up was another. He'd seen Anna console him too, and he was a bit annoyed that he'd gotten all of her attention. He'd killed someone, too, and just because he didn't let on so much didn't mean he wasn't also upset.

Once dancing began, Andier's mischievous nature apparently attracted its own kind of women to Eric, and while most were subtle about wanting amorous attention, others weren't. They seemed to think it was all right to be honest with Eric about their desire to be naughty, and he wondered just who this Andier fellow was. Maybe he had a reputation Eric needed to uphold. A glance at Ryan suggested the wholesome women had gone after him as Korrin while the sexed up ones went for Andier. Eric could live with that – or so he thought until he saw Anna's dance partner. It was the dashing man he'd noted earlier, and from the way he was looking at her, he clearly had naughty ideas of his own.

"My Lady Hope," began the man to Anna, bowing as he cut in on someone. "What a pleasure it is to meet you. I am Cirion of Ormund." One rough hand took hers while the other found the small of her back, both suggestive and possessive. She thought his mysterious, dark eyes seemed amused and probing, dancing a fine line between making it clear what he wanted and giving himself plausible deniability. He cut a lean figure in a green tunic that hugged his broad shoulders, black hair catching on the turned up collar of his black shirt. He seemed somehow nimble and quick, as if he'd never let himself be still long enough to get complacent. The phrase "a rolling stone gathers no moss" came to mind, his strong jaw suggesting he was in full command of his journeyman life and would have it no other way.

"To what do I owe the pleasure?" Anna asked, knowing a guy who wanted to bed her for what he was. She had to admit he was rather charming and she smiled despite herself.

"You waste no time, I see." He smirked knowingly.

Catching his meaning, she replied, "Well, you have until the dance is over to do your business. I'm sure that won't be a problem for you."

He laughed a rich baritone. "I assure you I can last quite a few songs."

"Perhaps, but maybe I'll be bored by then."

He laughed more genuinely. "Ouch! My lady, I had no idea you had such wit, and so cruel, too. Perhaps your title of Lady Hope is a misnomer, as you've surely tried to dash mine."

"But I haven't succeeded, I see."

"Well what kind of man would I be to give up on the first try?"

"Do you really want me to answer that?"

"Not really." Cirion paused. "Perhaps you'll be more amenable to other hopes of mine."

"Ah. Here it comes."

"Yes, you see, it's been some time since you visited Honyn and you might benefit from a guide on your way to Castle Darlonon, not to mention inside."

Her eyebrows arched. Was he a Dragon Cult member? "You've been inside?"

"Certainly. Not since the dragon returned, of course, but after your last visit."

She noticed he didn't say why. "And why did you go in? Didn't you know we strictly forbade such entrances?" This was a little tidbit she's picked up from Sonneri.

He smirked and ignored that. "I wanted to see this famed Dragon Gate, of course, but as you know, I couldn't reach it."

"Not man enough?" Anna asked, wanting him on the defensive as much as possible. Better him than her.

He grunted. "More like not wizard enough. I can cast a fair spell or two, but Soliander there can put up spells even an arch-wizard can't get by." He looked over at a young, red-robed wizard who was approaching Matt.

Curious what they'd encountered, Anna asked as if testing his truthfulness, "And what did you find there?"

Cirion seemed to catch her intention as he replied, "Well, for starters, the castle gate was unguarded, presumably to lure people to that courtyard, where the tiles burst into flames if you put your foot in the wrong place. Nasty trap, that one. We didn't get much farther despite getting by the main doors. The stairs were clearly unwise unless you wanted to visit for a rather long time, but the way forward was no better. We spent two days in the maze beyond it before escaping. After that, we were rather tired of the whole affair."

"Is that all it took to defeat you?" Anna asked, wondering how they would get past these defenses. "Why would you want to guide us? What's in it for you?"

He smiled, pearly white teeth dazzling her. She knew that in medieval-like times, such fastidiousness was rare. "Aside from the pleasure of your company and wicked wit?" Cirion replied. "Why, to see you slay the dragon. Few have seen the legendary Ellorian Champions in action."

Making up stuff, she replied, "We don't generally allow spectators. They might get killed. You wouldn't want that, surely?"

"Naturally not."

"Then why do you really want to go?"

He paused. "As I mentioned, I'd like to see this Dragon Gate."

"Why? For what purpose?"

Seeming put off, he sighed slightly. "Haven't you ever admired something purely for its beauty?" He looked her up and down suggestively.

"Yes, but not when it might kill me," she replied, giving her own suggestive look.

Smirking, Cirion replied sagely, "Without risk, there can be no reward."

"And what reward do you expect?"

"Well," he began expansively, "if you must know, being in the company of the famous champions when you seal the gate would allow me to say, and rightfully so, that I was partly responsible, and my improved reputation would allow me grander adventures of my own and all the subsequent fortune and happiness." He smirked at her. "Surely you wouldn't deny me this?"

Turning the tables, she pressed against him suggestively. "Don't be so sure of what I'll deny you. Why didn't you just tell me this before?"

He leaned close. "I didn't want to seem greedy," he confessed.

Anna feigned surprise. "You?"

He smirked again. "I do have pride, my lady."

"So I noticed." She rolled her eyes, then decided to cut this short as the dance neared its end. She felt comfortable to make this decision without the guys. "I'm afraid I can't allow you to come with us. We can't be sure what we'll face, and what risks we'd expose you to." Cirion nodded his understanding, and when the song ended, excused himself, to her relief.

As Matt watched his friends from beside the dance floor, he sipped from a wine glass etched with dragons and ogres. He tried to look unapproachable because he'd never danced a step in his life, but he was in luck, for Soliander wasn't the target of anyone's fancy, and therefore neither was he. He'd noticed big men who were probably knights talking to Ryan and had noted in relief that there appeared to be few wizards in attendance, though he wasn't sure. Were they required to dress like him? That made it easier to notice them, but if not, there could be more than he wanted. On one hand, he was eager to ask others about this, but he sensed Soliander was the one who'd get the questions, so he hoped to evade it altogether.

He fingered the ornate, mahogany staff in one hand, having sensed that leaving it behind was unwise, considering its nature and how powerful it could potentially be. Elegant gold script he couldn't read flowed down it, a bluish-silver steel prong atop it holding a fist-sized diamond. In the cloth bag he'd arrived wearing over one shoulder, he'd found two tomes that had proven to be spell books. Inside his soft black robe, numerous hidden pockets held several vials, tiny bags, and oddly shaped items he couldn't identify by touch and hadn't had time to examine yet. Several rings, a bracelet, and a necklace beckoned his curiosity, since they might have been magical.

As he stood hoping for a chance to explore these items, a red-robed fellow a few years younger than him stopped beside him, looking every bit the young wizard, a wooden staff in one thin hand and several pouches hanging from a golden cord at his waist. Matt had noticed him before. Gold rings and bracelets peeked out from the sleeves of his well-worn robe, which depicted a magic wand and staff over his heart. Tall and skinny, he seemed awkward and nervous, one hand brushing the long brown hair from his thin face. His brown eyes were deep and intelligent, alert, but discreet.

"Greetings, Soliander," he said timidly, bowing his head.

Matt nodded at him and tried to use his best alpha male tone, which was pretty weak, to intimidate the guy into going away. "Greetings, wizard."

"My name is Raith," said the young wizard. "You begin your quest tomorrow?"

"That is correct."

"It would be most interesting to see you in action."

"Perhaps," replied Matt evasively.

"Um, well, I've, I've been thinking it might be a great help to Honyn, and yourselves, if you were not the, um, only one able to work the Dragon Gate. This way, the four of you would no longer be summoned simply to close it."

For a moment, Matt thought that was a great idea, but then he thought better of it and gave Raith a hard look, knowing where this was going. "It's not that much trouble," he said dismissively, "and we might have no other reason to visit your fair world."

"That is true. Hopefully nothing else would require your assistance, as much as we are honored by your presence." He paused. "Still, what if you are unable to come and no one can close the gate? You could be away on another quest, or... or..." He stopped.

Matt arched an eyebrow at him. Was he suggesting Soliander might be dead and unavailable? That was bold. "You needn't worry about that," he replied, feigning disapproval.

Raith hesitated and Matt had the impression he was choosing words carefully. "I'd very much like to learn how the Dragon Gate works," Raith began sincerely, "and accompany you on your journey. I could lend assistance, freeing you for more important tasks."

He wore such a hopeful look that Matt took pity and lightened the attitude. "I think it's best that no one but me knows how to turn the gate on and off."

Raith nodded. "Yes, and pardon me for remarking, but it seems that someone else has already figured that out, Great Magus."

Now there was a good point, but there was no way Matt could give this guy what he didn't have – knowledge of how the gate worked. It wasn't really his decision to make anyway, but that of the real Soliander, despite his apparent disappearance and abandonment of the gate and any other concerns. Fortunately Matt had a better point. "And you see how much trouble this person has caused?"

Raith bowed his head. "You are wise beyond me. Perhaps you could merely show me how to activate it, not deactivate it."

Matt conceded that was another good point, except it was possible the same thing turned it off and on. "That is possible, but I'll make that determination after the quest, not before."

"You are too kind. Perhaps if you saw me in action yourself, you'd entrust me with this task more readily?"

Matt shook his head inwardly. This guy didn't give up easily, but Matt was resourceful, too. Changing the subject without seeming to, he asked,

"Maybe. Why don't you tell me about your schooling? How did you become a wizard?"

Raith looked flattered by Soliander's genuine interest and soon became engrossed in relating his experience, which Matt helped with a barrage of questions to keep him distracted. A life as a wizard's apprentice or formal schooling sounded fascinating. Raith had been on his own a few years now, and it became clear he wanted to learn from Soliander, but Matt was having none of that. He skillfully avoided questions to the point of rudeness, but with such a deferential admirer, it was easy. He forgot to keep an eye on his friends, but he wasn't the only one getting distracted.

Awash in perfume, caresses, and flirtatious looks on the stone dance floor, Ryan felt the effects of so much feminine attention on him. Normally it didn't work, but the sheer volume of young women vying for him was unusual. The subjects they raised didn't help, like how much land their fathers owned as dowry, or what title he'd assume upon marriage, or their family's proximity to the throne. While they clearly wanted a husband and perhaps a trophy one at that, their looks promised no shortage of bedroom frolicking. These weren't just girls, either, but full-bodied women, all dressed to kill.

The only sobering aspect was that it wasn't really him they wanted, but Korrin, the Pride of Andor, and that his courage in battle was the reason for his desirability. It was the single greatest difference between them, and why these women found a violent man so attractive mystified him. They must surely be romanticizing the whole hero idea and ignoring the bloody truth they never saw. He was sure that the reality of a dead body would've taken the romance out of their looks in an instant. It had surely done so for him. Every dance step became a bitter reminder that the man he'd killed would never take another step again.

The women took turns with him, casting looks of thinly veiled hostility toward each other, though one seemed rather unconcerned with any dagger-like glances thrown her way. She caused a hasty retreat in the one she replaced, and from the muscles bulging under her golden gown, she could apparently take care of herself. Her gaze was direct like that of a man, and she seemed powerful, dangerous, and sleek like her jet black hair. Rough calloused hands added to the sense of vigor, suggesting she was a swordswoman, and an agile one at that, for her dance movements were smooth and nimble.

"What's your name?" Ryan asked, feeling a firm grip nearly crush his hand.

"Nola, the Fair Raven," she replied, her dusky voice stirring him. Her mysterious dark eyes lent weight to her nickname.

"You are strong," he appraised her, "and yet gentle."

"As are you, Lord of Hearts," she purred. "It is no wonder women throw themselves at you."

"I'm a good catch," he replied, but her blank look indicated the joke fell flat, so he moved on. "How did you develop such a physique?"

"Swinging swords at men who wouldn't take no for an answer."

"Then I guess I had better be civil."

"I'm sure my skill is nowhere near yours, Pride of Andor," she reassured him, "so you needn't worry. I *would* be grateful for the chance to cross swords with you, if only in jest, of course." She pressed against him suggestively, her bosom pushing up more in her low-cut gown, but even that couldn't take his mind from his conscience. The thought of pretend violence made him frown.

"I'm afraid time is short for swordplay," he replied quietly, "as I leave first thing in the morning."

Nola asked, "Are you headed straight to the castle?"

He paused before replying. "Yes," he answered, having remembered the side trip to Arundell with Lorian was a secret. "I don't know of anywhere else we'd want to go."

"Aren't you traveling with the elves?"

The accuracy of the question startled him. How did she know that? From her slight smirk, he suspected his expression, whatever it was, had answered for him, but he tried to lie anyway. "Uh, no," Ryan said lamely. "Why would you think that?"

She smiled. "My mistake. I saw you dining with them. I guess a big strong man like you doesn't need help from a bunch of scrawny elves to kill the dragon. You're the Dragon Slayer after all."

He looked down and away. Why did everyone have to remind him of the expectation to kill over and over? His thoughts strayed to Daniel back home, the loss of his smartphone and any way to use it a gnawing worry. He had to get back. He needed to quit dancing now and go blurt the truth out to Sonneri. Maybe Lorian was wrong and they could go home now anyway.

"Why the long face?" Nola asked quietly, breaking his thoughts. She seemed sympathetic and he realized he'd dropped his guard. "Does something trouble you, Korrin?"

Their eyes met and the kind look in hers disarmed him. He couldn't really tell her the truth, but did he have to pretend he wasn't upset? Did it matter? He shrugged noncommittally. "It's nothing."

She pressed against him more, as if offering herself as consolation. "If it dampens your spirit despite all these ladies pursuing you, then it must surely be something. Would you prefer to discuss it in private? I have a suite to myself here in the castle and you can unburden your noble heart to me." Her hand stroked his hair tenderly and she laid a sweet kiss on his cheek. Sudden, turbulent emotion welled up with him, threatening his self-control.

"You're very kind," he started huskily, intending to regretfully decline, but she interrupted.

"I've only just begun to show you kindness, Korrin," she replied gently, and with that she whispered sweet, compassionate words in his ear and leaned into him. It seemed that all his life he'd kept his torments to himself, for in those few moments when someone saw his angst, he'd kept quiet like so many men so often do. Culture demanded men deal with pain alone, but her embrace promised a release he increasingly felt unable to restrain. His guard fell. Even Anna, for all their friendship, hadn't gotten past his defenses, but he felt himself falling into this stranger's care. As the dance ended, she led him from the floor, past the guards and away, and he went readily if not eagerly.

Out on the dance floor, Eric struggled to keep his wits about him. Naughty thoughts raced through his mind every half second, in no small part because women put them there. Andier might be the Silver-Tongued Rogue, but now Eric was either tongue tied or it was hanging out of his mouth, figuratively speaking. It had been too long since he'd been with a woman and the desire they aroused was strong. It was all he could do to tear his eyes away to keep tabs on his friends, and this time he didn't see Ryan. His eyes searched again, less discreetly, and finally he dropped all pretenses on realizing the big man was gone. He caught Matt's gaze and moved his fingers behind his dance partner.

Did you see Ryan leave?

Matt put his wine glass down. *No. He's gone?*

Yes. Eric figured Anna was too distracted to have noticed and Lorian was too embroiled in conversation. The guards, he realized. They ought to have noticed.

He excused himself and sought one at the entrance. The young man snapped to attention. "Did Lord Korrin leave this way?"

"Yes, my lord."

Eric hadn't expected the title. Only Ryan had gotten that so far. "When?"

"Just a few minutes ago."

"Where did he go?"

Looking apologetic, the guard answered, "He did not say, but he was headed toward the Blue Crest Wing."

"Was he alone?"

"No, my Lord. He escorted Nola of Ormund, presumably to her, uh..." He faltered, looking pained.

"Her suite?" Eric finished.

The guard pursed his lips. "Yes, my lord."

"Where is that?"

"I'm not sure, sir, but probably in the second level of the Blue Crest, directly down this hallway." He gestured and Eric took off at a jog, worried and wondering what Ryan thought he was doing. It didn't occur to him that he'd allowed himself to be separated from the group as well, but someone else in the Great Hall noticed.

Watching Eric leave, Cirion excused himself from a different young lady who'd just been flirting with Andier at his direction. Like all the others, she didn't have anything interesting to relate about the rogue anyway, for Andier didn't give much away, but distracting him had been the real goal. To his surprise, Eriana had been a harder mark than he would have believed. He'd had other reasons for talking with her, one being the chance to bed her despite her reputation for chastity. He had conquered unattainable women before, but she had proven her womanhood wasn't the only thing she guarded well. He hadn't learned a thing from her, and that was rare. A glance revealed Raith still had Soliander's attention, and Nola had succeeded with Korrin where he had not, so if at first you don't succeed....

He headed for Eriana, but as he closed in, a familiar figure intercepted him.

"Cirion," began Lorian smoothly, offering a goblet of red wine. "I know your love of elven wines and have brought you a glass of our finest. You must try it."

The dashing man looked at him first in annoyance, then impatience, feigned cordiality, and finally resignation. "You're too kind," he replied politely, taking the glass and casting a regretful glance at Eriana. Elves were famous for subtlety, but he saw the knowing smirk on the elf's face and made a note to watch out for this one. How much did he know? He didn't have long to wonder. From the corner of Cirion's eye, he saw two elves moving quickly through the crowd, then take off running in the same direction Korrin and then Andier had gone. Cirion silently cursed and returned his gaze to Lorian, finding a look of barely hidden steel in the eyes.

CHAPTER SIX

LORIAN

It wasn't until he reached the door to Nola's suite that Ryan realized he was lost. He hadn't been paying attention, his mind a swirl of death and affection, blood and caresses, remorse and hope. Nola looked up at him suggestively as she aligned the gold key with the lock on her suite's door and slipped it inside. Her lips brushed against his so that he hardly noticed being drawn into her scented room, an odd mixture of steel and roses in the air.

Suddenly two hands yanked him backwards, breaking contact with her so fast that it startled him. He blinked in surprise and turned to see a short figure with black hair glaring at him. A moment passed before he recognized Eric.

"Didn't you hear me?" Eric snapped, pulling him further into the hall. "I must've called your name four times."

Ryan heard himself mutter something even he didn't comprehend.

"C'mon," said Eric the rogue, "we have a big day ahead of us tomorrow and don't have time for this."

"But–"

"No buts. Let's go." Eric pulled him by the arm and Ryan followed, still off guard and confused. "Goodbye, my lady," the rogue called to Nola. "He's not the sort to call the next day anyway."

As Eric led Ryan down the hall, two elves appeared out of the shadows ahead, looking alert until seeing them. They slowed, stopped, and became far more casual in demeanor. Ryan realized that not only had Eric come after him, but the elves, too, possibly at Lorian's suggestion. Suddenly he remembered the pledge to stay together, but even now, he saw no harm in going with Nola. He sighed in frustration, which worsened when Eric spoke again.

"What did you think you were doing?" Eric asked. The elves waited until they passed before trailing along at a discreet distance.

Offended, Ryan replied irritably, "You wouldn't understand."

"Try me."

"Bug me about it tomorrow. I'm not in the mood."

"But you were in the mood to get laid."

Ryan shoved him away with one hand and kept walking. "Asshole. That's not what this was about."

"Well, what then?" Eric asked, following.

"I told you later. Just leave me the fuck alone." He sped up to put distance between them, relieved that Eric seemed to let him go on ahead. He followed the noise toward the banquet hall and then wandered off toward their suite, fairly certain he could find it. Not until reaching the door and opening it did he look at his pursuers, seeing only the two elves. He sighed and closed the door, feeling lonely. Would they stand guard outside to keep other people out or him in? He didn't think it mattered as long as he got to be alone – and no one snuck in to try killing him.

Once inside, Ryan struggled for some way to calm down, but the lack of modern entertainments like television or the internet left no room for distraction. He stood alone with his dark thoughts, eyes moving from silken pillows to ornate, mahogany furniture and rich rugs. The lavishness seemed somehow shallow and empty, matching his outfit style for style so that he tore at the tunic to get it off. He soon found himself on his bare knees beside his bed, head bowed, hands clasped before him, smoke from the snuffed out candles curling through the dark room. He hadn't done this in a long time and didn't question whether the God of his Earth could hear him here or not. It didn't really matter, for the forgiveness he sought for killing someone had to come from within and he doubted that would happen anytime soon, if ever.

He wondered how Daniel was doing and if he'd ever see his brother again. In the strangeness of the arrival here, the attack, and the man he'd killed by accident, he'd hardly had time to wonder about Daniel. All these years of worrying about his brother and now it was his own life that might suddenly end. That was always true in a sense, but courting danger like this raised it to a whole new level. There was no easy way out of this. He went to bed and suffered through a restless night that left him tired in the morning, and the last to rise despite being the first to bed.

The next morning, Ryan entered the sitting room to find the others, dressed for the quest, talking quietly. From their glances and the sudden silence, he surmised the subject had been himself. His dark mood had lifted some, enough to pretend he was fine anyway. Trying to ward off any well-meaning remarks, he flashed an insincere smile.

"Does anyone know where I can get some coffee?" He scratched at his stubble, wondering what to shave with.

"I already asked," Matt complained. "There isn't any. They don't even know what it is. This is going to be miserable."

Anna chuckled, picking at some fruits. "You'll get used to it. I have to admit I was hoping this was a dream when I got up."

"Or a nightmare," Ryan added quietly. "I wish I knew how Daniel was doing."

Eric gestured to a ceramic bowl of water on a silver tray, a short blade for shaving next to it on green towels. "They dropped off this stuff earlier," he said, sitting down. If he harbored any resentments about the night before, Ryan couldn't tell and appreciated a lack of attitude. "We already used it, but you'll want to warm up the water on the fire. It's not the most sanitary thing, but I think we're okay."

Ryan took the bowl and left to shave, his thoughts on his problematic role of a knight. They would never return home if they didn't succeed, and the quest undoubtedly required all of them. Matt couldn't cast spells, nor Anna heal anyone with magic, which left him and Eric. If he refused to fight, it was all on the martial artist. As impressive as Eric was, he wasn't going to punch a dragon into submission. Ryan would have to help and be willing to use deadly force. Even if he didn't, he'd still be condoning whatever Eric did if he just stood there and watched instead of stopping him. It was unlikely they could seal the Dragon Gate at all, with or without a fight.

He couldn't do this. There had to be another way. If refusing meant living out his life on Honyn as a shamed coward, that was better than killing anyone else. He could live with that, but the others might share in his fate and he didn't have the right to decide that for them. Maybe he could just quit and let them go without him. If this Lorian guy could bring enough elves with him, Ryan wouldn't be needed. The idea brightened him. He'd talk to Lorian privately when he got the chance.

⚊ ✦ · ✦ ⚊

After a quick breakfast, they left the suite to see Lorian, following a guide through the castle halls. Matt walked more briskly than the others, his head full of questions about the summoning, wizardry, and anything related to magic. The elf was the one person he could ask about such things, since everyone else would expect him to already know. It wasn't that he wanted to cast a spell – well, he did, but that seemed as improbable as anything else – but the talk with Raith the night before had filled him with ideas. Besides, he needed to know how to fool people or give plausible excuses that he wasn't going to cast a spell when they expected him to. When they arrived, the elves wasted no time. Two let them through a door to Lorian's suite. The elf promptly greeted them and got right down to business.

"It is not safe for us to speak of your true identities in this place," he began, motioning them to sit on sofas embroidered with forest settings, "but my brethren have cleared the area of possible spies. We should have a few minutes, at least."

"So they also know who we are?" Eric asked, walking around the room and peering through doorways. Matt looked at the balcony and see an elf there, his head scanning back and forth.

"They know who you are not," corrected Lorian, slanted eyes watching him, "but only two of them, who would have discovered your charade on seeing you. It is important that such individuals be told the truth and cautioned to remain silent, else they might remark upon it aloud in front of the wrong company."

Eric nodded, remaining standing while all but Lorian sat. "And the wrong company would be everyone, except elves?"

"Elves who knew them, yes, and some dwarves."

"Dwarves?" Matt asked. What else was on this planet? Despite the danger that would get closer by the day, his curiosity was rising even more.

Lorian replied, "Yes. Elves and dwarves are likely to remember the details of the champions' appearance better than humans. Four years is long enough for your kind to forget, and it is not unreasonable to mistake you for them, considering the similarity of your appearance." He looked at them one by one. "I must say, the resemblance is remarkable, as you're each the same basic height, build, hair color, and have similar features. You are nearly the same age, a bit younger. This is undoubtedly why they chose you. Only those with whom they'd spent considerable time are likely to discover the deceit, and on most worlds, they acted very much alone."

"Chose us?" Ryan asked, looking like he hadn't thought of that before. Neither had Matt, who had assumed this was all some sort of accident.

"Yes," said the elf, leaning against a chair. "Those you impersonate. I'd very much like to know why the four of you have appeared in their place."

Ryan glanced at his friends. "We were hoping you could tell us that."

Lorian's slender, blond eyebrows arched. "You do not know? Didn't they tell you?"

"Who?" Matt asked, fingering his staff. "This Soliander and the others? You think they sent us?"

"Of course," answered Lorian. "How else would you come to be here in their place?"

"We don't have the slightest idea," replied Ryan in frustration.

The elf asked, "They didn't tell you?"

"No," answered Ryan. "We've never even heard of these people until we showed up in the court. We certainly haven't met them."

Lorian looked from one to another, measuring them. "Then they didn't send you."

"No," answered Matt, realizing Lorian didn't know what was going on any more than they did. "Not that we know of, anyway."

"And you haven't met them." Lorian paused, eyes troubled. "Then you do not know their whereabouts?"

"Right," said the wizard, sobered by the elf's reaction.

The elf sighed. "I was hoping we'd finally know where they've been since we last saw them."

Anna asked, "Are they missing or something?"

"Essentially, yes." He looked at them as if something had just occurred to him. "You say that you've never heard of them. How is it that possible?"

Matt glanced at the others, but no one answered. "Why is that surprising?"

"There must be some connection between this world and yours," started Lorian, "for the summoning spell to have brought you. Their existence must therefore be known there, and they are a legend on every world to which they are known. You therefore should have heard of them."

"Well, I don't think anyone's heard of them back home." Matt was tempted to make observations about the lack of magic and knights and all that, but decided not to get into it. He wondered how the champions could have ever been to Earth, not to mention recently. Magic, had it ever existed, had died out centuries ago. Then again, that was pure speculation as much as anything else. Maybe people secretly practiced it. "Are all these worlds they go to places of magic, knights, castles...elves?"

"Yes, of course." Lorian paused. "Is your world not such a place?"

Ryan snorted. "No. There's nothing like this on Earth."

The elf asked, "Earth? Is that the name of your world?"

"Yes," Anna replied more politely, frowning at the knight.

Lorian looked at the big man. "This would explain your disbelief that I am an elf?" Ryan nodded, and the elf looked at him curiously. "But you say elves don't exist there and yet you've heard of what an elf is."

Eric said, "Yes, we *have* heard of elves, dwarves, dragons, and magic, but they aren't real in our world."

Lorian spread his slender hands. "But then how could you have heard of them?"

A long pause followed that. Matt figured that the likely reason was that storytellers and authors had invented them, but elves were real on Honyn. How could they be real in one place and an invention of the mind in another, and yet be so similar? They had to be the same, which meant that somewhere on Earth, at least in the past, elves, dwarves, dragons and all manner of fabled beings had really existed. And maybe still did.

He remarked, "That's a good question, especially considering we were clearly summoned by magical means from Earth. Magic must work there after all."

"I don't know about that," disagreed Anna. "The magic was performed here on Honyn. Besides, it could've just been technology we don't understand, remember?"

Eric shook his head. "Whatever it was, I assume it had to work on both sides, so if it was magic here then it was magic there. You know, if magic works on Earth, people could hide that fact as long as they avoid doing it in public, but elves, dwarves, and dragons would be hard to hide."

Lorian suggested, "The dragons could have been banished from your world as well."

Matt perked up. "That's true."

Nodding, Eric admitted, "Yes. And technically, dwarves exist. There have always been little people on Earth."

Anna nodded. "They don't act like that, though, living underground, the long beards, being grumpy."

The elf smiled at her and turned toward Ryan. "But no elves?"

The big man spread his empty hands as if to apologize. "'Fraid not."

"There are a lot of deep forests that are seldom traveled," Matt started, "so they could always be hiding in there."

"I don't think that's so true anymore," Eric said, "but anyway this is all beside the point."

Lorian nodded. "Another thing I want to know is where you were when summoned."

"A place called Stonehenge," said Matt. "It's an ancient monument thousands of years old. No one knows what it was really designed for."

"Describe it, please."

"It's a circular monument in an open field, with giant monoliths of stone standing upright, some with other stones on top, connecting them."

Lorian seemed to think he'd said enough. "It sounds like a Quest Ring. Most look roughly the same, being circular monuments, similar to where you found yourselves upon arrival. Champions are summoned to a Quest Ring on every world and is usually the place from which they depart for home. Magic words are embedded into the material from which the Ring is made—usually stone."

Matt glanced at the others. That sounded a little too familiar. "There were words in the stone, but they usually weren't visible." He described what happened when the words of fire erupted and they vanished.

The elf gazed at him thoughtfully. "Interesting. That suggests they were on a quest on Earth, but you were sent back instead. Maybe they're still there."

Eric asked, "Do they need to be in a, uh, Quest Ring, to be summoned, like we apparently were?"

"No," said the elf. "They could be anywhere, be separate from each other, even on different worlds. The spell brings them together, delivering them to the Quest Ring of those summoning them. However, the summoning spell would fail if they were engaged with another quest. It may have been coincidence that you stood at that particular Quest Ring when summoned."

Matt absorbed that in silence like the others before the elf broke this thoughts.

Lorian said, "Something of more immediate concern is that Cirion of Ormund and his mercenaries spoke with each of you last night, probably to glean information." Matt saw blank looks on everyone's face except Anna's. She looked startled. Lorian elaborated. "Cirion danced with Eriana while his young wizard, Raith, spoke with Soliander at some length. Nola, an exceptional warrior in her own right, targeted Korrin and nearly succeeded with some design, from what I understand." His eyes met Ryan's and the knight flushed. Lorian turned to Eric. "Andier was not a target except as Cirion could get you distracted, as your predecessor's ability to spot trouble is legendary. A parade of lovely women sought your attention at Cirion's behest."

It was Eric's turn to look startled, then a little embarrassed, even angry. Maybe resentful. Then something seemed to occur to him. "The dashing man who danced with Anna?"

"Yes," said Lorian.

"Who is he?" Anna asked. "What does he want?" She blushed after asking and Matt knew what she was thinking because he'd watched them. Cirion couldn't have been more obvious about one desire and he stifled a smirk.

"One of this world's would-be heroes," began the elf, "who try to earn a name with quests. He hides his questionable ways well, understanding appearances. Others of his ilk have demonstrated their misguided attempts to reach the Dragon Gate, which is no doubt his aim as well. Cirion's mercenaries arrived hours before you and were no doubt unhappy with your arrival, for it should have signaled the end to their aspirations, but it seems they were intent on interfering with you in some way." He looked at Korrin pointedly.

The big man looked uncomfortable. "But I thought she just…" He trailed off and then flushed, seeming indignant, then angry. Matt had never seen the big guy mad before. He looked especially dangerous standing there in that golden armor, a sword on one hip. Matt knew he was a gentle giant, but if Ryan could learn to put on that face on purpose, that and Korrin's reputation might stop some people from messing with him.

Anna asked, "What happened? Did I miss something?"

Ryan and Eric exchanged a look, making Matt wonder what passed between them.

"She lured me to her rooms under the guise of…" Ryan hesitated. "Of making me feel better about having killed that man, but Eric stopped me at her door." Anna let out a slow breath through her nose. Ryan heard it and met her disapproving eyes before looking away. "I'm sorry for wandering off," he said sincerely. "I know we promised to stick together. It won't happen again."

"It had better not," Anna replied quietly.

Rescuing the knight, Matt changed subjects. "That wizard was asking me how to manipulate the gate, but I didn't know anything to tell him even if I'd wanted to."

"Cirion wanted to lead us to the castle," said Anna, "but I refused him. He also said he'd been inside, not long after the, uh, champions left, but he couldn't get by some sort of maze. Do you know what we might run into?"

Lorian nodded. "Mostly Dragon Cult members. I suspect Soliander's traps have been dispelled by whoever opened the Gate. If not, the way will be harder."

A nearby bird call prompted an elf to enter from the balcony, exchange a look with Lorian, and return. "Attention has begun to focus on your presence," said Lorian.

CHAPTER SEVEN

WIZARDRY

As he always did, the dark elf hesitated three strides from the richly carved mahogany door of his master. Fantastic scenes of dragons, knights, and wizards doing battle graced its surface, but none were more heart-stopping than what he had personally seen in the room beyond. Daunting forces had been summoned by the wizard within, and despite the ferocity of each, whether it be demons, wraith lords, or even minor deities, the wizard had commanded obedience. The thought reminded the elf not to falter in his devotion, for an urgent message had arrived at the black, looming castle.

He was a dark elf, so called to distinguish his kind from wood elves, those beings of light and goodness, the very thought of which made his lip curl in a sneer. There was power to be had in darkness, and it was his kind that sought to harness it. Long ago they had given themselves up to it and found their skin turning nightmare black, the hair whiter than the palest moonlight, eyes of blood red staring from their now sinister features. The same delicateness of wood elves remained, but what passed for a tender, supple nose there gleamed sharp like the blade of a dagger here. So, too, with their grace, no longer like a breeze through the trees but like a knife sliding into flesh. Dark things were their province, and yet what lay beyond the door was darker than anything his kin sought. All seemed still at the moment, but that could change in an instant.

Steeling himself for the unknown, he quietly rapped on the door, which opened silently, orange firelight washing over him from within. As he entered, a quick glance confirmed no magic was afoot, though the dark granite floor bore the residue of powdery markings inside a circle of still-flickering candles. Bookcases full of ancient tomes lined two walls, vials, jars, and jugs of every shape filling another. Bright flames roared in the hulking stone fireplace, and an enormous black desk seemed to cast a pall over the room. Behind it sat a slim figure in a dark robe, unremarkable in its lack of adornment, and yet anyone trained in magic would have taken notice of the man at once. The reek of power coming from him struck like a blow.

The sorcerer bent over a large tome, his features lost in the shadows, a gold orb of swirling colors on a small stand beside him. The room was far too dark to read, but the words and drawings were written in light. The dark elf waited for what seemed like an eternity, a line of sweat trickling down his back while he fought to remain still and silent. Only a fool reminded the wizard of their presence. Finally the wizard favored him with a glance.

In a quavering voice, the dark elf said, "My lord, I have important news."

The master commanded, "Speak it."

"The Queen of Alunia on Honyn attempted to summon the great Ellorian Champions."

The sorcerer interrupted in derision. "She's hardly the only one. Even children attempt this."

"Yes, my lord," the dark elf answered, knowing it was a common fantasy of children, "but she was successful."

The wizard's head snapped up. "What?"

"She was—"

"I heard what you said," the robed figure interrupted. "What do you mean? Be specific."

The elf steadied himself. "The four champions answered the summons and are embarking on a quest."

The wizard frowned inside the hood. "Four? Not three?"

The elf felt confused, wondering at that but knowing better than to ask. He'd seen those who didn't know their place burned to a crisp or frozen and then shattered on being toppled to the floor. "Yes, four of them."

"And they claim to be Eriana of Coreth, Andier of Roir, Korrin of Andor, and Soliander of Aranor?"

"Yes." The elf paused, then ventured, "There has been no suggestion in Olliana that they are imposters."

Only silence greeted this, for the dark magus was not one to share his thoughts. "What is the quest?" he asked, fingers touching on a newly fashioned amulet of priceless, bluish steel, made from a rare material that the dark elf knew no one else had ever possessed.

"To banish the dragons again. The device holding them—"

"Yes, yes, I know what happened." He waved a dismissive hand.

The elf wondered how the dark magus could have known, but he was often aware of things transpiring far away.

"When did they embark on the quest?"

"They have yet to do so."

"Leave me."

As the dark elf turned toward the door, his eyes darted to the rosewood cabinet in one corner, where no one dared go. Those with magic power could sense the foreboding protection around it, and those without power just felt unwell the closer they got. He suspected a demon guarded it, for he had a bracelet that pulsed when one was near and had discreetly tested it just by wearing it into this chamber. He knew better than to even look too long, for he'd seen a man killed for that. But this was the first time he'd been in here in some days and he had the unmistakable impression that the cabinet had been disturbed. As he closed the door behind him, he risked a glance at the wizard and saw glaring eyes on it, lips set in a resolute grimace.

—◆·◆·◆—

In the azure sky high above Castle Olliana, the white wizards' tower drew hopeful eyes to it like none other, for the tower's residents were known to practice their art from its highest reaches, creating fantastic displays for anyone lucky enough to be watching. Those within had a rare sight to behold, too, for the topmost windows provided view of the swaying green treetops of the Great Honyn Forest and the jagged, snowcapped peaks in the distance. In the last fortnight, Sonneri had spent many hours watching those peaks for dragons. Even with magical vision enhancements that put telescopes to shame, nothing unusual had appeared to magical watchers like the one he now stood instructing for a different purpose.

"I want you to discreetly follow them," said the wizard to the black crow, whose impassive black eyes stared back with unusual intelligence. "It's imperative you not be detected. The rogue is likely to be just as alert as the stories say, and the elves are wise to such surveillance."

"Of course," squawked the bird, impatient. This wasn't the first time it had spied on people.

Sonneri fixed it with a serious stare, used to more respect. "Keep your distance, for the wizard's magical sense is formidable and extends farther than you'd ever imagine. Change your shape each time you come near them."

The crow became a robin, then a mockingbird, and finally a peregrine falcon, and he nodded, satisfied.

"Report back often and don't dawdle in the elven lands."

The falcon bobbed as if bowing and turned on the pine perch before launching itself through the open window. Sonneri stepped to the window, reaching out for its bronze handle. A loud brass fanfare rang out far below and he peered down into the teeming courtyard, where a throng of people cheered. It seemed the Ellorian Champions were leaving.

⚬ ⚬ ⚬

Castles weren't designed with dragons in mind. That much was obvious. Even well-kept keeps kept their occupants only one step ahead of discomfort, the hard stones cruel surroundings. Drafty, ruined castles fared worse for the lack of upkeep, though they did have the advantage that if you felt compelled to knock down a wall or rip through the ceiling with your claws, no one would complain, but there was only so much you could do to one and leave it standing. Interior decorating dragon-style had its limits.

Even with her recent modifications to the long-abandoned Castle Darlonon, Perndara the dragon was grumpy. The Grand Hall was big enough for her enormous bulk, and the hole in the floor a good place to dangle her barbed tail, but she wanted to be outside. Dragons weren't meant to be indoors any more than castles were meant to be their homes, and she desperately wanted to fly again. She'd been spotted last time, however, and though she'd devoured most of those hunters, one had gotten away and Nir'lion hadn't exactly been amused with the result. Now their plans – well, all the plans were really Nir'lion's – had been ruined and Nir'lion was off dreaming up some way to turn the situation to her advantage.

In fact, just this morning, news had come that the Ellorian Champions were on their way. Perndara's spirits had soared for the first time since Nir'lion had practically torn her golden scales from her thick hide. Shortly after the pair first escaped through the Dragon Gate, Nir'lion learned of the champions' apparent disappearance, threatening the revenge she so badly wanted. But now that goal had returned.

Perndara had been so happy that she'd roasted the poor messenger and then slurped him down in one gulp, savoring the flavor of fresh human. That was a chief complaint about the land of their banishment, there being nothing but wild livestock. Dragons loved to play with their food, and nothing fought back like sentient races. Humans were good, dwarves not so much with all that nasty hair, but the elves were delicious, the marrow sweeter and more succulent than even their blood, which was like wine. She was pleased to know some elves were expected for supper in a few days.

She had to avoid eating too many of these Dragon Cult members in the ruin, however, though the stupid fools seemed to consider it an honor. The cult had never been bright. They knew enough not to flaunt danger, however, and had been avoiding her when in dragon form. It was one reason she changed now, her large body shimmering briefly as she vanished like an illusion. In her place stood an elegant woman of exceptional beauty, golden hair tumbling to her slender waist, full breasts straining against the silken gown, and jewels of shining brilliance about her sinuous neck. The only hints of her true nature were the golden eyes that faded slowly to pale green. As all dragons could, she snuffed the sensation of magical power emanating from her so as to pass for human. But as she had with those hunters, sometimes letting the power exude had its advantages.

Perndara slowly climbed a staircase at one end to look down on the Dragon Gate. A large oval nearly twenty feet high and twice as wide, it lay on its stand almost flat, tilted toward the blue sky. Dragons were pulled down into it through the ragged opening in the castle roof, the crumbled ceiling having made this an ideal spot for the gate. Newer rubble had lain scattered about the floor – most likely Soliander's doing when setting up this device – until she'd ordered the cult to move it to a corner. They had dutifully cleaned everything but the gate upon her order. The last thing she wanted was the door to their prison kept in good shape. If she could have destroyed it, she would have, but it was impervious to her magic or dragon fire. She had no idea what it was made of and hadn't seen anything like it. It was unadorned except for a peculiar looking hole above the three steps at its base. She surmised this related to its activation but wasn't really interested. Once the dragons were free, they'd bury the thing under tons of rock. For now, they waited, the force of Nir'lion's will strong enough to keep the remaining dragons on the other side despite the door being open.

The sight of the gate renewed her thirst for vengeance. She'd been told not to harm the champions too much, for Nir'lion wanted them alive. After all, these were the four who'd trapped them these long years, and revenge was to be had slowly. Still, accidents were known to happen, especially with such powerful forces being tossed about, and Perndara was in fact known to be somewhat careless. That's how she'd come to be seen flying over the tall peaks, so it wouldn't be too surprising if one of the heroes met an untimely end. Yes, that's how she'd put it to Nir'lion. The knight had simply not been fast enough. He was unable to escape her fiery breath, or a sweeping claw, or the clamp of her long fangs on his tender flesh.

She had healing powers, like all dragons, and was prepared to answer the question as to why she didn't heal the knight after accidentally wounding him. In the heat of battle, she'd say, she was too distracted and hadn't noticed the grievous nature of his wounds. Oh, and the priestess Eriana, well, she had been knocked unconscious during the melee and unable to heal the knight. By the time she roused, he had perished.

And it had to be the knight, if for no other reason than that title he proudly wore, that of Dragon Slayer. She would see about that. If this puny human thought he'd be slaying a dragon here, he was in for a surprise. More importantly, it was he who truly led them, regardless of any counsel or help from the others. It was that knight who had guided them into this banishment, she was sure of it, and for that he was to pay with his life. Nir'lion would have to settle for the other three and Perndara's best rendition of an innocent apology from a timid, careless, twit of a dragon who was nothing of the sort. She knew perfectly well what she was doing and the wrath that would come with it, but let it come. It would be worth it. Lord Korrin of Andor was going to die screaming in her fanged mouth.

CHAPTER EIGHT

AFFINITY

As the horses cantered into a stand of evergreens, Olliana disappeared behind them and with it, a kingdom full of hope. Ryan breathed a sigh of relief, settling in to enjoy a ride through beautiful country. He'd been an avid horseman for years, but his friends looked quite out of place. Anna had some experience, but the elves had taken the reins from Matt and Eric, leading them along for now. Some basic horsemanship lessons were in order.

An embarrassing fanfare had accompanied their departure. Beyond the blaring horns, crowds of people had lined the streets to see them off. Some threw bouquets of flowers to Anna and garter belts to the men, particularly Lord Korrin. Outwardly, Ryan had appeared to enjoy the attention, hiding his consternation. The number of people depending on them daunted him, and he'd settled for waving and concentrating on holding the lance in his stirrup, the deep blue banner snapping in the warm breeze. On it, a golden dragon breathed fire toward a fearless golden knight. He hoped the depiction was pure fiction but began to rethink his decision to stay behind, for all the looks of hope, especially on children's faces, made him realize all these people were counting on him in particular. The thought of letting them all get killed wasn't acceptable, his loathing of violence notwithstanding. He suddenly felt selfish.

There'd been no sign of Cirion, Nora, or Raith, which both worried and relieved him. An unseen troublemaker wasn't good. He doubted they'd simply turned tail and gone home. If headed for the gate as expected, maybe Cirion's mercenaries would spring any traps the cult had set for them. It would serve them right.

Cirion wasn't likely to arrive first, however, for his mercenaries couldn't take Lorian's shortcut, which shaved two days off the eight-day trip to Castle Darlonon. Lorian's family controlled that area, his estate in its center, and the elf sent a messenger to warn of wayward humans matching a certain description. Cirion, and anyone associated with him, weren't welcome in the elven woods, where borders had been tightened in advance of war. He could try anyway, but elves appeared to be far less amused by smart talking rogues than humans were. Since only the queen knew they'd visit Lorian's estate, they'd spend one day there, still arriving at Darlonon a day before expected. It gave them time to learn self-defense, at least.

For the first day, they rode in silence through open fields and peaceful autumn foliage, reflecting on the situation and what might be happening back on Earth in their absence. The days on Honyn seemed shorter, the nights longer – and the season happened to be the same – but Ryan's friends could have sworn this day in the saddle lasted forever. At times only the frequent moaning broke the quiet.

"Oh man," said Eric during a break, standing beside the horse and holding onto the saddle to keep from crumpling to the ground. "My legs are rubber. I would've thought all the martial arts would've had me in better shape. How am I supposed to fight anything when I can't even stand?"

"Nothing prepares you for so much riding except riding. You'll limber up after a few more days, Eric," Ryan advised. Despite his experience, his legs hurt, too, but he refused to admit it.

"I seriously doubt that."

Lorian asked. "Is that your real name? Eric?"

The rogue nodded. "Yes. I guess we had better tell you our names to avoid confusion."

The elf suggested, "On the contrary, you should use your assumed names, and only those, in case someone overhears you. And if no one else knows your real names, we can't use them by accident."

"Good point," agreed Eric, wincing.

The cobblestone roads near Olliana soon gave way to dirt as they pushed hard across rolling hills and wooded trails. Their band of armor-clad elves and humans attracted no attention until stopping at a roadside inn for the night. Firelight shone through ground floor windows, two chimneys pumping smoke into the starry sky. As Ryan looked for constellations he knew wouldn't be there, he thought the stars shone brighter, whether from the lack of city lights and haze or just proximity. Among the stars drifted three moons, the best evidence they weren't on Earth so far, the impossibility of faking that sinking in. He took a deep breath, noticing the fresh air. Everything seemed more natural, from the unprocessed foods to the handmade garments, though the lack of modern accommodations, especially toiletries, almost negated any pleasure derived from that naturalness. The idea of spending twelve days on the quest frustrated him, for that was two weeks of knowing nothing about Daniel.

As they filed into the inn, the elves stabling the horses, Ryan secured four of the bedrooms for the four elves and four champions, as they'd be sleeping two to a room. In doing so, he flashed more gold – courtesy of the court – than the innkeepers probably saw in a year. Eric quietly suggested more discretion. The innkeepers were quick to realize their identities. Korrin's golden armor and Soliander's staff didn't help.

They gathered for a meager dinner in the inn's cramped common room, pushing two well-worn corner tables together for a meal of day-old bread, slightly stale ale, and tough beef, with apologies from their hosts. Ryan hadn't eaten such poor fare since he'd tried cooking for himself on a few misguided occasions, but he expected it would get worse once camping. The generous tip he gave was more charity than deserved, but the owners looked like they needed a break. He asked that they not be disturbed and got his wish.

Lorian had introduced his three elven companions along the way, but only one, Morven, chose to speak with them. At one hundred fifty years old, he was still a teenager among elves, making Ryan wonder if it was awful to be a teenager for so many decades. Tall and skinny, he showed none of the awkwardness of human teens, being all grace if not poise, brown hair flowing freely to his waist and sometimes across his delicate features, hiding shy green eyes. He spoke quietly if at all, as if unsure of himself, but his words nonetheless conveyed conviction in his thoughts. The elf's specialty was archery, yet another skill they lacked, and the knight wondered just how many skills the champions had that they didn't. If Morven and other elves didn't come with them, they'd never succeed or see Earth again.

While the others made small talk, Ryan pulled out the vellum scroll the real Soliander had written about their previous time here, unfurling the painted case to see a scribe's bold and elegant script. After skimming a few lines in the dim lantern light, he whistled and said, "Listen to this."

At the time of our summoning by the King of Alunia's arch-wizard, Aurilon, the dragons of Honyn were rampaging. Under the leadership of Nir'lion, the dragon horde had laid waste to hundreds of towns across Alunia and the neighboring lands, with Alunia suffering the worst. No village was too small to escape their fiery breath, no town too sacred, no outpost too remote. Castles, temples, schools, homes, and farms were equal targets under their wrath, and the only reprieve came when they had gorged themselves on humans, dwarves, and elves so fully that they could not continue for a time.

"They *eat* people?" Anna asked.

Ryan nodded slowly, thinking he'd always avoided swimming in shark-infested waters or going other places where humans were considered food.

Eric asked, "So Sonneri was not the arch-wizard at the time, and there was a King?"

Lorian nodded. "Yes, the king died several years ago, and his wife became queen. Shortly thereafter the wizard retired and has since perished. Sonneri was an apprentice of Aurilon's and long a confidant of the royal family. His assumption of the role at the queen's request went unchallenged."

Ryan turned back to the scroll, trying to keep his voice down so the serving girl wouldn't overhear.

With the countryside in disarray, people fled to the cities. As if waiting for this very thing, the dragons set upon these fortified population centers en masse. The city of Trisune in Nurinor was razed to the ground in just hours. Across the sea, the Empire of Perthia lost the great port cities of Gharili and Tuunark, and here in Alunia, Vollunia, Hexia, and Ferralon fell in quick succession, inspiring our immediate summoning.

As is usually the case, many great warriors and wizards sought to solve the problem prior to our arrival, to no avail. Upon our briefing, we made our own determination after investigating. Rampaging dragons do not respond to reason and cannot be subdued, and with Nir'lion's leadership keeping them engaged, this was especially true. We suspected that even with her death, the dragons, now used to their rampage, would continue for an unacceptable time before reverting to their usual "every dragon for itself" attitude. Thus, we determined that something must be done about all of them.

The quest as stated indicated we must not only halt present hostilities, but eliminate the possibility of such actions in the future. This latter item is an aggressive request, so much so that its improbability renders it potentially invalid. Such invalid quest requirements may be safely ignored, meaning the questors can still depart at the conclusion of the quest's other requirements. However, it is difficult to know this will be the case and it behooves us to make some attempt at resolution, even if the solution does not satisfy the exact parameter as stated.

We therefore decided upon banishment.

Ryan looked up, several questions on his mind.

As if reading his thoughts, Lorian offered, "Some quests are impossible to perform, and the summoning spell knows this, in a sense, and will make the summoning fail. However, some quests have multiple requirements where only part of the quest is impossible. Such requirements can be ignored by the champions. Other times, a requirement cannot be met as stated, but some approximation of it can be accomplished and the questors are obliged to achieve what they can. Sometimes this impossibility results from a poorly phrased requirement where the intention was not stated accurately, and it is up to the Ellorians to determine the true intent."

Anna remarked, "It reminds me of those genie-in-the-bottle stories where the genie grants the wish but it's never what you meant."

Ryan nodded and returned to reading Soliander's scroll aloud once more.

In my own travels, I had previously come across an uninhabited world suitable for the cause. It is lush with vegetation and wild stock, mountainous enough for dragon lairs, and yet no sentient races exist there, or even non-sentient humanoids. The dragons could live and thrive.

However, this world was not without concern. On it I had discovered a unique ore I named soclarin, an ancient magic word meaning "vessel of power." In addition to being impervious to the elements, such as fire and ice, it also resists magical energy, and yet magic items created with it are of significantly greater power. It was this ore that allowed me to create the Dragon Gate, a device powerful enough to not only banish the dragons but serve as a lock on the planet Soclarin. Only the most powerful of wizards can fashion items from it, but I am its discoverer and only I know how to do so.

For the banishment to be effective, neither dragons nor anything else should be able to leave Soclarin, since dragons can change shapes and impersonate other beings. However, locking a planet in this way takes tremendous energy. Without the soclarin ore, it would be extremely arduous if not impossible. However, choosing Soclarin as the place to banish them presented a problem for me, as I have used the ore to fashion other items and would no longer be able to access it once the gate was active. For this reason, I traveled there one last time to retrieve a suitable quantity of ore for the foreseeable future.

Two gates were created, one upon Soclarin and another here on Honyn in the ruined castle of Darlonon in the Tarron Mountains of Alunia. The Soclarin gate does not contain a lock for the obvious reason that the dragons have no need of operating it, and the Honyn gate locks both. I formed the Honyn gate in such a way that only my staff – or a similar item made of soclarin ore, of which I believe there to be none not in our possession – could unlock it. Items made from soclarin appear bluish grey or silver if fashioned into a blade, being lighter than expected and virtually indestructible.

The description reminded Ryan of Korrin's sword, which was bluish silver, unusually light, and had been completely unmarked after the sword fight in their suite. His opponent's sword had been badly nicked.

Eric leaned forward. "This says only Soliander could open the gate, or someone with a soclarin item, which again means him, unless someone stole something of his."

"Well, with him being missing," added Matt, "it's obviously not him, and since he's not around to guard his stuff, someone might've tried to steal something of his."

Morven shook his head, a brown lock of hair falling off his shoulder, green eyes moving from one champion to another. "The magical protection around his dwellings is reputed to be truly formidable and includes demons and the like. It would be madness to try."

Fingering the staff, Matt said, "I guess all we need to close the gate is this."

"Possibly," agreed Lorian, "but the staff usually facilitates spell casting and does not replace it. There might be more needed still." He frowned. "Since you have it, and the rest of you have their remaining items, they clearly do not also have them. It does not bode well for them."

"Maybe the spell is in one of the books." Matt pulled out one bound in red and silver and started flipping through it despite the unfamiliar language. Archaic-looking symbols graced many pages amidst probable directions and maybe ingredients for potions, identifiable by the quantities listed. Depictions of dragons, unicorns, monsters, and other mythical beasts – or maybe not so mythical – adorned the pages. Most of the text was in one of two scripts, the first aggressive and somehow suggestive of being ancient, the second smooth, elegant, and flowing, beautiful to look at even if not understood.

Lorian, who sat next to him, said quietly, "It is written in elvish."

"Why elvish?"

"It is common among human wizards to write spells in another language so that ordinary folk cannot understand them, whether it be the incantations or the accompanying descriptions. Most humans cannot read elvish."

"Yes, it's working, because I can't read any of it. These books aren't going to help me much."

"I can teach you both elvish and the language of magic, , Nu'Eiro."

Matt perked up. "Really?" Then his face fell. "How can I learn anything useful in a few days?"

"There are magical means to acquire the ability quickly," replied Lorian.

"That reminds me," Eric began, "I've been meaning to ask how we can all speak English, our language back on Earth, and you guys do, too. I know the worlds are connected, but it seems a huge coincidence."

The elf nodded. "You are not speaking English. Just as I can cast a spell to allow you to speak and understand another language, the summoning spell has this built into it. Soliander added this to make it easier for them. Otherwise they might often arrive somewhere and be unable to communicate. The summoners must specify what language is expected and the spell adjusts accordingly."

"This summoning spell sounds incredible," Matt remarked.

"It is, and among the most sophisticated spells ever cast. It is one reason the soclarin ore was needed to enable it."

Eric asked, "So then what language are we speaking?"

"Vortunon, the common tongue of this continent, of the same name."

"But I feel like I'm speaking English."

"That I cannot explain, but I would imagine that, now that you are aware of the difference, you could speak in English and switch back to Vortunen if you tried."

They exchanged a look, with Matt the first to say something in English. The others followed suit, then switched back to Vortunen.

Eric asked, "So if we're summoned elsewhere, we might gain the ability to speak that language?"

"Yes."

"Is this permanent?"

"I do not know."

"So if elves summon us..."

"You gain elvish."

Matt said, "Wow. That's awesome. I want to learn how to do this kind of spell."

Lorian chuckled. "As would many. First, I must test your affinity for magic to see whether you have anything more than the rudimentary powers everyone possesses. Otherwise there won't be much point in instructing you. I brought materials to administer the test." Lorian looked around the inn and added, "Now would be a good time if you are agreeable to it, but not here. Let us go upstairs."

Matt nodded and rose, taking the books and staff with him. Eric got up to go, too, gesturing for the others to remain. Matt looked at him inquisitively.

"No going off by ourselves, remember?"

Matt shrugged. Lorian appeared trustworthy but being cautious didn't hurt. Neither would a witness. Minutes later, Lorian and Matt sat facing each other in the elf's room, Eric watching with his back to the closed door. The floor creaked as he shifted to brighten a wall lantern. They weren't used to it being so dark inside at night. They needed to maximize the daylight hours, rising early. Being a night owl lost its appeal when there was nothing to do and you couldn't see anything.

From a woolen bag, Lorian retrieved a rectangular tray of black metal divided into four recessed squares, a split, recessed circle in the center. The elf placed the tray on a three-legged stool before pulling six glass vials out, one holding a deep red sand he poured into one corner, where it flattened by itself to form a level surface. That got Matt's attention. They had yet to witness anything supernatural after the summoning. Sparkling light danced from within the next vial as Lorian poured it into an adjacent space, where the liquid softly glowed. Another bottle of clear liquid seemed unremarkable until he poured it and it ignited into a low, golden flame. The next glass held a swirling, smoky atmosphere that drifted down to the fourth quadrangle, softly stirring as if alive.

"The four elements," realized Matt, wanting to touch them.

"Yes," Lorian approved.

"And in the center?"

"The essences of magic and spirit." Lorian held up a glass with a thick, glowing, golden liquid. It wasn't smooth like a fluid, but multifaceted like crushed foil. It slowly oozed into one half of the center circle, looking for all-the-world like solid gold. The last vial held a similar, shimmering liquid like molten silver.

"Which is which?" Matt asked, staring.

"The silver of the moons is of the spirit, which is why silver weapons hurt the undead. Magic, the fire of the soul, is golden." He took the tray in both hands and uttered several phrases that didn't sound elven from they'd heard today as the elves spoke among themselves. The tray glowed briefly. Then Lorian pulled out a small knife and gestured for Matt's hand, which the techie warily extended. "I need six drops of your blood, one at a time for each test."

"Why?" Matt asked, feeling lightheaded as the blade approached his fingertip. He'd seemingly been born averse to the sight of blood.

"It is the gateway to the soul," Lorian answered, "for how is the soul released except by the shedding or stilling of blood? It connects body and soul, and being part of both, allows us to touch your soul's magic energy through the flesh." He reached for Matt's hand and chose one finger to hold steady. The knife snaked out to slice a small cut before the wizard-to-be could flinch. Lorian pulled Matt's finger over the sand and gave a short squeeze. A single drop fell to the sand. After a moment, the red sand rose to form an elegant house, which then dissolved into a village of many houses, then a city, a continent, and finally a small planet showing continents and rotating on its axis.

"What does it mean?" Matt asked, the blood forgotten.

Lorian's wide eyes fell on him. "You have a strong connection to the earth. The weakest would see only a hut form, or a house. The stronger see a town, a city, maybe a kingdom."

Matt wasn't sure he wanted to understand the implication. "But, this shows a planet."

The elf nodded slowly. "I have only seen one stronger, showing many planets. It was Soliander himself."

Matt whispered, "Wow."

Eric shifted and Matt glanced at him, seeing a look of concern he didn't share. The rogue said, "I'd like the results of your testing known only to us."

Lorian said, "Very wise. Agreed. Let us proceed."

He pulled Matt's finger over the tray again, this time to the fire, which had been softly crackling. Another drop of blood fell, landing with a sizzle. The flames turned dark red, then brightened to orange, yellow, and finally a white so bright it hurt the eyes. Matt leaned back from the heat as arcs of white flame lashed out like a solar flare. Though the test concluded and cooled, the globe still spun slowly. A sun had formed.

"That was awesome." Matt breathed, anxious to see what the other tests did.

"Great power over fire," observed the elf, gesturing for him to proceed.

This time Matt squeezed out a drop himself. The fog stirred as shapes began to form. First were archaic-looking symbols he didn't recognize, then a dragon flying through the clouds, and finally his own face staring back. A swirl struck the visage and tore it apart, a spinning vortex growing wider as others formed, the tornadoes merging to form a huge hole of swirling blackness, the roaring air and thunder audible as cracks of lightning flashed light upon the watchers.

Matt recognized a hurricane from TV. A glance at Lorian confirmed his high level of affinity for air, too. "What did the symbols mean?"

"Symbols?" The elf looked confused. "Where?"

"In the fog," Matt answered. "It was right at the start, before my face appeared."

Lorian and Eric exchanged a look. Matt realized from their glances that only he had seen them. "Describe them," commanded the elf.

"On the left was a circle with a man inside it, lightning surrounding it. In the middle was a square with each line bowed inward toward a little star-like point in the middle, with something sticking out of it. The right one showed one sword piercing two hearts, each with a drop of blood falling from it. What do they mean?"

"I'm not sure," evaded Lorian, frowning. "The first two are unknown. The last is bleak."

"Meaning?" Eric asked.

"Death," Lorian announced, "though that could be death of an idea or a cause, not necessarily the one who sees the symbol. It can also mean rebirth. Its meaning is possibly changed by the others, but I do not understand them. What seems clear is that two lives will be at stake."

Matt sighed. Things kept getting more complicated. Hopefully this wasn't some sort of omen, especially since his life was likely one of those at stake.

"Please continue," suggested Lorian.

Matt squeezed a drop into the crystal water, which splashed upward to form a fountain from the blowhole of a whale that materialized beneath it. As the water descended, it formed a wooden ship-of-the-line as the whale vanished. The ship's sails unfurled with a snap and it surged forward on the wind, slicing through the white-tipped waves. Dolphins leapt ahead of it.

"That's amazing," said Matt.

"You can master water, if you desire," said Lorian, appearing impressed.

Matt wondered if he was jealous and how much power the elf had. Something occurred to the young wizard. "These keep showing great things, but what happens when someone is not gifted?"

"It varies from person to person," the elf replied, green eyes thoughtful, "and can sometimes be interpreted as fortune telling, though that is not its purpose and it cannot be taken literally. In the case of water, I once saw a whirlpool open and swallow the ship depicted. The fog has shown someone lost within, walking in circles, unable to find their way. The fire has shown nothing but charred ash. The signs of weakness or failure can be subtle, since these can be overcome and are uncertain, but the signs of power are unmistakable."

Eric asked, "How much interpretation is involved. What is the chance you are wrong?"

"It's always a possibility, but I see only signs of great potential here."

Lorian nodded at Matt, who squeezed a drop onto the silver, which reached up to catch the blood, then lay still. Smoke stirred on its cold, silvery surface, forming a floating torso and ghostly head with wild hair, two arms reaching toward Matt as the figure howled and shrieked. Two pinpoints of hateful red light looked into his. Then it stopped as if truly seeing the wizard for the first time. It became a peaceful, hooded figure with a bowed head and arms outstretched in supplication. But when its eyes, now blue, looked at Matt again, the figure turned and hurled itself away, slamming into an invisible wall along which it desperately slid, searching for escape. A low, terror-filled moan filled the room and gave way to a whimper as it raised one hand as if to ward off a blow.

"The dead will respect and fear you," remarked Lorian in amazement, "not the other way around. I have never seen such a reaction."

Matt wasn't so sure about that. The first figure had certainly made an impression on him. Then again, so had the last.

Lorian gestured to the gold liquid. "The final test, for magic, is the most important."

Too distracted by the fantastic to be concerned about blood, Matt eagerly squeezed out a last drop. It landed with a clink as if striking solid metal, and there it stuck, still shaped like a droplet. The gold beneath it simmered as if melting, the blood drop smoldering, then oozing out across the now molten surface and sinking. A hooded, robed, golden figure rose from within, carrying a staff topped with a crystal that burst forth with golden light that swirled around the room before settling on Matt as the figure knelt and bowed. It wasn't as spectacular, but Lorian gasped.

"The master wizard has bowed to you!" The elf's eyes were wide and he looked from Matt to Eric with what seemed like alarm. "I would not tell even your friends of these results. Even if you trust them with your life, others have means of extracting information from even the most determined captives."

Matt raised an eyebrow at Eric and received a nod of agreement. The young wizard trusted his opinion above all others. Both leery and eager, Matt asked, "Will you be able to teach me anything between now and the castle?"

"Certainly," the elf replied, thinking safety had to prevail, more so in Matt's case than usual. "We must prevent witnesses, however. After all, Soliander is not in need of instruction. Keep this private as well. We must be very careful, not only with the knowledge of your potential, but of your need for training."

"How dangerous is Matt?" Eric asked, arms folded, and the wizard-to-be looked at him in surprise. A look at Lorian showed the elf wasn't surprised by the question. He pursed his lips and appeared to choose his words carefully.

"Right now, he is not, and we must ensure that only those he wishes to harm are affected by anything he does."

Eric nodded and seemed to have heard what he expected.

They returned to the common room long enough for Lorian to suggest everyone retire for the night. As they filed back upstairs, Matt realized they hadn't divvied up the rooms yet, so he suggested Eric stay with him. He wanted to talk about the test and what it meant. He also felt safer with Eric around than anyone else. He'd always respected his friend, but after that martial arts display when they'd met the elf, this had soared. If they had a leader, it was Eric, who was more decisive than everyone else and more able to handle himself. Then again, after what Matt had learned about his potential, maybe he'd soon be the strongest of them all. He went to bed intending to fantasize his way into sleep and dreams of power.

CHAPTER NINE

ARUNDELL

Across the hall, Anna couldn't say the accommodations surprised her. The low, rickety cot was a far cry from the previous night's lodging. Getting accustomed to the lack of amenities would only worsen once the camping started, as she assumed it would in a day or two. The idea that it was all downhill from here and that she should be pleased right now made her smirk. Ryan had closed the door and dropped a sack of supplies beside his bed.

"Do you need help with your armor?" she asked, moving closer in the dim light.

"Not really, but you can help."

"Okay, what do I do?"

He showed her how to loosen the straps and unhook pieces, and as she removed the big back plate, she placed it on his bed, across from hers. She hadn't shared a room with any of the four before but trusted them, maybe Ryan more than the others. Or at least Eric. When a guy flirted with you as much as the rogue, you couldn't help wondering if there was something to it, even though he did it to every girl. That didn't necessarily mean it didn't mean anything.

"I think you can handle the rest. I'm going to change out of this robe. Just don't turn around."

"You don't want me to step outside?"

"No. I trust you. And I don't think I want to be alone except when using a chamber pot, and even then..."

Anna quickly changed into a sleeping gown with one eye on her companion, who never peeked, as expected. He had the honor part of being a knight down, at least. He busied himself stowing armor pieces in the sack.

"Okay," she started, "I'm done. Do you need any more help?"

He shook his head. "A man should take care of his own armor."

She rolled her eyes. "You and your 'man's work'. When are you going to join the rest of us in the 21st century?"

Indicating their surroundings, he remarked, "It's more like 13th century, so maybe I'm just being hip."

Amused, she said, "Next you'll tell me that women want a man to take care of them. We can take care of ourselves perfectly fine, you know."

"Maybe, but women like it when a man takes care of them, whether they admit it or not, and to be honest, I prefer the kind of women who admit it."

"Would you feel better if this quest was to rescue a princess?"

"Actually yes, I would," he admitted, closing the sack of armor. "Not only would I not have to kill a dragon, but she'd be grateful instead of resentful or something."

She teased, "Ah, I see. You just want her to sleep with you after you rescue her."

"No, though that never hurts," he joked. "I just like it when a woman lets a man be a man and she can be a woman herself, instead of fighting it."

"And what does accepting it mean? Being barefoot and pregnant?"

He scowled. "I never said that, and that's not what I mean."

"What *do* you mean?"

He sighed. "Not dressing like a man, and being feminine, for example. Being seen as a woman is not the bad thing some women make it out to be."

Anna had to admit he had a point but decided to end the banter. She climbed under the grey, wool blankets and rolled away from him. "Well, you can change now and I promise not to look. That way I won't see you as a man."

With a chuckle, he asked, "Afraid you'll enjoy it?"

She turned back and looked him in the eye. "Oh, I'm sure I would."

"Turn around," he ordered, smiling.

"As you command, my lord."

— ✦ · ✦ —

In the morning, Eric stood on weak legs and knew it was going to be a long day. Soreness set in despite the stretching he'd done the day before and before bed. The others had watched in amusement, but today it would be his turn to laugh. He peered through the dirty window, seeing the sky lightening to one side. He'd risen near dawn without an alarm. Life without a timepiece seemed more relaxed as long as he didn't have appointments or a schedule. In the castle, people had come to get them or wake them as needed, and he suspected Lorian would set their schedule from here onward, but he longed for a way to be certain of not oversleeping.

With Matt asleep, he tried to discreetly use the black, wrought-iron chamber pot, but the sound of a liquid stream hitting metal woke the techie, who rolled over and groaned.

"My legs hurt and I haven't even stood up yet," Matt complained, pulling sheets over his head.

"Maybe Anna can heal you," Eric replied helpfully.

"She doesn't believe in God, remember? How's she going to heal anyone?"

Eric grunted and buttoned his leather pants, which he'd slept in, though he normally slept in the buff. Then again, he lived in a temperature controlled environment, not a heat-impaired wooden inn. The court had given them sleeping gowns, but they weren't really appropriate for traveling and corny anyway.

"That's a good point. I hadn't thought of that." He sat on the bed to pull on his leather boots. "I'll leave so you can pee. I wonder what time checkout is." Matt smiled at his reference to Earth hotels.

"Check the weather on the TV while you're up, and please, please, please get me some coffee. I'm dying here."

"I didn't see a Starbucks," started Eric, heading for the door.

"You'd be surprised," Matt interjected. "They're everywhere so Honyn has to have one somewhere."

"I'll be downstairs checking my email at the concierge desk."

"We *are* the news," Matt remarked, laughing.

Eric paused as the truth of it struck him. They were indeed. And when they failed, they were also going to be the news.

This was not going to end well.

— ◆ ∙ ◆ —

In the Great Honyn Forest, a buck stepped quietly through the underbrush, picking its way so silently that any humans or elves wouldn't have noticed had they been near. The estate of Arundell lay just yards away, but those inside paid no heed to natural things moving beyond the wall surrounding it, for it was enchanted to let wildlife pass through and onto the grounds. The wall reformed behind the buck as it entered the grounds and it glanced over its shoulder as if acknowledging the wall's anomalous behavior.

As for the buck itself, it was of unusual coloring, being dark black with white streaks through its fur, with wicked antlers of ebony, and bold demeanor. It strode with a purposefulness uncommon in wildlife, even passing elderberry, greenbrier, holly, and other delights without a glance. Nearby white-tailed deer took one look at it and bolted, for something never before seen was not to be trusted. The buck spared them not a glance as it reached a clearing. In the distance, the rooftops of Arundell's manor appeared. With a bound of energy, the buck headed straight for them.

⚊ ✦ ✦ ⚊

A winding dirt road brought the champions to the crest of a hill overlooking the Great Honyn Forest, green treetops and pines stretching away, the craggy, snow-capped peaks of the dark Tarron Mountains on the horizon. The peaks' distance made Ryan realize he had days before his trial truly began unless something happened on the way there. And it likely would, for Lorian confirmed that ogres, orcs, goblins and other fantasy creatures they'd heard about existed in the woods they now cantered into, on alert for trouble.

Hours later, only a tree blazed with a head of two pointed ears indicated they'd entered elven lands, no enormous trees with a city built high into them in sight, for only Noria stood this way. Ryan's desire to quickly get home to Daniel muted his hopes to visit later if they survived this quest; a bad dream about his brother had upset him.

As night approached, they stopped in the trail, Lorian turning to one side and speaking a strange word while flashing an amulet. The tall grass parted and low hanging branches lifted up and back to reveal a wrought-iron gate with the elven word "Arundell" carved in gold above it. The gates swung inward, and the elf rode his horse through, the others following. Ryan glanced behind to see the gates closing, foliage returning to position.

They entered a wide clearing with deer grazing, a herd of elk drinking from a pond farther off, and elves playing various war games on the lawn. Covering hundreds of acres, the property had a river, archery range, riding trails, its own farm and winery, plus separate buildings for staff, guests, and the manor house. The latter stood atop a hill, a garden twice its size surrounding it and threatening to consume it entirely, gazebos, trellises, and walking trails amidst natural spring fountains and fish-filled pools. Trees that seemed to stand behind the house from a distance were actually inside and poking through the roof.

Stopping by the stables, Lorian remarked, "I know you're weary of riding, but you three could benefit from instruction while here, preferably tonight." He indicated all but Ryan as elven stable boys took the horses away, house servants grabbing the saddle packs. Another elf tried to take Matt's staff until the techie waved him off. Then the elf went for the bag of spell books, and for a moment Matt let him before Eric caught his eye and shook his head.

Anna winced as she dismounted. "Can we start lessons tomorrow?"

Lorian looked amused. "Yes, but Andier should not wait. If there's to be fighting from horseback, you must be ready."

Eric's eyebrows rose as he and Anna followed the elf inside. "Is there expected to be any?"

"No, but you must be prepared for the unexpected."

"He sounds like a boy scout," observed Ryan to Matt, patting his horse farewell as they followed.

The wizard nodded. "He's probably light years ahead of any boy scout."

Ryan had been a decent scout but not taken it seriously, since practical application for all of it was hard to come by, but that was different now. "Maybe I can learn tracking from the elves or something," he said.

"Maybe you should," Matt began. "Eric, too, just in case something happens. We're completely dependent on them to get there and back. I mean, what if all the elves are killed?"

Ryan hadn't thought of that. How would they get back from Castle Darlonon? "I'll mention it to him," he answered, having a worse thought. *What if all of us are killed?*

Before dinner, they moved into separate but adjoining bedrooms with the softest pillows, comforters, and sheets Anna had ever known. After the attack in the castle and with so many people around, she had never felt comfortable there. Something about this elven estate was beyond peaceful, and she drifted off.

In the meantime, Eric suffered through some basic horsemanship lessons from Morven, focusing on forward propulsion and direction control. The fine balance he'd honed via martial arts paid off as he kept a good seat and control with his hands. Still, any experienced rider could see the mistakes, from moving his hands too much to poor leg position. Every time he focused on one thing at Morven's reminder, something else went wrong. As he got off, Morven suggested continuous lessons during the quest and the rogue quietly muttered to himself as he walked away.

Wearing the finery given to them by Queen Lorella, they were greeted by a surprise when they gathered for dinner. Before leaving Olliana, Lorian had sent for a dwarven friend to meet them here. Rognir of Vodavi not only lived in the dwarven community in the nearby Tarron Mountains, but knew the land around Castle Darlonon and had been inside. The dwarves had built it for Kingdom Alunia long ago, so he'd learned its layout and secrets the last time the champions came.

Rognir made an impression despite being just four feet tall. His bulbous nose was the most obvious feature of his rough-hewn face, which was so covered in bushy black eyebrows, a mustache, and a waist-long beard that his gray-as-stone eyes were almost invisible. The pointed steel helmet tucked under one arm had mashed his hair down more on his face, if that was possible. He wore a stained, grayish blue tunic over a chain mail shirt and stiff trousers that were tucked into hard leather boots, which had seen better days. They were covered in dirt, grass, and leaves, as if he'd walked through everything without discrimination.

Seeing their stares, Rognir scowled hard enough to split stone and gruffly barked, "Have you no manners? What are you staring at? Have you never seen a dwarf before?"

Matt was the first to recover. "Uh, actually, no."

"There are no dwarves on their home world," Lorian informed him, "or elves for that matter."

"What?" The dwarf was outraged, eyes afire. "No dwarves? Don't tell me it's all *humans*!"

"All humans," Ryan confirmed. "Not a bearded, short-tempered, hairy dwarf to be found."

"Short-tempered!" Rognir snapped, turning on the big man. "I'll show you short tempered." He reached over one shoulder as if for a weapon that wasn't there. Realizing this, he squared his shoulders and advanced all the same. "I don't need more than a fist to teach you a lesson anyway!"

Ryan remarked, "Careful, my knees can't take too much."

The dwarf sputtered as if struggling to think of a reply. Finally, he burst forth with a hearty laugh and slapped Ryan's arm. "Let's get some ale first, then we'll fight. My aim is better drunk." He turned toward the dining hall and headed off.

Ryan flashed a smile at the others. "I like him."

Eric nodded. So did he. Maybe having someone for Ryan to banter with would keep the knight from any dark moods, which seemed to come and go, a fact that struck him for how peculiar it was. Ryan had always had a sunny disposition, though Eric had noticed that there had always been something troubling behind it, though he could never figure it out. The sadness always surrounded Daniel, which wasn't surprising, but he got the impression there was more to it. But now Ryan clearly felt the weight of something on him, likely the man he'd accidentally killed. Eric wanted to talk to him about it but wasn't sure where to begin and had settled for just keeping an eye on the big guy, whose tendency to keep troubles to himself was more apparent now than ever. But maybe that wouldn't work, given their circumstances. They needed each other.

The group continued to a richly carved hall with a large oak tree growing out of one side. The sloping glass ceiling let fading daylight stream down while they feasted on wild boar, pheasant, fruits, spiced vegetables, steaming bread, spiced ale, and a rather strong elven wine. Rognir encouraged Ryan's drinking a little too much considering the quest before them, to Eric's unspoken disapproval. He exchanged a look with Anna, sensing she agreed. But they weren't going anywhere tomorrow and would instead focus on skill development and planning.

Rognir had been filled in on their imposter status, since he'd also known the true Ellorian Champions and wouldn't have been fooled. Lorian permitted no talk of this until after dinner, when they moved to a more private chamber, the doors locked. Eric surmised that even though elves were generally trustworthy and of good nature, the truth was a secret from the household staff. The oak-paneled room offered more privacy as they gathered around a long oak table with rounded corners and matching, high backed chairs with green cushions.

Getting right down to business, Lorian tried to bring the dwarf up to speed by remarking, "My understanding from Soliander and the scroll is that there is no way to free the dragons from the inside, so someone on Honyn had to do it."

"Who would do that, and why?" Anna asked, sipping her glass.

Rognir's grey eyes fell on her. "A better question is who *could* do that. The spells Soliander wove around the device were strong, and he was one of the most powerful wizards on any world. To dispel them and reach the gate would require equal skill, such as wielded by only three men on Honyn."

"Who?" Ryan interrupted, lifting his drink.

"Rohr of Marillon, Dieranon of Kianna, and Sonneri of Olliana," the dwarf replied.

Ryan's goblet stopped halfway to his mouth. "The queen's wizard?"

"Yes," answered Lorian. "Given the speed of the attacks on you after your arrival, he seems a likely suspect, for the others would not have learned of your arrival for days."

"But why would he summon us to stop the dragons if he's the one who freed them?" Ryan asked.

"Because they never meant the summons to work," Eric reminded him.

"Correct," agreed Morven, chiming in.

Rognir added, "You were attacked within hours, so whoever ordered it had to arrange it quickly, and know where you were staying. If it was not Sonneri, then it is possibly conspiracy from within the court, maybe someone secretly in league with the Dragon Cult."

"Great," muttered the knight, frowning, "we can't even trust those who brought us here. Maybe we should just tell everyone the truth."

Lorian shook his head. "I'm afraid that won't do any good. Whoever wants the champions dead would extend that to you now."

"Why?" Eric asked, not liking it.

"For any number of reasons, including an assumption you know their whereabouts. You have inherited their identities and now their enemies."

Great, the rogue thought. It had seemed a simple thing to play along until they knew what to say or do, but it was getting increasingly out of control. How many enemies did the real champions have after disrupting the world domination plans of countless evil bad guys on one world after another? Powerful people had powerful enemies.

As if thinking the same thing, Anna remarked faintly, "I hope we've inherited their friends, too."

Rognir winked at her. "You certainly have, my dear. You certainly have."

"You know," started Matt, "whoever stole the original scroll knows about this soclarin ore and has a motive to open the gate, to get the ore, so they can make strong magic items from it."

Ryan asked, "Yeah, but how would they open the gate unless they already have something made from soclarin?"

"Maybe they stole something of Soliander's first," the wizard answered. "You know, maybe someone stole the scroll, learned of the ore, stole something of Soliander's to access the gate, got past the spells at the castle, then opened the gate, and then went inside to get more ore."

"You might be on to something," Eric admitted. "Then again, if they can steal Soliander's stuff, why do they need to go through all the trouble to get to the raw ore when they've got his stash?"

"That's a good question," Matt admitted, frowning. "Maybe they wanted to make different items than what Soliander created."

Eric turned to Lorian. "Are all of these wizards able to travel between worlds? Maybe they went to Soliander's, uh, tower, or something, and tried to get in."

The elf nodded slowly. "Yes, they can."

"Sonneri had access to the scroll," observed Eric, "but no reason to steal it. He could've read it and just put it back, so in a way it suggests it wasn't him."

A brief silence followed before Anna observed, "Or that both he and another wizard know about it, so it could be either of them. He also could've arranged to have it stolen so he wouldn't be suspected."

"Very cunning," admitted Rognir, puffing on his pipe, "but not unreasonable."

Eric nodded but remarked, "We should focus on the most obvious explanation as being the likely one."

"The Dragon Cult was suspected in the theft," Lorian remarked, "since the scroll contains details on the gate and might presumably aid in opening it but does not."

"How many people knew about the scroll?" Eric asked. "That narrows the suspect list."

Morven replied, "We have no way of knowing."

"What about the other two wizards?" the rogue asked. "Have they been mysteriously absent or showing signs of powerful magic items that can't be explained?"

Lorian answered, "Not that we know of."

Frustrated, Ryan drained his goblet and said, "Okay, so we know the dragons are out but didn't release themselves, and there's one at Castle Darlonon. Has there been any word of some wizard walking around there? He'd be the one who did it."

Rognir cocked an eyebrow. "No, but we only know of Nir'lion because she was spotted flying. If the perpetrator is there, he has not revealed himself. It is possible that a wizard of great power is lying in wait for our arrival."

The four friends exchanged alarmed looks.

"Doesn't anyone have any *good* news?" Ryan asked in exasperation.

Lorian advised, "A complement of elves will take this quest with you, some quite well-versed in magic, and all skilled warriors. We also have a trained dragon slayer with us. You may not be the champions Olliana expected, but together we will fulfill this quest."

Eric wasn't so sure but was glad for the help. Otherwise they'd never see Earth again or return to their lives. All of this was far beyond intrusive, their lives put on hold in the meantime. It reminded him of something.

"I have a question," the rogue started, slouching. "The champions couldn't refuse a summons or a quest, but why would they put themselves in that position? How were they supposed to live their lives?"

Lorian nodded. "I have often wondered the same, but they did not discuss their reasons. I know they sometimes aren't happy with disruption caused by the timing of a given summons, but they put on a good face."

Ryan said, "It sounds like they didn't want to do it any more than we do."

Matt suggested, "Maybe someone forced them into the quests, just like us."

After a long pause, Lorian remarked with some surprise, "Four people of such power could not be easily compelled to do things they don't want to do."

Eric thought Matt was on to something. If they'd found a way out of it, that would explain why they weren't answering anymore. Maybe that was why he and the others had taken their place, but it didn't explain their disappearance, or the substitution really. More importantly, if they were true replacements, were they also now to be repeatedly summoned and unable to refuse? The idea alarmed him.

A soft knock turned their attention to the door and an elf discreetly opening it, carrying a pine tray of several wines and chopped fruits. Eric noticed that the intrusion surprised Lorian. He recognized the elf as the one who'd tried to take Matt's staff and magic books on arrival. The servant was unremarkable save for the white streaks in his otherwise black hair.

"Did they ever try to leave without completing a quest?" Eric asked, realizing too late that perhaps he should've waited until the newcomer left, but Lorian seemed unconcerned.

Watching the servant set the tray on the table, Morven replied, "Not to our knowledge. At the least, it would have looked quite unhero-like."

"I suppose so." Eric hadn't thought of that. "My point is that if they never tried, how did they know they couldn't?"

Lorian nodded as the servant began passing out the fruit bowls. "Assuming you're right and they were compelled against their will, it's possible that early in their adventures they tried and discovered it wouldn't work, but that is conjecture."

"I guess we'll never know," Anna remarked, sighing, "unless we find them and ask." Something seemed to occur to her. "Has anyone gone looking for them?"

"Yes," replied Morven. "But they have not been found."

Rognir said, "The fact remains that they disappeared altogether and have not returned to their home world. They have friends and family, of course. There have been no sightings of them anywhere."

"So they are missing," observed Ryan.

The dwarf nodded.

"Presumed dead?"

"No," answered Lorian, "it is not easy to presume such a thing about four such capable people."

"Imprisoned?"

"Also unlikely, but less so."

Ryan asked irritably, "Then what? What is most likely?"

Eric let the others do the talking, as the servant had caught his attention. He seemed to be taking his time. Something about the intensity of his eyes, the pointed way he looked at each of them as if noting their features, made Eric suspicious. As the elf reached him, their eyes met, and the servant's grey eyes reflected a quick and easy smile that exuded charisma and friendliness. Suddenly the rogue felt foolish. Maybe he was just letting things get to him when he shouldn't.

Matt broke his thought when he asked, "Could they be on a quest to a world where time moves at a different speed, so they've been there a short time but a hundred years has passed on other worlds?"

Rognir snorted. "I've never heard of such a world." His eyes sought confirmation from the elves and got it.

"Possibly because if anyone went to such a world, they'd be gone an awfully long time before you'd find out about the time difference," Eric noted. "Maybe they'll show up at home in fifty years."

Lorian nodded. "True, but before such a world could summon them, others would have traveled there and established contact, and when the extreme time difference was discovered, they would have warned people not to go there. Regardless, no one would tell such a world of the champions, build Quest Rings, and teach the summoning spell because once summoned to that world, the champions would be unable to help any other world for a long time."

"Good point," Matt admitted.

"How did different worlds find out about them?" Eric interrupted. Different lands on one world was one thing, but this interplanetary travel was quite another.

"Soliander sent an apprentice to most of the initial worlds," Morven replied, "instructing them on how to build the Quest Rings and use the spells. After that, other worlds shared the knowledge, as he had instructed them to do so freely. Also, it's accepted fact that Soliander sent the apprentice, so this assumption of the quests being involuntary is baseless." After a pause, he added, "In any case, no one would want them summoned to a world where they'd be for many years while only days passed everywhere else."

After a pause, Eric observed, "Unless someone wanted to get rid of them the easy way."

Lorian looked at him approvingly. "You are as clever as Andier himself. While they had many enemies who might wish that, they mostly earned those foes after the quests started."

"So it's not realistic?" Anna asked.

"No," Lorian replied, waving off the servant from pouring him wine, "for the simple reason that the four of you have taken their place."

"Why?" Eric asked. "Does that imply something?"

The elf answered, "Yes. If they were still on a quest, no one, them or you, could be summoned and you would not be here."

Anna summed up, "So regardless of where they went and for how long, the only current quest is ours."

"That is correct," replied Lorian.

They mulled that over in silence, picking at fruit, or in Ryan's case, enjoying more wine. Eric decided not to say anything.

"Does anyone know where the last quest was to, or what they had to do?" the knight asked.

The elves shook their heads. "Word tends to spread between worlds when they arrive somewhere," Morven answered, "unless the world has limited communication with other worlds, as is often the case. Some keep records of the champions' deeds, but their quests are often only related by the champions themselves when they return. Generally, no one knows where they go, only that they have vanished, sometimes before people's startled eyes."

"That's gotta take some getting used to." Ryan laughed.

Casting a sidelong look at him, Eric asked, "So they might not have been doing a quest when they went missing?"

Lorian nodded. "We don't know, but much investigation into their disappearance has been done and it was learned that each vanished at nearly the same time. The exact moment could not be determined for each, as they were apart when it happened and all but Eriana was alone at the time. She vanished in front of witnesses. The others did not."

"In other words," said Anna, "it was probably a quest they went on."

"Yes," the elf admitted.

Matt asked, "Okay, but the only quest is ours, right? Does this mean another quest was in effect all this time but recently completed, allowing us to be summoned?"

The elves and dwarf exchanged thoughtful looks.

"Possibly," answered Morven, stroking his long, brown hair.

"The important thing is how recently?" Eric asked, watching the servant finish up. The guy was certainly taking his time. "How often do people try to summon them despite this idea that they aren't answering anymore even though they can't refuse to?"

Lorian shrugged. "There is no way to tell."

"Guess," offered Ryan, and seeing the elf frown, suggested, "Once a week?"

"Possibly."

"Once a month?"

"Almost certainly."

"So then sometime in the last month, they completed a quest," Ryan offered.

"*They* completed a quest," repeated Eric, leaning forward. "If they completed it, where are they? There is no word of them returning home?" The servant was done, and Eric watched him head for the door, step out, and quietly close it behind him.

Morven answered, "No, all word is of them appearing here."

"Us," noted Ryan.

"They could've completed the last quest a long time ago, though," Anna disagreed, "and it was only now that we took their place."

"True," Eric agreed, "but then why did we take their place now, and why not someone else at another time?"

"Well," started Matt, "we were at the Quest Ring when a summoning happened."

"That should not have mattered," noted Morven, "for the Ring only summons champions to it, not away from it, though if your being there was connected with the previous quest, such as having just finished one, it might appear that the ring was involved in your summoning when it was not."

Lorian's eyebrows rose, clarifying, "If you were the real champions, and had completed a quest and returned to the Quest Ring, and another summoning happened at that moment, you would have come from there. The return spell, the one you witnessed, might have been triggered by the new summoning spell. However, on your way home, so to speak, you would have been diverted to the next quest. There were known instances when two quests happened in quick succession and they did not return home until the second was completed." Ryan began fidgeting with sudden energy as the elf concluded, "In your case, it would simply be coincidence to be standing at the Quest Ring, this Stonehenge, at that moment."

Ryan spoke up excitedly, slurring a few words. "Wait a minute. You said the return spell on Earth might have been triggered, so we might have been headed to *their* home world but came here for a new quest instead. Does that mean that if we complete this quest, we won't be sent to Earth on finishing it, but to their world?"

Anna gasped. "Oh my God! I never thought of that."

Neither had Eric. They might never see their families or friends again, their former lives over for good. The lack of response from the elves and dwarf suggested Ryan might be right. A sudden image filled Eric's head, of him returning to Andier's home only to meet the rogue's startled friends and family, likely demanding he explain what he'd done to Andier. He'd never get a moment's rest, especially when yet another summons took him away. And what if he and his friends were separated, living on different worlds, or in different cities, always far apart until a new quest thrust them headlong into danger? It begged a question.

"Did they all live on the same world? The same city?"

Morven nodded. "Same world, yes, but different cities, some on different continents."

"I suppose it could be worse. Did they have to be at a Quest Ring to be sent back?"

"No," replied Morven. "However, it made it much easier and required less spell casting power. The Ring bears some of this burden."

Probably smart, Eric realized. What if Soliander was exhausted and had to cast the spell without help, and with a bunch of monsters on their tail? He also realized there might be times when the quest was done but they couldn't reach the Quest Ring and yet still wanted to go home. It made sense.

"I have a better question," the knight started. "Can someone else satisfy the quest for them?"

Lorian nodded, studying Ryan's face so that Eric wondered if the elf also thought Ryan meant something by it. "Yes, though I don't think anyone ever did. Still, if the need goes away after they're summoned, they are free to return. Otherwise you could have a case where, say, they must kill a dragon, but the dragon dies of natural causes before they do so. The spell recognizes the quest is no longer valid, and releases them. Otherwise, they would be trapped forever on the summoning world."

Ryan frowned. "How could a spell possibly know something like that?"

"The Quest Ring acts a bit like an oracle," the elf answered, "due to the spells on it. It is like a living thing, watching for the outcome."

Matt looked impressed. "That's cool. Is that also why it knows if quest requirements are valid or not?"

Morven nodded. "Yes. It's also why a Quest Ring is needed for summoning. It performs necessary functions. What were you doing at the Ring on your world?"

That made Eric think of something else and he digressed. "Can there be more than one Quest Ring on a world?"

"Of course. There usually are."

"Okay. Well, we were just visiting it. The monument is of cultural significance even though no one knows what it's for, so people visit just to see it in person."

Anna clarified, "We were trying to find a pendant of mine that I had dropped earlier in the day."

The elves exchanged a look with Rognir, who asked, "What is this pendant you speak of?"

"Um, well, it was a family heirloom, hundreds of years old. It was passed down to me from an aunt."

"Is there anything special about it?" the dwarf asked, puffing on his pipe.

She opened her mouth to reply and then paused as if realizing something.

Eric figured out the reason and asked, "Didn't you say that the diamond had words written in it that no one could ever read?" She nodded. "What did the words look like?"

She shook her head. "I don't know. I never saw anything like it."

"Was it Norse Runes?" Ryan asked, "like the lettering of blue flames on Stonehenge?" Anna shook her head again. They'd all seen such writing before from playing Dungeons & Dragons.

Lorian eyed her closely, then went to a cabinet, pulling out a scroll, which he laid before her on the table and rolled out, watching her as the lettering appeared. "The words were like these?"

She nodded slowly as Matt leaned over to peek.

"Magic!" the wizard stood up excitedly. "The pendant had magic words inside it. No wonder no one could read it!"

Rognir scowled. "There is truly no magic on your world, and no one able to read it?"

"Yeah."

"But there must be. How else would the champions have been summoned there except by magic?" the dwarf asked. "It's obvious that they must have been, else you would not have come instead. You clearly have a Quest Ring."

"That's true," admitted Eric, "but if magic still exists, no one in modern society knows. I *think*."

Morven looked at them thoughtfully. "Perhaps this has been forgotten or turned to myth, just like your dragons, elves, and dwarves."

"Possibly," Ryan conceded, sighing.

"Getting back to this pendant," started Rognir, "it's possible that the champions' quest was to retrieve that pendant you speak of, and when you unwittingly brought it to the Quest Ring on your world, the quest was satisfied. Coincidentally, at that moment, a summoning attempt occurred and you were brought here instead of the champions because they were...indisposed in some way we do not understand. In any case, it allowed you to take their place for unknown reasons."

No one said anything as they mulled that over. Finally, Matt said, "So they could send themselves back, if they did the quest, and not need the Quest Ring? Soliander had a spell?"

"Yes" answered Lorian.

"Maybe that's the first thing I should learn," the wizard suggested.

"It's in your spell books," advised Lorian, "but it will take some time to master such a strong spell."

"All the more reason to get started," Matt replied.

Eric stifled a frown. They were at Sonneri's mercy, and he might be the one trying to kill them.

"My head is spinning," remarked Anna.

Eric gave her a smile. "Maybe you should lay off the wine."

"On the contrary," she replied, reaching for the decanter, "I think I need more."

The dwarf rumbled with laughter. "A lass after my own spirit. Drink up, my dear."

"Not too much," cautioned Lorian. "You have a long day tomorrow."

"All the more reason to forget about everything for tonight," said Ryan, agreeing with her. He took the wine and drained what was left.

Eric had to admit that maybe they had a point, but as safe as Arundell appeared, he decided that at least one of them should keep his wits about him.

ASPIRATIONS

The next morning started early for everyone, with a first day of training. They'd train all the way to the mountains as time and circumstance allowed. Ryan and Eric started at a grassy archery range just behind the main house, Morven instructing them in the cross bow – a bow mounted on a wooden block with a trigger like a gun, making it easier to use. Instead of an arrow with an arrowhead and feathers, it shot a bolt without either. To Eric, Ryan seemed unhappy about spending all day learning to use weapons, but they only fired at targets of straw, wooden blocks, or severed tree trunks. When he finally hit the latter, it nearly flew apart from the force.

Looking impressed, Ryan asked, "What's this bow made of?"

As Morven replied, Eric's eyes darted behind them toward the manor, seeing three elves watching them, one being the servant with white streaks in his hair.

"Ash wood, sinew, horn," Morven answered, "glued together with animal tendon. It is strong and resilient."

"A composite bow," observed Eric to Ryan. He'd heard of them but never seen one. More powerful than other bows, they could punch a hole through plate armor like Ryan's.

Their aim worsened with the long and short bows, though Eric was better than Ryan. Morven gave frequent guidance, criticism, and occasional displays of impressive skill, making them glad he would accompany them to Castle Darlonon. Otherwise they could only hope for bluffing cult members into laying down weapons before revealing how bad a shot they were.

———— •·• ————

"Leave the books," commanded Lorian from the doorway.

Matt reluctantly put down Soliander's bag and followed the elf for his first magic lesson, dying to know what he could do. Wouldn't it be great if he could fly, teleport, stop time, or best of all, make women fall for him not with a spell, but from admiration? A gleam appeared in his green eyes, excitement overcoming his caffeine withdrawal. Maybe he could make a cup of coffee appear, too.

"What's the plan?" he asked, carrying the staff.

"We will abide by the traditional approach, albeit accelerated," Lorian replied. "You will have my assistance on this quest, but if we are to assume your substitution for the true champions is perpetual, you must advance quickly but safely to perform on your own."

"Of course," Matt agreed. He had no desire to turn himself into a statistic, if such a thing existed for wizards who'd accidentally killed themselves. He wondered if a census bureau existed for that.

"I will explain the fundamentals of magic before you attempt to summon power from your staff."

"I thought magic items had the magic, not the person using it, so all you need to know is how to turn it on." He hadn't gotten any of his items to do anything yet, though he hadn't tried much, afraid to learn what they did the hard way and become that statistic. They hadn't come with owner's manuals.

Lorian nodded as they turned into another wing. "That is generally true, but wizards often make their own items more powerful, and if one fell into an untrained person's hands, it would be more dangerous, so for a staff like Soliander's, you must be able to summon the magic within or nothing will happen. This is true of most of his items, save those your friends have."

That surprised Matt. "They have magic items with them? Well, I guess I shouldn't be surprised. Hadn't thought of that. I wonder if there's a way to tell what the items are and what each does. But you say they can't use my staff?"

"Generally, no. However, it possesses simple spells anyone can access, such as casting light."

That made sense. The others hadn't been tested and Matt wondered if they'd show any promise, especially Anna, though Eriana's healing wasn't magic but a matter of faith and allowing the gods to use oneself as a vessel. She probably hated the idea.

"If work with the staff goes well," continued Lorian, "I'll teach you simple spells."

"Does that require me to read them?" Matt wondered. "I can't read elven or magic."

"When we reach that point, I'll cast spells to grant reading, writing, and speaking skill of those. The spell to do so for magic is very rarely cast because those who have earned the knowledge do not generally give it to those who have not."

"I bet," mused Matt, eager to reach that point. This was going to be cool.

While the boys received lessons, Anna contemplated their situation from a comfortable wooden chair in the ever-present garden. Today was training day and yet no one had plans for her. She wasn't expected to fight, thankfully, but healing hadn't come up either. Her friends not mentioning it didn't bother her, since they knew her inclinations, but the elves hadn't either. Had Eric told Lorian she was an atheist and not to bother with training her to channel gods she didn't believe in? She didn't want to be considered just baggage and unable to help. Worse, she'd be a distraction if they had to protect her all the time. Maybe she should just stay behind.

She sat biting her lip when the dwarf Rognir noisily approached, stomping on the loose gravel, metal items hanging from his belt clinking together. Judging from this dwarf, the race seemed as surly and grumpy as legend allowed. She'd picked up on an idea that elves and dwarves from different planets weren't the same, so she'd asked a few questions and learned that they preferred living underground beneath mountains, tunneling deep into them for pleasure and treasure, neither shared with outsiders. Humans often relied on the legendary stonecutting skills when building castles like Olliana.

"Mind if I join you, lass?" Rognir gruffly asked, voice so loud that he disturbed a flock of birds that took off en masse. He looked almost offended.

"Not at all," Anna replied, stifling a smile. Rognir hadn't been here long enough to know of her disposition on gods and healing, so she asked, "Do you know how people do healing here?"

Rognir pulled a pipe from a pouch. "The usual way, my dear. Pray to the gods and lay your hands on the person needing healing."

"Why does it work?"

He looked sideways at her. "Pardon me for asking, but shouldn't you know these things?"

"No, not really," she started, smoothing her priestess' robe and wishing once again she didn't have to wear it. "That sort of healing doesn't exist on Earth. We do it with medicine or surgery." He looked dubious.

"Why doesn't such healing work there?" Rognir asked. "Are your gods so displeased with your people that they do not answer?"

"No," Anna answered. "God doesn't exist."

He frowned. "Your gods don't exist? Why do people talk of them?"

She shrugged. "Mostly to make themselves feel better. People like to believe a divine being has a plan for them and that the bad things in their lives are not random, but will ultimately bear positive fruit. The idea gives them hope, but they're just reading what they want to believe into things and telling themselves it's God's will."

He nodded, the long beard rubbing across his plump belly. "Yes, humans are especially prone to interpreting everything. Sometimes a misfortune is just a misfortune, like a tree falling to block a road because it's old, not to thwart your travel plans."

"Exactly," she agreed emphatically, hazel eyes bright. It was always a relief to talk with someone rational about these things.

"But other times it is the will of a god," continued the dwarf. "It can be hard to tell when they act through intermediaries. How many gods are believed to exist on your world?"

"Just the one," she replied. "It wasn't always that way, though. The Greeks and Romans believed in many gods, but those religions have long since passed. What always strikes me is that once people stopped talking of them, the belief slowly died. Now most believe in one god, and talk about Him constantly, but if they stopped, down the road it would be accepted as fact that He never existed either. It's weird to me that more people don't see that."

He nodded sagely. "People often see what they want to see. Since these gods of yours are not real, they do not appear to people, I assume."

"Right. Sometimes people have what they call 'visions' of God, but there's no proof they aren't just delusional. Even so, it is exceptionally rare."

"Some gods keep to themselves," admitted Rognir, "so not appearing doesn't necessarily mean the god doesn't exist. Do you think that if people had more faith in this god of yours that he'd be more likely to appear?"

She shook her head. "No, because many people devoutly believe in God and yet He does not appear." She shrugged and added, "Mostly because he's not real."

"How are you so certain he is not real?"

Anna spread her hands. "There's no real unbiased proof He's any more real than any other notion of gods on Earth. See, the prevailing idea is that having *faith* in God's existence and plans for you is what's really important, so He purposely doesn't appear."

Rognir furrowed his brow. "What purpose does that serve?"

"I don't know. None, really, unless you consider that God isn't real at all and therefore faith in Him does indeed become everything."

The dwarf nodded, brow furrowed.

She continued, "Many religious leaders try to keep people from seeing this by discouraging such thoughts. They say things like people can't possibly understand the ways of a god, so we shouldn't ask such questions. If you're a humble person, you accept Him on faith, and to question is to be arrogant and therefore unworthy of God's benevolence. It's a social manipulation tactic, basically."

Warming up to her subject, she added, "If the priests were as benevolent as they pretend, they wouldn't need to use fear and coercion to make people believe. And why should belief be so important? Either God exists or He doesn't. Why does my belief matter? If I stop believing in Him, do I make Him disappear?"

Rognir grunted. "Fascinating. I've never heard of anything like that with gods, on this or any other world. Ours is a simpler scenario. Our gods simply show up as they desire."

That surprised her. "So then they really do exist?"

"Of course."

That set her back a bit. "How many are there?"

He puffed on his pipe. "On Honyn, the humans have fourteen, while we dwarves have nine. The elves have twenty-two. You'll find it is different on other worlds."

"Interesting. Are there any worlds where the gods never appear?"

"No," Rognir admitted. "I've never heard of that until you mentioned it, but there are worlds where they are quite fickle and only show up every thousand years or so, sometimes on cue."

Anna found that interesting but had trouble accepting people would expect her to call on the gods to heal them. A total lack of sincerity on her part would doom any attempts like a self-fulfilling prophecy. If she didn't believe, they wouldn't show, confirming her disbelief.

"How does a priest heal someone?" Anna asked again. "I know you said they call on the gods – a specific one, I assume – and touch the injured person, but what else can you tell me?"

He pursed his lips, thinking. "You must be familiar with the gods, their teachings, and personality, and have some affinity or love for what they represent. They can sense this when you call upon them and it influences their decision to help. If you only intend to call upon one god, that's the only one you must know intimately. It's best if you've spent some time speaking with this god first. Some gods, even benevolent ones, can be capricious. Have you been told the names of the gods here?"

Anna paused, realizing that was probably in the scroll she'd refused to look at. She confessed.

"You should read it," he advised, "if for no other reason than to make conversation with those wanting your advice. I can counsel you as we continue."

"You seem to know a lot about this."

He winked at her. "That's because I'm somewhat of a priest myself, lass, though my skills are meager."

Anna wished she'd known that before and wondered if she'd offended him at all, but she didn't think so. She'd been careful to discuss only God on Earth, not gods in general. She'd admitted her atheism in front of the wrong people before and had some turn on her rather nastily. Even less devout Christians could turn ugly over that. She called herself a "benevolent atheist," meaning she didn't go around denouncing believers. Sometimes she wondered if that was a mistake. If religions could crusade, maybe atheists should, too.

She decided to look at the religious scroll after all and left Rognir behind in a growing cloud of smoke from his pipe. On returning to their suite, she found Eric leaving for a swordsmanship lesson with Morven, Ryan sitting in a chair, looking bored.

"While everyone else is busy," she started, "can you give me a riding lesson?"

Eric spent the next hour learning to swing a short sword properly, focusing on defense, since avoiding death took precedence. To his surprise, the training included footwork that came easier with his background in martial arts, so the elf quickly focused on just the sword. Before long Eric's hand hurt from the grip twisting in his palm as the force of Morven's attack made it shift. He'd learned some basic skills that were in desperate need of refinement, and the elf had him work with his non-dominant hand, too. Morven dismissed him to give his hands a break. Eric left with his thanks and a promise to resume later.

As he neared the suite, he noticed the door was ajar and stopped short, the hackles on the back of his neck rising. Strange voices came from within. Something was wrong.

Lorian led Matt to an octagonal room with tall granite walls, a domed ceiling with two open windows, and a single, thick, mahogany door, which he closed but did not lock; there was a thick beam that could be lowered to do so. This was the first fortified room Matt had seen here, most others having no locks at all. Arundell reminded him of simpler times in the U.S. when people didn't lock their front doors, the degree of trust refreshing.

"This room affords supernatural protection through magical wards," the elf remarked, leading him to the center, where two red cushions lay on the floor. "Most are denied entrance here, but today we will allow it, as your talents are unknown."

"So if I put us in danger," Matt surmised wryly, "you want people to get in and save us?"

"Something like that," replied Lorian lightly. They sat on the cushions as a robin flew in and landed on a ledge. "You must understand where magic comes from or you're no different from those using magic items, except more dangerous. Magic is inherently perilous, so we use prescribed means to perform it."

"Spells," Matt guessed.

"Correct. Spells can be fundamentally different on other worlds, but here a spell is a combination of words, gestures, and on rare occasions, physical matter. Not all are necessary. A spell's outcome is either failure or success. There's no accidental outcome unless only force of will is applied, which is why this is ill-advised. Magic draws energy from both living and inanimate objects nearby, another way people can be hurt, so spells control and reduce side effects. In addition, the wizard's strength, skill, and talent determine the power of a successful cast. A staff can assist and protect against catastrophe."

The elf said, "You must learn to draw on this magical energy to make Soliander's staff react. We'll start with bringing light to the orb. The staff's optional word of power will help and is needed for stronger effects."

"What's the word?"

"*Enumisar.*" At Lorian's indication, Matt stood the staff on one end, the orb above them.

Lorian advised, "Close your eyes. Reach out with your senses." The advice continued quietly as Matt searched, sensing nothing at first, but then like a light appearing in the darkness, a warmth glowed nearby. He yearned and it grew stronger, nearer, warmer. His heart pounded with a sudden desire and fear.

"Speak the word of power," Lorian whispered, watching in approval.

"Enumisar," Matt intoned. The word echoed in his mind, spreading outward to reach the force, from where a brief flicker washed back over him, making contact. He smiled like a boy getting his first kiss. He looked and saw a soft, yellow glow filling the orb, the faintest flame flickering there.

The elf looked pleased. "Few succeed on the first try. You have made contact, but not enough. Let your will flow. Embrace the touch."

With Lorian's endorsement, Matt closed his eyes and again reached into the power, immersing himself in a kind of spiritual energy bath. He grinned and let himself go, casting caution to the wind. "Enumisar!" Matt repeated lustily, his voice hoarse. Suddenly the force rushed into him. A huge fountain of fire erupted from the staff's crystal with a whoosh, a wave of heat blasting them from above and setting Lorian's cloak on fire. Matt yelped and rolled away, breaking contact and dropping the staff, the flames dying. Lorian snuffed out the fire on him.

Startled, Matt asked, "Did I do that?"

"You most certainly did." Lorian looked impressed but concerned. And slightly ruffled.

Awestruck, Matt said, "Wow. That was cool."

Lorian raised an eyebrow. "On the contrary it was quite hot."

Matt chuckled at the misunderstanding.

"We must work on your control," said the elf, sternly.

Chagrined, the young wizard said, "Sorry." His throat felt parched and his skin seemed dry. Either it was the heat or he'd drawn too much energy from himself.

Lorian licked his dry lips. "Now you understand the need for control, especially with your potential."

Matt nodded. "Please teach me."

The elf gestured to the cushion. "Resume your seat."

As Matt moved to do so, movement caught his eye and Lorian followed his gaze. Something lay smoldering on the floor. They approached to find the robin lying there, feathers singed and smoking. Lorian was about to say something when the robin abruptly turned into a raven. Matt's eyebrows rose. The bird moved slightly, not quite dead, and soon morphed into a falcon.

Lorian remarked in surprise, "A changeling spy! Your presence here is known."

Matt stared at the bird, concerned. "Maybe it's good that it won't live to tell anyone."

"An oversight on my part. I apologize."

"No harm done, I guess."

"Perhaps," answered Lorian as the bird stopped moving. "Someone still knows you're here."

"But now we know that someone knows, at least."

"True, but not who."

The elf called for a messenger to alert the staff but otherwise resumed the lesson as planned. Other elven wizards here could see to the manor's defense and the incident only strengthened Matt's resolve to achieve something today.

The instruction continued for several hours with Matt proving an apt and enthusiastic student. Years of analytical thinking from writing software code helped him grasp details and techniques. Finally, Lorian cast two spells on him so he could permanently read elven and magic languages. After Matt commented on wanting to read the spell books, with an eager gleam in his eyes, the elf doused some of the fun by instructing him to memorize two spells for their second session later that afternoon. It would keep him busy and out of trouble.

⸻ ⁘ ⸻

Eric stood quietly by the door to their rooms, hearing two strange voices just inside, one sounding somehow distant, as if farther away than was possible in their rooms. The other sounded quiet, respectful, but somehow unnerving. Silently stepping to the opening, the rogue cautiously peered inside. A figure in elven clothing stood with its back to him, gazing into a black orb it held aloft. Soliander's bag of books had been spread about on a table and rifled through. While Eric couldn't see the figure's face, the black hair streaked with white was unmistakable.

"I have found the spell books, master," said the elf respectfully to the orb, where a face hovered. "They appear exactly as you described. Do you wish me to return with them?"

After a pause, a voice replied from the orb. "No. Do not betray yourself. I will tend to them. What of the staff?"

"It is not here in the room," answered the intruder, "but I have seen it and it appears like your description."

"'Similar' and 'appearing' are not good enough," snapped the orb coldly. "You must be certain."

"Yes, master." The elf bowed.

"What of their identities?"

"None of them are who they claim to be, master, nor do they know the whereabouts of the true Ellorian Champions."

Eric cursed himself for letting them speak with this servant present, and it suddenly occurred to him to stop this communication, not listen to it for intel. He stepped forward and pushed open the door, hoping to catch the spy by surprise.

"Fool!" the orb snapped. "You are seen!"

The intruder whirled and threw a punch that knocked Eric back, a kick to the chest sending him to the floor. The elf leapt over him and started down the hall with surprising speed. Winded but undaunted, Eric pursued him.

The elf disappeared around first one corner and then another as they dashed by startled servants and house guests. Eric was losing ground and reached for a throwing knife to slow the intruder down as they neared an open archway, green fields beyond. Suddenly Lorian strode into view between the intruder and freedom, looking concerned at the commotion. Matt followed, a smile fading at the sight of Eric chasing someone.

"Stop him!" Eric shouted.

The spy threw a knife at Lorian, who leapt out of its path. He spoke a magic word and made a halting gesture. A brief flicker of light surrounded the intruder, but he didn't stop. Lorian's eyes registered surprise before he jumped forward, one leg arcing through the air violently. The intruder rolled under the kick, sprang to his feet, and took off, casting an intense look at the staff in Matt's hand.

Running across the grass toward the forest, the spy turned into a black buck with silver streaks, wicked black antlers thrashing through low branches as it dashed into the underbrush. Lorian transformed himself into an even larger brown buck and bounded after in pursuit. Eric and Matt exchanged startled looks.

Ryan suddenly cantered up with Anna lagging behind on her horse.

"Get on!" Ryan shouted, having clearly seen enough from where they'd been riding.

"Take Matt," Eric said, running up to Anna and leaping belly first onto her horse. He awkwardly managed to right himself behind her. Then he wrapped both arms around her and kicked the horse hard. Battle-trained and excited, it took off so fast he almost fell off. Ryan grabbed a half-willing Matt by the arm and hauled the wizard up behind him, then followed and overtook the others, his expert horsemanship paying off.

"Down!" Ryan called out as they raced into thin branches at a gallop. Matt scrunched down behind the knight's broad back as they leaned forward. Anna buried her face in her own horse's neck. Trying to shield her from the branches that slapped at him, Eric reached forward with one hand, feeling them sting his hands and face before they burst into daylight.

To one side, two bucks frantically raced through the thin forest, bounding over fallen trees and ducking low branches. The brown one had already halved the distance to the smaller black one. Ryan charged ahead and Eric realized he was looking for a good place to block the way. They soon slowed to a trot, moving into the woods ahead of the deer. Eric's horse followed more from training than from Anna's weak and confused commands.

"Everybody off," commanded the knight, "and spread out."

They clumsily complied before Eric realized this wasn't smart. The buck's antlers were fearsome weapons that suddenly appeared before them as the buck crashed into view. It came straight toward the undefended Ellorian Champions. The intruder saw the way blocked and an available horse, so he changed back into an elf and stepped toward it, something falling to the ground and rolling under some leaves as he did so. Ryan stood nearest that horse and slapped its rump so that it moved out of reach, the other horse following.

Seeing the false Lord Korrin, the elf sneered and stepped forward. Then the brown buck bounded up behind him and he turned to face Lorian, whose antlers were too close for the elf to transform before he'd be gored. With a snarl of irritation, the intruder turned back to Ryan but found Eric had replaced the knight. The rogue flashed an insincere smile of greeting and punched the elf in the face, knocking him down.

"Now we're even," the rogue remarked in satisfaction. To his surprise, the spy's nose had shattered, spraying blood everywhere. Eric didn't think he'd hit that hard.

Lorian morphed back into an elf and approached, hauling the spy up with Eric's help.

"Who are you?" Lorian demanded, receiving only a glare in response.

Matt stood watching the item that had fallen into the leaves, seeing its surface moving strangely. He went to where it lay and pushed aside the leaves to find an orb, which still swirled with colors as he looked into it. A partially hidden face stared back. At first he assumed it was his reflection, for it certainly stared with a curiosity bordering on his, but while his face shone with innocent wonder, nothing innocent existed in the cold, angry visage that appraised him.

"Lorian, I found something that guy dropped," he said, unnerved.

The elf's eyes widened on seeing the orb. "Bring it here, quickly."

The wizard did so, but as he neared the intruder, words of magic that he now recognized suddenly erupted from the orb.

"Rolinmor astorli nurarki a finta!" *Burning light, strike as fire!*

Crackling bolts of lightning arced from the orb to strike the spy in the head and chest, incinerating him. Eric and Lorian recoiled in surprise, letting the intruder fall as Matt dropped the orb in alarm. When the attack finally stopped, the smell of charred flesh filled the air. Anna choked and turned away to vomit. No one had to check the intruder's pulse to tell he was dead.

As they watched, the body shimmered briefly, and the countenance changed from beautiful to sinister. The skin turned black as night, the hair a dull silver. What had been pleasant elven features were now cold and foreboding. Even in death, a certain arrogance had seemingly come over the corpse's expression.

"A dark elf!" Lorian exclaimed.

Eric noted, "You're surprised? I thought dark elves were known to be up to no good."

The elf nodded. "Yes, what you've heard is true." He flicked a glance at the rogue. "Once again you seem to know all about a race that you believe does not exist on your world. In any case, dark elves live far from Alunia and have no business here." He cocked his head, examining the body.

"What is it?" Eric asked.

"I'm not sure," Lorian replied. "Something about this dark elf is different in a way I cannot ascertain. We will need to examine his remains."

"Lorian," Matt interrupted, getting his attention. "The orb?"

The elf retrieved it and Matt saw it had gone dark, looking like little more than a shiny black ball, and weighing several pounds. He told Lorian what he'd seen in it, getting a nod of recognition.

"It's a communication sphere," announced Lorian, slipping it into a pouch. "It is unfortunate we cannot learn what this elf was doing here or who he was communicating with."

"He was using it when I caught him," said Eric, watching Anna, who still looked pale. He related what happened prior to the pursuit.

"But I thought no one knew we were coming here," Ryan objected.

"No," disagreed Matt, "the queen's inner circle knew."

"Yeah, but she'd have no reason to stop us," observed Anna, grimacing, "unless it was Sonneri."

"Perhaps not," agreed Lorian, "but I have known Queen Lorella for years. She is trustworthy. But it is not unheard of for those close to a ruling body to have their own secret agenda." He went on to relate the bird spy Matt accidentally roasted. They absorbed that in silence.

Ryan remarked, "So two different spies. Does that mean someone was being cautious by making sure one spy succeeded if the other failed, or were two different people trying to get information about us?"

"I suspect the latter," Lorian replied, "based on what Andier has related."

Eric asked, "Is there any way to see who this spy was talking to last?"

"You mean like dialing star sixty-nine?" Matt asked, thinking of telephones and calling back the last number that called you.

Clearly not understanding the reference, the elf just said, "Not that I know of, no."

"We should warn the queen, for her own protection," Anna suggested weakly, "in case there *is* a spy in her midst."

"Agreed," said Lorian. "I will send someone."

Suddenly Matt noticed an elf silently step out from behind a nearby tree, then another and another. He'd heard of their legendary quiet in books but never witnessed it. They'd come right up on them without anyone noticing, save perhaps Lorian, who didn't look surprised. The elf directed the newcomers to take the body to the house as the rest of them followed, feeling like a funeral procession. The body count continued to climb and it was hard not to wonder if it would soon include them.

CHAPTER ELEVEN

THE ELLORIAN CHAMPIONS

Unable to stop his pacing, Ryan waited for Lorian to join him in a private meeting room. The time had come to get at least himself out of going to Castle Darlonon, as guilty as that made him feel about not helping his friends. He'd decided he could live with that, however, but not with causing another person's death. The scene of the dark elf's murder had shocked him, and though someone else had done it, even being on Honyn had led to that. It seemed that death would follow them until this quest ended, and he wanted his part done right now. He would not watch another man die.

When Lorian arrived with a questioning look on his face, Ryan turned to him almost angrily.

"Shut the door," he commanded, then realized his rudeness and softened his tone. "Please."

The elf nodded and did so, quietly watching Ryan continue pacing.

"How many elves are going to the castle?" Ryan finally asked, opting for small talk first.

"I haven't decided," Lorian began, "but sufficient numbers that the four of you should see little fighting or a need for magic and healing."

"Good." After a pause, he blurted out, "Because I don't intend to go with you at all."

Lorian's surprise shone on his face. "You will remain behind while your friends ride into danger?"

Ryan opened his mouth, then shut it. That wasn't fair. It made it sound like that was his goal. "Look, I can't do this. I'm not a knight and know nothing about sword fighting, and I don't like killing people! I want no part of it!"

Gesturing to a chair, the elf said, "Let us sit and talk. I understand your reluctance. You seem to know something of elves, but let me assure you we value life greatly and do not lightly end it or risk our own."

That sounded like elves, alright. Ryan reluctantly took a chair, trying to calm down.

"It is common among elves," Lorian continued, "to avoid a death strike and instead disable our opponents, but we also understand that death is sometimes the outcome of such violence. Even the gentlest among us must acknowledge that those who seek to do evil through violence are risking their own lives of their own volition. They must expect violent opposition, and it is foolishness for us to refuse self-defense."

"But I'm a Christian!" Ryan protested. "We're supposed to turn the other cheek because violence begets violence. The cycle will never end if we don't. There are whole regions of Earth that will forever be at war because they always retaliate."

Lorian held up a hand to calm him. "But what happens if you do not defend yourself? Are you not merely cut down, your life ended by those with an opposing view of what is right and just in the world? Is it right that your values cease to exist because you would not defend them? If they mean so little..." He trailed off.

Ryan sat at a loss for words, unsure where to start. Finally he said, "They mean a lot, but I don't want to have to kill for them."

"Understandable, but it is sometimes necessary. Something that you must understand, and this is of great importance, is that ending a life when that life is seeking to end yours, is wholly different from the aggressor trying to end the lives of others to further some cause of your fancy."

"Yes!" Ryan agreed, standing up in his passion. "But I'm going there to kill a dragon!"

Lorian shook his head as the knight paced. "No, you are not. That is not part of the quest. You are to *banish* the dragons, not harm them."

Ryan opened and then shut his mouth again, his emotions ahead of his mind. "But what if I have to kill this one in order to banish the others? Doesn't that make me the aggressor? This dragon hasn't hurt anyone since coming through, right?"

"On the contrary, it killed four men that we know of, but I'm afraid it is only a matter of time before it kills far more. It is the nature of these dragons."

"But preemptively killing this dragon before it kills someone else is hardly a justification. That's murder!"

"What if we are right about its intentions based on dragons' history? Would you prefer to wait until all the dragons are released and kill countless people before realizing they are indeed the killers history has proven them to be, and then act? Is that not a greater evil for all the lives lost while you waited for the dragons to prove their nature?"

Ryan's heart sank. The elf was right about that. He'd certainly feel worse. "The lesser of two evils," he muttered.

Rising and coming around the table to him, the elf put a hand on his arm. "Listen, Ryan," he started, using his real name for the first time, "I know this fight is not yours, but it is important that you accompany us. Your armor is protected against dragon fire. It is the only one of its kind available to us in the time allowed and it will not fit any of my elves. We are too slender. It might be needed to get at least you past the dragon and to the gate, or allow you to distract her while Soliander closes it. We need you. Honyn needs you. Your friends need you."

After a long pause, Ryan quietly said, "I wish they didn't and could just go without me."

Lorian shook his head. "I don't think you mean that. You say you cannot live with the thought of taking another life, but can you live with the thought of your friends dying while you remain safe here, especially when your presence might have prevented their deaths?"

Ryan hadn't thought of that and knew he would forever blame himself. His shoulders slumped in defeat.

The elf said, "I can teach you how to avoid delivering fatal strikes while defending yourself, and since this is your preference, I would like to see you enter into such training with vigor and not reluctance. You can do great good without causing death. We can also teach you how to use your lance to kill a dragon so that you will understand what not to do if you wish to only hurt it, or stop it."

Ryan looked up, seeing compassionate slanted eyes on him. He knew the elf was right, and while he didn't like it, there was no escaping it. He sensed a kind of kinship and suddenly felt grateful.

"So, if I stay behind, my friends might die," he said quietly, "and if I go, I might hurt or kill someone. It seems like no matter what I do, death is going to find someone."

"In all probability, yes. The important thing is that if you come along, you can help decide who survives, but if you remain here you are powerless to help anyone, including yourself."

Ryan looked up, realizing something. "With me separated, someone could attack me here while you're all gone, couldn't they?"

Lorian nodded. "Yes, though the estate is well protected."

The knight made a rueful expression, thinking of the day's events. "Not enough, apparently." He let out a big sigh. "I guess we had better get started."

———————— ✦ · ✦ ————————

Ryan wasn't the only one bothered by the spies. Both Anna and Matt found concentrating on their studies difficult, and the former finally went for a walk that didn't help because she no longer felt safe. She kept expecting someone to jump out from every corner or a staff member to suddenly become a threat. She finally secluded herself in Lorian's library with a few books on Honyn's religions and slowly became immersed in them, mostly out of curiosity.

For his part, Matt struggled to remain focused but more out of excitement than worry. He'd encountered two spies today and wanted to know how to detect them, and more importantly, put a stop to what they were doing. If he could cast a lightning bolt spell like the figure in the orb, someone would think twice about messing with him or his friends. He could now read every word of the spell books and couldn't believe the powerful spells in them. Only Lorian's expectations for him and the fear of something going wrong stopped him from working on them.

Lorian had taken the orb away and not discussed it with them beyond assuring them it wasn't something they wanted near. As Eric had observed, it was better not to have what amounted to a phone that someone could call you on and then kill you through. And people had once talked about cell phones emitting radiation.

As the day continued, both Eric and Ryan learned swordsmanship from Morven and Lorian respectively, and shortly before dinner, Matt succeeded in casting a spell under Lorian's watchful eye. The wizard could read the words on both his staff and Ryan's sword now, though he refused to tell anyone what the staff said, feeling some responsibility to keep it unknown as much for his sake as Soliander's. He discovered that even Lorian could not read it despite the words being in the language of magic. It seemed that only its true possessor could, which suggested Matt's ownership had more finality than he was comfortable with. The sword wasn't as complicated, however, and had the words "Brave is the Heart – True Flies the Steel" written on its two sides. The sentiment got a frown from Ryan, for the blade would never find its calling in his hands.

By nightfall they once again gathered in Lorian's private meeting room. Eric had finished reading the scroll Soliander had written and discovered no mention of how the Dragon Gate worked. There was probably good reason for that, but now their only hope lay in something being written on the gate itself. Otherwise they'd just have to wing it, and no one thought that would turn out well. Now he wanted more information on the Ellorians themselves.

The rogue asked, "What can you tell us about Andier and the others? If people think I'm him, some info on him would be nice."

Seeing four curious faces turned toward him, Lorian responded, "Andier comes from the kingdom of Roir on another world. Less is known about him than the others, even Soliander, because it's his desire to draw information from others, not reveal it about himself. Like all good men of his ilk, he knows that others' ignorance of him is to his advantage. Not only do they not know what to expect from him, but it makes his reputation larger than life, and such things go a long way in negotiations. Having details of your personality and past known can only be used against you, and the champions certainly have their enemies."

"From thwarting people's plans?" Anna asked.

"Yes," answered the elf. "For every group that sings songs of their deeds, there's another that curses their names. Each of the champions had enemies even before they started working together."

Before the elf could continue, Matt wondered aloud, "When did they meet? Why did they join forces?"

This time Morven answered. "Before that, each had done quests alone or with helpers who weren't up to the task, such as Korrin needing a wizard but finding only someone so unskilled that they became a second danger as a result. As the Ellorians started encountering each other and learned they shared a passion for solving the problems of various kingdoms, each realized the others were the competent comrades they desired."

Anna asked, "How many quests did they go on? How long were they doing this?"

"Several years, and hundreds of quests in that time."

"Wow. That doesn't leave a lot of personal time."

"Yes it is," agreed Rognir, puffing on a pipe that gave off a sweet scent. "This self-sacrifice is responsible for the respect in which they are held, and for the willingness of summoners to provide every comfort imaginable during their stay."

"What else can you tell me about Andier?" Eric asked, getting back on track. He noticed they spoke of the champions in the present tense, as if they still lived somewhere. Hopefully that was true, and it would be great if they showed up any time now to take over.

Lorian turned back to him. "Little. He is deadly with knives, swords, the bow and arrow, and with his hands and feet, much the way you are from what I saw in your suite. His balance is superb, and he's nearly as adept from horseback, even dragon-back. He can scale any wall, get beyond any trap, and solve any riddle. His ability to get others to unwittingly reveal information is legendary, and it's said he often knows people better than they know themselves, and within minutes of meeting them. He is called the Silver-Tongued Rogue with good reason. He is also rather charming with the ladies, as you might imagine."

"Well," Eric drawled, trying to make light of all that, "at least I have that last part taken care of." He glanced at Anna, who laughed a little too hard about that.

Morven added, "Andier is an only child and it is not known if any relatives live, though undoubtedly some do. He would not want anyone to know so threats to them cannot be used against him."

Eric nodded, thinking that being unaware of any living relatives was another thing he shared with Andier.

Morven turned to Anna, his face lighting up as he spoke so that Eric wondered if he had a crush on the subject of his words. "The Lady Eriana of Coreth is unusual in her peacefulness, which shines from her. Her presence alone lifts spirits, and she seems on first glance to have never known anguish, for many people assume such tranquility could not possibly lie on the far side of tragedy. They have never known it to be so, have never seen someone be at such peace after catastrophe, but Eriana has known deep pain.

"It is said she was shattered in her teenage years by a betrayal from someone close to her. It devastated her mind and spirit, causing great turmoil and leaving her desperate for kindness and care from others. Instead, she fell in with the wrong sort and received quite the opposite, making her confusion and anguish worse. It was in this darkness of the mind and soul that her power – and ultimately, her peace – were found. We do not know by what means she recovered herself, but the wisdom for which she became famous suggests deep introspection.

"Some time after this, she sought to help a gravely wounded friend and found herself begging the gods for aid, which was granted with vigor. So touched was she by this answer that she devoted herself to helping others, and the power she has wielded as a devotee of the gods is quite unusual. Her new calling gave her the serenity for which she is now well revered."

"We call it self-actualization on Earth," remarked Anna.

Eric thought she looked displeased, almost disapproving. Did she think she couldn't be that way herself? "How old was she?" he asked.

"Each was in their mid to upper twenties when they disappeared," answered Morven, "perhaps a few years older than each of you."

"However," started Lorian, "their experiences gave them gravity beyond their years so that they appeared older. You seem young by comparison, especially to an elf."

"So everyone should expect us to look a decade older," observed Eric.

"Yes," replied Lorian, "but few ever saw them for long. Casual encounters with you will leave most people fooled, and many will be too awestruck to question anything."

"That helps," remarked Eric. He noticed they spoke about this as if he and the others were permanent replacements, which he didn't like, but something else had his attention. "What can you tell us about Korrin?"

Morven set down his wine glass and looked at Ryan as he replied. "He received training as a knight from an early age and seems to excel with every weapon he touches. He even fights well with things that aren't intended to be weapons. His strength is impressive, and he's been known to shatter an opponent's sword or shield with a single-handed blow. The title Dragon Slayer is well-earned and initially caused his great reputation, for he was trained in killing them with both the lance and sword. You'll find that his armor there is fire-proof, to a degree."

"To a degree?" Ryan asked skeptically. He started to laugh. "What does that mean? I'll only get second degree burns?"

"It means you'll feel no effects from dragon fire the first few blasts within a short time," answered Morven. "Then the protection lessens until it has a chance to restore itself, which usually takes a day from what I remember. The magic is strong. It should be, as Soliander cast the spell."

"That was rather sporting of him," said Matt. "Do you know what magic items we all have?"

Morven replied. "Maybe not all, but many, yes." He went on to say that Soliander created various things for them. One was called the Trinity Ring, for it could heal someone three times before being spent, and all but Eriana wore one. Korrin bore another ring called the Dispersion Ring, which allowed the hand wearing it to pass through magical barriers and generally be unaffected by magic up to the shoulder. For Andier, another ring made his hand do more damage and act like a magical weapon, since some creatures could only be struck by one and he often fought with hand and foot. Lorian didn't know all their items, however, and remarked that all of them lost their power in certain areas where magic didn't work at all.

"What about Soliander?" Matt asked. "What can you tell us about him?"

This time Rognir replied. "For all Andier's silence about his life and wants, Soliander is the most mysterious of the four, not because the details of his life aren't known, but because they are. It is he who has had enough brushes with darkness to make some question his allegiance to matters of peaceful living, quietly of course.

"It has long been known that those of a dark disposition attain power more readily, due to the absence of a conscience to impede their progress. If their aspirations go awry and cause a death, for example, it is of no consequence to them, and while Soliander is not this way, he has always desired great power, and with good reason once the quests began in earnest. The champions are summoned to fight truly fearsome foes of often great magical power, and it is Soliander's own might that often defeats these opponents. Imagine needing to be the most powerful wizard on not only one world, but across many. As a result, he sometimes takes great chances with his soul, dancing a fine line between the light and darkness to achieve his goal."

"That said," interjected Lorian, "he is a good man, but one greatly preoccupied with other matters and not given to idle conversation. His reputation for being uninterested in social matters, to the point of rudeness, is well known." Looking at Matt, he remarked, "You are far more approachable so that some will be surprised by this, but you should expect to find yourself standing alone at social events. Soliander is a most intimidating man."

Matt nodded, and Eric remembered his account of Raith at the banquet and how nervous the young wizard had seemed. No one else had spoken to him all night.

"You had best turn in early tonight," advised Lorian, rising, "for the quest begins tomorrow and you will need your strength and energy in the days ahead."

⸺ ✦ · ✦ ⸺

The arch wizard Sonneri frowned at the black orb before him. A wizard of his power didn't fail to make such simple scrying devices work, so he knew it wasn't him. Something had happened, and while it stood to reason that the spy might be in an area of Lorian's estate where contact couldn't happen, he had a bad feeling that wasn't it. If Soliander had caught on, Sonneri didn't relish the ensuing discussion.

"Stupid bird," he muttered, throwing a black cloth over the orb and turning away. Queen Lorella expected a report on their progress to Castle Darlonon, and while he could still provide one, it would be the last. She had been rather demanding the last few weeks, which was unlike her, but she was under great stress after all. It affected all of them, but he'd noticed that no relief had come to the queen with the champions' arrival, which was odd. The last time they'd been here, the situation had been astronomically worse and the task far harder, so Lorella should've been as giddy as a girl. Not so. Wondering about that, Sonneri left the tower for her meeting rooms, something nagging at the back of his mind.

UNREST IN THE FOREST

The quest began in earnest the next morning as they departed Arundell in the company of Lorian, Morven, Rognir, and a dozen elves. They traveled light, with little more than grey, woolen bedrolls and long bows tied to battle-ready horses, the leather saddle packs easily carrying what little supplies they needed. The dirt trails offered few challenges, allowing them to ride side-by-side and talk idly, but everyone kept quiet. The apprehensive mood of the group made Ryan wonder if he'd cast a pall over them. His long face matched his melancholy heart, since he'd believed for days he wouldn't be going and yet here he sat. Since he agreed with Lorian's reasoning, there was no sense thinking about it, but it weighed on him anyway and he rode in resigned silence.

The quest wasn't anything like stories made them seem. He realized all those fantasy role-playing games were true foolishness and that there was nothing romantic about this. It hadn't seemed that way on arrival and when leaving Olliana amidst cheering crowds, but those people had no clue about death. Maybe it was always that way when people went to war. People who didn't do the fighting often had romantic visions of it while those doing the killing and watching friends die were scarred for life.

The thought strengthened his resolve to escape unharmed, for he had no intention of watching his friends die or spending any more of his life mourning those close to him — whether his actions contributed to it or not. And maybe that was the heart of the matter. He would fight to save himself and his friends, and that was about all. Never mind the quest. It was only important because they couldn't go home until it was done. He wasn't a hero and didn't want to be one now that he understood what it took.

Along the way, he decided to make sure they could find their way back if something happened to the elves or Rognir. When Lorian offered to teach him and Eric scouting tricks, he accepted, learning how to tell a footprint's age and subtle signs of passage, whether it be crushed grass, overturned leaves, disturbed branches, or the more obvious overturned stones and broken limbs. Deer, elk, rabbit, and elven prints lay on every trail, but eventually they came upon a print they hadn't seen before.

"What does *that* belong to?" Ryan asked, surprised by the print's size. Longer and wider than his by half, the single set of tracks lay half in the grass and half out. Even he could tell the creator wore two mismatched boots.

Lorian's eyes moved from one print to the next. "Nothing we have to worry about now," the elf answered, rising. He made a gesture to the other elves, who cast wary glances about their path. "I hadn't expected to see this so far from the mountains, but the marks are a week old."

"Okay, but what is it?" the knight persisted as the elf remounted. So many fantasy creatures were coming to life on Honyn that the footprints' size and spacing suggested names like giant, ogre, and troll. He wasn't looking forward to meeting anything like that.

"Let us ride." Lorian took the lead again and the others followed as the knight stood there frowning. It wasn't like the elf to be tightlipped, and he and Eric exchanged a look.

Anna took the opportunity to reposition herself away from Rognir, who had pressured her to choose a god to call on when the time came. The dwarf was a priest and her three friends each wore a ring with three healing spells, so they'd be fine and not need her to pretend. She'd find a way to be helpful when the action started, stopping short of any violence. Despite the run of films and TV shows with women kicking butt, she didn't have delusions of spinning kicks and the like. She'd leave that to Eric. Staying alert would be enough for now.

She pulled up beside Matt, who rode with his nose buried in a spell book. He'd long ago let the reins drop, prompting Morven to take them and lead the horse. The breadth of available spells amazed him into reading about all of them instead of focusing on a select few to learn. He'd expected restrictions on what he could learn, such as some spells reading like gibberish until he was powerful enough, but he understood all of it and began testing himself, reciting the words without looking at them, trying to get them right.

The first night, they'd camped in the elven forest, feeling vulnerable as darkness descended. They'd been attacked in a fortified, armed castle and in Lorian's estate, so being in the open seemed absurd even with the elves standing guard. Ryan lay awake for a long time, ears straining for any weird sounds, of which there were plenty in the alien forest. Most he recognized as bird calls or night insects, and while the howl of a wolf sounded familiar, a deeper growl far off caught his ear. Two elves exchanged a look and the knight lay back heavily. It was going to be a long night. His only consolation was the belief, however uninformed, that whatever made those big footprints would make enough noise to give him some warning if it showed up here. He'd never slept in armor before but felt more comfortable in it despite it being uncomfortable.

As the second day passed, the forest-covered mountains loomed larger through the treetops, the ground rising and falling as they entered the foothills. Tomorrow would see them at the castle, meaning one last day before seeing a dragon in person. Ryan had to admit the idea still excited him if he ignored everything else, but toward noon that became impossible. The big footprints had reappeared. This time the guides' unmistakable reaction prompted him to urge his horse up to Lorian.

"What is it?" Ryan asked. The elf rose from examining the tracks, one hand discreetly loosening his sword.

"Ogres," he replied, swinging into the saddle. "Three of them. One walks with a limp." He looked the knight in the eye. "The tracks were made yesterday."

Shit, Ryan swore to himself. Remembering the other footprints being older, he asked, "Did we catch up to them?"

Loran shook his head. "None of the prints match the other set exactly. Given the unrest in the Tarron Mountains from the Dragon Cult's activities, and those like Cirion trying to reach Castle Darlonon, and Olliana trying to stop them, the ogres have likely come down to the woods for sport and will not be returning soon." He indicated the prints and remarked, "These travel parallel to the mountains, not toward them or even away like the ones yesterday."

"So there's a good chance these three are still around here?" Ryan noticed the other elves quietly checking their weapons.

Lorian didn't answer, instead remarking, "We're a few hours from the elven outpost where we'll stay tonight. They can advise us on how things fare."

That surprised the knight. "Would the ogres have easily gotten by the outpost to reach here? Wouldn't the elves have stopped them?"

Lorian's knowing green eyes met his before the elf moved on. Ryan frowned, aware of the elves repositioning themselves to surround and protect them. If the ogres had made it by the elves, what would they find ahead? He didn't know how big a deal ogres were, but an elven guard station being overrun didn't seem like a minor event. Curiosity about the number of elves there and its fortifications ate away at him. They only had twelve with them.

Toward late afternoon they stopped on the trail, having twice seen more ogre prints at least a day old and moving in various directions, as if they wandered in search of something to do. An encounter seemed inevitable. Morven made a trilling bird call twice and they waited for a reply from somewhere ahead, but nothing came. Again he made the sound only to be greeted with silence. The elf looked at Lorian and, receiving a curt nod, dismounted. As he started forward, Eric decided to follow. He half expected Lorian to tell him not to, but instead he received words of caution.

"With stealth, Andier," Lorian advised quietly. "Learn from Morven, and be armed."

Ryan shifted in his saddle, indecisive about going, too, or telling Eric to stay, and when Morven gave the rogue a look of encouragement and they moved off, he felt a pang of jealousy. They knew Eric could play his part far better than Ryan could his. If he tried to go, their reaction would likely be different. In a way, they didn't trust him, or probably even Matt or Anna, to do their parts, but Eric seemed like the real thing. The idea of being a knight still appealed to Ryan despite the violence that came with it and he frowned at his hypocrisy. He couldn't want the admiration, respect, and celebrity without the killing and maiming that would earn it, and if death led to such esteem, how could he enjoy it anyway? And yet some desire for it remained, likely from his days at RenFest, which was fake, unlike this.

He looked down at the beautiful golden armor that made him feel so cool, even proud, every time he saw it. It wouldn't look so nice with someone's blood all over it, especially his, but that reminded him of its purpose, to keep his blood from being shed. That in turn reminded him what this was about – protecting people. This was the real reason knights received those accolades he apparently wanted. Maybe he should stop trying to be so noble and just accept that he wanted to be adulated. Was that so bad? Helping Daniel all these years had made him want to be a hero to his brother, despite his true nature: a coward. Perhaps he just had to find a way to help people without hurting someone else in the process. For now, he felt relieved to be out of it. Let Eric be Andier and find out what's going on ahead. He'd be Korrin another day.

Up the dirt trail, Morven quietly led Eric, careful not to disturb fallen leaves or snap a twig. The rogue had broken into enough places as a youth to know the craft of stealth, though the consequences here would be far worse than a stint in juvenile detention on Earth. He felt ready but nervous, especially when Morven pointed out several large footprints amidst smaller ones he recognized as elven. The pair moved off the trail into the woods, paralleling the path the others were on and stopping to listen every twenty paces.

The faint sounds from the horses behind them faded as they advanced, no sound ahead.

After a hundred yards, they slowed and crouched. Morven peered up into the trees, looking for something the rogue's eyes couldn't find. "The watch post above us is vacant," he whispered, eyes searching the trees ahead, "and should not be. I see no sign of a body or struggle. Let us proceed."

Worried, Eric asked, "Should we get the others?"

Morven considered before answering. "No. You will climb the watch tree for a view into the camp while I scout ahead to make sure you have time to come down if trouble arises."

The rogue had mixed emotions about that and thought the elf ought to do that first. He'd be vulnerable up there. "What should I expect to see?"

"Into the camp, just beyond the tall hedge, with elves inside."

Dubious, Eric looked for any signs of an outpost ahead and saw none amidst the trees and bushes. He'd never have suspected a fortified position lay there.

Handing him a pair of horn-rimmed glasses, the elf said, "Take these. They will increase your sight."

Eric nodded and they crept to the watch tree, but as they neared Morven stopped him, sniffing the air. He slowly pulled a sword from its sheath.

"What is it?" the rogue whispered.

"Death," the elf replied. "Much of it. And ogres."

"Where? From inside the camp?"

The elf sniffed the air again. "Something is nearer."

Eric cocked an eyebrow. "Which is nearer? Ogres?" After a pause, he added, "Or Death?"

Morven glanced back. It was an important distinction. "Death."

There wasn't much to say about that and the elf gestured for him to start climbing. Somewhere above them was a hidden platform. The tree's hand and foot holds were carved from the trunk, a piece of bark-colored cloth concealing them from a distance. Eric went up smoothly, for he practiced parkour and could've climbed without the aids. He stayed alert for anything odd but saw no signs of a hasty exit from a wounded elf, and no blood, even at the three-foot square platform, where one branch functioned like a chair. To one side, the trail below peeked out through the foliage, winding over the hills for some distance, and in one clearing a glint of light caught the eye.

Ryan's armor, he realized, getting his bearings.

A closer view of the trail just outside the camp showed Morven wasn't kidding about death. Out on the road lay an elf, face down as if leaving the outpost for Arundell, three carrion birds picking away at the remains. While gruesome, it paled in comparison to the outpost itself. Through the leaves, Eric saw carnage amidst the wooden tower and walls, enough to realize no one lived. He counted seven dead elves and nine dead ogres, more birds pecking away at them, their distant squawks the only sound. More bodies undoubtedly lay out of sight within.

Eric looked and saw Morven patiently waiting. The elf moved his fingers at him.

What do you see? the fingers asked.

Surprised by that, the rogue answered and came down while Morven gave another bird call. This was one was answered from behind them, and soon they gathered near the body of the fallen elf on the trail. He had been bludgeoned from behind. Eric expected the grisly scene to appall Ryan in particular, but if so, the knight surprised him, gritting his teeth, looking away, and saying nothing. No one else did either.

They quietly advanced, the smell of death growing as they entered the camp with swords drawn and arrows nocked. Nothing inside moved save the birds, which took to the sky with loud protests, all pretenses of stealth going with them. Anything nearby now knew they were here.

Lorian ordered scouts into the woods while others searched the camp. Barracks large enough for a dozen people stood badly damaged and an open stone fire pit with charred embers lay in the center. A simple wooden tower provided a high archery point. A raised walkway encircled the wall's interior. Only one doorway allowed entrance, forcing any threat from the mountains to circle the camp before finding it. After the scouts returned, Lorian ordered the broken doors barricaded against roaming ogres, though none were found and all footprints were days old. Thirteen dead elves and nearly as many ogres lay both within and outside the walls. A large band had defeated these elves, and Lorian sent an elf back to Arundell to warn them and send replacements.

"We're still spending the night here?" Ryan asked, wrinkling his nose. Matt stood leaning against a wall, covering his nose with a sleeve, eyes closed.

"Yes," Lorian admitted, almost apologetically. "It is the only wise choice."

"What about the bodies?" Anna asked. "We can't stay here with them. There's a risk of infection."

"We will burn them tonight when the smoke will not attract attention."

The priestess nodded. That was safe and much faster than burial, but the smell would be awful. She already felt like it was never going to be out of her mind. Fortunately, when the time came, Lorian cast a simple spell to mute their sense of smell. It was especially welcome considering all of them were needed to move the corpses, though they spared Anna in a show of chivalry that came not only from her friends, but the elves and dwarf. She wasn't complaining.

The same couldn't be said for Matt, who clearly felt no need to hide his distaste, especially when they handled the large ogres. They were nine feet tall with an almost reddish skin, bulbous, crooked features, and soiled clothing. They exuded filth even before death. The number of wounds required to bring them down daunted him, and all but a few had arrows in them. Touching their clothing wasn't much better than their dirty bodies and everyone felt disgusted.

It seemed like forever before the funeral pyre burned in the darkness, black smoke curling into the night sky as everyone settled in for a long night. The horses were stabled inside with elves stationed at each watch post, in and outside the camp. Their owl-like calls came through the darkness every few minutes. Soon Anna found it comforting because it never changed and she hoped that would continue till dawn.

She sat staring into the funeral pyre's flames without seeing them. The scene of carnage had cast doubt on her ability to help anyone here like she did at the hospital, where she could diagnose and administer the proper aid. She was out in the field, not a cozy building waiting for the wounded to arrive, surrounded by all the latest equipment. Even if she were an EMT riding around in an ambulance, she'd be stocked up and ready to go with basic supplies.

As it was, she had nothing, just an amulet around her neck and a scroll full of gods she didn't believe existed. It hadn't mattered today, but what about tomorrow? Maybe wanting to believe it would all be better in an instant was why people had believed in witchcraft and all the other superstitions she'd scoffed at. Maybe people were still just being suckered into false hope even today. She shouldn't be so hard on them.

She needed to lighten the attitude she'd developed, but it was hard when someone like Ryan spouted religious stuff, taking it literally. She saw him up in the tower now, looking out at the Tarron Mountains as if hoping for a sight of the castle. He'd seemed melancholy since the estate but there hadn't been a chance to talk alone since. She was about to go to him when Eric dropped in beside her.

"Hello," he started quietly. She got the impression that he was trying not to disturb Matt, who sat nearby with his nose in spell books again. "How are you doing?"

Anna opened her mouth to say she was fine, but then closed it. She needn't keep up appearances about this whole thing with him. If they couldn't be honest with each other here, they were even worse off.

"Worried," she confessed, frowning.

He nodded. "About anything in particular?"

After a moment, she admitted, "Everything but you, really. You're the only one who can take care of yourself in this. The rest of us are hopeless."

His dubious expression suggested he didn't agree and she felt glad that he didn't contradict her. She needed to believe it.

"I take it you aren't planning to heal anyone with prayer," he remarked without judgment.

"I doubt I could," she admitted.

"Since you're in a new reality, can you pretend and go through the motions of communing with these gods in case it turns out to be real? It won't be the first surprise on this quest."

She looked into the pile of burning elves and ogres. He had a point there, and while the carnage had made her guard drop, she wasn't ready for that. "Maybe, but not yet," she admitted.

He leaned toward her, remarking, "Not to rush you, but you're a little short on time."

She knew what he meant, that they'd reach the castle and trouble tomorrow, but in looking at the pyre, she realized they might all be short on time in a different way if they were all killed. Companionship for her friends made her lean against him for comfort, missing the days when he would joke with her. Everything had become serious and it seemed like all of them were changing. Eric put one arm around her.

Up in the tower, Ryan happened to look down just then and felt an unexpected pang of jealousy. He turned back to his sword, which stood point down before him as he sat on a bench, the hilt in his hand. Tomorrow he'd have to use it and he reminded himself of the reason – to defend himself and his friends so *they* wouldn't end up in a funeral pyre on a strange world where friends and family would never know what became of them. He resigned himself to the coming violence and would pray for forgiveness tonight before it even started. Seeing the elves in mourning, he realized his second lesson with the lance wasn't going to happen tonight and he hoped to never need it.

As he sat lost in thought, he didn't notice Anna climbing up to him until she sat down beside him. They exchanged a look before both turned their attention over the dark forest, the looming mountains a darker black against the night sky, two of the three moons visible overhead. Not for the first time,

Ryan stared at them bleakly for what they were – a reminder that they were far from home.

He seldom forgot to wonder what Daniel was doing back on Earth, but for the first time it occurred to him that Daniel was probably worried what had happened to him and the others. After all, it wasn't like Ryan to not check in. A search had likely started right away but not mattered. It wasn't like anyone would find them.

"Are you ready?" Anna asked quietly as he put away the sword.

He glanced at her, having wondered the same thing about her. "Are you?"

"Not really, no. I'm hoping I won't be needed."

He nodded slowly. "I couldn't agree more."

"There's nothing I can do to help anyone," said Anna, "so I feel kind of useless. I can't exactly heal people here."

He looked out over the woods. "Don't be so sure. Magic works here, and they believe in it. So do I, in fact. I've seen it now, and we've heard the stories Matt's been telling of his magic training. If magic works and people believe in it, it stands to reason that faith-based healing works, too, since they believe in that. No one's lied to us about anything. So far."

She nodded reluctantly. "Maybe, but that doesn't mean I'll be able to do it. And I'd have to believe it first, which I don't see happening anytime soon. I wish I had at least basic medical supplies like on Earth." After a moment, she added, "You know, there are people who believe in faith-based healing back home, too, but it doesn't work there."

Knowing they were tiptoeing around her atheism and politely avoiding an argument about that, he asked, "How can you be sure?"

She frowned. "Well, I suppose I can't be, but do you really believe that it works on Earth?"

He opened his mouth to say yes, then closed it. "I don't know. I've thought about taking Daniel to one of these guys, but they wanted a lot of money, which to me meant it was a scam."

"Right," she said.

Suddenly something occurred to him. "Wait a minute. If you could learn to heal people here, you could do it on Earth and heal Daniel!" He stood up in excitement. "Think about it. We know magic works there because the Quest Ring worked there, so it stands to reason that healing works, too. You just have to learn how and then you could heal Daniel!"

They stared at each other silently. "But Ryan–"

"No! No buts!" He grabbed her by the arms and lifted her to her feet. "It will work! I know it!" His excited shouts turned the attention of those in the camp to them. "How could I have not seen it earlier? *That's* the reason I'm here. *You're* here. It all makes sense now. This is God's doing. He has given me a chance, a chance to save Daniel!" His bright eyes turned back to her. "He's given *you* a chance. You can do it. I know you can!"

Finally Anna found words to stop him from going any further. "Ryan, just wait a minute," she started gently. "I understand your hope but you're getting way ahead of yourself."

"No I'm not!"

"Yes you are, and you're putting way too much pressure on me."

That pierced his excitement some, but not much. "Okay, that's true, and I'm sorry, but you have to promise to try for me. For Daniel. Will you? Please? I know it's against your beliefs and everything and I'm sorry for that, but we have a different reality here and I would be sooo grateful if you would just give it a chance to see what can happen."

He stared into her eyes, dimly aware of them darting away from his and back, like a trapped deer. He opened his mouth to say more when she finally spoke.

"Okay, okay," she said gently, "just stop. I'll look into it. I already have. Just stop, okay?"

He was about to try to convince her more but then thought better of it. "You promise? Please?"

"Yes, I promise," she said, looking around hastily. "To look into it, not to succeed."

"Okay. Okay, that's fair. But you have to have faith, Anna, or nothing happens. Please open yourself to it."

She said nothing more, turning to the ladder as if to escape, and he wondered if he'd gone too far. Probably. For the first time since they'd left Stonehenge, he felt calm, and with a renewed purpose. Now he regretted any time avoiding learning things that might benefit them, and ultimately, his brother, who was going to be amazed when Anna helped him. Ryan spent the rest of the night imagining it.

The night passed without incident from ogres or anything else and they left the outpost on horseback at dawn. As the day wore on, the foothills grew steeper, the trail narrowing to single file and the trees and underbrush growing denser. Anna kept her distance from Ryan, while Matt once again kept his nose buried in spell books. Morven and Eric rode ahead of the group, the latter in training for how to track and listen to the forest's sounds. Even his sense of smell received instruction.

"Ogres have a certain scent," advised the elf, long brown hair tightly braided. "You no doubt recall it from last night, though it was mixed with the smell of death."

"Yes, I remember," the rogue wryly admitted.

Toward noon they stopped in a small clearing for lunch consisting of elven bread smothered in fruit jam, downed with spring water that invigorated them more than Ryan would have expected. It tasted like sweet water. Both he and Matt had passed on breakfast due to nerves and nausea but both were able to eat this time.

Ryan hadn't stopped thinking about Anna healing Daniel since he'd thought of it. He felt renewed purpose and was chafing for something to get her motivated. He knew she liked his brother and would be happy to heal him once able. The trick was getting her to see that they lived in a new reality now and that she had to change her perspective. He wanted to talk to her more, but every time their eyes met, he saw her looking like she wanted to avoid him. A pang of regret filled him. Wouldn't it be ironic if his pressure became the reason she refused to open herself up to the gods of this world or of Earth? He wanted to laugh. Or cry. For now, he decided to bite his tongue, sitting over by Matt and studiously avoiding any hope-filled gazes at the medical student.

Ahead on the trail, a sharp shout preceded a hoarse bellow. Several thuds boomed ominously before a crack of stone striking stone and a scream split the air. Everyone rose and reached for weapons as Lorian issued commands, pointing up the trail where two elves ran with bows drawn. Rognir came to stand beside the champions, gesturing for Ryan to get out his sword. The dwarf's axe gleamed before them, its obvious wear and tear adding realism to their dread.

"What is it?" Anna asked, moving toward her horse. Ryan thought she looked ready to mount and go. The idea sounded better the second someone answered her.

"Ogres," replied Matt, able to understand elven thanks to Lorian's spell.

"Indeed." Rognir brandished his axe, taking warm up swings. "Battle is upon us. I suggest you remain behind me."

"No argument there," muttered Matt as angry sounds reached them.

He wiped both hands on his robe and Ryan suspected the wizard's palms were sweaty, like his. Ryan mentally reviewed what Lorian taught him about not hurting anyone much, though that now seemed less important than protecting himself. The assassin attack had happened so fast he never had time to think about it, but this time the waiting was awful and he eyed the horses. He would not be the first to run, but if someone else went for it, he was all in.

Suddenly a low rumbling began as the ogres charged around the bend, two elves retreating ahead of them. Morven and others stood at the trailhead with arrows nocked, and when the ogres came into view, he called out in elven. The elves let fly, all at the lead ogre, six arrows striking it in the head, neck, and chest. It tumbled in a heap, its huge, spiked club rolling ahead of it. Two other ogres tripped over it, slowing the pack and giving the elves time for one more volley. None of the remaining six or seven ogres fell.

Rognir moved a few steps ahead of the champions as if to bar the way to them and Ryan reluctantly joined him. An arrow soared overhead toward the ogres from behind the champions, via the other elf watching their rear. As the attackers reached the clearing, a line of elves tried to bottle them up on the path so that only one or two ogres could attack at once, but momentum carried four ogres into the clearing, their wooden clubs whooshing through the air, metal protrusions catching elven blades. They weren't kidding around and Ryan paled at the sickening crunch as an elf's shoulder shattered and he flew sideways. Lorian replaced the fallen one, sword bouncing right off a club that soon sent another elf to the ground with pulverized bones. Rognir clomped forward to drag the wounded elf back by the tunic before bending to heal him as Ryan watched curiously, but unable to see the result.

Suddenly Eric threw a knife over the heads of the elves, but the blade missed when the beast happened to move. The knife distracted the ogre long enough for Lorian to kill it. Eric's next knife flew true into another's throat, killing it instantly. As the corpse toppled backward, Ryan felt no regret, just relief. What did that mean about him?

A roar to one side startled him. An ogre had come around the thick brush and trees unseen. Its club hurtled toward his head and he barely ducked as it whooshed by. He retreated, eyes wide, forgetting everything Lorian had taught him. As the club came down like a hammer, he sidestepped and stumbled on a tree root. By the time he recovered, there was no dodging the coming blow. He raised the sword and met the club with a clang, nearly losing his grip. The ogre raised the club with both hands, lust for death on its face. Did it sense what Ryan did, that the knight stood dead center, too close to dodge, and had little idea how to use that sword? Realizing his peril, Ryan lunged and stabbed it through the stomach. The ogre squealed hideously and slid back off the blade, sickly red blood oozing out. Ryan blanched at what he'd done. His self-preservation instinct had overridden his dispositions as if they were nothing.

The ogre's expression promised such death and personal hatred that Ryan snapped out of it. It was still going to kill him, but he didn't have to do the same. With a grimace of resignation, he punched the ogre in the wound and it doubled over, screeching awfully. Then Ryan clobbered it in the jaw. The ogre toppled backwards and lay stunned and unmoving.

A moment passed before Ryan realized he'd done it. He'd stopped it, and without killing it. Or at least he thought so. Suddenly worried he ended a life, he looked at the Trinity Ring on one hand. Rognir had told him how to use it, so he put one hand on the ogre and focused his will on the middle stone. Tingling warmth spread from his hand, which glowed softly as the belly wound all but disappeared. He'd never seen magical healing or experienced it, feeling like an affirmation of God's power had occurred. Sighing in relief, he rose and moved over by Anna and Matt. Maybe he could do this champion stuff after all.

He saw that another three ogres lay dead, despite Lorian's comments that elves held all life sacred. Maybe elves weren't so pious after all. Or maybe they just understood something that he didn't. Rognir had meanwhile healed several elves and Ryan could tell that Anna hadn't moved from where he'd last seen her, far from the action. He couldn't blame her, but it meant she wasn't even trying. Even *he* was.

Anna had watched Rognir leaning over one injured elf after another as if helping them, but she hadn't seen anything happen. No glow of godly power. No wounds closing. Nothing. She wasn't even sure he'd helped them in any way, not to mention by laying on hands. His back had been turned each time. Part of her felt annoyed by that, but part of her was relieved that no proof she was wrong about gods had shown up. The medical student in her couldn't help thinking of how one wound or another would be treated back on Earth.

Ryan's fight with the ogre had surprised her a little, that he could fight back so well despite the whole non-violence thing. If she wasn't so consumed by fear she might've almost felt proud of him. She had no idea why he'd leaned over the ogre after. Still waiting beside Matt, she now watched Eric standing ready for another knife throw, when something caught her eye. The ogre Ryan had fought rose to its feet. Her eyes darted to its belly, wondering how that could be, and she stared uncomprehending at the belly wound that was now gone. For a moment, this distracted her into not realizing it was raising its club and swinging at the nearest target.

"Eric!" she screamed as the club flew toward his shoulder.

The martial artist was already turning, but Anna saw it wouldn't be fast enough. With a sickening crunch of shattered bones, the blow flung him five feet away, where he landed screaming and writhing in pain, the knife from his other hand sticking out of his thigh. Without thinking, Anna ran over to him, putting herself in danger as she knelt and tried to stop him from rolling back in forth in agony. Behind her, she heard Matt's voice speaking words that sounded like magic.

"Kertemor iafiirlompu terteli, uapiiltoko nukoorkel naakli." *Shards of ice like darts be thrown, strike my foe down to the bone.*

Anna looked up at the ogre, only now realizing her peril. She'd seen enough men ogle her to be surprised by a similar expression on its disgusting face. If Matt's spell had worked, there was no sign of it. She heard him saying it again, faster, more nervously she thought, and realized it hadn't worked. Then another voice spoke similar yet different words and she glanced over to see Lorian crumbling a piece of stone in one outstretched hand, toward the ogre. She looked up again. The ogre's face twisted in surprise, its movement slowing to a stop and a grunt abruptly cutting off. Its skin turned a deep grey as it turned to stone, upraised club and all.

Suddenly the noisy Rognir stopped beside her, examining the still writhing Eric, who continuously moaned in such pain that Anna fought back tears. "How bad is it?"

Anna shook her head, unable to speak. His shoulder had shattered. He'd never use the arm again and modern hospitals back home would never get all the bone fragments out. Even his neck had twisted from the tortured angle of his shoulder and he'd never be pain free again. The dwarf laid a hand on the rogue and spoke a word. Eric relaxed into a stupor, his head lolling to one side as if he were delirious, no longer groaning.

"He will feel no pain for a few minutes," Rognir advised her, "but you must heal him quickly."

She'd forgotten all about that, but now was not the time for half-baked theories. She opened her mouth to say so but what came out was, "But I don't know how."

"Lay your hands on him," he advised gently, "and ask your chosen god for help with all your heart and soul. I know you care for him. The gods will answer you."

She looked down at the rogue, his glazed eyes on hers as if dimly aware. Placing both hands on him, she honestly wanted him healed, but the gods she'd read about all seemed jumbled to her, their names and what they stood for confused. There were too many and she longed for one god to make it simple like on Earth, which only reminded her that this was all nonsense. She looked down at her hands, tightly clenched on Eric's clothes. Nothing was happening. It didn't surprise her. Her pleading eyes sought the dwarf's.

Rognir took her hands away and placed his own on the rogue. In dwarven, he spoke quietly for almost a minute, sincerity on his bearded face. Anna wished she could understand him, gain some insight into what he was doing. Finally, a golden light spread from Rognir's hands over Eric's shoulder before fading, like all signs of Eric's injuries. Even his leg had healed. The rogue blinked and sat up, clear eyes on the dwarf.

"Thank you," Eric said emphatically. "Words cannot describe..."

Rognir patted him. "Then do not strain yourself. There is no need." He got to his feet wearily. From what Anna had heard, the power she'd finally just witnessed used the priest's body as a conduit, an act that was draining. The dwarf had healed multiple people just now. He took a long pull from a pouch that Anna knew wasn't water before stomping away past a dead elf. The skull damage had killed that one instantly. Anna realized it was the one who knew how to slay a dragon and hoped Ryan didn't notice that. Only now did Anna realize the battle was over.

She turned Eric. "Are you alright?"

He nodded slowly, as if lost in thought. Then he began to smile. "You've got to try that," he said, and she assumed he meant healing someone, until he added, "It feels great."

"You're sure?"

"Yeah." He sounded surprised, but then he looked away and she followed his gaze to Ryan. Even from here, the big guy looked pale and shaken. The knight had healed the ogre, which had then nearly killed Eric. Wondering what he was thinking, she turned to the rogue, and the quiet anger she now saw in his eyes left little to wonder about.

"Not now," she said quietly. "Not when you're mad."

"I'm never not going to be mad."

She leaned over to hug him and sudden tears spilled down her cheeks, he put both arms around her and they stayed there for several minutes.

Though the ogres – and one elf before them – were dead, Lorian maintained high alert, making everyone mount and continue down the trail still armed. He said that once the sounds of battle had rung out, other nearby ogres would've come hot for blood if around, but other things more cunning could now be watching and waiting. All seemed eerily quiet as they advanced to the scene of the initial attack, finding the lead elf's body.

While the elves tended to the remains, Eric went to talk to Ryan, who stood on the far side of his horse as if wanting to be alone and away from everyone. The rogue patted Ryan's horse on his way around the back so it wouldn't get startled and kick him. He'd had enough blunt-force trauma for one day. Stopping next to Ryan, he tried to mute his anger.

"What were you thinking healing that ogre?"

Ryan's face couldn't have gotten much longer. "I didn't want it to die." When Eric didn't say anything, the knight added, "Is that so wrong?"

"Well no, not in theory, but when the choice is us or them, then yes. It was already knocked out. You didn't have to make it recover. I mean, come on, Ryan, that was ridiculous. If it had swung higher and hit my head, I'd be dead."

Looking at his feet, the knight muttered, "I know. You don't have to remind me."

Frustration mounting, the rogue added, "What is it with you anyway? Why are you so afraid of hurting anyone? I mean most people don't *want* to, but they can at least be rational about it when something's trying to *kill* them. You make such a big deal of out this to the point of letting someone else get hurt anyway, so it's kind of a moot point, isn't it?" When the big man just looked away, Eric continued, "Did you hurt someone once or something? Is that it?" Again the knight said nothing, just turning his face away. "That's it, isn't it? You act like you're all traumatized by it or something. Why don't you just get over it and move on?"

Seeming startled, some fire appeared in Ryan's eyes as he turned back. "Because *he* can't," Ryan replied before turning his back, "so why should I?"

"Who?"

"It doesn't matter."

"Oh yes it does. I almost got killed today over it so I think I've just earned the right to know whose life is more important than mine."

"Would you stop it? It was an accident. I didn't mean for you to get hurt."

"So? I *did* get hurt. Was you hurting this other guy also an accident? I can't imagine you doing something on purpose."

"*Thanks.*"

Eric wasn't used to hearing sarcasm from Ryan. That was *his* domain. But when the knight didn't answer the question, he repeated it.

Ryan sighed irritably and admitted over his shoulder, "Yes."

"Okay great. Now we're getting somewhere. So it was an accident. Why don't you forgive yourself and forget about it? And get on with your life. And stop letting it cause other accidents?"

"Well what right do I have to get on with my life if he can't get on with his?" Ryan snapped. He didn't mention that there was no forgetting about it, not with a daily reminder, but he didn't want to let on too much. He didn't think he could stand them knowing the truth. It was better to let them wonder at his preoccupations – even if they thought less of him for it – than to see their knowing eyes on him all the time.

"Why, is he dead?" Eric asked.

"No, he's not dead," Ryan answered in annoyance.

"Then what? Paraly–" Eric stopped in mid word. It made all the sense in the world and he didn't know why he hadn't realized it before.

Ryan had stiffened and silence hung heavy in the air. Suddenly the rogue realized that everyone was listening to their conversation.

"Was it Daniel?" Eric asked quietly. Ryan turned his head away again, fists and jaw clenched. In the silence, Eric asked more pointedly, "Did you paralyze Daniel?"

He didn't mean it to sound like an accusation, but Ryan now whirled around, his face turning red with fury. He visibly struggled for words before finally responding.

"Yes!" he shouted. "It was Daniel, all right? I paralyzed my brother, God damn it. Is that what you wanted to know? Does *that* make you happy? *I'm* the one who put him in that fucking wheelchair for the rest of his life. *I* was the one who was fucking around and knocked him off the trampoline. It was *me*, God damn it!"

Eric was suddenly aware of Ryan's size, having seen big, angry men take out trained martial artists before. If he'd known his questions would lead to this revelation, he'd have gone about it differently. Now he tried to defuse the situation. "It was an accident," he started.

"So? What difference does that make? He's still *paralyzed*."

"Intent matters, and you know it does. It's why I'm not mad at you for healing the ogre desp–"

"Oh really? You sure sounded mad a minute ago. Don't you fucking pity me, God damn it. I don't need that shit from you."

Eric opened his mouth to reply but Anna's hand on his arm stopped him.

"Ryan," she started quietly.

He glanced at her. "Oh what do *you* want?"

She bit her lip. "To see you happy."

He seemed to swallow a retort before thinking of something else to say. "Good, then you can learn how to heal by magic or whatever it is, and when we get back home you can fix Daniel. *That* will make me happy, and nothing else."

Politely, she responded, "You know I'm going to try for your sake as much as your brother's, but you should prepare for the possibility that it won't work and find a way to accept what's happened. Otherwise you'll be miserable for the rest of your life. Is that really what you want?"

"As a matter of fact, it is," he said snidely. "Why do I deserve to be happy when Daniel isn't?"

"Why are you so sure he's unhappy?"

"How can he not be?" Ryan interrupted incredulously.

"He's moved on with his life, adapted to the injury, and found a purpose, just like everyone else does with their lives. He finished college, got a job, and has a life, but you quit school, won't work, and you won't do anything with your life so you're available to him all the time. That's great in spirit, but he doesn't need or even want that. He wants you to live your life, too, but you're the one who's held back by what happened."

He glared at her, wanting this conversation to end. "Well you're going to fix that by healing him, and since you're all so determined to help, I expect to see everyone doing just that."

CHAPTER THIRTEEN

A RUIN ALIVE

The dark silhouette of a castle stood out against the night sky, a handful of lights twinkling in its black windows like stars. The moonlight showed no details of it or the surrounding mountains, but the path to it had been easy enough to follow. Below, the dark tree tops of the forest swayed in the night breeze, hiding whatever lay underneath and suggesting the forest teemed with activity. The rustling leaves were audible all the way up here and gave them the creeps.

As Cirion's mercenaries watched the castle, a sight they weren't expecting caught their eyes. Another silhouette, this time of two giant wings attached to a thick body with four legs and a long tail, rose up from within. With powerful strokes, the dragon soared into a nearby cloud to disappear. Relaxing, they realized now might be a good time to get through the gate before it came back.

The winding road into the mountains had hidden them from the castle's inhabitants, since trees had claimed what Darlonon abandoned. Likely knowing nothing of fortifications and keeping lines of sight open, the cult members, hired mercenaries, and a handful of ogres, had unknowingly allowed Cirion's mercenaries to get up here without resistance, but they weren't the only ones here.

A young wizard leaned against a boulder to save his strength, not at all happy with how much he'd been relied upon to get past the guards from Olliana. Stationed along the road, the guards barred the way to Castle Darlonon in such a way as to prevent anyone from simply going around them. While the magic he'd used to do so anyway had drained his strength, the exercise had been worse. They'd been running along the road the last few hours, having left the noisy horses behind in a ravine. The others seemed to think his struggles were an annoyance and that he now slowed them down, but without Raith, they wouldn't have gotten this far, and certainly not before the Ellorians.

How quickly they forget, he thought to himself darkly.

He'd enchanted their horses to gallop across the land much faster than biology allowed, moving from Olliana to the ravine far below in record time. Cirion's surprise at the show of power had been clear, but the wizard had foreseen that. He'd been toting around a new spell book and told their leader that such superior spells came from its pages. That part was true, but he'd really mastered the whole book long ago. Sometimes it was wise to be more powerful than people expected. In fact, it *always* was.

Whether stopping time for a minute, making the guards forget them, turning themselves invisible, or some other spell, Raith had shuttled them past everyone so that only the guards at the gate remained. He now claimed he was out of such tricks. Let someone else expend their strength, like Cirion, whose fighting and stealth could lead them forward.

The rogue peered around a boulder at the open space before the castle. He'd been here before and it hadn't changed much except for no longer being deserted. Between the tree growth and small landslides that hadn't been cleared, enough cover existed to reach the closed gates unseen. A big hole in one would let them in, though someone undoubtedly watched it from inside. Through it they saw two ogres pacing back and forth, with more likely out of sight, but there was only one way to tell.

Cirion gave the signal and they moved ahead.

——— ◆ · ◆ ———

He hadn't really known what to expect, but when Ryan finally laid eyes on the ruined Castle Darlonon high above, his stomach twisted. This was it. They were here. It was real. Lights even shone in some of the windows, though nothing could be made out from here. Maybe that was good. He didn't want to think about who, or what, waited for them.

No one had said anything to him about the earlier incident and for that he'd been glad, until now. Part of him felt something was warranted from someone, maybe even himself for his outbursts, but he wasn't ready. He'd been emoting a "leave me alone" vibe ever since, too, but maybe tensions should have been resolved before they headed inside. Now that he sat there with true peril awaiting, he regretted not smoothing things over. He glanced over at Anna, and on seeing her blank gaze, which seemed unfriendly to him, he flashed a half smile. She nodded and looked away and he sighed.

Only his family had known who paralyzed Daniel because they'd decided long ago to shield him from others blaming or pitying him. The omission was meant to protect him when he felt undeserving of that anymore. After all, as Daniel's older brother, it was his job to protect him, and in this he had failed miserably. His parents' protection had only made him feel more ashamed of what he'd done. That shame drove him to hover over his brother constantly, to protect him, to provide anything he needed. To make amends. He couldn't help it, even though he knew Daniel didn't like it. He sighed again, almost relieved the secret was out.

From the saddle, he watched as the others dismounted, secured their horses, and took what they needed from their packs. The dwarves who'd built the castle had used this tunnel entrance until construction ended, when they magically sealed and concealed it. Even now there seemed to be nothing but yet another jagged rock wall in the cliff face, but that could've been just the darkness of night. He took Rognir's blunt announcement that they'd arrived on faith. No one else seemed perplexed, so Ryan dismounted, remembering to take his helmet and the lance, wondering if there'd be any corners too tight to get the lance around. Maybe he'd have to leave it behind.

Eric stood gazing up as if looking for a route to climb it, his rock-climbing experience likely making easy work of it, but unless the elves could do that, too, he'd be going alone. The rogue had a sealed pocket in his clothes, with climbing chalk that he'd arrived with. He also had lock picking tools and other devices like a glass cutter in hidden pockets in the leather pants and jacket.

Matt had been preoccupied since the ogre battle, trying to shrug off his failure to cast a spell. There could've been any number of reasons for it, but he knew nerves had been the only reason. The words had been right. He'd looked at them again since and confirmed it. He'd just felt their eyes on him, people wondering what he'd attempt, whether it would work or not, and his mouth had grown dry. His eyes had sought Lorian's for approval but seen only alarm that he was doing anything. He'd tried to shut it all out, waiting for the power to fill him, but nothing had come, especially not the icy darts he'd expected to shoot through the air. The pressure to do it before the ogre crushed Anna's head hadn't helped. Thank God for Lorian, who had since favored him with a smile or two that suggested compassion that Matt resented because it resembled pity. But he wasn't holding a grudge. The elf meant well.

Lorian summoned him to the rock wall. "Remember, your staff can detect magic," remarked Lorian to Matt, who'd learned more about Soliander's staff, including that it automatically protected him from many things, which was a relief. "Use it to discover the door's location. It is hidden by illusion."

The young wizard nodded. He'd practiced this trick on his magic items in front of his friends so he wasn't worried. After a moment's concentration, a rusty and stubborn looking iron door materialized nearby in the rock. Only he could see it until he pointed it out to the others, tracing its shape and describing it to them. Lorian started to approach it when Matt stopped him.

"Wait," he said, aware that the detection spell hadn't abated. "There's more."

The elf cocked an eyebrow. "Can you discern its nature?"

Matt pursed his lips, but he wasn't the one who could sense something and the staff wasn't passing along impressions. "Not really, no."

"There is a spell for it. It is called the Omni-Eye and reveals the details of an existing spell. Did you learn it?"

The wizard remembered seeing it but hadn't memorized it. He shook his head and the elf made him stand back. Matt watched eagerly, hoping to learn something from the guy he considered the master to his apprentice, but aside from a few gestures, there wasn't much to see.

"Interesting," Lorian remarked. "Anyone who touches the door will be transferred inside the castle to the dungeon and an alarm beacon will light in several guard rooms."

Matt grunted. "You got all that from that? That's pretty cool. Could we use it to get inside? It would certainly save time."

"You mean trigger the spell on purpose?" Lorian asked, eyebrow cocked. "Yes, but we can't risk the alarm, though it's unlikely anyone inside would know what it means. Still, being trapped in the dungeon is a real possibility."

"True," the wizard conceded, disappointed. Being teleported places seemed like fun, but that really depended on where you arrived and who was waiting for you. "Can you disarm it?"

Lorian nodded. "Can you?"

Matt made a face. "Somehow I knew you'd ask that."

The elf stepped aside and added, "Nothing will happen if you fail, so do not be concerned."

Except I'll look stupid, thought the wizard. He shook his head, trying to block out the thought. He had just succeeded a minute ago and still felt good, so he closed his eyes and reached out to the staff. He'd done this many times now but finding the right impulse to awaken required concentration. He searched with his will, blanking his mind and letting his desire guide the staff. At times like this it seemed his lack of concentration helped him, for his mind picked up on the staff's subtle responses. Images formed in his head and he couldn't resist focusing on them, which helped him grasp the staff's power. Opening his eyes, he reached forward with one hand and a ray of light snaked out to engulf the door with a slight flash before retreating into his hand. A twirling ball of light hovered there for just a moment before fading to black and puffing out, smoke curling into the air.

"Excellent," Lorian congratulated him. Anna and Eric gave a smattering of applause. Pleased but embarrassed, Matt indicated no other spells were on the door.

Rognir took the lead, remarking, "This will lead up a slope, through storage rooms, and by several hallways we can ignore, though we had best be wary of anything that's taken up residence since the castle was abandoned."

His comments reminded Matt of role-playing games where monsters lurked in every room and traps could lie anywhere.

"What about traps?" Ryan asked, watching an elf hand out unlit torches. He donned his golden helmet, leaving the visor raised.

The dwarf put on his own helmet. "There shouldn't be any in the lower areas, not from dwarves anyway. I can't say what the humans did after we built it." Eyeing the lance, he added, "That shouldn't be a problem."

"Where will we come out?" Eric asked.

Rognir gruffly answered, "Let us not waste time. You will see soon enough."

After heaving the door open, Rognir and Lorian led the way with lit torches, the champions in the middle with Morven right behind, other elves bringing up the rear. Matt remembered to light his staff, experimenting with changing its brightness, radius, and beam. He was starting to think this was all very cool when they soon found their path blocked once again.

Anna observed, "Somebody really wanted to keep people out."

"That somebody was Soliander," noted Lorian.

Matt thought that the bluish metal door looked quite new; it had been fused with the stone all around it, not just cut into place. The walls, ceiling, and floor had even bowed inward as if to grasp the door. He saw no handle or hinge. Only a fist-sized, circular hole lay in the center, with several notches cut into the otherwise smooth circle of it. The door looked familiar, though he'd never seen anything like it. Not even realizing why he did it, Matt lowered the staff, placing the lit crystal into the hole. It didn't fit at first because he hadn't lined up the prongs holding it, but once he did it slid right into place. The door gave a brief pulse before turning transparent and releasing the staff. He put one hand against it, but his flesh passed right through it because it was now only an illusion.

"How did you know to do that?" Ryan asked.

The wizard looked blank, but then a spark of realization lit his eyes. "A hunch. The symbol on the door looks like one I saw during the magic test Lorian gave me, though I don't understand why." After a moment, he added, "It also doesn't explain how I knew what to do."

"Something to ponder later," advised Lorian, gesturing for them to pass through before it closed. They stepped into an empty storage room beyond and the door turned solid behind them. As the others followed Rognir, Lorian quietly observed to Matt, "Only Soliander could make it past that."

"Or someone with his staff," corrected Matt, wondering if the elf was trying to tell him something.

—— • • • ——

Like any good medicine, it tasted awful to prevent misuse, and so Cirion choked down the foul tasting stuff with a grimace until the blue vial sat empty. As he lowered the vial, the slash on his forehead disappeared, as did the more troublesome, bloody gash on his sword arm and a smaller one on a leg. Most of those around him were doing the same, for few had escaped the battle unscathed.

They had made it past the five ogres and the mercenaries beyond the gate but with a terrible price. Four of his men were dead and most of the others were hurt, but the rogue regretted it not. They'd known what they were getting themselves into when they signed up with him and he wouldn't tolerate any whining about it now. Still, he'd expected better swordplay from several, who at least paid with their own lives, but they had risked his as well. Their ineptness also caused an alarmingly quick reduction in their healing potions. After using up most of what they'd brought, he'd looked to Raith to see if any were hidden in those robes, but the wizard shook his head. Hopefully no more would be needed, but he doubted that. He wasn't entirely certain the wizard was telling the truth about that, either.

They stood in the castle's entrance hall, doors closed behind them. No sounds of running feet came their way thanks to Nola's quick aim with the crossbow. A robed cult member had gone sprinting between the curving stairs on either side and straight into the castle's further reaches, but the crossbow bolt had slain him in mid stride. For now, no one knew they were here except the dead, and Cirion intended to keep it that way.

The flaming tiles he'd encountered last time hadn't been active in the courtyard, presumably done away with by the current occupants. The stairways, however, were still out of the question due to what was happening on them and had apparently been happening for a long time. With swords, knives, and bows in hand, men dressed much like them stood on the stairs in climbing positions, and yet they moved not at all. Each stood caught in time, alive but forever unmoving. They'd all been here the last time Cirion had, and in fact two of them were his men, and yet they hadn't moved more than an inch in all that time. The rogue looked longingly at an ornate dagger in one man's hand, for it was his and had been borrowed shortly before the man became ensnared. He'd resigned himself to never getting it back.

Cirion gestured toward the guy with a bolt in his back. "That way."

Nola and Raith followed, their hired men following, weapons drawn. Ahead stood an archway with two hallways leading right and left to the rest of the castle. The main wing stood straight ahead, but the rogue hadn't been lying to Anna when telling her a maze lay there. He suspected traps waited everywhere, and while he specialized in getting past them, many would be magical and beyond his skills. A glance showed the young wizard's lips silently moving as he tried to detect magic along each path. At the very least, they wouldn't be going straight into that room.

"Anything?" Cirion asked, realizing the ogre blood dripping from his sword to the floor would leave a trail. He wiped it on an ogre's shirt.

"Yes," the wizard answered. "There's something in every direction, but more directly ahead. Still, I think we should go forward, even if by another route. The gate is bound to be in a big room in the main wing."

Cirion frowned. "Wouldn't it be hidden in some out of the way place where no one would look for it."

"No," the wizard disagreed. "Remember, the dragons had to be pulled into it, so it must be enormous, and the only rooms that big are public places."

"He's right," agreed Nola.

And Cirion knew she did so reluctantly. Neither of them trusted the wizard. Well, they didn't trust *anyone*, but they both thought Raith was hiding something. The show of strength he'd put on to get them here had surprised him. To agree with Raith now probably made her feel like she was playing a part in some machination of his she didn't understand. That's how Cirion felt. Beyond the outrage of being duped by someone they'd held in contempt, he knew such things usually ended with the ignorant person dead. It was too bad Nola hadn't managed to drug Korrin with that sleeping potion after the banquet; that damn Andier ruined that. It would've given them a head start of a few days, but thanks to Raith, it seemed they'd arrived first anyway.

"All right," Cirion started, "let's avoid the big halls unless we can see into them before entering. That dragon will be back soon, so let's get on with our search before we find it sitting between us and the Dragon Gate." He gestured to a side hallway that hopefully led in the same general direction while providing cover. "This way."

He and Raith took the lead, each doing their part to detect traps as Nola and their hired henchman followed. The way seemed clear as they paralleled the big room on one side via a hallway leading further into the castle. Doorways spilled into other rooms, some with spells upon them, but all were empty of life. Down an adjacent corridor lay several skeletons and a more recent corpse with flesh still on it, all with charred clothing. From the next doorway beyond it, a sliver of golden light streamed into the hall. Cirion motioned Nola forward as he listened to men speaking without concern of being overheard.

"The dragon's out for her nightly feast," said a gruff voice, "but she'll be back soon."

"Good thing it's not one of us," remarked another, chuckling.

Only nervous laughter greeted that, and someone asked, "Your service to the dragons stops short of being dinner?"

Before anyone could answer, Cirion kicked in the door. The nearest guard turned to find Cirion's short sword slicing into his chest. The guard went down with a grunt and the three other men stared in shock as the intruders charged. Nola's crossbow found its target across the room, piercing through a man's belly and pinning him to his chair. She was already swinging her sword at another man who soon fell dead. The last guard ran toward another door. Seeing this, the guard bolted to his chair yelled out, "No! Not that way!"

It was too late. As he crossed the threshold, the man turned to solid ice, his momentum carrying him sliding across the floor toward the stairs across the room, a wide-eyed expression frozen on his face. As he tumbled down it, the ice – and him along with it – shattered, cascading downward like ice cubes made of body parts.

"Nasty use for a transmutation spell," muttered Raith, smirking. "Anywhere that's safe to go, the guards know and have been. Either the dragon cleared a path through the halls or a wizard working for them did it."

Nola looked at him flatly. "Or the wizard who opened the gate."

"Or that," he admitted.

"So how do we figure out which paths those are?" Cirion asked, noting his henchmen keeping alert in the hall.

In the silence, the wounded guard whimpered and the intruders exchanged a look. Soon they had pried him from the crossbow bolt and chair and were headed back down the corridor, the guard in front with Cirion's knife to his throat. Unless he wanted to be the first victim of a trap, he'd steer them clear all the way to the gate, but it proved more difficult than that.

"Wait, wait," said the guard, and they paused near a hall's end.

"What is it?" Cirion whispered.

"Guards," the man replied quickly, "around this corner. They're always here. The gate room is up the stairs beyond it."

Nola cautiously took a look to confirm it. "A lot of them on a wide staircase, looking bored," she reported, turning to Raith coldly. "You better have something good ready."

Cirion knocked out the guard and quietly laid him aside, and when the wizard gave the signal, they launched their attack. As they charged forward and startled guardsmen fumbled for weapons, the flapping of leathery wings accompanied a loud roar before the floor shook hard enough to knock them all off balance. Part of a wall nearby crumbled and an arrow intended for them missed wildly. A disturbed look passed between intruders and guardsmen alike.

The dragon had returned.

———— ◆ · ◆ ————

They stood quietly in the dark, their torches doused, the wizard's staff dark. Just ahead sat an open room full of dust, cobwebs, and scattered crates, but no signs of recent passage. On the far side, an open archway revealed a stone staircase rising toward the castle's main areas, dim firelight dancing down the stairwell from above. A nearby noise had inspired their caution, but it didn't compare to the deep thud that now shook the walls, loose mortar falling from the ceiling, a rotting board dropping with a muted clatter. Anna cringed at the sound. Only a dragon somewhere above them could've made that thud. As the elves unsheathed their swords, she eyed the lance. Such a slender weapon taking out something massive enough to make that loud a noise seemed improbable.

Eric crept up the stairs with Lorian. After peering around the corner, they motioned for the others to follow. Anna made it there first, eager to see why the light above was so much brighter than expected on the floor below, and why the sound of flames was so deep, loud, and unusual. She leaned around Eric's shoulder and saw why. Before them roared a superheated wall of crackling flames barring the way. No wonder the area below lay undisturbed. Nothing could get by this.

Except Soliander. When asked, the techie had no ideas, his staff not helping.

"Something's hanging in the air there, guys," Anna said quietly, squinting at the fire. "It's a cylinder of some sort."

After a moment, Lorian remarked, "Ah, I've heard of this from Soliander. This device of his sustains a spell without wavering and is nearly impossible to remove, unless..." He trailed off, turning to Ryan. "Korrin, do you still wear the Dispersion Ring? You can reach the device without getting burned. Just grab it and the spell will end."

Anna had seldom seen such a dubious expression on someone's face.

"Are you sure?" he asked

"Yes. Another item of Soliander's, especially a magic resistant one, is the only way. Remember your arm will be unaffected up to the shoulder. It is magical fire, not real."

"It seems real enough to me." He began pulling out a gauntlet to don. "Wait a minute, I thought the armor was fire proof."

Lorian shook his head. "Only against dragon fire."

"Great," he muttered. He held up one hand toward the fire, remarking, "Well, I feel the heat everywhere except on this arm. Maybe there's some truth to it."

Anna bit her lip. There had better be more than *some* truth to it.

Taking a deep breath, Ryan pulled the helmet's visor down to protect his face, donned the right gauntlet, and carefully reached through the fire. The flames vanished as his hand closed around the device. Visibly relieved, he pulled up the visor with the other, bare hand, but the metal had become hot in just seconds and burned his fingers.

"Ow!" He jerked his hand away, seeing red blisters already forming.

"Let me see," said Anna, the medical student in her taking control. "Second degree burns. We need to wrap this."

Rognir cleared his throat. "Why don't you just heal him, lass?"

She looked at the dwarf uncomfortably. Rognir's healing of Eric had deeply impressed but troubled her, weakening her resolute disbelief in gods. She'd reconsidered this whole business with more seriousness than the hollow promises she'd made Ryan. Following Eric's suggestion to start pretending, she'd chosen a goddess to call on, identifying with Goddess Kiarin's philosophies. She'd imagined a pretend conversation with her but gone no farther, feeling silly. She wasn't ready and couldn't open her heart to this.

"I have a better idea," started the knight, rescuing her. "I'll just use the Trinity Ring."

With mixed emotions, Anna watched as the wound disappeared even as another opened in her heart. She'd seen it twice now. The proof could not be denied. Her upset eyes met Rognir's disappointed gaze, which stung.

Perndara the dragon beamed with pleasure. She'd resumed nightly flights after learning the Ellorian Champions were coming, since pretending she wasn't here made little sense now. The exercise kept her from feeling imprisoned yet again, this time in the ruin. She had to settle for sticking her head in a waterfall instead of a dip in an ocean or lake like on that other world. Of course she could have gone back through the gate for a while, but...

Never again! she thought.

Standing by the Dragon Gate, she snarled at it before overhearing the sounds of steel on steel. The Ellorians were here! Afire with excitement, she impatiently waited for them to get past those amateurish cult members. Her preparations were in order – both her own and those directed by Nir'lion. She bellowed a small spout of flames to get warmed up but didn't waste it. The bile that fueled their fire breathing only lasted so long. Days would pass before a full supply built up again.

Soon quiet descended and she waited expectantly for the door to open, but the minutes ticked by. Finally a familiar knocking preceded a cult member timidly entering. Behind him, two others dragged a man with fresh blood staining his leather tunic. They dropped him to his knees and walked out, shutting the door. It seemed that her legion of admirers – or at least, that's how she chose to think of them – had captured someone, but not a champion, just a mercenary.

The man gazed at her with suitable horror, the ghastly wound in his belly more than just oozing blood. She asked a few questions he seemed too terrified to answer, which was just as well, for she wasn't much in the mood for conversation herself. She was quite hungry and topped off her recent snack of mountain goat. Her fanged mouth engulfed him and his screams.

There had clearly been a battle, and recently. A rivulet of deep red blood still flowed across the floor from the nearest slain man, whose sightless eyes stared at them as they listened at an archway. Ryan stared just as unseeing, reminded of the lives at stake but surprised to feel little pity. Maybe he was getting used to death, however horrible that seemed, but his distaste for cults likely contributed. He only felt pity on realizing that some of these zealots might not be the ones who coerced others to their vision, but the ones who'd been coerced.

"What do you think happened?" he whispered, putting a comforting hand on Matt, who looked like he was going to throw up.

Rognir's eyes moved over the bodies. "We're not the only ones in the castle uninvited," he observed. The bodies were all human, but two looked like cult members from their matching attire while the rest were mercenaries, each dressed in his own unique fashion.

Lorian retrieved an arrow, noting its craftsmanship. "The fletching style is of Ormund. Cirion is here."

"How?" Anna asked. "We were supposed to get here first."

"When we find them," started Eric, frowning, "we can ask." Any chance at surprising the cult or dragon had vanished and there was no telling where Cirion's mercenaries were now.

"Good plan," Rognir gruffly approved, "except we'd better forget them and head for the dragon immediately."

"Wait," said Ryan, "one of them moved." He indicated which one and Lorian crept forward. The wounded cult member stirred when Lorian touched him but lay unconscious until Rognir healed the man enough to come out of it. Anna pursed her lips.

"What happened here?" Lorian sternly demanded.

His tunic torn and bloody, the young cult member glared back, no love lost for those whose allegiance didn't lie with dragons. "Why would I tell you that?"

"Because your future is in our hands," started the elf, "and we'll be more forgiving of what you've done here if you cooperate."

Sneering, the cult member muttered, "Unlikely. I would show *you* no mercy."

"Then how about because I'll bash your head in if you don't," barked Rognir, scowling and raising up his well-used axe.

The man blanched. "We fought intruders, some captured, some killed."

"Where were the captured taken?" Rognir demanded. "To the dragon?"

"No. Only one. The others went to the dungeon."

"And which way is that?"

Gesturing with his head, the cult member said, "Back that way."

"It had better be." Without warning, the dwarf slammed the butt of his axe into the man's forehead, knocking him out.

— ◆ ◆ —

As they were shoved along a crumbling corridor, Cirion failed to hide a look of concern that convinced Nola how grave their situation was this time.

They'd been captured on other exploits and gotten out of it, but not with a dragon involved. Taking one on wasn't why they were here. He suspected the most gravely wounded of their group had been taken to it moments ago and met a gruesome end. The rest were likely headed to a cell, at least for now.

Guards forced him, Nola, Raith, and another survivor down several flights of stairs through increasingly damp areas, the signs of disrepair mounting. Cirion hoped the dungeon locks were poorly kept and easily picked, or the bars were coming loose from the crumbling walls. He'd used that to his advantage before. Few torches lit the way and he suspected they'd be the dungeons' first inhabitants in a long time, his hopes rising. Unprepared jailors were the easiest to escape from.

Their weapons had been confiscated, but they might have less need of them if just fleeing. Too few of them had survived to reach the gate now unless the champions' arrival distracted the dragon, or it flew out of the castle again. The glory of closing it had vanished. Saving his own skin, and to a lesser extent, Nola's, was all that mattered. Everyone else, including that suddenly capable wizard, Raith, was expendable. It wasn't that Raith had done anything wrong, but people with unexpected strength were dangerous. He and Nola had shared a look or two of agreement. It was only a matter of time before one or the other stuck a knife in the wizard's back – maybe right after he helped get them out of here.

The guards rudely shoved them into a dank cell and Cirion expected Raith to follow, but the wizard was shoved into a cell across from them. A sign on the wall showed a broken wizard's staff and the rogue nodded to himself. Of course. A room with magic protection so that spells failed. The wizard wouldn't be helping them escape anywhere.

"What's this?" the guard grunted, yanking down the nape of Raith's robe far enough that even Cirion could see the symbol tattooed on the base of his neck from across the way. It hadn't been there before, the rogue was certain, having seen the wizard's nape more than once. Had Raith been using an illusion spell to hide it? The spell would've stopped working once in that cell. Most people would've recognized the symbol at once. The guard turned Raith around, and Cirion saw the wizard caught between a frown, a smirk, and a glare. With a knife to the throat, the guard led the wizard away again and this time Cirion suspected he knew where they were going.

CHAPTER FOURTEEN

CONFRONTATION

The shimmering portal that hung in the air before him differed from those that others used to travel across or even between worlds. He could, unassisted, make it appear anywhere, such was his power. This took great strength, so he sometimes used more mundane avenues, especially if he'd recently experienced battle to sap his energy, but years had passed since anyone had been foolish enough to challenge him. Most wizards used permanent portals created by someone else to travel to a fixed location, but he always chose his own destination and often visited places that few others dared. Fixed portals were usually guarded, though, like any skilled wizard, he could make people forget he'd arrived.

The black robed wizard looked over at the rosewood cabinet in one corner, now empty after years. He hefted the staff, its weight familiar, the crystal atop it held by a bluish steel few had ever seen. Memories of happier times returned, but so did painful ones best left forgotten. Companions long lost had once given his life greater dynamics if not pleasure, and his was a life devoid of trust since separating from them. Still, the choice had been his, and it wasn't one he consciously regretted.

He brushed aside the thought to focus on the task at hand. The time had come to learn who these champions-apparent were. His spy had learned enough before foolishly being caught, forcing him to incinerate the dark elf so Lorian couldn't learn anything. A corpse only revealed so much. He had blocked the communication orb from reaching any of his other orbs. Still, he had a secret to keep and to that end he'd planned how best to deal with these imposters. Death was of course the ultimate option, as always, and this time there'd be four bodies for people to mourn over, not just a memory of heroes vanished.

"So tell me," purred Perndara, her deep, husky voice rattling the loose stones nearby, "why is a member of my Dragon Cult sneaking into a castle guarded by the very same cult?"

Raith hadn't thought of a good reply for her question despite knowing it was coming. With a mixture of defiance and awe, he regarded the golden dragon silently. She loomed more massive than any depiction in literature and was far more beautiful than he'd imagined dragons could be. The foul scent of death on her breath had never been mentioned. Nor had the giant, smooth intakes of breath, or the hot exhale that carried the reminder of flames, or the floor rumbling with her shifting weight as dust fell from the ceiling, the ruin adjusting to her. Only the folded leathery wings, the barbed tail curled around a pillar, and the great fanged mouth were common features of every story, and they were enough to induce amazement. The dragon's piercing, malevolent gaze chilled him. Even without its other advantages, its intelligence and magic were fearsome. It was little wonder the champions banished them—the dragons of Honyn weren't given to good deeds and peaceful living.

"Unless, of course," continued the dragon, "you are not a true member of the cult but an imposter. I wonder how best to determine your loyalty in the absence of an explanation."

The wizard's heart skipped a beat. Honyn's dragons had inventive and nasty ways of getting answers and demonstrations of devotion, sometimes resulting in a loyal but dead follower. Cirion would have thought lesser things would scare him, but Raith was quite a different man than Cirion knew and had faced far worse threats than his supposed leader would have imagined.

"The intruders I was with want to close the Dragon Gate and I needed to be certain they could not," he started, hoping this turned out well.

"Then why not simply kill them?" Perndara interrupted, unimpressed. "You needn't masquerade as one of them."

Thinking quickly, Raith said, "They have a scroll written by the Ellorians who imprisoned you. It describes how the gate works, or so I believe. They have not allowed me to see it or know its location. If I kill them it might fall into the wrong hands again."

"I see. Go on."

Realizing the dragon was baiting him, Raith stifled a sigh. Did she know better than to help people explain themselves? Getting them to say too much was always a goal, one he'd used himself. He chose his elaborations carefully.

The dragons couldn't know why he'd really come here. Not only would they kill him, but they would do for themselves what he intended to do for himself, and that would be disastrous. His loyalty to the cult – to anyone but himself, really – had ended the moment he read the scroll's contents.

"I needed to locate and destroy the scroll," he began, "but before I could, they insisted on coming here in an attempt to seal the gate for their own idiotic glory. I came along, hoping to discover what they'd done with the scroll and stop them."

"And did you learn this thing?"

He feigned a frown. "No." He knew exactly where the scroll was and had been all along – in one of his robe's pockets. Cirion didn't even know it existed.

The dragon was disapproving. "And when were you planning to stop them? It was getting rather late."

Raith nodded, still feeling a bit charmed by the magnificent beast despite his new allegiance to himself. They saw you in the sky and thought to work the gate while you were gone. I thought that would be my opportunity."

"But they have failed," stated Perndara flatly, "as have you. How did you come to know they possessed the scroll?"

He paused and decided to bolster his lies with some honesty, since he wasn't coming off as well as he'd have liked. "Dragon Cult members stole it from Olliana at my direction long ago," he confessed, "so it could be destroyed, but it was lost through foolishness." He smiled slightly. The thieves had indeed been foolish, for if a man won't reveal his identity when he hires you, you should expect your death instead of gratitude for a job well done. "When I heard this group had paid a huge sum for a scroll, I surmised they had it and convinced them I could help them here. They soon admitted to the possession but that was all."

He didn't admit to hearing rumors of Cirion's mercenaries having come before but encountered all manner of traps, which was a principal reason he'd used Cirion to get here. Better his men get killed than Raith. Every wizard needed warriors to do grunt work. Even Soliander paraded around with those other champions.

Perndara contemplated and he knew she wasn't entirely convinced. A long pause followed and he projected a desire to be helpful and pleasing, mixed with fear and awe.

"I sense magic power in you," observed Perndara approvingly. "You can be of service to me."

The wizard bowed, wondering where this was headed and flattered despite himself. *Stop it, you fool.*

"My sources tell me the Ellorians are on their way. I want you to challenge Soliander and keep him occupied."

Raith hesitated. He might be far stronger than Cirion's group knew, but he'd not win a direct challenge against *that* wizard. He only sought a way to achieve his goal before anyone knew what he was doing. He just hoped that whoever had opened the gate hadn't beaten him to that goal. It clearly wasn't Soliander and he was ready to fight whoever had done it to the death to get what he wanted. There was no graceful way to refuse this request, however, and he'd long ago learned the immense value in making empty promises to gain trust.

"Certainly," he replied, bowing as if honored, and with some annoyance he realized he wasn't entirely faking it. "I will keep him from disturbing you."

"See that you do." She then instructed him on where to be and what to do and he moved to the far end of the hall, so near the open gate that he struggled to keep from staring at it. Once the champions distracted Perndara and he had a moment alone with the gate, he would seize his destiny.

— ✦·✦ —

"Are we going to rescue them?" Anna asked, dubiously.

Eric frowned at the idea. Across the hall from the unlit room they stood in, a descending stairway led to the dungeon, the faint sounds of men talking and laughing drifting up from below. No one was looking forward to visiting it. If they weren't careful, they might get to visit anyway. A patrol of guards had already passed by once. Enough torches and lanterns flickered along the stone walls that they knew company lurked everywhere, and they had doused their own.

"I think they can wait," remarked Eric. "I don't want them along while we're facing the dragon. It's like having another enemy in our midst."

"Easy for you to say," muttered Ryan, gripping the lance. "You don't have to do much."

"I don't know," started Matt, "they've got another wizard with them and he could be a big help."

"I agree with Soliander," said Lorian. "Though we will have to fight our way to them and it might arouse guards elsewhere, the addition of another wizard is worth the risk."

Rognir grunted as a loud clatter rose up the stairs. Shouting followed. "No one will think twice about a commotion down there, as long as we are quick."

"True," agreed the elf, "the mercenaries are typically amateurish. Let us proceed before someone comes." With that he peeked into the hallway and then ventured across and down the stairs, other elves and Rognir following. Before joining them, Eric frowned at his friends.

"Keep an eye on Cirion and the others when we get them out," he suggested. "I expect nothing but trouble from them and am surprised Lorian wants them along."

"Maybe he doubts our ability to help," remarked Matt.

"Probably," Eric admitted ruefully. "Just don't trust them with anything, especially our safety."

"Agreed," said Ryan, wondering what Nola really had planned for him that night.

Eric peeked into the hallway and quickly leaned back. Guards were coming, this time from another direction that provided full view of them. He ushered the others back, but the empty room provided no cover and wasn't nearly dark enough. He tried the only door, which opened to reveal a large, empty room, two torches burning. Motioning for everyone to go in, he barely followed as the guards reached the opening. Shutting the door quietly, he turned to the others and stopped short. They were gone. So was the large hall, a much smaller one in its place, brightly lit by lanterns. Confused, he turned to the door and discovered it was gone, too.

—■ ❖ · ❖ ■—

Ryan blinked in the bright light, which, along with the lack of dust and cobwebs, suggested a well-used room they had better leave. Suits of armor and weapons lined the walls, gleaming as if new. He turned to the others and found himself alone. Maybe they hadn't come through the door after him, but then he saw that even that was gone, too. In its place stood a solid wall.

Maybe the door is camouflaged, he thought, pulled off a glove to feel for a seam, but his fingertips felt only the natural pits and chips in the limestone. He was about to call out to see if they could hear him on the other side when a door creaked behind him.

He turned as a warrior in dusky black armor strode in, malice in every step, a short plume of white feathers atop its helmeted head. The raised visor revealed a dark elf's cruel features. The elf unsheathed a black sword, metal ringing with the motion as it advanced on him, its metal-shod feet clanging with every step like the tolling of a bell. Death had come for him at last.

Ryan fumbled for his own sword, stepping forward to avoid being cornered and looking for an escape, but he saw only the door beyond his attacker. As if reacting to his thoughts, it slammed shut, locks clanking furiously on the far side. The elf struck at him, their blades clanging once, twice, three times. Ryan's defenses steadily pulled his sword to one side, exposing his front, and the dark blade struck at his chest, bouncing off the armor.

Stepping back and regrouping, Ryan parried several blows imperfectly. He got the impression the elf was testing his defenses, for the elf didn't take every opening, instead looking for all the faults to form an overall strategy. Lorian had taught Ryan how to do it and now he knew the ploy was being used on him.

And so Ryan went on the offensive to disrupt him. At first the elf seemed surprised, but a few strokes later Ryan stepped back with a gasp, holding his side, where a deep cut oozed blood. His poor assault had let the elf's blade slip between the plates.

No more attacks unless something comes up, he decided, sobering up. It's my turn to test and evaluate.

Time after time the swords crossed, the elf faster, the knight better protected, Korrin's armor impervious to the elf's sword unless a stabbing blow made it through the chainmail. Ryan's strikes badly dented the other's armor but happened too infrequently. The elf's blade stabbed him again and again, a half dozen cuts oozing blood, and yet the elf had only one meaningful wound to his unused arm. Ryan was losing and not getting more blows to land.

As if realizing this, the elf began striking the same wounds over and over but not making them worse, just causing more pain. Being tortured to death wasn't on Ryan's agenda and he grew angry. He suddenly realized the elf had become predictable. Sacrificing his left leg to the next attack, he didn't bother with the expected defense, already swinging hard at the surprised elf instead.

Both blows struck home, Ryan's only stinging while the elf received a deep gash that likely cracked ribs. Wild relief and anger surged within Ryan and he pressed forward, hammering down at the retreating elf's sword arm. And suddenly he realized his strength made up for his skill. He'd been afraid to use that strength since hurting Daniel so long ago, but now rage set him free and he slammed the sword down again and again. It forced the elf to hold his blade with both hands, eliminating any one-handed maneuverability. Still using only one arm himself, Ryan punched the elf in the face with the other, feeling grim satisfaction as he knocked the elf backward.

It was a mistake, for the elf regrouped and returned to the fight meaning business but seeming wary as they circled each other. A flurry of quick strikes kept Ryan from delivering a big swing. Cuts began to appear on him, a terrible wound causing him to limp and poorly support his weight, another making his left hand unresponsive. He grew lightheaded from blood loss, his judgment slipping.

Maybe that's why his sword arm dropped suddenly. The elf lunged and Ryan hauled the sword upward, blades crashing together and rising above their heads. With a crash he head-butted the elf's face with his helmet, knocking him back and then slamming the sword into the elf's thigh, down to the bone.

With a shriek, the elf fell to one knee but still tried to stab the knight through the belly. Seeing it coming, Ryan brought his sword down on his foe's neck, cutting deep through armor, bone, and sinew, nearly beheading him. Blood sprayed all over Ryan, whose anger abruptly vanished at what he'd done, the ghastly mortal wound spurting blood with each heartbeat. The elf would be dead in a minute, but not if Ryan used the last and most powerful healing spell in the Trinity Ring. He bent to use the ring but then stopped short.

The last time he healed an enemy, Eric nearly got killed. This time it would be himself. His wounds weren't life threatening but he'd lose another fight if not healed. His friends, Daniel, and everyone on this world were depending on him. Besides, he wasn't ready to die. And Lorian was right. An aggressor brought death upon themselves. The choice had been made. Seeing the dark elf's still angry eyes on him, Ryan snapped out of his particular brand of foolishness after a lifetime of it. With a coldness that surprised him, he brought the sword down one more time, finishing the elf.

— ✦ · ✦ —

On stepping through the door, Anna spied an elaborate mural and turned to examine the depiction of a battle winding down and priests kneeling among the wounded, helping, caring, and healing them. The looks of gratitude made her realize patients didn't care how you made them better, just that you did. All of this healing stuff wasn't about her, and she blushed at her selfishness. If appealing to a god was the only means to heal such terrible wounds, then wasn't she obligated to try?

But then why her? Surely not just anyone could convince a god to heal someone through them. She wasn't a logical choice and knew that pretending to be Eriana wouldn't convince anyone of her merits. Rognir must have gone through some training or somehow been found worthy. Having not done either, Anna didn't expect a god to answer her even if she tried. One never had before, since the god of Earth wasn't real, at least to her.

She became so engrossed in her thoughts and the mural that she lost all sense of time and only slowly became aware of the clanging of metal behind her. She turned to see Ryan fighting a warrior in black and the others were gone. On trying the door she came through to get help, she discovered it wouldn't open no matter how hard she pulled.

Helplessly, Anna turned to watch, wincing at every wound inflicted on Ryan, her medical training helping her assess each. His fierce expression convinced her this was a fight to the death, but the sight of Ryan beheading his opponent shocked her. For a moment she was too startled to move, but then she rushed to him.

"My God, Ryan, are you alright?"

Dazed, he looked right through her, woozy and disoriented. Then he crashed to the ground with a clatter.

"Ryan, stay with me," she begged, kneeling beside him. She had to stop the bleeding but saw nothing to use as a tourniquet except her robe's hem. Struggling to tear off a piece, she finally used his dagger to do so. She tried to bind the worst wound on his leg, but the thigh plate stood in the way until she got it off, remembering how from their night at the inn. She pulled tight but knew it wasn't enough, the chain mail that was covering his leg making it too hard to stop the bleeding.

"Ryan." She leaned over him, patting his face to wake him, getting blood all over his cheek. "Ryan, please stay with me. I need your strength." Even as she said it, she knew he was too weak to pull the tourniquet any tighter than she had. She desperately tried again, pulling with all her might to no avail. He was going to die right here in front of her if she didn't find another way.

Feeling like a fool, she remembered Eriana's method, and only a moment passed before she brushed aside her disposition about it. She placed one hand on his forehead and another on his chest, trying to remember what Rognir had told her. She didn't know the words he used but surely the Goddess Kiarin would answer to save Ryan.

"Lady Kiarin," she began, struggling for words, "please spare this man's life. He does not deserve to die here today. He shouldn't even be here and –" She stopped herself. That probably wasn't a good line of thought to follow. Maybe if she admitted how important he was to her. Surely her personal connection mattered.

"Please Kiarin. I don't want to lose him. He is a good man, the best I've known, and such men are rare and deserve long lives. Please spare him." Shaking her head in uncertainty, she continued, "I don't know what else to say to you. Please forgive my methods and look into my heart instead, to see my words are true. Please answer my call."

Even as she said it, from somewhere deep within her the memory of unanswered pleas to God surfaced and along with them anger about never being answered. She tried to snuff the resentment and uttered another plea to Kiarin, but her heart also carried something akin to an insistence that she get a reply. She'd never have expressed the sentiment aloud but it lived on in her still, and that was enough. Nothing was happening.

Ryan's head rolled to one side and she gasped, checking his pulse with a trembling hand, begging Kiarin for help. She found no heartbeat and the flow of blood from his wounds faded, his skin white.

"Oh my God, no. Please no."

She begged Kiarin again but it was too late. Ryan lay dead. Several minutes of desperate CPR followed with nothing changing. Tears poured down her face as she clung to his body, a blur of emotions raging in her. Looking heavenward, she screamed, "Why won't you answer me?"

But there was no response. Unable to look at Ryan's pale face any longer, she staggered to her feet and stumbled into a corridor she hadn't noticed before, not knowing or caring where it led.

⸺ ❖ ⸺

Even as the wizard stepped across the door's threshold, he knew something was up. The staff sent a pulse up his arm and he found himself standing somewhere other than the large hall he'd briefly seen. Either he'd been transported or he now saw an illusion. Since the staff no longer alerted him to magic, he suspected the former. It still looked like Darlonon, but he easily could've been teleported anywhere on Honyn – or even off world. It wasn't a pleasant thought.

Matt stood in a ten by ten room with a corridor to one side. It offered the only way out, though he wasn't sure he wanted to go wherever it led. The teleportation had undoubtedly been Soliander's doing like all the magic they'd encountered inside. He wondered if something similar had happened to the others or if he'd been treated differently on account of the staff. So far Soliander's spells had recognized it, so perhaps only the arch wizard himself would have been transferred to where Matt stood now. The idea piqued his curiosity but stood little chance of being verified.

The room stood bare save for an oval mirror that hung in space across from him. Aside from its lack of support, it was unremarkable. He examined his reflection, not having seen himself in the Majestic Majus' black garb yet. The overall impression was intimidating and made worse by the black hood obscuring his face, its shadows suggesting something sinister. With a start, he realized he wasn't wearing the hood, and no sooner had that difference registered than the reflection stepped from within the apparent mirror and into the room, the portal vanishing. Matt gasped and stepped back, but it was too late. With a curt gesture, the figure spoke a word and Matt could no longer move. It grabbed him by the robe.

"Who are you?" the figure demanded, piercing eyes glaring.

"Uh, Soliander," Matt stammered, frightened.

The glare hardened. "No, you are not. What is your *name*?"

Unsure what to say, Matt repeated with more confidence, "Soliander."

The man's eyes flashed. "*Soranumirae,*" he intoned, and sudden pressure crushed Matt's chest. His eyes bulged as he struggled to breathe, his face turning red. Merciless eyes stared back and only when Matt started to black out did the figure speak again. "*Earimunaros.*" The pressure released and Matt gasped for air, dizzy and weak. Before he'd finished recovering, the figure looked ready to do it again.

"Matt!" he blurted between gasps, in over his head and wanting out. "My name's Matt. Sorenson, from Earth."

The figure's eyes intensified as if recognizing the name, surprised by it, or both. "Earth?"

"Yes. My planet. Where I came from." Matt squirmed as the figure stared at him silently. Maybe he'd said something wrong.

"And who travels with you?"

Matt figured little harm could come from giving their real names, since this man clearly knew he wasn't Soliander. "Eric, Anna, and Ryan, all from Earth, too."

The man cocked an eyebrow, eyes boring into his. "Not Andier, Eriana, or that lumbering idiot Korrin?"

"No. We're not really them, just pretending to be."

The man seemed satisfied and thoughtful before returning attention to his captive. "Who sent you?"

"Uh, Queen Lorella."

The figure scowled. "Not to this castle, to this world."

Matt wasn't sure how to answer that. "We were summoned by Sonneri."

The man frowned and paused, rephrasing his question. "Did Andier, Eriana, or Korrin somehow arrange for you to arrive in their place during the next summoning?"

"No, I don't think so. I don't know." Matt noticed he didn't ask about Soliander, and with a start the significance of their identical possessions registered, right down to the supposedly one of a kind staff each held. His eyes widened in excitement and fear, but he dared not ask the question, instead focusing on how he was going to get out of this. He couldn't move his arms but wondered if his magic items might work. His eyes turned to the staff.

"It is no use," the figure said, seeing his gaze. "You cannot cast a spell. I have seen to that. Your magic devices will also not work." Suddenly the figure paused, wide eyes on Matt's staff. "You...you have a copy of the staff! This should not be." Suspicious eyes turned on the techie, a glint of new menace appearing. "Well, no matter. You won't live to use it. You will remain until I am done with you, and you will reveal what I want to know."

With that, the man put one hand on Matt's forehead and spoke magic words he understood. "Be open and true, your mind laid bare, safe and secure, your secrets treasured, honored, and shared. Let all be revealed in the comfort of benevolence, kindness, and trust, for to free yourself of your fear is to free your heart's woes. Be open to me, in all your beautiful glory."

Despite the soothing words, Matt resisted as the man probed his mind, control of his thoughts wrested away. As if his memories were television stations and this man held the remote, his thoughts leapt from one thing to another, randomly and without regard for Matt's privacy. He flushed at being violated, embarrassing moments mixing with what anyone knew about him, secrets of no value to this man devoured as readily as their time on Honyn. Matt's life flashed before his eyes, anger building as he sensed amusement and scorn about his life and identity from the man.

He could still think for himself, it seemed, and in the back of his mind an idea lay hidden, his eyes on the identical staves. If he could control his staff, then in theory he could control the other one, too. Matt's staff might have been disabled by the wizard, but the other one likely hadn't been.

In desperation, Matt focused his will on the figure's staff, reaching out to it with all his might. At first it wouldn't recognize him as if uncertain that two people could connect to it at once, but then Matt felt it react. So, too, did the figure, realizing Matt's intent and surprised it was working, which Matt sensed due to their connection. But it was too late. With a burst of hope, Matt embraced the energy and spoke the word, "Enumisar." Flames erupted from it to engulf the man and in an instant Matt fell free of his grasp and the spell binding him. Scorching heat washed over him as he turned and ran, screams of pain and rage mixing with the crackle and whoosh of fire behind him.

— ◆ · ◆ —

Standing with a knife in each hand, the rogue looked around warily. He'd come through the door last and seen his friends in the room before him, but now they and the room itself were gone. The knives had come out when he realized he wasn't alone. Across the room stood a tall woman in a silky, golden robe, voluptuous curves tempting his eyes away from her striking face. A vision of loveliness, she looked at him expectantly if not pleasantly, hands folded behind her back. The room stood otherwise empty of even an exit. All four walls, the ceiling, and the floor were solid, unless the way lay hidden. Searching might yield something, but he suspected the woman held the answer and stepped a little closer. They stared at each other silently and when she finally cocked an inquisitive eyebrow at him, he spoke.

"Greetings," Eric said, deciding on diplomacy. "I don't mean to be rude, and would love to stay and chat, but I need to get out of this room and back to where I was."

"That you may do," she replied in a vibrant, alto voice.

"How?"

In response she simply smiled. He got the impression that she was amused by the possibility that he thought it would be that easy. He paused to get his bearings. Since rooms normally didn't behave this way, he had to assume this was Soliander's doing and not something the former inhabitants had left behind. Then again, assumptions were never good, especially now. He needed to know who and what she was and why she was here. Then he could figure out how to get out of here.

"Are you real?"

She paused. "Yes."

He looked at her shrewdly, knowing the hesitation meant something. It had been a bad question. She could be a real illusion.

"Are you a being of flesh and blood?"

"No."

So she was real but not physical. He realized these questions weren't really getting him anywhere and changed subjects. "Did Soliander summon you?"

She smirked. "No."

Again her demeanor tipped him off that she wasn't entirely honest because that hadn't been a good question either. Technically the wizard was nowhere to be found and yet the spell had still gone off. In a way, Eric had caused her to be here. "Is Soliander responsible for you being summoned to this room when I entered it?"

"Yes."

He nodded, satisfied. This could take a while if he wasn't specific. He wondered if there was a limit on the number of questions he could ask, or a time limit, like many of the computer games he'd played. How was he supposed to know? He could ask, but she hadn't been forthcoming and only given yes or no answers. Still, Soliander must have meant this as a test, not an execution or imprisonment, so there had to be rules and it wasn't sportsmanlike to prevent him from knowing them. She hadn't answered his general question on how to get out, however, so he thought long and hard before opening his mouth again.

"What are the limitations imposed upon our interaction?"

She beamed as if pleased at the leap in his logic. "You may ask ten questions."

His eyes widened. How many had he already asked? Five or six, at least.

Seeing his reaction, she winked knowingly. "You have four left."

What? Shit. If he'd known that he wouldn't have asked half of them. Maybe he should be grateful he found out now. He wanted to ask what happened after that but of course that would waste a question. He muttered, "After that I guess I'll be stuck here."

A glint of steel appeared in her eyes as her arms slid out from behind her back, a short sword gleaming in each hand. A shiver ran over him. She might have looked like a woman, but she was clearly something more deadly – if that were possible – and her motion suggested great skill and willingness, both of which he lacked. He was no match with the sword, and he suspected a knife or two wouldn't take her out before she – or it – reached him. He had to say something to get out of this, but it could have been anything. Asking a question probably wasn't going to do it. That would just allow him to figure out what to say. He knew what he wanted to know but thought about how to phrase it for several minutes before finally asking.

"How can I convince you to let me gain my freedom from this room?"

"You must prove your freedom is wise."

Finally, he thought, *a real clue. Okay, so why is my freedom wise? I'm here to reset the gate, but this spell predates the gate being open again, so that can't be it. The spell was created by Soliander, probably to stop people from reaching the gate, but not himself, of course. So I could say I just want to leave and maybe it would let me go, but if I was Soliander, I wouldn't fall for a lie because I could just try to get in some other way.*

The rogue stopped there, biting his lip. He wondered who Soliander would let reach the gate but drew a blank, since only the other champions were likely, but maybe that was it. The only people who could be trusted were those who'd been involved from the start, and they were probably the only ones Soliander thought would try to reach the gate with good intentions. That had to be it. Now Eric might be pretending to be Andier, but that wasn't enough. Maybe he had to prove he was one of the other three. It warranted a question.

"If I can prove I am Andier, Korrin, or Eriana, will you let me escape?"

"Yes."

Eric sighed in relief. He had two questions left and felt close now. There were only two ways he could think of to prove it. Either he had an item of Andier's he could show, and he should have everything with him, or he had to know something only they would know. He hoped for the former and thought about what he wore. None of the items were that unique, aside from being well made, but then he remembered the short sword and Ryan's observation that both of their swords might have been made of soclarin ore. His eyes lit up. That was something only the Ellorians had. He slowly pulled out the sword and held it up for her to see.

"This is made of soclarin ore," he began, "as only they would...." He didn't finish the statement, for the woman leapt at him with swords slicing through the air, a frenzy of slashing motion. Startled, the rogue barely had time to launch one knife, which she casually caught on a blade and flung aside. Then she was on him like a whirlwind of steel and he knew he was going to die. Their swords met only once before a blade slashed his arm, another his chest, and finally both plunged to the hilt into his belly. In agony, he bent forward over her fists, her sinister eyes looking into his with contempt. She then shoved him back and off the twin blades. He fell on his back, his abdomen a bloody mess.

It occurred to him too late that Soliander had described the ore in the scroll so anyone could have known about it, and that it was the worst thing he could've said. After all, that's probably why someone had opened the gate and Soliander certainly didn't want the ore falling into the wrong hands. Feeling like a fool, he looked up at his killer without blame as she straddled him with both swords raised above her head, ready to finish him. He suddenly remembered the Trinity Ring and that Soliander had made it and Eric knew the voice commands – something only the champions knew.

"Oonurarki," he choked out, and the woman vanished as the ring's strongest spell healed him. He sat up, finding himself in the room he'd seen before stepping through the door. An *illusion*, he observed without surprise, noting his injuries had been real enough.

Taking stock, he rose and decided not to open the door he'd come through yet. It had obviously triggered a trap and once had been enough. Maybe the others were dealing with something, too, and so he moved off to one side to wait. Not long after, a distraught Anna ran through another door, covered in blood. Seeing him, she buried her face in his shoulder before he knew it.

Momentarily speechless, he finally asked, "Are you hurt?" Her head shook. "Then whose blood? Matt?" Again she shook her head. "Ryan?" She nodded and he put her at arm's length. "Where?" He started for the door.

"No!" Anna said, grabbing him again. "No, it's too late."

"What? What do you...?" He trailed off, her distress answering the question.

Lone, steel-shod footsteps sounded from a hallway to one side and he moved to guard her, pulling out two throwing knives. A figure in golden armor stepped into sight, bloodied sword in one hand and a lance in the other. Blood covered much of the knight, who gave no indication of being in pain as he flashed a relieved smile.

"Ryan!" Eric let out a sigh of relief. Anna's head snapped up and her mouth fell open. The big man came forward, eyes looking for the wizard.

"Where's Matt?" he asked, putting away the sword. Anna suddenly rushed into his arms.

"I don't know about you," started the rogue, glancing around warily, "but I just dealt with an illusion that dumped me here when it was done. I think Anna did, too. She saw you die, I think."

"Oh," said Ryan, turning serious. "Well, I'm fine, Anna," he said to her, putting a hand on her awkwardly. "It's okay. I mean I did get hurt but I was able to heal myself with the ring."

She nodded and pulled herself together to step back. "So maybe you dealt with an illusion, too," she suggested, wiping tears from her face.

"Maybe," he agreed. They heard feet running toward them from another hallway and Matt ran into view, looking terrified.

"We've got to get out of here!" Matt yelled, looking back.

"What's the matter?" Ryan asked.

"There's a powerful wizard not far behind me. He's pissed!" He stopped to catch his breath. "I set him on fire."

"That would do it." Eric smirked.

The knight shrugged. "It's probably an illusion. We all just experienced one, separately, it seems. Yours is probably over just like the rest of ours."

A scream of rage sounded from behind Matt. "Did that sound like an illusion?"

"Actually, no," Ryan admitted. He looked at Eric. "Do you think we'd experience each other's illusions? We didn't before."

Eric took Anna's arm and started for a door across from the one that triggered everything. "Let's not find out."

With trouble coming from behind, they didn't wonder what lay behind the door as they jerked it open and stepped through, but only an ascending stairway greeted them. The others started up as Ryan bolted the door behind him. It wasn't until he saw them standing at the top and not moving that alarm bells went off in his head. He crept up quietly, hoping to get a peek without letting himself be seen by whatever had arrested their attention, but all thoughts of that vanished when a tremendous roar shook the walls. It was deafening and shocking in its massiveness and could only mean one thing.

As he watched, a sinuous golden neck rose high into the air, pulling an enormous head with it. Two gigantic, baleful eyes swept over his friends and then picked him out from down below them, not missing a thing as its prey arrived. Ryan heard a slow rushing of air he didn't understand until the dragon opened its fanged mouth and the sound reversed, accompanied by a huge spout of searing flames racing toward them.

⸻ ✦ ⋅ ✦ ⸻

"They did not follow?" Lorian asked, worried. He, the dwarf, and the other, remaining eight elves stood on a landing halfway down to the dungeon. The guards could still be heard laughing and joking below, unaware of the impending attack, but now the rescue of Cirion's mercenaries might have to wait. The absence of the champions didn't bode well. Lorian cursed himself for letting them come last. Something must have happened.

"We'd better check on them," Rognir muttered, starting toward the stair with a muted clatter of metal.

"No," started Lorian, fearing the dwarf would be heard. "I'll go. Continue on to Cirion. You should still outnumber whoever's down here."

The dwarf frowned. "This fellow isn't nearly as important."

"Yes, but the wizard can help us. The cult likely didn't expect prisoners and probably only diverted a few guards for this. Nine of you likely outnumbers them and one more won't make a difference."

"You underestimate yourself."

Lorian nodded thanks and hefted his sword as he cautiously retraced his steps. No fighting had been heard, which suggested the four had taken to hiding. While only Andier had skill in the role he played, Lorian doubted the group would give in easily. They'd shown a willingness to defend themselves at least.

Atop the stairs, he saw and heard nothing, their last known location empty. The far door seemed the most likely place they'd have gone, so he opened it, peered in, but saw no signs of them in a room with several doors and corridors. He pursed his lips, considering. They'd probably gone that way, but there were too many options to investigate. They could be quite far removed from here by now. Perhaps he had better look anyway.

He took one step in when a scream split the air. It came not from below where he expected fighting but off to one side and behind. He shut the door and returned to the hall, seeing no one but hearing rushed footsteps and a staff thumping on the floor, moving away, so he followed. At the first corner, he caught the scent of burned flesh and saw a figure in smoldering black robes moving away. Assuming it was Matt, he hurried after to help the wounded wizard, but the figure's aggressive gait was quite unlike the techie's, so he slowed in suspicion.

Around corners and down stairways, he discreetly followed the figure until suspecting he knew how to intercept it. The dust had been disturbed along the route, so any traps had likely been cleared. He descended stairs into the darkness, no torches burning along the way, and ducked behind a marble statue at the bottom, in a dark room adorned with pillars. Across the room, a dim light grew brighter and footsteps louder along with the thumping staff as the figure stalked into the room from a hallway. Despite the face being turned away, Lorian stared in recognition, questions swirling as he followed, wondering what to do or say. Something wasn't right.

Always waiting until the figure vanished around a corner, Lorian followed quietly until hearing magic words. He peered around it to see the robed figure standing before an ornate golden frame covered in dust, shimmering rays of light pouring from it to cast dancing shadows around the room. The figure took one step toward the portal and Lorian stepped out into the room.

"Soliander!"

The figure turned with such fierceness that the elf knew something was coming. He dove behind the wall as a blast of lightning scorched the hall and blew stones all over him, a dust cloud obscuring the air, a deafening rumbling all around. When it stopped, he couldn't hear anything and worried the figure would be standing above him when he turned, but it was not. A gash on one leg made it hard to stand, and on peering around the corner that, he felt no surprise that all signs of the wizard were gone.

⚔ ✦ · ✦ ⚔

Now that Cirion had inspected the jail, he felt confident of a quick escape. These cult members knew little about imprisoning someone and it had seemed an afterthought to take their weapons. Well, most of their weapons.

They knew even less about searching a man of his talents, apparently. More importantly, he had enough tools of his trade to do the deed with little trouble. He picked at the new lock on the rusting bars as Nola chipped away at the crumbling mortar holding them to the stone.

As he glanced over at her, looking fetching as always in her leather armor, the sound of fighting erupted out of sight but didn't last long. Elves and a dwarf soon appeared with weapons drawn.

Noting the missing champions, Cirion wryly asked, "Lose someone?"

The leading elf replied flatly, "Yes, one elf."

"You had better be worth it," barked the dwarf, who continued by the cell, leading several elves further into the dungeon looking for other threats.

Watching him go, Cirion turned to the elf and observed, "You look familiar."

"Morven," came the reply as he unlocked the gate and pulled it open with a screech.

"Ah, Lorian's friend. He is here then? With the Ellorians?"

"Yes. We had best return to them. I assume you are still interested in helping seal the Dragon Gate."

Cirion cocked an eyebrow. "They would let me?"

"Provided you are well behaved. Come along. Your weapons are this way." Morven turned to go as the dwarf returned without further struggle.

Cirion stopped him. "Wait. What of our wizard?"

The dwarf replied, "The dungeon is otherwise empty."

"I'd like to look for him."

Frowning, Morven replied, "No. Another wizard would be helpful and is the only reason we came for you, but we'll not further risk giving away our presence."

The walls shook from a tremendous roar that could only come from one thing.

Cirion smirked. "I think it's too late for that."

CHAPTER FIFTEEN

DESTINY SEIZED

As the wall of flames rushed toward them, Ryan waited in horror. This would be far worse than that little burn he'd gotten at the wall of fire. He couldn't bear to watch as it reached his friends and engulfed them, but when nothing got to him, he looked up in surprise, which only grew at the sight before him. Matt stood with one hand before him as if to stop traffic, the other holding the staff, its crystal shining brightly. The oncoming flames were striking an invisible barrier Matt had erected. Ryan could hardly believe it and almost yelled excited encouragement to the techie before realizing that doing so might distract him.

When the flames stopped, Ryan joined the others atop the stairs, catching his first sight of a dragon. The sight filled him with awe that would've had him gawking were it not for the terror of it having just tried to kill them for what was undoubtedly only the first time. Tendrils of smoke drifted up from her nostrils, two baleful, malicious golden eyes turned from the others to him, with what looked like recognition and renewed fury. Her torso was tall as a two-story house, golden scales flashing with reflected firelight. The giant wings lay folded, her tail uncoiling from a pillar behind her, four giant, clawed feet and fang-filled mouth formidable weapons. The floor rumbled with her every move and it was a wonder the whole place didn't come down around them. Behind her, where thrones had likely once stood, he at last saw the Dragon Gate.

It nearly filled the hall at that end, standing on a waist high platform with three steps. A giant oval, it was wider than it was tall to accommodate the outstretched wings of dragons in flight as it pulled them in. It lay almost flat, tilted up toward the gaping hole in the roof, its lowest point at the steps. And it was on. Like a still lake in the black of night, it reflected torchlight and the tapestries above it, wisps of smoke curling along its misty surface. Waiting near it stood Raith, lips moving in what Ryan assumed was a spell with them as its target. How could they fight off both a dragon and a wizard?

He tore his eyes away to Matt, who still stood with arms outstretched, breathing hard. The knight wondered if the barrier would remain up and how long Matt could do that. The dragon had similar ideas, it seemed, for with one foot she casually flung a bench at them. All but the wizard took cover but it bounced harmlessly off the barrier. Matt flinched as if the blow weakened him. His arm sagged and his breathing deepened. They needed cover and the knight looked around.

The wide hall stretched to either side in a long rectangle, for they hadn't entered from the nearby main doors at one end, though they were close. Along this wall and the one opposite stood other stairwells, a long row of balconies overhead. Tattered, faded tapestries hung in ruins everywhere while scattered torches and lanterns dimly lit the dark room. An enormous gaping hole in the ceiling revealed the starry sky overhead, with piles of rubble from the half-ruined roof lying shoved to one side.

Ryan ushered the others behind a nearby fountain with a low wall around it as Matt indicated his spell had ended. The dragon would come after all of them, but only he could withstand her fire if Matt felt too tired to do that again. Seeing the dragon moving toward them, he stepped out before he could think it through any further, lance in one hand and sword in the other. He had to at least lure it away from his friends, not only to keep them alive, but to distract it so they could reach the gate. He still didn't want to kill it and doubted he even could.

"Ryan!" Anna called out.

Eric said, "No, he's fireproof, remember?"

"So what?" she asked incredulously. "It's not claw or tooth-proof!"

"We're not going to let that happen," Matt put in, still catching his breath, "but I agree on not following him out there."

"You've got to reach the gate," Eric reminded him.

Matt eyed the distance to the gate. "How am I supposed to get over there?"

"I don't know," Eric admitted. "Ryan's probably trying to distract it. Stay ready for an opportunity and I'll do everything I can to help."

Ryan approached and the dragon reared up near the ceiling and slammed both front claws into the floor, the boom thundering deep into the castle, loose mortar cascading down around the room and a balcony tumbling to the floor with a crash.

"Dragon Slayer!" Perndara roared. "This is one dragon who will slay you instead!"

One giant foot swept toward him from the right and he swung the sword at it, though it was bigger than his whole body and he braced for the impact. Instead, red blood sprayed all over him as the sword cleanly severed all three toes and the dragon shrieked, the toes tumbling across the floor instead of Ryan. The dragon's roar of pain shook the walls and she shifted weight to avoid standing on the maimed foot. Then she turned on Ryan and unleashed a torrent of flames. At the last second, he slammed shut the helmet visor. Fire blasted him, the force making him step back. The others stared, looking for a sign that Ryan still lived among the flames, but all they could see was his planted feet still upright.

Eric pulled his arm away from Anna, who clung to him, and rose. He took two steps and hurled a knife at one of the dragon's enormous eyes. The blade twirled through the air and struck home, the fire stream abruptly ending in another shriek of pain. Perndara raised the injured foot to nudge out the blade but couldn't, finally shaking her head furiously until it went flying. Something yellow oozed from the eye as she turned to see Eric throwing another. This she deflected with a turn of her head, but the blade still sliced into her golden scales. She spoke a few words and the eye healed itself, her foot no longer bleeding but not growing back. Ryan began to advance on her and the dragon retreated.

"Matt," said Eric, "if she starts to cast a spell, you have to help distract her. Ryan won't stand a chance if she does magic on him."

"She's moving too far away."

The rogue looked at the archers now arriving on the balcony, most waiting for a good shot at them, some repositioning themselves to get one. This hiding place wouldn't last long. Before they could react well, he ran along the wall under the balcony on one side. The archers let their arrows fly at him as Anna yelled out a warning, but the archers were neither accurate nor well organized and he avoided the haphazard volley, diving behind a rubble pile nearer the gate, where the wizard there locked eyes with him. Raith began gesturing, his lips moving. Eric raised up and quickly threw a knife that ricocheted off Raith's bony hands, disrupting the spell and causing a shout of pain. He didn't get back down fast enough, for two arrows struck the wall overhead while another lodged into his left arm. He fell back with a groan and glared at the arrow there. Working himself up to pulling it out and using the Trinity Ring on himself, he saw Matt watching him.

Are you okay? the wizard's fingers asked.

Yeah. Good enough.

As Perndara retreated from the knight, her long barbed tail struck the Dragon Gate's shimmering surface and momentarily turned to smoke like anything about to pass through it would. She glanced back at it as Korrin called out to her.

"Back through the gate, dragon," Ryan hollered, "or you will die here today!"

Her head whipped back around to him, furious eyes flashing. "Never! Never again!" Her giant jaws thrust at him, snapping, but he kept the lance between them. She retreated and Ryan lunged with the lance, stabbing her deeply in the neck. Perndara yanked backwards off of it and roared while blood spurted out.

The main doors behind Anna and Matt flew outward with a loud bang as two cult members arrived with a dozen mercenaries. Matt turned and a wall of crackling flames erupted from the floor between them, stretching to each wall. A tapestry caught fire on one end and quickly spread to the second floor, igniting another.

"How long can you do that?" Anna asked.

"I don't know. I'm surprised I did it at all."

Another commotion broke out to one side. "Focus on the fire," Anna advised Matt, who didn't follow her advice, looking over to see the next threat. The flame wall began to lower, then vanished altogether as men leapt over it with swords at the ready. Fortunately, the new commotion was the elves, Rognir, Nola, Cirion, and Cirion's remaining henchman arriving to take on the mercenaries. Rognir and Morven stopped beside them.

"You all right, lass?" the dwarf asked, seeming relieved to see them.

"Yeah we're okay."

"Soliander," Rognir started, giving Matt a pat, "assist Korrin while I show these elves how to fight." He charged away with a clatter.

Morven had already let an arrow fly at the dragon's head, but it bounced harmlessly off the golden scales as Perndara moved. A second arrow flew true but also ricocheted. The elf turned to the archers and began picking them off one by one.

As an arrow killed their lone henchman, Cirion and Nola ducked into a stairway to take in the scene. He spied Raith standing by the Dragon Gate, eyeing it hungrily, unmolested and apparently trusted by the dragon, but as Cirion watched, the wizard ascended the gate's steps and cast a final look at the suddenly chaotic hall, making brief eye contact with the rogue. A flash of recognition preceded a condescending smirk before the wizard stepped onto the gleaming surface of the Dragon Gate. At once he turned to smoke, which retained his shape an instant before slowly dissipating across the portal, twisting around and down until it vanished. He was gone.

Nola cursed and fired her crossbow at the archers, picking off one before seeing movement from another balcony. She trained her bow on the lone figure but didn't fire. Lorian had finally made it to the hall, his leg healed with a potion, his position on the balcony letting him assess the situation.

"Ryan," he called, "it is Lorian. Do not take your eyes from the dragon. You have done well, but you must pierce her heart with the lance."

"I don't want to kill her," Ryan replied.

"You have no choice. She will never let you near the gate alive."

"I'm already closer to it," the knight disagreed, advancing again, but then he stopped as a hail of arrows suddenly rained down on him. They bounced off harmlessly, but they distracted him enough that Perndara's jaws snapped toward him and clamped down on the lance, yanking it from his grasp. She tossed it behind her where it clattered to the floor behind the Dragon Gate, with a triumphant glare returning to the knight.

"Shit!" Ryan cursed.

Eric saw this and began creeping along the wall. The archers didn't react to his motion, but Perndara had sucked in a breath to roast him when a crackling bolt of lightning filled the room. A charred black wound, oozing dark blood, appeared in the dragon's chest. Roaring in pain, the dragon changed her target and sent flames at the source of the lightning. Lorian saw the retaliation coming and ran back through the balcony door, diving to the floor and around a corner as scorching heat washed over him. The door and benches burst into flames as the former flew off its hinges and crashed against the wall nearby. He quickly patted his cloak to make sure he wasn't on fire, too, then got to his feet to find another view point. This one stood blocked with flaming benches.

Ryan ran forward and swung hard at her good front leg before she could get her weight off it. The blade sliced into it easily, flinging blood out the other side as the sword passed through. She reared up on her hind legs to get away from the blade, spewing more fire over him instinctively, like a cat hissing at a threat.

"The charred spot on her chest," Lorian yelled, "is where you must strike."

Ryan couldn't reach it without the lance, even if the dragon came down from her reared-up position, which she couldn't do without landing on his sword. She swung first one front foot and then the other at him, narrowly missing, but then she swiftly turned and slammed him hard with a back foot, sending him tumbling across the hall. The sword fell with a clatter and he didn't stop rolling until he was all the way back by the fountain, dazed and groaning. Anna ran to him as the dragon advanced. Eric crept toward the lance.

At the hall's main doors, one elf went down in a heap, fatally wounded. Morven and the other elves had nearly finished killing the remaining mercenaries, but one leapt over the body, charging ahead to strike down the legendary Soliander, who recoiled and fumbled for words or items to block the raised sword about to end him. The blow somehow stopped just inches from Matt as if striking an invisible barrier. With a shriek, the man fell over dead, bearing a wound just like the one he would've inflicted. The wizard gaped in disbelief.

Anna knelt beside the fallen knight. "Ryan," she started, hands on him, "where are you hurt?"

"Everywhere," he moaned.

Anna tried to block out the approaching dragon and laid her hands on him, trying to call to Kiarin. The blood from Ryan's illusionary death still darkened her robe.

Perndara saw the white-robed figure trying to heal the Dragon Slayer and swept her claws through the air. Anna never saw them coming, but Lorian did. He shouted words and thrust out his hand, sending shards of ice into the dragon's neck. Perndara flinched, the motion changing her claw's path so that it struck only a glancing blow that still nearly ripped Anna's arm off, sending her tumbling into a heap where she lay unmoving.

Ryan saw the flash of golden scales remove Anna from above him, a shower of awful red blood splattering his visor. He bolted up despite the pain, screaming her name and seeing a pile of white robes stained with fresh blood. He rose, favoring one leg, and started for her when an enormous growl made him turn, for the limping dragon loomed overhead, triumphant, ferocious eyes ablaze. He stood defenseless.

Watching this, a visibly livid Matt gripped Soliander's staff in both hands and closed his eyes. Moments later, a forked tongue of lightning burst from the crystal to strike each of the dragon's eyes, boring into them. The enraged dragon flung her head side to side, trying to escape, but the twin beams followed her every move. When they stopped, only two scorched holes remained of Perndara's orbs, and no amount of magical healing would ever bring them back.

A deafening howl shook the walls, drowning out the sound of the lance sliding under Perndara and across the dusty floor. Eric had retrieved it and now sent it right up to Ryan, who stopped it with his foot. The knight lifted the lance, concentrating on the black scorch mark on the dragon's chest. Perndara never even knew he had it back when the Dragon Slayer took two quick steps and slammed the lance's tip into the bull's eye Lorian had given him.

The blow went deep into the dragon's chest. She reared up as if startled, a small puff of smoke curling up from her nostrils, jaws agape. She paused there as if to collapse would acknowledge Death had come for her, but finally she crashed to the floor with a great rumble that knocked loose stones from the broken ceiling. The body twitched and slowly the weight of her giant corpse settled. After a moment of silence, the great lungs expelled a final breath that washed over him.

Ryan let out a deep sigh, unsure how to feel, but the dragon didn't matter now. His reluctance to do harm had gotten yet another person hurt, and worst of all, she was the one person who could save Daniel. The dragon wasn't the only thing that had just died, for something in Ryan had, too, and yet it set him free like he hadn't been since the day of the accident so long ago. The man who had recently stood in horror over the body of the slain assassin was gone, replaced by a man who could look at something he'd just purposely killed with little regret.

Ryan looked about the room, so preoccupied with the dragon that he only just now saw the bodies everywhere, most behind the fountain and some on the balconies. Many survivors bore blood. Everything about this mission was so important to everyone that they were willing to risk their lives either to keep the dragons away or assist in their return.

He went to Anna, seeing Rognir leaning over her, soft light fading from his hands as the priest finished healing her. "How is she?" the knight asked the dwarf, seeing her eyes opening.

"She'll be fine, lad," replied the dwarf, watching as Nola and Cirion emerged from hiding to take aim at the remaining archers, who'd been standing in shock. Now they fell lifeless one by one until some realized the battle was lost and fled. "A better question," began Rognir, "is how are you? You took a mighty blow."

Ryan had almost forgotten, the adrenaline having kept the pain at bay. He was about to reply when Morven came up to them, looking grim. Two elves had died and another lay badly wounded. The dwarf started to rise sluggishly, weakened by all the healing he'd done. He could only do so much before his own strength gave out.

"Maybe I can help," began Eric, having clambered over the dragon to reach them. He gently pushed the dwarf back down and went over to the wounded, using the last of his ring's spells on the more gravely hurt. One elf still had a broken leg, so the rogue had Matt come over and do the same. Ryan gathered his sword and lance, Eric retrieved his knives, and Lorian slid down from the balcony on a tattered tapestry. The sounds of men fleeing echoed from all corners of the ruin. Aside from a few dead, everyone was accounted for, with one exception.

CHAPTER SIXTEEN

A Hero's Welcome

Matt felt good as he watched the battle's aftermath. While he seemed a one-trick pony, fire erupting from the staff was a fearsome trick, and he had cast a few spells aside from that. Only now could he look at the dragon with the awe and fascination it deserved.

"Has anyone seen Raith?" Morven asked, interrupting his thoughts.

"I saw him go through the gate," Cirion admitted angrily. "I'm going after him."

"Not so fast," said Ryan coldly, clamping a big hand on Cirion's arm. "You've already caused enough trouble."

The rogue tried to pull free but got nowhere. He was no match for Korrin and knew it. He stepped back, eyes hard, while Ryan moved to stand between the gate and everyone else. If they wanted to get to it, they'd have to go through him, and for the first time in ages he was willing to use his strength to get his point across.

"Should we go after him?" Anna asked dubiously. "There's no telling what's on the other side."

Eric shook his head. "Too risky. There are thousands of dragons there, and whoever opened the gate can appear and lock it behind us."

Images suddenly flashed inside Matt's head; of the black-robed figure that attacked him standing here just weeks ago with his identical staff inserted into the gate's base; of that wizard fashioning the gate from soclarin ore; of a knight, rogue, and priestess in his company on a quest, dressed just like Matt's friends were now; of the figure's hand penning the original scroll describing their time here; of a rosewood cabinet opening to reveal the staff and robe locked within; of his own face as seen by the figure through the orb just before lightning flashed from it to electrocute the dark elf spy.

Matt's mouth fell open and he just stopped himself from blurting out his realization. He'd known it earlier but had forgotten during the fight. Now Nola and Cirion stood here and this was none of their business.

"You two," he said with such a commanding voice that he startled his friends, "get over there behind the fountain." When the pair hesitated, he barked, "Now!"

Lorian nodded at his elves and a few escorted a glowering Cirion and Nola out of earshot. The others gathered around Matt more closely, perplexed.

"Soliander did it," the wizard said in a quiet voice, amazed by the truth of it. "The real Soliander. He's the one who opened the gate, and he attacked me downstairs. That's who you heard screaming before."

Expressions of disbelief surrounded him except from Lorian.

The elf nodded, looking grim. "I suspected as much myself." Inquisitive eyes turned on him and he added, "When you did not join us in the dungeon I went looking for you and saw what I thought was you walking away, so I followed. It soon became apparent that it was someone else despite the identical staff, which was impossible. Or so I thought. It would seem that you each have a copy of it, presumably a result of the summoning spell always equipping the champions with whatever they need for the quest. I am not sure how that works, but since they could be summoned from anywhere at any time, they cannot expect to be dressed appropriately and the spell resolves this for them. I suspected the truth as I followed the figure, and when he opened a portal to depart through, he nearly killed me. I did not confirm his identity. You are sure?"

"Positive," Matt answered. "He attacked me downstairs and tried to pull information from my mind with a spell of some kind." He flushed at the memory. "He wasn't very nice about it. I noticed our staves were the same, too. In fact, that was how I got away. He made my staff stop working but I was able to reach out to his and make it burn him, so I did. I don't think he was expecting that. Anyway, I think I somehow got some of the info in his head by mistake," he concluded, realizing he now knew what the real champions looked like.

Lorian made a sound. "Interesting. It is a two-way spell unless the one controlling it prevents that, as was undoubtedly his intention. His control would likely have slipped given the injuries he sustained."

"So you learned things from him beyond his identity?" Eric asked intently. "Now we know at least one of the real champions is alive, which raises a ton of questions. What else can you tell us? Did you sense anything about the others?"

Matt thought for a moment and frowned, shaking his head. "I don't know. It's not like that, I don't think. I don't even know what I know. I just know for certain it was him that attacked me, and when you wondered who'd opened the gate, I just knew that, too, as if his memory was mine."

Eric asked, "Can you tell why he opened the gate?"

Matt paused but again shook his head. "I don't know. I'm not getting anything."

"Maybe because you're trying on purpose now," suggested Anna, laying a comforting hand on him.

Lorian nodded, looking concerned about the revelations. "Yes, that could be. Since the transfer was involuntary, the memories and knowledge may be difficult to retrieve. We have more pressing issues, however, and can talk more of this later."

Wondering if hypnosis might work, Matt brushed that aside and asked, "So we'll leave Raith on the other side of the gate with the dragons?" As he wondered what was over there, images of a thick forest covering a mountain range popped into his head, but that was all.

"Yes," said Lorian, indicating Cirion and Nola could return to them now. "We can discuss his motives later, but he'll be unable to cause trouble once you seal the gate. We should act fast."

Matt took the hint and started for the gate with everyone following, which made him a bit nervous. He may have struck at the dragon with people watching, but that had been emotional. This was different – everything depended on it. He glanced over his shoulder at the small crowd, prompting Ryan to make all but his friends and Lorian stay back. The image of Soliander standing here at least gave Matt some idea what to do. The staff sent a pulse up his arm, letting him know magic was afoot, though he assumed that was the gate itself.

He mounted the steps, looking at the gate's misty surface in awe and tempted to touch it, but then the thought of dragons rising up through it banished that idea. He could daydream later. Flipping the staff upside down, he inserted the crystal into a hole. At once, a cone of blue light shot up into the sky from the gate before extinguishing, the gate's glistening surface turning to smoke with a slight whoosh, tendrils drifting upward. He could now see through the empty oval to the floor beneath.

Matt sighed in relief and came down the steps. "I guess that was it."

The staff sent another pulse up his arm, but he didn't know what it meant. Maybe something else was causing that. With the gate off, he decided he didn't care what else lay around here. Besides, maybe the gate always gave off that reaction. Once again he lamented the lack of owner's manuals or general knowledge of how things were supposed to work. Maybe if he meditated or something, he could learn such ideas from Soliander's memories.

"Now we can go home!" Ryan gripped his shoulder in congratulations. He sighed in relief. "I can't wait to see Daniel." His bright eyes turned to Anna and she frowned, looking away.

"We should return to my estate," remarked Lorian, "on the way to Olliana. Let us depart."

As Matt left with the others, he suddenly realized Cirion and Nola were gone and remarked on this.

"Damn those two!" Rognir spat, unhooking his axe. "I bet I know just what they'll be up to when we leave, too. Looting this corpse!" He gestured at the dragon, which surprised Matt.

"Why?" he asked.

"These scales, teeth, and claws are worth a fortune," the dwarf answered gruffly. "Lorian, as much as I love Arundell, I will stay behind. I have two heads to bust open." With that, he quickly said his goodbyes and stomped off through a doorway, clanking all the way. He stood little chance of sneaking up on Cirion. Matt noticed Anna looking after him regretfully. Was she regretting not learning more from him?

Ryan sighed. "It's just as well. I don't trust those two and don't want them with us anyway."

"Agreed," said Eric and Lorian in unison.

They left Castle Darlonon, making an uneventful return to Lorian's estate, a group of thirty elves meeting the weary travelers along the way. The forest teemed with them as they hunted down ogres and restored peace below the mountains. Since many an elf stopped to offer kind words. The quest had finally become almost fun now that it was over, and their worries were largely forgotten as they gathered with Lorian in Arundell's meeting room one last time.

In discussing Raith's involvement, they concluded someone might have to return one day to deal with the wizard, assuming the dragons or any traps left by Soliander didn't get him first. If he learned to use the ore, he could lie in wait for someone to open the gate and spring a trap of his own, so coming back sooner rather than later was agreed upon. With the real Soliander on the loose, the gate could be reopened again, and were a duel to happen between the two wizards, with dragons eager to destroy them both, the consequences could be terrible for Honyn. They assumed Soliander had opened the gate to get more soclarin but had no answers for why he'd left it that way.

Due to his questioning of Matt, they surmised Soliander knew nothing of where the other champions were and wasn't involved in the substitution. It was now apparent that the summoning had been altered in some fundamental way, since Soliander lived and yet Matt had come in his place. The real Ellorians could refuse or were spared, but their replacements could not, which suggested they might be summoned again and again, which no one wanted to think about.

Soliander's behavior concerned Lorian most, for it was quite unlike the man he'd known, raising serious questions. What had he been doing all this time? Where had he been? Did anyone know he still lived? It seemed unlikely, but then why was he hiding his existence? Did he have a new identity and a new life to go with it somewhere? Why was he acting this way? If the other champions lived, were their personalities so distorted as well? Soliander seemed to think they existed somewhere. Was he looking for them? And why? His actions suggested sinister intent, not a man searching for his friends, so finding them might spell trouble for the others.

Matt hoped answers would come soon so they could also escape the quests, but Soliander didn't seem amenable to polite conversation. It seemed likely that the Ellorian Champions were free as well, and despite no reports of them appearing home, perhaps they had done so secretly so they'd be left alone. A chance to speak with them might come sooner than they wanted because the real possibility existed that, instead of returning to Earth, they would be returned to their counterparts' homes instead if the spell couldn't tell the difference between them and the real champions. If so, Lorian promised to visit. He recommended telling the truth of their masquerade to the elven court, which had the power to send him across worlds as needed. Such aid would be invaluable and the elves would certainly keep the secret.

They decided to keep the truth about Soliander from Queen Lorella and the rest of Honyn, however. It would raise too many questions about not only the real arch wizard but the four new champions, though this did pose one problem.

"There's one more thing," started Matt, "the queen will want to know who opened the gate and we can't very well tell her it was Soliander if she thinks I'm him."

"True," agreed Anna, frowning. "So what do we tell her? I'd rather not lie, so can we just say we don't know? Is learning the truth part of the quest?"

"No, it is not," replied Lorian.

"Failing to admit it is still a lie, by the way," Eric interjected, "but I think we just go with a better lie than not knowing. Let's blame it on Raith. We think he's a cult member and involved in the stolen scroll anyway, so this isn't a stretch. As a cult member, he would have wanted to open the gate anyway but it was already open."

"The queen might not know a soclarin item is needed to open the gate, but if she asks if he had one, we'll just duck the question," added Matt. "He went through the gate before we could have asked him that."

Ryan nodded. "I think that is the way to go."

"There's something I should mention," began Matt. "When Soliander did his mind meld spell on me, he learned our real names and that we're from Earth, a name he seemed to recognize. I'm concerned he might track us down there and finish what he started."

Everyone's expressions became sober and serious.

Eric observed, "He could go after our families."

"Daniel," Ryan whispered, paling. Looking at Matt, he remarked, "I sure hope you can cast spells back home because if he shows up, you're our only real chance."

Matt exchanged a concerned look with the others.

They soon turned to drinking the night away in the safety of the elven estate, trying to forget the worst parts of the quest or what might lie ahead. On their way back to Olliana, each had their own preoccupation.

With help from Lorian, Matt practiced spells every day, hoping they still worked on Earth. He didn't know what to expect but suspected he wouldn't have the staff or books. He tried to memorize everything and spent all day with his nose buried in books to the point of rudeness. The others understood and left him alone.

Eric and Ryan both learned tracking from the elves and took seriously elements of horsemanship and wilderness survival that might be needed if they ever did another quest. Both expressed an interest in learning elven, so Lorian just cast the spell on all of them, then dwarven. Learning other languages like ogre came up but the elf said with a smile that they needed to absorb what they had already gained. There would be time enough for more later.

Anna had lapsed into quietness that prompted more than one to ask if she was feeling okay. She would nod and smile serenely but not say much about her inner world. She didn't understand what she was feeling and had something to sort through on her own. When Rognir had healed her, she'd felt the powerful effect of a god's compassionate touch in her. Part of her felt deeply shaken by it, but this was mostly psychological, her mind struggling to accept what had happened. Emotionally, she had never felt more at peace. She sensed that she'd been changed forever by it, and while that scared her a little, she felt eager to leave behind her old disposition and embrace something new. She been reading everything she could about the gods here, face buried in a scroll almost as much as Matt.

As they neared Olliana, people emerged from roadside homes and inns to offer congratulations, flowers, and even their chastity. Ryan exchanged knowing looks with Eric and Matt about the bounty of female flesh offering itself up, and how unfortunate it was that they had to be going.

"It's good to be the champions," remarked Eric, pulling up beside Ryan.

Ryan laughed, his banner snapping in the breeze atop his lance. "Yes, if only we had time to enjoy it."

Chiding them, Anna remarked, "Just think how many diseases you could bring back with you."

Undaunted, Ryan suggested, "You could always cure us." The boys laughed aloud while she failed to suppress a grin. The return to joking was nice.

They trotted through Olliana's main crowded cobblestone streets with Lorian and surrounded by elves, though Morven had remained behind at the estate. The escort Queen Lorella had sent out to meet them led the way, steel-clad knights riding in formation. The crowd's roar of appreciation greeted the champions and flowers flew, gifts were given, and ribbons were strewn around their necks.

From a balcony, the queen gave a suitable speech, declaring the day a holiday and that a festival of celebration was to begin immediately. Yet another banquet in their honor would be held that night, but first the champions gathered in the War Room to tell the queen, her wizard Sonneri, and the Prime Minister the details of the quest.

"I understand you were successful in sealing the Dragon Gate," the queen observed, smiling from her seat behind the hexagonal table. "Please tell us precisely what happened."

With a look at Eric to see which of them would speak for them, Ryan received an encouraging nod and replied, "Certainly, Your Majesty. When we arrived at the castle, we discovered that Cirion's group had arrived ahead of us, but they were captured with some loss of life. We freed those remaining and set about dealing with the dragon."

Queen Lorella asked, "And were you able to chase her back through the gate before sealing it?"

Resignation on his face, the knight replied, "No, my queen. We had hoped to subdue her, but her hostility was too great, and in the course of battle she was killed."

The queen's eyes widened in shock, a flash of anger appearing before she relaxed and assumed a look of resigned acceptance. "While I don't agree with the Dragon Cult's methods," she explained, "I do understand their desire to see the dragons live well and prosper. I had hoped bloodshed could be avoided and the dragon spared, but I'm sure you only did what was necessary."

Ryan hadn't realized she had a preference but wasn't surprised. He responded warmly and genuinely. "I can assure you I made every attempt to spare the dragon's life and avoid her death. It was very regrettable."

The look she gave him made it clear she didn't believe a word of it, her knuckles white from clenching the arms of the chair. "What happened when you sealed the gate?"

Matt responded, "Very little. No dragons were pulled into it, so Nir'lion was the only one here."

The queen nodded. "But you're certain the gate is now closed?"

"Yes."

One hand on his big belly, Sonneri asked, "What did you learn about who opened the gate?"

Ryan replied, "We believe that a wizard named Raith opened it. He is the one who stole the scroll and learned its contents, which gave him motive."

Queen Lorella asked, "What motive is that? I thought simply freeing the dragons was the reason."

Realizing his mistake, Ryan admitted, "Yes, it was, since Raith was a Dragon Cult member, but in reading the scroll he discovered the existence of soclarin ore on the world where the dragons are imprisoned."

Seeming satisfied, she asked, "Will this wizard be able to open the gate again?"

"No," Matt answered. "He was present during the battle and stepped through the gate before we shut it. He is now trapped on the other side."

With arched eyebrows, the queen considered that in silence.

The next morning, the champions made their final preparations for leaving, saying goodbye to Lorian. Word of their success had spread so that those armies threatening war against Kingdom Alunia had stood down. Castle Darlonon and the forest had been cleared out by the elves and Alunia's forces. Everything was returning to normal here and they hoped their own lives were next on the list. They suspected they'd been reported missing.

It was standing room only as they ascended the steps to the dais and turned to face those they'd saved from destruction. As before, only the rich and privileged attended, but many more such people gathered now. The queen bade them farewell with a last speech, and in the applause that followed, Sonneri cast a stern look at the crowd to be quiet. Turning to the book before him on a podium, he began to speak so quietly none could hear, but Matt tried to read his lips, another skill he'd picked up for his deaf mother because she often read his. He tried to memorize the words and gestures, realizing he'd lost the opportunity to learn that spell and should've thought of that, but hopefully he'd never need it.

The stone pillars around them began to glow with words of blue fire, the decorative markings on the floor turning white beneath their feet. Soliander's staff sent a continuous pulse up Matt's arm, letting him know magic was afoot, and the wizard knew he'd miss the power he'd come to wield here. Of the four, he'd done the most amazing things and would return to a life far more ordinary, and only his eyes were sad as the pillars burst into flames with a loud whoosh and the room around them disappeared.

CHAPTER SEVENTEEN

RESOLUTIONS

Jack Riley stood just inside the door of Anna's condo in Gaithersburg Maryland, not sure where to begin but sure he didn't want to start at all. No friend would want the task before him and it felt premature. It certainly didn't offer hope. Packing Anna's things as if she was never returning just felt wrong. He wasn't ready to let go and didn't understand her father's decision. Maybe he just wanted some action to break the frustration of getting no answers, no resolution, nothing to change, even if this particular action suggested an abandonment of hope. The weeks of waiting and wondering were unpleasant, certainly, but this wasn't the way to go. What would Anna say if she returned? You waited just weeks before deciding I was gone forever? Gee, thanks.

He smiled at the thought. They went back a long way – he and Matt, too – growing up in the same neighborhood. Unlike with many friendships, time had not forced them apart, and while he wasn't part of the foursome, he certainly knew the others, too. It was hard to know one but not all, they did so much together, but Jack had a life elsewhere. A less secure guy might have felt he was a fifth wheel with all the inside jokes and you-had-to-be-there references, but he was fine with that. They had shared adventures with him as well, but for weeks he'd been wondering if they were now sharing some nightmare instead.

More than two weeks had passed since Anna Lynn Sumner, Eric Foster, Matt Sorenson, and Ryan LaRue had disappeared in England, their van found abandoned by the side of the road. A motive for their return to the monoliths after hours remained unknown. No security cameras existed at Stonehenge and the British authorities had found little to help their investigation. No witnesses or signs of foul play turned up and the volume of footprints nearby eliminated any signs of theirs. Only the digital camera found in the car, with its few pictures of the happy friends in their last moments, proved they had really been here, but they shed no light on the situation. The best guess – and that was all they had – was that they had been abducted and taken away in another car.

A ransom had first been suspected, with the wealthy Ryan the target and the others just bystanders, but one never appeared. Nor had any bodies, thankfully. No terrorist organization or anti-American group had claimed responsibility, and no signs of mental instability or unhappiness existed among the four. There had been nothing to go on and nothing had changed since finding the abandoned SUV.

The mystery had captured not only England's imagination, but the world's, due in no small part to Ryan's family. The considerable wealth of the LaRue estate had been brought to bear on the investigation and broadcasting of each police report, but it had aided them little. Scores of press conferences and both television and radio appeals had resulted in only false leads. The offered reward money had simply swamped the resources available to handle those leads. Daniel had personally appeared on TV to appeal for help, remarking on how much his brother looked after him and would never disappear this way. That situation had added to the world's sympathy that yet another tragedy of some kind had befallen the family.

Candlelight vigils had been held both in England and the United States with speeches by friends and tearful pleas from parents. A prime time TV special had even detailed their lives, disappearance, media storm, and the international investigation, with the typical stock footage of friends in happier times and how bright their futures were – or had been. The four lost friends had become famous for the wrong reason, and if they were ever to turn up alive, a worldwide media storm would greet them, questions flying. Everyone wanted answers, but those closest to them really just wanted them back.

With the apparent exception of Anna's father, thought Jack.

He stepped further into the condo, seeing the cats come out from hiding in expectation of food. He'd been taking care of them and was supposed to take them home soon, once he cleared out the place. Anna's father hadn't put it on the market yet, but it couldn't be far off. It seemed he wanted to put the whole mess behind him and move on. Still feeling like this was a terrible mistake, Jack picked up a cat and headed for the kitchen. He would start tomorrow.

Autumn leaves rustled under the horse's hooves as the elf cantered along the road from Olliana. After much toil and danger, he rode with less alertness than usual, for there was little to worry about so close to the city. He needed to relax anyway after all the recent fighting and stress. It was why he'd freed the other elves with him to stay or go on alone, for he wanted some time to himself. He breathed in the fresh air and scents of the forest as he entered a wooded stretch of road. It reminded Lorian of home, his destination.

He could enjoy the comforts of Arundell for the first time in months, a crate of rare wine waiting for such an august occasion as the second banishment of the dragons and, even better, the death of Nir'lion. While elves valued life, some lives were bent on the destruction of all others and were best extinguished for the greater good. She wouldn't be causing such trouble again even on the uninhabited Soclarin, a thought which reminded him of the ore.

It was just as well that the gate had been sealed and that ore locked away. The ore was a dangerous thing for anyone to learn the existence of, and it pleased him that Queen Lorella, her Prime Minister, and Sonneri had agreed to destroy the scroll copy. No one else would learn its contents, and it could be safely forgotten. Hopefully Soliander would never open the gate again, or if he did, the new champions could lock it swiftly next time. They had done very well, very well indeed.

Thoughts of Soliander troubled him. The wizard he'd known would never have let the dragons loose to cause such damage or been so careless about leaving the gate unguarded. Where he had gone to and what he'd been doing all this time troubled Lorian as much as the attempts on both his and Matt's lives. It raised fears about what had become of the real Andier, Eriana, and Korrin. Something told him the wizard had something to do with their disappearance and he rode along thinking of every detail he could remember from their time together, looking for clues into this destructive behavior. Lost in thought, he never saw the net falling until it was too late. It swept him from the horse's back to the ground, where someone delivered a blow that knocked him out.

⸻ ⋅ ⋅ ⸻

Queen Lorella strode into her private chambers, leaving her guards outside and breathing a sigh of relief that this whole affair with the Ellorians was over, at least publicly. There were reconciliation meetings to occur between kingdoms via messengers and other intermediaries, but she'd leave those details to others as befitting a ruler of her stature. Now the armies threatening war had backed down, their warriors going back to their regular lives, unmindful of any danger that might turn up in the next days. Everyone's guard would drop and no one would think to watch the skies any longer.

She smiled. This was perfect, even better than she had planned. For a time, there she'd been rather angry, and more importantly, at a loss for how to salvage the situation. Then the champions had come against all odds and a new plan was born, one that left Honyn even more unsuspecting than before. It had unfortunately cost the life of the same foolish dragon that had caused the problem by being spotted, and there would be a hefty price to pay for her death, but in the end, disaster had not only been averted but turned to her advantage.

She turned to a map of Honyn on a table, eyeing the nearby kingdoms and recalling what Olliana's generals had told her about troop movements and battle tactics in the event a dragon horde emerged from the gate. No one had been willing to share plans due to suspicion about which kingdom's wizard had unleashed them, but knowing they wouldn't cooperate with each other was worth knowing, too. The fools didn't deserve the peace they now enjoyed, but sometimes fools got what they deserved. Their lack of loyalty to each other and to the kingdom that had now twice saved them would cost them.

A sound behind her indicated someone had entered through the secret entrance and now waited quietly, obediently, like a respectful servant should. Unlike some, she commanded authority and didn't tolerate abuses to respect, though one had disobeyed her recently and caused no end of trouble.

Irritated by the memory, the queen asked sharply, "Have you received word from the castle?"

"Yes, my queen. They arrived safely just as you intended."

"And what of the elf?"

"He will join them shortly."

She turned toward him menacingly, eyes turning to red fire as a glint of her power surged. "See that he does...or I will devour you alive."

A feeble, "My queen", was all he could muster as he bowed and backed out of the room.

Heading for a tall shape covered by a golden cloth in one corner, she decided to see for herself, for these spies couldn't be trusted despite their sincerity. She pulled the cloth to the floor, revealing a shimmering portal that seemed to show a portrait of herself. Her depiction wore a soiled gown that had known better days. Time had a way of changing such finery for the worse without good care. The woman's body had fared only slightly better, dirt smudging each cheek, her hair dirty and matted. Some might have thought the queen gazed upon some impending future reality, but she wasn't even really looking at herself at all. Smiling grimly, she put one hand to the mirror's edge, spoke a magic word, and stepped through, vanishing from Olliana.

After a moment of flashing colors and whooshing air, he stepped onto blackened and charred earth, blinking in the sunlight. Mountains loomed all around and deep green forest covered everything but the area just before him, which looked to have been blasted with fire so severely that nothing grew here anymore. His eyes searched the sky for threats, but nothing appeared. No signs of movement came from the slopes' craggy shadows and cave openings, but that didn't mean he wasn't being watched. He'd maintain a constant vigil lest his death appear on wings, but for now everything seemed fine. He was alone.

As he glanced about to get his bearings, he noticed a faint trail leading away from the Dragon Gate behind him. Raith's eyes lit up and he set off at a jog, his distaste for such exertions forgotten. Time was short, for the champions wouldn't take long to kill that stupid dragon. While he'd long admired the creatures, he'd never met one before the banishment. He knew some dragons were smarter than others and was certain that this dragon hadn't been the famed Nir'lion. He'd probably not have gotten past that one. Curiosity as to her whereabouts lingered, though it occurred to him that perhaps she had died here somehow. It was something to ponder later.

Now he had to get to the soclarin ore, retrieve a healthy supply, evade the Ellorians when they arrived, and get back through the gate. Then he'd find his way back to the horses and eventually reach his secret tower in the crags of the Naken Peaks. He would learn to fashion magic items from the ore as Soliander had done, and once ready, would bring all of Honyn to its knees.

With lust for power distracting him, he made quick progress up the winding path, shadowed by the thick canopy of trees. The dragons wouldn't see him now unless one shape shifted to human form and followed, but he doubted they would. Dragons didn't care to remain in that form long and had little reason to suspect anything was here. Soliander had undoubtedly not told them of the ore, and unless they'd discovered it on their own, they were none the wiser.

The trail ended in a thicket that only someone in armor could pass without getting shredded, and while it looked natural, he suspected otherwise. He murmured a quick incantation, but nothing happened. Gripping his staff for more power, he tried again. This time the brush parted to reveal a short path. He smirked and set off.

The winding trail soon deposited Raith in a narrow, sloping ravine of rough stone that rose sharply toward a natural cave. Feeling clever for getting this far, he started for the mine opening, pulling a fist-sized bag from a pocket. It would hold far more than it appeared, being enchanted to be nearly bottomless and hold tons of weight without burdening the one who carried it. It neatly eliminated the need for help, which was just as well. He'd never have gotten assistants here anyway and it spared him the trouble of killing his hired help yet again, not that he really cared.

He'd taken no more than a few steps when the rock wall beside the entrance broke apart. It didn't fall to the ground as expected, instead forming itself into a humanoid shape taller than him, two powerful arms and legs attached to a muscular torso. The menacing head turned to him with a sound of grating stone, two hollow eyes narrowing as it stepped in his direction.

"A stone golem," he muttered, disappointed. "I should've known." Only blunt force could defeat one but his staff would snap like kindling. Magical power was his forte anyway. His eyes on the heavens, he focused his will on a cloud and spoke.

"Uusrolinip, uusrarkitor!" *Two arcs of fire, two blasts of light!*

With a loud boom that echoed off the mountains, a forked shaft of lightning struck the golem in the head and leg, but it continued forward as if nothing had happened. Raith realized too late that it wasn't the force of lightning that blew things apart, but the effect on the material's composition. Earth was largely immune to it. He had wasted energy and had only so much time before it reached him.

The stone golem stopped to touch the rock wall and a large boulder rolled out of seemingly nowhere. The golem lifted it and then hurled it at Raith with startling speed. Thinking fast, he continued to cast the next spell on his mind – levitation – but changed targets from the golem to another boulder, which he lifted into the path of the one hurtling toward him. They collided with a horrible crack, showering the ravine with jagged fragments. One struck him hard enough to dislocate his shoulder and he gasped at the pain, blood running down his arm. Quickly he pulled out a vial and tore the stopper off with his teeth, draining it in one gulp. The injury healed like it had never been, and when he looked up again, movement behind the golem startled him.

A figure dressed in black robes sat upon a rock, a staff in one hand. For a moment, an unexpected and yet likely name came to mind, but it couldn't be. Even great wizards couldn't be two places at once. Then all thought of the black figure vanished as the golem lifted another boulder, this one smaller and more easily targeted than before.

Raith barely dodged it before another followed. He wasn't the most agile fellow and couldn't keep this up, so he tilted his staff forward and focused. With a loud bang, the next head-sized boulder shattered two paces from him on an invisible barrier, the shards scattering. Dust cascaded around him as Raith trembled from the impact. Another rock did the same, then another and another, each one testing his strength, each one pushing the barrier closer to him.

The golem advanced, still hurling boulders as it came, pulling stone from its own chest and throwing it. As if made of liquid rock, it filled the hole in its chest from its own body as it absorbed more stone from the ground while walking, reforming itself spontaneously. The distance between them quickly shortened and a surge of panic struck Raith. He had one chance to drop the barrier and destroy this thing and then run for his life, for the robed figure would go next and his strength was spent.

Suddenly an idea hit him as the golem loomed overhead. He dropped the shield and again used the levitation spell, hurling the golem backward straight at the robed figure, hoping to kill two birds with one stone. The figure never even moved as the golem shattered on him and fragments flew everywhere. A cloud of dust obscured the result, but the golem's head rolled straight toward him, between his legs, and came to rest a few feet behind. He had done it!

Then movement caught his eye. The cloud faded to reveal the robed figure without a mark upon it, for it had erected its own barrier. It rose to its feet and as Raith fumbled for a magic item, the sound of stone moving came from behind. He turned and saw in horror that the golem had reformed and was swinging a crushing fist at him. Ribs snapped like twigs as he was flung to the ground, the last healing vial breaking with the impact. The golem took one step and hurled another rock down at him, smashing his pelvis to bits. He would have screamed but for the stabbing pain in his lungs that left him gasping at his murderer.

The golem raised a final boulder.

"Stop."

The golem halted.

Soft footsteps signaled the approaching figure, which wore a badly singed robe but walked without pain. The figure stopped and gestured for the golem to move aside.

"You," Raith wheezed, more certain of the identity now that he recognized something he'd seen at the banquet in Olliana. He'd seen drawings of it many times before and would know it anywhere.

"You no doubt recognize my staff," answered the figure in calm approval, "as all serious wizards should. And of course, you're presence here is a great sign of your seriousness. You have come for the soclarin."

Raith didn't bother to confirm it. The voice sounded different than he remembered, but then his senses were beginning to fail him. He'd already lost feeling in his legs.

"It was you who stole the scroll," observed the figure.

"Yes," Raith confessed, seeing little reason to hide his secrets anymore. He would soon have no need of them.

"Personally, or did you hire someone?"

"Hired."

"And then killed them upon delivery?"

Raith nodded slightly, suddenly overcome with sorrow for what was happening to him. The figure could heal him but clearly wasn't going to despite this going against everything Raith knew about the man whose voice he heard. Then again, so did allowing a golem to bludgeon him to death.

"Excellent. And you have the scroll with you?"

Again Raith nodded, but the figure made no move to retrieve it.

"Did you not wonder why I left the gate open?" the figure asked. "Or did you, like everyone else, assume I had gone forever and perhaps someone else had done it?"

Raith struggled to acquit himself well but relinquished his pride as a spasm shook him and blood trickled out his mouth. "I don't know," he confessed.

"That's because you are a fool," replied the figure coldly, watching without compassion as the young wizard slumped further. "You, my dear boy, are the reason the gate is open. I needed to know who had the stolen scroll, who outside the court knew about soclarin, as the individual would come looking for it. You triggered the spell I put on the gate to alert me when you stepped through, and you have met your end via the golem I left waiting for you. For all your ambition, you are, like so many, blinded by it, and therefore come to the pathetic end that is your destiny." The figure chuckled. "And in the process, your ambition has caused the dragons to be free to doom your world."

Feeling a haze overtake him, Raith said quietly, "But I *want* the dragons free."

"And so shall they be."

Surprised, Raith asked, "You won't close..." His breath failed him.

"No. Only you knew of the ore, and you'll not leave here alive. No one else knew to come looking for it, but I suspect others may know now. The trap must remain." He cast a glance toward the gate, visible beyond the tree tops. "And I care nothing for what becomes of Honyn."

The figure pulled back the hood, revealing black hair and a cold expression. The face was similar to the one Raith anticipated but not the same. His surprise was plain.

"I am not who you expected?" the figure asked.

"S-s-s," stuttered Raith, confused as blackness overtook him. "Soliander?"

"Indeed," confirmed the wizard, "the *real* Soliander."

CHAPTER EIGHTEEN

END GAME

Right from the start Eric had his suspicions. He'd only traveled via worm hole – or whatever it was – once before, but the vivid memory remained. There had been lots of flashing lights, roaring sounds, wardrobe changes, that sort of thing, but none of that happened this time. Maybe the spell sending them home was different, but they still needed their clothes back. Granted, all this magic stuff was rather new to him, but something didn't seem right. It wasn't just his lingering fear that they weren't really headed home either. His suspicions only deepened when the spell stopped almost as soon as it began.

His first thought was that something had gone wrong. For one, he still wore the leather armor and weapons, Matt still looked like a wizard, and Ryan and Anna hadn't changed either. They also weren't standing in a field surrounded by the stone monoliths of Stonehenge, but in the center of a dusty chamber with cobwebs on the walls. The stone work, general disrepair, and odor of decay seemed familiar. Through a dirty, stained-glass window off to one side, forest-covered foothills sloped away for miles. A nearby wooden door stood closed, but another was open enough to reveal a tall, swiveling mirror with the looking glass removed. The room was sparsely furnished, but what little remained lay covered in filth and mold, mildew having rotted cushions and curtains. The only newer items were a wooden tray with an empty plate and drinking cup on the center table, and a rough cot in one corner. Upon this sat a woman about twice their age. She looked to have seen better days, for the dirtiness of the room had clung to her gown, face, and hands, as if the room's disrepair were slowly consuming her, making her a part of itself.

Anna turned to him. "Where are we?"

It was the woman who answered. "Castle Darlonon. I assume from your astonished expressions that you did not come here to rescue me?"

"No," Anna answered. She peered curiously at the woman. "You look a lot like Queen Lorella."

"That's because I *am* Queen Lorella," she replied, rising with a natural air of authority her surroundings hadn't changed.

"You do look a lot like her," Ryan admitted, stepping closer, "enough to be her sister maybe, but we just came from where she is."

"Olliana? That is an imposter and has been for some time."

"How do we know you're not the illusion?" Eric asked.

"The staff isn't telling me there's anything," Matt observed. Suddenly he looked surprised and opened his mouth to say something when Anna spoke.

Anna asked, "Why would someone impersonate the queen?"

"Because the queen learns all," said a bold female voice from the other room, "and that's just the sort of information I need."

They stared as another Queen Lorella stepped into view wearing a smug sneer and a tight-fitting leather outfit showing a dragon's head emblazoned on the breast, every tone and movement hinting at danger and cunning, not elegant benevolence. Behind her stood a swivel mirror shimmering with light. Eric noticed that Matt looked less surprised than the others. Had the staff warned him that magic mirror was on?

"You have no doubt noticed," continued the new arrival, stalking into the room in black, heeled boots, "that you have not been safely delivered to your precious home world, wherever that may be – and I intend to know. A visit there seems only fitting once I have terrorized Honyn, a joy for which I will wait no longer. When done I will return to tear answers from your hearts, one by one, until there is nothing left of you. And what I want most to know is where the real champions are."

Looking back and forth between the two queens, Ryan objected, "But the spell was supposed to send us back. We finished the quest."

"Did you now?" the imposter interrupted, snidely amused. "You accomplished nothing more than what I let you believe, fool! The gate stands open even now. Its closing was an illusion, as was Sonneri's attempt to send you home, though he thought it was real, but he saw what I wanted him to see while another spell of mine brought you here." She laughed cruelly.

"Nir'lion," Eric said in realization. *Two* dragons had come through. Who had they killed?

"But we killed Nir'lion," Ryan protested.

"No!" the dragon snarled, slapping him so hard that he crashed to the floor with three bloody gashes on his cheek. "You killed my daughter,"

Nir'lion growled as Anna bent down to him, "and for that I will roast you alive!" Tendrils of smoke drifted up from her nostrils, a reek of power from her engulfing the room like a smothering weight.

"What now?" asked Eric, hoping to distract her from more violence.

"Oh, I want a great many things. My brethren will be arriving in minutes to take back this world that belongs to *us*."

Hoping for answers and to stall, he asked, "Why didn't all of you come back before? Why just you and your daughter?"

She gave him a withering look. "What point lay there in that? Unless I found and killed every wizard able to close the gate, someone could just send us back. I had to find and execute them all first, before anyone knew we'd returned. Perndara ruined that by being seen."

"You didn't know only Soliander can do it. Or someone with the ore."

"Yes, not until I replaced the queen here and read the scroll, but then I learned someone had stolen a copy. I had to kill them. I cannot allow knowledge of how to close the gate become commonplace."

"Why did you summon the champions? It wasn't supposed to work."

She rolled her eyes. "That's *why* I had them summoned. Empty gesture to silence the kingdoms threatening war, which could interfere with finding out who could close the gate."

"You knew we weren't them at once, didn't you?"

"Of course. I would never forget *those* four. The question now is how you came to be here in their stead and where they are. Giving me the answer is the only reason you're still alive."

Eric wasn't looking forward to being tortured, however she was planning to do it. He had to stall for time. "Why didn't you just do something to us then? Why let us complete the quest, or appear to?"

"I wanted to know who you were. My spies soon assured me that you were not up to the quest's challenge, which meant that by fooling you into believing the gate had been closed, I could undo the damage that Perndara had done to my plans. And it worked. Armies have already stood down. You even found out for me who stole the scroll."

They had indeed. But Raith was on the other side of the gate, still alive, unless the dragons over there had gotten him, which seemed likely. "What of Perndara? She fought us and if we'd done the spell to close the gate, she would've been pulled through. Since we weren't doing it for real, we would've known it didn't work."

"She was supposed to pretend she couldn't handle you and fly back through it before you tried. As it turns out, she couldn't handle you for real."

The dragon looked at him as if realizing he was a bigger threat than believed. Maybe they could use that to their advantage, but he had no idea how. The entire quest had been a trap. They'd achieved nothing, would not be going home, and Honyn would be destroyed. They had snatched defeat from the jaws of victory.

"So now what?" Ryan asked from where he still sat on the floor.

Nir'lion sneered. "Now you will wait for my return, when I will learn from you and your elven friend in the dungeon how you have come to be here instead of the Ellorians."

"Wait for your return?" the rogue asked, relieved she was leaving.

Nir'lion turned to the window, smashing it and sending shards of glass to the floor. "The armies of Honyn are unsuspecting once more, and the time has come."

She climbed onto the window ledge and leapt into the sky as storm clouds rolled in. She dropped out of sight at once. Eric raced to the window to see her morph into an enormous golden dragon bigger than the one they'd killed, her wings snapping out to catch the wind. As she soared away, a great rumbling shook the room, sending loose mortar falling from the ceiling and dislodging blocks from the walls. From the gate room, dragon upon dragon soared into the sky, some slamming claws into the ruin in a first swipe at the world they would destroy. The darkening sky filled with death on wings, silver, blue, red, green, golden, and black dragons headed in every direction and roaring with bloodlust. As if at one with the impending dragon storm, the sky unleashed a crack of lightning and torrents of rain began to lash the tower.

Eric turned around, glad to see Ryan rising now that Matt had used the Trinity Ring on him. It now had only one spell left and the other rings were spent, so if Anna didn't start healing people soon, someone might stay hurt next time.

Anna interrupted his thoughts on asking, "How did you come to be here, Your Majesty?"

The queen sighed. "She came to me in human form as an emissary from Nurinor, bearing the gift of a golden mirror she placed in the royal suite. One moment I stood alone with it, and the next something invisible wrenched me through it. I've been trapped here since. I heard the fight with the other dragon and had hoped to be rescued, but no one came."

Eric said, "I assume you heard the part where we're not the real champions and have somehow been substituted for them. Before you ask, we don't know how or what's going on. We've learned a lot and done okay on the quest, aside from being fooled by Nir'lion."

"Yes, I've known for some time. And there's no shame in being fooled by her. I was. The magic of dragons is very powerful."

"So what do we do now?" Matt asked, eyeing the portal mirror in the other room.

Eric saw his gaze and said, "I doubt she would have left us here with that if we could use it."

"We've got to get out of here," answered Ryan. "She made a mistake bringing us here because the Dragon Gate is downstairs. We just have to get to it."

"Right," agreed Eric, surprised by that, "but that means it's probably really hard to get out of here or to it." He listened at the door but heard nothing. "I'm not sure where we are, though it seems like a tower from the view."

"The northwest corner," offered the queen, looking skeptical. "There are guards outside and at the bottom of the tower."

"Okay," said Ryan, lowering his voice, "assuming we can get out of here, let's plan what we're doing. Do we just close the gate or go get Raith, too?"

Eric said, "It's been a week since he went through. Do we have any reason to believe he's still there? He could've come back. The gate has been unsealed all this time. Or the dragons could've killed him."

They looked at Matt to see if he was getting any images in his head. "He might still be there," the wizard admitted, "but there's no way to tell. Soliander has an earth golem guarding the place."

"I think we have to be sure," said Anna, "because if he's *here* with soclarin then it's our fault and we need to go after him. If he's there we need to stop him."

Eric frowned. She was right. "Okay, let's go through the gate, but we have to hurry. Nir'lion probably won't be back soon, but there's only so much time before she knows we're gone." He started examining the door's lock, pulling tools from various pockets in his black leather pants.

Ryan observed, "She'll never suspect we went through the gate unless someone sees us."

"What about Lorian, or whoever she's got downstairs?" Matt asked. "Should we get him now? He could help us."

"I think we just run the risk of being caught," answered Eric, inserting a tool into the door and fumbling around with it. It had been years since he did this and it brought back bad memories. "Let's get Lorian when we come back."

Anna interjected, "Okay, but what about the queen? She can't come with us. It's too dangerous."

Ryan exchanged a look with Lorella. "Yeah, but leaving her here isn't wise, especially once we take out the guards. Who knows what else is still in this place? The guards are keeping her in here but also protecting her in a way."

That was a good point that no one had an answer for until Matt reached for his spell book. "I have an idea," he started. "There's a spell of invisibility in here somewhere. She can just stay here until we return and no one will realize she's still here."

Ryan remarked, "That might work. Do you know how to cast it?"

The wizard made a face. "No. I have to find it first. Ah, here it is. It doesn't look too bad." He spent a few moments practicing the words and gestures. Then he gave the staff and book to Ryan before approaching the queen, who arched an eyebrow at the idea of him casting a spell on her. He faltered.

"I, uh, beg your pardon, your honor," Matt started, and Eric smiled at the title, "but I need to, uh, cast this spell on you, if you don't mind."

At that, Eric chuckled, prompting Anna to smack his arm. It jostled the tool in the lock, which clicked. In surprise, the rogue pulled on the door and it opened with a creak. He waited before going any further.

"Your Majesty," Anna started confidently, "we're certain this is the best way to protect you while we're gone."

"If I didn't agree I wouldn't still be standing here," the queen replied with muted humor. Turning to Matt, she asked pointedly, "Are you sure you know what you're doing?"

Projecting confidence, he replied, "Yes."

Queen Lorella held his gaze a moment. Eric watched, knowing she was judging Matt, who managed to hold her gaze without flinching. "Then proceed."

He nodded and went over the words and motions again, but just when he was about to do the spell, he paused. "Um, would you mind closing your eyes?" She complied without comment and he visibly relaxed and began the spell. One moment the queen stood there and the next she had vanished.

"Good work," said Anna approvingly.

"I think you four had better be going," remarked the invisible queen.

"Right," Eric agreed.

Ryan and Eric unsheathed their swords before opening the door a crack. Golden torch light filled the hall. The rogue opened it wider, ready for anything, but nothing happened. He stuck his head out a bit further, but his forehead bumped into something invisible.

"Ouch," he said, rubbing it. Then he reached out to feel the opening, discovering it was blocked from top to bottom with an invisible wall. Two guards to one side stepped into view, smug grins mocking him. Frowning, he turned to Matt and gestured for the wizard to do his thing, even though the guards would be ready. Matt focused his will on the staff and blockage but didn't have any luck dispelling it.

Disappointed, the wizard remarked, "I can't get rid of it. The other ones I did were by Soliander, and his staff helped a lot with his own spells, I guess. These are by the dragon, I bet, and they're supposed to be very strong in magic. I guess I'm not much of a wizard," he concluded.

Eric sighed and closed the door so they could talk in private. He wondered why the queen hadn't mentioned it, but she had likely assumed Matt could get around it. Or maybe she hadn't known. The dragon had known they were coming, clearly. Looking around the room, his eyes fell on the shards of glass.

"The window," he said, starting for it. "She probably didn't plan to bust through it like that so maybe it's not protected." He stuck a hand through it without trouble, then his head, peering down into the dark gulf, gusts of wind tearing at his black hair. The courtyard stood to one side far below, dense treetops to the other, and nothing but boulders directly beneath him and a window thirty feet straight down. Descending that would be tricky even for him, despite his years of rock climbing. He had none of the usual safety gear except chalk, but if he could make it to the window, he could come back up and take out the unsuspecting guards.

After hearing the plan, Ryan asked, "Even if that works, how are the rest of us going to get out? The door will still be blocked."

"They can turn it off," said the queen. "One of the guards has a little device that removes it and puts it back. It's how they bring me food."

"Great," said Eric, projecting confidence he didn't really feel. "See you in a few minutes."

As the others exchanged worried looks, he clambered onto the window ledge, dangling his legs over the side. Rain soaked them quickly as he put chalk on his hands. The rain might wash it off, but it was better than nothing. He rolled onto his stomach and eased both legs out and down, searching with the leather boots for a foothold. The castle's disrepair proved a boon, for chips and holes had been left unrepaired and he soon disappeared over the side, making his way down. Despite the rain and wind lashing at him, the rogue descending steadily until the ruin revealed its dangers. As he lifted one foot, the other foothold suddenly gave way, blocks of stones tumbling into the darkness and leaving him swinging by one wet hand.

"Eric!" Ryan called out, wanting to help, but there was nothing he could do. Then Matt appeared beside him, lance in hand. The knight extended it down to the rogue, who grabbed it in relief, able to trust it more than the castle. There seemed nowhere to hold onto the tower anymore except the one handhold he already had. Water dripped down the lance and over his hand as wind tore at him, but he was halfway to the other window.

"Hold on tight!" Eric yelled up to Ryan. "I'm gonna let go of the tower for a second!"

Ryan swore in protest and Eric had to just hope the big guy was as strong as he always seemed. This was a bad idea that wasn't getting any better. Eric reluctantly let go of the wall, all of his weight on the slippery lance. He moved down the lance as fast as he dared, slipping once before finding the next handhold. He was past the trouble spot and soon made it to the window ledge without further incident.

Unfortunately the window was closed, with no handle on the outside for the obvious reason. Breaking the window might make too much noise, but among Andier's tools he'd found a small glass cutter in one pocket. In short order he'd cut a hole big enough for his hand, unlocked the window, and climbed in, shutting it behind him.

He paused on the musty carpet, taking stock. He was alone, drenched, but free, and thankful to be alive. He reached a wooden door that seemed to lead into the castle and tried the handle, but it was locked. Out came the lock-picking tools once more, but this one was jammed, which might have accounted for why the room was still furnished. Fortunately he knew how to get around that and soon creaked open the door carefully. The dimly lit stairwell on the other side was empty and quiet.

⎯ ❖ ⎯

The moons had glistened on the smooth surface of Lake Isinia when Joril and Siarra first rowed out into the beautiful, calm night. Their parents wouldn't let them be together for reasons youths often chose to ignore, and this seemed the only way to consummate their love in private. No one on shore could see what they were doing and so it was that they lay together under the peaceful sky, not noticing the storm clouds gather overheard until the first drops roused them from a dreamy, post-coitus sleep. Joril sat up, realizing how far they'd drifted and that they had to get moving, and fast. And yet he sat still, for the first flash of lightning revealed something he thought impossible. He stared into the sky so intensely that Siarra asked what was the matter, but then another flash revealed their fate and his reply turned into a scream. A black dragon swooped down upon them, an ear split-ting shriek accompanying the giant boulder it let fly. The stone smashed the boat to kindling and dragged them deep down to the lake's depths, burying them together in death.

Not too distant, the trees rustled quietly as Morven rode along, eyeing the sky above the next ridge when he could. The stars seemed to fade in and out strangely when the tree tops parted. The elven village of Yulin lay over that ridge, and on cresting its top, he stopped in amazement at the sight be-low. The village stood ablaze, black smoke curling into the sky to obscure the stars, the smell of death and charred flesh heavy in the air. The cause made itself apparent when a red dragon landed before him with a thud, two hostile eyes afire with malice. Only instinct saved him as the dragon's head snapped forward. Teeth covered in blood clamped down on the horse just as he rolled off. The dragon couldn't spit it out fast enough to reach Morven, who fled into the woods as fast as mortal legs would fly.

In the kingdom of Nurinor, Lord Neelim sat astride his horse, watching the battle unfold below as his knights crushed ogres and trolls in a rampage to rid the region of them. His domain held no place for such uncivilized crea-tures. And so it was that suitable horror filled him on seeing another night-mare soaring across the plains below his cliff-top vantage point. Not one but a full score of death on wings came toward his realm. First one and then an-other roared from a distance until a chorus filled the air and all those below stopped to stare. Some dragons descended among the melee to roast men and beast alive while others soared past the carnage to his kingdom's heart. Among them, one silver dragon headed straight for him, his armor catching the light and its attention. It plucked him from the horse and flew onward, crushing his bones with the force. His scream ended when the dragon bit him in half and swallowed him, armor and all.

A cargo ship on the Lisen Ocean found fire raining down upon it, setting it ablaze so that it burned to the waterline, all hands lost. A wizard's tower on the Peaks of Normin toppled to the crags below, shattering into as many pieces as the dragons tore the wizard within. On the walls of Castle Roinin, men sounded the alarm to no avail, weapons of war unready for the on-slaught of tooth and nail, fire and malevolence, might and magic. All of Hon-yn burned in disillusionment and despair. The Ellorians had failed them and hope disappeared as fast as life.

The mastermind of it all, Nir'lion flew over the still pristine city that was surely on everyone's mind, for Kingdom Alunia had claimed the dragons were gone. That deception demanded the worst revenge humans could mus-ter, but when she was through there'd be nothing left for humanity to destroy. She had warned the dragons to leave this gleaming city untouched, that had so prospered from their banishment. Its destruction was hers to enjoy, and relish it she would. The time had come. With a shriek that put other dragons to shame, she swept down from the sky, blasting the royal tower with fire before landing atop its battlements. Let all those below see her, know her, and fear her. This world belonged to her now.

In another castle not far away, Ryan figured he'd given the rogue enough time, having seen him disappear through the window below. His turn to help with their escape had come. He opened the door to see two men grinning as if particularly amused by his captivity. He'd seen looks of jealousy flung at Lord Korrin before and used it to his advantage, hoping to distract them for Eric. The bigger, blond guard seemed in charge from the way he carried himself.

Giving his own smirk, Ryan poured on the cockiness and said, "Why don't the two of you and I settle this like men? Let me out of here and you can both take me on. Neither of you could hope to beat me by yourself, of course, but together you have nothing to lose except your pride."

The blond guard spat on the floor. "I don't need help to beat you, Korrin. You're no champion. If it weren't for all that magical armor, you'd be nothing more than a dandy."

The other guard laughed as if to ingratiate himself with the other one and Ryan replied, "A fist fight, then. I should've known better than to expect something more sophisticated from you. Let's get started, unless you're afraid a dandy will beat you." When the guard didn't take the bait, he added, "Maybe when I'm done mopping the floor with you, I'll enjoy your women, too, assuming you're man enough to get any."

The guard came closer, scowling. "I have more women than I know what to do with and—"

"Or do you prefer men?" Ryan interrupted with suggestive look at the other guard. "This one seems willing to please you."

"You son of a bitch!" the guard yelled, coming up to the opening. "I know what you're trying to do and I'm not pulling down this wall just to have a go at you."

"You don't need to," replied Ryan before punching the unsuspecting man's face, sending him flying backward into a crumpled, unmoving heap. Amazed silence followed and no one moved. Suddenly the other guard fell to the floor and lay still. A dripping Eric stood behind him, the blow to the back of the head having done its job.

"How did you hit the guard through the barrier?" Anna asked, looking shocked.

"I've got that magic ring, remember?" Ryan replied, holding up the hand with the Dispersion Ring, which made his arm unaffected by magic. "I forgot about it."

"You seem to be getting past your aversion to violence," Eric noted, using a small rod he found on the blond guard to disable the spell. Ryan frowned at the sense of approval but didn't say anything as they filed out of the room, leaving the queen behind and giving her the rod so she could manipulate the barrier herself.

Matt and Eric quietly led the way down the stone steps, the wizard saying the staff should warn them of spells, and the rogue looking for more traps, though they doubted any existed, since the guards went up and down. They might have known to avoid a certain step or two, though footprints indicated they put their feet everywhere in the dust and dirt. He motioned for the others to follow the path just to be sure. Everyone kept quiet and Ryan in particular once again appreciated how quiet his armor was.

Halfway down the curling tower stairs, the rogue stopped, motioning for the others to remain still. He began a sign language conversation with Matt, and not for the first time, Ryan wished he knew what they were discussing. If this summoning thing became a real issue, with them being sent on quests again and again, both he and Anna had to learn this valuable skill.

The conversation finally stopped, and the wizard reached into a pocket, pulling out a small bag he stuck one hand into as he crept forward, Eric retreating to give him room. Finally, the wizard seemed to whisper something before throwing sand from the bag forward. The sound of someone falling with a small clatter reached his ears, but then Eric and Matt rushed forward.

"Stop him! Stop him!" Matt fiercely whispered, alarming Ryan, who made it to the corner just as the sound of something metal bouncing down stone stairs began. The guard that Matt had made fall asleep had collapsed and was now starting down the steps, his dislodged helmet already disappearing around the corner. Eric just missed grabbing an arm as the man followed with a horrible racket that just kept going and going as he went seemingly all the way to the bottom. Ryan exchanged a look of alarm with the others and shot Matt a glance.

"The whole castle probably heard that!"

"Sorry. I didn't think of that."

"I think we had better be going," said Eric, who was still dripping with water and leaving a trail.

On reaching the tower's bottom, they discovered the still sleeping guard. Eric hid the man's weapons in case they encountered him again. Then he and Ryan dragged the man around a corner and left him there.

"Let's keep moving," Eric suggested, eyes assessing which way to go. "Remember we have to stay in halls that look like they've been used."

They continued through the castle with only one minor fight, Eric's flying feet and fists taking care of it quickly. Again they hid the unconscious men to avoid leaving a trail of bodies. Soon they stood at the gate room's main entrance, hesitating. The huge carcass of Perndara still lay where it had fallen, the smell overpowering them, its teeth and scales harvested by Cirion or someone else. It sickened all of them.

"It's too bad we didn't find another door," Ryan quietly remarked, eyeing the room. "We have to walk the entire length of the hall to reach the gate."

"True," agreed Eric, watching the rain fall in through the roof, "but finding another door might cause more problems than just heading across. I don't see anyone, do you guys?" Aside from some sort of guard, it stood to reason another dragon might be here, but there wasn't, at least not in dragon form.

"No," replied the wizard, "but the staff feels something. I just don't know what."

"Then you go first," suggested the rogue.

"Very funny."

"I wasn't joking."

"Let's head along the side where we came in before," suggested Ryan, "since we know what's over there. Hopefully no one is hiding in here somewhere, but there's bound to be something guarding the gate."

They headed off, Matt and Eric in the lead again as they skirted the dragon. Anna pursed her lips on stepping by the place where a god had first touched her. Why had it needed to be at a scene of such pain and death? Was that just the way of it? She'd long known people found god when in their darkest moments. Until now, she'd never realized she'd revisit the place where it happened again, but it hardly felt like a special moment given the rotting corpse overpowering her nose and the fear of more death being imminent. She found herself whispering a prayer to the goddess Kiarin as they went.

They soon came around to the gate, which no longer looked as if it was off. Smoke curled along its surface just like when they'd first seen it, and it seemed unguarded. Together they mounted the steps but didn't get far. Something began to form in the air above the top step. The shimmering figure of light and darkness resembled the ghost of a dead knight that had decayed in the ground for years. A wicked sword appeared in one hand as two hollow eyes swept over them, stopping on Anna. Before anyone else could react, it leapt from the steps to land before her, one ghostly hand grabbing her by the throat.

"You will be mine!" it said in a hollow voice. She stared in horror, drawn into its eyes and unable to look away. What she saw in them she couldn't name, but she knew death would only be the beginning of a new existence beside this thing for eternity. And yet a longing overcame her, one so deep and urgent that she whimpered in terror, her will to live fading as a will to be its bride came over her. She heard the others shouting but their voices seemed far away as if she'd already left her body behind.

She became dimly aware of Ryan's hand trying to grasp the spirit by its own neck, but his hand passed through it. The eyes that had bored into hers turned toward the knight and the mesmerizing lure of them left Anna. Ryan was gasping in pain as she reached for the medallion at her own neck, seeing the spirit's head turning back toward her. As her fingers closed around it, urgency compelled her to scream out in her mind to Kiarin for help, all doubts or hesitation gone.

The goddess' face appeared in her mind at once, a brief look of outrage preceding a wave of strength that filled Anna. Still gripping the medallion with one hand, she grasped the death knight by the forehead with the other. Bright light engulfed the ghost, which screamed as the darkness within it exploded with light. When Anna could next see her surroundings, nothing of the figure remained and her friends stood staring at her. Ryan's arm was covered in frost and he stood wincing in obvious pain. She took it in both hands and thought to Kiarin with genuine thankfulness, *Just a little more please, for Ryan.* The touch came again and the frost melted away, leaving the knight's hand warm and refreshed.

Ryan lifted the hand before him, flexing the fingers and turning to her with a smile. She suspected she knew what he was thinking. They had argued so many times about the existence of God and now she had used the power of one to heal him. She couldn't deny it now, not after this, not that she felt much inclined to. This time she hadn't just seen it, or been on the receiving end of it, but both, asking a god for help and being answered. She felt jubilant, but when Ryan swept her into a bear hug, she knew he'd expect her to do it back on Earth and there was no telling whether it would work.

Eric pulled them apart, casting a sharp look at Ryan as he asked Anna, "Are you alright?" She only nodded, and he wondered aloud, "I wonder why it went for you."

"The medallion," she said. "It saw the medallion. Something about it attracted its attention."

"What was that you did there?" Ryan asked.

"Talk about it later."

Eric said, "Yeah, we don't have time for this." He took her by the arm and they mounted the steps. "Then let's go before something else shows up."

Anna gazed at the whirls of smoke on the Dragon Gate's surface. They were already one world removed from Earth and now it would be two. Aside from Matt's assurances that little probably awaited them on the other side, no one wanted to go through. The gate's lock lay right there and all they had to do was seal it and this would all be over, which caused a brief argument. Ryan just wanted to go home to Daniel. He and Matt tried to persuade Eric to forget about Raith, but it was Anna who finally made them do it. Whether they wanted it or not, they had a responsibility despite the risk of Soliander appearing and locking them on Soclarin forever.

"I guess I'll go first," Matt volunteered despite his concerns, "just in case the staff wards off anything over there." Even as he said it, something seemed to occur to him. "I know what's over there," said the wizard, looking surprised, "and why Soliander opened the gate in the first place. He did it to lure whoever stole the scroll there, not to get more soclarin. The gate being open is a trap, and stepping through it sounds an alarm, but as long as the staff is present, it doesn't do anything. That's how he sets up spells to affect everyone but him. He obviously wasn't expecting a duplicate of his staff to exist." The wizard indicated that the staff no longer alerted him to the presence of magic, which meant what he'd felt last time had been Nir'lion's traps, not the gate itself.

Anna cast a final glance about the room and noticed the tower from which they'd come was visible through the hole in the ceiling. Hopefully, Queen Lorella would be fine up there. "I think we should all go through at once," she suggested, taking Ryan and Eric's hands so they were all touching. They agreed, steeling themselves for the unknown as they stepped onto the surface.

— ❖ · ❖ —

Nir'lion reveled in the destruction she had wrought. Buildings lay in ruins around her, towers had collapsed like dominoes, and only shattered windows remained in castle walls. Amidst the inferno ran screaming people frantic to save their lives. Their desperation healed the wound in her heart. Their suffering had only begun. She'd eaten the Prime Minister who had so often gotten on her nerves, but so far Sonneri had eluded her. He could run, but he'd not be able to hide forever. Now she had other things to attend to, however, and rose back into the sky, signaling other dragons to continue with their onslaught now that she'd taken the best prizes for herself.

The smoke disappeared behind her as she glided to Castle Darlonon on powerful wings, other fires raging on the horizon, where her kin soared in the rain-filled sky. All of Honyn must tremble, she knew, and the fear that preceded her arrival anywhere was like a red carpet thrown before a gala affair. She had missed that terribly, for her only joy came in the anguish of others, and as the mountains grew larger before her, the anticipation of tormenting those false champions grew and grew.

On arriving at the ruin, she roared to the heavens and dug her claws into the tower, sending blocks tumbling to the ground while she held onto her perch. One great eye looked in through the windows but saw no sign of champions or queen. The door stood open, the guards unconscious on the floor. Her nostrils flared in anger, and that's when the fresh scent of fear caught her senses. Someone was still here.

A spoken magic word later and the truth stood revealed, a frightened Queen Lorella flattened against the far wall and edging toward the open door. Nir'lion snarled and sent one razor sharp claw smashing into the room, grabbing the screaming queen and pulling her from the now crumbling prison, blocks of stone tumbling into the trees below. The dragon pushed off into the sky, sending the tower swaying dangerously as the top collapsed in on itself, half burying the room Lorella had been in.

"Where are they?" the dragon demanded, tossing her through the rain-drenched sky like a rag doll. Lorella screamed as the jagged peaks rushed up to meet her, but Nir'lion snatched her from the air, baring bloody teeth as she snarled the question again.

"The gate!" Lorella cried out. "They are at the gate!"

Nir'lion had suspected that. "How long ago?"

"An hour," the queen blurted, slipping.

Nir'lion snorted a puff of smoke as she turned toward the tower. An hour was enough time to have closed the gate, so either they were unable to do it, or they'd gone through for the ore. In either case, she knew what to do.

"I'll deal with you later," Nir'lion warned as she deposited the queen in the crumbling room. Then she leapt away and soared up, giant golden wings beating the air as Queen Lorella lost sight of her. Moments later a great rush of air signaled the dragon hurtling toward the gate.

The crumbling walls of Castle Darlonon disappeared into blackness that slowly faded, revealing forest-covered mountain slopes all around the champions. In a small valley, another Dragon Gate sat alone, tilted up at a sky where two suns shone. Many of the trees stood burnt to cinders, some long ago, some so recent they smoldered even now, as if the dragons had taken one last vengeful blast at their prison on the way out. Scorched and blackened earth surrounded the gate and nothing moved anywhere. It looked both new and familiar to Matt, who eyed the sky for dragons but saw none.

Ryan hefted his lance and stepped off to the top step first, nudging the wizard. "Which way?"

Matt looked for the faint path where he expected it to be. "There."

Like Raith before them, they followed the trail to the ravine, the sight of the young wizard's broken and battered body greeting them. Matt suspected he knew why and the golem that emerged from the rock wall confirmed it. As it approached, he went forward, unsure what to do but sensing this was his battle. He held the staff before him, intending to summon fire, but the golem abruptly stopped and bowed.

They stared in silence for a moment.

"It thinks you're..." Eric started before stopping himself. "Soliander, why don't you ask your servant here to recount what happened for us?"

Mat nodded. This impersonation thing had its advantages. "Of course. Golem, tell us what happened to this man."

The golem straightened, looking at him and ignoring the others. "But master saw," it said. Its voice sounded like stones grinding together.

Matt felt his skin crawl at the confirmation that the arch wizard had been here recently, their encounter still fresh. "Tell me."

"Him came," it said, indicating Raith. "You said so. Hurt him. You said so. Left him alive! You said so!"

Digesting that, Matt quietly muttered to the others, "When he comes, hurt him but don't kill him so he can be questioned. Those were the orders." Turning to the golem, he said, "Very good. You have done well," he reassured the monster. "What happened next?"

Looking confused, it replied, "You saw. You spoke."

The wizard glanced at Raith's body but didn't see any obvious signs of spell craft. If Soliander's words had been magic, the golem likely wouldn't have understood, but that didn't seem to be the case. "What did I say? What did we discuss?"

"Scroll. Ore. Stealing!"

They exchanged looks before Eric said, "Raith stole the scroll and came here to steal the ore, as we suspected."

"No surprise there," remarked Ryan.

Matt turned to them, eyes narrowed. "So if he opened the gate and left it that way to lure whoever stole the scroll here, why is it still open? He could've closed it."

"He could close it with us inside, so we should go," Ryan said, looking toward the trail.

Anna put a hand on his arm. "That's true, but Raith's been dead about a week, I'd say, so Soliander got what he wanted and could've closed the gate by now and didn't. I don't think he's intending to."

Matt frowned, unable to scrounge up a motive from his connection with Soliander. Maybe the decision to leave the gate open had come after their encounter.

Ryan asked, "When do you think Soliander came here? It had to be after the fight with the dragon because Raith went through during that and that would've set off the alarm, but we didn't see Soliander go through after him, so he had to do it after we left."

"Right," said Eric. "He must've known the gate wasn't really closed despite the illusion that it was."

Anna observed, "Which means he knows we never completed the quest and are therefore still on Honyn, or were until coming here."

Ryan asked, "Do you think that's why he left it open? To keep us from leaving?"

Eric looked at him pointedly. "Or is it to keep us from returning to Earth?"

Matt grunted. "I suspect you're right. All of you. Because he wanted to know how we took the champions' place and that obviously happened on Earth. We could be there now but we're stuck here."

Ryan said, "That's got to be it then. He's trapped us here, not on Soclarin, but on Honyn, by leaving the gate open. We have to get home."

Eric nodded. "And quickly, though I'm not sure how much we could do back on Earth."

"True," said Matt, turning to the golem. "What else happened?"

It shrugged. "You take. You leave."

"What did I take?"

"Scroll."

"Ah," said the wizard. "Of course. He wanted the scroll back so no one would know of the ore. He probably doesn't know there's a copy."

"Let's keep it that way," suggested Ryan.

"Right," said Matt, not intending to communicate with the arch wizard again. Once had been bad enough. "Maybe we should get some of this ore while we're here. We can't take it to Earth, I don't think, because we can't bring anything back with us, I assume, but the elves can hold onto some. Items made from it have already proven useful."

The others weren't so sure about that and a brief conversation led to a compromise. They took no more than a few pounds of soclarin, putting it into the magic bag Matt found on Raith's body. Like all magic items, the bag had continued giving off a magical vibe after its possessor's death, alerting him to this and other items left on the dead wizard. He didn't know what the other things did but would give them to Lorian or Sonneri. It was too bad he couldn't take them to Earth or start creating his own private stash.

They made their way back toward the gate, intending to end this quest for real, but as they left the trees to see the gate gleaming in the sun, a golden dragon burst through it and spread its wings, soaring up and arcing to view the ground. Nir'lion turned sharply. They had been seen.

"Run for the gate!" Ryan yelled, running with the lance. "We don't have to fight her, just seal it!"

Eric ran after him. "No! We'll never make it!"

Matt yelled, "No, Eric! Stay with me! Ryan is fireproof and I can block her fire and anything she throws at us at least once."

Eric swore and came back to stand behind him with Anna. Ryan stopped a dozen strides from them, looked back, and then stayed where he was, hefting the lance and loosening his sword. Matt nodded to himself. It gave the dragon two targets instead of one. Three problems for her was even better.

"Eric, get a knife to throw, even if you miss. She might, too, because of it. Ryan!" he yelled, seeing Nir'lion closing fast, "be ready with the lance. Even if you can't hit her, make her think you can."

The dragon opened her mouth. So did Matt, words of magic, and fire, erupting with equal fury. He saw Eric's knife fly over their heads from behind and heard the rogue get closer to him after throwing it. Nir'lion rolled slightly to evade the blade as she neared. The shield went up around them moments before the flames arrived and blinded Matt to everything else. A roar of flames. A loud shriek of pain. A whoosh of air buffeting them. The dragon breath stopped, Nir'lion having passed them. Matt glanced in concern at the knight, who stood unmolested, the lance on the ground ten paces from him. The dragon rose back into the sky and banked, blood dropping from a gash in her side. Ryan picked up the source of her wound, red on the end. His eyes met the wizard's.

"*Got* her," he yelled in satisfaction.

"How bad?" asked Anna.

"Not enough. Just pissed her off, I bet."

"She's coming after you this time," predicted Eric. He ran for the tree line.

"What's the plan?" Ryan yelled to them.

"The same," said Matt, wondering what the rogue was doing but trusting him, "but expect her to go for you. She knows about the armor. It will be a blow, not the fire. Dodge to the ground."

Ryan nodded. They all looked for Eric and saw him keeping out of sight, two throwing knives ready. Nir'lion was approaching lower this time, as Matt expected if she intended to physically strike any of them. Would she use more than her fire on Ryan?

"Watch for the claws and tail!" he yelled.

The knight didn't react, the dragon headed straight for him. As she reached the clearing, mouth agape with flames swirling within, first one and then another knife from Eric flew toward her. The first bounced off into the trees. The other pierced her side. The dragon breathed fire all over Ryan, but at the speed of her passage, it didn't last long. A claw didn't lash at him. Neither did the tail as she passed, but suddenly it slammed into Matt's shield as Anna cried out. The shield held firm.

"Didn't expect that," Matt observed, feeling weaker. Did Nir'lion know that every blow took some of his strength away? Probably. And every spout of fire at Ryan weakened his armor's fireproofing. Eric changed positions near the trees, closer to Ryan.

"We have to attack, not just defend," he yelled.

The knight threw his lance to the rogue and drew his sword. Eric moved to the tree line as if to hide from the dragon, who was circling again.

Matt asked, "Anna, does the goddess have any ability to protect us with a shield of some kind?"

"I don't know," she admitted. "I think so."

"Eric's right. We need to attack. I can't as long as I'm protecting us. If you could do it, that frees me to do a spell."

"Okay, let me try. I need to concentrate."

"Right. I'll shut up. Maybe close your eyes. Hold on to me. You don't need to watch."

"Easier said than done, closing my eyes to this." But she put one hand on his shoulder.

Nir'lion appeared to be focused squarely on the knight again. Had she realized Matt was no danger with his shield up? They needed Anna to succeed in shielding Matt herself so the wizard could nail the unsuspecting dragon with *something.*

As she soared just above the low trees and reached the clearing, Ryan yelled, "Now!"

With one hand on the butt and another on the shaft to guide his aim, Eric threw the lance upward at Nir'lion's unprotected belly, his entire body behind the motion. Matt thought it couldn't possibly reach or do much, but it must've been lighter than he thought for how high it went. Even as Nir'lion blasted fire toward Ryan, the thrown lance flew high enough to strike, the angle causing it to puncture her belly. The fire abruptly stopped as Nir'lion grasped it with a hind leg and yanked it out. Her tail fell low enough as it passed Ryan that the knight slashed with the sword and cut a gash near the tip. Nir'lion roared as she rose into the sky, throwing Ryan's lance far into the trees, blood cascading from belly and tail. She spoke a few words and the bleeding stopped.

"Lower your shield," said Anna.

Matt turned in surprised. "You're sure?" She nodded. "Because if you're wrong – "'

"I'm not. Trust me."

Their eyes met and he saw only strength and clarity in them. He turned toward the dragon. This time Nir'lion seemed focused on him. What could he cast that didn't involve gestures until the last second? He mentally flipped through Soliander's spell book, a choice surfacing. As the dragon neared, he didn't see the telltale fire swirling in her mouth. Claws? The tail? Her magic? Trusting in Anna, he began his own spell, the words coming easily as he relied on the trusty staff and his most fearsome trick. He hardly saw Eric throw a knife. Then the dragon's spell sent a hail of large boulders raining down on Matt and Anna even as flames blasted them. One rocked the ground next to them, half buried in earth. Another bounced off Anna's shield as she grunted. A third slammed into the ground before them and bounced over, a cascade of dirt showering them but ricocheting off the shield. Another struck a glancing blow as dragon fire obscured the rest, though from Anna's moan it seemed that another scored a direct hit before deflection.

When the flames vanished, Matt retaliated as the dragon soared away, a focused beam of fire bursting from the staff's crystal to burn deep wounds in the dragon's back and one wing. She roared and nearly flipped over in the air to plummet toward the clearing, rolling in the sky to land on all fours with an incredible thud. Nir'lion took a few steps forward, swung her backside around, and then kicked out at Ryan, clobbering the knight so that he flew into a nearby tree and didn't move again. She looked back and sucked in a breath. Flames appeared in her open mouth, eyes on Matt and ablaze with fury. Even as the fire began to rush forward, a knife from Eric struck her neck and she swung the tail across the ground at him. He leapt over it. The flames hung in her mouth. The tail came back and he rolled under it, then threw another knife that bounced off her head. Mouth agape, she brought forth the flames toward the rogue, who ran for the trees.

"Saarilmor nukal o nusaak taasili kuniase mu'unia a rolinmor purta!" *Flying metal, hot as fire, seek head and heart as I desire!*

The words from Matt caused a hail of metal shards to pelt Nir'lion, whose head swiveled from Eric to him, a blast of flames roaring around him and Anna again. When her flames stopped, Matt conjured his own from the staff. Even as the fire raced toward the dragon, she kicked out at the priestess and sent Anna tumbling across the ground. Matt's spell faltered, but then fury tore through him and the flames strengthened. The dragon leapt into the air, wings beating furiously as she escaped his attack. Eric ran across the ground to reach Anna, who wasn't moving. Looking for blood, Matt saw none on her white robes and wondered just how badly she was hurt. Ryan hadn't moved from where he lay. A growing anger grew within. The dragon flew over the nearby peaks and disappeared, but he knew it wouldn't last.

Matt heard Eric quietly calling Anna's name while holding her. That meant she was unconscious. "Get her out of sight," he called, watching for Nir'lion. Eric seemed to agree, for he carefully picked her up over one shoulder and made for the tree line. Matt raised his shield.

Where is she? he thought, eyes scanning the sky. He looked at his friends and all of them were seemingly out of harm's way. Matt was the lone target remaining and felt confident his shield would hold. He stood alone in the clearing, the Dragon Gate off to one side. If Nir'lion had been smart, she would've brought help, for they'd never have beaten two dragons at once. It didn't look like they were going to beat *one.*

A subtle sound of a wing flapping caught his ears, but he still saw nothing. He checked each mountain around them, wondering which one she'd come out from behind. He gazed straight up. Nothing. A sound of rustling leaves caught his ears to one side, but there was nothing there. The wind? He felt no motion. The sound grew louder and he turned to the direction, suddenly seeing the treetops sway violently right at the clearing's edge.

Invisible! he realized. A blow of some kind. That had to be the reason.

He ran to one side as a whoosh of air reached him, the snapping shut of giant jaws just feet away. The dragon appeared to him now, for the illusion of invisibility only worked if he didn't know of her spell. The sight of her golden body passing overhead, claws haphazardly swiping at him, stunned him.

As she passed him, the staff in one of his hands violently flew away. He watched in horror as it tumbled end over end, up and above the trees for a hundred yards before falling among the boles. The dragon's tail had struck it. The way to close the gate was gone. The way to shield himself was gone. The source of aid he needed for every spell that stood a chance of stopping Nir'lion was gone. Matt watched in terror as the golden dragon turned, a whorl of fire already brewing in her opening mouth, a look of triumph dawning in the golden eyes.

"Time to die," she growled, banking toward him.

Matt eyed the distance. Ten seconds, if that, before he died. Then Anna, Eric, and Ryan died. Then everyone on Honyn. And maybe everyone back on Earth if the dragons figured out that's where they came from. Or thought that's where the Ellorians were hiding. Andier. Eriana. Korrin.

Soliander.

Before he understood why, his hand reached into a pocket and pulled out a dagger, images of a spell he'd never seen before popping into his head. As if he'd cast it before, the words came to his mind and out his mouth, the hand with the blade held up, pointing toward the dragon that was hurtling at him. He saw her lungs expand. He saw the words on the page of a spell book. He saw what was supposed to happen when he finished the words. Matt searched around him for every source of energy to draw from. With the staff gone, that meant everything that lived. As if the staff had blinded him to other sources of power before, he suddenly saw and felt them all, trees, plants, insects, birds, mammals. With a rush of ecstasy mixed with fury, the power roared into him.

"Kuniali mu'unia a narosmor likaa a rarkimor kiapan. Mu'oste aatsum!" *Fly true this steel, as light as air, as fast as light, a fate you seal/steal!*

The dagger in his hand erupted into flames and leapt from his outstretched hand. Leaving a trail of fire behind it, the blade arced through the air at Nir'lion, who began spraying her own fire toward Matt. She turned to evade the flaming dagger, but it moved with her like a heat seeking missile, slamming into her chest and passing right through the golden scales. With a look of shock, surprise, and horror, Nir'lion stopped flapping her wings. The flames in her mouth drew back in as if she'd inhaled them. Matt began to topple backwards, his last sight an enormous golden dragon that appeared to be dead in the air slamming into the clearing with a thunderous crash and tumbling into the trees, where she burst into flames.

CHAPTER NINETEEN

FIRESTORM

Eric shielded himself and the unconscious Anna from the roaring flames as Nir'lion burned. He finally tore his eyes away to see Matt on his back. None of his friends were moving. He ran to the wizard, stopping above him in shock. Matt's hair had gone grey. Deep lines creased his face like he'd aged forty years. His breath came in ragged gasps. Thinking quickly, he knelt and looked at the wizard's Trinity Ring. It had one spell left. He knew that his and Ryan's were spent. Rather than healing Matt, he removed the item and ran to Anna, whom he used it on. Her eyes fluttered open and he quickly filled her in, noting that her protective spell must have shielded her quite a bit from the dragon's blow. She nodded and felt strong enough to stand. He helped over to Matt.

"Oh my God!" Anna said, kneeling and laying her hands on the wizard. "What happened to him?"

"You've got to do something," Eric urged her.

She closed her eyes. While Eric waited, he looked over at Ryan, the dragon, and then finally noticed several dead birds on the ground. The grass that hadn't long since been burnt by dragon fire had withered and died. So had all the trees near the clearing's edge. Everything nearby but them appeared to be dead. The mostly untrained wizard had drained the energy from everything, killing it all. What had kept him from drawing energy from them, too?

His gaze returned to Matt. The lines in the wizard's face disappeared as his features returned to normal and his eyes opened. Anna looked fatigued. Being a vessel of a god's power was not without its drawbacks.

"You're getting better at this," Eric remarked.

"It's getting easier to reach her each time."

Eric helped her up.

Matt sat up slowly, eyes on the nearby flaming dragon, then the knight. "What about Ryan? Is he okay?"

Eric extended a hand and helped him to his feet. "Time to find out."

They headed over and found the knight on his back, awake, and in tremendous pain.

"Can you tell us what's wrong?" Eric asked him.

"I'll be able to tell," said Anna, closing her eyes as she knelt beside him. It started sooner this time, Eric thought, but took longer, for Ryan had been more badly hurt. Several bones had been broken and the armor had to be loosened to prevent the dents from digging into him. Anna was so fatigued that she refused to get up. Knowing she needed rest, Eric suggested the others remain together while he went in search of Soliander's staff and Korrin's less important lance. It took more than an hour to retrieve them, and by then, Anna felt well enough to walk with assistance. They headed for the Dragon Gate, eager to put all of this behind them.

Matt couldn't help eyeing the dragon. The dagger spell wasn't supposed to include fire. It just should've sent the dagger at his target and followed any evasion until the blade pierced the heart. He had clearly overdone the drawing of power and nearly killed himself. If he ever had the chance to do magic again, he really needed to learn control. But he'd killed Nir'lion. He'd outsmarted her, too, much of that improvised battle plan being his. He'd never felt so formidable and proud, the memory of that power coursing through him and its utter destruction on someone trying kill him and his friends bringing a smile to his face.

Burn, bitch, burn.

With a final look at the scene, the champions left Soclarin, disappearing through the Dragon Gate to find the great hall of Castle Darlonon on Honyn empty, rain still pouring through the roof. Matt wasted no time putting the staff into the gate, having no idea how to close it for real, but then words formed in his mind as if he'd said them all before. His arm gestured before he understood what he was doing, the gate reacting like a finely tuned instrument. A rainbow of colors swirled across its surface, a ray of light shooting into the rainy sky. As if striking an invisible layer in the stratosphere, it burst into a ring that spread outward as if to encircle the planet.

For a few moments, nothing else happened and they stood exchanging glances at each other and back at the sky. Then the first dragon came into view, being pulled backward by an invisible force, its wings beating uselessly. It looked back then, the motion making it tumble over so that it now appeared to be flying forward, but all four legs and its wings showed signs of fighting the inevitable. With a roar of defiance, hatred, and anger, it hurtled down toward the gate and then disappeared with a whoosh and a puff, air buffeting the amazed champions. Eric suggested everyone but Matt step away in case a stray wing, claw, or tail managed to hit one of them. That's when Matt realized a shield protected him, so he felt safe, having a front row seat to the spectacle.

Dragon after dragon lost control as the gate wrested them from whatever act of destruction they were engaged in. Pulled across the sky, they shrieked in defiant outrage as they plummeted into the castle and through the Dragon Gate, a blur of silvers, reds, blues, and other colors. Matt lost count of how many as the numbers rose to the thousands, the champions their last sight as they were violently flung from Honyn once more. No sooner had the last of their kind gone through than the gate closed with a flash. The champions stood breathless, eyeing each other wordlessly until Matt pulled the staff free.

"Wow," said the wizard. "That was the most incredible thing I've ever seen." He turned away and saw the queen's collapsed tower through the ceiling's hole. The others followed his gaze as he added, "We'd better get up there."

"Let's get Lorian first," suggested Eric.

And so they did, finding an empty prison, the elf abandoned inside by mercenaries and cult members who'd already fled, no one wanting to face those who'd closed the Dragon Gate. They gave him the bag of soclarin ore for safe keeping and wasted no time climbing the queen's tower, giant cracks in it raising fears that worsened on seeing blocks of dislodged stone on the stairs. The fallen guard had disappeared, but the two unconscious guards remained at the top. Anna knelt beside each and with a quick prayer brought them awake, Ryan's sword point indicating they ought to flee down the steps as fast as their legs would allow. They quickly disappeared.

As Matt watched, Eric and Lorian clambered over the loose stone blocking the doorway, the outside wall of the tower in ruins, a gaping hole revealing the quieting storm outside and wind tearing at the walls. The fallen ceiling had buried almost everything but the adjacent room with the mirror. As Eric stepped into the opening, a wooden table leg came straight at his head. He barely blocked it with his hand.

Queen Lorella, no longer invisible, gasped. "Oh! I thought you were..."

"I know," he replied, relaxing. "It's over. Let's get out of here."

"Gladly."

Lorian saw the portal the dragon had used to visit her captive. "An elven Mirror of Sulinae," he said in surprise, moving toward it. "Do you know where it leads?"

"Yes," answered Matt from the doorway, "to Castle Olliana somewhere."

"Good. Then let's use it." The elf stroked its edge and spoke magic words as the others joined them. It had never occurred to Matt that Lorian might know how to use it. In moments, the frame filled with an image of the queen's royal chambers, empty. The elf gestured for them to go through, Eric first, then Anna, the queen, and Ryan, all disappearing from Castle Darlonon in relief. Even as Matt left the ruin, the tower began to tremble ominously. Lorian shoved him through and leapt after as the tower collapsed in a shower of debris, taking the other mirror with it. This one shut off abruptly. A moment of silence followed before everyone realized they were safe.

⚊ ◆ ◆ ⚊

The next day, Ryan felt a mixture of relief and regret that they were going home. For the most part, he was eager, but he'd finally had time to think about the reality of this quest, for the first time since arriving. Dragons. Elves. Magic. It was all real. It seemed almost strange to finally marvel now, but danger, fear, and the unknown had taken any potential fun or amusement right out of this whole thing. He'd heard himself sighing repeatedly since arriving back in Olliana, where they'd taken care of various issues, including a good bath, warm meal, and a little too much wine and mead, followed by a long sleep.

They reached an agreement with Sonneri and the queen on how to deal with Honyn's questions about why the dragons had appeared after the quest's apparent completion. The story was that the Ellorians needed to spring Nir'lion's trap on purpose as the only way to discover and rescue the queen, held prisoner in an unknown location with the dragon taking her place. Revealing this also helped Queen Lorella avoid explaining some questionable decisions Nir'lion had made while posing as her, even as she quickly reversed those orders. Since they couldn't admit the real Soliander opened the gate, they claimed Raith had done it without giving his name so that neither Cirion nor Nola would counter this. The pair hadn't been seen and couldn't be trusted to keep secrets either way. To prevent further trouble with the Dragon Gate, a protective force would guard what remained of Castle Darlonon indefinitely.

Most of Honyn had seen the dramatic display of dragons pulled across the sky, knowing what it meant, but few cheers had erupted due to the devastation. Months, even years of rebuilding and burying the dead lay ahead. This time no fanfare accompanied their quiet departure, everyone feeling it was inappropriate. It almost seemed like they'd failed Honyn and were skulking off in secret, their accomplishment diminished by destruction.

Now Matt stood in the throne room with the others, atop the dais, the Quest Ring around them beginning to light up with words of blue fire. They hadn't seen the ring since arriving and hadn't previously noticed the hole on one pillar, for the top of Soliander's staff, which would trigger the return spell if the quest was done. In the back of his mind, he prayed they were truly headed home, not to the home worlds of the four champions they'd replaced. It would be especially bad in Matt's case, arriving right into Soliander's grip. They hadn't spoken of it, but Eric had quietly told him not to speculate aloud about it so as not to worry the techie. If it happened, it happened, and there wouldn't be much they could do about it. There was only one way to tell what was going to happen.

Hoping for the best, Ryan let his thoughts turn to home. Were people looking for them? What should they say about their absence when asked? More importantly, what, if anything, had Soliander done to their friends and family while they'd remained here?

Moments later, the vortex of light and sound ended and the four friends stood in the dark countryside, a black sky above, a familiar moon to one side, and giant stone monoliths beside them. Stonehenge looked just like it had when they left and caused an audible sigh of relief from all of them, which made them start to laugh.

"We're home!" Ryan said, noticing that Eric was not only dressed as before, but holding the SUV's flashlight in his hands. It was on, too.

"Thank God," said Anna.

"It's cold," Matt observed.

Ryan nodded. The air seemed a bit too cool for what they wore – the same Earth clothes they'd been wearing several weeks earlier. "I don't think we're dressed for the weather anymore."

Eric remarked, "I guess the spell just returns you to how you were before the quest, not change your clothes to something appropriate like it does when you're summoned."

"I hope we're never summoned while naked," Matt joked. "That could be awkward on returning."

"Let's hope we're never summoned again," said Anna.

"I'm just glad to be back in my own clothes," remarked Ryan. He pulled out his iPhone but still had no signal. Checking in on Daniel, or giving him the good news that they were back, would have to wait.

"It's good we didn't return in those outfits we had on," said Matt. "That might've been hard to explain. I wish I had the spell books, though."

"Speaking of explanations," started Ryan, "we need to get our story straight."

"Can we get out of here first?" Anna asked, shivering. "I'm freezing."

Ryan gestured to where the SUV had been parked. It was gone. "Yeah, but how? We need to start walking, I guess."

"Then let's go," she replied, starting off and looking at the pendant in her hand, unable to put it on because the necklace clasp had broken. "I'll guess we'll never know if this pendant had anything to do with the quest. Matt, maybe you can look at the words within it to see what they say."

He agreed to do it once they had a chance. They compared suggestions on a story about their disappearance as they walked, from alien abduction to getting lost in the countryside, but each invited more questions and lies they all had to keep straight. It wasn't going to work and they knew it.

Finally Eric suggested, "Maybe we should just say we don't know. We came back for the necklace, found it, and when we turned back to the SUV, it was gone. We didn't hear it leave and just don't know what happened. We still had the keys." He looked at Ryan. "You still have them?"

The big man felt in his pockets and pulled them out. "Yes."

"Okay," Eric continued, "so we started walking back, hitched a ride or whatever, and only when we got to your aunt's house and your aunt freaked out did we know something was wrong, besides the SUV being stolen, I mean. That's when we heard we'd been gone however many days it turns out to be. I think I lost track."

"That might be a good idea," Ryan conceded. "It keeps us from getting into a bunch of lies."

Matt agreed but added, "The only problem is people will want some sort of answer."

Anna offered, "We can just say, 'so do we'."

Eric nodded. "The best lie is a simple one."

After a few minutes, Ryan stopped. In the excitement of returning he'd forgotten something. "Anna, let's see if you can heal me here."

The others stopped, exchanging a dubious look. Before they could talk him out of it, Ryan used his keys to scratch a cut into his palm. It wasn't much, but it would have to do. Grimacing, he held it out to her as she sighed.

"This really could have waited for a better time. Don't get your hopes up," she reminded him.

"C'mon," he replied, "think positively. You have to believe in it. You've done it before. You can do it."

She sighed and he suspected she wasn't really into it. Did he have to be dying before she tried? Apparently not, for she took his hand in hers and closed her eyes. She appeared to be making an effort, but nothing was happening. She opened her eyes.

"I'm sorry, Ryan," she said. "It's not working. I don't know why."

"Try again!"

"I did. I don't know what's the matter. Maybe none of that works here for some reason." Seeing him about to protest, she added, "Look, you know I would love to heal Daniel as much as you. You believe that, don't you?"

He opened his mouth to urge her to try again, but then stopped himself. "Yes, I do, but–"

"No buts," she replied. "It isn't working. Maybe it will work some other time, but not today. Okay? Can we just leave it at that?"

He sighed heavily. It couldn't have all been for nothing. There was no way God would do that to him. To Daniel. He'd try again with her later and see what could be done, but he couldn't just give up. Maybe they could somehow take Daniel with them on another quest, if it came to that, and she could heal him there. Surely that would work and if he came back with them, he wouldn't return to being injured. That would just be cruel.

As they continued, Eric kept the flashlight shining, hoping a car would soon stop for them, and one finally did. The friendly driver asked too many questions about what they were doing out in the middle of nowhere, and Anna, seated in the front, did her best to fend them off. She spied a newspaper folded up between seats and read the date aloud. Two weeks had passed. Desperate to get away from the questions, she asked for the nearest place to catch a taxi and they soon had a quieter ride, suspecting the questions would get a lot worse, and they were right.

⎯ ◆ · ◆ ⎯

A covered lanai was the ideal place to wait out an afternoon thunderstorm, and warming her bones was another reason Erin Jennings had moved to Florida. Once one past a certain age, such things made the hours easier. She chuckled to herself. She hadn't aged all *that* much since learning to call this world home, even though it sometimes felt like it inside. She had other ways to make the signs of time's passage vanish, but there was a limit on how much she could do before people started talking, and so here she was.

She put her legs up on the recliner and watched the rain fall over her screened-in pool, sipping a favorite zinfandel, for wine was one of the few things of her youth available here, everything else having been modernized into oblivion. The ornate wine glass was etched with an armored knight atop a charging steed, a sight that reminded her of a friend long lost. She hadn't seen him in many years and didn't know his whereabouts despite many fruitless searches. These days it seemed everyone could learn anything about anyone, thanks in large part to the internet, but try as one might, some people simply never surfaced. She didn't know if she'd recognize him anyway, for nearly twenty years had passed since they and two other friends had last been together.

They might not recognize her, either, especially with a different name and a new life as a banker's wife. Despite starting over, she was a student of history and spent time researching medieval times, becoming something of an expert, albeit unknown. She was a private person and chose not to advertise her scholarly findings lest it attract attention, but had anyone known the truth, she'd have been known as one of the foremost scholars on the period. At times she wondered if she should come forward, for that might draw forth these old friends if they were still around, but it would also raise scrutiny. She hadn't covered her own tracks as much as she probably should.

With her mind so much in the past, she often missed the news and so hadn't heard anything about the four friends who'd disappeared from Stonehenge. It wasn't until just now that she caught the early afternoon telecast of the frantic rush to bring the story to the world. She frowned at that, as always, not pleased with the speed of modern living. They knew nothing of a quiet day without television. She was tempted to turn it off until a pretty young woman appeared onscreen, talking about their reasons for visiting the monoliths. Around her neck hung a pendant she kept playing with, drawing the eye as the camera zoomed in on it.

"By the gods," Erin whispered, staring at the recognized stone, her wine glass slipping unnoticed to shatter on the lanai, the wine draining away like a rivulet of blood. Her face grew paler as the girl spoke of visiting the monument, vanishing for weeks, then returning as if nothing happened. She professed to have no recollection of the missing time, but Erin had been reading people in tough situations far longer than this pretty girl had and she knew a lie when she heard it. The spark of untold adventure in the girl's eyes said it all and Erin rose from her chair with a light in her own.

"What have they done?"

⸺ ✦ · ✦ ⸺

A week after the firestorm started, it quieted to a dull roar as the media moved on to other stories and the flow of interviews trickled off, but all was not well with their lives. On the surface, little had changed for Ryan, whose parents had displayed more affection for him in a few days than in his whole life before that. In theory that was good, but the departure from their regular indifference and established lack of attention made him uncomfortable and didn't seem to be letting up. In fact, it got worse, as they wanted to know his every move and even suggested assigning a 24/7 bodyguard. Their monitoring of where he drove the GPS-equipped car made him disable that and the tracking app on his phone. He was starting to feel like a prisoner in his own life and didn't know what to do. When Daniel remarked on how annoying such hovering can be, the big guy finally understood his brother's need for space.

Their reunion had been the happiest moment of his life, and seeing that Daniel had survived without him the greatest relief. While he'd come to grips with the violence he'd experienced on Honyn, the first sight of Daniel had made him flush with renewed guilt he couldn't explain. He had to lie about his whereabouts to the one person who most deserved the truth, and since Ryan had never lied to Daniel before, he wasn't good at it. His brother didn't believe him, some awkward moments following. His friends watched with more understanding than ever and Ryan was glad he'd told them the truth about the accident.

Ryan's initial call to Daniel had led to his parents knowing of their return and soon, the world did, too, via a press conference they arranged. Amidst police reports and interviews, they'd finally flown home to meet their relieved families and friends. The question dodging had become painful, but the four friends stuck together, their ordeal creating a bond.

Things hadn't turned out quite so well for the others. All of Eric's martial arts students had moved on to another teacher in his absence, and the guy who had first been a temporary replacement during his "vacation" had taken his job. The owner, Kim Jung, was less than kind, asserting that Eric had abandoned his position and students and wasn't welcome back. The students and even his replacement were more forgiving and understanding, but ultimately it didn't matter. He had lost his job, a fact that made headlines. The backlash on Jung worsened after he stupidly aired his opinion on camera. Many of the school's roster went elsewhere, a move that both pleased and embarrassed Eric, who wasn't used to such shows of loyalty. He received a dozen offers from other schools, and many of his former student's parents withdrew their children to follow Eric to his new job.

Matt took a few days off and then reported to work as usual, though he got little done the first week with geek co-workers jokingly asking what being abducted by aliens felt like, or similar half-baked theories. Being at work dealing with irritating tech problems felt wildly uninspiring and he increasingly longed for more in his life. Not an hour passed without dreams of the power that was once his. He could be a different man with it, and life just wasn't the same without that energy coursing through him, like his black-and-white life had been infused with color only to cast him back to greyness. He'd tried to perform magic here without success despite his clear memory of the spells, which he'd written down in his own book. He hadn't yet been hypnotized to see what of Soliander's memories he retained and wasn't sure if it would matter now anyway. Besides, he'd need someone he trusted to do that.

Perhaps the biggest change had been for Anna, whose position at the hospital had been filled by necessity, though a similar one had become available. Jack Riley had never packed her things despite her father's request, but she learned of the intent anyway and was quite upset with being written off so quickly. Her father's lukewarm response to her return, not even offering her a hug, had surprised her. A few pointed questions later had revealed he'd investigated collecting her life insurance policy, too, and now she wasn't speaking to him, to her mother's consternation. She was starting to feel lost, her world so different from before. When she saw a patient near death or in agony that no medicine could alleviate, she wanted to reach out and heal them, but it was impossible. *God doesn't exist here. He isn't real*, she told herself, but the same assertion lacked the strength it once had, though her failures to reach Him had kept her atheism intact. She didn't want to think about any of it but it was always in the back of her mind now, her job a constant reminder. She felt relieved when the next weekend came.

The four friends gathered in Anna's condo Saturday night, enjoying some quiet and privacy. They hadn't been alone for long since their return, but they'd invited Jack to let him in on the truth. They had discussed the idea at length, the deciding factor being that someone needed to look after their interests if they were summoned again and he was the only one they could trust. The threat of Soliander's appearance was another reason to tell someone. If he showed up while they were on a quest, they wanted at least someone to be aware of who and what he was.

Now Jack sat quietly, trying to digest what they'd told him. He had laughed at the start, assuming it a joke, but the more details they'd revealed, the less funny it had become. Efforts to ask a question they couldn't answer had proven fruitless. The details were sobering in their complexity, and he'd tried catching them in lies to no avail. It had become clear that the level of planning needed for them to get all their stories straight, if they were lying, would have been a flattering amount of time to waste just to play a trick on him, and he had never known them to possess such imaginations as this.

But the pendant was the thing that got him. They'd acquired a loupe and taken turns looking at the words inside, but only Matt could understand them. They were indeed in the language of magic and read:

Within the jewel magic resides
Creatures, too, and all abide
To keep Earth safe from she who lies
The prison here keeps hope alive
The henge of stone shall set them free
Good and evil, equal be
Undo what's done and come what may
Risk the price all life could pay

They'd discussed this privately and now let Jack see for himself, and though he couldn't verify what it said, he'd never seen script like it and thought it would've been going awfully far to get that inscribed in there just to fool him. And there was no escaping the reality that they'd disappeared and returned weeks later

As for the pendant, no one knew who "she who lies" was but they assumed that bringing the pendant to Stonehenge had set something unpredictable in motion. This had been one reason to tell someone the truth, for if anything odd began happening on Earth, like dragons appearing over Manhattan, they wanted someone besides them to know. It was possible they'd be off-world on another quest. They wanted Jack to be their eyes and ears while they were gone.

"So you haven't seen any sign of this Soliander on Earth?" Jack asked, focusing on what they wanted, though he didn't know what he could do against such a wizard if one appeared.

Ryan shook his head, his hand diving into a bag of Chex Mix. "No, thank God. We all asked our families if anyone strange had been hanging out around the houses or neighborhood, but they said only reporters."

"What do you think he might do if he shows up?" Jack asked.

They exchanged a look before Eric stopped himself from swiveling back and forth in an office chair. "Go after Matt, first, unless he tries to be sneakier by going after a less obvious target, for bait or something."

"What can you do to protect yourselves from this guy?" Jack asked, shaking his head.

"Move," suggested Matt, looking up from the laptop before him on the table. "I've already been looking into apartments. There's no sense in any of us staying where we are except maybe Anna, since you can't sell your condo as easily."

"That's actually not a bad idea," admitted Eric, "especially for you and me. We should get an apartment together."

"Absolutely," the techie agreed. "I don't want to be alone when he shows up."

"When?" Jack asked. "Not if?"

Matt shook his head. "I think it's only a matter of time."

Ryan said, "Maybe I can join you. My parents are driving me nuts. The only drawback is leaving Daniel, but my presence might bring Soliander to our doorstep and that's certainly worse. I can't let that wizard get to Daniel."

"Even better," said Matt.

Looking at Anna, Ryan added, "I don't think we should leave Anna alone, though."

Anna nodded, sipping a glass of zinfandel. "I agree, though I'm not sure I want to share an apartment with three guys, especially you three."

Eric replied, "You already shared space with us in far less modest circumstances."

"True," she admitted, playing with her pendant.

"Ryan," Jack started, "if the apartment is registered in your name, people may be able to find you. Maybe you should do it in mine."

Eric perked up. "Great idea. I knew it was smart to tell you. None of us should do a forwarding address for mail, either."

As talk turned to arranging such details, Jack took the opportunity to get another beer and excused himself for the kitchen. His head spun with crazy thoughts and he needed a moment alone to get a grip. They had never lied to him before but all of this suggested the world was a far different place than he knew. He wouldn't truly accept any of it unless he witnessed something with his own eyes. In the fridge sat the remains of a welcome back cake, and he dipped a finger in the icing before grabbing a drink and shutting the door. As he licked off his finger, a bright flash came from the room behind him, followed by a glass breaking, and sudden silence. He popped the beer can open and started back, saying, "Did a light burn out or...something." He stopped in the doorway, staring.

Matt's laptop still lay open and unlocked, when the techie was paranoid about not signing out if he stepped away. Anna's wineglass had broken on the floor, red wine spilling across it. Ryan's bag of Chex-mix had fallen over on the couch. And the office chair Eric had been sitting in was slowly spinning, empty.

They were gone.

THE LIGHT BRINGER

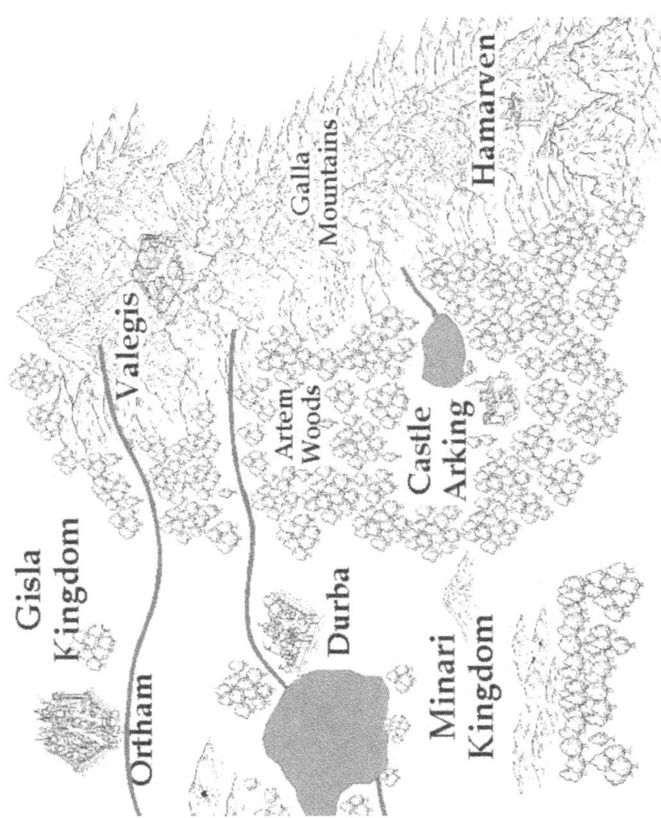

Map of Minari Kingdom, on Rovell
Color map: http://bit.ly/DGS2Map1

CHAPTER ONE

To Quest or Not to Quest

A vortex of multi-colored, changing lights, swirling wind, and a thunder-ous whooshing noise surrounded Anna. Powerless to stop what was happening, she noticed a knot of dread and worry replace the tingling in her stomach. Her eyes darted down, seeking the surface that she felt her feet standing on, its invisibility adding to her disorientation. Across from her stood Ryan, with Matt and Eric to the right and left, all facing each other in a circle, their shocked expressions likely matching hers. Eric mouthed "shit" at the shared realization that, just as they had feared, they were being sum-moned from Earth for another quest they could not refuse, and which could get them killed.

Barely in time, she remembered to put one arm across her breasts and the other over her privates as her Earth clothes vanished and she stood nude a moment. Then a long white robe covered her, matching boots on her feet, an amulet that showed one person healing another replacing the usual pen-dant she wore around her neck, her long blonde hair in a tight braid. She was once again to be the priestess Eriana of Coreth, the Light Bringer. Her gray eyes went to the others, seeing Ryan in his golden armor and helmet for his role as a knight, a large sword on one hip. Eric wore dark leather, a bandoleer of knives across his chest, and a shorter sword hanging from his belt, where a rope was tied around his waist. And Matt stood in a black wizard's robe, a bag of spell books slung over one shoulder, a staff in one hand.

It had been a week since the planet Honyn had summoned the "Ellorian Champions," as they'd been called, to save them from dragons. The episode had already started to feel like none of it had really happened, a feeling that had grown when they told their friend Jack minutes ago, his face registering disbelief on hearing about their quest with elves, dwarves, dragons, ogres, gods, magic, and supernatural healing all being real—at least on another planet. But he had just seen them vanish from Anna's Maryland apartment. And there was no denying that a quest was happening again right now.

As the summoning spell ended, Anna simultaneously noticed the circle of fading blue light surrounding them and a thunderous banging on wood to one side, the cacophony reverberating in a large, dark, enclosed space she could not make out. A sense of immediate danger filled the air. Her white robe caught the light and made her feel like a target, a feeling that worsened when an arrow struck nearby and bounced to her feet with a clatter. She thought it seemed poorly made for reasons she had no time to ponder.

Words etched in blue fire faded from the gray stone beneath her boots. Around them stood the rest of the Quest Ring that had summoned them, chest-high pillars of stone also covered in fading, glowing runes. Beyond them stood a red-robed wizard in his twenties, his long black hair disheveled, intense, wide eyes moving from one of them to the next. No one else seemed nearby except for whoever—or whatever—was violently pounding on doors somewhere beyond the wizard. Then Anna saw torchlight through a wide crack in a splintering door as intruders came closer to breaking it down. From the racket, several other doors were nearby and nearly breached.

"Ellorians!" said the wizard, stepping toward them.

"What is happening?" Eric raised a throwing knife he'd yanked from his black leather, seeming as in command of what to do as ever. Anna trusted his judgement and martial arts skills more than the other two. If anyone could get them out of whatever was happening, Eric could. Hearing his matter-of-fact approach provided the first sense that they would get the chaos around them under control.

"We are under attack," the wizard replied, stopping his advance.

"By what?" Anna asked, backing away. As the blue light faded, her eyes adjusted and to see that a large, dilapidated hall of grey limestone stretched from left to right before them, scattered oak furniture casting shadows, torn but unfaded tapestries hanging askew from the walls. They appeared to be standing in an alcove set aside for the Quest Ring, with no exits from the big hall except those that had something bashing in the barred doors.

As if noticing what she had, Eric asked a better question. "Is there a way out of here?"

The wizard answered Anna instead. "Ogres. Goblins. They found me before I could summon you. I am surprised I made it this far."

"The exit?" Ryan demanded, sword in hand. Was he more willing to use it now? He had hesitated to fight so much on the last quest that Anna wasn't sure he could be trusted to help. But she saw only alarm and determination on his handsome face. An aggressive posture, instead of a cringing one, further reassured her. Maybe he had changed after all.

The wizard who summoned them shook his head. Anna noticed he looked exhausted and beaten, his robe stained with mud. "You will have to kill them. I have spent my energy getting here and casting the spell to summon you."

As he said it, he pitched forward to crack his head on one of the pillars, an arrow protruding from his back. Eric jumped forward faster than Anna and helped drag him inside the Quest Ring, which had now gone dark.

"Enurarki," said Matt, and the crystal atop his staff shone with light that surrounded them. "Still works," he said, sounded as relieved as Anna felt. Only now did she fully realize her fears that few of them would be capable of playing their unwanted roles again. Matt could cast some spells, but the most fearsome he did came from the staff.

"Good," said Eric. "Ryan, stand in front. Your armor can shield us. Matt, can you do something to make them back off?"

"Let me think," replied Matt. Ryan took up a position in front of them.

The injured man looked up with painfilled eyes and clutched Eric's leather sleeve. "The quest. I must tell you why you're here."

"In a minute."

Anna knelt, wondering how to heal this man. She didn't know the gods of this world and said as much when Eric asked her to do it. How could she call on a god to send healing power through her into this man? "Wait," she said, looking at his hand, where a silver ring with three diamonds curled around one finger, indicating how many healing spells were still in it. "The Trinity Ring."

"Good call," said Eric. "Hold on. Gotta pull the arrow out or it won't do much good." He made an apologetic face at the injured wizard and then pulled the arrow from his chest amid a cry of pain, which mixed with the hoarse bellows of the attackers and a shattering of more wood. He spoke a word and a soft glow spread from his hand over the man. Both the arrow wound and the gash on his head vanished. He sat up, looking grateful and relieved. Another arrow struck nearby.

"Matt?" Anna eyed the intruders as they opened more of the door. She saw greenish skin, half naked bodies, and hideous faces with extended jaws, two large teeth jutting up like on a wild boar, bulbous noses, and random tufts of unkempt black hair over thick, menacing brows. Equally crude cudgels, maces, and swords threatened maiming and death.

"I'm trying to think of a good spell." Matt fumbled with the bag and pulled out a thick spell book with black leather binding and gold lettering on it.

"Try faster," said Eric, rising to join Ryan. Anna saw herself and their summoner in the line of fire and backed away so that Ryan's body shielded hers. She gestured for the man to join her, but he spoke from where he was instead.

"The quest," began the wizard, "you must succeed to restore peace. You are to–" An arrow struck him in the eye and flung him on his back.

Anna gasped. "Eric!" The rogue looked back and came over to drag the man to her. Sightless eyes stared at the ceiling. "The ring. Use the most powerful spell." All but her wore an identical Trinity Ring.

"Yeah," he said, yanking the arrow from the wizard's skull with a grimace and then spoke the word. The same soft glow lit the wounds, but no healing occurred. He swore.

"What?" Ryan asked, not looking back an arrow bounced off his golden armor.

"Ring didn't work. He's dead."

"Most powerful of the spells?" Ryan asked, as the ring was named for having three of them, each of different strengths, a specific command for each.

"Yeah."

"What does that mean about the quest?" Anna asked. "He didn't tell us what we need to do."

Eric met her gaze. "Then I don't think we're bound by it."

"We can go home?" Ryan asked over one shoulder.

"I think so. Only one way to know. There's no one else here to tell us."

Anna wondered if he was right. If no one told them the quest, they obviously couldn't do it and were not trapped here by the summoning spell until it was complete like usual. She remembered something about there being a time limit in that they needed to be told the quest shortly after being summoned, but she thought it was an hour or more. They didn't have that much time. As if to prove her point, a loud crashed heralded the arrivals of the goblins, bellowing as they charged, several eight-foot-tall ogres with two small horns and mottled red skin among them.

"Matt!" Eric yelled. He rose and quickly threw small knives that flew into the darkness to disappear. The only indication of success was a body, then another, falling face down on the floor to be trampled by the mob coming to kill them.

"Going with the shield instead!" Matt yelled.

Anna wished he had done it sooner, but the shield would only prevent them from being reached. Whatever spell he had been thinking of before may have offered a chance to repel the attackers and a chance to escape this place. Now they were about to be trapped within a shield, but it was better than nothing.

White light sprang from the top of Matt's staff, outward, and then cascaded down around them just outside the circle of pillars to touch the floor, giving them ten feet of protection. The shield was transparent save for the soft white glow. They didn't have to wait long to see if it was working. Two arrows bounced harmlessly off, then another. A second door shattered open and more foes arrived, charging. A third door would soon break down. They were not getting out of here easily. The goblins and ogres, and a few other creatures Anna couldn't identify, slowed as they neared, coming to a standstill. The four Earth friends backed up to the center of the ring. Anna stared at the disgusting attackers and shuddered, looking away from one creepy killer to the next. Assuming the remaining door held an equal number at bay, she guessed a hundred were here.

As they silently stood, the last door crashed open and the crowd deepened, nearly filling the hall. The room grew brighter for the additional torches, which allowed her to see the mob parting as someone pushed forward from the rear. The individual finally stopped before them, taut black skin under the black chainmail with silver engravings on it, a long bow over one shoulder, a sleek narrow blade on one hip. Haughty, red, slanted eyes stared coldly at them in a face that was as sinister as it was beautiful, long white hair pulled back into a ponytail that let the sharply pointed ears be visible. He bore a long scar on one cheek. No one had to say it out loud, for they all recognized a dark elf from their last quest.

The dark elf's eyes jolted Anna on meeting her gaze, as he appraised first one of them and then another. He nodded in apparent satisfaction while looking at the dead wizard behind them. Then his eyes alertly scanned the perimeter of Matt's spell and Anna went cold. He was planning something, she knew, and it didn't take long to learn what. With a gesture, he indicated they were to be surrounded. The goblins squeezed themselves around the Quest Ring, which stood only a few feet from the walls on three sides. The ogres were too big to fit and instead came up beside the dark elf. Anna looked at Matt. The wizard was the only way they would survive this.

"What now?" Anna whispered to Eric, who had proven himself a more efficient planner than the rest of them.

"Attack," said the dark elf in elven, which they all understood thanks to a spell cast on them on their last quest. Those surrounding them began slamming their weapons into the shield, which showed no signs of failing. The elf silently watched, not taking part, a grim smile of anticipation growing. He withdrew the sword from its sheath.

"All those blows are weakening me," observed Matt, his arm shuddered.

Eric nodded. "I think that's what they're counting on."

"They're not intending to capture us," Ryan remarked, speaking loud over the dull thudding of weapons hitting the shield.

Anna knew he was right. Would they just kill her or do something worse than death first? She trembled again.

"Matt," began Eric, fingering a throwing knife, "do we think things can get out through the shield but not in?"

"I'm not sure."

Ryan met Eric's gaze and said, "You know, you and I could easily stab every single one of those on these three sides, especially, because there's no room for them to back up. That would make them stop."

"Wait," said Anna. She had noticed something. "The Quest Ring can send us back if Matt sticks the top of the staff into the hole in one pillar. I just saw it. There." She pointed to a hole with a shape matching the prongs and crystal. The pillar was the one at the back, opposite where the dark elf stood. This didn't surprise her. While the Quest Rings appeared similar, minor variations were apparent, but what they all had in common was a tallest pillar at the rear, opposite the opening they usually arrived facing. They had seen this hole before on the last Quest Ring but never tried it.

"Okay," said Matt, wincing as the blows continued, "but I'm not sure what happens to this shield when I move the staff to do that. It kind of reminds me of an umbrella right now, and if I tilt the staff to do this, maybe one side lifts up? What if it doesn't stop them anymore and they get to us before I can send us back?"

Eric spoke confidently. "It's our only chance. But I have an idea. Matt, get ready to put the staff in the hole. Anna, help and stay in the middle. Both of you. Ryan and I will protect both of you. Ryan, time to test whether we can strike them, but they can't strike us. If it works, we need to attack all the ones back near the hole first."

"Got it," the knight said.

"Hurry," said Matt, voice strained.

"Hold on," said Eric. "Need to demoralize." Anna watched him flick the throwing knife with one hand. It passed through the shield and struck the dark elf in the chest. The elf took a step back, wobbled, and then fell back. Eric pulled out his short sword.

"Wait, start at the front corner," said Ryan. He didn't wait for agreement and thrust his sword between two pillars into the belly of a goblin, which squealed in pain and fell back. Eric began doing the same on the other side. Anna saw the wisdom of the knight's suggestion. The dead bodies would keep those farther back from escaping over them. The two made quick work of it, twenty goblin bodies now surrounding them just outside the Quest Ring, some dead or about to be. Knight and rogue then moved to the front of the alcove and began stabbing at ogres that came within reach.

"Now!" yelled Eric.

Matt began tilting the staff and Anna grabbed hold of the end. She cast one frantic look back and then guided the staff head into the rearmost pillar's hole with both hands, resulting in an audible click. The words of blue fire abruptly ignited, causing the ogres to step back.

"Stay on guard!" Eric yelled to Ryan as he stabbed forward again. "We don't know how fast we're safe from–"

The room disappeared, the now-familiar vortex pulling them into some unknown space between worlds. Anna covered her body with her hands again, since the robe would soon vanish, leaving her nude before her Earth clothes replaced it. Her eyes studiously stayed on Eric's so they didn't wander, especially as the rogue made no attempt to cover himself, not for the first time, and unlike everyone else. She saw looks of relief and something on their faces, maybe satisfaction that they handled it well enough to survive. Time seemed to pass quicker on the return, and she sensed she was sitting down as a final flash of light momentarily blinded her.

CHAPTER TWO

MASTERY

Jack jumped to his feet and stepped back twice, brown eyes darting between the four new arrivals, then around as if to make sure no one else was present. He cut an athletic figure, his brown hair short enough to not move with his activity. A paper towel in one hand, wet and red, dripped onto the hard floor. "You guys scared the crap out of me."

Matt blinked to clear his eyes, noticing that they had returned to Anna's Gaithersburg, Maryland apartment as expected. Everyone was back in the exact spot they'd been in before the summoning. He still sat on the edge of the couch, a laptop before him on the table and still open to the webpage he'd been perusing. Ryan sat on the couch's other side, one hand in the bag of ChexMix he'd been munching on. Eric was back to spinning around in an office chair, though he was stopping himself. Jack had apparently been kneeling beside the dining room chair that Anna now sat in, the glass of red Zinfandel she had been drinking broken on the floor, the red liquid half cleaned up. All of them now wore the same clothes as they had been before disappearing. They were breathing harder, which made him realize he was doing the same.

Adrenaline drove him to his feet. Ryan and Eric rose, too, the former beginning to pace. And yet Anna stayed down, lifting one foot like a cat that had stepped in something. Matt saw spilled wine soaking one white sock, shards of glass in a pile nearby. The symbolism of it struck him. Had their lives become just as fragile?

"Jesus," said Eric, dark eyes assessing them one by one. "Glad that worked."

"Language," Ryan admonished him absently, blue eyes far away as he ran a hand over his face and through his blond hair. He didn't look as big without the golden armor, but he still intimidated. Matt let Ryan's comment about taking the name of the Lord in vain pass. Ryan could have his faith in God if it helped him deal with what they were facing. Besides, maybe everything they'd heard about their entire lives was real after all, including God.

"Everyone okay?" he asked.

Anna sighed and removed the wet sock. "Physically? Yeah. Not sure about the rest of me."

"Yeah," agreed Matt. "That was messed up in so many ways, from the guy getting killed in front of us, to that creepy dark elf. This wasn't anything like the first time. Could you imagine if that had been that way?"

"What happened?" Jack asked, coming to help Anna step away from the broken glass. Before anyone could answer, Ryan stepped up to the kitchen table and grabbed the beer, drinking a little too much. Jack started, "Hey that was—never mind."

Ryan lowered the bottle and flashed an apologetic glance. "Sorry. I need it more than you."

"You guys weren't gone more than five minutes."

Eric filled him in, concluding by observing, "We never even got the name of the wizard who summoned us."

"We don't even know what planet we were on," added Anna, sitting on the couch.

"It could have been Honyn," Matt began, "like the first quest, just to another kingdom or continent. But there's no way to know."

"Mostly," began Ryan, "I'm just glad we're back again, but I feel like we let down whoever needed us. Besides the wizard, I mean. Even though it's not our job to do this stuff. Or it's not supposed to be."

Matt didn't agree out loud because he knew he didn't have to. The real Ellorian Champions were missing, except the wizard Soliander, who he was pretending to be, and who had attacked them on Honyn. They never found out why and might never know. It topped their list of unanswered questions, such as where the real champions were, how he and the others became unwilling substitutes, and what they could do to stop the quests. He had thought about this many times and knew no answers were coming anytime soon. Maybe if they told everyone the truth, they would be left alone.

Eric sat, brow furrowed. "It's been a week since we returned from Honyn, and we've been wondering if that was a one-time quest. I think we have our answer."

Ryan said, "I didn't want to say it out loud."

Matt did. "We've been permanently substituted for the Ellorian Champions and will continuously be summoned in their place, for quests we don't want, can't refuse, and are likely to get killed doing."

He felt bad for saying it out load, as an awful silence descended on the room. He sensed he was the only one who wasn't all that upset by the idea. His life was okay. All of theirs were, too, but none had the potential that he did. The elf Lorian had tested his affinity for magic on the last quest and revealed how naturally talented Matt was. He had never felt powerful before. Of course, he'd never been terrified either. Not like that. He'd been bullied and beaten up a few times growing up, just like Eric, but while his friend had become a martial artist who could now kick seemingly anyone's ass, whether on Earth or not, Matt was no such thing. Thin, wiry, not exactly strong like Ryan, Matt had only intelligence as a natural asset. And it led to him getting beaten up.

He sat and began furiously typing on his laptop.

"What are you writing?" Anna asked, peeking over his shoulder.

"The spells I just looked up, before I forget."

"Not sure it will do you any good here."

"You never know, and I hope you're wrong."

Ryan said, "I hope you won't need them."

"Me, too, but I need to start memorizing spells on these quests and writing them down once here. Honestly, you guys should, too. I wish those spell books would come back with me."

Eric said, "I'll wait until it matters, like after magic works on Earth."

Matt shook his head. "We already know it does because we wouldn't get summoned without it."

"True, but it appears to not be quite the same thing. Someone is casting it elsewhere, and the Quest Rings are pulling us or sending us back. Maybe it's only one-way."

"That would suck," Matt blurted out. "I mean, how am I supposed to get better at it if I can't practice? As we just saw, there may be no chance on a quest."

Jack had put the wet paper towel in the trash and now asked, "What if you could stop people from telling you what the quest is? Then you could send yourselves home without having to do it. I mean, I realize it makes you look bad, but you're not the real champions anyway. Why do you have to maintain their reputations? It's not your problem. In fact, why not just admit you aren't them?"

Eric sighed. "You have a point, but I'm not sure it would be wise to say we're imposters. It raises questions we can't answer. During the Dragon Gate quest, everyone was clearly impressed and gave us a lot of respect, maybe even leeway. I think we might end up in danger if we confess. I mean, these guys have a fearsome reputation that might keep some people from messing with us, if they thought to try."

"It didn't stop Cirion," Anna remarked.

Matt agreed with her. The dashing rogue had led a band of mercenaries to Castle Darlonon to try closing the Dragon Gate before they could do it, causing problems for them. While Eric was right, there would always be people who weren't intimidated by the Ellorians. He said as much.

"Fair enough," admitted Eric, "and I agree it might not be our job to maintain their reputation. I just think it's safer right now. Maybe I'm wrong."

"Maybe Jack is right," Ryan suggested. "Let's think this through. What would happen if we refused the quest by not letting them tell us about it?"

Jack offered, "Run out the clock? How long do they have to tell you? Do they know? Do you?"

"Not really," Matt admitted. "We didn't exactly get an instruction manual. I don't think Lorian said much about this did he?"

Eric pursed his lips. "I thought he said something like an hour. I would imagine it gets awkward keeping us from knowing so most people might tell us immediately. This guy certainly tried. Just wasn't fast enough. But not knowing this makes it harder to stall after we arrive without seeming weird about it. It's also likely that everyone who does a summons knows this and it's only us that do not. They would likely be in a hurry to bind us to the quest by telling us what it's for."

Anna remarked, "That wizard who just died seemed urgent."

"Not urgent enough," said Ryan. "Could you imagine if he'd said it? We would have been stuck there with all of those... what were they? I recognized ogres, and the dark elf. I'm not sure we would have gotten out of there."

Matt smiled without humor. There was no way Ryan was ever forgetting what an ogre looked like after their encounter on Honyn.

"I thought the other things might be goblins," Eric said, and images suddenly flashed in Matt's head.

"Yeah, they were goblins," he asserted.

Jack asked, "How can you be so sure?"

Though Jack hadn't been there, they had told him about the Honyn quest, but Matt reminded him, "Remember, when Soliander attacked me, he did that mind meld spell on me and I ended up with a bunch of his memories. Most of the time I have no idea what's in my head from that, but sometimes when we're talking, images, scenes, and info pop up. Those were goblins. Now that I think about it, there was actually an orc or two in the back, but they never got close enough for me to really see them."

"A motley group of monsters," muttered Anna, shuddering.

"Let's go back to this idea of refusing a quest," said Jack, sitting at the dining room table and ignoring the mess he had been cleaning. "Maybe you can tell them that something urgent is going on back home and you really need to return."

Eric said, "They would just summon us again and the excuse would be unlikely to work a second time. Besides, they have their own urgency that brought us there."

Anna said, "Lorian made it clear the worlds interact with each other, so if we do this, everyone will hear about it soon and they'll know we're lying."

Matt nodded, more memories surfacing as he pictured the real champions arriving on one world after another, some of them saying they had heard about a quest on another planet. It was common knowledge that some traveling across worlds happened. "I can confirm it's true. The worlds interact."

Jack suggested, "Tell them not to say anything."

Eric shook his head. "Wouldn't work for long. I mean, we could try it a few times, but I don't think it's a long-term solution."

Matt had to agree. It would make them look bad. Protecting the reputation of the real champions was one thing, but now they were it and would give themselves a reputation. They were benefiting from the real reputation now and would create a new one that would do more harm to themselves than anyone else. The risk wasn't worth it. Not yet, anyway.

"What *is* a long-term solution?" Anna asked.

"Getting out of the quest cycle," said Ryan. "We just don't know how they did it." He looked at Matt. "Anything pop into your mind?"

The techie searched his thoughts and impressions. "No. I don't know how we were substituted."

"In the meantime," began Eric, "I think we need to prepare as much as we can. After we returned to Stonehenge, we only had so much time to quiet everything down here, and we weren't sure we'd be summoned a second time. Now we know this is ongoing. We have to train for whatever comes up. There isn't much we can do about magic or healing, but we can all learn swordsmanship, martial arts, how to handle a knife, and just basic self-defense. How to use a bow."

"And ride a horse," added Ryan. "I've been riding for a decade, and all the stuff I do at the Renaissance Festival acting like a knight made me even better. But you guys only have basic skills. No offense. If we're fleeing at a gallop or have to jump over even something small like a fallen tree, you're probably falling off and getting hurt or killed."

"Maybe I have a spell for that," Matt joked, and they all laughed, which felt like a welcome relief from the tension. Sometimes it didn't seem like they had much to laugh about anymore, and if this continued, which was likely, that might just get worse. He wasn't catching up on things like TV shows he was missing episodes of, not that this was important, but that was the point to him. When were they supposed to have down time and just relax, get some escapism?

"Well," Anna began, "I've always wanted to ride, so I'm game. I'm not sure I can afford it, though."

Ryan shook his head. "No, look, I'm paying for everything we need, lessons, gear, whatever. We can't let money get in the way. You know I've never used my parent's money for much, but that's changing. They don't check my credit cards anyway. They may never even notice."

"I agree," Eric said, always practical. "We don't have time to care about anyone's feelings about Ryan picking up the tab, okay? We need each other and we all have to take this stuff seriously."

Everyone agreed aloud. Like the others, Matt had never asked for anything from Ryan, whose parents were rich, but he'd never turned down something either. He wasn't going to start now. Eric was right. He usually was.

Ryan said, "I need somewhere to send things we order online, which is probably most of it. Anna?"

Her eyebrows rose in question before falling. "Of course. Send it here. Not a lot of room, but we'll think of something."

"A storage unit. I'll get on that."

"There's an archery range at Lake Needwood," offered Jack. "I pass it all the time. I don't know if they do lessons, but I can look into stuff like this, especially while you guys are gone."

"Great. What else might we need?" Matt asked. "Gear doesn't matter because we can't take it with us, so it's only stuff we can use to train ourselves."

Eric, who worked as martial arts instructor, said, "I can teach everyone hand-to-hand fighting and self-defense. That's an easy one."

Matt asked, "Can you teach us at your job?"

"Good question. I think so, but that would require Ryan paying for it when that isn't necessary. The owner wouldn't let me teach people who aren't paying."

"We'll think of something," said Ryan. "I could teach a lot of the horseback riding, but I probably can't unless I have my own horses and a ring. I do have a horse, just the one, but it's stabled elsewhere, and I doubt they would let me teach there with going through some sort of approval process that we don't have time for. Besides, it would be a job, and I would just keep disappearing, getting myself fired, so it doesn't make any sense. I want each of you to have one-on-one lessons, but if we do lessons every day, it might also raise questions."

"Every day?" Anna asked.

"The faster the better."

"Okay, I can't disagree with that. It's just a lot."

Matt agreed. Maybe they were getting carried away. How were they supposed to live their lives and keep jobs? And starting all of that physical training wasn't something he was going to handle well, but he didn't want to admit it. He had complained about physical exertion enough times to them that he felt like Eric was smirking at him even though he wasn't.

He said, "I think we have to pace ourselves. Some of us aren't exactly in good shape. I guess we need to change that."

"Physical conditioning," began Eric with a straight face. "Strength training, at least a little. I can handle some of that. We might need gym memberships or something."

"Adding to my list," said Ryan, typing on his phone. "There are some great gyms in the area."

Anna suggested, "The fitness training classes I took means I can help with conditioning. We might want to start a jogging routine, for example. Get our cardio better. We will never be in control of whether we have horses or something. We might have to do a lot of walking, even running at times."

Eric observed. "I think we need to be prepared for anything, as much as we can be."

"You know," began Ryan, "on the first quest, Eric and Matt knowing sign language seemed pretty useful for communicating when we needed to be quiet. How hard would it be to teach us?"

Matt nodded. He had learned it from his deaf mother and taught a curious Eric years ago. That hadn't gone smoothly, but they'd had time, unlike now. There was no real crash course in it. They would have to work on it often. "Not hard, but it may take a long time to get good at it, and there's no spell for it, I don't think, like when Lorian cast one to teach us all a bunch of languages at once. We should definitely get started for at least the basics."

Anna admitted, "I'm feeling a little overwhelmed, guys. How will we have the time for all of this?"

Matt liked his career as a software developer, but maybe it needed to wait. He was only a few years into it anyway. "Yeah, I was thinking the same thing. Ryan doesn't need a job. We aren't so lucky."

"Do you think you should quit?" Ryan asked. "I can pay bills and other stuff."

Seeing dubious expressions, Eric shook his head. "I don't know. I think it's premature. I mean, someone has now summoned us twice, and we have every reason to believe we will be again, but what if it's a week? Or a month?"

"My gut tells me it won't be," Anna said.

Eric sighed. "I know. But we can't quit yet. That might cause scrutiny we want to avoid. That said, we could request some time off, as if we're bothered by some of what happened when we disappeared from Stonehenge. The world knows about that one, but not this one tonight, and they never will. But you know something? None of us would handle more than a few hours of something like horseback riding at first anyway. Our bodies have to get used to it over this first week, especially. It was rough when we were on Honyn. I think we're fine for now, and we have at least a couple days of making arrangements to do. I think we need to get started and not go overboard too fast."

Matt agreed and kept some of his worries to himself. Except for Eric pretending to be Andier of Roir, the Silver-Tongued Rogue, each of the others had struggled with their roles on the Honyn. Andier's ability to smooth talk people, read situations, and use his street smarts to his advantage had fit Eric's past as a juvenile delinquent, when he broke into places, stole for food and money, and lived by his wits until being jailed. It made him believable as Andier, a man skilled at disarming traps, picking locks, and scaling walls. Eric's rock climbing, parkour skills, martial arts aptitude, and knife throwing ability—honed at RenFest—had made him almost oddly suited for the role of Andier, but the others hadn't been so lucky.

On the first quest to Honyn, Ryan had nearly gotten Eric killed over his own issues. An expert horseman who played a knight at RenFest every summer, Ryan gave the appearance of being suited to play a knight. Muscular and tall, he knew how to don armor, swing a sword, use a lance, and speak in a commanding voice meant to impress. But it was all a show. Now he had to be a real knight on their unwanted quests, playing the role of Lord Korrin of Andor, the Dragon Slayer.

Aside from knowing nothing of real swordsmanship and tactics, Ryan had been afraid of actual violence or hurting anyone since they had known him, but they had never understood why—until the ogre battle. His fear that he had nearly killed one ogre in self-defense led him to heal it with the Trinity Ring on one hand. It had risen and almost killed Eric. Only in the aftermath did he finally admit that he was the one who had paralyzed his brother Daniel when goofing around as children, the guilt haunting him ever since—and causing his attitude.

He had gotten past that as that quest continued, finally killing the dragon who posed the greatest threat to them, but Matt still wondered if the big guy had really conquered his phobia. On this second quest just now, Matt had felt relieved to see Ryan stabbing the goblins threatening them, so maybe they didn't have to worry about Ryan's conscious putting them at risk anymore.

Anna was another problem that might have been resolved, but he couldn't be sure. An atheist, she had been visibly annoyed to discover her own role – the Priestess Eriana of Coreth, the Light Bringer, a healer who channeled the power of gods to save the dying. How could a woman who didn't believe in such things change her heart so fully that a god chose her as a vessel for their power? Her transformation had been slow and nearly as deadly in its delays as Ryan's, but Matt was the one she had finally healed at the end, so he knew she could do it. But every time they arrived on a planet, she had to reach a god she had never heard of to make contact. Someone had given her a scroll of information and help with this the first time. Just now, that wizard who summoned them had died partly because Anna had no idea what gods to ask for help from. Without these Trinity Rings all but she wore, this could be a serious problem.

And Matt wasn't fine in his role as the Majestic Magus, Soliander of Aranor, one of the most powerful wizards on any world. He hadn't known a thing about magic. Only training from the elf Lorian had made it possible to summon power using Soliander's staff. Matt had relied on it right up until the end when it had been knocked from his hand and failure to cast a spell had meant death. Not having the staff on Earth had hindered his ability to perform magic here. How was he supposed to practice? Did he need to be terrified to do anything without it? Was magic even working here? He sighed and tried to ignore his worries.

For the rest of the night, they sat together, often not speaking, each with an agreed upon aspect of training to develop on behalf of them all. While Matt had taught sign language informally and leisurely to Eric, they needed something faster, and he soon used Ryan's credit card to purchase a number of manuals for him as a teacher and the others as students. Jack researched archery locations, instructors, gear that matched the medieval or Renaissance periods, and ordered more supplies, including practice targets of their own. Eric planned a curriculum of karate and other disciplines to teach them, then purchased some training equipment they could use away from his job as needed. Ryan researched horses he could buy, for the "school horses" typically available were not good enough and would not compare to the battle trained mounts he would expect them to be given. Anna looked into physical conditioning and strength, including endurance, running speed, and flexibility, which Eric's training would help with.

She finally asked, "Where are we going to do some of this, guys?"

They sat in silence for a minute, and then Ryan said, "I have an idea."

Ryan pursed his lips, waiting for Eric's response. They stood inside the partially empty guest house at the estate of Ryan's parents in Potomac, Maryland, where mostly rich people lived. Outside, tall trees loomed in nearly every direction, just far enough away from the house to prevent falling leaves from clogging gutters. The shade they cast moved with the breeze so that sunlight danced across the hardwood floors inside, never staying constant. There were no curtains or hardware to hang them, or furniture. His parents had renovated the place years ago, having all the walls painted, new cabinets added, the whole bit, but then they stopped short of finishing it when Ryan had paralyzed Daniel so long ago. The thought made him sigh, for the building was frozen in time back to that period and it always brought unpleasant memories back. Even so, it seemed the best option for what he and his friends needed.

"I think this will work," Eric admitted, looking around.

Ryan felt a little relieved at the reaction. He admired Eric even before this business with being champions arose, but his friend's critical thinking skill wasn't something he'd really noticed before. Eric would find the flaw in just about anything. While the others had good ideas, no one picked them apart like his former juvenile delinquent friend.

Sometimes he wondered if that past was where Eric got the skill from. Had breaking into places, stealing, and making his way by his wits made him not just street smart, but savvy? Eric thought things through with a speed and precision that would have made Ryan jealous if he really cared about being that way himself. In his mind, Eric was their leader, though Ryan was supposed to act like it on arriving for a quest, or any other time they needed to impress on people how important and powerful they supposedly were as the Ellorian Champions. He was the most imposing for his height and muscular physique, the golden and gilded armor of Lord Korrin of Andor an impressive sight.

More people wanted to talk to him, too, for Eric was supposed to be Andier of Roir, the Silver-Tongue Rogue, with a reputation for swindling people or tricking them into revealing too much. Matt as the Majestic Magus

Soliander of Aranor just scared everyone. And Anna as the Light Bringer Eriana of Coreth, who saved countless lives by channeling a god's healing power through her, inspired reverence, respect, and awe, much of it causing people to be very polite and keep some distance.

All of this left Ryan to receive the exuberance of desperate people grateful for their arrival to save them. He was the showman, too, having played a knight for years at the local Renaissance Festival for fun, so beyond knowing how to don armor and swing a sword (just not for real), he was best suited to the apparent-leader role. That Eric held that position behind the scenes was fine with him. They just had to stay on the same page.

And so Ryan sighed in relief on hearing Eric accept the use of the guest house as a training area. On the same property where his parents and he lived with his brother, the building stood two stories and had its own three-car garage, driveway, and gate with unmanned security. An acre of land, with a line of thick pine trees, separated it from the main house. As long as they kept quiet, everything but the horseback riding could be done here without his family even knowing they were using it. The property had some empty acres where archery could happen, too.

Looking at some old Persian rugs the family was storing stacked atop each other in the living room, Ryan said, "I think we have to clean it up a little. Use the dining room for storage due to the chandelier being in the way anyway. Can't swing anything in there. We can move some of the other unused furniture there, create the spaces we need."

"Is there a basement?" Eric asked.

"Yeah. And it's got some big open space, depending on what's been put down there."

"Let's have a look."

They soon decided the first floor would have minimal equipment in case anyone happened by, like the gardeners and others who maintained the property. They didn't want suspicions forming. Gym mats and exercise gear would occupy the basement that would be kept dark when not in use. They realized that, if anyone did catch their cars here, that maybe they should pretend they were using it as a place to hang out, and they would need somewhere to sit anyway. Some couches, tables, and an entertainment system would help convince anyone they weren't up to anything weird. Matt, being a techie, could set up a security camera to alert them to anyone dropping by if they were downstairs. The need for such a ploy became apparent sooner than expected.

The front door opened with a bang and Ryan's younger brother rolled his wheelchair over the threshold and into the foyer, then the living room, from where he smirked at them as they sat on the pile of Persian rugs in the adjacent dining room. His long black hair lay in a ponytail over one shoulder, tattoos visible on his arms, one of which he had full use of. He was a quadriplegic thanks to the accident Ryan had caused when they were kids, but he never seemed to bear his older brother ill will. If anything, Ryan was the affected one, his guilt a frequent shadow on him, except that now that they knew supernatural healing existed, Ryan was determined to help Anna figure out how to do it on Earth and heal his brother.

"I can't imagine what you two are doing in here," he said, using the wheelchair's controls to position himself to see them better.

"Daniel," said Eric by way of greeting.

"Hiding from you," Ryan said. "How did you know we were here?"

Rolling toward them, his brother replied, "I was playing with my drone just now and the camera picked up the cars out front."

Ryan silently cursed. He hadn't planned on using the garage but now they would need to. That might require more cleaning out depending on what was in there. He wasn't even sure they had working garage door openers. Part of him wanted to tell Daniel the truth, but so far only Jack knew. No one else had been discussed and Ryan hadn't raised the possibility. It might be better, really, since Daniel could keep their parents and anyone else from prying while they were gone. But how do you tell your younger brother that you are being magically summoned to other worlds full of magic and fantastic creatures? Having been an avid *Dungeons and Dragons* and Tolkien fan, Daniel would have loved it and been supremely jealous. But he also wouldn't have believed a word of it and thought Ryan was making fun of him.

"What *are* you doing in here?" Daniel persisted.

"Checking out the place," said Eric, and Ryan realized his friend was a better liar and should do the talking. "The press has been a pain, so I was thinking to move. Ryan suggested here."

"Not seriously though," said Ryan, not sure he liked that lie. Daniel would invite himself too often. "Just showing him around. The media will die down."

Daniel looked skeptical. "Yeah, maybe. Did you see that report today of someone being healed in Argentina somewhere? With new stories of weird shit cropping up all the times now, you guys and the Stonehenge thing should be forgotten before long. All you did was vanish for three weeks without explanation." He paused. "Still waiting for you to tell me what really happened."

Eric and Ryan exchanged a look, and on a sudden instinct, Ryan told the truth as if he was lying. "Someone summoned us to another world for a quest to save the planet from a horde of dragons. I fought off some ogres, too."

"Me, too," added Eric, sounding flippant. "Matt and Anna tagged along but were only so much help. It was really us."

"Yeah, and then I killed this dragon. It was freakin' huge. Breathing fire and everything, but my armor was fireproof."

"Well, *mostly* fireproof," Eric corrected with a grin.

"Yeah. It doesn't work so well against dragon fire, just other kinds. And 'almost' only counts in horseshoes and hand grenades."

Daniel smirked. "Did you get to deflower a virgin while you were at it?"

Ryan pretended to consider. "Come to think of it, no."

"I think we got screwed," Eric suggested.

Daniel's shrewd eyes appraised them. "You know something? Reports of weird shit going on around the world started right about the time you guys went missing. You probably missed a few of them, and it took a while for them to really start catching on in the news, like about two weeks, which was a couple weeks ago. Be straight with me. What the fuck happened out there?"

Eric opened his mouth, but Ryan knew he was going to joke and adopted a more serious tone. "Seriously, we don't know. It surprised us when everyone said we had been gone three weeks."

The martial artist added, "That *did* explain why the SUV we'd driven there was gone. We were wondering where the hell it went because we would've thought we'd hear someone driving off with it."

Daniel rolled closer on the hardwood floor. "So, are you suggesting it was some sort of time dilation shit? I mean, that only happens in sci-fi."

"Yeah, but all this other stuff is supposedly happening in the real world," said Ryan, "so maybe we were just the first of these incidents." He looked at Eric because he hadn't thought of this before, but now was no time for discussing it. *Had* they been the first?

"Do you guys feel any different after?"

They exchanged a look and shrugged. "Like what?"

"I don't know, like the ability to do magic or heal people like some are saying? I assume you would tell me *that* at least."

"Come on, man," started Ryan, "Of course, I would tell you if that was going on. Besides, the first thing I would do if I could heal people would be get you out of that chair I put you in."

Daniel frowned. "What makes you think I *want* out of this chair?"

That brought Ryan up short. He had never thought of that. He had just assumed Daniel wanted to be healed, which he wanted Anna to do the moment she was able. This was the first time he'd broached the subject because there hadn't been a way to do so before without being weird about it.

"Why would you not want to?" he asked. "Don't you want to walk again? Run? Go swimming?"

"Yeah, sure, those are all fine. Why not? Ryan, just because people are talking about being healed lately doesn't mean it's not a bunch of bullshit. I accepted being in this chair for the rest of my life a long time ago. Don't get your hopes up about this crap. That's all it is."

"Yeah, okay. I didn't mean it like that. I just thought that if you had the chance, you would take it." He hesitated to ask. "Would you?"

Daniel turned around and started rolling out. "Ask me when it's possible and you know a cute girl who can do it."

Anna breathed a sigh of relief and started her white Kia Optima, driving away from her apartment complex. It had been a long few days. Her thighs and butt still hurt from the first hour-long horseback lesson she'd shared with the boys, with another scheduled in a few days when they recovered. Eric had given them all some initial karate lessons that hadn't been so bad. Matt's sign language work was less painful, at least. She was a little sore from her first jog as well, but things were coming along. She just needed a break from it all.

A girl's night out was just what she needed. She had avoided her girlfriends a bit since the reappearance at Stonehenge, partly because everyone had so many questions and fending them off was the opposite of relaxing. She expected a few more queries tonight, but felt more comfortable dodging them now. As much as she enjoyed the boys, she had to get away from everything involving them now. She had spent all of her free time on preparing for their new reality. The worst part was the pressure—the feeling that every minute counted because someone could summon them without warning. They needed years of expertise but had no time to gain it. And they felt lucky to not have already been taken again. The stress was getting to her.

She put it from her mind with an effort. Five minutes later, she picked up her dance instructor friend Jade, an Asian woman who wore her jet-black hair in an asymmetrical bob, the front past her chin on one side, a dash of green through it. Ten minutes after and they met roommates Heather and Raven, who piled into the back. Anna headed for the highway, a night of dinner, dancing, and drinking with them ahead of her.

"So girl," began Raven from the backseat, "Anna, what's up with you hanging with these boys all the time? You doing a foursome and not inviting us?"

Anna blushed as they all laughed. "I don't have that much stamina."

"I do!" said Raven. She lifted up her phone and started videotaping their conversation, as she liked to do, sometimes posting it online with faces blurred out. She had a decent online following.

"I would go for Ryan," said Heather, putting blush on her white cheeks. "I like my men big."

"Who doesn't?" Raven asked, cackling.

"I think average is just fine," said Jade from the front seat.

Raven said, "That Eric is supposed to be a karate guy or something? That's hot. I like flexible men."

Laughing and already feeling her stress melt away, Anna asked, "Is there anything you *don't* like in men?"

"What about Matt?" Jade asked, turning to look in the backseat, which is when Anna realized her friend hadn't put on a seat belt and told her to, but didn't get a reaction as Jade added, "I think he's cute. I like smart guys."

"That's because you're Asian," began Raven. "Your boys all got big brains."

"Seriously, though," started Heather, "first you disappeared with those guys in England for three weeks and now you're hanging out with them all the time. Come on, what's going on?"

Anna sighed, noticing Raven's camera recording. She'd ask her not to post anything about what Heather just said, or her response, because it would reveal her identity.

"We've just been hiding out from the press. They were driving us crazy and the only people who understood what it was like was them. I didn't have to explain anything to them, or answers questions I can't answer."

"You really don't know where you were all that time?" Jade asked.

Anna repeated the agreed upon lie that Ryan had told Daniel.

"I don't know where we were during those three weeks," Anna concluded. By now, her car had reached the highway and they were doing 70 mph in a big block of vehicles, heading south on I-270 against rush hour traffic toward Rockville.

"Maybe you need one of those healers that people keep talking about," began Jade, still not wearing her seatbelt. She was making Anna nervous. "They could get your memories back or figure out how three weeks of time went away for you."

That was just what Anna needed, someone poking around and forcing her to make up more lies. She felt stressed by it, but she knew they were just making small talk and would likely drop it soon.

"I think you mean a hypnotist," Heather corrected.

"No. I don't. We could find one of these people and they could answer the mystery."

"That shit ain't real, girl," said Raven, still taping on her phone. "Come on. And you know Anna don't believe in that."

"Yeah, but they showed that one on video," said Jade. "The guy's leg was mangled and it just went back to normal."

That surprised Anna. She hadn't heard of that story, but then she'd been too busy and not really catching up on these stories as much as she should, especially when it sort of concerned her. She would get on that tomorrow. "Seriously, Jade, please put your seatbelt on."

"Come on, that video was fake, like the moon landing." Raven let out a cackle, since she wasn't serious.

"Would you let someone heal you?" Jade asked Anna, putting her seatbelt on with an eye-roll.

Seeing that, Anna relaxed. "If it actually worked? Yeah, sure."

"See?" Raven asked. "She had to qualify that."

"I would want a hunky doctor type to heal me," began Heather, "and then I could show him my gratitude."

They erupted in laughter and Anna said, "I've really missed you guys."

Her face hurt from the grin, and then she felt a tingling in her stomach. A moment passed before an awful realization struck. Her wide eyes went to Jade beside her, then the cars hurtling along around them. A glance in the rearview mirrored showed a freight truck a little too close behind. White light blinded her, but it wasn't coming from the headlights there, just around her body. She frantically looked to the left to plow through the HOV lane to the median and stop, but cars blocked her way. She began screaming "no" as her foot plunged for the brake pedal and passed through air, her hands no longer around a steering wheel. The faces of Ryan, Matt, and Eric appeared before her, their resigned expressions turning to alarm on seeing her screaming.

CHAPTER THREE

UNEXPECTED COMPANY

Soliander of Aranor felt nervous. Some would have been surprised that a man of such power could feel that way, or that he would admit it to himself, but he was no fool. Refusing to acknowledge it could lead to death, and worse. He had summoned sentient forces to do his bidding many times, and some of them could detect such a feeling and exploit it. That would lead to first one mistake and then another. All but one of his apprentices over the years had resisted acknowledging their feelings and potential impact, so he usually made the most prideful summon a demon, inevitably lose control of it, and have it take them away to eternal damnation while the other candidates watched, aghast. He smiled. Either their willingness to heed his advice soared or they left his tutelage for good.

That lone standout apprentice had always been the most promising. Soliander had been trying to find him for years, but the former student knew it and was in hiding. Far worse than being a demon's slave awaited Everon for betraying Soliander. Tracking his whereabouts had been especially difficult during Soliander's years as one of the Ellorian Champions. Any pursuit was doomed to fail when you could disappear from the trail without warning. His spies had turned up little, and in the years since breaking free of the quest cycle, Soliander still hadn't found Everon, though he'd come close.

His eyes went to a window, beyond which lay the darkness of night and a tower, golden light twinkling from its windows. A prisoner occupied the top room, guarded by the supernatural and dark elves. Diara's capture had been fortuitous. She had refused to give up her lover Everon's location, but the *Mind Trust* spell had solved that problem. All ethical wizards respected that forbidden magic and wouldn't use it. But it had its uses.

Magically sifting through her memories had yielded much, including Everon's hide-out, but Soliander had acted in haste and cost himself his quarry. He should have taken time to plan an ambush, rather than immediately arriving via magic portal and laying waste to everything in his path. Everon was not there. If Soliander's vast network of spies asking questions about Everon had not made it clear that someone dangerous was after him, the destruction Soliander wrought on his home had. He knew from Diara's memories that Everon was unsure if Soliander was behind the inquiries. After all, everyone thought Soliander was missing, just like the rest of the Ellorian Champions, and yet dark elves with bluish-steel blades had often done the asking.

Only two people knew how to create such items made from the soclarin ore. And Everon only knew because he'd stolen the secret from Soliander. Those items were how they were inadvertently tipping each other off as to their activities, whereabouts, or both. One of Soliander's spies had captured a man with such a blade, which Soliander knew he hadn't created. The *Mind Trust* spell on the man led to Diara, and then to the home she shared with Everon. Since Soliander's attack, Everon abandoned every place he'd been with Diara, who he was sure to notice had gone missing. The degree of abandonment—and the fear it revealed—told Soliander that Everon knew it was him, even if the former apprentice did not understand how that was possible. Setting traps might be the only way to get him now.

It was one reason Soliander had opened the Dragon Gate on Honyn. Not only had he needed more of the ore, but he wasn't sure if Everon knew the gate led to the only place to get it. Had the apprentice run out of what he'd stolen from Soliander's stash? If he knew where to get it, learning that the gate was open would lure him there, Soliander's *Detect Presence* spell triggering an alarm that would bring them together once more at last. These betrayals about the ore were minor except for how they had enabled the betrayal that really mattered, the one for which Everon was to pay for eternity once Soliander got him. It was all arranged. He just needed his victim.

But now another mystery beyond Everon's whereabouts had Soliander's attention. Somehow his life had become all about finding people. First Everon. Now Ryan, Anna, Eric, and Matt. And maybe Korrin, Andier, and Eriana. He didn't know where his fellow Ellorian Champions were any more than anyone else did. He had assumed they were dead or trapped on Earth. But he hadn't been able to find Earth with any locator spell since he had returned from there years ago, and last seen the champions. He had never heard of Earth or seen it before someone summoned all four of them there, or since. It was as if Earth had never existed.

But now the locator spell found Earth on the first try. And second. And third. Even his apprentice Darron could find it. Soliander knew why, even how. Magic had returned to working on Earth, rendering the planet detectable. And the pendant being returned to Stonehenge had triggered this. He knew this even without the images in his head from the brief *Mind Trust* connection with Matt. Stonehenge looked about the same as when he'd last seen it in person, but the stones appeared considerably weathered, far more so than a few years would have suggested. This wasn't the only sign that the world had transformed. When he had been there, it hadn't been noticeably different from any other world he'd been to, but the images in Matt's memories were startling.

Vast buildings and cities of glass, steel, and precisely carved stone. Little boxes with moving images and sound. Enclosed, moving wagons of metal. Portable, long range communication devices. Handheld devices that fired deadly projectiles. An enormous mushroom cloud that obliterated an entire city. And more. So much more. He knew the names of these from Matt's thoughts. Computers. TVs. Phones. Guns. Nuclear explosions.

All of them revealed a world far different from the one he'd visited years ago with his friends. The images of Stonehenge had included a flashlight, a phone, an SUV, and a visitor's center that certainly hadn't been there before. Someone could have added it since, of course, but the technology apparent in it suggested that only a few years having passed was highly unlikely. A suspicion had formed and seemed the obvious explanation, but he had to go there to find out.

There were two names he would have expected to find in Matt's memories of important people, but there had been no trace of them. Maybe it wasn't surprising and meant nothing. Everything he had learned was unusually disjointed due to the way the *Mind Trust* spell had been abruptly broken. That had apparently scattered the retained information, and the thought made him feel lucky. Sometimes it isn't the memories gained that are scattered, but the caster's mind, leaving the wizard infantilized, a useless, drooling idiot. This was another reason the spell was forbidden. He had dodged a bullet, to use an Earth expression he now knew. Matt had nearly destroyed both of them when he escaped the *Mind Trust* spell.

It gave more reason to visit Earth. He needed to understand what was happening there. That he might find some sign of his lost friends compelled him to go, even if nothing else would have. He certainly wanted answers to the mystery of why Matt and the others had impersonated him and the real champions. He sensed from Matt's memories that there was little they really knew. There were no images of Korrin, Eriana, or Andier. But he'd seen Lorian, the elf who had shouted Soliander's name at him in the ruins of Castle

Darlonon. He had been considering grabbing the elf for information, but Lorian was less important. What really mattered now was this visit to Earth.

He needed to know so many things, including who truly controlled the nuclear warheads. Only he and a few others held such power, and he had purposely destroyed most of the others. That wasn't a power any mortal should have, only the gods. As far as he knew, only he could do it now, but he sensed from the spell Lorian had done on Matt that the latter was unusually strong in magic. Perhaps he had the power, if not the skill. Matt was no wizard, he knew. Not really. And yet he had taken control of the staff in Soliander's hand and burned him with it. He was caught between grudging admiration and irritation about that, but vengeance on Matt wasn't a priority, not that he wouldn't take the chance if it arose. But he had more pressing concerns. He wanted to know who controlled these warheads.

But even that paled compared to understanding the changes on Earth and what had happened since his departure from there. The latter had been eating away at him for years. And now he could finally learn a great many truths, not the least of which might have been where his former friends were, and where they went. The fate of Korrin and Andier concerned him, but not like that of Eriana, the Lady Hope, her disappearance crushing any hope—or even goodness—left in him. Had she seen the look of fear and awful realization in his eyes the last time they were together? He was certain she had, as their eyes met one final time before they disappeared in a flash of light.

His eyes again went to the window and the tower where Diara sat in chains. What would Eriana think of him having imprisoned her younger sister? He wanted to laugh. If Eriana still lived, she would likely be furious. But she would also understand. After all, if it hadn't been for Diara, Everon could not have betrayed them all. While Soliander was certain the Lady Hope was dead, he could never fully resign himself to the idea. And it was the primary reason he hadn't killed Diara. Eriana might understand imprisoning her sister, especially to gain information on his former apprentice, but she would never forgive killing her, even if Diara had it coming. If Soliander ever found Eriana alive, he would have some explaining to do, but stating why he'd locked up her sister was a lot of less troubling than why he'd killed her.

And so Diara lived, and in good health, at that. He had made no secret to his prisoner that Eriana was the only reason he kept her alive. Besides, he didn't need her cooperation when the *Mind Trust* spell bypassed all of that, so telling her the truth affected nothing. He had long since learned everything he needed to know and had not visited her in some time. Maybe he would after his trip to Earth, depending on what he learned of Eriana's whereabouts.

The possibility that she still lived caused his heart to pound. And he knew that this was why he was nervous. Never mind the strange visions of Earth, and what Matt and his friends might know, or that magic had resumed working there once more, possibility heralding an extraordinarily dangerous situation, made all the worse by the existence of nuclear warheads, among other inventions. No, what threatened his self-control was whether or not Eriana was alive. He calmed himself and summoned his current apprentice, Darron, a dark-skinned dark elf who would excel at the excursion now planned. The black hair would hide the pointed ears, but something would have to be done about the red eyes.

The apprentice wizard entered his chambers wearing clothes neither had seen anyone wearing before, except in Soliander's memories from Matt. Blue jeans, a t-shirt, and sneakers covered his lithe form. He carried a black back-pack in one hand. It had taken implanting the idea in someone's head to get her to create these replicas, which would have to do for now. Darron fidget-ed quietly, as if tying to get used to the attire.

"Must I really wear this, Master Zoran?" Darron asked, tugging at the tight jeans and using the false name Soliander had been using since even before the Ellorian Champions had vanished. No one knew that Zoran the Devasta-tor was really Soliander of Aranor, the Majestic Magus, hero wizard from among the missing Ellorian Champions.

"Yes," Soliander replied. "It is the fashion there. You must fit in, as will I if I can join you. You will carry your wizard's robes and other items in that bag."

The apprentice lifted it awkwardly. "Its design is strange, but I must ad-mit the many pockets seem quite functional."

"What I have seen of this world is strange. You must not gawk upon arri-val."

"Yes, master. What is it you want me to do?"

"You will arrive near the home of the man named Matt. It will be night. You will ensure no one is watching. I need you to act nonchalant while find-ing a quiet place to contact me via the orb, while no one can observe you. You must avoid suspicion."

"Of course."

"This world does not know magic, from what I understand. Once you can contact me, I will ask you to perform a simple spell while I watch via the orb. If the spell works, I will join you."

"And if the spell does not work?"

You will be trapped there forever instead of me, Soliander thought. "We will deal with that at the time. You may have trouble getting the orb to work as well, but keep trying."

He didn't get into what would happen next. The apprentice would likely find fitting in difficult and would get stranded or apprehended on a strange world without magic to help him. Soliander didn't much care. If that befell the apprentice, they'd never see each other again. He didn't think it likely, however. Matt and the others could not have been summoned from Earth unless magic was working on Earth again. Even the spell Soliander was about to cast to send Darron there would fail if the planet was still locked, but he had to be sure. If the spell worked and the orb functioned on Earth, and the apprentice performed magic while Soliander watched, then and only then would he feel comfortable casting himself there personally.

He sighed. The time had come. He rose from behind the stone table with its spell books, scrolls, and magic runes carved into its surface. Along the way, he stopped at a table to place a soft, black cloth over a golden orb that had been glowing softly, various images fleeting across its surface. Then he went to stand before Darron. The apprentice didn't seem as nervous as Soliander felt, but then he had little idea how important this moment was. That inspired Soliander to calm himself and place one hand on Darron's shoulder. Words of magic slithered from his mouth as the power began to course through him, enveloping the apprentice, who seemed remarkably trusting as Soliander made him vanish from before him. Strange how the disappearance of someone so unimportant to him might lead to the reappearance of those who mattered so very much.

Erin Jennings tightened the top of the white thermos she'd brought from Florida, a comfort from home just like the tea itself. She seldom went for designer flavors or even coffee, just regular tea, mostly because the taste was a holdover from a life long gone but never forgotten. How could anyone forget such a life? The only equivalent in this world were fictionalized stories. Sometimes it all seemed like a dream, but she knew better. And everything she had done since helped her prepare for today.

Twenty years had passed since it ended abruptly in what she had surmised was an explosion, but she didn't really know. One moment she'd been standing with her dearest friends and the next she stood in a rural field somewhere by herself, a little dazed, very confused, and apparently not at all dressed for the fashions of the day, as she learned when she went to the nearest home for help. The style of the house had been as strange to Erin as her clothing to the occupants, who had initially assumed she was taking part in a nearby festival.

Erin had learned to be quick thinking from many moments of being thrust into new, unexpected situations. At those times, she had sometimes counted on her reputation to get by. People were often too intimidated to cross her or her companions, but this time no one seemed to recognize her. Taking her cue, she had played along, having mastered the art of asking questions to control the conversation's flow, as one of her friends, who was infinitely wilier, had taught her. And so she came to understand that this place was different from any other she had visited.

Those elderly homeowners had been a stroke of good luck, she now knew. It was late afternoon when she knocked on their door and she accepted their invitation to dinner. Seeing an opportunity as the night wore on and she professed to not knowing who to contact to come get her, she had asked for a room and been given one.

Her hosts were forgetful but kind, and a little clueless about modern technology. They had a missing, and presumed dead, granddaughter Erin's age, and whom she reminded them of. The result was treating her like family and doting on her, especially on learning that she was lost. They didn't ask too many questions, to which they sometimes didn't remember her awkward answers anyway, and that had allowed her to give a better response when they asked again. They didn't begrudge the ignorance she struggled to hide, for there were so many things so alien to her, from the TV to phones, computers, and the internet, that pretending she had familiarity challenged her. With wide eyes had Erin taken it all in.

And so her month-long stay with them had begun, as she discreetly pumped them for information, gorged on TV news programs, and used the internet on their old computer once she figured out how from watching them struggle to do so themselves. Hour after hour had she immersed herself, slowly learning one important idea after another.

She was on the south island of New Zealand. She needed a passport to get on a plane to England to find Stonehenge, which was still standing since she'd last seen it. It had changed since then, but then it seemed like everything had and this place was no longer recognizable, not that she had seen much anyway. While people believed in a lone god, there were no confirmed reports of Him answering anyone. Magic didn't seem to work, and no one believed in it. An internet search of her friend's names turned up nothing, but two other names brought up a lot, and yet all of it was considered a myth from a thousand years past. Had she been flung into the future? All signs pointed to it. Ever since, a kind of grief had lurked in the back of her mind, that everyone and everything she had ever known was just gone.

Eventually she left behind the elderly couple who had given her a wad of cash and a suitcase of old clothes and other knickknacks as she set off for Christchurch, a nearby city with international flights. She promised to repay them, but they told her not to worry about, as they weren't using any of it anyway. Getting the documentation she needed for international travel would have been impossible were it not for their missing granddaughter, whom they had been raising after their own daughter died. She bore just enough resemblance for Erin to get a nerdy young man she flirted with to issue her a new driver's license in the girl's name, which she adopted, becoming Erin Jennings. Similar machinations finally got her the passport, credit cards, and a new identity, all of it helped by those sweet grandparents having done little to formalize the girl's death. They hadn't had the heart to go through that again and hoped they might find the real Erin one day, but it had been years and they seemed resigned that it wouldn't happen.

She finally stood before Stonehenge, which had weathered considerably since she last saw it a month earlier. A nearby visitor center looked decades old but hadn't been here before. Something was clearly amiss. She stayed in Britain for a year, working as a server and making new friends to avoid suspicion, hoping for a sign of her true friends, but it never came. When it became apparent that she was in this brave new land for the rest of her life, she moved to America and married someone a few years older and with a promising future. Nearly twenty years had passed.

She spent those years preparing for today, acquiring supposed magic items from around the world, a few of which were upstairs in her hotel room. None had worked, but she had heard reports of random people being able to do one thing or another. And the Stonehenge disappearance could never have happened without magic. Some people could also heal others. Most dismissed that as nonsense, but Erin knew it had been possible in her old life, which was about to collide with her new one. She felt nervous. So much depended on this conversation with the Stonehenge Four. It was important to have this talk in person. Their expressions would tell her more than words ever could.

As she sipped her tea in a hotel dining area in Gaithersburg, Maryland, the loud, excited voices of two approaching teenage girls broke her thoughts. The first words she could make out got her undivided attention.

"The guy vanished right on camera!" said the blonde one as they swept into the dining area, moving around the small tables and chairs, the afternoon sun streaming across the floor.

The brunette asked, "Do you think that's what happened at Stonehenge, but no one was there to see it?"

"Could be. Damn, the TV isn't on. Where's the remote?"

Erin's eyes went to it on the counter, from where one girl grabbed the TV control and furiously pushed buttons to no avail. "Damn thing is busted!"

"Grab a cookie and let's go. Come on!"

They ran from the room and Erin strode right behind them, her long skirt snapping as she marched to the nearest stairs. She ascended three flights, taking two steps at a time. She finally burst into the hall and swiftly unlocked her room door, then headed straight for the TV, which came on, already set to the news from her viewing it earlier today. Words gushed from an excited black reporter as Erin read the chryon across the screen's button, "Man Magically Vanishes on Camera."

"Lisa," the reporter continued, addressing a news anchor on the split screen, "as you can see from the footage, I was right in the middle of our interview when he disappeared."

Lisa replied, "I know some people are speculating that this is just a special effect, added afterward."

"Yeah, and I'm here to tell you this is absolutely not the truth. I saw it right in front of me and there are a dozen witnesses to this, some of whom caught it on their cellphones."

As the two women talked, a silent replay of the moment began repeating, sometimes in slow motion. The techie, Matt, stood shyly talking into the microphone held toward him, green eyes on the reporter as he only rarely glanced at the camera as if uncomfortable before it. A light breeze touched his shoulder-length, wavy brown hair. And suddenly the smile left his face as he stopped talking mid-sentence, one hand going to his stomach, those eyes widening in a clear look of alarm, and a soft white glow surrounding him. A murmur slowly began from those near, and the camera tilted a moment as if the holder was startled out of position before recovering just in time. A glow enveloped Matt and then disappeared along with him.

The anchor interrupted the reporter, "Hey listen, we're going to have to switch to another story, possibly related, that is just coming in. There are reports of a very serious, multi-car accident on I-270 near Gaithersburg. Initial reports suggest that a bright flash of light, similar to the one that occurred nearby during the interview of Matt Sorenson, happened just moments before the collision, which has involved several cars, one of which has overturned. We currently don't know if this is related to Matt Sorenson's previous disappearance with Anna Sumner, Ryan LaRue, and Eric Foster."

The screen switched from showing Lisa to a helicopter view of wrecked cars along a four-lane highway, traffic snarled in both directions. Several people outside vehicles were frantically trying to help one person thrown from a car and others who appeared trapped inside. A white sheet covered a body that lay a considerable distance from the wreckage.

The anchor added, "There are initial reports of serious injuries and one fatality. All lanes of I-270 south are blocked. Police and ambulances are approaching the scene now and we will keep you updated on this breaking story."

Erin hit the mute button and flopped heavily on the bed's edge, an awful realization going through her. She had been wondering if it was possible for a week and now had her answer. Anna, Matt, Ryan, and Eric had somehow become a kind of new Ellorian Champions, replacing the real ones. The stakes had risen. Questions swirled. She had to help them.

Now it was absolutely critical that she find them the moment they returned.

Daniel knew something wasn't right, but then it didn't take a genius. It wasn't easy to control a drone with one hand, but he did well enough. He just had to give up performing elaborate tricks. And tricks were on his mind when the display camera showed his brother's car in front of the guest house, the trunk and passenger door open. He had first felt relieved and buzzed around the building for signs of what Ryan was doing, but there was no sight of him, so Daniel landed out of the way with the camera aimed at the house and the motion sensor on. He'd see when his brother reappeared. If he did.

The police had shown up last night, looking for him. Neither Daniel nor his parents had been surprised, having seen footage of Matt vanishing on camera and confirmed reports about Anna's car on I-270. Those first moments with the cops had been awful. Daniel wasn't the only one who had feared the worst, his mother nearly collapsing at the possibility that the police had arrived to tell them their oldest son was dead. But the fatality had been a female, as were the other passengers, though no one had been publicly identified, pending the families being informed. They hadn't even been willing to say whether the bodies came from Anna's car or the dozen other vehicles involved.

They had been calling Ryan all night and trying to track his phone with no luck, which didn't surprise Daniel. Their parents had installed GPS trackers on Ryan's car and phone after the Stonehenge Four had returned from three weeks of being missing. It had led to some arguments with Ryan complaining that he felt like a prisoner. He had finally disabled them.

Daniel had assumed that his brother was gone, like Matt and Anna. Eric hadn't been found either, his last known whereabouts being his job, where he had finished for the day and was apparently planning to leave, according to his boss. And then suddenly he was gone, with no sign of actually walking out. His disappearance had not been witnessed or reported until the police noticed that two of the Stonehenge Four had gone missing and they tried tracking down the other two, leading to Ryan and Eric. The police found the latter's car at work, his boss showing the officers the abandoned belongings, as Eric had just finished teaching a class in his karate clothes and not changed yet. He was now presumed missing. So was Ryan.

Now Daniel called to his nurse, Susan, a young brunette he enjoyed flirting with. He wanted help and a witness for their excursion down to the guest house. It was time to see what his brother was up to down there. He hadn't believed anything Ryan and Eric had said the other day due to their joking tone. His older brother was hiding something but had never lied to him. Or he didn't think so anyway. The big guy could be irritating like any sibling, but Daniel trusted him. He wasn't hard to get a read on, really, unlike Eric.

"What do you need, hon?" Susan asked as she arrived from another room. He never grew tired of the East Baltimore accent and predilection for calling him that.

"Keep this between us, but I just found Ryan's car at the guest house. We need to head down there."

"Um. Okay. Are we expecting trouble of any kind?"

They had discussed the situation. "Pretty sure no. I don't think he's there, but I want to see what's going on and I can only get to the first floor."

"Sure. I'll get my purse, by which I mean gun."

"I love it when you're sexy," he called as she walked away.

Within minutes, they were beside Ryan's black Dodge Charger, where his car and house keys lay on the pavement beside it. Exchanging a wary look with the nurse, Daniel had her tell him what was inside the backseat. He could already see that the trunk was empty.

"Just a couple boxes." She pulled a long, rectangular one out. On the side were pictured arrows with red fletching.

"What the hell does he need with those?"

"Taking up archery?"

Daniel put his hands on the drone's remote and made it start up again, piloting it into the open front door of the guest house. That Ryan had not meant to leave was clear, but Daniel still didn't expect foul play. Even so, sending in the drone with its camera was better than going in personally. He saw more boxes inside but no people, including the second floor as he moved it around everywhere but the basement, as the door was closed. He landed the drone there.

"Okay, let's go in."

He had wondered if he'd been seeing right through the camera, but there was no denying it now. Someone had stacked books on medieval customs and warfare on a table. A dozen swords of varying lengths lay atop the Persian rugs. Several round and rectangular steel or wooden shields leaned against a wall. Three Western-style horseback riding saddles were in one corner where helmets, crops, horse blankets and more were stacked. Four boxes held what looked like long bows, and another four were crossbows, each of slightly different styles and none of them looking modern. That contrasted with a big screen TV hanging on the wall, a make-shift entertainment center filled with electronics that weren't plugged in, the boxes everything had come in still here. The tables for a living room set were haphazardly placed, possibly because they were waiting on missing couches.

"Is this all for RenFest?" Susan asked, picking up a sword by the hilt.

Scowling, Daniel replied, "I doubt it. I mean, he's been doing it for years and never needed all of this stuff here."

"What's with the TV? It's like he's setting up to hang out here or something. Is he moving down here?"

"No. I don't think so. He didn't say anything. And I doubt he would start with all of these things. I mean you don't furnish a house with weapons, then go furniture shopping."

"True, but your brother is weird."

Daniel saw light from under the basement door. "Can you open it? I'll send the drone."

Wordlessly, Susan did, and he piloted the device down the stairs to the wide cellar. His first priority was again verifying that no one was here, which he did. He was dying to go down himself but had her go without him, as she confirmed what the camera showed him. A punching bag hung in one corner, as did another, maybe for kicking. They had set two treadmills and a stair climber up. Several gym mats were stacked in one corner, but nearly half the floor had been covered with them. Someone had stacked several archery targets along with their stands. The biggest surprise was two armor stands, one holding the suit of plate mail that Ryan wore at the Renaissance Festival, the other empty.

Now Daniel knew his brother was lying. The last 24 hours had proven it, but he'd been certain all along that they weren't telling the truth about what happened at Stonehenge. "We don't remember" is such a lame excuse and exactly what he might have said if something odd had happened. But what he really wanted to know now was why it looked like they were preparing to train in using these weapons? Where had they gone? And why?

He couldn't help saying it aloud as Susan returned to his side. "What the hell are they doing?"

THE ORBS OF DOMINION

Thoughts rushed through Anna's head with the same chaotic intensity as the roaring of sound and light that accompanied a summoning. Her friends. The car. The highway. Speed. And no one at the helm. She still clenched her hands before her on a steering wheel that wasn't there anymore. Her right foot wasn't placed against an accelerator, but beneath her as she stood, yelling "no" over and over. The concerned faces of Eric, Ryan, and Matt before her made another round of thoughts tear through her. A quest. Danger. People watching. Their expectations. The ruse of being the Ellorian Champions. Their startled reaction to her arriving screaming. She stopped herself just as the summoning ended.

Her breath came hard, eyes darting around for peril like the last time. The Quest Ring stood with its light fading. A dozen calm people outside it. No weapons drawn. A gray partly cloudy sky above, the sun nearly overhead. A castle in the distance. Mountains behind it, dramatic hills and a river between. A hill beneath their feet. No more people. No creatures. No danger. Not yet.

Anna twisted her back to those who had summoned them, trying to slow her breathing, calm her face, and wipe the panic from her eyes. Eric came around to her, one firm hand on her arm through the now familiar white robe of Eriana.

"What happened?" he whispered.

"I was driving."

"What?"

"70 miles an hour, the highway." She heard Ryan step closer in the golden armor, his boot scraping the smooth stones beneath their feet.

"Were you alone?"

She shook her head, too afraid of what was happening back on Earth to say it aloud.

"Oh shit," muttered Ryan.

"Okay," started Eric, "we can talk about that in a minute. There are people looking at us. We need to act like heroes and—"

"I can't," she said, shaking her head.

"You don't have to say anything. Ryan."

"Right." The big guy turned away, his voice regal and cheerful as he said, "I apologize. We needed a moment to discuss something urgent that was happening before your summons."

A gravelly voice replied, "Of course. We understand that we have pulled you from your lives and you may time to adjust. We are deeply sorry for any inconvenience, but our matter is most urgent."

"The quests always are!" Ryan said heartily, and Anna thought his time playing a knight at the Renaissance Festival had prepared him well for what he was doing. He sounded convincing. The thought made her pull herself together, and she turned to face their summoners, forcing a smile. There was nothing she could do about her friends now anyway, but she felt sick. Only now did she notice Ryan didn't have Lord Korrin's lance with him, so at least they wouldn't be facing dragons. From what they knew, the Quest Rings supplied them with likely weapons from whatever stash of them the real Ellorian Champions had somewhere, presumably on their own world of Elloria.

Gesturing toward one side, away from the river valley below, the speaker said, "If you are ready, lords and lady, it is important that we quickly get out of sight."

"Are we in danger?" Eric asked, scanning around them.

"Not precisely. All will become clear in a moment. Please follow us."

Ryan and Eric went first, leaving Anna beside Matt, whose concerned eyes were on her. She hooked one arm with his as they followed.

Amid the summoning spell, they were always facing each other so far these three times, and sometimes they arrived in that position, but once they had been turned in the same direction so that they faced what she thought of as the opening of a Quest Ring. This is where they went now, and she noticed this ring was once again different from the others in various details. It reminded her of Greek architecture, with white pillars of equal height all around, each one standing on a stone wall and supporting a matching, circular top that was open to the sky. Three steps at the front led them to a marble path. The way continued straight, where the castle waited in the distance, a town before it, but they turned away and followed a branching path into the trees. Twenty paces away awaited a two-story stone building, vegetation partially overgrowing it.

No one spoke on the way, giving Anna time to assess their companions. Her eyes went to a tall, regal, striking woman in tight-fitting red leather that matched her wavy, red hair. She oozed intelligence, sophistication, and strength as she strode ahead of them. Two similarly dressed men trailed her. One wore deep blue, his hair stark white. The other man wore dark green and had brown hair. They seemed to defer to the woman. None of them carried anything, and yet Anna sensed they were very dangerous. She was certain they were magical in some way they would likely reveal.

The wizard who had summoned them had a gravelly voice, a balding head of graying black hair, and walked with a slight limp, but she couldn't tell much else from behind. His brown wooden staff thumped on the marble as he went, a purple robe brushing the stone.

A slender but muscled man in silver plate mail sauntered beside him, a sword at one hip, a dagger on the other. A helmet with a white plume of feathers had been tied to one waist. Short brown hair and a close beard framed a rugged face with sharp eyes. Anna sensed he held a high rank compared to the dozen, less ostentatiously dressed warriors behind her and Matt. No one else was present, including anyone who seemed like royalty. Due to this and the attempt at getting them out of the castle's line of sight, she questioned whether someone did not approve of their summoning.

As they approached the building, Anna saw several very large saddles on the ground, similar to ones for horses but so large—the size of a compact car—that she wondered what enormous creatures they could be for. The leather-clad trio entered first without a sense of danger, followed by the wizard and the silver-armored knight, the four Earth friends, and finally most of the other warriors, two remaining outside and guarding the doors, which were left open.

The building's interior seemed comprised of a single principal room, two open doors leading to smaller ones not much bigger than a closet. A staircase ascended to the upper level, old tapestries flying from the walls, no other decorations in sight. The room was functional and from the proximity of the Quest Ring, she wondered if it had been designed specially for them, and whether they had ever summoned the real Ellorian Champions before. No one seemed to second guess their identities, so maybe not.

They remained on the first floor, where a broad, rectangular table with cushion-less wooden chairs around it filled the center. Everyone stayed standing but the champions, wizard, and silver-armored warrior, who spoke first.

"I am Novir, Commander of the King's Guard," he began, voice confident until he added with a frown, "or what's left of it. The wizard is Derin. You stand in the Kingdom of Minari, on the planet Rovell, near Castle Arking."

Ryan said, "I assume you know us, but I am Lord Korrin." He then introduced the others and asked, "What happened to the King's Guard? How many of you are left?"

Novir answered, "The rest of the guard still live, we think, but their minds are not their own anymore. More will become plain as we tell you what has led up to your summoning. Those you see with us here are not the King's Guard, but the most trusted men from among our other forces."

The wizard Derin spoke up. "First, I must apologize for our haste in leaving the Quest Ring. The king has not been informed of your summons and would not be pleased, but we have done the right thing and he cannot see it, with good reason."

"Is his mind also not his own now?" Eric asked.

"Yes. The Orbs of Dominion have enthralled him."

Anna grew alarmed. Would they find themselves similarly enthralled, whatever that meant? They had already lost control of their physical lives, but now their minds might be taken over, too?

"We are not familiar with these Orbs of Dominion," Ryan said. "Please tell us more."

Derin nodded. "Of course. No one is certain who invented the orbs, but there are believed to be two, a master orb and a slave. Legend says that the creator, a wizard, kept the master for himself and sent his apprentice to ensnare rulers with the slave orb, which was mounted atop a staff. This allowed it to enthrall individuals or large groups if it was raised high enough for them to see. Somehow, both the wizard and his apprentice came to ruin, and the orbs passed through various hands before disappearing. Today, it is unknown who has the master, but it has clearly been activated. We know where the slave orb is, and this is what you are here to retrieve and deactivate, by destroying it if possible."

"How do they work?" Matt asked, leaning forward, green eyes intent.

"The master orb is like a communication orb, allowing the one controlling it to interact visually and verbally across great distances. But it only works with the slave orb, which is called this because anyone looking into the slave can have their mind taken over by the one who controls the master."

Matt asked, "Does this control continue after the slave orb is removed from their presence or deactivated?"

"Yes. It is permanent or can be until the master orb releases the individual. This happens if the one controlling the orbs dies or relinquishes control somehow."

Eric observed, "And the Minarin King has looked into the slave orb and is now under someone's control."

"Yes."

"And you do not know who controls him?"

"We do not. But your quest does not include determining this, though it would be helpful to know."

Eric asked, "How did this happen?"

The warrior Novir answered, "The slave orb was being kept in the nearby dwarven Kingdom of Hamarven, deep beneath the mountains. Only a few dwarves knew this. It was among various rare, precious, or dangerous items under heavy guard. We do not know how long this has been true, and there has been so little mention of the orbs for centuries that many do not believe they are real. Many have never heard of them.

"According to the dwarves, the slave orb suddenly turned on after so many years of inactivity. The dwarves guarding it were so surprised that they mistakenly stepped closer and became ensnared. Whoever took control convinced them to bring other guards nearer, and one by one, those under its control grew in number so that they could walk out of where the dwarves kept it, carrying it before them, ensnaring more as they went."

Anna inwardly groaned at how easily more people could be affected. It was brilliant and awful. "I can see why these are so dangerous."

Novir nodded. "Yes. They brought it before the queen and captured her mind. The king passed years ago. We do not know how many among the dwarves the orb enslaved, and there is some question as to how many people can be controlled. It is unknown how the orbs really affect someone, but we suspect that the enslaved just become willing to take orders. We aren't sure how much they are aware of."

"Maybe it's like the orb hypnotizes them," mused Matt.

Novir didn't seem to understand the remark and continued as if Matt hadn't said it. "Before long, the dwarves arrived in our kingdom with the orb. We are not sure what their intent was, whether they came to ensnare our king or if they only did so on their way north. The result is the same."

"They succeeded." Eric surmised.

"Yes. We are on friendly terms with the dwarven kingdom, and so no one thought any harm would come from their request to meet with our king. Once the audience was granted, they unveiled the orb, and all were lost to it. I was not on duty or else I would have been among them. I had heard of the request and was en route to the throne room when I learned something was amiss. There are ways into that room, known to only a few, and I used one. I saw the thrall the orb had cast over everyone. I also heard a voice commanding King Orin and him obeying."

"What was the command?"

"To assist in the orb's travel further northwest to a place known as Bolin Hill, where the dwarves were to give the orb to someone else."

"Who?"

"It was not specified, but we now know, as you will see. The power of the slave orb allowed the dwarves to leave unmolested, due to the King's Guard members enforcing the king's orders. The orb did not enthrall all of my men, as not all were on duty. Regardless, in their departure, the dwarves ensnared anyone they encountered, leaving some behind, and taking others with them. Some who departed with them were our finest warriors. I sought Denir at once and on learning of my description of the orb and what occurred, he surmised we are dealing with the Orbs of Dominion."

Denir spoke up. "As you know, we must attempt to solve our own problems before attempting to summon yourselves, or the Quest Rings do not bring you."

"What do you mean?" Anna asked. She thought Lorian might have explained this, but she wasn't sure. So much had happened that she couldn't retain it all. Then she realized others expected to know and struggled to justify her question, making up something. "What I mean is that there are variations in the way the Quest Rings work. They are not all precisely the same. We prefer not to assume but get confirmation on how a specific one is performing, especially if we use it to return."

Denir looked intrigued. "I was unaware of this. Thank you. Quite interesting devices." He looked at Matt, who nodded as if to thank him. "I cast the summoning spell and answered the questions I was asked about the quest and what we had done to resolve the matter ourselves. Upon completion, the Quest Ring's oracle, I believe you call it?"

"Correct," said Matt, though the expression was news to Anna and likely him, too.

"The oracle agreed the quest was valid and brought you here moments later."

"I see," said Anna, wishing she could see this in action but suspecting she never would. "Thank you."

"Of course. As I was saying, we explained to the Quest Ring our previous attempts to resolve this. Our first attempt at securing the slave orb was as the dwarves fled, but this led to nothing but more enthralled warriors and we had to back away. We lost over two hundred good men and women to the orb. Our second attempt was another failure, but one that provided insight into how dire the circumstances truly are."

"What happened?"

Novir said. "We sent a handful of men and one wizard to the rendezvous point, Bolin Hill. They arrived first because the dwarves and our captured men were on foot. It gave them time to see who they were meeting."

He exchanged a look with Denir, and Anna sensed they had debated whether to reveal something. "We need to know everything you can tell us," she said.

Denir sighed heavily. "We learned that the Orb of Dominion was bound for the Lords of Fear."

The Earth friends shared an inquisitive look, and Novir spoke up. "As you were, uh, missing for a few years, you may not have heard of them. They began making a name for themselves since then."

"Who are they?"

"An assassin, a necromancer, a sorcerer, and an undead knight."

Eric smirked. "Sounds like a charming group."

Anna knew he was kidding but had a terrible feeling about this. She had already encountered one undead knight on Honyn when it grabbed her and announced she would be its bride after death. Her skin prickled with goosebumps from the awful cold that had settled in her bones. The memory was one of many that sometimes kept her up at night. She brushed the thought aside with an effort, just as she kept trying to ignore her fears about what had happened to her friends when she vanished from the car. Focusing on the details of the impending quest helped her some. "Why are they called the Lords of Fear? Are they actual lords?"

The wizard said, "Yes. Or they were. Some have been stripped of their titles."

"Why?" she asked.

"Nothing good. They sometimes assassinate royalty or other prominent figures, or extort them. They have started wars between kingdoms. They have assisted others in achieving evil. And they go after powerful supernatural items like these orbs, so much so that people on various worlds have taken to hiding them from this threat."

"So they operate across worlds. Are they from this one?"

"They are not, and we believe that, now that they have what they came for, that they are attempting to leave with the orb. It cannot remain in their hands. It is dangerous regardless, but with the Lords of Fear using it, there is indeed much to fear. Their methods are nightmarish and true to their nickname. The assassin is not above poison, for example, whether this is given directly, in food or drink, or on her weapons. Should you fight her, you must be certain not to let a blade slice you."

"It's a woman?" Anna asked in surprise.

Denir said, "Yes, and she was the daughter of a countess, her father being an Earl who has since disowned her."

Eric leaned forward. "Do you know anything else that might help us understand her? We might be able to use the details to our advantage."

Novir spoke up. "She is known to love both men and women, but same-gender relations carry a penalty of death in Nysuun, even for royals. As teens, her and the princess she loved were condemned. After watching her love die by fire, Kori escaped the same fate and disappeared. There has been much speculation about her history since, but we know she joined a secretive group that trained her in hand-to-hand fighting, weapons, and other skills an assassin needs. But they would not let her seek revenge. It appears she was bound, perhaps supernaturally, by a pledge to them, but she freed herself from it and got her revenge. The organization tried to kill her for this, so she did the same to them, but whereas they failed, she was successful. The group is no more."

Anna couldn't hide her disbelief. "She killed *all* of them?"

"Yes. Kori of Nysuun is among the most ruthless women alive."

Anna tried to mute her intimidation. If the others were just as deadly, she and her friends might be in worse trouble with this quest than it seemed. Not sure she wanted to know, she asked, "Who are the others?"

"The sorcerer is Lord Garian of Ormund."

Ryan perked up. "Ormund? On Honyn?"

Novir turned to him. "Yes. We understand you closed the Dragon Gate there recently."

"We did. We met someone from Ormund along the way."

"Cirion," muttered Anna, remembering the dashing man who first tried to seduce her, then interfered with their quest to close the gate. He was trouble of more than one kind. "Hopefully, he won't appear. Who is Lord Garian?"

Novir answered, "He was the prince and heir to the throne, but no longer. His father stripped him of his peerage."

Anna cocked an eyebrow. "What did he do to cause *that*?"

Denir replied, "While magic is not quite forbidden in the kingdom, it is viewed with suspicion and not openly practiced. When Garian discovered he had the talent in his teens, he secretly sought training and received it, but his master had plans of his own."

A scowling Matt asked, "To control him?"

Novir answered, "He wanted power over Garian once the prince became king. I suspect the master treated Garian poorly, knowing the prince could tell no one."

Denir interjected, "Yes, and it is this, coupled with learning dark wizardry, that seemed to alter Lord Garian's heart. His personality was seen to change even before the truth of his secret life and talent was discovered. Having a member of the royal family practicing magic was not well received, and perhaps it was the impetuous nature of youth that led him to publicly flaunt his skills. We believe he did this to show that it was of no danger to anyone, but the king, his father, did not view it that way."

Matt finished, "And so they stripped him of his titles."

Denir nodded. "And banished. I expect he will one day return to claim the throne and abolish laws against magic."

Matt said, "I can't say I blame him. He doesn't sound like he's that bad of a guy."

Denir sighed. "He enjoys sympathy in some quarters, but his actions since then leave little doubt that he can only be a hero to unsavory people. He is very charming, as if the spell he weaves is one of seduction more than wizardry. You should know that you will not identify him by a sorcerer's attire, for he seeks to hide his talents and skills, I think more to surprise people than from shame, though perhaps his past inspires it. Do not look for a wizard's robe or staff, but a well-dressed man of royal refinement in a tunic and trousers, the ingredients for spells discreetly on his person. He keeps a wand up one sleeve should he need it. Beware the Dragon's Fire Wand, for it is powerful."

Eric observed, "You refer to him as a sorcerer, not a wizard."

"Yes, but there is no difference, though sorcerer has a connotation of using dark arts."

Anna wondered what he was willing to do. She recalled that Matt had two of Soliander's spell books in the bag he always arrived with. The techie had said one had seemingly more innocent or benevolent spells, while the other tended toward dangerous and possibly immoral. She thought of it every time her friend was looking in that one, wondering what he was learning. She had wanted to look through it herself, but Matt tended to find excuses for secrecy, which only made her more curious, but not quite concerned. Still, when he performed a spell, she sometimes wondered which book he got it from.

"Speaking of dark arts," she began, "who is the necromancer?"

Denir began, "Lord Areon the Soul Stealer was a priest who married into royalty, but lost his title when his wife was murdered. He was too late to heal her and began practicing necromancy to not only resurrect his wife, but to get revenge on her killers, as they were executed too mercifully for his tastes."

Grimacing, Anna asked, "Did he succeed?"

Denir looked unsure how to answer. "Stories conflict as to whether he was successful, but I believe he did not reanimate his love in satisfactory condition, and they remain apart."

Novir added, "They banished him for this. There is a bounty on his head. His god forsook him so that he cannot heal anymore."

"Did that push him further into necromancy, so he still had power?"

Denir looked at her approvingly. "Yes. He has since shown little regard for life, or death, and has become powerful in his quest to restore his love."

"That's tragic and very creepy," Anna remarked, shuddering. No one should love so deeply as to become corrupted throughout their being. Sometimes letting go was better, however painful. But then she had never known such love for another or herself. Could it really be so wonderful, then so awful? Part of her didn't want to know, but she was sort of curious. She supposed she couldn't really judge this lord, but if he was doing unholy things to others, that would be enough to condemn him in her eyes.

Breaking her thoughts, Matt asked, "What sorts of things is he capable of? Raising the dead? Defying it himself? Controlling them?"

Denir replied, "All of that and more. Communication with the departed has given him vast knowledge found in no library. That may have been how they knew of the orb. That said, this communication is difficult to achieve, as not all deceased are accessed as easily as some. We will never know."

"Novir," began Ryan, "Do you have a mace or flail I can borrow? My sword may be of limited use against the undead, assuming he has a bunch with him."

"Of course." He gestured to one warrior, who had a spiked, black mace on one hip. They gave this to him.

"Thank you," said Ryan. "This may also be useful with the undead knight, as well. I don't suppose he became that way because of the necromancer?"

Denir fixed him with an appraising look before turning to Matt. "Indeed. And this story may be of special interest to Soliander."

Matt cocked an eyebrow. "Why is that?"

"The undead knight is technically King of Aranor now. That is your home kingdom, is it not?"

Matt nodded slowly. "Tell me."

"Lord Voth was an ambitious knight, second-in-command of the knights, in service to the king. Some in the knighthood believed the king had grown weak, spoiled, and uninterested in the greatness some wanted of their monarch. And so they staged a successful coup, killing the king and much of the royal family."

"That is a betrayal of their oath as knights," Ryan observed, frowning.

Novir smirked. "There was worse to come. Voth's commander assumed the throne, but not for long. Voth killed him and took his place."

Denir added, "Yes, but he miscalculated. The population had supported the coup due to the popularity of the commander he had just killed, and they were irate at his murder at the hands of Lord Voth."

"Good for them," Ryan said. "What happened?"

"They swarmed the castle, and when Lord Voth, now King of Aranor, ordered his knights to slay the mob, they refused, seeing him as a worse ruler than those they had executed. And so they opened the gates and let the mob have Lord Voth."

Eric laughed and held up one apologetic hand for his reaction. "No honor among thieves, we say on... we've heard said on another planet. Seems like he caused his own downfall."

"Yes," agreed Denir. "He does not elicit much sympathy, only terror. The royalty had access to an ice dragon, and so his punishment was to have it breathe on him, encasing him in ice and killing him. This resulted in one of his nicknames, the Ice King."

Matt asked, "And he somehow escaped from this?"

Novir nodded. "With help. He was on display in the throne room of Aranor by the new king. An unknown wizard and the necromancer Areon reincarnated him as undead. Lord Voth had his vengeance and reclaimed the throne, the room now perpetually covered in ice, the kingdom ruled by a prime minister because Lord Voth seems to have interests elsewhere."

Denir added, "All that he touches dies, for the power of the grave is the only thing flowing in his veins. Aranor is now called the Kingdom without a King, though it technically has one."

"Is he bound to the necromancer?"

"That is unknown. He appears to have his freedom and voluntarily works with the other Lords of Fear. Together for several years now, we saw them meddling in many kingdoms on quite a few worlds. Sometimes they work alone, in which case it can be harder to determine whether they cause something, but they are unmistakable when together."

Anna asked, "Who was the wizard who freed Lord Voth along with the necromancer?"

"There are many rumors about this, but no one is certain."

"Is it safe to believe that this person is the one who has the master Orb of Dominion?"

Denir replied, "No, though it may well be. We could find out if we let them succeed in their journey, but we cannot allow that."

Anna agreed but said nothing. These Lords of Fear sounded like the evil version of themselves, but without quests binding them. Did they always work for the same person, doing missions? Were they genuinely bound or only by a promise? The difference mattered because the latter can always be broken. Maybe these Lords of Fear weren't as well understood as the Ellorian Champions. Perhaps there was more to them. Now she was curious but doubted they would sit down and chat about it all. How could they get information directly from the lords?

"What is happening now?" she asked.

Denir answered, "Our second attempt at recovering the orb failed because our men recognized the Lords of Fear and knew they could not possibly beat them. When the dwarves and other enthralled arrived, they gave the orb to Lord Voth, then went with them. They and the rest of our captured forces are heading toward Ortham, a large city in the Kingdom of Gisla to the north. It has a portal to other worlds. We cannot be certain this is their goal, but we suspect it is."

Novir interjected, "Our contacts in the city have confirmed that the lords arrived on this planet via this gate some days prior to all of this. There was strong suspicion about it, but it only seemed known after we learned their identity at Bolin Hill."

"Wait," started Ryan, "how could an undead knight just walk through? Isn't either side guarded? Wouldn't someone see him and stop him? Or did people try to get killed?"

Denir answered, "We can easily identify most undead because of their appearance. However, Lord Voth does not look undead. Being frozen in ice killed and preserved him. Once raised from the dead, he does not decay, which is common of undead, as you know. Their bodies remain as they were at the moment of reanimation, likely by the design of the forces used to raise them. Otherwise, they would continue to fall apart and the problem of their existence would soon resolve itself as they become a pile of bones."

"Good point," admitted Ryan, then added apologetically, "Eriana and Soliander likely knew that, but I forget that sort of thing."

Cocking an eyebrow about that, Novir said, "They arrived and walked away, as the others give no casual observer reason to be concerned. But people noticed the cold from Lord Voth, and his startling blue eyes, rumored to be made of ice. Guards followed, and eventually he walked on grass that died under his feet. Between that and his healthy appearance, and the known description of the others, the Lords of Fear were identified even before we contacted Ortham to ask."

"Is it known in Ortham that they are returning to the city and have the orb?"

"Yes," Novir answered. "We consulted with them on this and agreed that the path from the city gates to the portal must be evacuated, but it is unknown how successful they will be. The population likely doesn't understand the danger. We must assume the lords intend to hold the orb aloft and ensnare anyone who sees it."

"The guy controlling the master orb has to be watching through it, though, right?"

"Yes. We are assuming he is keeping close watch on matters as they unfold."

Matt remarked, "I assume those in Ortham can close the gate."

Denir replied, "Yes, and they have left it open until the last moment, if needed. We are on friendly enough terms with Gisla Kingdom, at least on this front. Our plan is that all of you will arrive before then so that closing the portal is unnecessary. It takes some effort to reopen it, though perhaps less so if you will help, Soliander."

Matt said, "Of course. Is this the only portal they can use?"

"No, but it seems the likely one. As you know, travel between worlds requires more power than most can afford or wield, if they are wizards. We do not know if Lord Garian has such power, but maybe not. We expect they are attempting to leave the planet this way. They must be stopped, the orb taken away, preferably destroyed."

Novir said. "As the king knows nothing of your quest, you can expect no real help from the kingdom, sadly, as our king has issued orders to not interfere with the lords. And no one should be told who you are. Only those in this room know the truth."

"We understand," Ryan said, but Anna thought he said it unconvincingly. These men were risking their lives to free their king and kingdom, and their understanding of the gravity of the situation needed to be conveyed better. She was going to say something when the king's guardsman spoke first.

Novir added, "While we are doing the right thing, it would be treason until the king's mind is his own again."

Anna sensed the weight on him and wanted to reassure him. "He will see that it is good then. No one will learn our identities or purpose from us. We already have other names we can use, such as Anna for myself." Hiding the truth in plain sight seemed bold but obvious.

"Thank you, my lady." Denir placed four small bags on the table, each clinking. "We do not expect you will need to purchase supplies, but we know the unexpected happens. Please accept these coins and gems to satisfy any needs that may arise."

Ryan and Eric sat nearest him and took a pouch each for themselves, giving the others to Matt and Anna. She knew better to look inside, as did Ryan. She suspected Eric did too, but he did it anyway, and Matt dumping the contents on the table did not surprise her. She thought it was just boyish greed, but then he asked a smart question that made her feel sorry for doubting him.

He asked, "How much is this in these kingdoms? Is it enough to attract attention? Should we be careful showing this much?"

Denir said, "We thought of that. The coins are not platinum, which would be noticed at once except among royalty. There is only a little gold, one piece each, because they would also notice this in poor quarters. I recommend finer places if the need arises, which we do not expect. You should use the silvers and coppers."

"And the gems?"

"Emergency use only, and only in a city at a reputable trader. Use them out of sight, not in a main room where others would see the transaction."

Eric nodded. "Got it. I've been meaning to ask, how big are these orbs?"

"Half the size of a human head."

"How do we stop ourselves from being ensnared by them?"

Matt regarded him. "I think I might know a spell." He lifted the bag with Soliander's spell books in it and pulled out one in black leather with gold writing, the one Anna knew to have "nicer" spells in it, as opposed to the one with silver markings. Everyone waited quietly as he flipped through the pages. "Found it. It protects against any attempt to read the mind. I remembered if after what happened on Honyn, when I, uh, ran into that wizard who tried to do that. If I had cast this spell on myself beforehand, he may not have been able to learn anything."

Anna asked, "Can it be cast on more than one person?"

"One at a time." Matt's eyes scanned the page. "Wait, I can do it on a group."

Denir asked, "May I ask the name of this spell? I don't believe we have such a one on Rovell."

"*Mind Shield*," replied Matt. He let the wizard look at the spell and Anna wondered if sharing like that was a good idea or not, but then it wasn't an offensive one. Maybe they needed to talk over something like that, and establish some grounds rules before giving a dangerous spell to a world that didn't already have it. It might be like introducing an animal into an ecosystem that developed without it, destroying a delicate balance.

The wizard looked over the spell. "It says you need eyes from a blind fish, two eyes for each person. Do you have any with you?"

Matt shook his head. "I don't think so. I will have to check my supplies."

Denir said, "We have similar fish. This spell looks like it would work here on this planet. You are more experienced traveling between worlds than I, but most spells from other worlds work here as long as you have the needed materials, or can substitute them."

"The substitutions typically work?" Eric asked.

"Yes."

"Where could we get these fish eyes? I don't suppose someone sells them?"

"No. They are not commonly needed. There is an underwater lake to the southeast in the mountains, from where you could get them, but it is in the opposite direction from where the Lords of Fear have gone. I'm afraid that puts us under great pressure, but it might be needed."

Novir spoke up. "I know of another place north of Valegis, a mountain town. It is on the way, less of a detour, but it is more dangerous."

"How so?"

"The Kirii Cave not only has the large, batlike Kirii in it, but there is a leviathan in the waters, which is why I have heard of the place, as have most. We would have to be careful to not disturb any of kirii, but I think it is worth the risk. Four champions of your power could easily defeat anything we awaken. It lies within another dwarven kingdom, in a valley of the Galla Mountains."

"How do we get the fish?" Anna asked, imagining the famous Ellorian Champions standing around with fishing poles, the idea almost making her smile despite all of her worries. "Is there something faster than a net?"

Derin responded and turned to Matt, "A simple cantrip can round them up with little trouble. You know of it?"

Matt appeared to think for a moment and shook his head. "Perhaps you can show me."

"It would honor me to teach the great Soliander the merest of spells."

Eric said, "Okay, so given time being an issue, how do we get to this cave and then the city quickly?"

Novir gestured to the three leather clad companions, who had remained silent as they leaned against a wall listening to all of this. "The dragons will take us."

CHAPTER FIVE

THE KIRII CAVE

Ryan arched an eyebrow and turned to look at the humans that were apparently shape-shifting dragons, just like the ones on Honyn, except that none of those had been civil, just murderous toward any that were not their kind. The male in blue smirked at him, the one in green looked bored, and the female in red sauntered toward him, her intense gaze locked onto his. She seemed fiery and sexy, powerful and sleek and dangerous. He had only seen two dragons before, both golden, and each had tried to kill him. She had no obvious weapons with her, but he doubted this would matter. Only the calm with which Novir revealed their nature kept him sitting still instead of rising to face a potential threat.

She stopped before him in an aggressive yet alluring stance that made the word "vixen" pop into his mind. "Fear not, Dragon Slayer," she said in a rich alto. "We know your reputation, but we also know you only kill the ones who deserve it. And there are none such here." She leaned over and ran a finger along his jaw, leaving a trail of heat as the scent of roasted embers filled his nostrils. "We're not even offended by your nickname."

Clearing his throat uncomfortably and amazed that a dragon was hitting on him, Ryan said, "I have others, like the Pride of Andor."

"And do you feel pride, Lord Korrin?"

"To be talking to you? Absolutely."

She smiled then, all the way to her stunning eyes, and he felt certain that, by some miracle, he had just flattered a dragon. A freakin' dragon.

She added, "You will ride me, Pride of Andor." Hearing Eric quietly laugh, Ryan shot him an amused yet stern look to keep his mouth shut. "One other can accompany you, as we each can take two."

"Eriana, if it pleases you."

The dragon looked at her and nodded. "It does."

Denir said, "The dragons rarely involve themselves in the affairs of others on Rovell, but they recognize the threat that the orbs pose for all, including them. Three have agreed to assist us."

The red dragon strode to the head of the table as the other two came to flank her. She rested one arm around the neck of the one in blue leather. "I am Jolian. My brother Brazin here will carry Novir. The others will ride with our green friend, Sebast. We should leave now. I am curious to see this leviathan up close and see how she compares to us."

Eric caught Ryan's eye and said, "We would like a moment alone to discuss our plans."

Denir nodded. "Of course. We will step outside and prepare the saddles and what supplies you may need. Please join us when ready."

"Thank you."

Everyone filed out, Jolian the last to go with a last look at Ryan before closing the doors. They waited a moment for the voices to move farther away, and within a minute, the sound of enormous wings snapping in the air reached them, the ground shaking slightly from the steps of dragons.

Anna smirked at Ryan. "I think she likes you."

He tried to put her on the defensive instead of himself. "Jealous?"

She chuckled. "I can't compete with that."

They all laughed a moment before turning serious, with Eric, as usual, being the one to get down to business.

"Anna," he said, coming over to her, "how are you doing?"

Ryan thought she looked like she didn't want the reminder of what had happened on Earth as she pursed her lips. He shared her concern. The car had almost certainly crashed. The only question was how hurt her friends were. It might also cause another round of attention from the media, as if they needed more of that.

"Worried," she admitted. "There's nothing I can do. It's already too late."

Ryan came around to her, wanting to make her feel better. "Try to have faith. I know we've argued about God and all, and I'm sorry about that. You don't need faith in Him so much. I know it takes an effort, to just trust that everything may have worked out fine, nothing but minor bruises and scrapes. We can't know and letting our minds go to the worst possible outcomes... well, it won't help us all get back to find out the good news that everyone is fine."

She smiled, putting a hand on his arm. "Thank you, Ryan. You're right. I need to focus on our own problems right now."

"Yeah. Just, if you need anything about all of this, we're all here. You'd do the same, helping us if it had been us instead of you, so don't think you're being a burden or something. We're all family now."

"Yes," said Eric, "just physically protecting each other isn't enough. There's a lot more going on with all of us. Fear, uncertainty, not knowing what the hell we're doing."

"I hear you."

Ryan watched as Eric turned to the table and gestured for them to come over. "Memorize the map in case we get separated. Keep your own money bag, too."

They studied the map, noting roads and the compass direction, anything that might be useful should they be on their own to find their way back to the Quest Ring. The importance of not becoming lost or separated hung in the air.

To the east loomed the Galla Mountains that they had seen outside, the dwarven Kingdom of Hamarven toward its southern end and directly east of their position. Most of the Minari Kingdom lay west, but they'd never see it. To the northeast, past the Artem Woods, more of the mountains awaited with the town of Valegis nestled between the peaks. And nearly due west from there, outside the peaks on a plain, lay their ultimate destination of Ortham just over the border with Gisla Kingdom. If they got lost, it looked like all they had to do was walk south, parallel to the mountains. They had three options for that. Walking along the foothills risked attack from anything in them. Walking through Artem Woods to the west of the peaks offered the same. But still further west, miles from the trees, lay a road all the way from Ortham down to Castle Arking and the Quest Ring. As long as the mountains were on their left, they were heading south when coming back.

With the map memorized, Eric asked Matt, "Are you certain you can cast this *Mind Shield* spell?"

"Yeah, it doesn't look hard. Getting the fish eyes will be the issue."

"Without it," began Anna, folding her arms, "this Orb of Dominion really worries me. This may be our only protection against it."

Ryan had tried not to think what would happen if they became enthralled because the idea gave him the creeps, so he changed the subject. "Even with the spell, this sounds pretty difficult. I don't like the sound of these Lords of Fear at all."

Eric sighed. "Yeah, we should think about this on the way to this Kirii Cave. We need ideas, plans. The mace was a good idea, Ryan, but don't discount that soclarin sword you have. There's no telling what advantages the real Soliander gave it for fighting undead."

"True. I'll keep the mace as backup."

Eric asked, "Matt, Anna, what do we know about curing poisons? This assassin woman, Kori, sounds like serious trouble with poisoned blades."

Anna said, "In theory, I can heal that. I need to spend some time trying to communicate with a god. I must ask Novir and the others before we leave, if they have any choices for me, so I can try while we travel. I wish there was a way to do that as soon as I arrive on a quest. It's a lot of pressure to quickly know a god and reach out to one, get an answer."

"Yeah," agreed Matt. "At least the spells I remember will still work. My ability to shield us may be crucial. I suggest we stick together when we encounter these guys. They make me nervous already."

"Good idea. On the plus side, they don't know we're coming or that we have dragons with us. Oh, I just had an idea. When we get near the orb, we should pretend that we're enthralled by it and are under their control. This would gain their trust that we aren't a threat and maybe allow us to get close before they realize the truth."

Ryan clapped a hand on his shoulder. "That's brilliant. Love this idea."

"Do we need anything else before we get going?" Matt asked, as another thud shook the building.

Ryan smirked. "Yeah, dragon flying lessons. I think we should ask when we get out there, you know, like we usually do, as if like we're just confirming how things are on this world."

"That's good," Eric agreed. "They're intelligent, so it's not like we have to give commands from reins or something. Let's check that. Everyone ready?"

Ryan let the others go ahead of him as they left the room behind. He was undoubtedly the one to take on this Lord Voth, but the undead knight didn't concern him as much as the assassin and her poisoned blades. He imagined her targeting Anna or Matt. Maybe he and Eric needed to get Lord Voth and the assassin away from the other two as a tactic. He sighed, not sure what to do. The Lords of Fear had worked as a team, doing whatever they were up to for far longer than him and his friends. The dragons might be crucial, and after they finished at the Kirii Cave, they needed to discuss what options they provided. Surely they would do more than fly them around. They could affect the success of this quest.

The truth of this became apparent after they stepped from the building and followed a warrior around the corner, away from the Quest Ring. They walked onto the grass, a light autumn breeze stirring the pine trees. The season was the same as on Earth right now.

Behind the structure was an open field, shielded from the distant castle's view by trees, and it was here that the three dragons awaited in their natural forms. Rays of sun broke through the overcast sky, and Ryan saw that a sheer cliff drop awaited anyone foolish enough to venture too far to one side. A wide crevasse ran perpendicular and away from Castle Arking, a rushing river audible below, or perhaps it was a waterfall out of sight. Mist rose from the cliff, and in the distance, the thick Artem Woods stretched for miles, the leaves turning red, gold, and brown.

He turned to gaze at the dragons, the sheer size and mass of them as intimidating as the wicked talons, white teeth taller than him, and powerful wings. Not counting the necks, heads, and tails, each was bigger than a two-story, single-family home. He'd once seen a video of a jet engine flipping a car upside and hurling it away. The impression that the air blast from one stroke of a wing could send him off the cliff made him uneasy. Just one dragon could more than level the playing field against the Lords of Fear. He also wondered how a brother and sister dragon were different colors, and whether anything else about them was unique, but there was no time to ask.

The blue dragon stood nearest and was ready, silver eyes cold and indifferent as he gazed down at Ryan. Maybe he was imagining it, but he felt some disdain. Brazin's sister had been flirting with him. Was he irritated about it? Did dragons even fool around with humans? Was it possible? Or was the idea just insulting to one such as Brazin? Ryan wasn't sure but didn't feel comfortable with him and was glad to not be riding him.

Past him, Jolian rose to her feet and stretched her wings, a saddle now affixed to her, the warriors who had assisted with it stepping away toward the green dragon beyond. Jolian was noticeably larger than the other two, red scales gleaming as a ray of sun broke through the overcast sky to touch her. She took a deeper breath, the saddle girth expanding and contracting snugly as she did so, before a small burst of flames erupted from her nostrils, smoke curling up from them after it was over. She seemed satisfied and rested on her hindquarters, massive head turning to regard the Ellorian Champions. Her red eyes seemingly met Ryan's. It was hard to tell, given that they were bigger than a horse. But he saw kindness in them, which Brazin's baleful gaze made easier to recognize.

Warriors were now saddling the green dragon, Sebast, as he crouched to make it simpler for them. Ryan tried to watch in case he needed to do the same thing, but he couldn't see much from here. Was saddling a dragon noticeably different from a horse? It almost had to be.

Approaching Novir, who stood beside Denir, Ryan said, "So we've ridden dragons before, of course. It's just different across worlds."

Novir smiled. "Say no more." He led him toward Brazin, who cooperated by crouching and moving the nearer blue wing back. "You see the saddle is before the wings, of course. These may differ from others, but unlike a horse, dragons can at least tell you how to saddle them, if you must. They know where we are going and will largely take care of direction, but if you must, you can use the four straps to control the flight path. One each left, right, top, bottom. Use two at once as needed and flying straight and level means pulling on the top and bottom at together."

"Got it."

"I will lead the way, but they know where the Kirii Cave is, generally."

"Generally?" That was hardly good enough. What if something happened to Novir?

Novir winked and used a small rope ladder to climb the side of Brazin, settling into the seat and strapping himself into the saddle with a wide belt that he hooked to it once before and behind him. As he started pulling up the ladder, he yelled down. "Of course, I don't need to tell you to always strap yourself in first in case they decide to take flight. Things like a rope can wait!"

"I just wanted to see if *you* knew that!" Ryan joked. He wondered what other "obvious" tips he would not think of and learn the hard way. If he fell off a dragon high in the air, would it realize and be able to catch him? Finding out wasn't appealing.

As Anna went to get a scroll with information about gods from Denir, Ryan walked to Jolian. Was he supposed to pass in front of or behind Brazin? With horses, you avoided going behind unless you put a hand on their rump to let them know you were there. A startled horse had been known to kick and badly wound or even kill a fool. Would a dragon do it by accident, or would Brazin do it to Ryan on purpose? He wasn't sure what would happen as he neared the giant head, but the blue giant suddenly rose and let them pass under his neck.

"I think you need to go up first," Ryan said to Anna when she joined him. He took her hand to the rope ladder. "I can be in front for control, if I need it. I'm more used to, well, horses anyway."

"Yeah," she muttered, looking apprehensive. But she climbed the ladder and clambered into her seat behind his. Ryan followed, grinning. He hadn't been this close to a dragon before, except after he'd killed it. The expanding and contracting dragon body as she breathed him feel like he was dreaming, and despite the danger awaiting them, for the moment he didn't need to face it and marveled at what he was doing.

At the top, he found Anna trying to adjust the straps and so he briefly helped her, figuring it out. A wide belt opened on one side and had to be tightly cinched around the waist. Then two hooks fastened it to the saddle. She had already gotten her feet into two stirrups that were unlike those on a horse in that it firmly attached them to the saddle. This meant no trying to control the dragon with the feet. The stirrups seemed more like another way to brace yourself.

Keeping his weapons out of the way, he soon had himself situated and tested his own security of position, feeling reasonably satisfied, trying to ignore the forty-foot drop to the ground. It being so much worse than falling off a horse made him chuckle nervously. He thought that if he was going to get killed or worse on this quest, at least he was getting one hell of a ride first. He looked over to see Eric helping Matt get seated in the rear spot of Sebast's saddle, the two of them arguing a little. Jolian shifted beneath him the way horses do, the motions stronger because of her size, and he suddenly wondered if the others might get sick. That would be very un-champion like, puking from the back of a dragon, especially if Eric did it and Matt caught a face full as they flew. At the last minute, he untied his helmet and put it on for some protection from the wind. Or maybe it was for Anna behind him.

Jolian's neck twisted as she turned her enormous head back to him. "Are you ready, Pride of Andor?" Her voice boomed but sounded similar to when she was in human form.

"I was born ready," he said.

"Good."

With no other warning, Jolian took several giant steps forward, smote her wings once, and lifted off just enough to get past the cliff edge. And then they dove over it, the feeling like the first incredible drop of a rollercoaster. He heard Anna scream behind him like girls always did at the amusement park, but then Jolian straightened out and turned into the crevasse to soar just below its top. Wind buffeted Ryan's chest in a steady rush. The great snap of leathery wings was intermittent as they glided. Trees roared by on either side of them, above the canyon, and white water splashed hundreds of feet below among rocks, more trees, and a brief shoreline beside the river, the occasional four-legged animal startled into fleeing at the sight of them hurtling by. Jolian's head lifted a bit and the amount of wind striking Ryan suddenly dropped. Was she doing it on purpose, creating a pocket of calmer air?

After the initial exhilaration, Ryan took stock of himself and realized he was gripping the reins hard but not pulling on them, probably from many years of good horseback riding habits. He jammed his feet into the stirrups, his body tight. But he made himself relax and start gazing around. Turning in the saddle revealed Anna looking a little tense, but she smiled. Not far behind and gaining was Novir on the blue dragon, and just behind, the green one with Matt and Eric. He really wanted a GoPro to capture this experience for forever.

Moments later, the crevasse ended, the cliffs disappearing as they emerged from it, a shimming blue lake below, more forest all around it, snow-capped mountains in the distance. The sun streamed out in places, lighting up a fleet of fishing boats to one side. Suddenly a shadow appeared on Ryan and he looked up as Brazin overtook them, four enormous legs closer than comfortable, especially when he dove toward the water, the tail coming perilously close. Jolian followed him down, both dragons skimming their feet across the calm waters. The spray from Brazin struck Ryan, who stayed dry inside his armor. He laughed as they climbed again, the powerful wing strokes propelling them up faster than he would have believed. The ground fell away, and he wondered just how many thousands of feet in the air they were now. It became quieter, more peaceful, colder, and even boring as they disappeared into the clouds.

And then suddenly they were above them, bright sunlight all around, nothing visible but the sky above, the white moody clouds below, eddies from Brazin ahead of them whisking up. Nearer now than before, the tallest mountains poked above the serene view. Wanting to share it more, he reached behind him with one hand and after a moment, felt Anna's hand grip his. They rode this way for a long time, and as they went, Ryan considered the task before them, reminding himself of what training he had received in swordsmanship and battle tactics.

The batlike kirii at the cave, and the unknown leviathan, concerned him less than the Lords of Fear. But right now, something bothered him about Brazin that he couldn't quite identify. He sensed his own distrust and that the friendliness of Jolian was the only reason he didn't outright dislike her brother. Novir seemed to think nothing of it, so he wasn't sure what to believe. He felt certain that Brazin was only doing this for Jolian, and that if the red dragon somehow fell, Brazin would leave them behind. He didn't want to be alone with Brazin, or give him a chance to abandon them. He decided that as long as someone monitored the blue dragon, maybe everything would be fine. Not being able to trust those who've summoned him away from his life and into danger made these quests even more troubling.

Ryan wasn't sure how long they were above the clouds, but it seemed like over an hour. They passed between the nearest mountains, and when they dove beneath the clouds, he saw they were quite a distance into the range. He realized their flight had made it harder to mentally follow the map he'd memorized. But then he saw a town off to one side and wondered if it was the one he'd noted. Were they getting near? The green dragon came up beside them with Eric and Matt giving them a thumbs up and huge grins. Ryan didn't really have anything he wanted to say, but he realized knowing more sign language as those two did could help in situations like this. The idea of riding dragons so often that he needed that made him laugh.

Brazin banked sharply, which was the only warning Jolian was about to, and now it became concerning as they tilted wildly to the left, a dragon no longer directly below them, but the ground far below, just like when a roller-coaster takes a sharp turn. They glided in circles, the earth rushing up. Ryan began visually searching the area for threats and the cave they needed to enter, but he saw neither, just a cleared area barely big enough for three dragons to land one-by-one, moving aside so another could arrive. Jolian dropped last, powerful wing blasts sending loose leaves and dust into the air. The landing was surprisingly smooth for a creature this size. Ryan exchanged looks with the others, noticing as he did that the dragons appeared on alert but relaxed as if they sensed nothing amiss. He took a long drink of water from a flask in the saddle, seeing Eric doing the same.

Novir was already grabbing a crossbow and quiver of bolts from the saddle pack, then a cloth sack before dismounting. Ryan got himself unbuckled, then helped Anna. He took the quiver and crossbow from his saddle despite not being sure how to use them. Then he climbed down the rope ladder to the ground, almost sorry to be standing on his own two feet again after that ride. Everyone soon gathered in one place, near the heads of the dragons. Even Jolian, with her benevolent attitude, was simply frightening this close to that gigantic mouth. Ryan could have walked straight into it and been swallowed whole.

"Where's the cave?" Eric asked of Novir, looking around. Ryan didn't see it either, just pine-covered, snow-capped mountains all around, the foothills covered in thicker foliage, boulders of every size gathered in old rock falls. They stood on uneven earth with more stone jutting up, most of it smooth from weathering. He had seen a trail leading past this spot and a way to climb down to it, and it made him wonder what had made it. Whatever it was wouldn't be much of a threat to dragons, and likely wasn't dumb enough to try something. They were taking a chance trusting the dragons, because if they left while they were underground, they would be lost without adequate supplies with who knows what nearby and a town a few hours away. He at least felt confident which direction it was from here, the trail leaving only two options.

"That way," Novir replied, pointing past some trees. But when Ryan looked, he saw nothing. "I think it could be best for Brazin and Sebast to remain here. Jolian can change form and come with us? Good. I think one dragon might be helpful inside, just in case we run into more trouble than expected. When we come back, only having to put one saddle back on is better than three."

Ryan was about to ask if they needed to at least loosen the saddle on Jolian when she whispered a few words he didn't catch and morphed into the leather clad vixen he'd first seen. For a second, she had appeared as both, the humanoid form where the dragon head was like an illusion, close to the ground. She dropped a few feet to land nimbly and straightened. The saddle, reins, and halter fell to the earth, the bulky saddle landing with a thud and rolling sideways. He assumed they were designed for such impacts and for the first time, wondered how they got it up there, as he hadn't been watching Sebast get saddled, and the others had already been prepared.

"Is there any chance of Sebast and Brazin being seen while we're inside?" Eric asked.

"Some," Sebast responded, his rumbling voice deep, "but boredom is our greatest threat."

Novir added, "There are trolls and ogres in these mountains, but they are smart enough to stay far from dragons. It's a long walk to the nearest town, and a deadly one. There's a reason few come to this cave." He gestured toward the faint trail leading up into the peaks for what seemed like an arduous climb.

Ryan scanned around them but saw no signs of movement. "What should we expect inside?"

Novir pulled a cloth sack off his shoulder and pulled two torches from it, tossing one to the knight. "A walk down a narrow tunnel. We can talk about the cave itself as we go. Let's move."

He started toward some trees and the others followed, Ryan and Jolian in the rear as they stepped around boulders and over the random fallen trees always lying in the wilderness. Ryan had no tracking skills to speak of, really, though he had learned some from Lorian, but he saw no signs of recent passage, including near the ten-foot-wide cave opening that was low so that he had to duck into it. After another few feet, it rose just high enough to straighten.

And part of a humanoid skeleton was the first thing Ryan saw. A glance around showed another set of bones from something bigger, then a pair of skeletal wings with some of the leathery part still on it. Most of the remains were partial, and he wondered if animals had gotten to the rest, as something had moved various bones around. The bodies not being fresh gave him some comfort that a threat was not imminent, but they left no doubt that danger lay here.

Novir lit his torch and then Ryan's. Matt made the top of his wizard's staff glow with a spoken word.

"I assume we should keep our voices down as we descend," Eric said.

"Yes." Novir stepped deeper into the tunnel, Eric right behind, then Anna, Matt, and finally Ryan and the dragon. "There is little to concern us until the cave at the end, but sound travels here and we want to silently do this so as not to disturb anything."

As they followed on what looked like a natural passage, every surface rough and uneven, Eric asked in a low voice, "What is at the end, and is it really the end or just our destination?"

"The Kirii Cave is at least a hundred yards high, less wide and deep. And it is not the end. There are several passages deeper into the mountains, or in other directions. Some of these are above in the ceiling, and that is how the kirii fly out into the sky to hunt. They are nocturnal, which means they will be sleeping, hanging from the ceiling above the water. They should not disturb us. The leviathan is our concern."

"What is it, exactly?" Eric asked.

"No one is really sure. Hard to get a good look at in the darkness, and partly because it has long tentacles and can pull you from the shore without showing its body. These appear to grow back, so wounds do not easily deter it."

"Do normal weapons hurt it?"

"Yes. It is not supernatural. Our best tactic, aside from not waking it, is to retreat into the tunnel, or near it, and fight from there if we haven't gotten what we need."

Ryan had a thought and asked, "Disturbing it means disturbing the kirii, doesn't it?"

"Yes, it does. One will awaken the others."

They stepped around loose rock that had fallen from a wall. "And what will they do?"

"Attack."

"Us or the leviathan?"

"Everything that isn't them."

They entered a natural cave with the ground falling away to one side. As they skirted around, Eric asked, "How dangerous are they?"

"Very, especially because we are where they live. They do have young to protect and will see us as a threat. Expect a vicious, nasty battle if one happens."

"Are they animals or smarter?"

The passage continued, tightly closed on all sides so that they had to turn sideways to continue, but it didn't last long. Ryan wasn't feeling quite claustrophobic, but a little uncomfortable when the passage got too tight.

Novir answered, "Oh, they're smarter. They have weapons. Small crossbows, slings. They understand tactics. One of them is two or more of them grabbing you and carrying you away. You are as good as dead if this happens, whether they tear you to pieces in the sky, drop you to your death, or save you for food. It is more reason to retreat if needed."

Ryan asked, "Will they follow us through this tunnel? I saw the one skeleton outside."

"Not sure, but they know where the tunnel leads. The one we saw probably flew out and came around to the opening."

"So they could trap us inside."

"Yes, they could, but they don't fight well in small spaces. And they aren't likely to enter the tunnels very far."

"Still leaves you trapped. They can wait you out."

Novir said, "Let's not worry about it. We have a wizard and a dragon in here with us and two more dragons outside. The kirii would see Brazin and Sebast and turn around at once."

They descended in silence from there, the tunnel sometimes getting wider or taller but seldom much smaller. They passed through several small caves and a cave-in, which made Ryan wonder how stable all of this was. The possibility of getting trapped or lost underground wasn't something he had considered until now, and the number of natural tunnels branching out from caves made him want to concentrate and memorize the way. Only a few looked to have been created manually, as evidenced by chisel marks and scattered debris, but they sometimes came upon multiple openings of different sizes and leading up, down, level, or in other directions. It was not obvious which way to go, and their reliance on Novir bothered him. What if something killed him? Ryan had been making a point of always looking behind him when they reached a cave, to visually identify whether other openings were there and which one they had just exited. He couldn't see Eric up ahead until then, but his friend was doing the same. They finally stopped, gathering close.

"We are near," Novir whispered. "Around the next turn. It is best to ready ourselves here."

He wound the crossbow he had been carrying, as Ryan did after watching to see how he did it. He needed to learn these things back on Earth and practice everything related to it. He hadn't opened the weapons that had arrived. He'd been loading them into the house when he was summoned. Confidence that he was an excellent shot would have eased his nerves, and maybe those of his friends. Eric had already drawn a throwing knife, and Ryan knew his friend was deadly accurate. He wanted the others to rely on him the same way he did on Eric right now. As he stood thinking about this, Matt was fumbling in his robes for what turned out to be a vial he held up, nodding that he was ready.

Ryan turned to Anna, asking, "Have you been able to reach a god?"

She nodded. "Yes, on the way here."

"Then I guess we're ready."

Seeing agreement, Novir quietly led them another ten paces and around a curve. A bit farther and it appeared to end in blackness. They continued forward, Novir the first to step out a few paces and then aside as the rest joined him. Ryan exited last and looked around, but there wasn't much to see in the dark. Seeing Novir put a torch on a wall sconce someone had fastened beside the opening, he looked for a second on his side and put his there. The light being in his hand wasn't helping his eyes adjust, but now they all stepped forward on the stone, which extended twenty feet out and to the sides as the cavern opened around them. While most of the lake appeared to be directly ahead, some of it lay to either side of their position.

Two dim shafts of light above revealed two openings to the outside. Against them, they could see dark shapes hanging from the cavern roof, scores of them by one shaft and more by another. Given the room's size, Ryan guessed that well over a hundred kirii were here, most out of sight, and he knew that the number could be far higher. They seemed small from here, but he knew they were four feet tall. None appeared to be moving.

One small, somewhat flat island lay off to one side, but a large, rockier, and taller one stood farther away, jagged spires of rock straining upward. Both seemed to have various shiny items laying on them, and he wondered if they were "treasure" to lure people out there. A rowboat lay on the shore. Another rested off to one side of where he stood, available to them if needed. A third floated aimlessly on the still waters, and the wreck of a fourth jutted up from beneath the dark surface nearer to them. He saw no bodies, but from what Novir had said, maybe the leviathan or kirii carried away anything left here. Nearby, he saw a rusting sword, broken arrows, and loose stones that might have been fired from a sling.

"You're up, Soli," Eric whispered.

Matt sighed and moved carefully on the dark, slick stones, stopping at the water's edge and resting the crook of his staff in one arm. Ryan moved toward him in case Matt needed physical protection, but his eyes were on the kirii, not his footing, and he stepped on a loose rock that slid out from underfoot. He nearly fell with what would have been a loud clatter, but caught himself. The rock wasn't so fortunate, rattling over the other stones and into the water with a small splash. He cringed and watched helplessly as ripples of water spread out and away. He knew Eric's incredulous eyes were boring into the back of his head without bothering to turn around to confirm it.

Ryan asked in a whisper, "Any chance you can direct a focused beam of light from the staff? I'd like to know what is out there."

"What if I wake something up?"

"Good point. Maybe right before we leave. Or maybe not."

"Hold the staff, please."

Ryan took it as Matt crouched to the water, opened the vial in one hand, and emptied it into the waters as he spoke words of magic, which Ryan only understood thanks to the spell Lorian had cast on all of them on Honyn.

Into the waters you seek and find
All the creatures, make them mine
Bring them here, all of one mind
Caught like a fish on hook and line

Matt made a gesture as if to spread the liquid out, and then another toward himself, as if bringing back fish. Only now did the knight realize he hadn't noticed Matt getting the fishing cantrip, as he thought of it, from Denir. Matt straightened and took the staff back.

"How long does it take?" Ryan asked.

The wizard shrugged. "Not sure. A couple minutes?"

They waited in silence, Ryan casting a look behind. Eric and Anna stood together as far from the water's edge on three sides as they could, and the opening behind them, as if concerned something might come from there. Or at least, that's what Ryan suddenly thought of. But Novir stood just before the torches, as if expecting it, too, so he had their back. Jolian had walked to the water's edge and crouched, eyes staring off into the dark as if she could see things they could not. She sniffed the air several times, making Ryan wonder what she smelled.

His thoughts were broken when a surge of water a few inches high moved toward them from out in the lake. It came in waves, something under the surface clearly moving closer to them, as if undecided about doing so and starting and stopping, each time causing a new rush of water. Ryan gripped his crossbow and loaded a bolt into it. Another surge started to one side, closer to Jolian, who turned toward it. The first surge came again, this time larger and with an audible sound of moving water. Ryan's eyes darted up to the cavern roof, and he thought several red glowing eyes were visible, but maybe it was his imagination. The earliest waves reached their feet, lapping at the stone shore, but so far there was no sign of the cause.

"I wonder what else is in these waters," he whispered to Matt, watching the source draw nearer. "What if it's not just the one type of fish and this monster?"

The wizard looked back at Novir, who was too far away to ask. "Wish we had thought of that earlier."

"Let's get away from the edge."

"Brilliant idea."

They cautiously backed up, and as they did so, more waves came from the side near Jolian, one being noticeably deeper than the shallower ripples. He couldn't see her face, but Ryan had the impression she was watching intensely.

"Soliander," began Eric, who had approached them silently and startled Ryan, "how exactly does this spell work?"

"It brings nearby sea life to–" He stopped, a look of alarm on his face.

Seeing that, Ryan asked, "What is it?"

Eric asked, "Does the spell specify fish?" Matt's wide eyes turned to him and Eric swore.

Ryan began, "Why does that... oh shit."

"What?" asked Anna.

Eric answered, "The spell summons sea life. That might include the leviathan."

Suddenly splashes came from the first source of movement and a few silvery fish broke the surface as they approached chaotically. Ryan relaxed at the sight. The rush of water grew louder and more intense, which made him look up again. For a moment, he thought one of the kirii that had been a silhouette against the dim ceiling lights had disappeared, but then he realized he was the one who had moved. A quick step to one side to change his angle and he confirmed it was still there.

But now the noise grew uncomfortably loud as a swarm of fish surged toward them, the shallow water causing waves to crash and echo in the cavern. And it only got worse when the hundreds of silver fish reached the shore and began flopping both in the water and on land. Each was about as long as his hand and narrow, but together they were making Ryan nervous with the noise. He saw other fish among them, red and smaller, and large black ones. Something that looked like a turtle was hard to see with the other fish flopping around on top of it. No leviathan, at least.

"Which ones do we want?" he asked Matt, who was pulling out a pouch. A glance at Jolian showed her still watching the other, unseen source of movement, which had come closer, too.

"The silver ones. Just grab a bunch and throw them in here."

The sound of rushing water near Jolian made them turn. A two-foot wave surged forward, and she stood up, her wary posture showing alarm. To the left and right of the surge, two thick, black tentacles broke the surface, one lashing out at Novir near the exit, but missing. The other swung at Jolian, who did a backflip over it, and when she landed, long nails had sprung from her fingertips. Novir fired his crossbow at the place where Ryan suspected the body of the leviathan was, the bolt slicing into the water to vanish. And then several more tentacles sprang from the water.

Ryan hefted his crossbow and wondered where to aim. The tentacles were moving too fast, but then Jolian spoke a word and they slowed to half their speed as if stunned. He fired into one and it recoiled. Novir did the same, but Ryan shook his head. Crossbows would not deter this thing.

"Ryan, back away from Matt and get your sword out," said Eric, coming closer. The knight turned and saw him leading Anna to the wizard, telling her to scoop up some fish into the bag and quickly get to the exit and wait there. Eric was right. She had to get out of harm's way and wasn't much help in a fight, as far as he knew. Just then a tentacle flew toward him and he swung the sword, cutting deep into it as black blood splattered around him and on his armor. The wounded limb came back, and this time he cut it clean. And then a horrible screeching sound erupted from the roof of the cavern, and Ryan turned in realization. The kirii were coming, dozens of flying silhouettes against the rays of dim light from above.

"Matt!" he yelled. "Light this place up!"

The wizard gripped the staff and turned toward the flying menace. "Oonurarki!" he yelled. From the top of his staff, the dim light became blinding and hurtled outward with such force that a shock wave struck everyone and hurled back the kirii. Scores of them had been flying toward them and were so disoriented that several fell all the way to the water and splashed around. Suddenly the jaws of something rose to clamp around one and drag it under. There was another lifeform down there. And above them, the kirii seemed in chaos, but it was hard to tell.

Ryan yelled, "Matt! We can't see."

"Sorry!" The wizard laughed and dimmed the light. Ryan got the impression he loved the power.

Jolian dodged more tentacles, swiping at them with her nails and drawing more blood. But only his sword looked like it was going to help, unless Matt did something. Anna had filled the sack and now scampered toward the entrance.

"Time to go!" Eric yelled.

But then everything seemed to happen at once. The kirii closed in, stones fired from slings clattering on the ground and cavern walls behind them. Eric threw one knife, then another, two kirii dropping to the water with a splash. Matt sent a jet of flames at others, setting a dozen of them on fire, before retreating. A tentacle flew toward Jolian, but she dodged it only to be grabbed by another and hauled high over the water upside down. The leviathan finally rose to the surface, a huge, black, oblong head appearing with a mouth opened wide, multiple rows of teeth as big as a person ready to clamp on Jolian. It dropped her toward its gaping maw, clearly expecting a meal but not the transformation that came. The dragon assumed her true form as she fell, wings snapping out as her mouth stretched wide and a torrent of flames roared down on the leviathan. Deafening screeches filled the air as Jolian landed atop the beast, which tried to submerge only to have Jolian dig claws into its head and beat the air furiously, lifting it from the water more and more.

Ryan stood transfixed until a stone struck his helmet with a loud bang, dazing him. Hearing little flapping wings near him, he swung upward without looking and felt his sword bite into something. He turned, swinging again, slicing through a kirii that he saw up close this time as it hovered before him. A snout like a dog jutted between yellow eyes, a drooling mouth of fangs snapping at him even though it was much too far away to matter. A knife from Eric struck that one in the face and it fell, another kirii replacing it, brown leathery wings pounding the air as clawed arms reached for him. He cut into one of them and retreated as more kirii closed in. They smelled of rot and seemed intent on grabbing him, to fly away with him as Novir had suggested. An energy pulse hurled them back, and he looked back to Matt and nodded.

Suddenly a thundering roar of rumbling stone and earth came from the exit behind Anna and they looked over in new alarm, not seeing a cause, but

Ryan sensed it was farther up. Had the passage out crumbled? They gathered at the opening.

Still holding the bag of writhing fish, Anna asked, "Where's Novir? I just realized he wasn't here when I got here with the fish."

Eric looked around. "The leviathan didn't get him, did it?"

"Pretty sure it didn't," said Ryan. "We need to get out of here. We just need Jolian."

They turned to see the dragon biting into the leviathan's head repeatedly, yanking giant hunks of it off and spitting them out. The tentacles had all stopped moving, and the creature seemed dead. Some kirii actually went for Jolian, who jumped off the leviathan and with one stroke of her wings, landed in the shallow water near them, being unable to get closer in that form because of the cavern walls. She turned toward the kirii, and Ryan thought she smiled before blasting them with fire. The smell of burned hair and flesh filled the cavern as bodies hit the water. The dragon changed form again and sauntered over to them.

"Ready?" she asked with a smile. She stopped before Ryan and looked him up and down, then wiped one finger across his armor. It came away thick with black blood, which she licked off her finger.

"Let's go," said Eric, grabbing the remaining torch. Novir had taken the other. "I have a bad feeling about this."

They hurried into the tunnel and jogged as fast as they could while not banging their heads or risking a twisted ankle. Whether Matt had summoned the leviathan by accident or not, they would likely never know, and Ryan put it from his mind. The thought of being trapped inside a mountain or having to find their way out through some other path, and then make it down to the dragons, worried him. And with good reason. They soon stopped at a rockfall that had blocked the path.

Eric said, "Unless Soliander or Jolian can do a spell, I don't see getting through this."

"Is going back easier?" Anna asked, frowning. "I don't like either option."

Jolian turned to Matt. "We may need two spells. One to move the rocks, another to hold up the tunnel until we pass so that it doesn't collapse more. My magic is limited and is for dragon-related elements."

That surprised Ryan. "You can't do other things?"

"We can but rarely learn them. The other races mostly use magic. My brother is an exception, spending enough time with humans, elves, and others to have learned. So we can. We just don't."

Seeing Matt thinking, they waited, Ryan feeling impatient. But finally, the wizard had an idea and coordinated with the dragon. The rest of them stood back as Jolian cast a spell to bolster the ceiling, and Matt cast a spell that vaporized ten feet of rock. He had to do this three times as they advanced and finally made it to the other side. Once everyone was out, Jolian let her spell end and another cascade of debris filled much of the tunnel, though not as much as before. As the others left, the dragon and wizard looked back at the collapse, Jolian studying the ceiling.

"This was no accident," said Jolian, turning around with a glare and striding toward the exit. "Novir did this."

"How?" Matt asked, coming behind.

"I'll find out when I strangle him."

They ran through the tunnels with Matt's staff casting light far ahead of them, Jolian taking the lead as she expressed confidence about their path. After another few minutes, they heard a faint roar ahead, then another. Ryan assumed it was Sebast and Brazin. Jolian picked up her pace, exuding rage. The roars grew louder amid the sound of ice shattering with a loud crack. Then it went quiet for a minute until they burst from the tunnel and paused. All except Jolian, who continued past the line of trees separating them from her kin. The others followed and came into view of a battle just as Jolian yelled her brother's name in disbelieving surprise or anger.

The green dragon, Sebast, lay on his side, one wing visibly broken, shards of ice embedded all along that side of his body, including his neck and head. Gashes that appeared to be from another dragon's claws punctured the body, and several evenly spaced holes that looked like bite marks were on his neck. A green liquid oozed from his nostrils, dripping on the ground and hissing as leaves emitted smoke from its touch. From the lolling head, gaping mouth, and unmoving, open eyes, he seemed dead.

Brazin reared up on two hind legs, his blue body showing burn marks from the green liquid that dripped off of him. Two gashes in his belly oozed red blood, and Ryan saw the body expanding as the dragon sucked in a large breath that heralded trouble. Two baleful eyes fixed them. On his back sat Novir, who lifted his crossbow and fired at the group just before a blast of frost from Brazin's throat flew toward them. Matt put up a shield, and the bolt bounced harmlessly away, but the ice struck the barrier and stuck to it, forming a dome over the invisible protection. As the blast continued, Eric stepped back and then ran away through the trees as Ryan watched, wondering what he was doing.

CHAPTER SIX

FLIGHT OF THE DRAGONS

Eric sprinted through the trees, using them to hide his intentions. Once out of sight, he chose another path and began creeping back toward the blue dragon, hoping to emerge where they neither expected him nor saw him.

"Brazin!" Ryan yelled, "you have a coward on your back."

Eric looked over at them but couldn't see the knight's position. Maybe it didn't matter as long as he kept up a banter, but then another dragon joined the distraction.

"Brother!" Jolian called out, voice anguished. "What have you done?"

"I have done what I am commanded, dear sister. Do not follow or your death is next."

In reply, Jolian transformed into a dragon, and in that moment, Eric threw a knife at Novir. The blade was halfway there as he took off at a run. It did not surprise him that his throw missed, partly because Brazin moved. Seeing the blade go by, Novir turned and fired the crossbow at him but didn't come close. Eric hurled another knife as he ran, then another as he adjusted the aim. The last blade struck Novir in the side.

"Fly!" the guardsman yelled in pain, pulling the blade out and dropping it.

Brazin leaped up and beat his wings furiously, lifting into the sky. Jolian looked ready to follow when Eric called out.

"Wait! Not without me!" He ran for the dragon, who turned with impassioned eyes. He thought she would refuse, but she lowered a wing as her brother continued a climb.

"Climb up the wing, Andier. My magic will keep you on."

He raced up the wing, the footing bouncy until he ran along the bone at the front, wondering why they didn't just use magic all the time instead of using saddles, which there was no time to put on. Reaching the spine, he straddled it and grabbed a handful of red dragon's mane, the insanity of what he was about to do filling him with adrenaline and fear.

"Eric!" Ryan called. "We shouldn't separate!"

"No choice!" he yelled down. "Wait for us!"

He nearly bit his tongue as Jolian leaped up, wings beating the air. The time for talk had passed. She climbed effortlessly, Eric hanging on with effort. The idea of letting go to find out how well she was keeping him there with magic made him laugh, but he knew that if she failed for even a second, he was plummeting to his death. He didn't need to look down to know his knuckles were white. He squeezed her enormous body with both legs, but as he did so, he had the sense that they were almost attached to her back, as if it and him were magnetic. He tried to lift one knee away and found he couldn't.

"You will feel better if you trust me," Jolian said, and he wondered if she felt him struggling despite what he assumed was a preoccupation with gaining altitude. Brazin had turned away, high enough above the peaks to soar for escape to the west and Ortham, but Jolian needed a few more seconds to pursue. Eric looked down and saw that his friends were growing smaller beneath him, a half dome of ice still standing behind them, since they had come out from behind it. With a pang, he sensed he might never see them again.

He yelled to the dragon, "Just tell me why people normally use a saddle and I will relax."

"Because they are as terrified as you if they do not. It is not actually necessary and is frankly a nuisance."

He laughed despite himself. If that wasn't a believable answer, nothing was. He first relaxed his legs and found himself secure there despite the wind tearing at him. He tried to lift his butt but learned he was unable, as if strapped into an invisible saddle. He finally took a deep breath as she turned for pursuit, and he relaxed his grip bit by bit. By the time they were soaring away, he had almost let go but remained leaning forward to shield himself from the wind.

Jolian was bigger and more powerful than Sebast, whom he had last ridden. She was also larger than her wounded brother. As they flew, it felt like they would inevitably gain on the blue dragon. It was just a matter of time, which was wasting. But what would they do? He had no real say in this, he knew, but would Jolian attack her own family? Nothing could answer that, and he realized worrying about it was senseless. He could better use his time to assess what had happened.

Novir was a traitor. Had the Orb of Dominion compromised him? It seemed plausible. But then why had he taken part in the summoning of the

Ellorian Champions? If he wasn't enthralled, then he was doing this for another reason. Was he in league with the Lords of Fear? Or the one who had the master orb? Was that why he was not enthralled? It wouldn't be necessary if the orb had already gotten him.

But what of Brazin? The dragon said that he had done as commanded. Who had ordered him? It seemed unlikely that he gave a damn what Novir said. That coward giving orders to a majestic dragon seemed implausible. Had Brazin come under the orb's spell? Eric didn't know how that could have happened and cursed his ignorance. Everything he knew had come from Novir and the wizard.

Could they trust Derin? How much of what they'd been told had been a lie? He wondered if the Orbs of Dominion even existed, or worked as described. Was there even a king enthralled, not to mention a dwarven queen? Maybe there wasn't, and this was why the summoning happened out of sight. What about these Lords of Fear? How could he and the others prepare for a fight against an enemy they have only heard of and when they aren't even sure about the identities or capabilities? He couldn't remember how much of that information had come from Novir, or who said what, but no one in the room had contradicted anything. The only person he trusted right now, aside from his friends, was Jolian.

He remembered the spell Soliander had cast on Matt to read his mind. It was horribly invasive, beyond unethical, but it seemed almost like a good idea. A single lie could get them all killed. How else could they know who they could trust? Supposedly the Quest Rings had an oracle-like quality that validated some of a quest before bringing them, but how much did it really know? And there was no way to know how well was it working. After all, the rings weren't bringing the real champions, just them, by mistake. What else were they wrong about?

Eric had never been the trusting type. That was Ryan, maybe even Matt, for different reasons. Ryan wanted to believe the best of others as his faith in God guided him. But Matt was just a little naïve and didn't see bullshit coming.

Eric had neither. Juvenile delinquency, some time on the streets, and a few poor foster parents had given him street smarts. He needed to rely on them more now. He had gone soft, his last foster parents being good to him, his dark past behind him, a steady job and brighter future ahead. He hadn't needed his suspicion or calculating mindset in years. But now it was crucial, and he vowed to ask far more questions from now on. Never mind if someone felt offended by an improper question. He imagined Anna frowning at him. He would have a talk with all of them about it. No one was supposed to admire or like Andier of Roir anyway, and Eric would take being feared and alive over being liked but dead any day of the week and twice on Sunday.

And the first person he would try out his new probing mindset on was Novir once he caught up to the little shit.

They hadn't thought to ask when the dragons had come into the situation. Where had the orb been then? Was it long gone before the dragons arrived? How could only one of them have been taken over by it? He sighed in frustration. Maybe the dragon had been compromised some other way. The only way to know was to capture both of them.

Jolian was gaining ground with every mile, the plains beyond the mountains visible in the distance. Novir frequently looked back, Brazin less so. Eric smiled. They had to know it was inevitable. Then he realized his disadvantage. Neither of their quarry would think twice about hurting Jolian, who likely didn't want to hurt her brother if she could avoid it. And Brazin had some magic, more than Jolian. Maybe Matt should have been here instead of him. Too late now.

Not sure if she would hear him, he yelled, "Do you have a plan?"

"I know my brother."

"Are you sure?"

"We used to play this game as children. He will not triumph. I know better than to teach even family all of my tricks."

He had to take her word for that. Suddenly there was no more time to worry about it. With only fifty yards separating them now, Brazin dove. Jolian continued forward instead of following, banking sharply just as her brother rolled sideways onto his back, already spewing shards of ice upward at where he clearly expected his sister to be. The shards flew past into the sky, striking nothing. Had she seen it coming? Jolian banked again and hurtled downward as Brazin rolled onto his stomach, snapping out his wings to continue, but he'd lost forward momentum and Jolian gained with terrifying speed. Eric felt certain she could kill Brazin with little trouble as they neared. What was she going to do? Driving him to the ground had to be the plan.

With Brazin ahead and below them, Jolian soared down and blasted fire into her brother's path, but slightly to his right. It came as no surprise that Brazin banked left, right into his sister's trajectory. She was clever. Eric braced for the collision as Jolian kicked downward with what felt like all four legs, striking Brazin's body with a jarring thud so deep that she knocked the breath from the dragon's body with an audible grunt from him. Eric heard the cough-like whoosh of air from him, a mist of frost expelled as if by accident. Now Brazin fell as if knocked off balance or struggling to regain control, his legs kicking wildly, wings jerked by the wind instead of used skillfully. He pulled himself into a ball as he plummeted, then spread his wings again, once more in control as he looked around for his sister. Eric thought he saw fear.

And it was too late. The trees and a lake weren't far below now and Brazin looked helpless as he beat the air to gain speed and altitude. Jolian closed in from above again. This time she breathed fire directly at Brazin, who heard the flames and rolled once more, countering them with ice, but again the red dragon saw it coming and had already banked left, then right, reaching Brazin just as he completed the roll. At the last moment, Jolian slowed herself and grabbed her brother's neck with her front claws, one back leg clubbing down at his body so that Eric wondered if she had just knocked off Novir. But he had no time to care. The lake rushed up at them until both dragons spread their wings to slow the impending crash near the shoreline. A huge fountain of water hurtled into the air, their momentum making them careen onto the short sandy beach, a line of trees near.

When they came to rest, it amazed Eric that he was still alive. Jolian was turning to stand on the ground more firmly, her front claws still around her brother's neck, and it gave Eric a clear sight of Novir having unfastened himself and sliding down the blue dragon's side to splash into the water. The sound of footsteps plunging through the shallows told the rogue that his quarry meant to flee.

"Jolian," called Eric, "let me go."

"Done."

Eric felt the spell holding him to the dragon's back release, and he smoothly pulled a throwing knife out as he raced down the wing that the red dragon lowered like a ramp to the sand. He kept a running count of lost throwing knives and still had roughly half of the dozen. He turned after Novir, who had a thirty-yard head start on him, heading along the beach instead of into the trees. Behind him, Eric heard Jolian take a deeper breath and wondered what she was doing until something crackling went over his head. He barely saw the man-sized fireball that landed in the sand a few strides ahead of Novir, who stopped in visible surprise, then turned and ran toward the woods.

Eric smirked and changed course to intercept him. He took a chance and slowed to throw a knife at his prey. He had already resumed course when the blade sank into Novir's hip to create a second wound. The King's Guardsman staggered a few paces toward the trees, pulling out the blade and throwing it down as he turned to Eric, ripping a sword from its sheath. The rogue stopped ten feet away, certain he wouldn't win that way. Instead, he threw another knife that Novir deflected.

"Coward!" he shouted. "Pull your sword and fight me!"

Eric threw two in quick succession, the first intended to distract and then second going for the sword arm. It worked, Novir wincing, his sword lowering as he tried to remove the blade with the other hand. Eric charged to make Novir think they would land in a heap, but at the last moment he leaped up, delivering a kick to the jaw that sent Novir on his back, the sword falling. And Eric was on top of him in an instant, another knife to his throat, Novir's arms pinned between his body and Eric's legs. The trees were just strides away, and he briefly scanned them for danger he didn't see before returning attention to his captive.

"Why?" Eric demanded.

Novir spat at him, but the rogue saw him getting ready to do it and leaned to dodge it. "I'll tell you nothing."

Eric punched him in the face, not bothering to wipe the spit from his ear. He sometimes forgot that one hand had a magic ring that did far more damage than might be expected of a blow, but Novir's broken lip and shattered teeth reminded him. He almost felt bad for the damage but said, "Normally I'd say I can do that all day, but I don't have time for this. Are you under control of the orb?"

Snidely, his mouth bloody, Novir asked, "Would it make you be civil if I said yes?"

Eric hit him again, but not as hard. "Answer and you'll find out."

A glare of anger appeared, and Eric felt Novir's arms struggling to slip free. Novir said, "I am going to kill you."

"Not likely. Why did you betray your king?"

Novir smiled, bloody teeth making him sinister. "My allegiance is not to him. I betrayed no one." A hint of pride surfaced, and Eric used it.

"For what? Money? Whores? A pint of ale?"

Sneering, Novir jerked his arms more and snarled, "Your petty pleasures are not mine."

"You betray a kingdom for a night with a slut you'll just get another disease from."

Novir shouted, "I betray no one! My master is more powerful than any of you! Even your Majestic Magus."

Mocking him, Eric asked, "Then why does he need the Orbs of Dominion? True power means not needing a magic item to control others."

Laughing bitterly, Novir said, "Oh, he knows how to control people without it, trust me."

"Trust a man who can be so easily bought? You will live your life in chains if I don't kill you first, beneath Castle Arking in the dungeon."

"I will sit on the throne of Minari! It is you and your friends that will rot beneath *my* castle!" He again tried to move his arms and while he'd succeeded some by now, he wasn't getting them free.

"You betray your king for nothing more than a *promise* to take his place? What a fool you are."

Smirking with condescension, Novir asked, "Am I, Silver-Tongued Rogue? If I am such a fool, then why am I the one who cannot see?"

Eric scowled, not understanding.

Novir spoke a word and Eric's sight went black.

CHAPTER SEVEN

VALEGIS

Novir violently bucked a startled Eric, twisted, and yanked both of his arms free. Eric swung but had his blow blocked, a fist finding his jaw as he fell back into the sand onto something long, flat, and hard.

His sword, Eric thought, rolling off and grabbing it, the edge slicing his finger until he found the hilt. Using his other hand, he swung fast twice, just hoping to ward off Novir, whose movements he heard. He advanced, swinging wildly, feeling disoriented. His own sword was on his hip, which meant he didn't need to see to keep the man away or save himself. That gave him an idea and he pulled out a knife. Novir cursed and ran toward the trees. Eric listened intently, trying to gauge distance and the path. Then he threw the knife, which sounded like it struck a tree. Novir continued crashing through the foliage as he escaped.

Eric turned toward the lake, or the direction he thought it was in, stumbling. He first needed to get the sand off his hands. And the blood. He wished Anna was here to heal him so he could see. All he saw was blackness, and having his eyes open but seeing nothing disturbed him. Hearing his booted feet splash, he dropped the sword, crouched, and cleaned his hands, rubbing one over the other, which is how he felt the Trinity Ring on one finger. He cursed himself for a fool. It had three healing spells. Surely one was strong enough to restore his sight. He didn't really know how much strength was needed but saved the strongest spell for something more serious.

"Enurarki," he said. Blackness lifted as light crept in, his sight blurry before slowly clearing. He sighed and picked up Novir's sword, glancing toward Jolian as he straightened. For a moment, he thought both dragons had left, but both had shifted to human form. He turned back toward the trees, which were quiet now. Either Novir was hiding or he was far enough away to be unheard. Eric wasn't sure if he should go after him, but the surprise spell made him decide against it. There was no telling what the man was capable of. Eric didn't like surprises. He was lucky to be alive.

He went to collect his knives, since he had thrown pretty much all of them. He kept an eye out for danger. Seeing some fruit made him realize his hunger, but there was no way to know what was safe to eat on this planet. There had been rations in their gear. Had Novir put it there? It no longer mattered because Eric wasn't eating it in case it had been poisoned. His face fell. What if the others were snacking on it now? He found several of the knives and hurried back to Jolian, noticing as he neared that Brazin seemed unconscious.

Eric asked, "He changed form?"

"Yes, trying to get out of my grip, but I just knocked him out after he did it."

The rogue looked back toward where Novir had disappeared. "I don't know if I should go after him."

"What did you learn? Was it enough?"

"No, only that he was promised the throne of Minari. He didn't say how he would earn it."

"That's a hefty reward for trapping us in a cave, however briefly. There must be more to him."

Eric nodded. "Maybe he was responsible for the king being enthralled. If so, he has delivered Minari to whoever has the master orb."

"That might be enough, assuming that person doesn't want the throne for himself, which seems likely only because he has already ensnared two rulers. Why stop there?"

Eric agreed. These Orbs of Dominion were far too much power in one person's hands. Part of him wondered if a James Bond-like villain was behind it all, believing he would create peace across an entire world, or multiple worlds, by enslaving minds so that everyone just agreed with everything. The problem with that was the adage that absolute power corrupts absolutely. The sort of person who would use "evil" means to reach a "good" end could not be benevolent, because that required ethics they clearly didn't have.

Jolian looked out over the forest and mountains. "We needn't worry about Novir. He has no escape that will occur in time to interfere with us again. There are many things in between here and civilization. He is unlikely to survive, especially wounded and with no sword. His scent and that of the blood will bring trolls."

"Good for him. Maybe he can be *their* king."

"Their next meal is more likely."

Eric hadn't seen a troll and wondered how big they were. Did they really eat people? Though cannibalism was about eating your own kind, sentient species consuming each other was nearly as disturbing. On Earth, only animals ate people, and usually by accident or in desperation, but then there weren't any other sentient species. Only a few animals like crocodiles ate humans on purpose. He supposed it didn't matter if you were already dead, but the truly awful thing about crocs was the way they twisted a limb rapidly until yanking it off while you were still alive and going into shock. It had to be one of the worst and most terrifying ways to die.

Just today he'd seen a leviathan try to eat Jolian. Being reduced to food felt ignoble and wasn't something he'd ever considered as a likely end to his life before these quests began. Had he entered a new food chain where he was a few notches down from the top of it? How did one go about making themselves unappetizing? The thought made him want to laugh, but maybe he really did need to look into it. How do you convince a predator that eating you in particular will be disgusting or make them sick? Did he just have to run faster than his friends? He smiled at the realization that he was already the fastest.

As for Novir, he felt some sympathy at the idea of being eaten. Traitor or not, it wasn't a good way to go. Hopefully, he'd be dead instead of boiled alive in a stew or something. The thought made Eric realize how dependent on Jolian he was to get out of here. He turned to her.

"I don't suppose you knew he could do magic?"

She frowned. "I did not, but that may explain the cave in. I saw nothing that looked like physical force had been used to cause it, but I thought perhaps such evidence had fallen with the rocks. He appears to only know simple spells, which is not a surprise. He would do more with his life with more power."

Eric sensed she was taking some responsibility for not realizing Novir could do magic, but he had something else on his mind. "What if he can do a spell that could help him contact someone he's working with? That would still interfere with us."

Jolian considered that. "The spell he cast on you was simple, as would be the one for the cave in. It might mean he cannot do much more."

"What if he has a device we don't know about?"

"I think the only one that could matter would be one that allows him to communicate our plans to reach Ortham." She looked down at her brother, frowning. It seemed clear that they had been trying for the city and the Lords of Fear.

Eric observed, "True, but if he had that, he presumably would have already used it. Otherwise, why bother fleeing at all when we came out of the Kirii Cave? He could have just contacted them and remained a hidden traitor among us."

"I think we can safely ignore him." She looked at Eric, eyes on his hips. "We must bind my brother. The spell will keep him in human form until I release him, but he is still dangerous when he awakens."

Eric nodded and began removing the black rope he always had around his waist. When neatly placed, it looked like a belt so that he hadn't actually realized its nature the first time he found himself changed into Andier's clothes. He'd seen Jolian eyeing it.

He had little experience binding people but knew how to tie various knots from his rock climbing days. Apparently, tying people up was another skill he needed to gain, but no bind would matter if Brazin woke and cast a spell. "What about his magic?"

"I have suppressed that with a spell that is normally forbidden among our kind, but it will only last so long."

"Long enough to complete the quest?"

"Unlikely. We will need to think of something."

Maybe this was a problem Matt could help with. That was one of several reasons he said, "We have to get back to the others. What about Brazin? I assume you don't want to leave him, but did he say anything about what he did, like why he did it? Do you think the orb has compromised him?"

She sighed. "He said nothing I care to repeat before I silenced him. His behavior and the way he looked at me left no doubt the orb has enthralled him. This must have been before the orb left Castle Arking."

"I was wondering about that. How do you think that happened? How did the dragons get involved? And when?"

"My brother was already at Castle Arking because he spends time among the races, unlike most of our kind. He must have become enthralled. It wasn't until after Bolin Hill and the Lords of Fear became involved that Brazin asked me and Sebast for help. I am not sure how Brazin encountered the orb and yet did not go with those taking it. He would have been the fastest way to Ortham. It is something to think on. We must go." Jolian gazed at her brother. "You can ride upon my back. I will carry him in my talons."

"Where are you going to take him? I assume you don't plan to leave him at the cave entrance."

"The town, the one we passed on the way there. Valegis is the only safe place for him. He will remain bound, but trolls and others would get to him if left without a guard. He is still my brother and I do not want harm to come to him."

"You think he'll be safe in the town in human form? Will they know the truth? What do they think of dragons?"

She appraised him. "All good questions. I think we must return to your friends, leaving my brother there for now, under their guard. Then you and I will go to the town, landing out of sight and walking the rest of the way. If I fly in, they will almost certainly attack us. Dragons don't appear often among such places, and people fear us. That we mean them no harm would mean nothing. The best way to gain their trust is for us to make our way to the town's leader and convince him of our quest."

Eric smirked. "That should be an interesting conversation."

She smiled. "I'm sure you'll think of something."

That would be a lot easier if he knew more about this world. He would need to think quickly. And he wondered why she thought it was all on him. Should he take it as a compliment? "What then? We admit to the guy that you're a dragon?"

"Yes, once we convince him we're no threat. I hope that you and I can arrange for him to keep my brother under guard and to ease the town's fears so that I retake my true form outside without causing a panic. I can fly back to the cave, and take my brother back to town, no one afraid of my return."

"What about if he awakens and regains magic?"

"The town should have wizards. Everywhere does. Magic is common here. Hopefully, they will subdue him. Several wizards working together could handle him. We will have to ask these questions."

Eric thought was a good idea so far, assuming it went according to plan. "What then? Can you carry all four of us to Ortham?"

"Yes, but two of you would not be in a saddle. You would need to choose one other who handled it as gracefully as yourself."

Eric started laughing and Jolian smiled. "Oh no, I'm not making that decision. We'll let them choose. Anyway, how long do you think it will take to do this whole thing with Brazin and be on our way?"

"Hours. I know we must move quickly."

"Can you hear me well enough while we fly? I must ask you something."

"Yes. Let us proceed."

Jolian stepped away from him and Eric made sure to not get slapped by a suddenly appearing dragon wing as she transformed, both the process and the result once again filling him with awe. She was always more massive than he remembered. That so much bulk could be reduced and then expanded like that made him assume magic made it possible. He wondered if a dragon ever spontaneously returned to their true form unexpectedly. That could be interesting.

He tucked Novir's sword into his belt in case they needed it, since the current plan meant Jolian and him walking into a town, and she might need a weapon that would not reveal her nature. Then he climbed up one offered wing to her back and felt more relaxed this time as she stepped toward Brazin, gently folding a front foot around him. She took to the sky with powerful strokes. Eric hoped the others were safe outside the Kirii Cave entrance, but Ryan and Matt were good enough at their new roles by now, he thought, that he wasn't too worried. They could fend off whatever came for them. Hopefully, they hadn't eaten any of the food, which they could replace in Valegis.

"What is your question?" Jolian asked, her voice rumbling like thunder.

Eric looked out over the forest-covered mountains as they soared between the peaks. He hadn't exactly been paying attention earlier. "After Novir's actions, I am not sure who to trust."

"I am also questioning what we thought to be true."

"Is there any part of the story that you are certain about? Like these Lords of Fear? Or even the Orbs Dominion? Do they exist?"

"Yes, the lords are well known. Whether they are involved or not, I do not know. Preparing to face such dangerous people will have us prepared for many lesser threats. And the orbs are legendary. Enough people saw an item matching the description, both in Hamarven and Minari, that I do not disbelieve this. I am more concerned about the destination."

"Ortham?"

"Yes. It seems unlikely that Novir would lead us to where the orb is truly headed."

She was right. Only a fool would have done so. Still, Novir had to make the orb's destination plausible. He said as much and asked, "Where might they be going that is in the same direction? And is there any proof that they are headed this way?"

"From what I learned, all proof about the orb's location was from reports that came to Novir. There is no way of knowing what they truly contained, and we must assume that they were not entirely accurate."

"Great. So he could have lied."

"Yes, but this may be another reason to visit the town. They are presumably not under his influence or that of the orb, which would not have come this way. Perhaps they are aware of its movement. I heard nothing that led me to believe the orb is not headed north, so it may be headed this way, just not to Ortham."

"It's a long shot, but we will ask the town, assuming they cooperate."

"Yes. As for other destinations, I know of nothing as plausible as the portal at Ortham. Novir did not strike me as a clever man, and he may not have thought of a compelling lie."

"Maybe he expected that leviathan or the cave-in to stop us."

"Unlikely, given your reputations and my presence. It seems clear that he wanted Brazin and Sebast alone, as it was his idea that I accompany you to the cave, which made it easier to defeat the leviathan."

"Do you think he just wanted to injure or delay us? He seemed in a hurry to flee."

"Possibly. I noticed his haste, but I thought it was fear. Perhaps not."

"Maybe the Lords of Fear don't know we're coming, and he hoped to warn them. He knew our plans at least."

"This is likely."

"Do you think we can trust Denir?"

"I think so, but perhaps he is compromised. Let us get to the town and see what they know. From there we visit Ortham and possibly gather more information along the way."

Eric sighed. It was as good a plan as any. He and the others were bound to the quest, and if the orb was going in a completely different direction, they would have to track it down. That would take considerably longer. And that meant more time away from home. The possibility of never returning always hung in the air. The price of failure was steep, even if they lived.

That mind reading spell of Soliander's seemed more and more like a good idea. He knew Matt better than the others and wondered if they should discuss doing it. The techie was as pragmatic as himself and could be persuaded with a good line of logic. Neither was as principled as Anna or Ryan. If they ever used it on someone, it would have to be when the other two weren't around or Eric would never hear the end of it. Matt would likely admit it was Eric's idea, sparing himself the judgment. Or at least some of it.

Besides, everyone knew Eric was the calculating one who would bend ethics when required. It came with his former life and he didn't mind his friends knowing it. He sometimes felt they needed to accept the situations they were now in with these quests and that being honorable was great and all, but not if you ended up dead over it. He was the first to ditch such ethics and didn't feel bad about it in the least. No one knew they were unwilling imposters ripped away from their lives without warning, and while the summoning wasn't unethical by intent, it kind of was for the result. Being ignorant of a crime doesn't make you not guilty of it, and while a summoning wasn't a crime, it was still a great wrong done to them. If they had to bend ethics to survive, then so be it. They didn't ask for this. Didn't want it. Weren't qualified. They just wanted to go home and back to their lives.

There was no sense in worrying about that, so he turned his mind to Novir. Why didn't Novir just take the orb and fly to Ortham on Brazin's back? Instead, he had taken part in summoning the Ellorian Champions. Eric went cold. Was Novir trying to bring them to the orb so they would get enthralled? They would be an enormous prize, one that might warrant being awarded a kingdom for it.

But then why would Novir help them get the fish eyes they needed for the spell that would prevent it? Because that spell didn't exist on Rovell, so he hadn't known about it when they were summoned. He must have been improvising, taking them to the dangerous Kirii Cave, hoping something happened to them. He got Sebast killed, but he must have known that Jolian could carry all four champions if necessary and it would only slow her. That must have been the intention. If he had gotten out of sight in time, they would not have known where to track him. The cave in and flight would have given him a head start to reach Ortham and tell the Lords of Fear that the plan to enthrall the Ellorian Champions would not work. This meant Eric and the others now had an advantage. They could pretend to be ensnared long enough to get close to the orb. It all made sense but was conjecture. He sighed but felt he had made sense of it, but he knew that he may have just been fooling himself.

Jolian soon banked to begin her landing, the tilt helping Eric see the ground. Sebast's green dead body still lay where it had been among the trees and bushes. Nothing seemed to move. He saw no sign of the others and hoped this meant they were just staying out of sight. He looked for signs of fighting and saw none. Jolian landed smoothly despite carrying her brother in a front foot. She laid him down as Eric scanned for danger and saw his friends emerging from the tunnel entrance, unscathed. He climbed down to meet them and quickly filled them in.

"Did anyone eat the food they gave us? It may be poisoned," he concluded, taking a few of the throwing knives that Ryan had collected for him. He had a half-dozen.

Ryan grunted and replied, "No. Didn't think of it. We arrived a little before noon and the Quest Ring always makes us feel like we just ate a solid meal an hour earlier."

Matt said, "If Novir knew that, he would have known we wouldn't eat soon. Poisoning our water would have made more sense, but we all drank some before entering the cave before."

"Nothing since?" He looked over at the saddle for Jolian, which sat upright on the ground. The one for Sebast was still on the dead dragon, half of it under the giant corpse. They wouldn't be reaching anything they needed from that side unless Jolian moved the body. He wondered what was where. "Okay, listen, we'll just replace everything in town."

Looking at the unconscious Brazin, Ryan asked, "You're sure he won't wake up while you're gone?"

Jolian responded, "He may but is well bound and cannot do magic for now. Keep a close eye on him. I suggest Soliander be ready with a binding spell if needed."

Matt nodded, but Anna frowned at Eric and said, "I thought we agreed not to separate. Now you want to again."

Eric assured her, "You guys should be safe here like before, just a little while longer."

She persisted, "And what about you? I mean, sure, I understand that you have a dragon to protect you, but we know nothing about this town."

Jolian, still in her natural form, interjected, "I am familiar with its reputation and we should have no trouble. There are far worse that we could visit, and they would be cause for concern."

Anna didn't look convinced. "What can you tell us? I really dislike not knowing about the places we go."

"Yeah, I know," Matt agreed. "I wish I had a spell that would help with that sort of thing."

To Anna, the dragon replied, "Humans built Valegis before knowing the dwarves were here underground, but the dwarves knew of the town and kept an eye on them. Valegis exists to mine these peaks for metals and gems, and the dwarves weren't interested in sharing what they might find. They believe the mountains belong to them."

Ryan asked, "Are these the same dwarves of Hamarven?"

"No. We are too far north, and if their territory spread all this way, Harmarven could claim the entire mountain range. But the dwarves in one place are much the same as another for not sharing. They are good-natured and came to the rescue of Valegis during a troll attack long ago. There has been an alliance ever since, with agreements on where the town can mine, and how deep, in exchange for dwarven help with safety, gem cutting, even tunneling. Valegis is where the dwarves barter with much of the outside world, so it is a trading town. We will find many dwarves there. This may reassure you we have little to fear. Still, the guards will be surprised to see Andier and I approaching on foot."

Matt asked, "Do you need a good story to get into town? Or to see the leader? Do we know his attitude?"

"I do not know who it is. I am trusting our Silver-Tongued Rogue to get us where we need to be."

Everyone looked at Eric and he admitted, "I will have to improvise. The big question we need an answer for is where did we come from? Why are two apparent humans walking around in the mountains?"

"Speaking of that," began Anna, turning to the dragon, "your appearance when you look like a human is pretty striking. Do you have control over that? I knew when I first saw you that you probably weren't human despite your shape."

Jolian nodded. "Yes. That is how I choose to look, but I will choose something more appropriate."

Eric gave Anna an approving look and turned his thoughts to what to tell the guards. If he and Jolian lied to get past them, and that became obvious while talking to the mayor, or whatever his title was, that could prevent cooperation. But what of the truth could they say? Talking about the Orbs of Dominion might not work if people didn't believe they were real. Remote mountain town guards might not have heard of them at all. But being on a mission from King Orin of Minari would get their attention and likely get them an audience quickly. But what mission could they admit? Maybe he refused to say it to anyone but the mayor. That might work.

But why would anyone believe them? He couldn't even claim to be Andier of Roir, one of the Ellorian Champions. For all he knew, this town thought the champions were still missing, and no announcement of a quest went out because King Orin was enthralled and would have interfered, so no one would expect this. That truth would not pass the smell test. Besides, with only himself present, being one of the champions was hardly convincing. How often did the real champions go around alone? He imagined saying his title and getting a snide response that the guard was really the King of Gisla.

And Andier was a known smooth talker not known for honesty. Admitting to their identities didn't seem like a good move, or at least, not to some guard at the gates. Jolian could prove she was a dragon and impress upon them that something serious was afoot as a result, but that would just get them shot with arrows.

But he had an idea the others agreed to, and with time precious, he helped Ryan carry Brazin into the mouth of the tunnel to Kirii Cave so everyone could stay out of sight while he and Jolian were gone. Eric walked up the dragon's red wing and sat on her spine again. Scattered leaves and dirt filled the air as she lifted off. He felt like he was getting used to this, but he didn't have long for this ride.

Valegis was hours away by foot, partly due to steep and challenging terrain, but they were near within a few minutes, Jolian flying low so that no one from the town saw them. She also didn't fly directly at it, but toward a wilderness area suspected to have fewer witnesses. For their story to hold up, they could only approach on foot from one direction—that of Kirii Cave—and this limited their landing options to that side of town. She glided between the peaks, just above the trees, and finally touched down with surprisingly little sound halfway up a mountain. Then she crouched down behind the trees and transformed to humanoid to get out of sight, hopefully no one witnessing the change.

Jolian looked more human this time, her red hair in a tight ponytail and less fiery. Looser, black leather that seemed functional, worn, and used had replaced the sleek, form-fitting red, her boots appearing scuffed. She gave the impression of a well-paid and skilled warrior who could pass for someone on a mission from a king. She took Novir's sword from him to complete her disguise.

"There isn't much of a path from Valegis toward Kirii Cave," Jolian observed, "but it is there. The town is around the next mountain over. I did not think getting closer in the air was wise. We should move quickly."

"At a run."

"Agreed."

They carefully ran across the bare earth, where small stones and boulders jutted up. The pine trees were sparse enough that they did not need a trail. Eric kept alert for signs of trouble, which could have just been animals, not ogres, trolls, and similar threats, but the way became more dangerous once they reached the way toward Valegis simply because traffic, however rare, might be expected there. It was just wide enough for one person. As they went, they sometimes had to walk because a rising cliff wall or boulder obscured the sight of any trouble ahead. Even when they could see for fifty yards because only smaller boulders dotted the landscape, the stray tree or bush near, they knew a traveled path invited scrutiny. Was anything waiting to ambush travelers? It seemed unlikely only because, as Jolian observed, few went toward the Kirii Cave. But just because they didn't go all the way there didn't mean the path wasn't used at all. An abandoned guard tower suggested the area was largely deserted.

They descended from their landing spot into a valley and took a brief break before resuming. When able to, they left the trail to stay near a line of trees, or even a cliff wall that was away from the trail. Anything to minimize being in plain view of something watching. But they faced no trouble as late afternoon began casting darker shadows. Danger would increase before long, so few breaks preceded them ascending again on widening path, the trees of a valley dropping below them on one side as they climbed toward a pass between two mountains. A pair of guard towers with black flags snapping in the breeze lay ahead. Eric assumed that the town lay beyond.

"They have seen us," Jolian observed, her eyes keener.

Eric had suspected as much and badly wanted some water and to catch his breath, sweat creasing his brow despite the air cooling. Once back on Earth, it was time to resume the jogging they had only just started. Anna and Matt would complain, but their lives could depend on it.

They continued jogging up the path until they saw a group of warriors doing the same in their direction. Giving a sense of urgency would just get the guard's tension up, so they slowed to a walk. Jolian tucked the spare sword into her own belt, having carried it because it had no scabbard, and running increased the odds of hurting herself with it. Now they did their best to seem non-threatening as the dozen warriors came to a halt ten feet away, most wearing studded leather and carrying a rectangular shield, swords of various lengths on their hips in scabbards. Only a few had a helm at all, each of steel. A tall, black-haired man in front was the obvious leader because of his chainmail shirt and finer tunic atop it. It bore the same insignia that seemed to adorn the flutter of black flags—a mountain with a sword and hammer crossed before it. Eric thought he had seen it before on a corpse in the entrance to Kirii Cave.

"Ho there!" said the one wearing chainmail, taking two steps toward them. "What business have you with Valegis?"

"We seek the town's aid. I am Eric of Arking in Minara. This is Jolian. Are you important?"

The man cocked an eyebrow, seeming amused but disdainful. "I am Talis, Captain of the Watch. And I am more important than you at this moment." His men laughed.

Eric smirked, feeling he had a handle on them. "Letting you think that amuses me, so I will allow it. Who runs the town?"

Talis scratched his stubble beard. "That would be Ogren, not that you'll be meeting him, except in chains."

Eric offered his wrists. "Would you like to try putting them on me? I'll tie one hand behind my back to make the fight fairer."

Talis smiled. "Well, I haven't had an offer that tempting in about two hours."

Jolian stepped forward. "If you boys are through playing, we urgently need to see Ogren. Will you take us to him?"

Talis appraised her with an obvious appreciation for her beauty, which did not appear to sway him. As if he meant no offence, he pleasantly re-marked, "If I took every mongrel that wandered in from the mountains to see Ogren just because they asked, I wouldn't be Captain of the Watch."

Eric drawled, "And if you don't take us, you won't be Captain of the Watch much longer when he finds out too late why we're here."

Talis's green eyes hardened, and he stepped forward, one hand on his sword hilt. "I am not accustomed to threats."

Eric took a step forward so that they were within arm's reach. "Yes, you are, or you wouldn't be Captain of the Watch."

Talis looked flatly at them. "Enough games. What do you want? Why are you walking around out here with no supplies? Where did you come from?"

Eric felt like this had gone as far as it could. Time for his story. "Our sup-plies are back at the Kirii Cave. Maybe you can go back and ask the leviathan to return them."

Cocking an eyebrow, Talis frowned. "I don't believe you."

Eric pulled a dead fish from a pocket, having brought one from Matt's bag. "Well, do you know anywhere else I can get a fresh one of these? It would have been handy to know before going there."

Talis appraised him with new respect, and Eric saw that he'd gotten the captain's attention. "What were you doing at the Kirii Cave?"

"The King of Minari sent us to get these fish for a spell we need."

"You are not wizards and do not wear an insignia of any kind, not to mention one of Minari."

"Our wizard is still at the cave. Listen, a force of men left Castle Arking some days ago and is headed for Ortham in Gisla. We mean to stop them, but as you noticed, we are short on supplies."

Talis's eyes looked away for a moment and Eric thought the man knew something about this, but the captain only smiled at him next. "You plan to purchase our falcons to get there sooner? With what? Dead sparis?"

"No, that was for you." Eric tossed him the fish, but the captain let it strike his chest and fall to the rocky trail between them.

"Just two of you are going to stop a force of men over one thousand strong? Oh right. You have a wizard. Why is he still at the cave? Fishing, you said?"

Eric adopted a more conciliatory expression and tone. "Look, if you real-ly want to know the answers to your questions, then escort us to Ogren and convince him to let you listen. Otherwise, and I mean this nicely, please get out of our way. We do not have time for this."

Turning toward his men, Talis mused, "The King of Minari, hmm? If we can't confirm your story, we can always feed you to the leviathan."

"Not after we killed it."

Talis stopped and turned back in visible surprise, eyes intently locked on Eric's. The rogue stared calmly into the captain's eyes and saw his matter-of-fact gaze register. The next question did not surprise him. "*Who* are you?"

Eric gestured up the trail. "Ogren?"

Talis sighed and turned toward Valegis, Eric and Jolian following as the warriors stood back to let them pass, then encircling them. As they continued up the path, the captain barked at one of his men, indicating the fish with a jerk of his head, "Pick that up!"

Eric eyed the forty-foot gray towers as they neared, archers clearly visible but relaxed. He saw little damage to show attacks had ever taken place. A wall extended out and partially up into the mountains. Torches and lanterns were already burning as dusk came early in the mountains, making Eric feel the need to send Jolian back as soon as possible. He didn't like the idea of the others waiting in the dark. They had cleared the area before this gate of brush, and from this vantage point he confirmed an impression he'd had—another path approached from a different direction so that one could continue that way by the gate instead of going in. But now they passed between two wide doors made of vertical wood beams, the gates closing behind them.

To either side as they continued were small barracks and more guards, who eyed them with either indifference or curiosity. A few were dwarves, who paid them no attention. Talis led them forward with only four of the guards accompanying them now, the rest remaining behind. Ahead were trees and a widening path of natural stone that had been chiseled and carved to be smooth. Two mountains loomed beside them, a host of archery towers there. Anything that made it through that gate would get slaughtered. The new road led between various small buildings that seemed disposable, as if necessary, but expected to be destroyed in an assault. As they ventured farther across this pass between mountains, the people increased in number. An archway of stone awaited, two more doors opened wide until they passed through.

And now Eric saw the valley where they had built Valegis. A thirty-foot tall, black stone wall enclosed it in a rough oval, uneven in various places, as if going around obstacles no one had been able to remove. It was wide enough, like the Great Wall of China in places, for wagons to be pulled along the top, as he saw several there now. Towers periodically rose from it for another twenty feet, each with an open top for archers. The wall stood back from the mountains and all trees had been cleared from around it up the slopes. He expected a castle or other fortification but didn't see one. From here, Eric could only see part of what looked like a wide moat that he assumed surrounded it, and from the snow still atop the peaks, he suspected it served as a defense against flooding during spring as much as against an attack.

Inside the wall, the land appeared to have been left alone, buildings alternating with trees and a few boulders so big that he could see them from here. Several very wide towers were inside and didn't seem defensive. Each had several long, horizontal beams sticking out at least thirty feet from the sides from large holes. Beyond it all was another mountain pass that seemed similar from here, except that the sun was shining through it and into their eyes. And for that reason, Eric did not immediately see the giant falcon flying toward Valegis. It bore a rider and circled one tower before landing on what he now realized was a perch. He couldn't see what happened to the rider after that, partly because he and the others began descending a narrow stone staircase. It reached the moat and a wooden drawbridge they walked over to enter the town.

Eric tried to take in the sights. It occurred to him that this was the first time he'd been in such a place without the others, but he was the most street smart and felt comfortable. Jolian had been right. The place didn't have an unsavory feel. He could hear children playing nearby, the smell of fresh breads and meats hung in the air, and the humans and few dwarves he saw watched them curiously but without malice. He guessed the town held about five-thousand people.

They marched straight to the center, past a strolling flautist he'd been hearing for several minutes, a fountain, and men who were skinning something that looked like boar, more of the animals roasting over a fire. A wide lawn that he guessed was used for gatherings stood near the mayor's manor as they neared, and with any luck, Jolian would leave from there as a dragon in under thirty minutes, with the mayor's blessing. He felt urgency. And the town seemed safe, not like some den of thieves.

When they reached a mansion in the town's center, Talis made them wait outside as he ascended the gray stone steps and disappeared inside for several minutes before returning and gesturing for them to follow, the guards still with them. They soon entered a dining room with a long mahogany table and eight high-backed chairs with green velvet cushions. At the table's head and looking unimpressed stood a tall, red-bearded man who calmly appraised his visitors. Eric felt there would be little fooling this man, but he didn't intend to anyway. They placed two mugs of ale on the table as the man gestured to sit. He joined them, Talis and the guards remaining in the room as the door closed. A fireplace cast flickering shadows around the room.

"I am Ogren," the man began in a deep voice, "mayor of Valegis. I understand you are in something of a hurry, and I have no interest in kirii dung, so speak plainly and we can see how we may assist each other."

Eric already liked him. "Forgive me for not being more forthcoming with Talis and your guards, but there are things we mean not everyone to hear. You trust those in this room to not speak of what we discuss?"

Ogren looked at them one by one, and Eric had the impression he was silencing them by doing so before turning his eyes back to the rogue. "Yes."

Eric held his gaze. "I am Andier of Roir, one of the Ellorian Champions. My companions, Soliander, the Lady Eriana, and Lord Korrin, are nearby and awaiting help. You know that there is a Quest Ring at Castle Arking? They summoned us to help this world and now we need some help from you if we are to succeed."

Ogren stared silently at him for several moments and then leaned back in his chair. "I heard the champions have been missing."

"No longer."

"I heard this as well. What proof have you?"

"None. And it doesn't matter. You know that a force of men recently left Castle Arking for Ortham in Gisla. We are here to stop them."

Ogren studied him. "And you believe sparis from the Kirii Cave will help this? How?"

"Do you know what this force of men carries with them?"

"Perhaps."

"One orb of Dominion. They have already enthralled the dwarven queen and King Orin of Minari. We require the fish for a spell that will prevent us from being similarly affected by the orb."

"And yet you are on a mission from that king to stop this orb from reaching Ortham?"

"Not exactly. His wizard Denir still thinks for himself and summoned us without the king's awareness."

"So then you are *not* on a mission from the king, as you told Talis. Why should I believe a man who lies?"

That was a fair question, and Eric thought quickly. "We are here on behalf of the Kingdom of Minari, and the rest of Rovell and other worlds, *despite* the Minarin king being compromised. It is at my discretion what to reveal to a man of Talis' authority as compared to your own."

Ogren seemed to appreciate that answer and looked at Jolian. "And who is she?"

"A dragon."

A murmur from the guards caused Ogren to hold up a hand to silence them. "Will you honor me by proving *that*?"

Eric turned to Jolian, who slowly rose from her seat to stand near the fireplace and a window that was partially open to the darkening sky outside.

"Listen for the sound," she began, "of your falcons screaming. I have done what I can to prevent them from sensing my presence, but know that they have no predators save my kind, and they will react when I let them know I am here."

She whispered something Eric didn't hear and morphed from her current appearance into the red leather-clad vixen he had become accustomed to. At the same moment, a horrible screeching of many birds erupted outside along with the shouts of men that Eric assumed were trying to control suddenly terrified giant birds. And Jolian's shadow on the wall stopped looking humanoid, the silhouette of a dragon replacing it. Several of the guardsmen put their hands on swords' hilts until Talis told them to stand down. Eric turned to Ogren and saw a sobered expression on his face. He gestured for her to sit, a glance at the window suggesting he wanted the reaction to stop. Jolian nodded as she resumed her seat, the disturbance outside ending.

Eric said, "We knew we would terrify the town, so we stopped nearby and hiked the rest of the way here."

Ogren asked, "Why is a dragon involved?"

Eric answered, "It speaks to the seriousness of what is happening. The Orbs of Dominion are real and are a threat to the world order on Rovell and other planets. It is being taken to Ortham to the portal in the Hall of Worlds. Once it leaves, we may not be able to find and destroy it. Many kingdoms would end up under the control of whoever has the other orb. We need to prevent this and you can help."

"How?"

"First, we need you to let Jolian transform into a dragon outside and fly back to the Kirii Cave entrance, and bring the rest of our group here without your people getting upset, or the guards attacking her."

"How many are we talking about?"

"Just three, and another dragon that is in human form and bound."

Ogren cocked an eyebrow. "Explain that."

"It is my brother," answered Jolian. She revealed how the orb compromised Brazin and the measures they had taken to ensure he was not a threat for now.

"And you would leave him here?" Ogren's frown left little doubt as to his feelings about it.

"Listen," began Eric, "it is getting late. My priority is to arrange for Jolian to go get the others before dark, which is any minute now. We can decide what to do with Brazin after. Will you let us do this? What can you do to calm everyone as she comes and goes?"

Ogren sighed but ultimately agreed to this much. He sent Talis out to spread the word and getting people to gather at the town square, where he soon stood before them as Eric and Jolian listened to him answer questions and concerns as darkness quickly descended. Eric wasn't sure how well all of it was going, but it no longer mattered. He watched with a mixture of apprehension and amusement as Jolian walked through the throng to a clear area on the great lawn, where she assumed her true form. The wave of audible fear that swept through the crowd had hardly begun when she took to the sky with powerful thrusts of her wings. Several people hastily left as she rose and flew out of view.

"First time I've seen a dragon," Ogren remarked, watching her go.

Eric commiserated. "It takes some getting used to. Thank you for helping us."

The big man turned to him. "Just be mindful that people here have simple lives. All of this will easily overwhelm them. I would like you and your friends to keep clear of everyone, for their peace of mind and yours."

"But not you?"

He chuckled. "I've seen a few things in my time. I am not given to fanciful thoughts. Listen, it is getting late. I think you will need to stay here overnight, unless you're really determined to go."

"Let me see what they think once they return."

"Sure." He nodded at the mansion. "This is the best we have. I'll be here, and we can have the place surrounded to keep the curious away. I'll get some food brought over. I assume there's more to discuss, including what help we can provide."

"Yes. And thank you again."

Ogren waved him off. "If you're right about all of this…"

He didn't finish, and they waited in silence. It didn't take long for Jolian to return, the saddle attached and Anna riding her back, a struggling and awake Brazin clutched in Jolian's front claws. Those who hadn't cleared the lawn by now scampered aside. Eric helped Anna to the ground and learned everything was fine back at the tunnel entrance, though the sounds of something moving in the growing darkness had alarmed them. Jolian left again as Eric and Talis carried Brazin up to the mansion's steps, where they waited again. Jolian had squashed his magic powers a second time, and the dragon remained bound.

Even less time passed before Jolian returned with Matt and Ryan, morphing into a human again and leaving the saddle on the lawn as they gathered inside with Ogren. They had laid a meal out for the five of them, Ogren, and Talis, the guards told to leave, Brazin lying in the corner. But a knock on the door preceded Talis letting someone in. A guard appeared, quietly reporting something to him as Eric wondered if something was amiss. Then Talis sent him out and closed the door again.

CHAPTER EIGHT

THE LORDS OF FEAR

Matt's stomach growled at the smell of fresh bread, brown rice, and something that looked like pork, the raw vegetables attracting less of his attention. The bitter ale he'd already sampled made him want more, but the danger of intoxication in unfamiliar surroundings had him wishing for water that wasn't there. Did these people know about staying hydrated while drinking alcohol? The room seemed pleasant and even cozy with the warm fire and torches, the scent of burning wood reminding him of the few camping trips he had endured growing up. Sometimes all of this just seemed like one big adventure, and moments like this were pleasant compared to the terror of the Kirii Cave, the fear of Eric not returning, or the awful bellows and screeches he'd been hearing in the mountains while awaiting Jolian's return with Ryan and Anna. Something had been out there and getting closer. Now it didn't matter, and he wanted to relax as much as that was possible, given the circumstances.

"What did he want?" Ogren asked his captain of the guard.

Taking his seat, Talis replied, "He followed their trail as per protocol. He found it began away from the path at Mount Dorun. Several large footprints and claw marks were present. It suggests that their story is true."

"I think we're past that," the mayor admitted. "Now that you're all here, what else do you need? Let me start by saying that we're aware of this force of men moving toward Ortham. You know who leads them?"

Eric helped himself to bread and answered, "The Lords of Fear. You know of them?"

"Yes. We are a trading town and so news reaches us daily. They are north of Durba and should arrive in Ortham tomorrow midday."

Matt remembered the town from the map. Having more time relieved him. He wasn't normally afraid of the dark, but flying through the night on a dragon to a strange city on an alien planet wasn't appealing. Who knew what else flew at night and might suddenly attack? What if they ended up on the ground camping overnight? The security of Valegis made him grateful, and he hoped future quests had far less traveling, though he doubted they would be so lucky. He had seen teleportation spells in Soliander's spell books but wasn't sure he could do them. He really needed time to memorize these things and find out if they could work on Earth. He intended to study tonight once this meeting was over.

What if they were on a quest somewhere and, instead of risking danger while journeying over land, sea, or air, he just cast them to where they needed to be? Fear of camping suddenly seemed a genuine issue because of being exposed in the dark wilderness, vulnerable sleeping, and trusting your equally inexperienced friends to stay awake when it was their turn to stay on guard. Or trusting strangers to do it. Trust was becoming an issue, but the normalcy of their dinner and a secure town had him dreading their departure the next day.

As Matt ate and listened, Eric recounted what had happened with Novir and Brazin, getting reassurance that they would replace any food supplies. He offered some coins Denir had given them, Ogren waving that off. With Jolian able to carry them all, replacement food and a place to stay tonight was all they really needed. Talk turned to how the Lords of Fear could be defeated, even with the group using the *Mind Shield* spell on themselves.

"Our plan," began Ryan, "was to get close and then pretend the orb has ensnared us. That will hopefully let us get close enough to take it."

Putting down a mug, Talis asked, "What if the orb isn't on?"

Ryan sighed and lifted his own drink. "We'll have to keep fighting our way to it."

"I think it will be on," said Matt, fingering some bread. "Whoever is controlling the master orb can check in with the lords and may expect trouble as they get near the portal, so they would have it on to both watch and assist by ensnaring more people and making everyone compliant."

His eyes on Brazin, who lay glaring at all of them, Talis asked, "How close does someone have to be to this orb for it to work on them?"

"We don't know," Matt admitted, having wondered the same. "My impression is it works up to a hundred yards away. I base this on what Novir told us about what happened at Bolin Hill, but he could have been lying."

"From the reports of what has happened near Durba," began Ogren, "that seems correct. The number of people with them has grown to over a thousand."

"Great."

"Even if you get the orb," began Ogren, "then what? They won't let you just walk away with it."

Eric said, "I am hoping we can do this near the portal and then convince them with violence that they had better leave through it."

Ogren laughed and refilled his mug from a decanter. "Convince them with violence. I do not disapprove! But it would be easier if you outnumber them. Right now, they badly outnumber you."

"I think we need to separate them from the enthralled," suggested Eric. "How?"

The rogue looked at Jolian. "Sustained blasts of dragon fire."

The dragon smiled. "Without hurting them, yes, but this would mean getting in between the lords and the enthralled first. That may not be possible."

Anna asked, "Why do we think they have all these enthralled people with them? Are they planning to take them through the portal? I don't see why they would. They can enthrall people on other worlds."

"Good question," said Matt, but he thought he knew. "Maybe they are just using them to get to the portal. Save their energy for any trouble there."

Anna asked the mayor, "Do you know where the portal is? Knowing that might help us. Maybe we can get there first and be waiting for them."

Ogren put down his ale. "The Hall of Worlds. They heavily guard it because of its nature, letting people from other planets reach Rovell, and this is the likely reason they have the enthralled, as you say, to save their strength. The lords could probably get inside and to the portal without it, but why take the chance? And this also suggests that the orb may not be on when they arrive. If it was, they could simply walk up and do what they want."

Matt said, "Then maybe the enthralled are a backup in case the wizard controlling the orbs is not paying attention." That seemed reasonable.

Ryan asked, "So how do we get into this hall? If we told the city why we're there, I assume they would let us?"

Talis exchanged a look with Ogren. "Yes, but that may take some convincing, and from someone they know. This would take time. I am thinking I might need to head there tonight."

The mayor nodded. "I will draw up something and seal it with the town's seal. You will take two others with you, each with a copy."

"Is that dangerous," Anna asked, "traveling at night, even with those giant birds?"

Talis said, "Yes, but it is a risk we should take. The kirii are actually one of the bigger dangers, but we can head away from them for a few miles."

"You will not land until you reach Ortham?"

"They can make it without stopping. If we evade the kirii, we should have no troubles the rest of the way."

Ogren said, "I will send more men with you until you are clear of their territory, and then they will return."

Anna asked, "So if we're successful in getting the orb and driving the Lords of Fear through the portal, what is to stop them from returning?"

Talis said, "They can turn the portal off. The city doesn't like to do it because opening it again is difficult, but this is a good reason. You would have time to get away with the orb before the lords could return."

She asked, "Does it make sense to turn off the portal before they arrive there so they can't leave?"

Talis smiled. "Do we really want them to stay on Rovell?"

Matt didn't much care which planet they were on as long as it wasn't Earth, but that made him see Talis' point. "When trapped, people are more dangerous. I'd rather convince them to leave."

"I have a concern about letting them get that close to the portal," began Anna, her brow creased. "What if we're too late or they get through? Then we have to follow."

"Yeah," Eric said, "that is a big risk, and I don't want to go to another world. How fast can they turn the portal off?"

Talis frowned. "I do not know."

Matt had an idea and said, "A few seconds, I would think, but it depends on how they are keeping it open. Are wizards actively casting a spell, or is a spell just in effect and needs to end? That was rhetorical."

Eric asked, "Would Ortham provide some wizards who can help?"

Talis suggested, "I will try to persuade them. They certainly have wizards. More so than us."

Eric said, "It sounds like we have a basic plan."

Matt agreed and raised an idea he'd been thinking of, and when they thought it sounded like a good idea, he asked for some parchment and began copying one spell from Soliander's books. The four of them cut a small lock of hair from themselves, put each in a sealed envelope, and gave those and the spell to Talis to take with him to Ortham. The Lords of Fear had a surprise awaiting them.

"By the way," the wizard began, "while we were waiting for you at the cave, I grabbed get a few things that might be useful, like the green stuff that Sebast had spit on Brazin. I'm not sure but it seems like acid. Never know when that could be useful. Had to be careful about getting it. The other big one is dragon ice."

Eric asked, "What's that good for? Won't it melt?"

"Yes, but I can reform it as dragon ice, which differs from regular ice. I don't know how, but some spells call specifically for it, and that's where it gets interesting. Dragon ice killed this Lord Voth. I may be able to use one of several spells on him because I now have this. I had some time to choose spells, based on what we know of the Lords of Fear."

The rogue asked, "Like what?"

"Something to slow poison if the assassin strikes with a blade. And this sorcerer might freak out if I make him covered in boils or something. I might need something better than that for him."

"Yeah. Keep looking."

Anna cleared her throat. "I used my time as well to reach Aryll, the Goddess of Life. She understands we are facing a necromancer and an undead knight, neither of them from this world, and she is not pleased. We can expect her help."

Ryan asked, "Any idea what form it will take? More than healing?"

"Yes. I sense I can be a, uh, weapon this time, if I see something and call on her and she doesn't like it."

Eric smiled at her. "Time to get your hands dirty."

Anna rolled her eyes and quoted an old line. "I'm a healer, not a fighter."

Ryan turned to Ogren and asked, "What about Brazin? Are you okay with him being here?"

The mayor looked to Jolian, who said, "He cannot shift back to dragon form and his magic is suppressed. He should be no trouble, but I would keep the truth about him known to only those who must know. One of your wizards may need to suppress his magic again. I will show them how."

Looking doubtful, Ogren agreed, and the conversation drifted to less important matters, the mayor drafting a few letters for Talis, who left to get ready and tell others to prepare. Knowing that the *Mind Shield* spell did not exist on Rovell, Matt made a copy of it and felt glad that they had captured far more of the sparis fish than they needed for themselves. Back outside the Kirii Cave, while they had been waiting for Eric and Jolian, Ryan had removed the eyes from all the fish and put them in vials. Matt hated handling them, prompting some good-natured ribbing from Ryan. He now had multiple small jars of fish eyes and had them and the spell brought to Talis, who would convince wizards of Ortham to use the spell as needed. This could significantly improve their chances of impeding the Lords of Fear and their approach to the Hall of Worlds.

"That's great," said Eric, looking him in the eye.

Matt flushed a little at the approval. Part of him wished he was as good at planning as the martial artist. He suddenly realized he loved his friends and would do anything for them. Maybe he should admit to how much he appreciated Eric's plans. What if his friend felt unappreciated and taken for granted?

As the night wore on, with another day of unknowns looming, Matt just wanted to be left alone to study. The four agreed to share one large room for safety reasons, extra cots being brought in, Jolian taking the next room over after some brief flirting with Ryan to see if he wanted to join her, but he looked both intrigued and intimidated and had demurred, to the amused smiles of his friends. That only prompted him to ruefully tell them all to shut up. He settled for cleaning the leviathan blood from his armor.

Matt went in early so he could memorize more spells either for use before returning to Earth or so he could write them down once home. This business of not being able to take the spell books back was an irritant. Sometimes he felt like every minute away from home, he needed to be doing this. He'd been tempted to pull out a book on the flight to the Kirii Cave but had known that was ridiculous and he might drop the precious book. But now he stayed up longer than he should have, the others going to sleep one by one until he finally blew out the lamp. He drifted off to thoughts of how to cause dread in the Lords of Fear. He and Eric especially needed to surprise these bastards.

In the morning, they ate a quick breakfast of porridge and bread with little fanfare and ensured they were ready. The *Mind Shield* spell only lasted a few hours, so they had already agreed to stop southeast of Ortham so Matt could cast it on all of them, including the dragon. They soon took to the sky, Matt feeling secure in the saddle behind Anna. Ahead of her was Eric, who made a show of being comfortable without a saddle. Matt suspected he did this to mock Ryan, who was behind the saddle and holding on to it for dear life even though Jolian's magic would keep him on. The big guy had looked suitably nervous, no assurances from Eric able to relieve his concerns.

With the morning sun behind them, they rose over Valegis and quickly left it and a crowd that had gathered to see a dragon behind, soaring over the mountains until the foothills and plains replaced them. The trip was quiet, a calm before the storm, and Matt spent his time mentally reviewing every spell he had memorized, the words, gestures, and which pocket a needed ingredient was in. Before Ortham came into view, they landed on an open plain and had a quick snack of fruit. He couldn't help wondering if it might be their last meal. They consulted one last time about the plan before taking to the sky again, and what they soon saw threw their plans into disarray.

Ortham stood just north of a river that flowed from the Galla Mountains, and they had been following this for some time before the walled city came into view on a plain. Towers jutted up from the battlements and among the stone buildings, a limestone castle south east of town looking over the rushing river. This attracted Matt's attention, for Talis should have already arrived and hopefully persuaded city leaders to clear the way to the Hall of Worlds or risk the population becoming enthralled. As the dragon banked overhead, he saw few warriors by the river crossing, but hundreds of horses milling around. Something seemed amiss.

They soared over the city, Jolian appearing to track the primary avenue across the river, past the southern gate and castle, and toward the center of town, where they knew the Hall of Worlds stood. And that's when they saw it—a force of warriors a thousand strong marched up the road inside Ortham unmolested. At their front strode four figures, one in a cloak that flapped in the breeze and holding a staff with a golden orb held high aloft. From this distance, they could not tell if it was on, but the Lords of Fear were already here. And they saw the dragon with its riders, the one with the Orb of Dominion pointing toward them. Jolian banked wildly just before a blast of lightning lashed the sky near them, but missed.

"Jolian!" Eric yelled. "Can you land near the Hall of Worlds?"

"Yes." She dove then, twisting and turning in case anything else struck at them, but nothing came as they plummeted toward the buildings farther north. Matt saw a large rectangular structure standing by an open square where Jolian touched down. They might have normally expected crowds, but the place was empty. It took several minutes for all four to climb down to the stone plaza one by one.

"How are they here already?" Anna asked, scowling in worry, her eyes going to the road from where the Lords of Fear were likely coming.

Eric replied, "They must have ridden through the night."

Still in dragon formed, Jolian rumbled, "It is the most likely explanation."

"That means they will be tired," Ryan suggested. "Hopefully. I'll take any advantage we can get."

"Yeah." Eric's gaze made Matt turn to see the familiar figure of Talis running toward them, from what he assumed was the Hall of Worlds. A dozen men followed, some wearing the insignia of Valegis, while others wore the red and black banner of either Gisla or Ortham. This was what might sometimes be helpful to know, but it didn't matter this time.

"Ellorians," Talis called as he stopped, "they arrived recently. But we are ready."

"Someone cast the *Mind Shield* spell?" Matt asked. "On how many?"

"Yes, on those few left in the hall. As many as we could."

"What about the illusion of us?" Matt asked. It wasn't hugely important, but the distraction of it might be the difference between success and failure. This was the reason they had given locks of their hair to Talis, as an ingredient for the spell.

"The wizards stand ready," Talis replied. "There are many more wizards than we could shield, so we couldn't risk others being enthralled by being here. They could just turn against us. We have a hundred and could only bring a handful."

Eric sighed. "Planning around this orb is getting irritating, not that we have a choice."

Matt had to agree. The orb could turn friend to foe in seconds. A few shielded wizards would have to do instead of a hundred that might become a problem for themselves rather than the enemy. He felt a moment of fear that the shielding spell might not work. The memory of Soliander mentally probing his thoughts would never fade. The orb wasn't much better. Anger strengthened his determination, and he turned to face the approaching threat.

"Is the orb already on?" he asked. "I couldn't tell."

Talis shook his head. "No. They haven't used it, maybe because they didn't need to. Like you had suggested, we cleared the streets to prevent their numbers from getting even larger."

Eric said, "Talis, head back to the Hall of Worlds. I assume that is it behind us? Okay. Jolian, any chance you can duck behind that big building over there as you are? If the lords are far enough in front of the enthralled, maybe a blast of fire in between will keep the mob back. They are innocent and should not be hurt, but feel free to singe the lords."

The dragon lumbered over that way, the ground shaking with every step, and the four Earth friends stood alone, silently looking at each other. Ryan loosened his sword and placed the golden helmet over his head, the act triggering the others to make similar movements. Eric checked his knife supply, finding nearly a half dozen left. Anna put one hand to Eriana's amulet at her neck, closing her eyes and whispering. Only Matt stood as he was, as ready as he'd ever be. The sound of footsteps approaching en masse became clearer, but there were no shouts that one might expect from a force of warriors. Instead, they marched silently, the crowd finally appearing around a corner between two-story buildings of stone.

In front strode the Lords of Fear, the undead knight Lord Voth on the left, black mail plate seeming to devour the light instead of reflecting it like Ryan's golden armor. He looked human from here, not something risen from the grave. Beside him strode a blond man with a waist-length cloak, trimmed in white, the underside of it royal purple. It swirled and flapped with the brisk steps of his booted feet, and even from here, his attire seemed elegant. He held a half-staff with the orb atop it, and the device did not appear to be on. Next to him walked a woman clad in black leather, with a ponytail of bright red hair, one hand on a short sword at her hip. She moved nimbly and efficiently, with sleek, dangerous confidence oozing from her. And beside her walked the black-skinned necromancer, in black pants and a matching tunic that appeared covered in silver symbols Matt couldn't see from here. He wondered if they should adopt intimidating stances, but the time had passed. No one on Rovell knew they weren't the real Ellorian Champions; maybe they could intimidate from borrowed reputation.

The enemy continued to advance until they reached the plaza, and by now the lords were twenty paces ahead of the enthralled warriors behind them, most wearing studded leather or chainmail. They bore an insignia of Minari, if anything, but a few showed signs of being from Gisla, a mixed mob of threats. Matt flicked a glance at Jolian, her massive red bulk crouched down by a building and wall out of view to one side. The lords reached her position and strode into the plaza and past the wall she hid behind. A few seconds later, just as the warriors came near, she rose, a blast of flames roaring toward the Lords of Fear, who whirled at the sound. The sorcerer Garian raised one hand and Matt saw the flames strike an invisible wall. Jolian seemed to sense it, too, for she turned to aim the blast at the ground between them and the warriors, who stopped and pushed back into the crowd, the sheer mass of them inhibiting their escape. The dragon could have roasted all of them alive if she had wanted to, but she let the flames die.

"Welcome to Ortham!" shouted Eric, and the lords half-turned to them. "Your fight lies with us."

The sorcerer, Lord Garian, seemed to consider that and Jolian, who glared down at him but made no move to attack again. When Matt saw the sorcerer move toward them first and the others follow, he knew which one led them. They advanced until twenty paces away. Behind them, the warriors appeared to advance again until another spout of flames changed their minds, but one ran forward before slowing to a walk, Jolian letting him go but glaring at the others not to try it. So far, this was working as intended. He noticed the necromancer's lips moving and wondered what he was doing. He could now get a much better look at them.

Lord Garian was young and wore a haughty sneer that ruined his otherwise handsome face, a neatly trimmed blond mustache and goatee adding refinement to his oval face. Green eyes glittered with intelligence and power lust, maybe a kind of eagerness that made him seem a little unhinged, dangerous, and unpredictable. Until the sorcerer smiled at him, Matt hadn't realized a grin could be so malevolent. Instinct told him to look away as if bored and unimpressed, so he did.

Matt's eyes fell on Lord Voth, who didn't look the least bit like undead, but then he had died by being encased in dragon ice that preserved him until the necromancer awoke him. If someone hadn't told Matt that Lord Voth was undead, he might never have known, and yet a sense of foreboding lurked in that direction. The knight's eyes were black and flat as if truly devoid of life, and he stood coldly surveying those before him without the passion Garian showed. He had trimmed close a black beard on his square jaw. Someone had broken his nose, which poorly healed judging by the crook in it. Only now did Matt notice the frost along the edges of Lord Voth's armor near his white skin. The symbol of Aranor, Soliander's home world, adorned the chest plate.

Movement drew his eye to the assassin Kori, whose beauty would make any man stare. Did she use it to kill them? Many a man might stare helplessly until she plunged a knife into them. Large hazel eyes, an upturned nose, and full lips would mesmerize, the depth of her gaze riveting for the mystery it promised within. It might even draw attention away from a sexy figure that her attire only accentuated. For someone dressed to kill, she had still painted her fingernails blood red, neatly bound her hair with a lace tie, and applied makeup. He wondered if she poisoned her ruby lips for a kiss of death, and he knew that he only saw the menace of her because she wanted him to, not because she couldn't hide it with ease. This was the most dangerous woman he had ever seen.

And beside her stood a man who spoke with the dead, raised them, and had their allegiance. Aeron's deep set, pale blue eyes shone from a black face that he had ritually scarred using something circular and hot and the size of a pencil, curving patterns of welts on his face and hands and rising over his bald head. They stole any charisma that his round face might have given, and when he blinked, Matt saw his eyelids had eyes drawn on them in white and blue. Did it help him see into the underworld? What role did the scars play? Similar designs on the tunic were now close enough to be seen but still not understood. And Matt didn't want to know.

"Are you wondering what happened to Novir?" Eric taunted them, breaking Matt's thoughts.

For an answer, Kori threw a knife toward him with a flick of her wrist and the rogue barely dodged it. She was as fast as him, Matt saw, remembering her blades were poisoned. She cast a brief glance at the lone enthralled warrior who had reached them, hanging back.

"I'll tell you anyway," offered Eric. "We fed him to trolls, just like we're going to feed you to the dragon."

The sorcerer remarked, "I see you are short two dragons from when you started. Pity. But no more of you shall fall, by our lord's order. We will ensnare your feeble minds for him after we amuse ourselves with you."

Matt nodded to himself. So it *was* a trap to ensnare the Ellorian Champions. As if they didn't have enough to worry about, now people were trying to capture them. But at least they did not face death. Garian was a fool to admit that, but anger at the threat grew. Matt began gathering magical energy.

Eric continued baiting the lords, for reasons Matt didn't really understand, but he trusted the rogue. "Like he ensnared yours?"

Garian smirked. "He already has our allegiance and needed no orb to gain it."

"Was it like Novir? Did you sell your soul for a pint of ale, or maybe a petty fiefdom somewhere?"

The smirk deepened. "We're already lords, fool. And we will take what kingdoms we want."

"Yes, but if you or he were so powerful, you wouldn't need the Orbs of Dominion to do it, now would you?"

Lord Voth pointed an imperious finger at Matt. "Bow before your king, Soliander of Aranor."

Matt tried to stay in character, amazed he was about to have a conversation with an undead knight. "You are no King of Aranor. You bow to another. Care to share who has enslaved you?" Lord Voth ripped his sword from its scabbard in one smooth motion. Maybe pissing them off wasn't a good idea after all.

The rogue asked, "Are you sure you don't want to rest a minute before we kick your butts through the portal? You must have traveled all night to get here. You look like you need a nap."

Kori answered in a rich alto. "We have ways to get our energy back. Show him, Aeron."

The necromancer gestured for the nearby enthralled warriors to approach, and once the man did so, he put one hand on the man's shoulder and began whispering words Matt couldn't hear but which made his skin crawl. Rather than light appearing as when Anna channeled a god's touch, a darkness gathered around the necromancer's black hand and spread over the warrior, whose face registered horror. He moaned, soiling himself as his hair turned white, his skin wrinkled and became spotty, and his posture stooped. His life's energy drained away into a ball of shimmering darkness in Aeron's hand. The warrior fell face first to the stones, dead. Glittering blue eyes turned toward them as the necromancer made a thrusting gesture with that hand. The ball of blackness separated into three, one absorbing into him and the other two racing toward Lord Garian and Kori, striking both and disappearing inside them. The assassin looked at them with a renewed blaze of energy.

"That's fucked up," Ryan muttered, scowling.

Matt had to agree and thought Aeron needed to be destroyed. He decided the time for chatter had ended. According to lore on Earth, ice had no effect on undead, but fire was another matter. Given that dragon's ice had killed and encased Lord Voth, and Matt had melted ice in a vial from Brazin, he wanted to test a theory. He opened a vial of ordinary water and poured some as he spoke.

With ice and frost I bind your flesh,
May time stand still, in peace you rest

He thrust the vial toward the target and watched as the water soared toward Lord Voth, growing expanding in volume. That it chilled in flight became apparent from the tinkling of ice shards that dropped on the stones as it flew on, finally striking Lord Voth, who hadn't bothered to move. Would arrogance be his downfall? Matt saw the water freeze around the undead knight's entire body, encasing him in inches of ice like he was a sculpture.

"Fool!" said Lord Garian, chuckling. "So much for the Majestic Magus."

Matt responded by putting the vial back in his pocket and retrieving the one with dragon's ice water. He wasn't surprised by what happened next. A crack in the ice appeared, then another bigger one. The knight was flexing his limbs inside it, and a third crack made a huge chunk fall to the stones and slide away. With a final wrench, the undead knight freed himself, sending ice pieces scattering.

Far behind the lords, Jolian breathed another round of flames to keep the enthralled away, and Matt's glance revealed their numbers had greatly reduced. Where had they gone? The obvious answer was to find another way to the plaza. Countless other entry points existed, but he had more pressing concerns. He repeated the spell, this time more hopeful of the result. Once again, the undead knight had been encased in ice as Garian and Kori stood smirking at him like he was an idiot. They waited. And waited. And waited. But Lord Voth did not appear to be moving. Not until he yelled with his mouth frozen shut did anyone realize he wasn't getting out this time.

Matt returned their smirk until a sudden gesture from Kori toward him made his breath catch. He barely saw the blade flying, instinctively raising his hands, words of magic struggling to form as the twirling knife reached him—and fell with a clatter at his feet. Kori screamed and doubled over, a splash of blood already leaking between her fingers at one shoulder. She staggered and fell to one knee, reaching for the necromancer and calling his name as she tumbled to the pavement, body going limp. Matt had forgotten one benefit of Soliander's staff—any physical blow intended for him caused the wound to appear on the victim instead. It only worked so many times, but sometimes once was enough. Whatever poison Kori was using didn't give one long to live, apparently. Aeron kneeled over her.

A roar of flame attracted Matt's attention, but Garian directed it at Lord Voth, his Dragon's Fire Wand rapidly melting the dragon ice. Matt hadn't thought of that. Were the flames truly like that of a dragon and therefore an effective counter to his spell, or would regular fire melt the ice, too? Once Lord Voth had been thawed enough to crack the ice on his own, Garian turned the wand toward Jolian despite the distance. She didn't move as the flames reached and struck her, giving Matt the impression that she knew nothing would happen to her. And it didn't. When flames stopped, she bared her teeth at him as if smiling.

Having healed Kori, who rose with fury on her face, Aeron again seemed to whisper, one hand rising to the sky. That surprised Matt. A necromancer would reach for the earth to get dead things to rise from it. What was up there to care about? He found out when a loud screech split the air and a green dragon flew over the courtyard, barely above the buildings, a rider upon its back. Both were close enough to see that they were dead, large puncture wounds in the dragon's neck, ghastly ones in its body, and a broken wing hampering its flight. Just as Matt recognized Sebast and the missing Novir, they turned toward Jolian and spat a fountain of green liquid at her. The red dragon ducked behind a building as steaming acid began melting everything around her. She seemed unscathed and leaped into the sky to pursue the undead dragon.

"Holy shit," said Ryan, turning to them. "Did you see that?"

"More like unholy shit," said Eric, reaching into a pocket. Matt saw one vial of green acid he'd collected from Sebast's corpse hidden in the rogue's reappearing hand, so he turned and sent a blinding flash of light from his staff at the Lords of Fear, who shielded their eyes. Eric threw the vial, which smashed on Garian's leg. Horrible screaming erupted as it ate away the sorcerer's flesh so quickly that the bone had already appeared. Lord Garian staggered and fell, Aeron running for him even as the sorcerer's blazing eyes turned toward Eric, the Dragon's Fire Wand raising. Matt ran to Eric and put up an invisible wall just as sustained blasts of lightning struck, crackling the air amid thunder that deafened him. From the corner of his eye, Matt saw movement, as did Eric, but neither were fast enough to dodge the knives that Kori threw at Eric, one hitting his shoulder, the other his leg. The lightning from Garian cut off. Anna ran to Eric. Matt swung the top of his staff in anger, causing a half circle of fire to roar up from the ground in between the combatants.

He glanced down at Eric, relieved to see Anna succeeding at healing the rogue, but there was no time to feel satisfaction. The sound of heavy footsteps preceded Lord Voth running through the wall of flames directly toward Ryan, who advanced.

"Matt," yelled Eric, "drop the flames. We can't see what they're doing."

"Right." He killed the spell and swore. With Jolian gone, the enthralled warriors had advanced, and the ones that had gone around were now entering the plaza from the sides. Undead would soon surround them except from behind. Aeron had healed a livid Garian, who now strode toward them, the dark Orb of Dominion in one hand and the wand in the other. To one side, Kori had drawn her sword and ran at Eric, who quickly drew his.

"Fall back!" shouted the rogue. "To the hall! Anna! Matt! Keep the enthralled away."

The loud clang of Ryan's sword blocking Lord Voth's split the air as they traded blows, Ryan steadily backing up and risking glances at the others to as if to measure the pace of their retreat. A flurry of more frequent and lighter clangs sounded on Matt's other side as Kori and Eric fought. Garian raised his wand at Ryan and Matt threw a brief shield up, so close to the sorcerer that the energy wave meant to strike the knight rebounded and knocked Garian into Aeron so that they fell in a heap. Matt smiled despite the tension in the air. Somehow, Eric and Kori were now fighting without swords or knives, each spinning, kicking, punching and sometimes throwing the other, still moving steadily toward the Hall of Worlds. Matt thought to get Eric's dropped sword for him, but there was no time.

A scream of warning from Jolian made him look up as Sebast bore down on them, a blast of Jolian's fire into his path making Sebast bank to avoid it, his spray of green acid missing the champions and striking the stone behind them. The green dragon had fresh burn marks on his head and one wing, but Jolian seemed unhurt. On his back, Novir was too small to see much of from here.

As Garian and Aeron tried to rise, green grass rose from between the stones beneath them, wrapping around their arms and legs, pulling them down. Startled, Matt turned and saw Anna with her arm extended toward them, fist closed and surrounded by white light. He moved toward her to protect the priestess as the grass grew longer, blades encircling Aeron's throat but not Garian's. This suggested that the necromancer was the true source of ire for the goddess of life Anna was channeling. But Aeron shouted a word he didn't understand before being strangled into silence. Some of the enthralled who were approaching ran at them, and Matt realized that each was undead.

Anna saw it, too, her eyes wide. Matt thought maybe she could just make more grass spring up and grab each of them, but she dropped her hand before turning it on the undead to one side. Those undead staggered as white light suddenly shone from their eyes, mouths, and ears. They stumbled and fell face first, unmoving. Anna whirled around and did it again to those on the other side, and then the ones running up behind Garian and Aeron, who had freed themselves and began to rise.

"*Thank* you," said Matt, reaching into his pocket for the vial of dragon ice water. Then he saw Sebast circling back toward them, Jolian once again in pursuit. "Anna, do you think you could hit the dragon with that?" To one side, Ryan appeared to be holding his own against Lord Voth, retreating steadily.

With a gleam in her eye, Anna said, "Let's see."

She made the same gesture at Sebast as he neared. The white light appeared in his eyes for a moment and caused him to turn sharply just overhead, but it seemed Anna wasn't strong enough to take him down. Something fell from his back and Matt recognized Novir's corpse as it plummeted, white lights shining from within his orifices until he smashed into the pavement yards from them, bounced once, and stopped moving.

Matt turned toward Garian and cast another spell of dragon ice, this time foot-long shards of ice hurtling at the sorcerer, who waved his Dragon's Fire Wand and melted them. But one struck a glancing blow off his shoulder and made him drop the wand. Matt struggled for a spell to levitate the wand to himself, but couldn't think of one as the sorcerer picked it up and looked at the sky. Matt followed his gaze, and this time only Jolian was coming, a jet of flames whirling in her mouth. He was about to run for the Hall of Worlds when Garian shouted behind him.

"Enough games, Ellorians! Meet your new master!"

Matt turned and saw that the Orb of Dominion now glowed with a golden sheen along its edges, a darker image within and moving but too hard to make out from here. Then a voice spoke from within it, far louder than he expected.

"Obey and serve," the voice commanded, and Matt wondered if those words acted like a spell to ensnare minds. "Fight no more. My will be yours. Follow the Lords Garian, Voth, Aeron, and Kori as your masters after me."

"Thank you, my Lord," said Garian, gazing at them in triumph.

Jolian flew past without breathing fire, and Matt saw that his friends had stopped fighting. Had the *Mind Shield* spell worked? He didn't feel any different. How should they behave? He looked at the enthralled to see what they did, as he was supposed to be one of them now, but they had just stopped advancing and stood idly by. For a moment, he wondered if the others were ensnared or safe like him, but then Eric caught his eye and the knowing look in them calmed him. Neither Anna nor Ryan was looking at him, and he sensed he should stop looking around like that or risk attracting attention.

"Ellorians," began Garian, glaring as he advanced, "stand together."

Since Matt stood in the middle of everyone, he didn't move as his friends moved toward him. He tried to seem complacent and just hoped they quickly went to the portal so he didn't have to pretend for long. The others stopped beside him and turned to face the Lords of Fear, who came within arm's reach before halting. Waves of cold from Lord Voth made him shiver, the hand closest to the undead knight feeling numb, but the sorcerer directly before him got his attention. Garian handed the Orb of Dominion staff to Kori without looking, his gaze fixed on Matt's staff.

"The famous staff of Soliander," he said, eyes alight despite the anger still on his face. "I have always wondered." He reached for it.

"Do not touch that," said a calm, menacing voice from within the orb.

Garian's hand instantly stopped as a look of fear took hold. He retracted his hand. "Yes, my lord."

"Bring them and the orb to me without delay."

"Yes, my lord." He raised his voice for all and said, "To the Hall of Worlds. Follow." He pushed past them, leaving the orb with Kori, who slipped her hand into Eric's. As Matt turned, he caught Ryan's eye and saw the big guy wink at him, sword still in his hand. The other enthralled all waited until the eight of them passed by, then fell in behind, a growing legion of warriors approaching the nearby hall. He listened for Jolian and thought he heard a distant whoosh of flames, but that was all.

"I think I'm going to make you my consort," purred Kori to Eric. "You disappointed with your sword skills, but the rest was great fun. Maybe you'll do better at poking me with something else."

"It is the Lady Eriana who should be a consort," said Aeron, his voice deep.

"Yes," agreed Lord Voth, in smooth tones. "Aranor needs a queen."

"I will raise one from the dead for you," suggested Aeron, "but she is mine."

Sounding amused, Lord Garian said, "You will wait in line. I understand our master has a special interest in her."

Despite the risk, Matt took Anna's hand to lend a supportive squeeze and found his hand being crushed by the strength of hers. The lords were in front and couldn't see, but he disengaged as they stepped into the shadow of the Hall of Worlds, a white building painted with planets of blues, yellows, and greens all along it except the tall wooden doors. These now swung open slowly, as if heavy, pulled by more enthralled. Matt suspected the lords knew that the path before them had been cleared so that they couldn't use the orb on more people, but were they surprised to meet no other resistance to accessing the portal? Garian commanded all but two dozen enthralled to wait outside. As they entered, Matt looked around. Where was Talis hiding?

The Hall of Worlds reminded Matt of an airport lounge stretching before them. They had entered one end of the long, two-story rectangle. Lining the walls were various supplies travelers might need, such as blankets and torches. A few weapons and light armor were also for sale, but much of it was food and drink. A six-foot high wall separated one from the next, each having an open storefront. They all stood empty of people. The hall's center stood bare except for murals of fanciful beasts on the floor and a stage in the center, a lute and several handheld drums lying discarded. Behind it all against the far wall, dancing golden light shimmered from the nearly two-story portal, its surface rippling as if made of a standing wall of liquid gold. Tall and wide enough for wagons to pass through, it stood unprotected, the guard stations to either side of it empty of life. Or so it seemed. They marched unmolested toward it, stopping twenty paces away when Lord Garian held up one hand as he and the other lords continued forward a few strides before turning to face them.

Garian looked at the enthralled. "You are to remain here on Rovell. Live your lives until word comes that we need you and then obey. Tell the same to those outside." He looked at Matt and the others and smirked. "It was not hard to defeat the famed Ellorian Champions after all."

"Maybe that's because that isn't them," said a voice to one side. Another Andier and Korrin stepped from inside a guard station to one side as the Lords of Fear turned sharply. A second Soliander and Eriana walked out of the other station on the other side, the wizard beginning to cast a spell. As he yanked the Dragon's Fire Wand from up his sleeve, Garian's piercing gaze swept over Matt and the others, none of them having moved.

"What is this?" he asked of no one in particular.

"A trick," said a dismissive voice from the Orb of Dominion. "It is no matter. Obey and serve!"

Eric yelled, "Now, Ryan!"

Chaos erupted.

The knight ran toward the assassin as the lords turned in surprise. Kori was too slow to stop Ryan's blade from cleanly slicing through the staff just below the Orb of Dominion, which dropped as she reached to catch it. Ryan swung again and cut her arm off at the elbow. She screamed and dropped the useless staff from her other hand to clutch at the wound as blood spurted from it. The orb struck the stones with a whack but didn't break.

"Kick it away!" yelled Eric as he backed up, throwing a knife at Garian and striking him in the chest. The knight complied, sending the orb tumbling at the rogue, who stopped it with one foot. Kori staggered toward Aeron and Ryan backed away. The second Soliander completed a spell that sent a hail of fist-sized stones pummeling the lords. Lord Voth leaped at the wizard, sword slicing the man in half and leaving a trail of frost along the wound.

"Rise," said Aeron, gesturing toward the now dead wizard.

"Burn!" yelled Anna, and pointed at the corpse, which burst into flames instead.

As if they had standing orders to protect the lords, the enthralled warriors moved to attack them. Anna turned and held up one hand, palm outward, as if to stop them. And it worked, to Matt's surprise. Had she suddenly become a partner in battle, more than just for the undead? If so, she was a welcome addition. Matt saw Lord Garian's eyes on them and knew something was coming. He struggled for another spell he could cast first.

"Try hitting it with your sword," Eric suggested to Ryan.

"Worth a shot," the knight said. He swung the blade high above his hand and brought it slamming down onto the orb with a clang. A shock wave knocked all of them back and onto the ground, Matt striking his head on the stones. He sat up, trying to ignore the pain, eyes on the Lords of Fear, who had also been felled. He followed Garian's shocked and angry gaze to the orb. It had split into the three pieces, two of them rocking on the floor on their spherical part, the other face down on the broken side.

"No!" said Garian, rising. A glance around the room revealed the enthralled men starting to sit up, their faces no longer intense and enraged, but calm and bewildered. "Attack them!" Garian commanded. But no one moved to comply.

Matt saw his chance and gripped Soliander's staff in both hands, willing as much power as he dared and not bothering to waste precious moments getting to his feet. "Enuminsar!"

A fountain of flame roared from the staff's crystal toward the lords, the scorching heat making Matt's lungs hurt and his eyes sting as if it would incinerate anything in its path.

Just before the wall of flames reached them, he saw both the wizard and necromancer raise their hands and speak words he couldn't hear over the roaring. The flames shot upward and out as if hitting a wall. With a swirling gesture, Matt directed the fire to the right, left, and up to go around any barrier there, and as the flames complied, they cleared his view of the enemy. Both Garian and Aeron stood with hands forward to protect themselves. Matt watched in satisfaction as their horrified eyes watched three tongues of fire rush around the invisible barrier toward them. Aeron turned to block one and succeeded, Garian did the same with the one above, but the other one engulfed Lord Voth and soared past for Kori, who dove out of the way toward escape.

Suddenly a knife flew at Garian and struck him in the arm. He gasped and stumbled toward the portal, the flames above diving closer at him, as if his barrier had nearly fallen, one hand still raised to keep it there. He shot a look of hatred toward Eric, his eyes then widening. From the corner of Matt's eye, he saw the rogue pulling back his arm to throw again. Garian turned and ran through the portal, Kori close behind. Eric's knife flew at Aeron instead, and the necromancer barely dodged it before running for escape, too. A thunderous crash outside suggested one dragon had plummeted to the ground.

Lord Voth stood alone before them, seemingly unfazed by one spout of flames engulfing him, only his legs visible. Wondering if three would be worse, Matt directed the others spouts into one unified blast, now that no magic shield stood in the way. No sooner did all three converge on the undead knight than a scream of pain split the air from the burning creature. Matt kept the flames going for another minute as the knight tried to get away from them. Matt made the torrent follow him, the smell of burned flesh growing. He finally wanted to see what had happened and not kill the fire in case he needed it again, so he made the flames form a low ring around the knight's lower body.

The knight stopped screaming, two blue pinpoints of light gleaming from where his eyes had been burned out in a bone-white skull. All visible flesh had melted away except for what still dripped off, steaming, hissing, and popping. Any cloth had burned off, and parts of him were still on fire. He now looked every bit the undead knight he was. A skeletal hand gripped his sword, the other pointing at Matt.

"You will die by my hand," he said in a voice shaking with fury or pain.

A moment of fear struck Matt before anger took hold and he engulfed the knight in flames again. He heard the metal boots take several steps before the portal gave a pulse and the sound stopped. He let the flames die. As expected, Lord Voth was gone. He turned back to his friends.

Eric flashed a smile. "I don't think he likes you."

Trying to sound unfazed, the wizard said, "He was dead already. Not sure what he's so upset about."

The rogue joked, "Maybe attracting an undead bride is harder now that he's not so handsome."

"Oh, I don't know, I think he looks better now. He should thank me for the makeover. The flaming flesh has a nice, romantic quality to it. Wouldn't even need to light candles on a hot date."

They all laughed and Ryan came forward, giving him a surprise hug. "Remind me not to piss you off. That's some spell you have."

"It's mostly the staff," Matt admitted.

They turned to take in their surroundings, and Matt saw that a pair of wizards that had emerged from hiding had shut the portal off. In human form again, Jolian strode up behind them, looking grim, determined, and irritated but unharmed. The formerly enthralled people had risen and seemed to be no threat, many having put away their swords. He wondered how much they remembered. Did they have any idea where they were or how they had gotten here? Part of him didn't care, but he thought that, as the Ellorian Champions, they should address it. He was about to say something when the pieces of the broken Orb of Dominion began to tremble, then vibrate. He gestured for the others to stand back as the pieces slid toward each other on the stone. Eric took a step toward them as if to stop one.

"Wait," cautioned Matt.

"Are you sure?" the rogue asked, stopping.

"No, but I think we need to see what happens."

Eric didn't look convinced. The three pieces came together on the floor and turned toward the others, each rising on one edge. Matt knew they were reforming before the three put themselves together as if someone were holding them. Was the wizard who controlled the master doing this? It seemed unlikely with the portal closed. He glanced around the room to see if anyone appeared to be doing magic to cause this, but no one was, and half weren't paying attention. His eyes returned to the orb just as the three pieces fused together, a brief burst of golden light shining from the cracks that disappeared. The Orb of Dominion appeared to have healed itself.

"Great," muttered Ryan. "Now what?"

Anna sighed. "Well, the good part is that everyone has been released. Now we just have to prevent it from being used again."

Matt asked, "Yeah, but where do we put it?"

Eric looked at him with a gleam in his eye. "I have an idea."

Night had fallen and Anna felt slightly tipsy from the wine, the gait of her white horse doing little to ease the feeling. Behind her rode the others in single file, the Quest Ring on a hill in the distance, Castle Arking behind them. The time had come to return to Earth, assuming no one summoned them in the few minutes remaining here. The idea of going from quest to quest without respite bothered her, but the moment they completed this one, they had become available to anyone else summoning them to solve their problems.

And what of their own? How were they supposed to live their own lives when they had to keep saving someone else's? It wasn't fair, but it wasn't like they could complain about it to anyone but each other. No one on Rovell knew they weren't the real Ellorian Champions. At least on Honyn, the elf Lorian and many of his closest friends, like Morven, had known. They could be themselves. Not pretend. Admit that they were scared and confused. That they didn't know how to do one thing or another that they would be expected to know. Somehow, they had succeeded at another quest. But it seemed like only a matter of time before they failed or got themselves killed.

The thought reminded her of home. Fear about what had happened to her friends when she had vanished from behind the wheel of her car had receded with their more direct concerns, but now that everything had been resolved, there was no escaping learning their fate soon. Even if everyone was fine and escaped serious injury, she would have some explaining to do. They had all seen her disappear. How does one explain such a thing when telling the truth is likely to get you locked in a padded psych ward? She would worry about that later. Her immediate concern was her own safety.

They now knew that they returned to exactly where they had been before the summoning. Matt would end up on a sidewalk where his interview had been taking place. Ryan would reappear in the guest house at his parent's estate. Eric had been at his job. But Anna had been in the middle of I-270, south of Gaithersburg. They all assumed she would arrive in that exact spot. With no car around her. No air bags. No seat belt. And possibly cars hurtling toward her. They had left Earth in late afternoon but arrived on Rovell before lunch. Based on this, they had agreed to leave Rovell a few hours before midnight. Hopefully, Anna reappearing on a major interstate in the middle of the night would dramatically lessen the chances of a car hitting her before she ran off the road. It certainly beat appearing in rush hour traffic. She knew that even with this plan, nothing was guaranteed. It was going to be pure luck. Either a car struck and likely killed her, or she got out of the way before one could. Maybe she should have had even more wine. It was the reason she had drunk so much.

They had also talked of the likelihood that they were famous again. Matt had disappeared on camera, so they expected significant attention. By arriving so late, they might sneak home before anyone knew. If reporters were camped out at their homes, which seemed likely, this was a problem. They had been gone three weeks the first time, but now it had been three days and that wasn't enough for people to stop watching, they assumed. For now, the plan was for Ryan to get his car and go get Anna. Matt and Eric suspected that their own vehicles might have been towed by now. Their priority was assessing their situation and then calling each other. Anna sighed, not wanting to deal with it.

Before and behind the supposed Ellorian Champions, a train of other riders accompanied them on their way to the Quest Ring. This included King Orin of Minari, his wizard Derin, the dwarven Queen of Morcanon and her retinue, and a host of revelers they had just partied with at a banquet in their honor at Castle Arking behind them. Enjoying such an affair was hard when she knew, at any second, they could suddenly vanish to another quest, but she had pushed it from her mind as best as she was able. It seemed she had to do a lot of that these days. The thought made her sigh.

Just in front of her rode Jolian and her brother Brazin, both in human form and in their preferred tight leather of red or blue. The group had told no one of Brazin's mental capture by the Orb of Dominion, to spare any humiliation or damage to his reputation. Once free of it, he had shown a level of humility and sorrow she didn't expect from a dragon, not that she knew much about that. They had collected him at Valegis and rode him and his red sister back to the castle, leaving all others behind at Ortham. Farewells to Talis and anyone from the city had been brief, but they had earned more friends that they would likely never see again, as much good as that did them.

It had taken hours to implement Eric's plan. First, he had Ryan try to break the Orb of Dominion into three pieces again with a different sword, which had shattered the blade instead. Only Ryan's weapon, made of soclarin ore, could do it. Once broken, Eric, Ryan, and Matt had each taken a piece and walked away from each other in the Hall of Worlds. Twenty steps apart hadn't been enough, because the shards tried to pull together once more, but doubling the distance prevented it from happening again. Eric had wondered if that was true, and with it proven, he told them his idea.

Leaving Anna and Ryan to heal people, and provide leadership, he and Matt had climbed aboard Jolian with one piece and been gone for two hours before returning without it. Then they experimented with bringing the two remaining pieces close together. The parts showed no attempt to merge, so they turned their attention to other matters. This had included a meeting with the rulers of Ortham to inform them of developments. They also arranged for those who had been enthralled to be sent home with necessary supplies for their journeys, whether to the town of Durba, Castle Arking, or wherever they lived. They offered Ortham some gems from King Orin for this, but in a show of appreciation, he had refused it.

And so they returned to Valegis for Brazin, who had proven to Jolian's satisfaction that he was of his own mind again, not that they doubted this. They had questioned various enthralled victims before and knew most had only been dimly aware of having been compromised. Most spoke of feeling an agreement with orders given to them, as if they had long thought of doing the very thing they were commanded to do and now felt certain of its rightness. When the orb had shattered, they had suddenly come to their senses and been disturbed by what they had done.

And for this reason, Brazin seemed genuinely ashamed that he had killed his friend Sebast. Anna had felt bad for him, having seldom seen such troubled eyes in her life. Brazin was haunted, and she wondered if the same thing would befall her on returning to Earth and learning the fate of her friends. Inspired by a dread that this would be so, she had spent most of the night with the blue dragon, trying to help him and gain some understanding of what this might be like. In doing so, she admitted to some fear of what had happened in her absence without going into details, and he seemed to understand that they had this in common. The kiss he had given her had surprised and delighted her, the tingling feeling of a dragon's kiss not something she'd soon forget. Had he just ruined her for regular guys? She laughed and looked fondly at his back as he rode before her.

That night in Valegis, with Brazin recovered, they had filled in Ogren and spent another evening in town. That had been the first celebration, where a small feast had been done in their honor, there not being much time to anticipate a bigger one. She didn't really mind, and the others had clearly enjoyed the attention. Eric had not returned to their rooms that night, and the smirk on his face the next day erased any doubt he'd been in a woman's room overnight. Ryan had returned late with something of a sloppy grin that had irritated her. She'd had half a mind to go find Brazin and get another kiss, but she wasn't really sure what that would do to her.

Instead, she had spent the night with Matt, memorizing spells with him. She had noticed women intrigued by the wizard, but also intimidated by Soliander's reputation. Matt had seemed little interested in them, but she suspected it was his new obsession with learning magic. She agreed with his desire to commit these spells to memory and write them down on Earth if magic became available to them.

In the morning, they had flown on Brazin and Jolian to the Kirii Cave. Eric seemed fine without a saddle, the crazy boy that he was, but Ryan had seemed concerned by the experience. Once there, they found another way into the cave itself and hid a second of the orbs' three pieces in the bottom of the underground lake. In doing so, they discovered that the leviathan wasn't entirely dead, though it didn't attack, and they returned to Valegis to ensure Ogren and the townspeople knew. This would prevent anyone from seeking the orb shard. Before leaving the cave, they had removed the saddle from the dead Sebast and placed it on Brazin, who had paid his respects while the others were below. His own saddle had been left behind at the lake where Novir had disappeared.

After this, they flew to Morcanon, the dwarven kingdom. It had taken some convincing to get to the queen, mostly by using the remaining piece of the Orb of Dominion to convince anyone of their identities. She had been freed of her enthrallment and been in contact with King Orin, and thus were they given an audience. It was here that they wanted to leave the other piece, figuring the dwarves had learned a hard lesson. This had resulted in their second feast, this time for lunch and once again haphazardly arranged. The dwarves had reminded her of Rognir, her Honyn friend and mentor, but their offered tours of their underground world seemed too much of the Kirii Cave, an apprehension that vanished before long. Their stonework skill had her and the others in awe, but there was little time to enjoy it. They soon departed for a short flight to Castle Arking.

They told King Orin a riddle that Eric and Matt devised. No one was to know where the three pieces of the slave Orb of Dominion lay in case someone brought them together again. But since it was possible that they might need this and the four Ellorian Champions were no more, they decided on leaving a clue. The result was a quest they devised for someone else to complete. Even Ryan and Anna didn't know where the first piece lay and found the clues to be suitably cryptic.

In ruins lies the first of three
Where once stood man but nothing be
Entombed in stone for none to see
In high noon's light it can be free
Where monsters swim and darkness lies
The second piece it does reside
All arms and wings, two deadly foes
Beneath the waves that one must row
The third lies in the tunnels of stone
Among those who were once overthrown
Now free again they have all sworn
To hide the shard and keep it torn

Anna wasn't sure which of the two came up with text because they looked equally proud of it when reciting it the first time, and they had cared little for her suggested edits. The thought made her smile. With danger over, they had returned to being like two boys playing *Dungeons and Dragons*. She wasn't one to stifle someone's entertainment anyway, and certainly not after everything they just went through. On the first quest, they had thought they would just go back to their lives after some initial attention, but this time they knew better.

Now Eric and Matt had created a quest instead of solving one. Maybe one day someone else might go on the quest to recover the slave Orb of Dominion, but hopefully it wouldn't be the Lords of Fear, or anyone else during their lifetime. The orb pieces would not unable to come together on their own, and only someone who knew the location of each piece could find them. Only Eric, Matt, and Jolian knew. They trusted the dragon.

Anna grew nervous as they neared the Quest Ring, the path to it lined by torches, an honor guard lining the way. The ring itself had been lit with more flames that illuminated those standing near it. Despite efforts to keep the crowd at bay, they were getting a hero's send off, and she got the impression the guards had given up on keeping people away. The mood was positive but quiet, as if the night sky hushed everyone, kids jostling for position. She had learned that the champions had never been here before and with their summoning happening in secret, no one had seen the spectacle. They weren't going to be denied this time.

The group dismounted and said their farewells, accepting some gifts despite knowing they wouldn't arrive with them. What happened to them they didn't know. Did they just fall to the ground here on Rovell? They would likely never get an answer. This was the first time they were supposedly bringing something they hadn't arrived with back. Before going, Anna asked Jolian to please come find them if she heard that they had arrived on Rovell again. They could use a friend.

Then they mounted the dais as people cheered, Ryan turning to them and assuming the role of a heroic knight that he played at RenFest. Who knew he would ever get to do it for real? He might have been the only one who truly enjoyed the pomp and ceremony of it all. And his wealthy upbringing had sort of prepared him for it, with the fancy balls and other stuff his parents had made him go to. Anna couldn't relate, but she could admire the way he worked the crowd. Better him than her. They hadn't really talked about it, but they knew Eric was their actual leader, the man with a plan, but that Ryan was the public face of the group. It seemed to work for all of them. The shy Matt could hang back as the intimidating Soliander while Anna could smile and try to soften their fearsome reputation. Taking the edge off boys and their sometimes-unruly leanings was something girls did anyway.

But she was faking it this time. It wasn't until they had said last goodbyes that everyone but them stepped off the dais. King Orin made a final brief speech, the dwarven queen did the same, and a shout went up from the King's Guard. Then everyone fell silent, Matt having decided to use Soliander's staff to trigger the return spell. He did the deed as people watched, then resumed position, the floor beneath them lighting up just as the pillars did. The crowd cheered and for the first time, Anna felt the weight on her lift. She hadn't let herself feel the gratitude or happiness until now and tried to cut herself some slack. Maybe Raven, Heather, and Jade were fine, and all this anxiety wasn't worth it. Then the Quest Ring and people disappeared.

The familiar vortex of light and sound roared around her. This time she remembered to cover herself as Eriana's robe vanished, making her nude before her Earth clothes returned. She felt the lump of her smartphone in one pocket and briefly wondered what would happen if she tried to make a call. How soon would it get a signal to let her know how many texts, calls, and emails she hadn't seen? Across from her, the others looked excited, if tense. Whatever happened to feeling safe now that they were going home? The three of them disappeared before her along with the noise, but the bright light remained, blinding even more, the sound of a car horn blaring, followed by the screech of skidding tires.

Then the darkness took her.

CHAPTER NINE

In the Dead of Night

Soliander held up a plastic card with numbers embossed on it. "What's this?"

A credit card, he suddenly realized, knowledge from his previous mental contact with Matt surfacing. Pieces were falling into place, but many of them weren't particularly useful. Still, he needed to know how to get around in this world. No magic portals existed, not that he couldn't cast him and his apprentice somewhere. But he grew eager to experience this place he'd only seen in Matt's memories before arriving on Earth himself. And then there was the question of seeming like they belonged here while avoiding suspicion. He had admonished Darron not to gawk, but part of him knew he was doing it, too. It was one reason they were in a Gaithersburg, Maryland hotel room now, gathering intel out of sight, with fewer bright lights and fantastic sights to make them stare.

"My credit card," answered Joe, a middle-aged, portly man who seemed typical of those encountered so far. He sat before them on the lone chair, tan slacks and a white button-up shirt at odds with their jeans and t-shirts. Darron had asked about the differing clothes, but Soliander wasn't inclined to explain trivial details, which he only sensed the significance of from Matt's memories. The fourth-floor hotel room had two queen beds and furnishings that the wizard suspected were normal. Joe's bag, or suitcase, lay open on one bed, the contents already rifled through.

"How does it work?" Soliander asked, images of using it to pay for goods flashing in his head. "You purchase things with it?"

"Yes."

"What sorts of items?"

"Almost anything. Food, hotel rooms, merchandise."

"Homes?"

"No, that requires a mortgage, a home loan."

"Explain."

Soliander and his apprentice listened as Joe explained about credit, banks, and the housing market. They had been at this for ten minutes, the spell Soliander had cast on Joe making him compliant and honest to a fault. This world was unlike anything he'd known. By morning, they'd likely know everything they needed. The information was overwhelming, and Soliander was growing impatient, because there was so much that was so different. He finally made Joe stop talking, grabbed his apprentice's hand, and cast the *Mind Trust* spell on Joe. It allowed both of them to sift through Joe's memories, which they did for hours, gorging on intel. They had previously done this to a hotel maid, then made her forget the encounter.

It had not taken long for Darron to contact him via the orb from a local park, then cast a cantrip to make a ball of light appear. Soliander had arrived moments later, but as strong as he was, magic was not without a cost and he felt a little weakened by the exertion. He recognized the sight of Matt's house, or that of his parents, technically, but he didn't go in. The lights and movement inside had not deterred him so much as the recollection, courtesy of Matt, of what lay inside. The memories returned more concretely now that he was here, his eyes going to one house or another, to places where Matt had experienced pain or pleasure, or where childhood friends had lived. And that's how he realized the parents of Anna lived next door. That could also be useful.

It was partly for this reason that the pair had spent hours walking around town and sometimes sitting on a bench, watching people, and quietly remarking on observed details great and small. Everything became more distinct for Soliander, as if the disjointed nature of his *Mind Trust* spell with Matt was undone by being in the places where those broken memories had originated. It was all more fantastic than Soliander had envisioned. Darron had been less prepared for it and so wide-eyed that Soliander had finally cast a spell to calm the dark elf.

Arriving at night had been helpful, as fewer people had been around to encounter, and they had spent until morning getting a feel for life on Earth. The need for sleep and a quiet base for further exploring had led to this hotel and Joe, who was in town for business. The right spell had resulted in Joe going about his day job while the wizards slept in his room with the "do not disturb" sign on, with breaks for exploring, then Joe dutifully returning to them for the night. Tomorrow would include trips to Anna's condo, Eric's place, and the home of Ryan's family, with much information falling into place. But one subject Soliander most wanted to know, he found nothing on, so he returned to the inquisition to ask directly.

"What do you know of Merlin?" he asked.

"Merlin?" Joe asked with a frown.

"The wizard."

Hesitating, Joe asked, "You mean the legend guy? From Arthur's Court? Knights of the Round Table? That's just a myth."

Soliander scowled in frustration, for his spells had rendered Joe helpful, and yet here he was not being so. It suggested the information was beyond his reach. "From what year is this myth?"

"I'm not sure. The 11th century maybe."

"And it's... the 21st century?"

"Yeah. It's after 2000."

Soliander stepped back. "A thousand years."

He had half-expected something of this sort, but not nearly that long. It explained the weathering at Stonehenge, which he was curious to visit, but it could wait. Matt's memories were quite clear on that one, being so recent. He asked Joe about the myth but learned little until Joe offered to look it up on his laptop, so they did. But for all the legends, there was nothing about Stonehenge in them, or Quest Rings, and no mention of himself, Eriana, Korrin, or Andier. And while Morgana appeared in quite a few of the tales, he found nothing about the Ellorian Champions. Or Merlin's Pendant. Or faerie creatures vanishing along with magic to their own world. It was as if none of it had ever happened.

Soliander sighed in frustration. No answer would come soon, he realized, so he turned his mind to practical matters. He wasn't sure how to go about acquiring his own credit card or smartphone to pay for things, and with cash still acceptable, he soon magically robbed a nearby bank by turning himself invisible, casting himself inside, and removing a small fortune in bills before leaving. Similar stunts helped prepare himself and Darron for further escapades, but with the Stonehenge Four, as he had learned they were called, gone on a quest, he had time.

He had seen news reports of Matt vanishing on camera, and the stories about Anna's disappearance, the others reportedly missing as well. The footage of Matt had been important for understanding one thing—they weren't going voluntarily. The expression of surprise on Matt's face had made it plain. This came as no real surprise. After Everon's betrayal, he and the others hadn't been doing it willingly either. The real question now was how the four Earth friends had been substituted for them. He had wondered if Korrin, Andier, or Eriana had somehow done this, despite it being improbable, but now he knew they had not.

Like him, they had railed against the forced quests and having to pretend they were happy to solve someone else's problem for them when no one could solve theirs—how to escape the quest cycle that only Everon and Diara knew was undesired. His friends would never have forced others to take their place even if they had known how, and if Soliander didn't know, they couldn't. He was the wizard who had invented everything about the Quest Rings–with a little help from Eriana for the healing elements—until Everon altered them.

His curiosity about them had only increased on learning of the quest on Rovell. They had somehow defeated the Lords of Fear, who had earned their nickname. The victory was impressive and unexpected. They seemed a threat to anyone up to no good and had surprised him twice now. This warranted respect and caution, maybe a little more reconnaissance. Had his old friends somehow trained them, or were they just getting lucky? It took more than good fortune to defeat the lords.

Aeron had suffered a loss of pride, and Garian had recovered from his wounds. Kori's severed arm had grown back with supernatural help, but there was no way to restore Lord Voth's previously handsome appearance. Soliander liked him better this way anyway. An undead knight who looked like a normal man wasn't nearly as frightening as one with bones and bits of charred flesh hanging from him.

The quartet had been suitably concerned about their future well-being after the failure, but they didn't have to explain what happened. He had seen their collapse himself, right until the moment "Lord Korrin" had slammed his sword down at the orb. After that, he lost contact, but he knew what must have happened, and the Lords of Fear had confirmed it. The slave Orb of Dominion had broken, leaving only the master. And now the subservience that had ensnared two kingdoms of the many to come had been lost. He frowned as he gazed over at a black velvet cloth atop a round object. When he caught up with these supposed Ellorian Champions, he would make them reveal what they had done with the other orb's pieces.

The moment he sensed he had returned to Earth, Eric dropped into a defensive crouch and scanned around him. Then he relaxed and straightened. He was alone. And he had arrived where he'd expected—back at work, which was predictably deserted. He once again wore his karategi, its white pants and jacket too bright for his comfort as he stood there in the dark. A glance at the clock showed just after two in the morning, so their guess at the time had been close. He turned to where his clothes should have been but weren't. His shoes, car keys, wallet, and phone were all gone. He searched for them, thinking his boss might have moved them, but then he went to window and looked for his car. Gone.

"Damn it," he said, not surprised. Someone might have called the police. He had a bad feeling they were about to be famous all over again. He went into the office and dialed Matt from the landline. To his relief, the techie picked up.

"Hey, it's Eric. I'm stuck inside at work because the alarm is on and I don't know the code."

"Just let yourself out anyway. Who cares if it goes off?"

Eric laughed. "Good point, but there is a problem. A couple. I don't have my regular clothes, or my wallet, and that stuff. And my car is gone."

"Yeah, so is mine. Is that why you're calling from another phone? I almost didn't pick up but figured it was you or Ryan."

"Yeah. My parents likely have it all. Listen, I forgot I was wearing karate stuff, which is what I'm in now. If I set off that alarm, and I'm walking the streets in this because I don't have a car, I'm going to draw attention."

"Yeah, you'd get picked up for sure, though I'm not sure how quickly they'd know a guy in a karate outfit is the one who set the alarm off there."

"Me either." But an alarm at a karate place going off and a guy walking around in a karate outfit would be too much coincidence for the police to not quickly put it together, then confirm it, all after arresting him. Technically, he had done nothing wrong, but that wouldn't stop the arrest or cause problems he wanted to avoid. It seemed obvious that his disappearance was known, so he might not get out of custody easily if apprehended. He felt like he didn't have time for that anyway.

"Why don't I come get you?" Matt asked.

"Still risky. I was just going to spend the next few hours here and try to sneak out in the morning or something. Hopefully, the owner won't notice. You could pick me up then, assuming you find your car." Eric sighed. This was getting irritating.

"Yeah. What time does the place open? I'll try to be there with clothes."

"Good idea. I need shoes, maybe sandals as they'll fit better since they aren't mine. Anyway, I think my boss gets in by 6:30."

"Then I'll be there by 6. It'll give me time to go by my house for some stuff."

"Okay. Listen, try Anna next. I will call Ryan. It's important none of you try to call my cell. If it's at my parent's house, they might see you calling and if everyone knows we all disappeared, they'll know you guys are back, and me."

"Why does that matter?"

"Just don't do it. I have to call Ryan before he calls my phone. Bye."

He wasted no time, dialing Ryan and having it go to voicemail, where he left a long message and a number to call back on until 6:30, anyway. Then he settled in. He wanted to hide their arrival as long as possible and control the narrative of when they returned. They had to lie, of course, but they had to know what people were thinking in order to do that well, so keeping quiet about their return was a good idea for now. He settled in for a few hours, being refreshed as usual by the spell and not needing sleep. He suspected a long day awaited him.

Matt wished there was no flash of light when he returned to Earth. It was especially troubling at night, not only for attracting attention, but momentarily blinding him. Despite his impaired night vision, he quickly glanced around and didn't see anyone near him as he stood on a sidewalk. He wasted no time dawdling and began walking away just in case he'd been seen, pulling the hood of his hoodie over his head, though doing this at night might have made him look suspicious. He sighed and pulled it down. The roads had been empty, but the first car headlights appeared up the street as he took his bearings.

He was still outside the office building where he worked, as expected. The longer they could keep people from realizing they always returned to where they'd been, the better. He wasn't sure what would happen then but imagined being tasered by police or something. That would be an entirely different blinding light and hardly a warm welcome after having saved another planet, kingdom, or whatever. He laughed.

But the sound died in his chest as he rounded the corner of his employer's building to see his car was gone. Then his phone rang from an unfamiliar number, but he assumed it had to be one of his friends at this hour. He found Eric on the other end and had their talk while walking away from the building to create more distance. He would need an Uber, and after he hung up, devised a plan, his ride appearing minutes later. Before entering the car, he put the hood up again and tried to disguise his voice a little, while keeping his face averted. Then he just put his head down and pretended to be tired.

"What brings you out so late?" the twenty-something Indian driver asked.

Matt drew a blank and then said, "Fight with the girlfriend. She threw me out."

"Oh! That's terrible! The woman is always right. That's all I know about dating. It's so hard."

"Tell me about it." Matt recognized a talkative guy and hid behind someone else's wall of words, but within minutes, talk turned to his own disappearance days earlier because he'd just been picked up near there.

"Yeah," the driver said, "now the police and even FBI, the CIA, are looking for this guy."

"What? Why?"

"There's a rumor that he can just come and go whenever or wherever he wants, so what's stopping him from showing up in the White House and killing the president?"

"Holy shit."

"I know! It's crazy."

"But why would I... uh, he do that?"

"Oh, I don't know. People are all over his Twitter feed and all that, Facebook, but there's no report of him being like that, so I don't know."

"Do people think he's dangerous?"

"No. I don't think so. But I don't know. I guess they'll catch him at some point, I mean if they can. How do you catch a guy who can disappear when he wants to?"

Holy fucking shit, Matt thought, mind racing. He couldn't go home. Not like this, pulling up in an Uber to be arrested? And of course people thought he had vanished on purpose. That was great. Nothing like a misunderstanding to make this even worse. He couldn't go back, or at least not pull up in a car.

"Hey, there's a Denny's on the way. Can you drop me there instead? Kinda hungry."

"Yeah, sure thing."

"Great. Thanks."

Within minutes he had gotten out and left a tip for the guy via his phone app. He went inside and straight to the bathroom, trying to get a minute to himself. Then he studied his phone, wondering if it was being tracked even now. He furiously looked up how to turn off any tracking features. Not for the first time, he wondered what happened to anything he was holding or wearing when summoned. Did it go into some sort of suspended animation between worlds until he returned? Maybe he'd ask Jack what he saw in a tracking app when they went away. For now, he didn't feel comfortable bringing it but needed it, so he turned it completely off and left the nearly empty restaurant, trying not to look suspicious as he glanced repeatedly over his shoulder. He was a mile from home and ducked into a neighborhood to get out of sight.

Hugging tree lines and bushes while trying to act like he wasn't, Matt approached his parent's two-story, single-family house from the next street over, cutting through a back yard to reach it. In the deeper shadows of a maple tree he stopped, carefully eyeballing every hiding place he'd ever used as a boy, not for himself to go into now so much as to see if anyone was in one. While Anna had moved out to her own apartment, Matt had not, and her parents still lived next to his. They had been friends most of their lives, she being among those who had played those games with him. Who knew those childhood adventures would turn all too real?

He saw nothing suspicious and entered the property, mindful of the motion-detecting light he knew was above the backdoor. He had a plan for that and was staying clear for now, but first he wanted to check the front yard and cautiously reached the corner behind a tall evergreen shrub. He scooted into the opening between it and the house and looked out.

The first thing he noticed was his own car in the driveway, so at least it wasn't impounded or something. His mother's was beside it, which meant his father's was somewhere else. His parents were pack rats, the two-car garage full of boxes and other crap. Across the street were townhomes, which prevented on-the-street parking and resulted in two sets of parking spaces, on one either side of the town row, and his father's Prius sat in one of them, sandwiched between two SUVs.

No one seemed to be out there, and his eyes went to each car in a driveway or in the parking spots. All were familiar except for one that sat in the set of spaces where his father's car sometimes sat. It immediately drew his attention because he saw the orange glow of a cigarette inside as someone took a drag from it. The dark silhouette of two heads were visible. The house was being watched. His Mazda 3 was out of the question. So was the front door. Thank God for that Uber driver or he'd be face down in handcuffs right now.

He leaned against the house for a minute. Did people really think he was a danger to national security? He was suddenly glad that he had never gotten involved in any political commentary online. What would he say if apprehended? If he told the truth, they'd put him in a psych ward somewhere, and lying would not work. Even Eric, who was pretty good at that sort of thing, probably wouldn't acquit himself well. He realized he needed an attorney—like he could afford that. Life as a software developer could be lucrative, but he was at the start of his career, not yet raking in six figures. He sighed. One problem at a time.

He went to the back corner of the building and looked around, then scooted toward the rear door with his back against the house. Stopping at the first window, he tried to peer inside, wondering if his parents knew the place was being watched. Would they cooperate with the FBI or whoever was out there? Would they let someone stay inside to grab him? Would they let him be arrested? He wasn't a criminal, had done nothing wrong. His mom and dad would be worried about him, just like when the Stonehenge disappearance happened, but he doubted they would help someone other than him.

Suddenly he realized that his credit card, which was associated with his phone and Uber account, and which he had just used to pay for the ride, had likely triggered an alert that was probably set up.

"Fuck," he whispered. "No time for this."

He moved past the window quickly without worrying about it, making it to the door just under the security light. He had argued with his parents about its positioning when his dad set it up, pointing out this exact flaw, but his father hadn't listened or cared because they really had no reason to worry about it. Of all the times his mom and dad didn't listen, now Matt was suddenly glad for it. He unlocked the door, which swung inward, and stepped inside. He didn't wait to see if anything happened and instead went straight for his room upstairs, moving as quietly as he could in the dark. Sneaking into your own home has the advantage of knowing exactly where everything is, despite the blackness. Thinking quickly, he grabbed a phone charger, clothes for Eric, sandals, and an extra change of clothes for himself, stuffing them into his backpack. He also stripped and donned darker clothing, then grabbed two baseball hats and some sunglasses. It suddenly occurred to him that it didn't look like they had searched his room. They would have needed a warrant and a reason.

He was about to leave when the sight of his big remote-controlled car gave him an idea. He took it and the remote with him, stole his father's car keys from where they hung downstairs, and wrote a brief note to his parents.

I'm okay. Sorry for worrying you. I had to take Dad's car. Don't report it stolen. If an unknown number calls, it might be me. Pick up. Talk soon, I swear. Matt. P.S. Destroy this.

He put it inside the microwave and then exited the rear door carefully. Then he put the remote-controlled car on the ground, facing away from the house, and carefully exited the area the way he'd arrived. He went down two blocks, crossed the street, and then returned near his father's car so that those watching the house wouldn't see his approach. Once beside it, he fired up the remote and made the car move a few feet. From the house's front, he could still see the white glow of the security light's beam as the car triggered it. As Matt crouched down, the guys in the car got out and jogged toward the house, both holding up a gun that made Matt go cold. He waited until they were out of sight, got into his father's car, turned it on, and backed up without the lights on. Electric cars had a significant advantage of being quiet and the men never seemed to hear it as he put the car in drive and crept away, turning on the headlights once far enough out of sight.

Ryan's eyes adjusted to the dark night as he stood outside the family guest house, beside his car. Someone had shut both the trunk and door, which didn't surprise him. They had been here. The house door was also closed. He went up to it, finding it locked. All the gear had been seen. The question was by whom. Daniel would likely have not said anything to anyone. Gardeners would have, especially given that he had been missing for days. Patting his pockets, he found his wallet and phone, but no car keys, which he'd been holding when he vanished.

He tried Anna, knowing she was at risk, but the phone just kept ringing and then went to voicemail. As he prepared to try for the third time, getting worried, the phone rang with an unfamiliar number, but he answered it.

"Yeah."

"It's Eric."

After being filled in, Ryan said, "I can't get Anna. Just keeps going to voicemail."

"Can you get to her location?"

"I'm not sure. No car keys. I have to see if I can get into the house for the spares."

"Okay. On the off chance that your car is known to police, maybe grab another."

"Not sure it's worth it, but sure. I mean, someone knows it's here and may have told the police, so I don't think they'd be looking for it, but maybe they are."

"Call me back on this number when you find her."

Ryan agreed and hung up. Then he went for his car just to see what was still inside it from the supplies he'd been unloading. The door was unlocked and a piece of paper sat on the front seat along with a house key. He picked them up.

Alarm is set for delay. Beware pigs.

Daniel, he realized, recognizing the handwriting. He owed his brother one. Now he knew who had been back here to see the gear.

He ran for the main house. His family always set the alarm overnight, but with it set for the 30-second delay, he could get inside and turn it off before it called the police. This was the usual approach when no one was home, but overnight, his family used the no-delay setting. Whether or not his parents were doing it, Daniel was making sure it was that way. Arriving at the door, he let himself in, turned off the alarm, and went for his room, quickly changing clothes before heading to the garage but being intercepted by his brother.

"Glad you're back," Daniel whispered from his wheelchair, pajamas bottoms below his bare torso. "Had a motion detection camera on, in case you're wondering."

Ryan felt relief to see him again, but no time for, well, anything. And Daniel was a little too smart sometimes, so the days of keeping him in the dark were not meant to last. "Yeah, listen. I owe you a huge favor, but I need you to trust me. I have to leave right now, and no one can know that I'm back. Cover for me and I swear I'll tell you everything."

Daniel's eyes grew intense. "Okay. Do you need anything?"

"To find Anna." He started for the garage again, Daniel following.

"Is she hurt?"

"I really hope not."

They entered the six-car garage, Daniel rolling down a ramp, and Ryan went for the rack of car keys. He ignored the vehicles that would attract attention, like the red Lamborghini Countach, a silver Aston Martin convertible, and a yellow Ferrari 308 GTS.

"Take a bike?" Daniel suggested. "Faster and she's been on the back if you are planning to pick her up. The cops are looking for you. Easier to lose–"

"Yeah, got it." Ryan went for the Ducati motorcycle and quickly grabbed a spare jacket for her, cramming it into a saddlebag, putting on his and zipping it, then attaching a helmet for her to the back seat and pulling his on.

"Your intensity is starting to worry me."

"I'm just worried," Ryan said, getting on and starting it, as his brother hit the garage door opener. He decided to stop hiding things because his brother had probably put together a lot already. Everyone had to know Matt had vanished, and the rest of them, too, so he admitted, "Look, she disappeared on the highway, which means she reappeared on it, but without a car, and that means she might have just been hit by a car."

"Jesus. Call me if anything has happened. I'll stay up."

"Love you, brother."

"Yeah. Be careful."

Once the door was high enough, Ryan hit the gas and flew out of the garage. As he neared the estate gates, they were already opening courtesy of Daniel and he blew past them long before they completed opening. Gratitude for his brother's help mixed with fear for Anna. He had a bad feeling about this.

River Road was empty as he hurtled onto the two-lane road, heading away from the Capital Beltway. He expected ten minutes to reach Anna's general location, but there was more than one way to get there, and if Daniel was right that the police were watching him, the back way offered many ways to lose them. And as it turned out, his brother was right. Within moments of hitting the road, red and blue flashing lights appeared behind him. He gunned it and turned up one road, rolling on the throttle and hoping they didn't follow.

But they did, and he sped up more, going over several hills at 90 mph before slowing and veering off another way and gunning it again. He could not turn the lights on a motorcycle off, unlike a car, and he roared over two hills before dropping out of sight. The flashing lights didn't follow, and he slowed, opting for several more twists and turns that made it unlikely he'd be found. He finally turned back toward I-270 and reached an overpass that made his heart sink.

More lights appeared, but this time they were below on the interstate. Police, a firetruck, and an ambulance. And a lone car with significant damage to the front. Heart in his throat, he made his way down to the partially blocked highway and used the mobile bike to get around snarled traffic. He also went around the first few cops who tried to stop him before he slowed to get off, other police rushing toward him.

"Sir," an officer began, running up as he pulled off his helmet, "Back behind the cones!"

Ryan was hardly listening, his eyes seeing a stretcher that lifted up as EMTs wheeled the person on it toward an ambulance. It was a young woman, long blonde hair in disarray and bloody, a torn shirt dangling from one limp hand, her neck in a brace. He couldn't see her face. The cop grabbed his arm and Ryan yanked it free.

"I know her!" he shouted, anguished and trying to get past him. "I think I know her."

"Well, you need to stay here and let the EMTs handle this. We can get your name and–"

"Stand back!" demanded another officer. "Hey wait a minute." His eyes scrutinized Ryan's face and went to the bike before one hand moved to the gun at one hip. "Are you Ryan LaRue?"

"What? Yeah. How–"

"Down on the ground!" he yelled, and the first officer shoved Ryan while tripping him, several pairs of hands forcing him down, painfully yanking his arms behind his back. Before he knew it, cuffs were on him and he struggled to glimpse the stretcher again from his stomach, the pavement inches from his face.

"Is it her?" he asked frantically as hands began searching him, removing his wallet, phone, and more. "Is it Anna? Let me up. Let me see!"

"The only thing you're seeing it the back of a patrol car."

"He's clean," announced another officer.

As they hauled him upright, he fought to turn and look for the ambulance, but the doors had been closed and it began to drive away. His eyes scoured the highway nearby for any sign of any other blonde woman in the vicinity, desperate for this to be a coincidence. But the search ended when they shoved him into the back of a patrol car and slammed the door, ignoring his questions about who the victim was.

CHAPTER TEN

THE PRICE

Matt sat behind the wheel of his father's Prius as it sat parked on the upper, empty level of a public garage. "I feel sick."

Eric looked over to make sure he didn't mean it literally, seeing his own worry mirrored on the techie's face. Both of them had changed their clothes and wore hats and sunglasses. He'd left his job without his boss realizing he was even there, mostly because the business had several rooms, and setting up for the day meant his boss going into more than one, giving Eric time to slip out. The front door had beeped when he opened it, but a quick jog to a stairwell had gotten him out of sight before being seen.

Now, a handful of tall hotels loomed overhead in two directions, shorter buildings closer and across the I-270 highway. Few people were out yet, so they didn't have to worry about anyone finding it weird that they were just sitting there in the car and never getting out.

The radio was tuned to WTOP and gave yet another update on the accident investigation on I-270, noting that a man on a motorcycle had been taken into custody hours earlier. Neither knew how that related to anything. All that really mattered is that neither Anna nor Ryan were answering their phones. Every time they tried, Matt drove around while Eric turned Matt's phone back on, dialed, failed to connect with them, and then turned the phone back off. They didn't know how cell phone tracking worked, but after what Matt had told him, Eric wasn't taking any chances and made sure they weren't sitting still to be tracked to an exact location. Then they returned here to park again. Now the sun was up.

"You're sure that your parents will find that note in the microwave before realizing the car is gone?"

"Yeah. My mom likes to know how warm her morning tea is, so she uses that, not the stove."

"I have a plan."

Matt sighed. "That took longer than I expected. You usually think faster."

Eric smirked. "Since neither of us can go home or risk using a credit card for a hotel, we need somewhere to stay tonight, assuming we don't hear from Ryan. Even if we don't, I think I know how to get onto his parent's property and to the guest house. Ryan was showing me the grounds. The security is okay, but it's not like they're really expecting intruders. They aren't a drug cartel or something, with armed guards and all of that. I can scale one wall away from the road, in case the cops are watching the house, as I assume they are."

"I likely can't climb a wall. You can do that with sandals on?"

"No, barefoot. We need to add rock climbing to our list of skills to train on." Eric had been doing it for years along with parkour, so getting into the LaRue estate wasn't an issue for him. His feet would get scraped doing it, but rock climbing shoes that let your toes grip were a help anyway.

"What then?"

"For food today, you have enough cash for us, and maybe we'll get some for tomorrow just in case. And we've got the car with a half tank of gas. Once we're at the guest house—I'm thinking after midnight we do this—then tomorrow, I'll see if I can get Daniel's attention at the main house, by going to the back door or something. We'd just keep an eye out for his parents, making sure they already left."

"You think we can trust him?"

Eric watched a red Toyota Camry pull into the lot ahead of them. "To not tell the police we're there? Yeah, I do. We might have to tell him more. He already saw the gear. He doesn't believe Ryan about the Stonehenge disappearance, and he's too smart. He would be a good ally."

"Okay. Are we ready to try the phone again?"

"Yeah. This time let's go near Ryan's house. I want to see what's around there and find a good place for you to drop me off tonight."

Matt started the car, and they drove off. This time, when Eric turned on the phone, he found a voicemail from someone named Quincy King.

The metal door opened, and the rarely seen Quincy, one of the LaRue family attorneys, stepped inside. A former football player, he was tall, muscled, black, and had a direct, piercing gaze from brown eyes that now looked grim. With it being before sunrise, he didn't have an expected suit and tie, just a hastily thrown on button-up shirt and jacket and jeans, and a shoulder-slung tote.

On seeing him, Ryan jumped to his feet from behind the small table in the police station holding room, knocking over the metal chair he'd been sitting on. It fell with a clatter.

"Anything on Anna? They won't tell me shit because I won't tell them anything."

Quincy closed the door and the sober look on his face made Ryan's heart sink. "Have a seat."

"Just tell me." The lawyer gestured for him to sit again, and Ryan irritably picked up the chair and sat down, the table before them, Quincy's bag on top as the attorney sat and looked him in the eye.

"There's no simple way to say it," began Quincy, his face resigned. "A car hit her. From the look of it, she wasn't in one herself. She's in terrible shape. Both legs are broken, one arm. Her spine."

Ryan felt a horrible pain in his chest and could feel the blood draining from his face. Knowing all about spinal injuries from Daniel, he just stared, too horrified to speak.

"She has a skull fracture, punctured lung. She's in surgery and will be for a while longer. She's stable, but there's no telling how well she will recover, though they do not believe she is at risk of passing."

Ryan held still, as if to make any motion, including breathing, would be to accept what he had just heard. All this time, they thought that being on a quest was such terrible peril and getting home meant safety. They could relax. Not worry. Be ordinary. This illusion had just shattered, just like Anna's body. The image of her on the stretcher stuck in his mind, as if refusing to get out of the way to make room for another picture with that list of injuries. He didn't realize he had stopped breathing until Quincy shook his arm and his eyes refocused on the attorney.

"Are you alright? Hold on."

Quincy got up, opened the door, and yelled for some orange juice, coffee, or something else sugary or caffeinated, saying something about Ryan being in shock. Ryan supposed that was true. He felt dazed, his head foggy. Not until the bottle of OJ sat before him and Quincy made him drink it did that start to clear. He gulped the drink until it was gone, coming back to the world a little more.

"Okay," began Quincy, "some color back in your face. Listen, I know you've just had a big jolt. We're not in a rush. Just listen a minute. The police, FBI, CIA, and probably a couple other acronyms have been looking for you, Anna, Matt, and Eric, because Matt disappeared on camera. They slowly figured out Anna did the same from the car she was driving on 270. They assume you and Eric can do this, too. They think you guys can go anywhere at any time, including into the Oval Office to kill the President of the United States."

Already in shock, Ryan reacted with confusion, the absurdity bouncing off him. "Why would we kill the president?"

"I assume you wouldn't, but they aren't certain. I've been on this a couple of days now, since your family called me, so I've looked into things like your social media presence, and there's nothing that would raise suspicions. We're already fighting with these agencies, who are trying to say you guys are a national security threat, but we've shot that down. I ended up coordinating with the parents of the others a little, and their attorneys, taking point on this."

Ryan had a thousand questions, but urgency to get away from here led him to ask, "Can you get me out of here?"

"Yes, but it's going to take a while. They think you evaded them on a motorcycle, and this gave them enough reason to arrest you. They also say you went around cones to get to the accident scene, then tried to push past them."

"That last one, at the crash, isn't illegal, is it? I was just worried. With good reason."

"Depends. They can spin it. It's mostly stuff like moving violations, so they can't really hold you over that. Did you flee from them, though? They are saying you did."

"Sort of. I saw cop lights far behind me and sped up, but if Daniel hadn't told me the police were looking for me, I never would have known from the lights that it had anything to do with me. I lost them immediately. It wasn't like some prolonged chase or something."

Quincy let out a breath. "Okay, that's something I can work with. You'll have some stuff to explain at some point, but I should be able to get you out. The police aren't the real issue here. NSA and all that shit is. They're outside and they're being difficult, but your family has clout. And you haven't actually threatened the president or U.S. or something, so they really have nothing. Besides, no one saw you personally disappear, so what they think they have is thin. They are calling you a person of interest and known associate."

"Of Matt?"

"Yeah. And Anna."

Ryan frowned. "Are they going to arrest her or something?"

"I don't know, but they're over there now, waiting for after surgery, like she'll be in any.... Look, don't worry. I won't let them pull any bullshit there.

When you talk to your friends, you need to tell them not to tell anybody anything without talking to me first. And on that note, I need you to tell me what is going on." Quincy's gaze hardened. "And don't tell me I won't believe it. I saw the footage. I also saw the stuff you guys bought and which is at the guest house. Daniel told me in private. Your parents know nothing about it. I'm already covering for you, you understand? You're my client. Never mind that your parents hired me. And from where I'm sitting, I suspect you have far bigger problems than car accidents, the media hounding you, or even these agencies coming after you. Your friend Matt looked surprised and afraid when he disappeared. You aren't doing it on purpose, are you?"

Startled that the attorney figured this out, Ryan met his eyes and saw certainty. He relaxed, wanting to get a load off his chest. "We have no control over it. We have no idea until it happens, and we can't control where we return to."

"You just go back to the same spot?" To Ryan's startled gaze, Quincy added, "Daniel told me you were at the guest house when you disappeared and again hours ago. Anna obviously reappeared where she was. Look, you need to tell me what the fuck is going on. That includes whether I am in danger, because while I'm determined to help you and your friends, I'm not getting killed, not to mention over some shit I don't even understand."

"You're not in—" The statement died on realizing Soliander might come to Earth for all of them. Quincy saw the look, and Ryan knew the attorney was sharper than he'd realized. He would rather have someone like this on his side than against him, certainly. Having decided, he almost laughed in relief. "Okay. I'll tell you, but you have got to get me out of here first. They would lock me up if they heard, and I don't trust that this room isn't bugged or some shit."

"They can't do that. It's illegal."

"Don't care. If they are that worried, they would do illegal shit and worry about the lawsuits later."

Quincy sat back and looked around. "Okay, fair enough. You're gonna need to hang tight a bit."

"I need you to do something. Call Matt and Eric. Tell them where I am and that we'll meet up soon. Don't tell them about Anna. Let me do it."

"Sure. Do you know where they might be? I know where they were when they disappeared, but where would they be now?"

Ryan shook his head. "Honestly, I don't know. I think the better question is where do we go once I'm out? Where can I meet them?"

Quincy thought for a moment. "Your parents' place is the best option, at that guest house, but you can't stay there. The media are already going berserk now that it's known that Anna returned on the highway like that. Let me think of something."

He stepped out and Ryan put his forehead on the cool metal tabletop, thoughts on Anna. How were they going to get in to see her with media and worse hounding her? He needed to visit her for his own peace of mind, and to let her know they were around. They had thought the situation with summoning was serious on learning she'd left while driving the car, but now it had skyrocketed, their worst fears about her return realized. It suddenly occurred to him that he hadn't learned what happened to her friends when she vanished.

Jack wasn't sure what expression he was supposed to be wearing, a concern so trivial compared to the day's other worries that he might have laughed if he'd had the heart. And that was the issue, really. Should he show the fear consuming him or project an optimism that everything would be fine? Anna's parents slowly paced back and forth nearby in the Intensive Care Unit of Shady Grove Hospital. Maybe they could have used some faith from him, as theirs was clearly rattled. But then he would have been faking it. Was he supposed to do it anyway? Would reflecting their worry on his own face make theirs boil over into tears so that his presence wasn't helpful?

They had known him for years. And since the accident—well, the first one on I-270 with their daughter—he had talked to them several times. He had tried to find the exact spot where the crash happened and hang out somewhere nearby with a view of it, waiting for the moment Anna reappeared, but the police were sometimes called, making him leave. It was unfeasible anyway. He couldn't just stay there all day, and being on the road was impossible. Crazy ideas like getting a jackhammer and destroying the pavement so that cones were up for a week and blocking the lane had gone through his head, but he didn't even know which lane she'd been in. Now it didn't seem so crazy after all. He'd woken this morning to the news on TV.

Anna was out of surgery, but the ICU staff hadn't let them see her yet. She was still unconscious. Jack wasn't sure what was more devastating—the concern about when she might wake up, or that she was paralyzed. Her mother had asked how they could know that if Anna wasn't awake to try moving, but they knew from the spinal damage and the way her body failed to react to stimuli. Bleakness threatened to consume Jack except that his mind kept going to those reports that had been going on around the world, of people having the ability to heal. There had to be a way to get her in front of someone like that. Whatever it took. Ryan would pay for it, he was sure, if he had to.

Suddenly he wondered if those people were being hounded with requests for healing by the rich and famous, whether to cure their cancer or something else. Were they as sought after as the Stonehenge Four? The media crush outside had been easy for him to dodge with a side door because no one knew who he was. Not until getting to the ICU did he have any trouble, with police and stern-looking agents from one agency or another trying to bar his way until Anna's parents let him through. The FBI had briefly interviewed him days earlier as a kind of character witness and friend of Anna's, asking about her politics, and he assumed that's who these people were.

Now he sat out of sight from them, overhearing Anna's father suggest to his wife that they go downstairs to the chapel. As they departed, Jack wondered what Anna would think of her parents praying for her. Was she still an atheist after her new ability to call on gods on other worlds? Would she be pleased or annoyed with her parent's decision? He knew she hadn't been able to heal here on Earth, but would it work now? What if she could finally call on God and just heal herself, then walk out of here? These thoughts gave Jack hope, and he wished he could tell her parents something to give them the same, and so he sat in turmoil in the waiting area, lost in thought and wondering where the others were. He hadn't had a chance to call without being overheard. He knew he would have to tell them what was happening because they'd never make it past the media or authorities.

An Asian nurse stopped before him and said, "I'm sorry, I forgot your name?"

"Jack," he said, rising. "Is there news?"

The woman smiled. "Yes. Anna is awake. She has been for a few minutes and the doctors are talking to her now. I know you're a friend of the family, so you should be able to see her shortly. Are her parents still here?"

"Yeah, they went to the chapel."

"Okay. I can call down for them." She turned to go as relief consumed Jack, but then he saw several doctors and nurses exit a room, and the woman turned back. "Oh, I think they're done. Come on over and let me check."

Before he really collected himself, she showed Jack into Anna's room. Light streamed in from outside to fall on a yellow, upholstered chair, causing a mild golden hue to light the white walls. White and blue cabinets and closets lined one wall, an open door to the bathroom off to one side. In the center lay her wide bed, the curtain pulled back to reveal the occupant and all the outlets for wall attachments, many plugged into a machine on either side of the bed. A sheet and yellow blanket were pulled up to Anna's chest as she lay nearly flat, her upper body raised a little. An IV was in the one arm not in a cast, an ID badge around the wrist.

For a moment, he hesitated at the door, but then he saw her open eyes blink and a sudden desire to rush over brought him to her bedside. This time a smile came naturally because he was so happy that she was at least awake. With an effort, he tried to ignore the bandages around her head, the cuts on her face, the casts on her legs and one arm, and the noises of machines beside the bed.

"Hey," he whispered, leaning over her partially swollen and bruised face. Her eyes seemed clouded, but maybe it was just the result of waking from anesthesia and a concussion. "Can you talk? You don't have to say anything."

Anna licked her lips and nodded a little. It was hard to tell, but she seemed pleased to see him. "Jack. Yeah. Just weak. Confused."

"Okay. Let me just give you some updates before your parents get back." He glanced back at the door for signs of her parents, seeing nurses walked by. "They went downstairs for a few minutes."

"What happened?"

He took a deep breath, unsure what to say. "You don't remember?"

"No. Last thing was being in the Quest Ring."

"Okay. You came back around 2am and it's now about 8 in the morning, the same day. You arrived on 270 and were hit by a car. The media are all over this because they know it was you, and Matt was caught on camera when he vanished before, so it's been crazy with media attention. I don't want you to worry about that, though. They can't get in here, okay?"

"I can't feel my legs."

Jack didn't have the heart to tell her the truth, partly because he was hoping they were wrong despite the gravity of her injuries being impressed upon him now that he saw them. "Well, they have you pretty heavily sedated, and you just came out of a lot of surgery, so that might be normal. I don't know. Don't worry, okay? You know Ryan's loaded and he'll do anything to help you. The best care anywhere, I swear."

"What about my friends?"

Apologetically, he said, "I'll keep trying to reach them."

"Not the boys. The ones in the car. When I disappeared."

"Oh." Jack's face fell. He didn't want to tell her the news. Not when she was like this. But he knew it had been days, and she had almost certainly been wondering the whole time.

"Please," she whispered. "I see it in your face. You have to tell me. The waiting...."

Their eyes met again, and resignation settled on him. She had a right to know, and wondering wasn't going to help. He whispered, "I'm so sorry, Anna."

"What is it?" she said. "Please."

He licked dry lips. "Jade lost both legs. Raven also survived, but she's paralyzed." He paused and felt awful as he admitted, "Heather didn't make it."

Tears welled up in her clouded eyes and spilled down the sides of her head as she blinked furiously. Jack wiped them away, whispering that he was sorry over and over, that it wasn't her fault. This was all too much for anyone to deal with and sudden anger struck him. He hid it by closing his eyes and putting his head on her shoulder, whispering for her to remain calm because of her punctured lung. She seemed to hear him, for her breathing became shallower.

He straightened and looked her in the eye, "You know I am here for you. Whatever you need."

Anna looked at him calmly, eyes clearing, and after a few moments, said something he wasn't expecting.

"Get me a priest."

If there was anyone Daniel trusted, it was Ryan, and yet part of him thought that his brother, Matt, Eric, and even Jack were bullshitting him and Quincy, with whom he had just shared more than one dubious look. And yet their demeanor suggested they were telling the truth about these Ellorian Champions and their disappearances. And of course, he knew about the various vanishings and footage. And reports of healing or magic working around Earth. That they were having this talk in the family guest house, surrounded by the swords, shields, crossbows and more that his brother had purchased, added a welcome, tangible sign that this outlandish stuff was real. Or at least, they certainly believed it. If he had only just seen this stuff now, he might have still thought it was an elaborate put-on, even though Ryan had never done anything even remotely like that. Accepting it was still an adjustment.

Quincy had gotten Ryan out of the police station, then picked up Matt and Eric somewhere. Someone grabbed Jack away from the hospital, and it was from him that they had learned of Anna's situation. Arriving at the LaRue estate, they had avoided the media mob outside the main gate, but Quincy's SUV with its darkened windows was seen entering the grounds, though too late to be intercepted, at least this time. They finally reached the guest house where they were now, calling Daniel down to it without his nurse, Susan.

Daniel felt a weird kinship with Anna on hearing she was paralyzed. It was one that he didn't want. He had also never felt it for another person destined to live their life in a wheelchair like him, maybe because he didn't know them, and he resisted much of the sentiment about this because too much pity had come his way over it long ago. Never before had he understood—not really—the depth of Ryan's concern for him, having just assumed guilt at causing Daniel's paralysis was behind it. Now he knew that personally caring for someone so grievously wounded was enough to make one want to hover. His heart ached for Anna and he already knew he would give her all the emotional support and encouragement he could muster, whether or not she wanted it. Resisting that seemed to come with the territory, at least for him, but he wouldn't let her get away with it for long any more than his physical therapists had let him.

Daniel's thoughts returned to the silent men awaiting his reaction and Quincy's to their story. He sighed. "Okay, I believe you. I think. But don't push your luck. No fucking with me."

Ryan sighed from where he sat on the pile of rugs in between Matt and Jack, Eric comfortable on the floor. "Fair enough."

"So what now?" Quincy asked, leaning against a wall. "We need some priorities."

"We?" Eric asked with a small smirk. He sat barefoot, sandals near.

Quincy nodded. "Yeah. No one but the people in this room, and Anna, know what's going on. *We* need to keep it that way. On one hand, I'm representing the Stonehenge Four, and this is something that only you guys are going through, but it's clear you need a team helping you, both while you're here and while you're gone." He paused. "I'm pledging you this help, more than as your lead attorney. Let me be your coordinator. You need continuity here and can't do it when you're gone. No offense, Jack, but you're not enough."

"Yeah, none taken. I'm glad for the help at least."

Quincy continued. "You guys are all pretty young and out of your depth, like anyone would be with all of this going on, just the stuff on Earth. You have enough to worry about when you get summoned. Let me take care of shit here. You need someone covering for you. I'm already doing it with the police and all of that, but you need a person who knows the truth directing a spokesperson who *doesn't* know the truth, at least not yet. I will get someone to handle the media on your behalf. I also know all of your parents to some extent from these last few days and can run point on that as well. Speaking of, officially I'm only Ryan's attorney. Technically I'm working for your folks, but we need to change that, too. You all need to make it officially me."

"Why?" Matt asked.

Daniel answered. "Attorney-client privilege."

"Right. The police, FBI, whoever. They can't make me say shit."

"What about me?" Jack asked. "Should I do this?"

Quincy nodded slowly. "I'll have something drawn up for both you and Daniel, ready to be signed. You may not really need it now. Technically none of you have committed a crime, but there are reckless driving charges and a few others pending against Anna."

"Great," muttered Ryan.

Daniel felt himself glowering. She didn't need more problems. They needed to make that shit go away, even if it meant an expensive settlement he and Ryan paid for. His eyes went to his brother, Matt, and Eric, seeing a seriousness and muted strain in their eyes, faces, and body language. This was all real. He suddenly felt like an unsupportive asshole and vowed to drop every last thing to help them. How that would manifest, he wasn't sure, but the surrounding gear caught his eye. Research. Buying stuff. Planning. It was a start.

Eric asked, "What about civil stuff for her? Are the families suing?"

"They haven't yet," Quincy said, "but I expect them to. Wrongful death. That sort of thing."

Daniel frowned. "She can't afford that kind of shit."

"She won't have to," said Ryan. "I think this is where you come in, Daniel. If mom and dad put up any resistance to anything, I need you to get them to back down. We are paying for all of this. We have all this money we don't need and I never use. That's changing."

"Yeah, totally agree. I can do that."

Quincy warned, "This is going to get expensive."

After a pause, Eric said, "Not nearly as pricey as not doing it."

"So I have a question," Matt started, looking at the attorney. "Can they track our phones and all of that? I've been leaving mine off."

Quincy said, "They don't have a reason, as much as the government people were trying to claim they do, but they may still do it."

Daniel knew how to solve this one. "New phones. I'll buy them and new numbers today."

Eric nodded and said, "Yeah, I was about to ask if you can get my phone from my parents. I assume they're the ones who have it."

"They do," Quincy replied. "They got all of your stuff when it became apparent you were missing with the others, and your boss cooperated with police, who initially took it, but I made them give it back after they checked it for evidence."

Jack asked, "Evidence of what?"

"Exactly. There's nothing, so they couldn't hold it all despite trying. Maybe they figured you'd want it so bad that you'd walk into the police station and they could interrogate you."

Daniel interjected. "Clothes, other stuff. You need all of that." He turned to Jack. "Can you go to each of their places to get whatever they want from home?"

"Yeah, of course."

Eric shook his head. "Jack, I think I'd like to keep you a silent, unseen partner. We don't want anyone thinking they should follow you because you'll lead them to us. You need freedom to move." He paused and then joked, "What I'm trying to say is that I don't want to be seen with you."

This met with muted laughter, and Daniel had an idea. "Listen, you guys need a break. Take a couple hours off from this bullshit. I hooked up the TV and other stuff while you were gone. Well, Susan did. I can bring the Nintendo Switch down from the house and set it up in a few minutes. Later, I think each of you needs to call your parents, preferably on video, but it can wait. Mom and Dad are at the house, Ryan, but they don't know you're here yet, I don't think. I'll keep it that way for a bit. I'll order pizza for lunch in a few hours. Quincy can set some shit in motion. Me, too. Let me think of some ideas on what you can tell the parents so you can just forget about it for a while, and we'll take it over later. I think we need to be on the same page, keep the story the same, as simple as possible. I think the lie you were telling before, that for you no time passes at all while you're gone, is the easiest."

The claim would be that one minute everything was normal. Then a white light surrounded them, and when it faded, they were in the same place. But sometimes the time of day had changed. Or the weather. Or the people who had been there were all gone. And if they were holding something in a hand, it was missing. They subsequently learned from someone else how much time had passed and were shocked. That was it.

The others agreed and split up. Quincy got in the van and left the property. Daniel went to the main house, having Jack come along to grab some chairs for himself, Matt, Ryan, and Eric, who stayed in the guest house. It took a bit of time and multiple trips for Jack, but the four of them soon sat playing Minecraft Dungeons, a game that bore some resemblance to their quests. Each player had a character, armor, weapons, special items, a bunch of zombies and other "mobs" to kill, and needed to work together to survive, get treasure, and complete a level. The similarly caused a brief conversation about whether they should play a game father removed from reality, but all expressed interest, remarking that it might give them ideas. "Splitting the difference," Eric called it, between all playing and all thinking about their situation.

Hours later, Daniel returned with pizza and new cell phones and numbers, having raided two local stores to get them all set up ASAP. They finished connecting the devices, adding emails and each other as phone contacts. They had a spare for Anna, and Daniel had gotten another for himself and Jack.

Then it was time to deal with their parents. By then, Quincy had already contacted all of them except Anna's, leaving her folks out of it for now. They aimed for brevity and even doing parts of the call together, Jack and Daniel staying silent and off camera. They didn't mention quests or other worlds, and they purposely kept the swords and other gear around them out of sight.

Matt's call went first, Eric and Ryan making a show of agreeing with his account and being supportive so that the parents didn't think their kid was going through this alone, with the police, media, and other stuff. Matt apologized again for taking the car, but his father was fine with it. His older brother and sister lived in Charlottesville, Virginia and Manhattan, and weren't on the call, but had been asking about him. He promised to call them but wouldn't anytime soon. The fewer people he had to lie to, the better.

Eric went second, and his was easier, shorter, and done alone, the others again off camera but in the room, no one opting for privacy. He knew nothing about his birth parents, had no siblings, and had been raised by foster parents he kept in touch with, albeit infrequently. As a result, they didn't really know who his friends were until the Stonehenge disappearance. Now they knew their names, so when Matt and Anna vanished, they once again suspected Eric had, too. And then the police had arrived with his car and belongings after this last quest, as he still listed them as an emergency contact. They offered to help him in any way they could, but he just told them not to talk to the media.

Ryan was up next, but they handled it differently. He and Daniel went to the main house alone, because they wanted to hide the others and the use of the guest house. Their parents argued at length for him to use the GPS tracking features of one thing or another so they could help when this happened or he returned, but he said the FBI and others would just follow him, even with Quincy running interference. They didn't agree, as Ryan evaded the subject with his brother's help. He told them Jack was helping Quincy with anything they needed, like using his car so the media wouldn't know to follow, and asked them to cooperate with him. They didn't want him to leave, however, and he realized there was no going back to the guest house for now.

But then Quincy did a conference call with all the boys at once, Ryan and Daniel in their rooms to escape from parental hovering. They reached a decision. The guys wanted to be free to move around the world, at least incognito with hats and sunglasses, rather than feeling imprisoned at the guest house. And Ryan's parents were already smothering him, worse than the media presence outside. Quincy arranged for a hotel suite on his corporate credit card for Ryan, Eric, and Matt. He would get Matt's father's car brought there for them to use. Jack would help as needed, and Daniel would assist from afar, not tagging along. The wheelchair just made him too conspicuous. Things like clothes would await them there, though Ryan was bringing a stuffed duffel bag. They would take things one day at a time.

In late afternoon, Daniel distracted the parents while Ryan and Jack carried a ladder from the garage down past the guest house and to a distant corner of the property, Eric and Matt joining them. Both houses were far enough back from the road, and enough trees stood in between that the media did not know. Leaning it against the wall, they climbed up and over, dropping onto the neighbor's yard before tipping the ladder back onto the grass out of sight. Daniel would get a gardener or someone else to deal with it later. Some estates in Potomac, Maryland had decent acreage, and they could stick to the distant rear of properties, most of which were not as walled off. A half mile passed before they turned in between two houses and headed for the street, where Quincy picked them up and soon dropped them at the hotel, giving them the room keys. Jack left to get his car, visit Anna once more, and return later with Chinese food and beer.

For only the second time since returning to Earth, the boys felt like they could relax a little. Matt had wisely brought the Nintendo Switch, controllers, and the box and cables to hook it to the TV, and they intended to amuse themselves later. They sat around a round kitchen table now, having settled into the rooms where they meant to spend at least this night, if not quite a few more. Talk quickly turned to Anna.

"How is she?" Eric asked, dripping soy sauce on his white rice. He really wanted to see Anna, but neither he, Matt, or Ryan could get there yet. Maybe tomorrow. Jack had scouted the hospital and learned just how many entrances there were and that most of the reporters were at one of them. But it also seemed like the police were keeping them back so that other patients and their families could come and go without a media circus in the way. But if the boys got inside to see Anna, they needed permission from Anna's parents, who Quincy and Jack would try to convince, but they worried this would cause a conversation with them about what was going on. They owed her parents that, but one reason Jack had just gone there was to bring Anna up to speed.

"No real change," Jack replied.

"What did she want with the priest?" Ryan asked. He had asked earlier but got the same answer as now—she wouldn't say.

Matt asked, "Do you think she's going through a religious experience or something?"

"Hard to say," Eric asked. "It's certainly enough to cause that sort of thing, from what I know, which isn't much. Ryan is our expert on trauma making you religious."

Ryan grimaced, spearing a piece of orange chicken. "Yeah. I mean, her guilt has to be astronomically worse than mine. I only paralyzed Daniel. I really wish I could be there for her."

"I know you will be," Eric assured him. "We'll get to her soon, hopefully on Earth before we get summoned–" He paused, eyes lighting up. "Jesus! We forgot about something. When that happens, the summoning spell is supposed to heal us."

He watched their faces as realization sank in, which was obvious from the smiles and Ryan jumping to his feet.

"Holy shit!" the big guy said. "It should heal her!"

"Oh my God," said Jack, as Ryan paced in excitement. "Are you guys serious? You all forgot this?"

They all looked caught between relief and feeling stupid, this being a minor detail they may not have told Jack. Eric put down his chopsticks and said, "Well, we've never tested it. I mean, we only went three times, and we were already fine. We only know this because Lorian told us."

"Do you think it would really heal her all the way?" Jack asked.

"It almost has to," said Ryan, turning toward them, eyes bright. "I mean, what would be the point of summoning a paralyzed healer?"

Eric observed, "Even if it doesn't do it, she should be able to heal herself once there, if she can reach a god."

"Right!" agreed Ryan. He picked his beer for a celebratory drink.

"I have to get to the hospital to tell Anna this," said Jack, looking like he meant to do it now.

Eric shook his head. "Well, I agree, but let's not get ahead of ourselves. I don't want to give her false hope. We should not be too excited to tell her in case we're wrong. I think right now we're all a little too keyed up about it."

Jack laughed. "Yeah, sure. I hear you. I wouldn't be able to say it calmly and her parents might ask questions."

"Exactly."

Matt said, "And here all this time I've been worried about being summoned again, and now I *want* to do it." He let out an enormous sigh that mirrored the room's mood. "Do you guys get nervous when we get into a car now? I mean, what happened to her could happen to any of us."

"Yeah," said Eric, having thought the same thing all day, since he'd spent far too much time in one. He had kept thinking to stay off a highway, but even the back roads were at least 35 mph and being hit at that speed was still enough to kill anyone. Driving through neighborhoods meant less traffic, but it could certainly take forever to get anywhere that way, though it was worth it. They were lucky Anna was not dead, as no healing would change that. "I think we need to limit our travel."

"Imagine being in a plane at thirty-five-thousand feet," started the techie, "and you get summoned. When you come back, this time there's no plane."

"Geez," said Jack, opening a beer. "I should think through more of this."

"Yes," said Eric, taking a beer for himself. "Speaking of summoning, the next time it happens, Anna will return to the hospital room she's in at the time. Jack, that means you may need to hang around the hospital for a sign of her."

"Sure, whatever you need. How am I going to know she's back?"

"Keep your phone on and charged. We all need to make a point of having our phone in a pocket. When we get back, our first action aside from getting out of sight and safe is to call or text Jack."

"Good plan," said Ryan, coming back to the table and sitting down. He grabbed a fork and dove into a dumpling.

Eric turned to Jack. "You can be in the hospital lobby, or cafeteria. Just keep changing places so no one sees you hanging around too much for too long, and when you get a message from one of us, you head straight for her room to help her. I would have a change of clothes for her, a hat to hide her hair in, that sort of thing. She might need shoes."

Jack nodded. "Yeah, I still have the key to her place and will head over there, keep a bag ready." He pursed his lips.

"What?" Eric asked, sensing another problem he would need to solve. Fortunately, he enjoyed being analytical and creating plans, especially when they worked, but there seemed to be an awful lot of issues coming up all the time now.

Jack let out a breath and looked apologetic. "You know, today is a day off, but sometimes I kind of need to be at work."

"No, forget Starbucks," said Ryan, shaking his head. "They have other managers. I'm hiring you as my personal assistant at four times your current wages, maybe more." To Jack's raised eyebrows, the big guy softened his tone. "I know it's a good job, but we need you, desperately, and you're the only one qualified for what we need, you know."

"Sure."

Eric saw that Jack wasn't too happy, but was willing to do it anyway. He also knew the job wasn't supposed to be forever anyway, as Jack was still trying to figure out what to do with his life, but it was a good gig in the meantime.

"You know," he said, "we really appreciate everything you've already helped with, and this might be the most important thing of your life, just like with us. Many things are happening in the world now that weren't before, and you'd be on the front lines, so to speak."

Jack nodded. "Yeah, I know. I get it. Sorry if I don't seem excited. I just hadn't thought about it before. It's just a piece of my life I'm giving up, but you guys are losing so much more."

Ryan added, "Financially, you will not have to worry about anything in return for your help. I'm thinking to get you a credit card for you to use, so you can buy things we need. We seriously need you for so many things."

Ryan called his attorney, letting Quincy know he needed a discreet way to access his money. He also told him to set up something to pay Jack a salary, a large "signing bonus," and creating an expense account and credit card for his use. He made a point of all of it being as untraceable as possible.

Eric had been thinking of something else that usually took a while to arrange, so they needed it to start immediately. "I think we're going to need somewhere to stay long term. We have to assume these quests are indefinite. I'm talking a house."

Ryan offered, "I'll pay for somewhere."

"I want to focus on a home base to set up," began Eric. "This is a priority. We can use this hotel room for a few days, but we need a long-term location, one we never have to leave, with Jack getting things for us, or delivery service. Jack can live there, too."

"So we need five bedrooms," mused Matt.

"We're thinking too small," said Ryan. "We need an estate, somewhere up on Route 28 near Sugarloaf Mountain, where all those large farms are. They have a bunch of land. Some have multiple buildings, like a guest house, or an older house before a new one was built. We need a barn where all of you can practice your riding. We need a martial arts training room like what we were setting up at the guest house. We need an archery range no one can see from the road. We can do swordsmanship in an indoor riding ring. We need a place where Matt can do magic, where no one sees it, if it's really working here. Maybe we need a set of locks we all learn to pick, or a rock-climbing wall so we can get experience with that, too. We need to cross train each other and get private lessons when we can, though doing that with no one knowing it's us might be an issue."

Eric's intense gaze fixated on him. "That was good. You are right. How much are those estates?"

Ryan shrugged. "Don't worry about it."

"How much?"

The big guy smirked at the insistence. "Two to four million."

"How do we get your parents to do that without asking questions?"

Ryan lifted a beer bottle wryly. "That is a great question."

"I think he's right, though," added Matt. "That would be ideal. We need good security but not so good that it looks like we're fugitives or something."

"Too late for that," Jack joked. "But seriously, if no one knows about it, you'd be freer. Not looking over your shoulder all the time."

"Right," admitted Eric, "and it's exactly why we need it all done discreetly, which is another problem. If your parents buy an estate up there, people will wonder why. Places like the FBI would know."

A moment of silence followed that before Matt suggested, "Maybe there's some sort of shell corporation your attorney can set up and they buy the estate. I don't know how that works, though."

The others seemed to agree, but no one said anything for a few minutes.

Ryan suggested, "Maybe in a bit, you can show me more sign language."

Matt agreed and opened his mouth to respond, when a knock on the door stopped further conversation. They exchanged a look.

"Does anyone know we're here?" Eric whispered.

"Shouldn't," said Jack. "Quincy?"

Ryan nodded. "I'll check."

"Peephole," Eric suggested.

Ryan went up to the door and peered through the hole. Then he turned back with a scowl and motioned for Eric to come over. The others followed. "It's a woman, about forty years old."

Eric looked and stepped back. "I don't know her." Matt and Jack looked, too, but they didn't either, so he thought a moment and then asked loudly, "Who is it?"

The woman answered, "Eriana of Coreth."

CHAPTER ELEVEN

A New Friend

Erin waited in the hall for a sound from beyond the door, her long skirt swaying with her fidgeting. She smoothed her blouse and tried to calm herself. She had good ears and heard furious whispering. She had to play this right or it might quickly go south, and she had a lot riding on the next several minutes. Many years of facing horrific danger had made her serene in the face of just about anything, but she was nervous for the first time in forever. All for a conversation.

But the information it might reveal was so devastatingly important to her that it had literally kept her up at night since the moment she'd seen that pretty girl—Anna was her name—playing with that pendant... *that* pendant... and talking about her reappearance at Stonehenge after three weeks of being missing with the young men on the other side of this door.

Erin had been following the news before they returned this week, and she knew about the three girls in the car accident, one maimed, one dead, and the other paralyzed. She knew the police had been looking for Anna and now patrolled the hospital where she lay. And she'd certainly heard about Anna then reappearing on the highway and being struck by a car. That wasn't supposed to happen. Something was terribly wrong for several reasons, mainly because no one on Earth should have been trying to summon the Ellorian Champions a thousand years since the last time they did. All of them would have been long dead by now. But the Ellorians had also never just returned to where they had been before a summoning. They had always gone to their Home Rings from a Quest Ring. This modern world offered a horrible danger that all of them had just realized with Anna's fate now caught in it.

After the recent events, the private investigator she used had grilled her a little about her persistent interest in the Stonehenge Four. He had helped her collect supposed magic items from around the world for years, making inquiries about a purchase on her behalf. Now he had asked her to explain about the pendant the girl Anna wore. She only said that it might have once been magical. This was true, except that she—and likely she alone—already knew what it was and what it did. Or had done. If she remembered right, the pendant's power should be spent by now. She couldn't tell this to her investigator because he would never understand.

Before now, she had only asked him to find addresses and biographical information of the Stonehenge Four, not hack into financial records to figure out where people might be staying. So Erin wove the truth through a story that the girl's pendant was partly responsible for the four disappearing. It was dangerous to them and she had to warn them, but with reporters and now people after them, she couldn't find them and needed his help. All of this was true, except that the pendant itself posed no danger. They had already set the effect of returning it to Stonehenge after a thousand years in motion.

He had grudgingly accepted the explanation, wanting to know what she was looking for. Trying to think like an old friend of hers, who was far better at this, she had reasoned that the rich one, Ryan, was likely paying for lodging somewhere but under another name. None of their parents could lend support because if the police opened an investigation into Anna or the others, the same financial records Erin wanted to use would track their whereabouts. It had to be someone else.

Her hunch had been correct, but it wasn't until Ryan's attorney bailed him out, revealing his identity, that they got another name to check and learned of the hotel room reserved under the lawyer's name. She had to promise her investigator that she would pay every legal bill if anyone ever found out, arrested him, and destroyed his business. That had only made him more suspicious, but there was a good reason she had spent considerable time with him over the years, earning his trust, even having a long affair with him to bewitch him as much as she could. And it had worked. She could tell he still loved her. She wondered if that would remain true once he found out who she really was.

Now she waited for that hotel room door to open, trying to look unthreatening and pleasant, which on one hand was easy because she was both. But her mind raced, for the reaction to her true name had told her something. She just wasn't entirely sure what it meant.

Then a voice she recognized from the TV interview spoke from beyond the door. "Can you repeat that?"

"Eriana of Coreth, one of the Ellorian Champions."

After a pause, the same voice asked, "How do we know it's you? Eriana is in her mid to late twenties, from what we understand."

That brought her up short and her mind raced. "Honestly, Eric, I do not know how to answer that. I have lived here for twenty years, but by my reckoning, you should not expect me to be alive at all, or I would be a thousand years old." After a pause, she added, "I would very much like to discuss this with you, and learn what you know of me, Andier, Korrin, and Soliander, and how you came to be substituted for us. It appears clear that this has happened from the news reports, and your friend Anna in the hospital, and–"

"Open the door," said another voice from inside.

Eriana thought it sounded like the techie, Matt. Andier had long ago taught her to memorize faces, voices, and more to aid in dealing with the considerable intrigue that had sometimes dogged them. She heard some arguing before the door suddenly opened to reveal four young men, three that she recognized. Her eyes moved between and stopped on Matt because of the intense way he was scrutinizing her face. This went on for several seconds of tense silence as she waited, eyes drifting to Eric and Ryan, then lingering on the other man, who expression spoke of attraction to her more than curiosity. Matt finally broke the silence.

"It's her. She's older, like you said, maybe twenty years, but it's her. We found her. We found Eriana!"

She smiled, comforted because they were looking for her, and they seemed excited, not the least bit threatening. She relaxed a little. "It's more like I found you," she observed.

Eric turned to Matt. "How can you know that it's her?"

"Soliander's spell, remember? I recognize–"

"You've seen Soli?" Eriana interrupted, stepping forward. "How is he? *Where* is he? When did you see him?"

More questions surged in her mind as relief and excitement filled her. It had been twenty years with no sign of them. She stopped looking long ago, convinced they were dead or possibly flung to another planet, like their home, Elloria. With magic no longer working here, had they been looking for her and unable to reach her, like the Earth was a phone giving a perpetually busy signal? And now there was an answer. Or maybe Soliander somehow was here all this time. Had they given up the search for her? She had to know if it was only him or the others, too.

Eric held up one hand to stop her and then gestured for her to enter. "I think you had better come inside."

She followed them as they moved toward the table where leftover food remained, the unknown guy locking the door. Being in a hotel room with four young men she didn't know might have given many women pause, but Andier had taught her a thing or two about self-defense long ago, and enough of her healing power had returned in the last month that she knew a quick word would render all of them unconscious. Well, normally it would. In her weakened state, it might only weaken *them*, but it would be enough to escape.

As Eric gestured to an upholstered chair, the guy she didn't recognize said, "I'm Jack, by the way. You seem to know everyone else."

"Yes," Eric began as they sat, "how is that? News reports?"

"Yes," she admitted, deciding not to admit that her investigator had turned up everything he could find on them. It would cause distrust, and she had to gain their trust first. As if reading her mind, Eric spoke again.

"Well, we've exchanged some names, and Matt thinks he recognizes you, but is there anything you can do to prove you are Eriana?" After a moment, he asked a similar question in elvish.

She smiled at that, thinking he was clever and quick. Eric picked up a sharp knife, holding it over his hand. She sensed his intent and replied in elvish, "My healing powers have begun to return, but you needn't do it to yourself, and don't do too much."

He returned to English. "A small demonstration is fine with me, and I can't let a lady cut herself for my sake."

He sliced the top of his hand, a line of blood rising but not dripping. It wasn't deep and would hardly need a band aid, but it was enough for her to get the point across. She placed two fingers on either side of the wound. "Please heal this man, Almighty One."

A soft light filled the wound, which closed, though it wasn't apparent until Eric used a white napkin to wipe away the blood, leaving smooth skin. His eyes met hers then.

"I also have this," Eriana began, reaching into her bag. She pulled out something in a soft jewelry bag, laid it on the table, and unwrapped the item. It was a gold amulet depicting one figure kneeling beside another that was rising from a supine position. From their expressions, she saw they recognized it. She had been wondering if they would and asked, "Do you know what this is?"

"The Amulet of Corethian," Ryan replied, looking a little confused. "It belongs to Eriana of Coreth."

So they did recognize it. She wasn't sure how that could be, given that she'd had it since arriving in New Zealand two decades ago. She had never let it be captured on film. The technology for photos or video didn't exist on the other planets she had worn it to before that, so if they were journeying to them, they wouldn't see images of it there unless someone had drawn it. But she had shown it on a hunch. And while it seemed to confirm her identity to them, it only raised more questions for her. How could they know what it looked like?

Eric had been smiling since she revealed it and laughed. "Well, it's extremely nice to meet you, my lady. We have tons of questions for you, and I think I speak for everyone when I say we are elated that you're here."

"Wow," said Jack, still looking at Eric's hand. "That's the first time I've seen any of you do something like that, the healing or magic."

Eriana raised an eyebrow at the others. "You've been trying?"

"Yes," admitted Matt, fingering an uneaten spring roll. "I have gotten little to work. Neither has Anna. In my case, it's partly difficulty remembering the spells, and maybe having none of the ingredients if those are needed. But for Anna and the healing, well, she's an atheist, so calling on God is a stretch for her. It's a bit of a sore point, really." He hesitated. "You know, you're already a legend to us. Sorry if we're all staring a bit. Part of me can't believe you're here."

It had been a long time since anyone knew the truth of her identity, or that anyone looked at her with awe, though their gazes weren't quite that fascinated. They had likely seen amazing things already. She saw respect and maybe some intimidation, though not from Eric. He seemed pragmatic and less impressed. She reassured the techie, "It's okay."

Matt continued, "You should know that when we get summoned, everyone thinks we are the four of you."

She had been wondering about this, even though she did not know how it could have happened. She had seen the surprise on Matt's face when being summoned. They had clearly been taken more than once, just like her and the others. She knew they had returned the pendant to Stonehenge, unlocking the Earth. But she also knew something had gone wrong long ago and the side effects might be unpredictable. Now she had to confirm the details.

"So you are arriving in a Quest Ring?" she asked, seeing them nod. "The ring is lit up with magic words that fade? And someone has cast the summoning spell. They welcome you as the Ellorian Champions, meaning that this is what they expect, four people."

Eric said, "All correct."

"Are you wearing all our clothes? The armor?" She paused. "My amulet?"

"Yes."

"And it happens each time? That's interesting."

"Why?"

"The summoning spell is supposed to outfit us, as it appears to be doing for each of you, but it takes the original item, like my amulet, and makes it disappear from its current location before putting it on me, for example. I arrive with it on even if I was not wearing it before the spell summoned me."

"That's what we're experiencing."

"Yes, but I have kept the amulet with me since your return to Stonehenge. You have disappeared at least once since then."

"Twice," Eric corrected. "No one but us knows about the second one, partly because it was very short. A few minutes."

She frowned. In their years of quests, she and the others had seldom experienced a quest nearly that short. It usually took hours, if not days, sometimes a week or more. If a quest was so easy that it could be accomplished quickly, the summoning spell would not bring them because others could likely handle it. After all, the Ellorian Champions were the heroes of last resort, brought in when no one else could handle the challenge. Still, a quick quest had happened, and she wanted to know how their second one proved to be that kind.

"Why only a few minutes?" she asked.

Eric said, "Goblins and ogres killed the wizard who summoned us before he could tell us the quest, so we could come back without doing it."

"Hmm. That happened to us once. They have to tell you within an hour. Less, I think. Anyway, the point I'm trying to make is that you've been summoned two more times, with one of you having the amulet on your quest, and yet it has not left my side during this time. The Quest Rings appear to have somehow created a duplicate."

"That *is* interesting," commented Matt, looking intrigued, "but I think we already know this, as I have a copy of Soliander's staff when I'm on a quest. Just to clarify our roles, they think Eric is Andier, and he is wearing his gear. Anna is you. Ryan is Korrin."

"And you're Soliander," she finished. Unable to resist her curiosity any longer, she asked, "You said you've seen him. I assume he is twenty years older like me? What of Andier and Korrin?"

Eric interjected, "We haven't seen or heard a word about the others."

"As for Soliander," said Matt, "I don't think he is twenty years older. I didn't get a good look, really, but I have some of his memories in me and they include his face in a mirror. No images are past mid to late twenties. I think it's only been a few years for him, though I'm not sure that makes any sense."

"Not much does," Ryan said sourly.

Eriana leaned forward, wondering if far more substitution had occurred than she would have imagined possible. Did they all have shared memories? That could be rather invasive and unsettling. What did Anna know of her life since before arriving in New Zealand? Her thoughts drifted to the troublesome parts of her past that she had never shared with anyone.

She asked, "How could you have his memories?"

Matt looked unsure how to explain and Eric interjected. "I think we need to exchange some history for the answer to make sense, because it's just going to cause more questions. It will get confusing out of order like that."

"Yes," she reluctantly agreed, then offered, "and as much as you have questions about me, I think your situation is more urgent."

"Do you have a situation going on?" Ryan asked. His eyes went to the hotel room door, beyond which they could sometimes hear people passing by, unaware that three of the famous Stonehenge Four were hiding on its other side. His thoughts went to Anna.

Eriana shook her blonde head, leaning back into the chair again. "No. Only to find out what is happening with all of you and how I can help."

"No one is after you?" Eric asked.

She cocked an eyebrow. "Not that I know of. I suppose it is possible now, but it wouldn't be someone from Earth, I don't think, only one of the many enemies we earned during our quests. You've given me something to consider, but no one knows that Erin Jennings of Florida is Eriana of Coreth from the planet Elloria. You are the ones everyone is after right now. And this is partly my fault."

"What do you mean?"

Eriana sighed, unsure where to begin. Too much history existed, so she focused on what would be useful to them at once, especially if this somehow proved to be their only conversation for a while—or maybe ever. "You went to Stonehenge while Anna had the pendant with her, right?"

"Yes," answered Ryan, playing with his fork. "We figured that's involved but only after the first quest, because we saw the poem inside it, the one written in magic words. Matt can read them now. Well, all of us can. Someone cast a spell allowing us to read various languages."

Jack looked at them jealously. "Kinda wish someone would cast that on me," he remarked.

Matt smirked. "If you're nice, and I learn it, maybe I will."

Eriana knew the lines, even though she had only heard them once. They had become a critical part of her life's course. She said them now to make sure everyone was familiar. They were part of an explanation she sensed she had to give.

Within the jewel magic resides
Creatures, too, and all abide
To keep Earth safe from she who lies
The prison here keeps hope alive
The henge of stone shall set them free
Good and evil, equal be
Undo what's done and come what may
Risk the price all life could pay

"What does it mean?" Matt asked, leaning forward on the table, eyes intense. "Who is 'she who lies'?"

Looking concerned, Jack said, "Better question. What is the 'price all life could pay'?"

Eriana looked away, collecting her thoughts as they waited with naked eagerness. "One thing at a time. You might find this hard to believe... okay, well, maybe not anymore."

"There's a lot we'd believe today that we would've laughed off a month ago," observed Eric.

She sighed and helped herself to one beer. It was that kind of tale. "Magic is real on Earth. It is always has been. What you would call fantasy creatures like elves, dwarves, dragons, and more are also real."

"Then why don't we see them?" Jack asked. "Are they still here?"

"The quest that brought us to Earth has hidden them from view, you might say."

"All four of you, right?" Eric asked. "Soliander, Andier, Korrin, and yourself were all here?"

"Yes. We were always summoned as a group and this was no exception."

"Who summoned you?"

Eriana paused, wondering if they would recognize the name. "Morgana."

She saw Matt cock an eyebrow before he asked, "As in Merlin and Morgana?"

"That's the one," she admitted, pleased that they knew some history.

Matt asked, "You're saying they were real? That was a thousand years ago, I think."

"Yes. Historical records are a little thin and people think they are a myth, but they were both real. We met them." She paused, letting them absorb that. Too much too fast wouldn't go well.

"So Morgana summoned you. What for?" Matt asked. "She was supposedly a, uh, good character, not evil, though modern TV shows make her out to be evil."

Pleased with his remarks, she observed, "You seem to know some of this."

"Yeah, I watch and read a lot of fantasy, even tried to write a book once. Sometimes I get curious about whether someone was real or not and google them. Now I'm really curious what's real and what isn't."

She said, "Well, these modern shows may have been more accurate. We only know what she and Merlin told us. Morgana summoned us to get that pendant and return it to Stonehenge. She is the one 'who lies' from Merlin's poem, the words inside the jewel."

"I'm guessing there's some backstory to the quest, like usual," mused Ryan. He took a swig.

"Yes, and hopefully it isn't too much to absorb." She took a sip and dove into it. "The faerie world is where dragons, elves, dwarves, goblins, and more are from on Earth. Magic exists in that world more than on Earth. That world intersects this one at key points, like doorways, and it is at these locations that faerie beings can cross over into this world, and the people of Earth can sometimes pass into the faerie world."

"Are these doorways just open all the time?" Eric asked.

"No. And they are sometimes guarded, and the character of the guardians can differ, of course, meaning obey laws, others not so much. The guards may exist on either side, Earth or there. There are times during the year when the openings are easier to pass through, as if the barriers between worlds are thinner. At other times, it is reversed. We celebrate some of these occasions as holidays, like May Day and Halloween."

She took another sip, gauging their reactions, which didn't seem skeptical, so that was good. Eriana continued.

"As you're likely aware from stories, dwarves and elves are benevolent, despite any personality quirks, and trolls, dark elves, and others are more nefarious. Dragons can be either. There are many more. What the so-called evil ones have in common is that they are often aimless and with little purpose unless they have a leader who encourages cooperation. This is where Morgana comes in.

"Both she and Merlin were half-human, one parent being fae. It is the reason both were so strong in magic, the strongest among humans, anyway. Some saw them as belonging to both worlds. Others to neither. Most humans did not know the truth about them, but fae can tell. From what Merlin told us, he did not approve of Morgana's growing influence among the so-called evil fae. They were like her, being interested in creating trouble for fun, some turning deadly. That turned humans against the fae world more."

Matt remarked, "I guess all of it being real is where these stories have come from, and somehow it turned to myth."

Eriana nodded. "Humans have always been fearful of what they do not understand, and making everything a myth might have eased fears. There were countless stories of humans attacking faerie folk of whatever kind, which caused some like goblins to decide humans are evil. Humans sometimes found these doorways between worlds and built barriers to keep anyone from entering Earth through one, or if the fae did, they would just find themselves imprisoned underground. This is what various mounds found around the world, especially in England, are really for. Each is over a known opening between the worlds. At other times, bolder humans would do a raid into the fae world, killing and even capturing those they found, bringing them back for evil purposes. This included making magic items from the remains after they killed the captured. A war was brewing."

"I have a question," began Eric. "You're saying that faerie folk are from this alternate world, or whatever. Is this true on other worlds?"

"Sort of," she answered. "It once was, but it appears that on other planets, integrating them was much more complete so that they effectively merged into one. There are sometimes what we think of as leftover magic doorways to supernatural places, or even between non-magical ones."

"That's incredible," said Matt, eyes bright.

Eriana continued, "I'm not sure why, but this merging hadn't taken place much on Earth when we were brought here, and the quest from our summoning ended it altogether, forcing near total separation of what appears like a natural process everywhere else. I guess that this separation is unnatural."

Jack asked, "Why did it happen? Was that the quest? To cause this?"

"Basically, yes. At some point, Merlin aligned himself with the more benevolent faerie folk, but some among the elves, dwarves, and others who supported Merlin did not believe the lengths to which Morgana might go until it was too late. Ultimately, as matters escalated, Merlin decided there was only one solution to protect everyone on Earth—a spell to banish all faerie back to their world, drain all magic from the Earth back into the Land of Fae, and seal the doorways."

Eric remarked ruefully, "That's one hell of a spell."

Eriana nodded, amused. "I imagine it was, but Merlin cast it, with the help of other fae, from what he told us. And yet there was a problem with such enormous forces at work. It takes time. And after he cast it, in the week that it would take for all magic to flow from Earth into the fae world, and all the creatures to be pulled there, too, Morgana learned of what Merlin had done. She also learned that there was a key to undoing the spell should that ever need to happen."

After a moment, Matt guessed, "The pendant."

Eriana confirmed, "Merlin's Pendant. It just had to be returned to Stonehenge, the most powerful doorway between the worlds. With that done, magic would resume working on Earth, albeit slowly, the same way it faded slowly, though there's no telling how quickly it will fully return. It has already been a month since Anna unwittingly brought Merlin's Pendant to Stonehenge and the spell was undone. Now, the doorways between worlds are opening."

Eyes intense, Eric asked, "Does that mean we will begin to see fantasy creatures here?"

"Yes, for two reasons. The first is that the ones associated with Earth should arrive once they know the spell is undone. The second is that, with magic not functioning, this world could not be reached by magical means, and all other planets that I'm aware of, like Elloria, could not reach us here. Now they likely can, assuming they know to do so. I don't know how long it might take for any alien fantasy creatures to arrive here. Or what they might think of this place, with its technology."

She paused again, giving them time to absorb this. For weeks, she had been running through all of this, rehearsing it in her head and trying to figure out what to reveal when, not because she really wanted to hide things so much as not overwhelm them. They had already seen much themselves, but learning some truths about your world like this could be unsettling. Life was not what they had thought it was.

Ryan turned to Eric. "I think we only told Lorian, on the first quest, where we were from."

Eriana's eyebrows rose. She recognized the name, though more than one such elf existed, she was sure. "Lorian, elf from Honyn, near Olliana?"

"Yes," Eric answered. "That was the first quest. We can get to that in a minute, but we trusted him. He was the one who filled us in on you guys. In fact, almost everything we know is from him."

That relieved her. They had spent significant time with him, and she liked the elf. "Unless he has changed, and elves seldom do, we can trust him. However, he may not have known to hide your origins."

"Yeah, why is it important?" Ryan asked, concern on his face.

Not sure she should admit it for fear of worrying them, she said, "I'm only speculating, but if people think you guys are the Ellorian Champions and have been on Earth for years, it may cause visits from both good and bad people. We had a lot of friends. Enemies, too."

"Like Soliander," said Matt, frowning. "He knows we are from here. I'm sure of it."

Eric observed, "But he also knows we aren't them."

"True. Not sure how much that will stop him from coming here."

"Neither do I," Eriana agreed, keen to see her old friend, but before she lost her train of thought from earlier, she added, "Before I forget, another effect of Merlin's spell being undone is that the connection to the gods of this world has been restored."

Ryan leaned forward. "Wait, are you saying that God has not answered prayers in a thousand years because of this, and now He will?"

"Yes, all the gods that people did not invent. There's no telling which is which, really. Not yet, anyway."

Looking dubious, Ryan said, "It seems unlikely that Merlin would have the power to stop God like that. It's a little hard to believe."

"He's got a point," agreed Eric, who then smirked at his friend, "unless, of course, God isn't real."

Ryan rolled his eyes. "I should have known you'd say something like that."

"In fairness," Eric continued, smiling, "maybe God agreed to go silent. He could have been like some of the fae, feeling that humans couldn't handle the supernatural wisely. Look what we do with nuclear weapons."

Eriana asked, kindness in her eyes, "I assume you are religious, Ryan?"

"Very," he proudly answered.

"Well, I don't have a real answer for you. Merlin only had time to explain so many things to us."

The big man rose, pacing back and forth. "This is interesting." He pointed a finger at Eric, grinning. "You had better believe now, my friend, or it's the lake of fire for you!"

The rogue replied, "I have more pressing concerns right now, but for the record, my atheism has everything to do with there being no proof of God. If He gives proof, I'll be happy to acknowledge He is real. And maybe now we know why there has been no evidence, not for a long time, anyway."

Eriana patted his healed hand. "You already felt the proof now. Who do you think I channeled earlier?"

As Ryan grinned at him, Eric conceded, "I can't really argue that."

"Let's get back to the quest that brought you to Earth," Matt interrupted, not seeming interested in any of the religious subjects. "So Merlin cast the spell to get rid of magic, and Morgana summoned you four to get the pendant and return it to Stonehenge, but you didn't."

"Right," Eriana confirmed, wondering what else to tell them, but so far everything had gone well. "There is what I think of as a morality matrix in the Quest Rings. It prevents us from being summoned to do evil, but Morgana could bypass it."

"How?"

"Well, the separation of the worlds might be considered unnatural, and we were summoned to stop it, so this could be seen as a good quest. Morgana certainly seemed to think so. But according to Merlin, Morgana had done many bad things and had plans for new ones, which was the whole reason he cast the spell."

Matt noted, "So her summoning should have failed. Any guesses why it did not?"

"Yes. I think part of it was the ambiguity of this, but the principal reason is that Stonehenge is not a real Quest Ring. Merlin implied that the builders were both humans and fae during an earlier period of cooperation, and that the goal was to establish a stronger foothold for fae here on Earth. They built Stonehenge at a doorway between the Earth and fae worlds."

Looking at her intently, as if fascinated, Jack asked, "It's not a proper ring, but she still summoned you to it?"

"Yes. Morgana turned it into a kind of makeshift Quest Ring. It bears some resemblance to one. But Earth had no genuine rings. Still doesn't. I don't think we had ever heard of the world."

Eric asked, "How did Morgana know to do this with Stonehenge, or the summoning spell, or even who you guys are?"

She had wondered the same thing and only had partial answers and some educated guesswork. "According to Merlin, both he and Morgana had the power of prophecy, and we don't know what they saw or how it has played out, but Morgana could learn the summoning spell this way. After we arrived and had a moment alone, Soliander revealed having seen Morgana's face in his dreams days earlier. He thought nothing of it until after we came to Earth, when he recognized her. We surmised she had gotten the spell from his mind during the dream and turned Stonehenge into a Quest Ring, one that is missing certain aspects."

The rogue said, "Like the morality matrix that would have prevented her from summoning you."

"Yes. And the keystone."

"Keystone?" Eric asked.

Matt's eyes suddenly lit up. "The keystone! Of course. It is made from so-clarin ore." He turned to the others. "Remember when I stuck the end of Soliander's staff into that hole in the Quest Rings? That's the keystone I'm inserting it into. Only Soliander's staff works on that. The rest of the ring is not of soclarin."

Eriana nodded. "Yes. Morgana summoned us, and in theory, they bound us to the quest just like any other. That part of the summoning spell worked. She told us the quest was to return the pendant to Stonehenge, because if we didn't, Merlin's spell, already cast, would remove magic and fae creatures from Earth. The way she said it, it certainly seemed compelling that Merlin was the bad guy. We went to confront Merlin and get the pendant, but he told us what was really going on, all the stuff I just told you. We sensed he was right.

"And we realized we had a problem. We couldn't return home unless we did the quest, as this is always true. And magic was about to stop working, trapping us here for good. But Soliander realized that there would come a moment when the magic had drained from Earth. And at that moment, we might theoretically be free of the quests. Not just that one, but any further ones."

She noticed Eric's shrewd eyes on her. "You weren't doing them voluntarily, were you?"

"No," she admitted, not at all surprised he knew this. "This isn't something you can tell anyone except Anna. It was a closely guarded secret. Many worlds looked up to us. We gave them hope. It would not have looked good if anyone knew. We never really had a choice, forced to go on a dangerous quest to solve their problems. I would ask that you maintain this ruse."

"Sure," he agreed. "It isn't really ours to reveal. Please continue."

Eriana sipped at the beer again. "We were trapped and had no way to get out. But now we had our chance. But it would leave us trapped on Earth, and none of us wanted that. We have friends and families back home. Merlin and Soliander had an idea. They would pool their remaining magic energy to combine their strength, which was fading. They would time Soliander's return spell to the same moment that magic stopped working and released us. In theory, either it would work and we'd all go home, or it wouldn't and we would just remain here forever."

Eric observed, "But neither really happened. You're here, and Soliander isn't."

She sighed, knowing she didn't have a good explanation for this. "I don't know what happened. I remember Soliander looked alarmed, right before the spell completed. And moments later I found myself in New Zealand. That was twenty years ago. I have seen no sign of the others since."

A long silence followed this. Finally, Jack turned to his friends and asked, "Twenty years? I thought you guys said that when you get summoned, everyone thinks you've only been gone three years? And Merlin was a thousand years ago. Something isn't right about all of this."

That caught Eriana's attention. "Three years? Are you saying only three years has passed on the worlds you've been to, since we went missing?"

"Yes," said Matt. "They were saying they've been trying to summon us for that long. And my impression from Soliander's memories is that this is how much time has passed. By the way, as you were talking, I could suddenly remember some of your quest here, from his memories in my head."

Eriana felt confused by much of that but smiled, then laughed. Sudden tears filled her eyes as relief washed over her, an old grief vanishing. The tears flowed down her cheeks. She had lost all hope long ago and resigned herself to an awful possibility that had just gone away. The others watched her curiously, smiling at her reaction without understanding it, so she took a moment to calm herself enough to explain.

"I thought everyone was dead," she admitted, wiping her tears as Jack handed her a tissue box. "I thought everyone that I have ever known was dead. My family..." More tears came and she stopped, her lungs heaving. New questions needed answering, but the boys had just given her something she hadn't felt in a long time—genuine hope of seeing those she loved again. She had been nursing some hopes since realizing the Stonehenge Four were being summoned repeatedly, but nothing like this. She wanted to just sit and laugh. She needed it.

"Well," began Ryan gently, "we don't know what is happening with your family, but it's only been three years everywhere but here. So there's hope. They're probably not all dead, certainly."

She patted his hand. "I have wondered before about the role of time travel in all of this, because when we were summoned, this world was like the Medieval Ages, and yet when I arrived in New Zealand two decades ago, it had changed so much. I thought Morgana had summoned us in the same time frame to Earth, and that I had been thrown a thousand years into the future. I didn't know that at first, only after researching about Merlin and Morgana and learning how long ago they had lived, according to what we now see as myths.

"Now it appears Morgana summoned us to a thousand years in Earth's past, and in all the worlds. And when the quest ended, and Soliander's return spell completed, something went wrong. It seems like I didn't quite make it back to the present, just close, the same way that I didn't make it home, but ended up somewhere else on Earth."

Matt nodded, eyes far away as if struggling to remember. "He sensed it. He felt something was wrong. His last look…" He looked at her knowingly, and she suddenly wondered how much the techie knew.

Eric observed, "So it seems like he was sent back to the right timeline, and the right planet, or close enough, but you were left here, and you arrived maybe seventeen years short of the right time. Another three have passed since then."

She nodded slowly, calming herself. "That seems accurate."

He asked, "And there's no sign of Andier or Korrin on Earth?"

"No. No sign of Soliander either, except for what you say. I have some questions about that, but I assume from our talk that you did not know what Merlin's Pendant really was until now."

Matt shook his head. "None. Sometimes info pops into my head, but there's no controlling it. Now I'm curious to know how Anna ended up with it."

Eric pursed his lips. "Yeah, and where it's been all these years."

Eriana remarked, "I have a private investigator that I use to track down supposedly magical items, and this was the first one I had him look for. But we have never seen or heard a word about it in all this time. Maybe when she is feeling better, she can say more about where she got it and we can track its history, but I'm not sure it's that important."

"You never know," said the rogue. "I wonder if it was a coincidence that she ended up with it. You said something about a prophecy. Was there anyone left on Earth who knew any of this and ensured she would end up with it?"

Intrigued expressions mirrored Eriana's own. "An interesting scenario. Merlin had a few Earth friends who knew what he'd done. It is possible one of them took possession of it when the spell completed."

"Any ideas what happened to Merlin and Morgana?" Matt asked.

Eriana frowned. "No, only what was supposed to happen. Both were to return to the fae world because any creature with that much fae in them would have died when the spell completed, if they were still here. Because magic is part of them, and they can't live without it."

Eric stood up. "Well, this is all beyond fascinating, but I have to hit the bathroom. Let's take a quick break. Eriana, if you need anything, please help yourself."

She nodded thanks and rose to stretch her legs, finding herself at the window, looking out over suburban sprawl as night gathered, lights twinkling on to brighten the dark. They mirrored how she felt, like a light had been lit inside her. Soliander was alive. And only three years older than she last saw him. This meant everyone else likely was, and a real possibility of seeing her friends and family again existed. She smiled as Jack came up beside her.

CHAPTER TWELVE

THE LADY HOPE

Jack remarked to Eriana, "Seems like an enormous weight off your shoulders. I'm happy to hear that you may see your friends soon, and that your family is alive."

He bit his lip. How much of one did she have back on Elloria before all the quests began? His curiosity about her was strong, and it wasn't just that she was physically attractive; she was old enough to be his mother. There was something charismatic about her. Comforting. Radiant. Sweet. And wise. Whatever was causing it, he wanted to know more, and to have her look at him. He sensed she knew he was attracted to her, and he didn't care that she knew, but not because he was a fool. He just felt a compassionate sincerity in her eyes and felt drawn to it. He'd seen the others, especially Eric, smirk about his interest and ignored it. This wasn't about sex. He didn't know what it was. He just felt good when she looked at him, somehow comforted, like everything would be alright, even though he wasn't the one who had any actual problems right now.

He added, "That must have been hard all this time, thinking they were gone a thousand years. They must have wondered if they'll ever see you again, too. That could be some reunion."

Eriana smiled at him and he blushed, then tried to make himself stop it. "Thank you. I don't even know what to think about it yet. Soliander, at least, would be shocked by how I've aged. The others could be even older for all I know."

"Hopefully, the guys and Anna will find some information on Andier and Korrin soon, on one of their quests. Like Soliander, they've probably heard the champions are back but know that can't be right, so I assume they'd be curious and investigate."

"That's an understatement," she agreed ruefully. "I want to get a message to my family, that I'm okay, but I'm not sure if we should keep my whereabouts and situation hidden for a while."

"Why? What kind of trouble do you expect?"

"I really don't know, but with these guys the apparent Ellorian Champions, news of another champion being elsewhere and doing other things will confuse people, and possibly cause problems when these guys are summoned. We have no way of knowing how people will react, but it's something to think about, maybe planning for."

"Gotcha. Well listen, if you need anything, let me know. I'm now like a full-time helper to them when they're gone, and that includes you. Ryan's literally paying me." He grinned. "I apparently just quit my job and got a new one working for them."

She laid a hand on his arm. "Thank you. I appreciate that, especially you stepping up to help them. They really need it. It's really important. We had many people who knew the truth and were helping. Right now, they just have you."

"I have some help now." He related his role so far, concluding, "We told the attorney the truth earlier, and Ryan's brother, so it's been nice to not be alone with this. And now I have you here, too."

"I can relate. I haven't told a soul the truth in nearly two decades."

He frowned, unable to imagine being that isolated with such a huge truth for so long. As secrets go, hers was beyond epic. No one knew anything about why God stopped answering people, so many believing He never had and wasn't real, and yet she knew. And everyone thought magic wasn't real, but she knew. Fae weren't real, but she knew. Her ability to keep quiet impressed him. She likely understood the padded walls awaiting her for admitting it. What a relief it must be now. He felt a mixture of regret for her and happy she wasn't so alone anymore.

"I'm sorry. That must've been awful, but now you can at least talk to us. I'm more than happy to listen." He was going to say more when the other boys gathered at the table and she gave him that warm smile of hers, laying a hand on his arm again before she joined the group to resume their talks.

"Okay," began Eric, who resumed his seat, "it's our turn to tell you what has been happening."

"Please."

As Eriana listened and held her questions, Ryan, Matt, and Eric related the quest to Honyn to close the Dragon Gate, and that Soliander had opened it, apparently not caring that the dragons might return and destroy the planet. Jack saw that the revelations, including Soliander's attack on both Lorian and Matt, concerned her. She said that this was not the noble, self-sacrificing man she had known. Had he, like her, believed that the rest of the Ellorian Champions were dead? She revealed that Soliander had always blamed himself for their being trapped in the quest cycle, but that had really been Everon's fault. To this, Soliander had replied that Everon was his apprentice, and it was therefore still his fault. They had endured countless arguments about it. And if the wizard believed they were dead, then he undoubtedly blamed himself.

Jack asked, "Do you think this was enough to turn his heart? It seems like he isn't doing, uh, pleasant things."

Eriana pursed her lips. "Yes, I think so. He was always troubled, and I knew he sometimes struggled to not give in to his demons. I helped him with that as I could. I'm afraid that what happened could have easily pushed him into the darkness he fought against. There's something else I wanted to ask about. When you guys arrive, you are fully healed and rested?"

"Each time, yes," confirmed Eric.

"And you are dressed in our clothes, and they fit?"

"Perfectly."

Eriana eyed them. "You three are about the right size. From a distance, you can easily pass for us. It may have been luck that, so far, no one who knew us well, besides Lorian, has been present at your quests."

"What do you think would happen if the truth were known?" Matt asked.

"I honestly do not know. It would really depend on the individual person's reaction."

The techie elaborated, "I guess what I'm getting at is that we haven't known how to react to the assumption that we're you guys, so we've been playing along. I think I can speak for all of us that we don't want to offend you by doing so."

Eriana smiled. "It's fine. I'm not offended and I agree with the decision, honestly. It's probably for the best. The reaction to learning you aren't us might not be a good one. It would cause disillusion with your ability to do the quest, for one. How has that been going?"

Eric smiled ruefully and replied, "It's been a little rough. We badly need training. We were just talking about that before you knocked. Some of it is easy enough, like horseback riding or swordsmanship, but for Matt and Anna..."

Eriana offered, "I can help Anna, certainly."

"Are you able to heal her now?" Jack asked, the images of Anna in the hospital hard to get out of his head. He didn't want to wait until she was summoned, and he really wanted her here with the rest of them. She was all alone over there, kind of like Eriana had been for two decades with her unknown truth. Maybe they had more in common than he had realized. "She really needs it."

"I know. I can help, but not all the way. I'm not that strong yet."

Jack offered, "I can take you to the hospital anytime. Her parents let me go in and I can get you in. The minute you're ready."

"Sure, I would be happy to. I would really like to meet her. One thing I wanted to assure all of you about, especially her, is that I don't think you need to worry about her health long term. Once you are summoned again, the summoning spell will fully heal her."

"We were talking about that earlier," admitted Ryan. "Are you positive? There isn't a limit on that? It even fixes paralysis?"

"Yes. As long as you're still alive, it will completely heal you. The spells in the Quest Ring are powerful. I put the healing ones in there myself."

Looking visibly relieved, Eric said, "*Thank* you. This is beyond great to know. We've all been so worried. What questions do you have for us that we haven't answered?"

Eriana looked away for a few moments and then admitted, "I'm not sure you can answer some, but together we might figure out a few things, either now or as this continues." She pursed her lips again. "I assume you know by now that your substitution appears to be consistent, possibly permanent. Ours was until a uniquely powerful spell and situation ended the cycle. I don't know how you can get out of it. We didn't know for a long time, and it wasn't for lack of trying. Soliander was very determined and is the smartest, most resourceful person I've ever known, and even he couldn't figure it out until the end. I'm sorry."

"The worst part," Ryan started, "is that based on what you've told us, we would need a spell to stop magic from working on Earth again, to once again break the cycle. I don't suppose it's in Soliander's spell books?"

Matt shook his head. "Saw nothing like that, and it was Merlin's spell, anyway. I don't have Soliander's spell books either. That raises a question for you, Eriana."

"Sure."

"We can never bring anything back with us, so I have been trying to memorize spells, then write them down here. We also never keep the items we're wearing or using. Is that supposed to happen?"

She shook her head. "No. We could bring things back whether the Quest Ring's spell sent us home or if Soliander personally brought us back. I don't know why that is happening, but it might be related to the other, more pressing issue, the one that resulted in Anna's hospitalization. You don't have Home Rings, I'm assuming."

"Home Rings?" Eric looked surprised, but Matt's face registered sudden awareness.

Seeing his expression, Eriana offered, "Each of us had one at our home. The Quest Ring sent us back to our individual Home Ring every time. Since the four of you don't have them, it appears to be returning you to where you were before being summoned."

Groans of realization came from all but Matt, who said, "We need to figure out how to create these immediately. Otherwise, this is a consistent, huge problem. It almost got Anna killed and certainly isn't great for the rest of us. We were just realizing we can never go anywhere in a car for fear of this happening."

"Or a plane," Ryan interjected.

Jack asked, "Was *that* spell in Soliander's books? How to create a Home Ring?"

Matt sighed. "Don't think so, but I feel like I understand parts of it. We need soclarin ore to make them."

"Yes," Eriana acknowledged. "You said Lorian took some on Honyn on your behalf. You should contact him when able and see if he can come here."

"Still don't know the spell really," observed a nodding Eric.

Eriana said, "Listen, I have a private investigator I trust, and he is the one who was able to find out you might be staying here. Ryan, when your attorney got you out of jail, we got his name and used it to look for credit card purchases, which led to this hotel. I'm sorry for snooping, but I had to find you guys, and you have been missing, whether you've been hiding from the police or press."

Ryan waved her off. "It's fine. But if you found us, someone else could."

"Yes," she admitted, "that's what I'm getting at. Now, my guy did some illegal things to achieve this and the police wouldn't be able to without a good reason, but you guys cannot stay here indefinitely. Check out sooner, even tonight. I could get a room for all of you within walking distance. It would not be traceable to any of you."

She saw encouraged expressions and Eric said, "That's an excellent idea."

"I can repay you," Ryan began, but she waved him off.

"Don't worry about it. I purposely married a wealthy banker who lets me do what I want, more or less."

"You're married?" Jack asked in disappointment. He hadn't meant to react that way, and her broad smile made him blush. "I just assumed... well, I don't know what. I guess you've been here long enough with little hope of your old life returning that you moved on? Settled down."

She conceded he was right. "No one wants to be alone forever."

Eric asked, "I assume your husband doesn't know the truth about you?"

"No. Not yet. Will cross that bridge when I come to it, probably relatively soon."

"Before you got here," Ryan began, "we were talking about setting up a long-term base where we can train, and not be bothered. Is this something you can help with? I mean, we don't know about buying estates and we were thinking my attorney can help. My family has the money, but I can't really arrange it if I'm disappearing all the time."

She nodded. "Absolutely. It's another thing that can be done in my name. If you like, you can always be a kind of silent partner where you name is not recorded on the deed or a mortgage, and no funds from you are involved in any way that can be traced, but you are an owner."

"Yes, something like that."

"There's always my apartment in the meantime," Jack offered. "It's not really big enough, but it can work before we get somewhere bigger. That way you're not in a hotel, which is kind of busy. Lots of traffic."

"I think that is a good idea," agreed Eriana. "Why don't you switch rooms tonight, and tomorrow you'll all go to his apartment. We can start planning a base for you. And I can go visit Anna with Jack."

No one disagreed with this and they set things in motion, their minds too full for more revelations. Eriana got them a hotel suite across the road and, with Jack's help, took over all of their suitcases so that they could essentially sneak in a side door, climb the stairs, and head inside while drawing fewer eyes. They walked over to do this to minimize the risk of being in a moving car when summoned, so Jack moved their cars. Then Eriana left for her own hotel.

In the morning, Jack loaded their bags into his trunk, Eriana arrived to check them out, and then she followed Jack as he drove the guys to his apartment. The twenty-minute trip made everyone nervous, but they weren't summoned along the way and finally relaxed once inside. They spent some time hooking up Eriana's phones to their new numbers and otherwise making some plans on what to do when they all disappeared again.

Now it was time to see what Eriana could do for Anna. She wouldn't predict the amount of healing that would come, remarking that her strength with it seemed to ebb and flow like a tide as magic slowly returned to Earth. The hope was to get Anna out of any remaining danger, but it relieved them to discover on arrival that she had improved overnight, enough that the hospital began considering if they should remove her from ICU. Jack hoped Er-iana would ensure this happened today. He felt grateful even before they reached Anna's room, her parents not having arrived yet, which Jack knew because he'd talked to them this morning. He purposely made it here first to minimize explanations about who Eriana was. They planned to do their thing and then the priestess, at least, would leave so that Jack could talk with An-na's parents. For now, he intended to claim ignorance about where Matt, Eric, and Ryan were. There were just too many things to explain.

"Let me go in first," Jack whispered to Eriana, who was peeking around the door at Anna. She nodded and Jack slipped inside the familiar room, with its whirring and beeping machines, various wires and tubes like an IV at-tached to the patient. A TV high on one wall, and which he hadn't noticed before, quietly played a movie that Anna didn't appear to be watching, her gaze far away until she noticed Jack, when she smiled a moment. He knew concern likely shone from his face but, with an effort, he forced it away, be-cause the woman he'd brought with him had brought hope with her.

"Hey," Jack began gently, gripping her hand, the one that wasn't part of a broken arm. Her fingers didn't react, and he wondered if she even felt it. "How are you doing?"

"Not great," she admitted, eyes going to their hands together. She met his gaze with a sad resignation, and he knew she didn't feel it.

"Well, I'm not going to waste any time with my announcement, because it's very important to me and the others that you feel hopeful about your future."

"I could use some good news," she admitted. "How are the boys?"

"Great, except they're worried about you, but we have reason to be ex-cited. There's someone very special I want you to meet. We met her last night, and she's a game changer." He looked back to see Eriana coming in to the other side of the bed. With any luck, that benevolent radiance exuding from her would work on his friend like it did on him, even before a healing spell. "Remember when you asked me to bring you a priest? Well, I found a better one."

"Hello Anna." Eriana gripped her other hand, smiling fondly at her. "It's so very nice to meet you."

"Who are you?"

"On this world, I'm known as Erin Jennings. But on my own and many others, I go by many names. The Lady Hope. The Blessed One. The Light Bringer. I am Eriana of Coreth, one of the Ellorian Champions that you and your friends have been impersonating without meaning to." As Anna stared up at her in a mixture of disbelief and curiosity, Eriana pulled the gold scarf from around her neck to reveal the Amulet of Corethian. "I understand you wear a copy of my amulet when you are summoned. And I'm sure you wear it well. I know you must have many questions, but your parents will have more if they see me in here, and so Jack and I have come before they arrive in a short while."

Anna's eyes went to Jack, who grinned at her and answered the question he assumed she wanted to ask. "Yes, it's really her. We've learned a ton last night, but right now, it's important for her to heal you before your parents get here." He saw sudden hope appear in her eyes, which went to Eriana with a desperation that hurt to see.

"Can you really heal me?"

"Yes," Eriana replied, "enough to get you out of ICU, anyway. For the rest of your injuries, you will need to wait until you are summoned again. I want to assure you, as I did your friends, that the Quest Rings will fully heal you. Anna, you will not be paralyzed for long."

Tears sprang into Anna's eyes and down her cheeks.

"We all forgot about that," Jack confessed. "And I think you might have, too." She nodded wordlessly, still crying, Eriana wiping her tears away.

"Thank you," Anna whispered, overcome. "Thank you. It is so nice to meet you."

"Rest a moment and I will do what I can to improve your health. Just close your eyes, sweet one."

Anna did as she was told, her breathing deep from emotion. They heard whispered words to a God Anna had never believed in, longer than what Eriana had said to heal Eric's hand the night before. The soft glow surrounded her as Jack watched in amazement, thinking he'd never tire of seeing this. The superficial wounds on Anna's face slowly faded, her complexion bore more color, and the fingers Jack held onto flinched, then curled around his. He squeezed in excitement and looked at Eriana, full of wonder. She had healed at least some of the paralysis, despite her earlier cautions. He wanted to ask Anna to wiggle her toes, but as he looked back at her, it was apparent that she had fallen asleep.

"Rest, Anna," whispered Eriana. "We will meet again soon. You are not alone and have much help."

Jack beamed at the healer and mouthed a thank you. She smiled in return and excused herself, leaving him alone with Anna, whose parents arrived ten minutes later to find him still standing there. They noticed the missing cuts on her forehead, but he quickly distracted them by observing that she had squeezed his hand. Her mother didn't seem to believe it until Jack replaced his hand with hers, and a sleeping Anna closed her fingers around it. Her parents hugged each other in relief and he gave them privacy and quit while he was ahead, so he left. He'd return later to fill her in on everything they'd learned.

In the meantime, he went home, where Eriana and the boys were jointly looking up real estate listings on a laptop hooked to his TV as a big monitor. They found several estates for sale north of Darnestown in a rural area that was still only minutes away from shopping centers. Some were better suited to their needs than others. One was especially nice, with an old house, a newer one, and a large indoor riding ring attached to a barn that had several apartments. There were riding trails and several open fields, one of which was out of sight behind a line of trees. That would make for a good archery range. The land had some forest on it, as well.

With Eric, Matt, and Ryan leery of going anywhere in case they were summoned or seen, Eriana and Jack called the realtor to see up a visit while they brainstormed things they needed to consider in a property. They also video-called Quincy and Daniel to introduce Eriana to get their "Earth team," as Eric called them, working together more. They made rough plans for a moving truck to grab all the gear at the guest house.

Just when it seemed like everything was moving in the right direction, Matt excused himself to the bathroom, and no sooner did the toilet flush than Eric and Ryan, who were seated neck to Jack, began to softly glow and then vanish. Jack sighed, then remembered that Anna should have just been healed all the way. He went to the bathroom to find the sink running and a soap bottle knocked over. As expected, Matt was gone, the toilet still refilling. He returned to the couch and sat.

Jack looked at Eriana and joked, "Does the summoning spell wash your hands, too?"

Darron felt uneasy. He had watched enough TV since arriving that he understood this world treated children with a far softer touch than anywhere else. Not being the fatherly type, he had no kids of his own and never intended to change this. Sure, he might father a brat or two, and probably already had, but they would be on their own, unless their mothers looked after them. He had no sense of how to handle a child and could not have cared less about it.

And so he stood on the edge of the park where children were playing on various metal bars, plastic slides, and a wide lawn, their parents standing idly by or slouched on benches, chatting together. He counted two dozen of the little monsters and amused himself with thoughts of which spells he could cast on them. The sleep spell was the more benevolent and therefore only brought a frown to his dark face, but fiery darts, a wall of flames, or making the Earth swallow them whole all cheered him. The thought of summoning creatures to chase and devour them made him laugh, the sinister sound chilling even a few adults nearby.

They were watching him, he knew. There seemed to be no help for that. Unless he had a child of his own to watch, he seemed to attract attention. Observation suggested no adults were here without one, and this had resulted in him being singled out. Why did these parents care? Something called an Amber Alert had been issued that morning, raising his awareness of kidnapping and worse. Where he came from, a missing child had typically been eaten by something. A missing kid on Earth hardly seemed worth getting upset over.

Maybe these parents could tell he wanted to do something to their brats. People were too sensitive. He wasn't going to actually *do* anything, of course. Zoran would've killed him for attracting any attention. And yet he was somehow doing that, anyway.

But he wasn't leaving. He had a job to do, and overprotective parents ranked last on any list of dangers he had faced over the years. The thought made him laugh again. They were like arrogant children if they thought they posed a threat to anyone, least of all him or those with whom he kept company. They knew nothing of being in genuine danger, and yet they had enough sense to be afraid of him. Exuding menace was a trait he had used to keep people in line before, but now it seemed likely to cause problems and he resented having to stifle his natural inclination for these people.

Darron turned his attention back to the apartment building across the two-lane street from the park. He and Zoran had now visited the homes of Ryan, Anna, Eric, and Matt, but not gone inside. Each time Zoran arrived at a location, the memories of Matt in his head coalesced into something more understandable, making entering unnecessary. From news reports, Darron now knew what the four looked like. His time lurking at the hospital had resulted in seeing a young man and middle-aged blonde woman exiting Anna's room separately. Not knowing their identities, he had followed the man for a time, turning himself into a raven once outside to more easily track his car from above. On describing the man to Zoran, his master unceremoniously cast the *Mind Trust* spell on him long enough to see for himself, announcing the identity of Jack.

"What of the woman?" Darron had asked.

Zoran waved him off. "I didn't look. A middle-aged woman is of no importance to me."

"It's probably his mother," Darron had mused, but he hadn't cared then or now. Still, Jack and the woman had gone into the apartment he stood watching, so perhaps Darron was right. Zoran's order to follow Jack had proven fruitful, but that came as no surprise, as his master was wiser than anyone he knew. Anna's location at the hospital since returning to Earth had been known, but there had been little sign of the others, though the news confirmed that Ryan had been arrested and released. They hadn't been able to locate him since, and Matt and Eric had also disappeared...

Until Darron's spying on Jack had revealed all but Anna were at Jack's apartment. Zoran would be pleased, once Darron informed him. The master had cast himself to England to visit some place called Stonehenge, the significance of which Darron did not know. But he had googled it when Zoran was otherwise preoccupied and noticed that pictures of it bore a resemblance to the infamous Quest Rings the Ellorian Champions had used. Since then, he'd been wondering if that's what all of this was about. But he knew better than to ask. Zoran didn't appreciate questions. Not for the first time, Darron wished he had the nerve to immobile his master and cast the *Mind Trust* spell on *him*. What extraordinary knowledge must be inside that man.

Like everyone, he had heard that the Ellorian Champions had returned, but that they never went home, unless this place was a new home after their long absence. He had never heard of Earth, nor seen anywhere anything like it. He wondered how Zoran knew of it, but it was clear his master had never been here before either. These four they were following didn't seem like any sort of champions. They didn't dress like them, or act like them. And the police were always after them, so they seemed more like fugitives than renowned heroes. Was that the problem? Had they been imprisoned on Earth all this time?

The bigger question was why Zoran cared about them at all. His master had seemed preoccupied since returning from Honyn with burn marks on him and a singed robe. It had taken an effort not to ask what had happened. He had never seen the master wounded before, however briefly. A healing potion had taken care of it. Surely these feeble Earth humans hadn't been involved in that, or had they? Like everyone else here, they didn't even seem to have magic, but then maybe it was just diminished. Zoran had said as much when cautioning him to never be seen using it on Earth, but the master seemed unaffected. Or maybe he was just so prodigiously strong that he could do things Darron could not. Not here anyway. Turning himself into that raven had been surprisingly challenging when it normally came easily, and yet Zoran could cast himself far away with little trouble. Perhaps the master held an enormous advantage over everyone else here. But then that was true, regardless of what planet they were on.

As he stood musing, trying and failing to not look conspicuous in his shorts, t-shirt, and Washington Nationals baseball hat, a pink, round, plastic disc some children had been throwing to each other landed near him. A little girl about eight-years-old ran toward him to get it but stopped short on seeing him turn to her. Darron smirked at her wariness. She was right to be afraid, but he stepped up his charade of civility. He stepped to the disc and bent to pick it up, the motion causing his hat to tip forward. He repositioned it with one hand while extending the disc to the girl, who did not try to take it. Instead, she was staring wide-eyed at him.

The girl excitedly noted, "Hey, you have pointed ears! Are you a Vulcan?"

Moving the hat must have made his ears emerge from under his hair, he realized. He didn't know what a Vulcan was and wasn't inclined to answer, anyway. Instead, he leaned forward, dropped the disc, and pulled the sunglasses away from his red eyes.

"Run away," he snarled.

The girl screamed and took a step back so suddenly that she fell on her butt. For a moment, Darron wanted to laugh. But then a man yelled something and began approaching aggressively, followed by other men. Kids stopped what they were doing, and women began holding up their phones, pointing them at him. Making videos, he knew. Zoran would not be pleased. Darron sighed, stifling the desire to just kill everyone as a crowd began to form. One man in a *Star Trek* shirt lifted the crying girl to her feet as another stepped closer to Darron than was wise.

"Did you push her?" he demanded.

"No," Darron answered, but then couldn't help adding, "but I wish I had."

"Well, why don't you pick on someone your own size, asshole?"

"Are you volunteering yourself?"

"Yeah! What the hell is wrong with your eyes? You some kind of freak?"

Darron put the glassed back on. "By the laws of this country, if you attack me, I get to—"

The man slapped the glasses from his hand and a jolt of anger tore through Darron. "Not if I'm defending a little girl."

The dark elf couldn't really argue the specifics, having only learned so much, but he didn't much care. It was obviously time to go. There would be no additional scrutiny of Jack's apartment today. He was dying to teach this man a lesson and struggling to contain the power in him.

He asked, "Are you hoping to impress this girl so you can do what you want with her, or perhaps her mother?" It was a fair question. He'd seen humans do that very thing, and goblins, ogres, and even his own kind, but from the fury that appeared on the man's face, he immediately knew that was not as neutral a question as he had intended it to be.

And then the man swung a fist.

"Kunia," Darron said instinctively, magic power filling him stronger than he had done on Earth so far. And the man flew backwards ten feet, colliding with several other people, including little kids, before they landed in a heap together. Cries of pain, fear, shock, and anger suddenly surrounded him. Darron dropped all pretenses and warily glanced around, quickly seeing the very thing he now worried about. He spoke another word and the gun in a man's hand burst into flames. No one else seemed to have another one as people backed away, but he had another problem. He cast a spell to emit an energy burst in all directions and heard the shattering of glass as the phones pointed at him overloaded and fried all footage of this encounter. Zoran would not be pleased any of this had happened, but at least Darron could destroy the evidence.

He strode farther onto the lawn as people scrambled to get out of his way. A line of trees beckoned and was the place from where he had emerged before. Now it offered escape as he left the mob. To his surprise, they followed, and he thought seriously about just killing all of them. Instead, he took off at a run, swallowing pride at the implication that they were a threat to him. They quickened their pace as well, but it would not matter. He disappeared into the trees, which was a thin line of them, and once out of sight spoke another word to turn himself into a raven that was already flying away. He circled above for a minute, watching everyone milling about in confusion as they tried to figure out where he had gone. One little boy seemed to know from the way he pointed at Darron, but maybe no one took him seriously.

Before long, the wizard landed on the balcony of a hotel room, changed back into a dark elf, and went inside. Fear of Zoran's reaction dominated his thoughts. By now he'd learned that news of such events spread quickly here, far faster than on any other world, and so he turned on the TV and sat waiting. Within an hour, the first reports of it were broadcast, with people he recognized claiming that he had struck the little girl. Humans were cunning with lies to cover their own destructive behavior. It was true on every world he had visited. Then security camera footage from a nearby eatery contradicted that account as they broadcast it. Darron frowned. He hadn't thought of that. The distance between him and the camera wasn't enough to hide that three separate moments happened, each best explained by magic. Reports of similar incidents from around the world were growing common. Would that make this incident less noteworthy to people? Would Zoran agree with that?

Darron didn't have long to find out. With a brief flicker of white light, his master appeared before him, the severed head of a dwarf dangling upside down from its beard in one hand. The dark elf rose and bowed.

"I hope your trip was fruitful, master. More than for just a head."

Zoran chuckled, the evil laugh pleasing Darron when it would have chilled any other. "This head confirms a door is open."

The apprentice did not know the significance. "I have news."

"Some of it I know," replied Zoran, voice hard.

Darron knew better than to ever play dumb with this man, who always seemed to already know what he wanted to say. It was a wonder he ever used the *Mind Trust* spell at all. He hardly seemed to need it. "Yes, I attempted to destroy the gathered footage but–"

"You did not think of the security cameras."

"Yes. Forgive me. There are fortunately many reports from around the world of similar moments and–"

"This may be considered one, yes. Why were you there? What have you learned?"

"The Stonehenge Four are dwelling with Jack and the middle-aged woman in Jack's apartment. The girl is of course still with the healers." He quickly related the success of his following Jack, hoping to bolster any punishment coming his way, but Zoran's next words crushed his hopes.

"So this incident happened across the street from the people we are hoping to ambush."

Darron went cold. Before he could reply, Zoran asked for the address. The elf gave it. Then one hand gripped his shoulder and words of magic he recognized paralyzed his mind. Horror. Desperation. Anger. Futility. Resignation. There was no besting the master wizard whose familiar words caused an expected burning sensation to rise from within. Darron had cast the spell before, never really imagining he would one day learn what it felt like.

"You have left enough evidence."

These were the last words Darron heard before he turned to black ash.

CHAPTER THIRTEEN

A Tale of Three Kings

As the priest left, Anna watched him go and still felt unsure what to think. She hadn't really expected solid answers, and yet she was still disappointed that she was no closer to knowing how to reach out to God and get an answer. Each of the priest's replies about interacting with God had suggested that he had never actually done it. Never had a prayer answered. Never heard a voice in his head. Saw a vision. Had his faith confirmed. He certainly hadn't been a vessel for God's power to flow through to heal the wounded.

And that was what she really wanted to know. How did God choose someone? Had he ever? She had wanted to ask if any stories about that were true, but suspected she wouldn't get a straight answer, just something about having faith. Or seeing that this guy believed it. That just reminded her why she had always been so cynical about religion. If it was real, you didn't tell people to just believe like it wasn't. Faith in something that had no proof was not the ultimate test of whether you were worthy. It just sounded manipulative.

She sighed, not wanting to rehash all the reasons for her atheism. She had accepted the gods on other worlds were real. She had heard reports of people healing others on Earth. And of course, Eriana had just healed her. An energy she knew to be the touch of a god had coursed through her. There could be no denying that He was real, but what concerned her now was what was true and what was not. Because it seemed like until that first quest from Stonehenge, it was all baloney. Why was God suddenly back? And how did Eriana reach out to him? She wanted to ask but would have to wait.

She had met with a different priest before, the first time Jack had fetched one. She had hoped for better answers from this, but no luck. Healing herself was certainly on her mind, but she needed to get out of here so she could heal her friends and undo what she had done to them. The fate of Heather, who had died, hung on her mind because she seriously doubted ever having the power to raise someone from the dead. She was no Aeron, the Lord of Fear necromancer. It seemed that even he could not raise his dead wife in satisfactory condition. Despite all the extraordinary things that had turned out to be real, even that one was pure bullshit. Raise the dead and they were still dead. Unless they were Jesus Christ? That was something to think about. But if he had been real, he still wasn't like the rest of people, being half god.

Her mind drifted often to her girlfriends and what had become of them. The grief loomed so large that she sometimes didn't feel it, but the drugs might have contributed to that. She should have known better than to drive—the source of her guilt. And she imagined her friends thought the same. Blaming questions likely awaited her when they met again, for those still alive. Would they even agree to see her? She felt a renewed interest in learning to heal so she could undo as much as she could, and this thought helped motivate her to not fall apart in tears. She had a solution, if she could only achieve it.

As she lay there pondering, a tingling in her belly made her catch her breath in anticipation. Never had she felt excited by a possible summoning, as they filled her with dread. But if everyone was right, a Quest Ring was about to fully heal her. As the room disappeared around her, the now familiar vortex of swirling light and sound replacing it, she began to smile.

Ryan, Matt, and Eric were now before her in their usual positions. And she was facing them, standing in a hospital gown. She looked down and saw her bare feet. She was never really sure what she felt beneath them while being summoned, but she felt *something* solid. And that was all that mattered because she hadn't felt her feet in days. She wiggled her toes, the gown suddenly vanishing. With a yelp, she covered herself and started laughing that she could, and a moment later the now familiar robe of Eriana, the Lady Hope, draped from her shoulders, down to her white-booted feet. She looked at the others, similarly attired in their adventuring gear of golden armor, black leather, and a dark robe. All smiling eyes were on her as the commotion stopped. She was so taken with her miraculous healing that she forgot to immediately scan for danger. Anna was quietly giggling, tears springing to her eyes and one hand reaching absently for the nearest of them, which was Eric, because he had stepped closer.

"Are you okay?" he asked.

"Yes!" she whispered, more because her voice was choked with emotion than because she was trying to be quiet.

"My Lords," began Ryan in his knightly voice, addressing the summoners, "thank you so much for inviting us. We are honored to be here. We would appreciate just a moment to confer among ourselves before giving you our full attention."

"Certainly, Lord Korrin," said someone.

Then her friends were all before her, asking how she felt and hardly letting her answer. That they were so genuinely concerned touched her and she felt grateful for them, suddenly realizing how desperately she had missed them when she most needed them, trapped in a hospital. Trapped in her own body. She threw her arms around each, not caring who was watching, though a quick glance past them showed a wide castle hall, the Quest Ring around them off to one side in an alcove. Scores of nobles, guards, and attendants waited, but the place was nearly empty, as if no one had expected them to appear, or few people were caught up in the possibility. Maybe there wasn't much riding on their success. That would be a welcome change.

She assured her friends that she felt fine, could feel her entire body. Indeed, as always happened when summoned, she felt fantastic, the thrill inside her adding to the sense of physical well-being. She finally insisted they get on with the quest business and everyone turned back to their summoners.

A lean middle-aged man came forward, putting one hand on the shoulder of the wizard who appeared to have summoned them, gently pushing him aside. Calm brown eyes shone with unexcited politeness, his thin lips curled in a smile that brought no life to his gaunt cheeks. Feathered brown hair covered his ears and touched the upturned collar of a cloak of purple and gold hanging to his waist. A boar had been emblazoned on it. A brown tunic covered his torso, tan, tight leggings disappearing into darker shoes. That this was a seasoned politician seemed clear.

"Ellorian Champions," he began in a smooth voice, "I am Prime Minister Othor of Kingdom Thiat, on the world of Eridos. We are pleased to host you. If you will follow me, some introductions are required."

"Thank you," replied Ryan.

As Anna walked out of the alcove with her friends, and into the two-story throne room, she sensed their overall mood was the best it had been so far at the start of a quest. Normally, being snatched from Earth upset them. She made a note of her own grin so she could at least fake it the next time. This is what it feels like to be thrilled with a quest. She doubted she would ever be so happy to start one again. The others seemed similarly affected, and their jovial mood may have inspired the men and women they passed as they followed Othor. Most bowed or made similar displays of respect, and she surmised that the boar silhouette several wore was the symbol of Thiat. Polished tile floors had inlays of fanciful beasts beneath their feet, while tapestries and giant, gilded mirrors hung from the walls, two unlit chandeliers evenly spaced. Enough light came in from the windows to not light them.

Ahead were several steps leading to a pair of golden thrones, one empty, the other occupied by a lounging, overweight, bored looking man in his fifties, with multiple jowls that were visible through his scruffy gray beard. A tall, gold, jewel-encrusted crown sat atop his round, balding head. A long purple cloak covered most of his wide body, gold fasteners keeping it closed. The King of Thiat sat frowning at them, watery-blue eyes unimpressed. The idea of summoning them clearly hadn't been his. Could they count on his support? It didn't seem like it. The two dozen others who had assembled remained standing like the champions, for no seats were here as they stopped before the steps, Anna wondering how many of them were royalty. Most were men.

"King Varrun," Prime Minister Othor began, "may I present the Ellorian Champions, Lord Korrin of Andor, Soliander of Aranor, Andier of Roir, and of course the Lady Eriana of Coreth."

"So, where have you been?" the king demanded, surprising Anna. At least he could be honest, and that was something. King Varrun waved a hand toward one group of standing nobles. "We could have done this years ago and gotten this lot out from underfoot."

Ryan bowed his head. "Our apologies, Your Majesty. We hope we are not too late to help."

"No, just too late to restore the peace of my home these last few years, but I suppose I should be grateful. You are about to do me a service worthy of earning a fiefdom. I should re-knight you just for giving me hope."

"I would be honored," replied Ryan.

"Yes, everyone is always *honored*."

Looking caught between amusement and embarrassment, the Prime Minister said in a conciliatory tone, "As you can likely tell, our matter is not urgent, though needed all the same. We will make preparations for a banquet in your honor this evening and a more proper welcome. We were not entirely sure you would arrive, given the number of kingdoms whose needs have waited while you were absent. We are thrilled that you have returned, both for our small matter and all the great ones in your future."

"Fine speech," King Varrun said with sarcasm. "If that's what it takes to earn power, then I'm glad I was born into mine and am spared the humiliation." He turned to a fidgeting man who was dressed in blue and green, the symbol of a bird of prey on his breast. He snapped, "Oh, stop shuffling your feet. It's like you have to pee or something. Show some dignity. And do it elsewhere. Othor take our guests and our restless friend away to tell them what is expected."

Prime Minister Othor bowed. "Yes, Your Majesty."

The fidgeting man bowed and said, "Forgive me, Your Majesty. I merely share your excitement."

The king snorted. "Well, *Your Majesty*," he sneered, "one day you'll learn that being king means not being so polite about everything. Now get out. Of my castle, and my kingdom. I have long looked forward to your departure from both."

Anna cocked an eyebrow. Was King Varrun just being snide or was this other man another king? He didn't wear a crown, but then she wasn't sure how that worked. It wasn't like royalty always wore one. She was glad to be leaving the curmudgeon's presence and didn't want to speak with him personally.

"Lords and ladies," began a smiling Othor, "please accompany me."

They filed out of the room behind him, several of the nobles coming along but the rest remaining behind. Passing through a short hall, they turned into a meeting room with a large oval table surrounded by high-cushioned chairs, a large map spread across it. Several youths were hastily laying out plates and goblets. Another stood ready to help beside a small table filled with pastries and crystal decanters, each filled with different color liquids. Anna wondered what time of day it was, but saw the sunlight coming in at an angle that suggested either mid-morning or late afternoon. They needed a list of things to ask about every time they arrived somewhere. As if expecting that, one young girl curtsied and handed her a scroll, presumably with gods in it.

They were shown to their places as the door closed, and everyone remained standing as Prime Minister Othor looked at them apologetically from across the table. "The king is used to speaking his mind, as is his right. Ironically, it is here without him that we can do the same. He is a good man but still smarting from our change decades ago into a constitutional monarchy where he no longer has the power he once held. And he quite chafes at all displays of ceremony. It is all worsened because he has been host for some years now to an absolute monarch, as he was once, but he enjoys pointing out that he, at least, still has a kingdom to rule over."

Othor turned to the man who had been fidgeting earlier. He was no older than them, tall, well-built, and confident. He wore a waist-length cloak similar to Othor but of different colors and style, being more ostentatious. His tailored tunic was embroidered, and he wore multiple rings on each hand along with a ceremonial dagger on one hip. Something about his brows and intelligent black eyes reminded Anna of a hawk, like the symbol on his breast. The pointed jaw and thin nose helped, as did the air of proud regality that shone from his bearing and mannerisms. And yet he seemed somehow uncomfortable, as if out of place or unsure what level of authority he held.

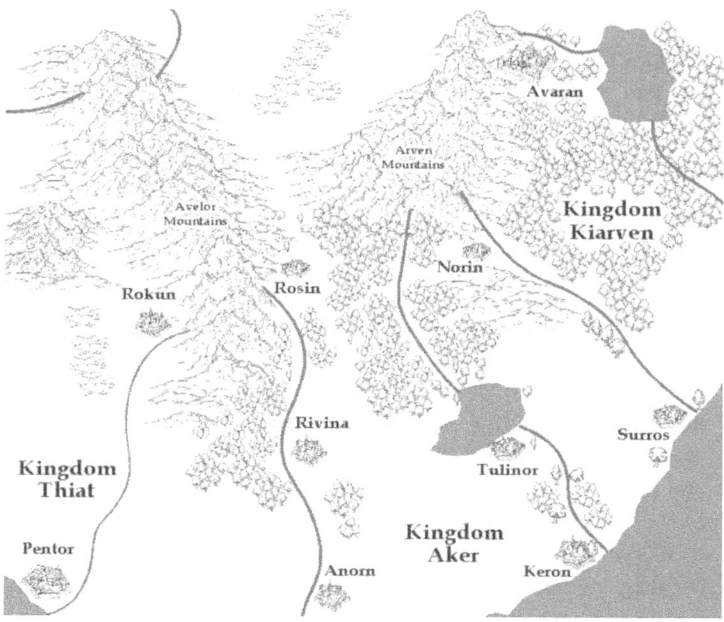

Map of Kingdom of Aker, on Planet Rovell

"Ellorians," began the Prime Minister, "this is His Majesty, King Sondin of Kingdom Aker. It is at his behest that we have summoned you, and as the quest is his, I will leave to him to lead our discussion."

King Sondin smiled graciously and with more genuineness than anyone so far. "I am so very grateful that you have come. Please be seated and be comfortable." Everyone did as he asked before he gestured to the young woman in the seat beside him. "This is my sister, Princess Miara. We have other members of our family here in Thiat, which has been gracious enough to host us for several years, but we're hoping you can put an end to the need for this."

As a servant put a plate of pastries before him, Eric asked, "What do you need us to do? Your Majesty."

The king waved that off. "We can be informal here in this room. I need you to restore us to our rightful place in Aker. I must assume the throne."

The champions exchanged a glance and Anna asked, "May I ask, why are you not there now?"

He gestured for goblets to be filled and indicated the map on the table. "This explanation will be thirsty work, but let us begin. Here we are in Thiat, across the Pumian River to the west. Beyond it, all this land you see is the Kingdom of Aker, a human power, though we have fair numbers of halfings, some elves, and a few dwarves. The river is our western border with Thiat, down to the ocean in the south, north to the mountains, and to near the eastern forests. That is where the dark elf Kingdom of Kiarven stands to our northeast. Years ago, the dark elf king broke a longstanding peace treaty and attacked Aker. I am sad to say we lost the unexpected war, and now all of Aker stands under dark elf control. However, we are still considered sovereign. No one recognizes Kiarven's claim to our lands."

Anna wasn't sure what that meant but suspected Eriana would be expected to, so she chose her words carefully. "This can be different across worlds, so we want to be sure we understand. Are you saying you are still seen as the King of Aker?"

King Sondin nodded. "I was a prince. My father, the king, died a month ago here in Thiat, and I have since become king."

"I am sorry for your loss. May I ask how it happened?"

"A tragic accident."

A petulant Princess Miara added, "He never should've been on a horse at his age, but I, for one, am glad it happened. Now perhaps we can go home." She had sorrowful brown eyes and a dreamy quality about her, as if she entertained romantic fantasies that had recently suffered a blow. Her freckles accentuated her youth, as did the braided hairstyle that exposed her round face and its remaining baby fat. She might have barely been twenty and gave the impression of impetuous emotion, whether born of immaturity, status, or frustration. Anna sensed the princess was restraining herself while silent, but then she spoke and said things she should not have, which she seemed to realize and then find herself caught between embarrassment and defiance about it.

"To an answer your question," began the king, laying a gentle hand on his sister's arm, which she pulled away, "other kingdoms must recognize sovereignty. While Kiarven is long recognized, their possession of Aker is not. We have found our kingdom to be contested territory, but there are no kingdoms who recognize Kiarven's claimed right to Aker. It is still seen as Aker, and I am the rightful king, living here in absentia and unable to return to my people, or to free them. As for my sister's remarks, our father wanted us to return but did not see it as possible. He has been content to wait for an opportunity, but my sister and I were more adamant about creating such a chance, which is why we have summoned you now that I am king. We should not wait longer to restore peace due to the conditions in which our people continue to suffer."

Fingering the food, Eric asked, "The dark elves are not peaceful rulers, I assume."

"Not to humans, no. They have plundered what they can of Aker. Our people have been enslaved. Terror rules them. It is not safe for any but dark elves to live there. Other powers have pledged their aid, including Thiat, in exchange for the peace and stability that comes with the restoration. There are trading and other issues that have arisen since the dark elf incursion. Others would also like this to stop."

Anna sipped at her drink to be polite. It was a little early for wine. Or maybe it wasn't. What time was it? "Does that mean you have an army?"

"No longer does Aker have one. But a force of others will drive the dark elves back. They await word from me and have recently begun more serious preparations now that I am king. I intend to invade."

Ryan asked, "What do these other powers get in return? What is to stop them from assuming control?"

King Sondin sighed. "I have conceded power. Kingdom Aker will no longer be an absolute monarchy, but a constitutional one with a Prime Minister as head of state. This is believed to give more governance to the people. I must admit that they have earned it after what they have been through."

"Why do these other powers want this?" Ryan asked before biting into a cream-filled treat.

Anna wasn't sure if they should munch on things to be polite or avoid it, since their hosts weren't eating, but once Ryan had done this, the princess nibbled on something. Were they waiting? She really wanted to understand protocol to avoid mistakes. Did Ryan know, or was he just clueless?

"Thiat has such a government. Nearby lands are similar or a democracy. We have been the remaining absolute monarchy, aside from Kiarven. Call it political vision. They would like to share one with us. Absolute monarchies are a dying breed in this region of Eridos."

The knight asked, "Are you waiting for us to do something before your invasion?"

King Sondin nodded. "I would prefer you to succeed first, but the assault happens regardless. When Kiarven conquered our lands, they put to death many of our royal family. Others fled here, but the rest were captured and remain prisoners. We are not sure of their whereabouts. I believe this to be on purpose. The dark elves use them to keep us from acting. We have long suspected this and recent events have proven it true."

"What do you mean?"

"A previous attempt at summoning you from the Quest Ring, that time in Aker, failed. We received the head of the Duke of Surros, my uncle, shortly thereafter."

Anna's heart had been sinking on hearing all of this because it sounded like they could be here for weeks, if not months. How do you restore an exiled king quickly? You didn't. She leaned forward. "You will risk the lives of the royal family?"

"No more than necessary. That is why you are here."

Eric asked, "What exactly is it you want us to do?"

"The quest is to restore us to power. How you achieve this is your decision. But my desire is for you to destroy the dark elf leadership so that they are more easily defeated. This would be one of two things, preferably both. Prince Kammer of the dark elves must be removed from power in Aker. He is the eldest son of King Erods and a ruthless tyrant like his father, who we would also like removed from power in Kiarven."

Trying to find a middle ground between being disapproving—of a king!— and polite, Anna asked, "Do you mean killing them?"

King Sondin pursed his lips. "As a king, I would not lightly condone the assassination of another sovereign."

"And we are not assassins," Eric observed coolly, and Anna tried not to look too approvingly at him. She would thank him for that later. Eric as Andier was the one who could get away with saying things like that to a king. Oddly, it was Eric's personality to do that very thing.

"Of course. But you have a long history of, well, stopping hateful regimes from continuing to inflict harm on a large scale. And from my understanding, this is often done by removing the leadership responsible. You need not kill King Erods or the prince. We would settle for capturing them, and a trial in either Akers or Thiat, where they can be made to answer for their war crimes. If the penalty is death, then so be it, but we do not seek their death."

"Speak for yourself," interrupted Miara.

"Sister..."

"No! They must hear this." Impassioned, she leaned toward Anna, appealing to the only other woman present. "My Gian was the one who tried to summon you. He did it for me. For us. We were to be... He went to Aker, to the Quest Ring. He was a wizard, a skilled one, and brave. We don't know what happened. All we know..." She turned angry eyes on her brother. "All we know is that it was not only our uncle's head that was returned to us!"

A moment of tense silence followed, Anna watching the princess with genuine sympathy. The girl's accusing glare at her brother hardly softened when looking elsewhere around the room. She clearly wanted a reaction from someone else, so Anna gave her one meant to calm her as her brother hid behind his goblet.

"I'm so sorry. That was very brave of him."

The Prime Minister spoke with some compassion as he observed, "Gian was a wizard of Thiat. He did not have the blessing of either king to reach the other Quest Ring and summon you. His action took place days after King Sondin was crowned. Discussions about the invasion and the need to somehow recover the royal family were underway when Gian took matters into his own hands. We assume for love. That can account for his... foolishness."

"Speak no evil of the dead!" Princess Miara demanded, eyes ablaze.

"I meant no disrespect."

Hoping to change the subject away from ones that upset the princess, Anna asked, "Why does Kiarven claim a right to Aker? Simply because they now occupy it?"

King Sondin lowered his goblet. "No. Many thousands of years ago, the forest spread to the river that borders Aker and Thiat, and that land belonged to them, so they say. We do not doubt it. There are still sometimes ancient buildings or relics of dark elf origin discovered within our borders. Kiarven extended beyond the river into Thiat, possibly all the way to the sea, and they are believed to want this territory back as well. King Varrun is unconcerned about this threat, however, as the dark elves have made no further moves. I suspect that they realize they will meet greater resistance now that multiple lands are on heightened alert regarding their activities. Also, while Aker still has forest, Thiat is less suited to their liking. I understand that not all dark elves have an interest in these lands anymore, and in fact, we are hoping a defeat will further sour them on the idea."

Eric asked put his own goblet down and asked, "These dark elves prefer the trees like all elves, I assume. How widespread are they?

"Not very. Before the war, they were in their lands, occasionally seen elsewhere in tiny groups. They cause distrust. Since the attack, they have largely withdrawn from all such places, so the conquest of Aker has increased their territory and yet shrunk how welcome they are elsewhere. We believe many among them are not happy about this and do not support further expansion or even holding on to Aker."

"And you believe removing the king and his son will cause a retreat?"

"That is our hope. If we are wrong, your quest is still done and you can return."

"The dark elf king is in Kiarven?"

The king replied, "We are not sure, as his whereabouts change, but yes. He is the lesser priority. You must eliminate Prince Kammer. He is in Aker at the capitol, Rivina."

Dreading the answer, Anna asked, "How far is that?"

"From here it is nearly a week by horseback, but with Soliander's powers, you should be able to cast yourselves there."

Anna stifled a frown. Matt didn't know how to do that. How were they to explain that? The idea frightened her anyway, unless he had a lot of practice. What if they showed up inside a wall? Instant death. Were there any safeguards against that? She had to admit, if Matt could master that spell, it would save them all sorts of time. Maybe it was time to practice, like casting himself ten feet away. Or did the distance not change how hard it was?

Eric asked, "Do you have a plan in mind for how we can reach and deal with the prince?"

The king nodded and talk turned to details on city layouts and suspected locations of royal prisoners. What stood out to Anna was the guesswork. They had few solid leads on where anyone might be, and she knew her friends were thinking the same thing. So did their hosts. Princess Miara excused herself in irritation early on, and the champions tried to be polite with King Sondin and Prime Minister Othor, who finally admitted that they only had rough ideas because they had felt certain that the champions would need to devise their own plans based on the information provided. This was true and Eric more than Ryan took the lead in assuring them they were right and not to worry. But he did say they really need to gather more information first. They agreed to provide various maps or anything or anyone else who could help give ideas. After several hours of this, they were shown to a suite of rooms and told what time they would be escorted to dinner.

Finally, they were alone together, ornate white couches and divans embroidered in elegant finery, numerous mirrors on the walls, thick curtains open to let the sunlight in onto the hardwood floors. The place reminded her of pictures of palaces in France. The sitting room had three suites adjoining them. But they would look it all over later. Right now, they all converged on Anna.

Eric asked her, "Okay, you seem fine, but are you absolutely sure?"

She put a hand on his shoulder. "Yes. I feel normal. Really, it's like a miracle, what the Quest Rings can do. I'm very grateful. Jack could only tell me a little about your talks with Eriana. I really need to get caught up. And read this scroll to find a god. Then we need a plan because these people don't have one."

"I know," he admitted, turning to sit in a chair that he seemed to think was uncomfortable from the way he kept repositioning himself. "One thing Eriana told us that you need to know is about your amulet. You can use it to find a god more easily. We didn't quite get into how. While the scroll and all of that will help, this is how she did it quickly, especially if that kind of info wasn't available."

"Yeah," said Matt, "like the last time we saw a dark elf. As they were talking, I was wondering if by some miracle that was the same guy. You know, that wizard who summoned us and was killed, and we went home with all of those goblins and ogres trying to get to us."

"And there was that dark elf I hit with a knife," he Eric.

"We never learned his name," admitted Anna, "or what the quest was."

Ryan suggested, "Maybe we should get a description. But I don't suppose it matters."

"It could," said Eric, turning to Matt. "Can one Quest Ring teleport us to another?"

The wizard cocked an eyebrow. "Well, that's an interesting idea. We could get to this city quickly if so, and it's the same place, or where we need to reach. It would save time at least."

Eric spread his hands. "Anything pop into your head from Soliander's memories when I said that?"

Matt thought for a second and shook his head. "No."

"Well," began Ryan, taking off his armor, "let's catch up with Anna here, get ready for this banquet, and then meet with whoever else we can talk to for ideas, either tonight or tomorrow morning. As we meet people tonight, grill them for info. You never know what someone might know."

Eric nodded. "I'd kind of like to talk to some regular guardsmen who've been to Aker. They often know stuff, but keep their mouths shut around official people like kings. Maybe you and I can hit some taverns tonight, dressed like normal guys."

"Yeah, I'm up for that."

Anna said, "That will give me and Matt time to prepare in other ways. Spells and gods."

With that decided, they changed into what Eric called "off duty" clothes that were brought to them, and which were more comfortable for everyone but Anna, who needed the help of a maid to get into a gown. It was more that she didn't understand how to do it than that it was too complicated.

She listened with great interest to everything Eriana had told them, but it was overwhelming after the details about the quest. Information overload had her asking for the simple versions, and they covered the highlights just before someone arrived to escort them to dinner. She could hear an orchestra long before they rounded a corner to find a crowd of well-wishers applauding their arrival, parting to let them into a grand hall that stood two stories high, empty balconies, chairs, and golden curtains above. Rows of tables and chairs had been laid out on the hardwood floor, where it didn't seem like any dancing was expected, to her relief. Anna almost wanted to add dancing lessons to her list of items to study on Earth, though she suspected it wouldn't help much. The dances had so far been unfamiliar, but then maybe that was normal. The champions couldn't be expected to know *everything.*

At the far end stood more steps to another pair of thrones that sat empty, and just before it lay what she assumed was the royal table. Prime Minister Othor indicated they would be seated there, two of them on each side of the king, who they had learned was a widower with an eye out for a new bride. Others in the room mingled with them as the group tried to stay close together, fielding questions, turning away amorous advances, and otherwise trying to be cordial. They had arrived before either royal, with King Sondin announced first before King Thiat joined them and the festivities began. Red wines, pheasant, boar, brown rice and steamed vegetables made the rounds along with several pies. Anna wondered if the Quest Ring could reduce the caloric content of what she ate when sending her home again, but she decided that eating sparingly was the elegant approach. Fortunately, their hosts weren't barbarians who expected them to belch to show approval.

During dinner, she listened to the King of Thiat complain about one thing or another, but sensed he wasn't as disagreeable as his first impression. He just seemed to find no real joy in life. She hoped to talk more to Princess Miara, who appeared sullen, whether about the recent death of her wizard lover or something else. Anna thought the girl might be trouble because she just acted intent on throwing a wrench into everything. It might have been better were she not around too much as planning went underway.

After dinner, the tables were cleared but not removed, with so many guests coming around to talk to each of the Ellorian Champions that a line had formed. They mingled as they could, with Anna discussing the gods of Eridos with those who held an interest in them. She hadn't tried to use the Corethian Amulet to contact one yet but planned to after returning to their rooms.

As Anna stood listening to a married couple, her eyes fell on Eric, who stood chatting with two noblemen. He was good at this sort of schmoozing, even if he pretended to not like small talk. Well, he didn't, as he liked to get to the point and for others to do the same, but maybe these alien worlds fascinated him. He certainly enjoyed trying to get information from people, and they sorely needed some. Hopefully, the outing he and Ryan would do tonight would help give them ideas because she really did not know how they were going to do this quest. Sneaking into an entire kingdom overrun with dark elves was far worse than their other adventures because the enemy was everywhere. Eric needed to find a plan.

She saw Eric's eyes go to a balcony and his face become serious. Following his gaze, she saw a curtain moving as if someone had just been behind it. She looked back to Eric to see that he was gone, and her eyes darted around the room, just catching sight of him stepping through the exit. She hurried after him, not liking the idea of getting separated, but when she reached the hall, he was gone. A concerned Ryan joined her, then Matt, but they saw no sign of the rogue.

Eric had disappeared.

CHAPTER FOURTEEN

THE PRINCE OF KIARVEN

Aside from no one having been on the second-floor balcony all night, something hadn't seemed right to Eric about the figure peeking out from behind a curtain. The movement had caught his attention, and then the dark skin and a hint of white hair made the words "dark elf" jump into his mind. The moment he'd seen the man, the guy turned away. Eric had seen stairs to that floor on the way here and left from the ballroom to the steps. He saw no one else as he climbed his way to the top, where he found several doors leading toward the ballroom and a hall that presumably led to the other side. He heard a door close that way and dashed after the sound on light feet. The first door he found led away from the ballroom, the sound of faint footsteps beckoning him to follow. Did the man know he pursued? Maybe Eric should have gotten others to come with him, but it was too late now.

He crept after and regretted that he didn't have Andier's leather armor on for the dozen throwing knives he could hide within it, and the rope belt that might help him bind someone if needed. Feeling exposed made him count on stealth and his hand-to-hand fighting if it arose. He still wore the Trinity Ring if he got hurt, but he always wondered how close to death he could get and it still save him. He just didn't want to find out.

Eric brushed another door open as he listened for sounds within, seeing dancing light from what he assumed was a torch he didn't see yet. He suspected no other escape existed. If he'd trapped someone, this would turn into a fight. He shoved the door wide and crouch, and as he did, he heard nothing fly over his head to strike the wall. But he saw someone standing to one side far against the wall.

"Andier of Roir," said the figure in elvish, "I am glad you came, and I mean you no harm, even after what happened the last time we met."

The room suddenly brightened as the figure touched another torch to the one on the wall. The figure remained still and Eric rose to his full height, casting one look back at the way he'd come. They appeared to be alone, and he stepped into the room for a better look. He had been right about the race, the dark elf before him wearing black plate mail with silver insignias on it. The black skin and white hair made him wonder how this one had gotten so far inside the castle, given that one look at him would have alerted the guards. It gave Eric even more reason to be suspicious. But recognizing the man, partly from the scar on one cheek, was what really put him on alert.

"You're the one who tried to kill us at the Quest Ring with the goblins and ogres."

The dark elf nodded. "Regrettable, but necessary."

Eric wanted to test his opponent before any blows and said, "I could say the same about killing you now."

From his smile, the dark elf seemed genuinely amused. "I did not come here to die or threaten others with death."

"Then why are you here?"

"For peace."

"Explain."

"I would rather do so to both King Sondin and King Varrun as well as you and your companions at once, but I understand you must agree to get me an audience. It is why I sought you out."

That surprised Eric. "You sought–" He cursed himself. This was a trap. He had been lured here. He needed to be smarter about that from now on. "Why don't you give me the short version."

"It is my intention to remove my king," the elf began. "I will take his place, withdrawing elves from Aker to Kiarven and brokering a peace between the kingdoms. In exchange for the help of the Ellorian Champions in achieving this, I will also release the royal prisoners. There is no need for the war that is brewing."

Now the elf had his attention. Maybe this was the guy who had information they needed to complete this quest, but there was at least one problem with this, aside from a serious trust issue, of course. "You do not have the authority to make such a deal."

The elf nodded. "And yet I can make it happen."

"Who are you?"

"Prince Dravo of the House of Alrond, former general of Kiarven. Some recognize my lineage. Others do not, for I am in exile."

Well, that was interesting, Eric thought. "And why are you in exile?"

"There are those who believe the elves should reclaim territory that was once ours. The king is among these. I do not, nor do many of my kin, and they made an example of me for being outspoken about this."

Eric wasn't prepared to take a single comment at face value. If this dark elf was going to lie, he would have to do it extensively and immediately. "Why didn't they just kill you?"

He frowned. "His son Prince Kammer wanted this, but I am royalty, or I was until they stripped me of my titles and land. The king spared me, to humiliate me, I believe."

"And yet you would kill him," Eric interrupted, trying to throw him off balance. He glanced back into the hallway again, since he still stood in the doorway and someone could see him.

Prince Dravo cocked an eyebrow. "I did not say I would kill him, though it is likely necessary. They thought they would suitably demean me to live among others not of my kind, but they underestimated me. I command a considerable force."

"Of goblins and ogres?"

"Among others. I had thought to use them to strike at the king, but then they invaded Aker. Since then I have been waiting for a good opportunity and often working beside the same elven forces I used to command. Many are still secretly loyal to me, I have learned. This does not surprise me."

"You are not exiled from Aker?"

"I was exiled from Kiarven before the conquest of Aker. Now that they claim Aker as theirs, some say my banishment should extend through it as well. Prince Kammer certainly wants this, but the king appears to find it amusing that I lead a band of brutes, as he calls it. He allows me to remain."

Smirking, Eric said, "So you just want to be king? Is that it?"

"No. That is a means to an end. I want the elves to withdraw to Kiarven and be done with these lands. We do not need them. Many of us don't want them, but the king wants to reclaim something lost a thousand years ago. He has done great harm to elven kind, and I want it to end."

Eric suspected something and had to ask, "Is there more to this? You must want your old life back, or family, or something."

"Of course I do. That life is gone, but my family still suffers on my behalf. This, too, must end."

Eric had a question that he expected would get a prepared answer, as the dark elf had to know it was coming. He already felt distrustful of an answer he hadn't even sought yet. "You seek my help now, and yet you tried to kill me just a week ago."

Dravo acknowledged this with a nod. "Things have changed."

"How so?"

"I was in Aker, the city Rivina, when we received word of that wizard trying to reach the Quest Ring at Castle Rivina to summon you. Prince Kammer ordered me to find and kill him, so I did. I had no choice but to try the same with you. You would have killed me and nearly did, so you cannot judge me for the attempt on your life."

Eric frowned. The guy had a good point, not that he wanted to admit it. In fact, throwing the knife at Dravo hadn't been necessary. Should he apologize? Instead, he wondered if he could provoke the calm dark elf. "How was the knife in your chest?"

Dravo smirked. "Painful, but I've felt worse. An elixir resolved the matter soon. I do not begrudge you."

Eric doubted that. He suspected something else had changed but wasn't going to suggest it, because it would only help the dark elf lie, if that's what he was doing. "Why didn't we have this conversation then?"

"Goblins and ogres have no patience for such a talk, so it would have gone poorly even had I wanted it. But more has changed. After my king learned I had killed the wizard and undone your summoning, he was pleased. He summoned me and my troops to Kiarven, the first time I have been there in the open since my banishment."

Something caught Eric's attention. "You've been there, but not where you could be seen?"

Dravo smiled, red eyes cold. "Several times, usually alone."

"Why did you go?"

"To plan a way to reach the king. To learn who my friends were. To remain aware of changes in the city. Anything to help my eventual return."

Eric couldn't really disagree with those reasons and didn't much care to. That the dark elf could get into somewhere he wasn't welcome was quite apparent, or they would not have been having this conversation. He glanced into the hall and back again. "What did the king want with you?"

"We were discussing how else I might be useful, given the need of more elves with my skills in military leadership. He intends to extend his conquest of Aker to Thiat, though this is not for some time. I soon learned that a new attempt at summoning you would take place, this time here. I came for your help."

"Not revenge?"

"I seek an alliance between kingdoms, brokered with your help."

"Why would we trust you?"

"I would prefer to reveal this to the kings. Have you heard enough to bring me to them? I, of course, will be disarmed, even bound if you like."

"I'm certain they would insist on it."

"We have an agreement?"

Eric sighed. He couldn't see why not, but who knew what the prince might be planning? He didn't like it, but it also wasn't his decision to turn him away. Only the kings should do that. "Yes, I will take you."

The dark elf nodded. "Thank you. One last thing. I am not alone." Dravo didn't pause long, maybe on account of Eric's eyes quickly scanning the room. "I have brought someone I do not want harmed. While you have a reputation for cunning, you also have one for honor. Will you do your part to safeguard her? We will both surrender."

Eric held his gaze for a moment, gauging him and sensing that if he seemed insincere, the opportunity would be lost. He nodded. "Who is she? *Where* is she?"

"My sister." He raised his voice and spoke in elvish, looking to one side. "Liera, please come."

Eric immediately noticed two doors he hadn't seen. One of them opened slowly to reveal another dark elf, this one wearing a dark gray, slender, ankle-length dress fastened with a gold belt. Two clips held straight golden hair back from her heart-shaped face. Her eyes seemed wary but inquisitive as she looked between Andier and Dravo, who gestured for her to step out of the small dressing room she occupied. She came to a stop nearer her brother.

After a moment of silence, Eric bowed his head at her and said, "Your Highness."

She flashed a wary smile. "Lord Andier. We have come at significant risk to ourselves. Our faith in humans is not strong, but you and the Ellorians are unlike most. We are trusting you with our lives."

Eric took a deep breath and let it out. He understood not being able to trust those you were with. "If you both behave, I promise no harm will come to you. Now I need to bind both of you."

Dravo removed his sword and a few knives from where they were hidden on himself. He came forward slowly as Eric took a sash from a drape and used it to bind the elf, who was slightly taller than him. He did the same to Liera. With them walking before him, Eric carrying Dravo's weapons, they made their way toward the balconies and then down the stairs, where they were seen at once, a shout going out and guards rushing in. Eric made them stand back as more important people arrived, including the Prime Minister, King Sondin, and Ryan, Matt, and Anna.

"Everyone remain calm, please," began Eric, doing his best impersonation of the commanding presence Ryan used as Lord Korrin. "This is Prince Dravo and Princess Liera of Kiarven. They voluntarily surrendered and seek an audience with both kings. I suggest that this be granted at once, with only those who must be there present. King Sondin, I would strongly recommend against Princess Miara being there." If the princess learned that the dark elf who had her wizard lover killed was here, this conversation wouldn't go smoothly.

The king nodded and turned an inquisitive eyebrow toward the Prime Minister, who said, "All of you present keep quiet about this. Take them to the throne room, which is to be sealed. Someone get His Majesty."

People began scurrying in various directions as the dark elves followed the Prime Minister with Eric and the others bringing up the rear, his friends giving him looks of frustration, curiosity, and respect. They soon waited for King Varrun, who waddled in looking irritable and slightly drunk. Eric suspected this conversation would go better without him. Princess Miara was fortunately not present. As King Varrun has no real authority, all of it being with Prime Minister Othor, he wasn't really needed, but keeping him informed was wise. He took a seat on the throne and turned to those standing before him as if impatient, when they were the ones who had just spent ten minutes waiting for him. The two dark elves stood in front beside Eric, his friends off to one side to watch the faces of the guests.

Eric summed up the previous conversation with Prince Dravo, and when finished, it prompted King Sondin to remark, "Beware of dark elves who talk of peace."

"We could say the same of humans, Your Majesty," replied Dravo. "I was not part of the forces that conquered your kingdom."

"No, but you are there keeping it under elven control."

"It was that or come to Thiat, and I'm sure you wouldn't want to be responsible for my presence here." He smiled as if trying to show he wasn't serious.

"Enough bickering," snapped King Varrun. "We have an elf who would be king, and king who has no kingdom, and a king who has no power. Why not enter into an agreement? It is as worthless as an empty wine goblet." He belched for emphasis and held out his empty cup for a page boy to refill.

"With apologies, Your Majesty," began Othor, "but I have the authority, as does King Sondin. But any agreement should be invalid until and unless Prince Dravo is successful. This means assuming the throne of Kiarven, releasing the Aker prisoners, and withdrawing troops at once."

Eric didn't particularly like King Varrun, but his bluntness could be useful. The king saw past bullshit with ease. Maybe he was more useful than expected. "There are a few more items we need to discuss. For starters, how did he and the princess get here?"

As if expecting that, Prince Dravo conceded, "There is an old portal deep beneath this city," he began, the statement causing a murmur of alarm from the guards present. "These lands once belonged to my kin, and what you likely do not remember, as your lives are far shorter, is that this city is built over the ruins of several previous cities, most of them human, but the oldest is elven."

"And how do you come to know such a thing, about this portal?" asked a snide King Varrun. "You just happen to know this now?"

"I have been aware for decades, Your Majesty, but I believe few know of it, or remember, or consider the knowledge useful, because the other side of the portal is in an abandoned area of Avaran in Kiarven. There has been little reason to use it, though I have before my banishment, mostly out of curiosity. It is how I knew the layout of this palace and could get in undetected."

"We need to find this portal and destroy it," King Varrun suggested, glaring. He seemed ready to say more when the dark elf spoke.

"On the contrary, Your Majesty," began Prince Dravo, "is it important to this mission. The Ellorians and I can travel to Kiarven and use this to both rescue the hostages and deal with King Erods."

King Varrun snorted. "Fine. *Then* we will destroy it."

"As you wish, but I think it would be more beneficial to guard it on both ends and use it to maintain our peaceful relations."

King Varrun frowned and then took a long draught from his goblet.

"What of your sister?" asked King Sondin, eyeing her with what Eric thought was appreciation. His eyes had returned to her again and again. "Why is Princess Liera here?"

The prince began, "I did not expect you to trust me, so—"

"Wise decision," interrupted King Varrun, leaning forward for emphasis.

"So I have brought her as a hostage."

Liera swiftly turned to him. "Brother!"

Eric heard genuine shock in her voice and wondered what Dravo had told her about the reason for her presence. That he had lied to her was apparent. How were they to trust him? Then he realized that maybe she would have been in danger in Kiarven had he left her and been discovered. He wasn't going to speculate about that aloud again to avoid handing the dark elf lies.

"Fear not, dear sister."

"How can you say that?"

"Andier has promised your safety." His gaze went to Eric, who nodded.

"No harm is to come to Princess Liera," announced Ryan in a commanding voice, taking his cue. Eric met his gaze in approval. People expected more honor from Lord Korrin, the Pride of Andor, than Andier, the Silver-Tongued Rogue. "She is under the protection of the Ellorian Champions."

King Varrun sighed. "Fine. We will accept your *hostage*."

"With respect, Your Majesty," began Prince Dravo, turning to King Sondin, "she is a hostage for Kingdom Aker, not Thiat."

King Sondin arched an eyebrow but nodded. "All disputes are between Aker and Kiarven. We must rebuild that relationship. What do we gain from having this hostage?"

"Hopefully some trust, Your Majesty. My sister is very important to me. I would not risk her safety. I need the Ellorians to accompany me to deal with my king or all of this is for nothing."

Anna spoke up. "He is trying to assure us that this is not a trap."

Dravo nodded to her as Eric frowned about her helping the prince's story be convincing. He might have to have a talk with her about making that sort of remark. Dravo met her gaze and said, "The Lady Eriana is correct."

"I don't feel reassured," Matt remarked, scowling. "You tried to kill us."

The prince looked him in the eye. "And you tried to kill me and killed many of my men. And this has brought us the opportunity we now have."

"What is your plan, exactly?" Eric asked, having already been over Matt's argument with him. "We go with you through this portal to Kiarven. And then what?"

"I do not need your help in reaching King Erods, and I could have killed him before now, but it would have cost me my life and been pointless. I can get to him alone but am then defenseless against all those loyal to him. I cannot possibly fight them off alone. What I need from you is protection until my forces can reach me."

"Where are they?"

"My forces are outside Avaran, where King Erods is. He summoned me to discuss a role I might play in further conquest. Once I am in power and call them to me, and I have their protection, you can leave back through the portal to here."

Eric said, "I assume they will meet resistance getting from where they are to you."

Prince Dravo turned to Matt. "I hope Soliander will resolve this. Perhaps an illusion to make the guards believe it is at the request of King Erods rather than myself."

Matt seemed to consider that. "I might be able to do that."

"All of my men cannot get to me without arousing suspicion, so I will need the most important of them. There are also dark elves loyal to me there, and I can summon them as well."

Eric surmised aloud, "You would have our help to take the throne first, then freeing the hostages?"

"Yes, because once I am king, I can order their freedom. If we free the hostages first, we must break into the prison, free them, get them through the portal, and then return to deal with the king. It will be impossible to reach him by then."

"How many hostages are we talking about?"

"Twenty-three."

"I don't like it," said Anna, her arms crossed. "We would find ourselves surrounded by the dark elves. What's stopping us from becoming four new hostages?"

"Good question," agreed Matt, frowning.

"My sister," Prince Dravo said.

"Sorry, but that's not enough," replied Anna. "We are considered a great prize in many places, and there are many who would think nothing of trading in a hostage for the Ellorian Champions. Dark elves do not have a good reputation for honor. For all we know, you are willing to sacrifice your sister for us."

"She's right," Eric agreed. "I want the hostages freed first. This way, even if we fail in dealing with King Erods, we have allowed the armies who want to reclaim Aker the opportunity to do so without fear of the hostages being killed."

Ryan observed, "Yeah, because getting you the throne only helps you with your goal. Our quest is to restore King Sondin in Aker, not a dark elf to the throne of Kiarven."

Prince Dravo didn't look pleased. "My price for freeing the hostages is helping me take the throne."

Eric stated, "It will have to be in the order we choose. Do you accept?"

The dark elf sighed and considered this. Eric could tell he was thinking, hopefully how it could be achieved, not how to betray them. Not for the first time, he wondered about that *Mind Trust* spell of Soliander's. Maybe now was a good time to use it. Was it wrong considering that being deceived might cost them their lives? Was it better to be honorable and dead or dishonorable and alive? He didn't know and wanted to ask their opinions about it.

Prince Dravo finally said, "I accept your terms. I propose we free the hostages tonight. No one checks on them when they are supposed to be asleep."

He was probably right. Eric observed, "We cannot remain on Eridos indefinitely. We need a faster way to restore King Sondin to Aker than letting troops slowly withdraw. I'm not saying your plan isn't sound, but your control of Kiarven or the army will not happen overnight. Would capturing King Erods, rather than killing him, make the forces capitulate more quickly? He would be a hostage of Aker or Thiat."

Prince Dravo considered and replied, "Yes, but we should do the same with his son, Prince Kammer. He is in control of Aker and the army. With both in custody and to be on trial for war crimes, change happens sooner."

Ryan asked, "So where is Prince Kammer? Somewhere in Aker? And how do we get him to Kiarven?"

After a moment, Prince Dravo smiled. "I think I know how."

CHAPTER FIFTEEN

KINGMAKERS

Anna said, "I don't agree with this. I will not be a part of it." She turned and strode out of the small meeting room.

Matt exchanged a knowing look with Eric but tried to not let on too much that this was what they wanted. Ryan went after her, his golden armor as quiet as ever as his feet thudded across the floor and out the door, which Eric closed behind him. This was a bonus, as the knight wasn't in on the plan either. It had been hours since the meeting with the kings, everyone having rested for their after-midnight mission to Kiarven. It was nearly time to go.

Now the wizard and rogue stood alone, the unrestrained Prince Dravo in a chair before them in the room's center, palms on his thighs and feet planted on the floor. The dark elf wore his sword once more. A podium stood near, with one of Soliander's spell books—the one with silver lettering on the black leather cover—spread open on it. Matt had already examined its pages in view of the others.

"Perhaps I erred in thinking you honorable," the dark elf remarked to Eric, who flashed an insincere smile.

"You heard our argument with Eriana, so you know what I think. Soliander, too. And we are asking your permission. There's a difference."

Dravo smirked. "I think that point was lost on the Lady Eriana."

"She also left before you agreed," observed Matt, pretending to look over the spell.

"I still have not agreed. It is not reassuring that the two most known for their honor have left in protest."

Eric observed, "Korrin only left to appeal to Eriana, not to protest."

"Ah, yes. Well, there's little sense in getting technical, I suppose."

"Listen," began Eric calmly, "you know time is short. While we appreciate the steps you've taken to gain our trust, I'm sure you understand it is not quite enough."

"I do not argue this. But what you propose is as invasive as the Lady Hope suggested. I am to be a king and yet you would have access to everything I know."

Eric remarked, "If you don't agree, you may not become a king at all, making your knowledge as useless as it is now."

Prince Dravo laughed. "Your silver tongue needs a little polish, my friend. Is there a way to limit what this spell probes?"

Matt said, "Not really. However, you can assist me by picturing the relevant subjects. The path to the portal below us here, how it works, what is on the other side, the prison where the hostages are, the place where the king is likely to be, and where your forces are outside the city. I will be able to tell if you are hiding something about it."

He wasn't sure if that was technically true. He had never cast the *Mind Trust* spell on anyone before and wasn't even sure how he would control what he saw. It was one reason he just said all of that, to get Dravo to help him without realizing it. A cooperative subject would likely make it easier the first time.

The thought made memories of Soliander doing it to other people besides him suddenly come to mind and he stood still for a moment, sorting through images, impressions, and feelings. The emotions were part of it, he now knew. This was how he could tell the subject was hiding something. Otherwise, getting what he wanted just seemed a question of searching through memories of events or time periods that were likely to produce them. The spell worked like putting a thought into someone's head, as if they were reminded of a subject Matt sought, unwittingly leading him right to it. Matt wondered if this knowledge would make it easier to resist someone doing it to him.

The idea gave him pause. He knew just how wrong this spell was, but that was why they wanted Dravo's cooperation. That, and making it easier on Matt. He and Eric had discussed the plan, which had included convincing Anna and maybe Ryan that they were going to do it whether or not the prince agreed. It was necessary. If Dravo agreed, they would not cast it, because the agreement would strongly suggest he wasn't hiding something. But if he refused, that likely meant the opposite, though there were plenty of reasons to say no. Still, a "yes" spoke volumes. The plan was Eric's, of course. Matt often wished he was half as wily as his friend.

"I have your promise," began Prince Dravo, staring into the wizard's eyes, "that you will seek only this?"

Matt stared back and tried to project reassurance, the dark elf's red eyes creeping him out a little. "You have my word. I seek nothing more. I won't have time for it anyway. The spell can last a long time, but I anticipate being done in just minutes, especially with your cooperation. You know we must do this raid on the prison tonight."

This was especially important because of Dravo himself. His absence might have already been noted, but according to him, he had left guidance for the trusted few who had been allowed into the city with him and were staying in his quarters. If anyone asked, the prince was entertaining a young woman and was not to be disturbed. Like the rest of his family, his sister had been kept close to the Avaran castle in a virtual imprisonment. Her accommodations had not been far from Dravo's. No one would look for her, in theory, but she was to be reported as unwell, if so.

Holding his gaze, Prince Dravo said, "I will accept."

Matt made a show of consulting the spell book one last time and approaching the dark elf, even putting the fingertips of one hand on his forehead. "Closing your eyes will help." Dravo complied and Matt stood still a few moments, looking to Eric, who nodded in satisfaction, so Matt stepped back. The elf opened his eyes in confusion.

"Thank you, Prince Dravo," said Eric. "We didn't need to actually cast it, though it would certainly help us. We only needed to trust you, and now we feel like we can."

Dravo turned to him with a pleased smile and direct gaze. "Well done, Andier. I trust you more for this as well, since you did not go through with it. I imagine the Lady Eriana was not aware of your ruse? I suspect she will forgive but not be as pleased as I."

"Our reputations have their advantages."

"Indeed."

When told of the ploy, Anna alternated between relief, exasperation, and acknowledgment that it was a brilliant idea. She seemed a little grumpy about it as the group made their way to the portal far below the city. They first left the castle with a score of guards accompanying them as an initial force to permanently guard the magic doorway—until or unless it was destroyed later. With over twenty prisoners expected to be coming back through it, several maids and healers were also coming. Dravo had reported that the dark elves kept most of the royals in poor conditions on purpose, and while they were alive, their needs were not exactly attended to. This included poor feeding, which had resulted in two sacks of food also being carried down to give the rescued more energy for the climb back to the surface. Two wizards, one of Thiat and one of Aker, were joining them, both under Matt's direction. The result was nearly forty people in the group.

The darkness provided little opportunity to see anything of the city as they walked across an empty square, where various seemingly temporary shacks stood, each closed up for the night, wooden signs indicating food or drink were sold there. Stone buildings that reminded him of an "old town" in Europe flanked the courtyard. He didn't see a moon. The night air smelled and felt like spring, making Matt wish he knew more about this world, from how many hours in a day there were, or days in a week, to which continent they were on. He knew from the map that they had seen that they were in the southern hemisphere. They needed to start asking about these things, but it was hard when more important details were thrust before them.

Prince Dravo led them a few blocks away through empty, narrow streets, the group moving quietly, but not enough to prevent curious citizens from sticking their heads out of windows to silently watch the procession go. A few saw the dark elf and cursed, one even throwing a piece of bread that missed. The group passed under a stone bridge between two hills, a doorway in the base of one, and this is where the elf led them, two guards remaining behind. Matt brought light forth from the staff, others bringing their burning torches, as they descended steps and into the cellar of a building. From there, a hidden door led into a roughly cut stone stairway leading down through earth and stone. It wasn't the most secure tunnel, but neither did it look like a collapse was imminent. Within minutes they had reached a level floor of dry earth, a puddle to one side of a room too small for all of them. Three hallways disappeared into darkness from it.

"The catacombs," remarked a guard.

"Yes," said Dravo. "The king may want to secure it more now that he knows it leads to a magic portal. This way."

They followed him through various branching corridors, through small empty rooms, and down flights of stairs, the air growing musty and colder than outside. Sometimes they passed a discarded item like broken pottery, an empty scabbard, and part of a skeleton, usually an animal but once a human. Matt suspected they were hundreds of feet below the surface and felt uncomfortable about finding his way back. Had the guards brought enough torches to light the way? Was someone marking the trail? They passed a sinkhole that had collapsed a wide area of earth to create a cavern, and here they had to climb over the fallen stones to reach a partially blocked stairway, which led to the buried dark elf city below it.

"No wonder no one knows it is here," remarked Ryan.

"There is little to see," observed the prince.

They followed him another ten minutes as they moved through crumbling rooms of what was obviously a long buried and abandoned settlement, the elegant designs apparent despite the age. Faded paint remained on walls and floors, carvings revealing they were in the elven city, whatever it had been called. They finally came to a wider room, the ceiling partially caved in to one side. The far wall had a carving of a doorway on it, with various symbols around it like a wide frame or border. Matt saw trees, stars, moons, castles, and a few animals he didn't recognize, but two silhouettes of elves stood out. He read the words carved around the door silently.

Here to the Land of Kiar this pathway leads
For elven kind or those in need.

Prince Dravo moved to stand before it as others kept their distance, but Matt joined him and spent a few moments learning the spell. It wasn't complicated, which was why a dark elf with limited magic talent like Dravo could perform it. The magic worked the same from this side or the other, and to ensure they could return even if something happened to the prince, Matt made sure the other two wizards also knew it before he cast the spell. The letters glowed green as the stone door faded and disappeared. Through it they saw bare earth with tufts of grass, a cascade of vines, and darkness that their torches pierced.

"We should go without light," said Dravo, Matt turned off his staff, others leaving torches behind.

The prince and wizard went first, Ryan, Eriana, and Eric following. A half dozen guards dressed for stealth came with them to assist the freed prisoners so that the Ellorians could fight if necessary and not have to worry about the hostages being led away while they did so.

The night air felt as warm as before when Matt stepped onto the earth. He moved to the thick, leafy vines obscuring anything beyond. He looked back at the portal as Prince Dravo spoke a few words and it closed, the soft green glow fading. They listened in silence but heard nothing, which didn't surprise Matt. The dark elf had explained their location in the cliff-side city of Avaran.

Only the royalty and those who served them likely knew of the ancient portal because it stood near an area reserved for them, which meant few others went there. But even the elves, who lived for hundreds of years on this world, didn't have memories that lasted forever. Overgrown and forgotten near a part of the royal enclave that had suffered a rockfall long ago, the portal hadn't been used in a thousand years. As he had told the champions, Prince Dravo only knew of it because he had long made a point of studying the defenses as one of the most strategic thinking generals of Kiarven. He had stumbled upon it. He had told no one what he'd found or of his explorations of the underground world on the other side under Thiat.

"Which way?" the wizard asked.

"Across the bridge, then left where the trail splits," answered the dark elf. "The prison is inside the mountain and reached via the town. With stealth, you, Andier, and I must lead, then the other wizards. Have your spells and wits about you."

"Yes." Matt had spent the last few hours memorizing them and raiding the local shops that catered to wizards. The two with them were among the more seasoned ones available, neither having any idea that they had far more experience in wizardry than Matt.

With the prince and rogue in the lead, Matt followed them out from behind the vines. The mountain's white stone loomed all around them in the moonless night. A mass of shattered rocks lay strewn to one side where they had fallen, some covered in vegetation, which grew untamed before them in what looked like an abandoned welcome area. An empty, cracked dais stood there, and beyond it, a curving stone bridge with small obelisks jutting from its railings. The earth fell away on either side.

Over the bridge, beyond the tall pines, rose one rear corner of the white-walled castle of Avaran, where King Erods likely slept right now. The castle was mostly below their position so that only the tallest towers were at eye level, but no lights twinkled in them. The odds of being seen were low, which was good, because the bridge was exposed. Beyond the castle, they saw some of the city, but very little. Pointed dark roofs topped white stone buildings, but they could see little else. They built Avaran along terraced cliffs so that it overlooked the forest valley below. Most of the mountain it lay on rose above their position.

As they crossed the bridge, Matt looked down into a rushing river far below. He wondered why they built the portal here where the destruction of the bridge would render reaching it difficult, but then maybe that answered his question. Anyone trying to invade from the portal's location could be more easily stopped. Stepping off the span found them on a stone path with grass overtaking it, trees all around and providing cover as the path quickly descended stone steps so that they were now level with the castle wall visible through the trees ahead. The path split, one heading right toward the royal grounds and another leading left and to the city. They headed that way, the castle on their right.

Matt and the other wizards cast a simple cantrip to mask any sounds they made, and the group crept along the underbrush off the path to keep any guards from looking down and seeing them. It didn't take long to reach the castle's front corner. The castle stood to the right, with more mountain and the river gorge to the left, for they built the structure in one corner of the available space. The settlement itself was ahead and to the right. They heard a waterfall tumbling down out of sight.

The path they weren't using was partially blocked by a crumbling wall, giving the impression that the way to where they stood had been walled off at some point and not maintained. The path curved around toward the front gates, where several buildings flanked a courtyard. Instead of heading there, they climbed over the debris and passed over the road. Then they hugged the rear wall of one such structure, edging their way down the steep rocks along the edge of the settlement. The hostages would never make it up this way, but they had a plan to use the streets by then.

They maneuvered past several buildings to reach the edge of a cliff. Matt gazed down and wished he could see better. Multiple terraces of buildings lay below toward the valley, none uniform in length, width, or vegetation, but even in the dark, a kind of loveliness was apparent.

"It is time," whispered Prince Dravo.

Matt knew what he meant and gestured for the other wizards to join him. He pulled a vial of cold liquid from a pocket in his robe, opened it, and whispered a spell. "Obscure all sound and light, a haze that blinds like night."

Then he began blowing across the bottle top. A mist formed in the air, slowly turning into fog. He made a fanning gesture with one arm and the fog drifted over and down the cliff face to seep into the city streets. He handed the bottle to the guard who would remain behind at this position, instructing him to continue blowing across the opening. The fog would spread on its own, rising and falling up and down the mountainside, growing thicker by the minute and appearing to come from the river gorge they had crossed. By the time the prisoners were in the open, seeing them would be far harder. The other wizards cast the same spell.

"Where exactly is the prison entrance?" Eric whispered.

Prince Dravo pointed to a location down one level from their position and a street over. "The one with the bell tower. The fog should reach it soon. We must be patient. Only the Ellorians and one wizard should come, so the other wizard can remain outside to assist. Once the fog has spread, the guardsmen we have brought should take positions where they can lead the hostages back up this way."

They waited in silence, hearing only the sounds of an alien world at night. Once, they heard footsteps and low voices as two dark elves passed the prison on the other side, heading from the castle to lower in town. The only other sign anyone was awake was the random golden glow from windows, but none were near them. Sounds became more hushed as the fog rose, covering the buildings near them so that couldn't tell what was happening anywhere else, including how far the fog had spread. They had to hope it wasn't localized, or anyone walking by might realize it wasn't natural because it only covered a small area.

Some of the group moved down to wait behind another building on the same level as the prison. Standing beside Ryan, Anna, and the other wizard, Matt watched Eric and Dravo disappear into the fog. He couldn't help looking around repeatedly, as if he would see something, and tried to focus on sound, hearing nothing, which was good. Several tense minutes passed before a short, dark figure began returning. It was Eric, who gestured for them to follow. As they reached the entrance to the prison, Matt stepped inside curiously, finding a small room with no one inside it, a lone hallway extending back into the mountain. To his raised eyebrow, Eric gestured at a closed door to one side and held up two fingers. Apparently, there were two unconscious dark elves over there out of sight.

"Ryan," began Eric, "I'd feel comfortable if you stayed here and guarded the entrance."

"Sure," replied the big man. Matt thought he didn't look comfortable being left behind. Who could blame him?

Dravo motioned Matt over and whispered, "At the end of this hall is a room with as many as ten people. Can you subdue them?"

Matt thought about what spells he had ready for that and made a quick decision, pulling out a pouch and fishing inside for a small marble he finally retrieved. He stepped up to the hallway and put the marble in his palm.

"How far?" he asked. The corridor wasn't lit. Only light from this end and the other filled it, but the flickering glow was faint at the other end and he wasn't sure what he was seeing.

Dravo answered, "Fifty feet."

"Straight?"

"Yes, but the room opens to the left for ten paces. There are several ways to leave that room, and if anyone does, it will be to alert others inside. We control the entrance, but they could reach the hostages before we stop them. They can also ring the bell, and then..."

Feeling like he understood the significance, Matt tried to ignore the pressure. It seemed like a long time ago when doing this or anything in front of others made him nervous. Now he only felt that way because failure meant people getting hurt, a different kind of pressure that made his old fears seem trivial. He shrugged it off, focused his will on the marble, and said the words of magic.

Safely fly through wind and air, burst with force, and strike what's there.

The marble rose above his palm and floated down the hall into growing darkness as he focused on its movement. He only had a general sense of how far it had gone and stared hard for some sign it had emerged into the torchlight at the end. It was too far, and too dark, but he thought it had reached the end. Hoping for the best, he made a hand motion as if to swat something to his left. Someone shouted in elven just as Matt said another word and a percussive blast of air walloped everyone in that room, sending bodies into walls and whatever else was there. While he couldn't see it, he heard the commotion of wooden furniture being overturned and metal falling to the floor. Maybe the noise made that an unwise spell. He nodded at Eric, who sprinted that way with Prince Dravo right behind and Matt following with everyone else.

Nearing the corner, Matt heard struggling and soon saw Eric deliver a kick to a guard's head as Dravo held another dark elf in a headlock that was making the victim lose consciousness. Both scuffles were soon over. Eight bodies lay on the floor, along with two tables and several benches. Anna pushed past him and checked several.

"They're still alive."

"They should be out for a while," Matt remarked, his voice still low. Suddenly he saw movement from a hall to one side. Eric saw his alarm and chased after a dark elf with one of their human guards following. A shout in elven rang out from there, and Dravo grabbed his arm.

"With me." The prince turned toward a stairway leading down and descended with Matt coming as fast as he could, lifting his robe with the hand that didn't hold Soliander's staff. A glance showed Anna coming, too. When they reached the bottom, they saw a dark elf trying to close a metal gate ahead until Dravo threw a knife that struck the bars and bounced off.

"Down!" Matt shouted. He didn't wait for Dravo to dive to the floor as he summoned a torrent of fire that hurtled down the hall from his staff and caused a shriek of pain. He stopped the flames to see two men on fire, the gate still swinging open. Dravo rose as they rushed forward and kicked his way in, their own guards moving to the left and right where other doors led elsewhere. A glance at once showed a water well inside, but then Matt was through the gate ahead, gagging at the burning smell of the two fallen elves. Behind him, Anna stopped to help them. He wondered if that was a good idea, but he also felt bad about what he'd done. The sight of white light surrounding and healing both men made him sigh in relief. As long as they didn't get up again soon and become a problem…

They heard a commotion ahead as the short hall opened into a wide room with several jail cells full of humans, many of whom were rising, sleepy eyed and fearful. The smell told him of their poor condition, the sight of torn clothing, dirty hair, and smudged skin confirming it. No jailers were here, and he counted twenty-two, one short of what they had heard. He wished Ryan was here to do the nice sort of speeches he gave, or even Eric. Fortunately, Anna saved him from having to do it.

"Hello everyone," she said, stepping toward the cells. "We are here to rescue you, but we need you to keep quiet and move quickly but cautiously with us. Do you understand?"

"Yes," said one middle-aged man. "But who are you? Why is a dark elf with you? They cannot be trusted."

"We are the Ellorian Champions, and this is Prince Dravo of Kiarven. He is helping us. We don't really have time to explain more. I need you to trust us."

The man pursed his lips. "You I can trust. Him I cannot."

"Fair enough. You speak for all?"

After a moment, he nodded. "I do."

Steady footsteps behind him made Matt turn to see Eric arriving.

"What's that?" Matt asked.

Eric tossed a thick rope in his hand to the floor. "The rope to the bell. He was about to ring it. I cut off enough to keep anyone from reaching it soon. I checked the other rooms on the way here. We're clear."

"There are more rooms back here," advised Dravo, moving toward them, Eric following. They came back a minute later, indicating that the only dark elf left was the prince. By then, the keys had been found, and the jails opened, the hostages all awakened. Some were just children, but none so small they would have to be carried. Anna crouched down to talk to them as Eric addressed the adults, telling them the basic plan. Anna did a cursory examination of anyone, healing a few of minor issues like dehydration, sores on their feet, and anything else that might inhibit the escape. It seemed they were ready to go.

Matt turned to the rogue. "Eri, um, Andier, why don't you tie up the two I burned?"

"Right."

"Catch up. We'll wait at the exit to the prison."

Within minutes, the group had gathered by Ryan, who looked relieved. He said that no one had come by. Matt and the other wizard, the one from Aker, cast another spell to muffle sounds, and the group left the prison with Eric in the lead. The fog had grown thicker, but the rogue led them right to the awaiting guard, who reported that two more dark elves had walked by minutes ago. Dravo took the lead, because this time they were staying on the streets and not walking behind buildings. They moved with good efficiency and stealth and reached the castle's corner sooner than Matt expected. They went over the crumbling wall back to the path, the wizard belatedly realizing they should have spread the fog here, too. So far, this was going fairly well. But no sooner had he thought it than the prison bell began tolling.

Prince Dravo turned to them and whispered, "Run! Quietly, but run!"

They did as he told them, moving to the path, Eric in the lead, his head turned toward the castle walls. Even if someone saw them there, they likely couldn't be stopped from reaching the portal now. Matt had seen no doors from the castle over here. He stayed at the rear with Ryan, gesturing for others to hurry. They heard shouts inside the castle now, feet charging on the other side of the wall, the bell still ringing. But the group reached the fork back over the gorge and went up the stairs, the healthy helping the women and children. Matt had the impression this was the most exercise they'd had in a long time. Their eyes shone with fear and desperation, but he felt calm as he crossed the bridge with the knight and looked back, everyone else continuing without them.

"I think we made it," he said, feeling excited by the adventure.

"Yeah, but now getting to the king is going to be a bitch."

"Can't argue with that. Go on without me. I need to do something."

"No, staying here to guard you at the least."

"Okay. Thanks." He pulled out the vial from earlier.

"What are you doing?"

"More fog. We need to get back across this bridge in a minute."

"I think we do it now, to be honest. We can do that out of sight at least and the others can catch up."

Matt nodded and glanced back to see Ryan gesturing to Eric where they were going and seeing Eric give a thumbs up. He and the knight went back into the shade of trees and Matt cast the spell from there, trying to speed up the fog's spread by gesturing more often and not sure if that helped any. He made sure it flowed in the other direction that they hadn't been yet—the one Dravo said led to a rear entrance in the castle. The royals who had long ago wanted to use the portal went that way, as did important guests. But any commoners had to go toward the city just like he and the others had just done. Presumably, no one would think to look back here at all.

They waited in silence, correctly assuming the rest of the group would join them once the fog was thick enough, and they did. Now the only ones left were the Ellorians, Prince Dravo, and the other two wizards. At the least, the rescue had been a success, the hostages through the portal and being taken care of in Thiat. But now they had to avert disaster. If they failed, getting King Sondin restored as the quest demanded would take longer.

"What now?" Eric whispered to the dark elf.

"The plan has not changed. We move to where my man waits for me. He may be delayed, however."

Matt frowned at the truth of it. While Dravo had been exiled long ago and many of his men dispersed so they could not operate together in any way, there were still those loyal to him. Some worked in the castle in various positions, and one such dark elf had helped him and his sister leave. They had climbed down a temporary rope ladder near the rear corner tower. Now he and the others would wait for that person to lower it again. He just wouldn't be expecting so many people to climb up. They headed that direction and, to even Dravo's surprise, the ladder was already lowered. He appeared to consider that a moment before ascending alone, pausing near the top to look over the wall. Several minutes passed as they listened to the sounds of activity inside, but virtually all of it was at the castle's front. Lights had appeared in far more windows.

The elf motioned for them to follow and disappeared over the top. Eric went first, then Anna, the other wizards, Matt, and finally Ryan. When Matt reached the top, he found a cart loaded with arrows, bolts, crossbows, and long bows had been left in the way so that he had to get on the wall and move over a few feet before dropping to the walkway. That's when he saw the cart had a broken wheel, preventing it from being moved. He gazed around and saw that the wall was about fifteen feet wide, the walkway they crouched on a few feet below the top. No one could see them unless from above, where his eyes darted to towers, but the fog had risen over the wall to obscure everything.

Dravo turned to them as Ryan finished arriving last. "The broken cart is a ruse, I'm certain. My man put it here so the rope ladder could be here all the time."

"How do you know this?" Eric asked.

"I don't, but it's too coincidental. He is smart. We must go down this tower, now, and head for the king's quarters. He is likely awake, as are far more guards, so we should expect a fight."

"Right. Lead the way."

They made it into the tower and descended the spiral stairs to the ground floor, where they could have stepped out into interior grounds. The fog was nearly absent there, having not seeped over and down the fortifications. Matt hoped they would stay within the castle walls, as they were not solid but hallways full of storage items like barrels and crates, but the prince led them onto the grounds. The castle itself stood not too far away, and they made it to its side wall, creaking open a door to get inside, where it was dark.

"Where do you think the king is now?" Eric asked whispered. "Throne room?"

"No. That's only used for formal moments, on the first floor. He is probably not in bed on the third, given that everyone knows who is in the prison and what the bell means. He will be on the second level, where business is done."

"So up this flight of steps?"

"Yes. There will be two chambers we must get through to reach the main one where he is likely to be. Expect a fight, and we must be quick to prevent them from sealing the other doors, the king inside. Soliander?"

Matt pursed his lips. "I'll be right behind you. See if you can create an opening for me to cast through to the next room."

The prince remarked, "Even if we make into that room, there is a way out the other side."

Eric sighed. "I don't like it. Can we go around and trap him? I feel like we don't have enough people to do that, but we have three wizards."

The prince agreed. "That is my concern as well. However, we have surprise to help us. If you take Soliander around to the other side, and the other wizards come with Korrin and I, this may work, but you risk being discovered."

Eric and Matt exchanged a look, and the wizard shrugged, remarking, "Even if we start fighting over there, and you start doing so over here, they will realize they are surrounded and that can cause confusion. Let's try it."

Dravo measured them with his gaze and then turned to Ryan. "I suggest we purposely make noise to draw them to us."

"Right." The knight didn't look too pleased with the idea.

They agreed to wait a few minutes before ascending, voices being audible above. Eric led the way along the hall that stood against the castle's rear wall, then stopped. Ahead were several guards at the rear exit, the one that likely led to the path toward the portal, though the door appeared to be blocked by more crates and barrels as if no one ever used the rear door. They wouldn't make it past the guards and retreated quickly to the others, telling them the issue.

The prince said, "Go up to the third floor here and use the same hallway there. You will not find the same problem."

Realizing they should have thought of that before, Matt followed Eric up the corner stairs, the same ones the rest would use in a few minutes. They reached the second floor and didn't bother peeking out to see what or who was outside the stairwell, multiple voices chatting idly about the fun they would have hunting the escaped humans if they weren't stuck inside guarding the king. Matt and Eric continued up to the third level, where the royal rooms were. Less noise was here, and they easily made their way to the other side of the castle, and then down the stairs just as the fighting broke out. They heard yelling from there.

"What is going on?" someone bellowed closer to them.

"Your Majesty," said another elf's voice, "we must get you to safety."

"Dravo!" someone yelled farther away.

"Dravo?" King Erods barked. "What is... Did he...? Bring that elf to me now!"

Several men screamed in pain, and Matt assumed one of the other wizards had cast something.

"Your Majesty! They will enter the room any moment!"

Eric peered in, turned back, and smiled. Then he pulled out his short sword and stepped into the room with Matt following, a spell on his lips. In front of them, the king stood facing away, straight white hair down his back from a balding black head, a disheveled red robe covering him. A wide oak table sat before him and on the other side of it stood a tall elf who faced them, sunken cheeks below red eyes that widened, his thin lips parting. He also wore a robe as if having hastily dressed and was apparently some sort of counselor. The rest of the room had chairs along the walls but was empty because whatever guards had been here had rushed to the fight.

"We're already here, King Erods," said Eric, kicking a chair out of the way and raising a sword. The king turned around in outrage that gave way to fear. "Soliander, make sure no one comes behind us."

"Right."

"Who are you?" demanded the king.

"The Ellorian Champions. Two of them, anyway. Don't try anything or I'll stick you with this sword."

The sound of two bodies falling made Matt look across the room, where Ryan and Dravo strode in, followed by Anna and the wizards. He saw Ryan was bleeding from his leg until the knight used his Trinity Ring to heal himself. They could hear yelling beyond them and barred the door against the reinforcements that were on the way. This was the part that the prince had needed them for. Matt knew he and the wizards were the key to keeping a considerable force of dark elves from breaking into this room and killing them all before Dravo's troops could get up here to protect him.

"How did you get in here?" the king demanded of Dravo.

"Why would I tell you that?" the prince asked as he approached. He shoved the table aside, then tore a long piece of cloth off the counselor's robe and ripped it in half. He roughly gagged King Erods and tied his hands behind his back, shoving him into a chair. "I don't have time for pretty speeches. Your hostages are gone. I will be king and I will try you for war crimes."

The counselor said, "But, Dravo, no one will recognize your sovereignty, just as other lands are refusing to acknowledge we control Aker."

The prince turned on him. "I have an arrangement with both Aker and Thiat for exactly that, and enough of our people agree that this war should never have happened that they, too, will support me. We will withdraw from Aker."

The counselor seemed taken aback but accepting of this news. "What of Prince Kammer? He will not agree."

"His opinion won't be needed much longer. Enough of this." He turned to Eric. "The tower bell has spoiled our plan to get my forces up here for protection. We need another plan."

Eric turned to Matt. "How good of an illusion can you do?"

Matt shrugged. "What do you need?"

The rogue smiled, and they got to work so quickly that it made Matt nervous of a mistake being made. The shouts and heavy footsteps of armored dark elves charging up the stairs didn't help. Eric threw open the doors to the room and everyone assumed their positions. It had taken some hair from the dead and living elves and themselves, plus the skills of all three wizards, to create the scene the rogue devised. The dark elves charged into the room to find the bodies of several humans scattered about, King Erods standing with a dagger at the throat of a kneeling and captured Price Dravo, who was the only person whose appearance was not an illusion. A half dozen elven guards appeared to be already in the room, having defeated the intruders and captured others.

"You're a little late!" snapped King Erods. "Next time try not to be asleep when someone is trying to kill me."

The lead elven guard looked aghast and bowed. "Your Majesty, we did not expect–"

"What?" King Erods interrupted. "To be hanged for incompetence? If you want to be useful, bring me every one of those disgusting ogre and goblin leaders from the prince's forces. And bring the biggest and meanest looking of the warriors, too. And their weapons still on them, so they suspect nothing. I'm thinking we'll have a little fun in the courtyard today with these traitors."

The guard nodded and turned on his heel, instructing his men to remain behind until the king barked at him to take them because he had his band of heroes already. He told them to guard the entrance to the castle, and no was allowed up here until the errand was complete. The humiliated guards left and everyone remained in their positions until they heard the sounds of them running across the courtyard.

From his knees, Prince Dravo looked up at the king and rose. "That was a fine performance."

"Thank you," said Ryan, stepping back and pulling the blade away.

"That went better than I expected," said Eric, looking like a dark elf guard. The real guards were all dead on the floor and disguised as humans. The actual king and counselor were among them, bound and gagged, though no one could tell. They talked it over and put into play Dravo's plan to deal with Prince Kammer.

Before leaving Thiat, Dravo had revealed that, while magic portals were rare, the people most likely to have them were royalty, of course, regardless of race. An elven Mirror of Sulinae was on the first floor of the castle and was part of a pair. The Ellorians had used one on Honyn when escaping Castle Darlonon. With King Erods not much interested in travel but recognizing the value of appearing in Aker as its new sovereign, he had made his son bring the other Mirror of Sulinae to Aker. Dravo had suspected they existed but been unsure where they might be.

But he learned the truth after he arrived in Avaran by horseback in the vanguard of his rebel band. The sneering Prince Kammer had made no indications of planning to travel from Aker to Kiarven, as Dravo had just done, and yet Kammer had somehow gotten here before Dravo, who then discovered the Mirror of Sulinae. This meant the other one must be in Aker.

Now the group staged a scene, most of them standing out of sight beside the Mirror of Sulinae. Dravo held a knife to the neck of Ryan, who was still pretending to be King Erods. Matt studied the words on the device. Memories from Soliander helped him understand how ones like this, though the design was slightly different. Everyone indicated they were ready, and he turned it on. The gold frame filled with a dark image that revealed very little. Eric, still looking like a dark elf, snatched a nearby torch from a wall and threw it through, the light from it showing a dark room that still told them little of where the other Mirror of Sulinae stood. They were taking a small gamble that it was near the bedroom of Prince Kammer.

"Kammer!" yelled King Erods in a panic. "Kammer! Help me!"

"Yes!" called Dravo, playing along. "Come watch your father die!"

They kept up the banter a few more moments before the alarmed face of a dark elf appeared in the mirror. He stood barefoot and naked from the waist up. The expression turned to one of outrage and fury.

"Dravo!" the dark elf yelled. "Traitor!"

Dravo pulled the king backwards, trying to create the impression that the king had activated the Mirror of Sulinae before he could be stopped, and now Dravo was dragging him farther away. The real goal was to create room for the expected arrivals.

"Save me!" yelled King Erods, but the face of Kammer disappeared. They heard him hollering for guards, as half-expected. It didn't take long before four armored reinforcements arrived and rushed through the Mirror of Sulinae and into the room, swords swinging. Pretending to be one of Dravo's elves, Eric drew some of them to him, and Dravo let go of King Erods to take on the other two. Matt wondered if Kammer was coming or if they would have to go get him. But then the prince stepped into the room with a wicked sword poised before him, his eyes catching sight of Matt to one side. Even as he turned, Matt spoke a word, and the prince collapsed.

Seeing this, King Erods said, "Stop in the king's name!"

The remaining four intruders hesitated, allowing Eric to slug one of them to the floor and Dravo to disarm another. The last two lowered their swords. It was over.

Ryan watched the late afternoon sun fall on the upper half of Castle Rivina with mixed feelings. He was glad to be going home, but the last time they were here, Dravo had tried to kill them. The scene had been among the more unsettling they'd experienced, one that added to a feeling that he and the others needed to make a plan for what to do once summoned. That included the moment of arrival and questions to ask about situations and even details about life. The day here was apparently an hour shorter than on Earth, and they counted the weeks differently. Would they one day arrive somewhere more drastically different?

After capturing Prince Kammer, the group had awaited Dravo's men, a hundred brought into the courtyard in Avaran and soon overtaking the surprised dark elves who had accompanied them. Some fighting had broken out despite Ryan, still pretending to be King Erods, having told the elves to disarm themselves. The order was dubious, and it didn't really surprise anyone that some had disobeyed, but with help from Matt and the other wizards, the castle had come under the command of Dravo, who waited until dawn to crown himself King of Kiarven from the castle walls as much of the city watched. It hadn't been up to the Ellorian Champions to help him secure the city or his kingdom, so they had returned to Thiat with the news.

Even the grumpy King Varrun gave them credit for the mission's success before pointing out that no one from the Kingdom of Thiat had benefitted from any of this so far. The Ellorians still needed to get King Sondin restored to the throne of Aker and out of Thiat. They had ideas on this, but first, they needed rest and slept into early afternoon, when they awoke to learn of various plans made in their absence. To secure peace, King Dravo had agreed to marry a human duchess from Aker. King Sondin was to marry the dark elf Princess Liera, Dravo's sister, who didn't look too pleased.

But her reaction paled to that of Princess Miara. By now, she had learned that the wizard Gian, whom she loved, had reached the Quest Ring at Castle Rivina in Aker a week earlier and summoned the Ellorians, only to be killed by Dravo's forces. Now Dravo's sister was to be Miara's aunt by marriage, and Queen of Aker. The fury had been impressive, and no one had to say aloud that if Miara were to remain in Aker with her brother, no peace would last. King Sondin was to marry his sister to someone in Thiat, to strengthen that bond as well, removing the princess from his kingdom. Miara hadn't exactly calmed with the news.

Prince Kammer was to stand trial in Aker for his war crimes, but Erods was to stay in Kiarven. Ryan wondered how that worked, when someone took over as monarch in a coup and the previous one was still alive, but they didn't have time to question it and it wasn't their problem. He just hoped that the elves didn't rise against King Dravo and do something that required another quest. Once was enough.

None of these marriages had taken place yet when the Ellorians traveled with King Sondin and Princess Liera, plus a few hundred soldiers, to Kiarven via the portal under Thiat. With King Dravo's blessing, all of them then used the Mirror of Sulinae to reach Aker, completing the quest.

As for Ryan and the others, it was time to go home. Rather than returning to Thiat, they would use the other Quest Ring in Aker, declining any attempt at a banquet or celebration. King Sondin had enough to worry about rebuilding his kingdom anyway, and no real staff set up to do such a thing. He settled for a procession that led them to the half-burned Castle Rivina. He could do nothing to restore it yet, but when they arrived in the room where their battle with Dravo had taken place, there were no bodies. They hadn't been sure what to expect. King Sondin couldn't keep the frown from his face as he surveyed the damage, vowing out loud to have it all restored.

Eric wanted a moment alone with the three of them, so they went to one side of the hall to speak. "The last time we returned to Earth, we aimed for nighttime. But this time, all of us were at Jack's except Anna. It should be midday, and maybe there is enough activity at the hospital that you can lose yourself in it on the way out. It depends on how well that room is being watched."

Ryan said to her, "We know that we always return to where we were, but we aren't sure if anyone else knows that, but I think they do because of you disappearing and reappearing on the highway. Someone may be waiting for you."

Eric looked concerned as he said, "There is probably still a warrant for your arrest. There might be someone in the hospital room you were in, either a patient or police."

Ryan frowned. "Yeah, the *bed* might have someone in it. I hope you don't end up on top of them or something. Not really sure how that works."

Anna asked, "What if something occupies the space we were occupying?"

Matt spoke up. "I know the answer to this from my talks with Lorian. You just get moved over to the nearest space. Most teleport spells have this sort of thing built into them. I think we can assume Soliander was smart enough to do this with the return spell."

"Good point," Eric agreed and turned to Anna. "Listen, regardless of what happens, you need to be ready."

"Yeah, I know," she said irritably.

"I'm not trying to boss you around. Just thinking out loud."

"Yeah, okay. Sorry. It just stresses me out every time we do this."

"I know. I'm sorry, but maybe we can start working on getting those Home Rings set up."

Ryan did not know how they were going to get that done, but it was definitely needed. So was a home base they could stay in and use for training. He wondered if his attorney or Jack had done anything for that in their absence, but it had been just over a day, so probably not. Sometimes it seemed like more time was passing from all the actions they had to take. Quests made for long days.

At least they hadn't been stuck on this planet for weeks, as he'd assumed would happen when he learned of the quest to restore a king to power. He just wanted to feel in control of his life again, but saw no sign of that happening soon. Anna was the more immediate concern this time, just like last time. He thought of something to help her.

"If people are in the room when you arrive," he began, "they will call security. I think you need to run out of there and hide. We can send Jack to get you."

Anna admitted, "Not sure I want to go back."

Eric pursed his lips in commiseration. "It will be okay, Anna."

"Will it?" she asked. "I've killed one of my friends, maimed another, and paralyzed one for life. I hurt several more and destroyed their property. I have all these lawsuits coming. There's an arrest warrant."

Ryan had almost forgotten all of that and put an arm around her, saying he would use his family's lawyers and money to fight everything for her if he could. She did not have to go through this alone or be financially destroyed. There were other problems, of course, but in the back of his mind was the possibility that she could heal those who had been hurt. They hadn't talked about it in a while because he didn't want to pressure her, but he never forgot it.

One day, hopefully soon, she would heal his brother Daniel, who could finally walk again. Anna could heal her friend, and as someone who had been paralyzed herself and knew what it was to walk again because she had been healed, the importance of it had to be apparent to her. Maybe he would talk about it with her soon, but not now. They needed to get home and be safe again, even if for just a little while. Anna, of all people, had felt this taken from her the most.

With the King of Aker waiting for them, along with those gathered to see them leave, the Ellorian Champions gathered inside the Quest Ring, confident it could send them home again even though it wasn't the one that had brought them. That didn't seem to matter, at least according to Matt. If it did, it wouldn't take more than a few hours to get back to Thiat and go home that way. But it worked. The familiar sights and sounds of a quest starting or ending enveloped them as another world disappeared from around them and they found themselves headed for Earth.

CHAPTER SIXTEEN

REUNIONS

Anna braced herself for arrival. She really hated not knowing what awaited her. Leaving Earth was one thing, but being able to relax on the way back would have been nice. At least a car would not hit her this time, although being arrested wasn't great either. Nor was shocking people who might scream and calling all sorts of attention to her. The idea of fleeing in a hospital gown with her butt visible made her smile. She tried to hope for the best as her friends assumed their Earth clothes before her. She felt herself wearing the thin gown, but she had forgotten having both legs and one arm in casts. Then the vortex of light ended.

The hospital room was empty, but the wooden door was wide open. She breathed a sigh of relief but had to grab the wall one with hand to steady herself. How was she supposed to get out of these casts? She felt healed and rested as usual, but walking without bending either leg had her wobbling toward the bathroom to get out of sight. If someone saw her like this, the attention would be immediate. She got inside and closed the door to remain hidden, listening intently. Her familiarity with hospitals meant she knew where to get a cast saw, but she would never make it there, even if she waited until nightfall, because plenty of nurses were still around then.

The guys had to come get her. And find a saw, plus some clothing. It was the only way. She cracked the door, looking for a phone she saw on the wall. A call to them would set that in motion, but they might see her doing it. She wasn't sure where her room was, near a nurse's station or farther away. Anna sighed. She was tiring of this whole thing. The likelihood of getting caught and arrested made her want to just walk out of there and not even bother trying to get away.

Footsteps sounded in the hall and she shrank back as a man and woman began arguing.

"Miss, you can't go in there." A guard. The room was guarded, after all.

"Oh, I'll just be a minute. I wanted to see what the rooms are like." The woman's steps came closer.

"This one is off limits. You'll have to–"

"I'll just be a minute."

More footsteps, this time from both, getting nearer. They had entered the room.

"Miss. Miss!"

"Does this one have a decent view? I so dislike not being able to see out."

"Okay, look, you've seen the–"

"Sleep."

The sound of a body hitting the floor made Anna's eyes widen. Had the woman just cast a spell on the guard? The woman's steps moved away and the room door closed with only a faint sound, but the lock turning made a louder click. Anna backed up as the woman's footsteps approached the bathroom door. There was nowhere to hide if it opened, but the steps stopped just outside it, a shadow visible under the door.

"Anna," said a woman's voice, "it's Eriana."

Relief washed over Anna, and she peeked out to see her smiling savior holding a white plastic bag. An unconscious police officer lay on the floor. She let out a big breath and laughed. "I am so glad to see you right now," she said emphatically.

"The feeling is mutual. Let's get you on the bed and out of that stuff. The officer will be fine and should wake soon, but we'll need to be gone, of course." She helped Anna wobble over to and onto the hospital bed.

"Do you know how to use that thing?" Anna asked on seeing the cast saw in Eriana's purse. She had never felt so happy to see one.

"Sort of. I've been watching videos."

Anna smiled, not reassured by that. "Well, I do. This is the hospital where I work, which means I really need a disguise to get out of here without being recognized."

"I have a hat and sunglasses for you, too."

"Okay."

They slowly cut through the cast on her arm first, and then Anna took over doing the upper part of one leg cast and teaching Eriana how to do the lower part. It took uncomfortably long to get them all off, at which point Anna changed into the undergarments, jeans, and t-shirt. She put her hair in a ponytail and pulled it through a baseball cap, impressed with Eriana's thoughtfulness. Then she donned the glasses she didn't really need and exited the room, which she now learned was toward the end of a hall, making it easier to be undisturbed. The officer was the only one here right now. They went down a stairway just a few steps away.

"You're a real lifesaver," Anna said, her voice full of gratitude, a feeling that was becoming common. That she needed a lot of help wasn't something she was accustomed to, but the devastating nature of her problems blew past any pride she might have felt about going it alone. Self-reliance was great, but she didn't care anymore. Let the help come by the truckloads. She was entirely happy to rely on others and eager to show her appreciation, which made her wonder how to do so for the woman she was so often impersonating now. What was an appropriate thank you gift for healing your paralysis, or knocking out a police officer, or rescuing you from impending jail time? Was a fruit basket not enough? She laughed a little, needing some comic relief even if she had to provide it herself.

Eriana smiled. "That's been the literal truth in my past."

"How did you know I arrived?"

"Hidden camera with motion detection," she said, slipping something tiny into her purse. "They have guarded the room since you disappeared, but I was able to flirt my way inside and plant one. I've been hanging out nearby or in the cafeteria or other waiting rooms since then."

They soon left the hospital by a side door and walked across the parking lot to Eriana's white BMW rental car. As the car started and they buckled up, they saw officers running into the hospital.

"I guess they've seen the guy you put to sleep. Or the casts. Maybe we should've hidden those."

"Maybe." The priestess handed her a red phone. "Why don't you call the others."

"Right." Anna called Eric first, filling him in, then asking her driver, as they headed down the road, "Where are we going?"

"Back to Jack's apartment, as quickly as we dare. I don't want you disappearing from a moving car again."

Anna had no argument against that. Along the way, they discussed the Corethian Amulet, which Eriana had in her purse. She asked Anna to take it out. She did, a weird feeling coming over her at the familiar sight of it. So far, they never saw something on Earth that they had seen on a quest. Though she had just been wearing a copy, seeing it on Earth brought a dose of reality to her. She shuddered, tears springing into her eyes before fading. The strict separation between quests and Earth had just ended for her, and though it had already been obvious that her life had changed forever, something about this brought it crashing in on her. She felt inexplicably lonely, frightened, and like the universe was infinitely bigger than she had known. And she was lost in it.

That reminded her of the trouble awaiting her, but when asked, Eriana said there had been no real developments. The police were obviously looking for her, but no one knew anything, though reports of her disappearance were all over the news despite it not being witnessed.

"Do you know how to create the Home Rings?" she asked. "I know Soliander did most of it, but the guys said you helped with the healing part of the Quest Rings."

Eriana turned off the highway into the even heavier side-street traffic. "I'm afraid I don't know enough, or have the power to make one. I just know what they're supposed to do. I think if we can get the four of you settled somewhere and you don't leave, you will be fine until we can create them. One thing I know is that you need soclarin ore."

That didn't surprise her. "That's interesting. We gave some to Lorian when we were on Honyn." She sighed. "If only we knew how to contact him."

"There are ways to send messages. Matt can look into it and either do it from here or the next time you are on a quest. It would be easier if you're already on Honyn, of course."

Talk soon turned to how to use the amulet, but there wasn't much to it. Anna would need to concentrate her will on it, and her emotions, opening herself to the touch of a god who might help her. The amulet would collect that energy and act as a kind of beacon to the gods of a world, whether she knew their names or anything about them or not. It facilitated an initial contact and all subsequent ones, but that was not all. The amulet helped channel power from that god under certain circumstances, mostly offensive ones, like when she had done things to the undead in Ortham.

For healing, the amulet didn't do that, as Anna's body was the conduit instead. It seemed to make sense to her, and Eriana suggested she try using it here on Earth to contact God for the first time. That seemed like a good idea, but she felt afraid of getting an answer. She still resisted the notion that He was real.

But she needed to get over it. And she wanted to. She had a friend to visit and see about healing because, inadvertently or not, Anna was responsible for what had happened to her. That was a conversation she badly wanted to have but was also afraid to do. And there was the issue of traveling there. There was too much risk to herself. Maybe she could send Eriana to heal Raven, but the real Light Bringer reminded her that even she was not strong enough to do it yet. Anna knew it to be true because Eriana would have healed her. Raven might have to wait.

The same went for Daniel. Ryan hadn't brought up the subject of healing his brother for a while, a fact for which she was grateful. But Anna felt a new appreciation for his guilt in causing the paralysis, a new sympathy and compassion that had made her want to hug him more than once and apologize, not for anything specific, but in case she had ever seemed dismissive or frustrated with his requests to heal Daniel.

She had paralyzed Raven by accident, just like he had done to Daniel. Having been paralyzed, she knew the fear and uncertainty of it. Raven was likely still in that same spiritual place. Daniel was not, having been in a wheelchair most of his life. How would he react to the possibility of being able to walk again? In theory, he would be all for it, but after so much time, there had to be some adjustments he would go through. While she assumed this would be positive, maybe he would resist such a tremendous change to his life.

Jade had lost both legs, and Anna didn't know if she would ever be strong enough with healing to fix damage like that. Even Eriana might not. That Jade would never dance again filled her with a different grief, because all of Jade's ambitions and dreams were about that, and Anna had killed them, probably forever. And even if it wasn't, Jade had no way of knowing that. Anna wasn't sure she could ever face her and the unspeakable loss she had caused.

Worse than all of this was that Heather was dead. She had had little time to come to terms with it, other than those awful hours in the hospital. The strong desire to visit her grave—if she had even been buried yet, and she didn't know—would have to wait. These Home Rings were everything and needed to become top priority. The random summoning was bad enough by itself, but having to be virtually imprisoned in Jack's apartment, or somewhere else, so they would be safe when they returned caused too many problems.

Looking at the phone in her hand as Eriana neared Jack's apartment, she wondered if she should call her parents. Would someone tap the phone? Would an email give away her location? What was happening with any lawsuits or other legal problems? She felt relieved as they parked. Jack hopefully knew these things. She badly needed an update and wasn't even sure where they had left off with any plans to create a home base that wasn't his apartment.

The champions soon reunited with Eriana and Jack being the only other two present. They dialed Ryan's attorney and Daniel for an update and planning session. The first surprise was minor; Eric and Ryan had been on the couch when summoned and had reappeared there, but Matt had been in the bathroom. Instead of arriving there, he was standing in Jack's kitchen. Anna had also not appeared on the empty hospital bed, but standing a few feet away. She hadn't actually noticed this. They didn't know what it meant, but clearly the return spell wasn't foolproof. Eriana speculated that the blast that had freed the real champions from questing had added some unpredictability to being sent home.

From Quincy, the lawyer, they learned that Heather's parents had filed a wrongful death civil suit against Anna, who just wanted to settle and get it over with. Both Jade and Raven were discussing legal action or their parents were. Ryan and Eriana both pledged to take care of it, financially, so Quincy would represent the matter and make it "go away" as she said. They could handle the other suits for various kinds of other damages the same way. The accidents had involved other cars.

Anna wasn't sure how to feel about all of it, from guilt over what happened to guilt that others were dealing with her problems. And part of her just didn't care, having too many problems as it was. She didn't want to think about it, didn't want to try talking to Heather's parents or anyone else, but she felt she owed it to them and that not doing anything was cowardice. But until they fixed this Home Ring situation, it would have to wait. And if the victims did not understand this, and they likely wouldn't given her inability to tell the truth, there wasn't much she could do about it. More powerlessness made her sigh in frustration and turn her mind to things she could resolve.

Jack and Quincy had moved forward with trying to find a rural estate to set up as a new home base. Jack had visited several for extensive tours with a video camera rolling, knowing they couldn't visit in person without unnecessary risks. One stood out and, while not perfect, would work. The group made a quick decision to gain it, Eriana footing the three-million-dollar cost and admitting she had to figure out what to tell Paul, but assuring them he would do what she wanted. Anna couldn't help wondering about that relationship and what the excuse would be, but Eriana believed it was best to start telling her husband some version of the truth.

Eriana had been collecting supposed magical items throughout their marriage, Paul well aware of the collection that they showed off in their house to wealthy friends. With the reports of magic and healing working around the world growing, he would believe that some items were real after all. With the friends back on Earth now, Eriana was booking a flight home to have this talk with Paul and, just as importantly, bring every last one of those items back here for potential use. She would tell Paul that Ryan and the others had some items of their own and needed her help to deal with them, and that the items were causing them trouble she wanted to help them with. She also intended to bring her private investigator for physical and digital security at the new estate. Anna felt beyond grateful for all of it. Maybe soon they would have less to fear while on Earth.

Daniel revealed that he had purchased tons of additional equipment for them—period appropriate clothes, crossbows, long and short bows, bolts and arrows, swords and daggers of every kind, suits of armor, shields, lances and more, and a small library of books about medieval life and culture, how kingdoms worked in various parts of Earth, and a copy of every supposed book about magic, including ones with spells. Some were about witchcraft, others about necromancy, and pretty much every variation on the subject. He had also ordered a ton of ingredients that were listed as needed for magic, whether or not any of it was true. They would soon have a lab set up.

On a more mundane level, Daniel was now going to shop for furniture for the estate with Jack. And it was time to buy horses, with Ryan placing an order for the related gear like tack. Eriana knew more about it than anyone but Ryan, who couldn't go, so she would take care of it once she returned, including hiring a barn manager. Ryan already owned the horse he used at RenFest but wanted a few extras, all transported to the new estate once set up. But this was going to take a while. Anna felt relieved to know that everything would progress even in their absence, and the others shared their appreciation aloud. They needed friends like never before.

Despite the return spell refreshing them physically, Anna felt exhausted by the night's end. She needed a mental respite but decided not to join the boys for a streaming movie to get their minds off everything. Eriana left to make preparations, promising to return in the morning and leaving the amulet with Anna, who sat on Jack's bed, where she would spend the night, the guys settling for the floor or couch in the living room. She felt bad about that and wondered which of the three other champions, if not all of them, she should get used to sharing a bed with. She trusted them, so it wasn't like one of them would behave inappropriately sleeping beside her, but she just had too many other things on her mind. And she felt violated, like she had no control or privacy, so she didn't want to give up one minor element of it sooner than she needed to. She knew the guys understood and didn't begrudge the uncomfortable night they would spend, but she felt guilty and was tired of that feeling.

As Anna lay trying to sleep, she had the Corethian Amulet beside her, one hand on it. Closing her eyes, she focused her will and tried to remember the feeling coursing through her when Eriana used the power of God on her.

It had felt just like any other deity's touch—firm, gentle, reassuring, power-ful, and a little intimidating, as if the god was holding back to avoid hurting the vessel—her. What would the full force of a god's will feel like? She doubted anyone would survive it. Pushing the thought from her mind, she reached out with her senses for long moments, her heart full of a desire to help those she had hurt and the wounded still yet to come. It had always been true of her, since she was a little girl, and led to her interest in medi-cine. It's just that in the apparent absence of God, she had resorted to other means of helping. Now maybe she had another way.

It took some time, but finally, she felt something, and the first touch of it made her smile. And somehow that made it rush into her so that she chuck-led, and then cry at the truth enveloping her. God was out there, and real, and He had answered. A new reality had finally dawned here on Earth, now in Anna, and she let go of the amulet, certain she didn't need it anymore. Not here. The power filling her felt strong enough to do what she needed, and she vowed that in the morning, she would find Raven and undo the damage she had done.

Anna would finally become the Light Bringer.

Jack turned away from Eriana to his kitchen sink to resume cutting an apple, having just explained that he'd woken to find the apartment empty of all but him. While they couldn't be certain because he hadn't seen it, both knew that Anna, Ryan, Matt, and Eric were not on Earth, having been sum-moned once more. Even Jack was feeling frustrated, and it wasn't even hap-pening to him. Eriana had mentioned that the rate of quests was higher than what she and the other real champions had experienced, but their prolonged absence had likely caused a backlog of them to accumulate. Maybe it would slow down after what, a few months? Every time they disappeared, there was a good chance he was never seeing them again.

"Ouch!" Jack yanked his finger away from the knife, expecting the blood that seeped from the wound. Pinching it tight, he ran water over it.

Eriana approached and put a hand on his forearm, her skin warm. "Let me see."

The feel of her hand and motherly instinct made him glad he'd cut him-self. There was something very comforting about this woman. A faint hint of perfume added to the feminine air that he sometimes felt was missing from girls his age, most of them wearing jeans or other clothes not far from that of a guy. He knew such attire was more comfortable for them, but he appreciated the way Eriana dressed—long flowing skirts and blouses that bore no resemblance to a man's clothing. Sometimes she had leggings on, like now, but then she had a smaller skirt atop it. He liked her style and had already recognized the signs of his growing interest in her. That they had spent some time alone lately had helped, and she had even seemed receptive to some gentle flirting.

Now Jack pulled his hand from the water and let her take it, the blood flowing more as he stopped squeezing the wound shut. She looked it over a moment and then whispered.

"For a kind soul, please."

Jack's finger tingled and the cut stopping stinging. A soft glow lit the inside as the cut vanished. A slight feeling of bemusement came over him, from the healing touch within him, as small as it was. He wondered how strong that would be if he was more desperately wounded. What had Anna felt? He turned to Erin, their eyes meeting. She pulled her hand from his, but he closed his fingers around it.

"Your touch is wonderful," he confessed.

She smiled. "It's the touch of your god."

"No." He held her gaze. "I felt it long before you did that."

Her smile broadened. "You're sweet."

He bit his lip, recognizing the sound of rejection coming, or so he thought. "I'm sorry. I know that you're married."

She gave his hand a small squeeze. "Where I come from, monogamy is not a thing. Not really." Jack tried to keep a hopeful look from his eyes and opened his mouth, but she laid one finger across his lips. "I honor it here because it is custom and expected, and I have made a promise."

He nodded and pulled his hand away. "Of course. I meant no—"

"A promise my husband made me, and which he has broken more than once."

That surprised him. Her clear eyes showed no sign of pain about her husband's betrayal, but it bothered him and he wanted to say he would not do such a thing. "He should not have."

"And yet he did. And it freed me from honoring the same promise to him, whether he knows that or not."

Startled again, he flushed at the implication, now noticing that her eyes held a smile. Unsure what to say, he murmured, "If you don't mind my saying so, your husband is a fool."

"I know."

Heat rising in his cheeks, he leaned forward when the doorbell rang and she put one hand on his chest, stopping him. "Good things come to those who wait."

Jack inwardly groaned as she turned toward the living room and front door, footsteps moving away. He turned back to the apple and bit into a piece just as he heard her open the front door. Then she gasped.

"Soliander!" Eriana said.

Jack almost choked on the fruit. *Oh my God..* His eyes darted for a way out, even though he knew the wizard stood at the only exit. *What is he doing here? How did he find...? If he hurts her....*

"Eriana?" said a man's voice, sounding confused.

Jack edged toward the kitchen corner, carefully peering around to the front door. Eriana had thrown her arms around a twenty-something year old man in blue jeans and a dark t-shirt, his wavy brown hair touching his shoulders. A pang of jealousy overtook Jack's fear. But neither overpowered his curiosity. He wanted to get out of there, but he wasn't leaving without Eriana, and he had to remain out of sight. Thinking of a security camera he had pointed at the front door from a corner table, he pulled up his phone, brought it online, and set it to start recording, watching via the phone and stepping back without a sound. Eriana had pulled back from Soliander and placed both hands on his cheeks.

"I can't believe it's really you!" she said. "I've been waiting. I've looked. I..." She paused as if to stop herself from gushing.

The wizard repeated, "Eriana? How? You look... older. How could you be...?" They stopped talking and stared silently for several seconds before he asked, "What happened to you?"

She took his hand and pulled him, closing the door, an enormous smile on her face. "It's a long story, but I've been here for about twenty years, Soli. And I just learned in the past few days that only three years have passed on other worlds. That's why you haven't aged nearly as much as me."

"That doesn't make... Wait. Let me think. Morgana. I have suspected that she summoned us to the past."

"I think so, yes."

"So there was already some time period alteration going on."

"I think something about the spell you did with Merlin threw us back to our own time, except I didn't quite make it, it seems."

"Twenty years." He sounded exasperated. "All this time, you've been *here.*"

"And now *you* are here. What are you doing here?" Then she seemed to realize something, and the same question in Jack's head came next. "Wait. What *are* you doing here, in this apartment? You didn't know I was here."

He glanced around the room and sighed. "I am looking for these four imposters. Do you know about this? They are pretending to be us."

"Yes. It isn't their fault. They–"

"Are they here?" He stepped past her toward the kitchen but stopped and turned back when she answered.

"No, they were just summoned overnight. Soli, what is going on? Do you know how they became us?"

"They are not *us*," he snapped. She recoiled a bit, and he softened his tone. "They are not the Ellorian Champions. The champions are dead."

Eriana shook her head. "What do you mean? You and I are alive. Have you seen Korrin and Andier?"

"It doesn't matter."

She approached and took his arm in one hand. "Hey, answer me. Have you *seen* them?"

Soliander shook his head. "I have not. No one has."

"Have you looked?"

"I... Yes. You think I would not have looked for all of you? I have searched everywhere that makes any sense, except here, because I couldn't find Earth until recently. Like it didn't exist. I suppose I should have been searching *when*, too, had I known." He shook his head.

Jack thought that would be impossible, having to re-search every place at different points in time.

"While I have been here," began Eriana, "where have you been? They tell me no one has seen you either. How can that be? Are you in hiding?"

A moment passed before he asked quietly, "What have they been telling you about me?"

She shook her head. "Things that concern me, frankly. You opened the Dragon Gate and left it that way after all that trouble we went through on Honyn to create and close it. You attacked Lorian and Matt. You cast that mind reading spell on him when it's forbidden."

He turned and stepped away from her. "Nothing is forbidden unless I say it is."

"Soli," she began, but he cut her off, turning back.

"Don't you disapprove of me. No one gets to disapprove of what I do, or how I do it. Not anymore. I will not be *powerless* again like we always were. If I have to cast a supposedly forbidden spell to be free, then so be it. I have done far worse."

She watched him quietly, putting one hand on her heart as he turned away again. "What happened wasn't your fault."

"Are we going to have this argument again?"

"Until I win it, yes," she said lightly, and he shot her a sideways look before sighing. She added, "It's nice to argue with you again, Soli. Really. I'm thrilled to get the chance. But I wish we didn't have things to argue about. I never thought I'd see you again, and I certainly didn't think that if I did, that I would have reasons to believe you've done terrible things. Or that I have reason to be afraid for you. Even afraid *of* you."

He turned toward her, sounded wounded as he replied, "I would never hurt you. You know that."

"The man I knew before would not have."

"He is dead." He said it with no trace of uncertainty.

"Then I have reason to fear you, and to grieve you." When he didn't respond, she asked, "What were you planning to do when I opened that door?"

For an answer, he only said, "I'm a wizard, aren't I?"

Seconds of silence passed before she asked, "Kill or immobilize?"

"I wasn't going to kill them. Not yet, anyway."

Listening, Jack wasn't sure if that was meant to be a joke. The wizard sounded blasé about it, and from what he'd heard from his friends, that seemed like the new Soliander, not the one of the Ellorian Champions. He had changed, and Eriana clearly knew it.

She asked, "What do you want with them?"

"I could ask the same of you."

"You didn't used to be so coy. I liked the direct Soliander."

"No one calls me that anymore."

"What *do* they call you? Are your deeds really so awful that you live under another name?"

"Some would say yes. I would say no. I have killed. I have tortured. I have destroyed entire cities. I have brought kingdoms to ruin. I rule several more and everyone fears me, just as I would have them do. And they do not know me. I do not want them to, out of respect for you." He frowned, and Jack heard bitterness when he spoke again. "I would not drag your memory down with me as Soliander, and there is value in the ruse. None know that the Majestic Magus is now the Arch Wizard Zoran the Devastator, the one who has made everyone afraid to cross him." He seemed caught up in his litany of exploits and hardly noticed Eriana's fallen face until now. Sounding resigned, he remarked, "You don't really want to know these things."

She sounded angry as she replied, "You might be right. I can't be with a man who does evil things. You know why."

In a low voice, he said, "Do not compare me to your childhood tormentors. I would never... not to you."

"Maybe. Maybe not. You don't seem to realize that you are breaking my heart anyway."

"Eriana," he began as if pained.

"I looked for you. All over this Earth. Anywhere I could think you might be." Her voice grew strained. "You more than the others. I eventually gave up hope, that you were lost and I would never see you again. And now after all this time, I heard there might be hope. I met these replacements for us. And they told me they had seen you, that you had attacked them without justification. I finally found hope again and can hardly believe it. And I just dreaded to find out that it was true, that you had changed in the worst of ways, and here you stand before me confirming all of my fears. I have found you only to find that you are more lost to me than I would have ever imagined you could be."

Imploring Eriana, Soliander said, "I am not *lost* to you."

"Then what were you going to do when I opened that door?"

"I... I was going to capture them. To get information from them. So I could find *you*. I thought them replacing us must have meant something, and there was hope to find you."

"That is the reason?"

"Of course. You have *always* been the only reason for me. You know this. Or have you forgotten in your new life here?"

"Am I the reason you have done terrible things? In the name of finding me? Avenging me?"

"No, that is not what I meant."

"Then what?"

He let out a breath. "Everything I have done since I learned you three were gone, and I was free of those damn quests, has been to make certain that no one ever makes me a prisoner again. I will be free even if I have to destroy a thousand worlds. I have tracked down some of those who helped Everon, and they are dead now. They cannot do anything further to any of us again."

"So it was for all of us?"

"No. No, it was for *me*, Eriana. You have your demons and I have mine. You can tell me as many times as you like that none of this was my fault, that it was just Everon and his band of vengeance seekers who trapped us in the quests, but it will always come back to me. You have never admitted that there is any truth to this."

"I'm sorry for that. I didn't want you to feel responsible. To valida–"

"It was too late!"

"None of us blamed you."

"It doesn't matter. *I* blamed me. If anything, you guys forgiving me just made it worse. Isn't anyone going to hold a grudge?"

"None of us want us to be like the Betrayer. Everon was wrong."

"Yes, I know. All three of you were always more noble than me. We all knew it. And I don't begrudge you for it."

"We were *not* more noble than you. I always knew you felt that way. It's why you always made snide remarks at Korrin. I don't know why you have a hard time admitting that you are a good man."

"Well, I'm not anymore. Isn't that what we're agreeing on here?"

She gestured futility and remarked with a light tone, "I'm mostly hearing us argue, not agree to anything."

He smiled insincerely. "Well, at least we can agree to *that*."

"So what now? The imposters, as you call them, aren't here. They are good people, Soli. They don't deserve what has happened to them any more than we did. Even less."

"Yes, so this is *also* my fault."

She sighed. "That's not where I was going with that. Stop that." He didn't respond, and she continued, "They would answer your questions without an interrogation. They answered mine."

His tone became aggressive. "What did they tell you?"

"That's between me and them."

"I can find out, you know."

She glared at him and softly observed, "If you *ever* cast that spell on me, me never forgiving you will be the least of your problems."

He held still and then laughed under his breath. "You are the only person on a thousand worlds who can get away with threatening me."

"I'm honored. But I think you need to leave."

Soliander shook his head. "Come with me."

"No."

"Eriana, please. I just found you. Do not make me leave this planet without you again. It was an accident last time and I'm certainly not doing it again, especially on purpose."

"I must help them, because you will not."

"They appear to be doing fine from what I've heard."

Eriana shook her head. "They are struggling, especially when they come back. They do not have Home Rings and it is causing very serious problems."

"Well, Matt seems powerful enough to create one. I'm sure they'll solve that problem soon enough."

"I know you are upset about the situation we were in, and yet you are so cold and callous about them being in one that is even worse."

Soliander sighed. "I am tired of ever caring about anyone other than myself, because all it does is cause me pain. And it is all because I lost you. No matter what you say, it was my fault. I thought I had *killed* you. Do you understand? Please, at least tell me you understand. All those years of protecting you, trying to stop this thing, trying to stop Everon and others from destroying our lives while we were gone on a quest we didn't want and couldn't protect anyone we cared about because of it. And at the moment we're about to finally be free, and we can be together without fear, I thought I had killed you."

"I'm still alive."

"I didn't know that."

"But now you do."

He made a gesture of futility with one arm. "It's been years, Eriana. How long was I supposed to keep the hate from my heart?"

Sounding concerned, she asked, "Is it you that you hate or everyone else?"

He laughed bitterly. "You always could see right through me."

"You don't have to hate yourself anymore." She walked up to him, very close. "I'm not dead, Soli, and it's because of you that I'm still alive. And free. You deserve credit for freeing us, not trapping us."

"Are you trying to save me?"

After a pause, Eriana said, "I *am* the Light Bringer."

Soliander put one hand on her arm. "Well, you can't save me if we're not together, and as you said, I should leave. Come with me."

"I can't."

"Then I'm sorry."

"For what?"

Somehow, Jack knew the intent and shouted "No!" as he ran from the kitchen and burst into the living room, heart pounding, a surge of adrenaline giving him speed. Words of magic reached his ears. Eriana's wide eyes darted from Soliander to him, and she held up one hand to ward off Jack, who suddenly realized his vulnerability. The powerful wizard shot him an icy glare that sent a jolt of fear through him, but he dove for them just as a soft light enveloped the pair. Jack braced for the impact—and passed right through where they were to land hard on the carpet. He turned back frantically, eyes racing over his apartment.

They were gone.

VOLUME 3

THE SILVER-TONGUED ROGUE

CHAPTER ONE

THE LAST ONE STANDING

As he woke to a roaring vortex of flashing lights and wind, Eric Foster thought for a moment that he was dreaming. He had been asleep on the floor of Jack's apartment, but now he stood on something invisible, feeling wide-awake and invigorated. Had he gotten a full night's sleep, or had the spell summoning him done that? The T-shirt, shorts, and underwear he was wearing disappeared for a few moments. He didn't bother to cover himself as he stood nude before the others, his short black hair rustled by the air. Then his expected black leather armor and boots appeared, snug and supple, a short sword on one hip. He had hidden knives throughout his clothing, lock-picking tools were in one pocket, and a black rope was coiled about his waist like a belt.

Across from him stood Anna Sumner. The summoning spell had braided her blonde hair behind her ears, and the gold Corethian Amulet hung around her neck. Those and her white priest's robe with its golden trim would have made her seem elegant were she not still standing with one forearm desperately covering her breasts, the other hand over her crotch. Now dressed, she relaxed her posture and saw him smirking. She flashed a rueful smile and seemed to sigh. It was so loud that even if she screamed, he'd hear nothing.

To one side stood Ryan LaRue in golden plate mail, a matching helmet tucked under one arm, a giant sword on one hip, and a gold lance in one hand as its butt rested on the invisible platform beneath them. As a big, tall man, he always looked huge in the gear, and he seemed far more comfortable with his role now as a knight than when they had started all of this. He flashed a resigned smile and ran a hand through his blond hair, likely mentally preparing himself to be their spokesman on arrival.

Across from Ryan stood Matt Sorenson, a black wizard's robe hiding his thinness. His wavy brown hair rustled in the air, one hand tightly gripping a staff, the crystal atop it dark because he wasn't using it. Eric caught his eye and arched an eyebrow, which Matt saw, nodding before his eyes drifted away and his lips began moving. They had previously discussed the possibility of him erecting a protective shield once they arrived, if they seemed to be in immediate danger. For the first time, Eric realized that he and Matt could communicate during this with sign language, which Matt knew because his mother was deaf, and had taught a curious Eric.

Suddenly the vortex ended, and Eric blinked in the bright sunlight, the sun high in a cloudless sky. His dark eyes darted past the expected stone pillars of the circular Quest Ring surrounding them, the glowing blue runes on the stones already fading. Outside the ring on one side stood most of the people who had brought them to whatever planet they were now on instead of Earth. Many wore armor of various kinds, but no weapons were drawn. A few more warriors casually stood to either side and behind. He noted two wizards—one behind them and another, who seemed like the one who had cast the summoning spell, before him.

Eric began to relax, noting the ocean all around them below. They stood atop one of the higher, grass-covered hills on a large island. The warm air smelled of spring, wildflowers blooming nearby. A small mountain range loomed nearby and blocked the view beyond, but on either side of it could be seen an expanse of sea. A port city with tall, wooden ships in the harbor lay miles away below them, with towers and a castle above it all. A winding path led down from their position to a clearing among the trees, where a dozen dragons sat patiently so that Eric knew they were steeds. Since horses could have easily been used to get them to the city, he surmised that they would be flying to a different continent. It lay in the distance in another direction, the shoreline visible from here. Behind it were taller, snow-capped peaks that pierced the clouds forming around them.

Beside one of the wizards stood a striking woman in black plate mail etched in blue, a sword at her waist. She wore it all well, seeming calm, assured, and unimpressed. Her close-cropped, jet-black hair hardly moved in the gusty winds, blue eyes dancing from one arrival to the next, a look of growing interest and menace surfacing in them. It seemed clear that she had expected something and hadn't gotten it—and Eric had a bad feeling he knew precisely what it was.

"Greetings!" Ryan boomed in the voice Eric had first heard him use while playing a knight at the Maryland Renaissance Festival. "We are the Ellorian Champions and are glad to—"

"No, you are not!" snapped the warrior woman, eyes cold. She yanked her sword from its sheath and the other warriors nearby did the same, the sound of metal ringing. She came closer and into the Quest Ring as everyone else stayed just outside it. Eric swore but didn't draw his sword.

Ryan faltered. "Uh, why do you think—"

"You think I wouldn't recognize my own *brother*?" she snarled, eyes turning to Matt.

Anna gasped.

What? thought Eric, startled. *Oh shit.* Ryan's uncertain eyes met his.

They had been impersonating the Ellorian Champions for two months, but not because they wanted to. It just seemed safer than admitting to being four people mistakenly summoned for quests they weren't qualified for, didn't want, and yet had to complete before being sent home. That someone summoning them would realize the truth was bound to happen eventually, but a relative being present had never occurred to him. Matt was impersonating the wizard Soliander, whose robes he wore, Soliander's famous staff in one hand. And apparently this woman was Soliander's sister.

"Listen," he began, holding up placating hands, "we can explain, if you just—"

"Where is Soliander?" the woman asked, turning toward Matt. She extended the sword toward his neck, though she came no closer. Eric wondered if she knew about the spell on the staff—the one that made any blow aimed at Matt strike the attacker instead.

"Taryn!" Matt said, sounding surprised. He didn't look afraid. "You're Taryn, his older sister."

She arched an eyebrow. "How do you know that?"

"Uh, long story. I have his memories in my head and—"

"What? How is that possible? What did you do to—" A look of menace appeared. "Seize them!" Taryn swung a fist at Matt's hand and knocked the staff to the stones. Then she slugged his jaw. He fell into an unmoving heap. Guardsmen closed in with swords raised.

"Wait!" Eric yelled, heart pounding. "We are no threat to you." He put one hand on Ryan's sword arm to stop him from drawing the steel. Magic incantations behind him made him look back. A wizard pointed at Ryan, who slumped to the stones with a clatter.

"Eric!" cried a panicked Anna, backing away, one hand on the golden amulet at her neck. She began crouching as if to surrender, but the butt of a spear struck her head from behind and she fell forward to Taryn's feet.

In sudden fury, Eric swung around and clobbered the guard who had done it, a spray of blood and teeth erupting. Another guard closed in, and Eric kicked out to stun the wrist holding a spear. A second kick and the man doubled over before an elbow to the back levelled him. He sensed Taryn closing in from behind and turned, one hand on his sword hilt, but her sword point was at his neck and he stopped moving.

"Yield," she commanded, blue eyes cold. They stared at each other. Eric removed his hand from his sword. Footsteps came from behind and several hands pulled his arms back painfully, a rope wrapped around his wrists. Someone took his sword, then patted him down for knives. He silently counted as they did so. Only he and the Silver-Tongued Rogue Andier, the man he impersonated and whose armor he wore, knew where every last one of the blades was, and his captors couldn't find them all.

"You didn't have to do that," Eric said, glaring at Taryn and indicating his unconscious friends.

"Maybe I just *wanted* to."

"What are you going to do with us?"

She walked away without answering as the guards forced him down on the Quest Ring's stone floor, where his friends' bodies lay unmoving around him. Despite the adventures they had already experienced, he'd never seen them laid out helpless like this—and so quickly! Maybe they had just gotten lucky before now. But the truth was that Taryn had surprised them with the sudden attack. He nodded to himself. She was wily, respectable. Neither was it surprising if she was really the sister of Soliander, the Majestic Magus, a man known for his intelligence. What would a sibling rivalry have been like?

He watched Taryn approach a tall, well-built man in a black and silver tunic, a ceremonial dagger at one hip and black trousers tucked into matching boots. He carried himself like a noble and had short black hair and dark eyes. Were they siblings? Soliander did have a younger brother, too. Eric regretted that he and the others knew so little about the real Champions, as their ignorance might be a serious liability right now.

As Taryn stopped beside the man, he said, "I will reluctantly concede that you handled that expertly."

"Nothing pleases me more than your praise, Lord Dari, especially when it's so sincere." Taryn glanced back to meet Eric's gaze.

A brief frown appeared on Dari's face. "The more time I spend with you, the more I understand why my old habit of snide remarks was not viewed favorably, as much as I enjoyed making them."

She favored him with a smirk. "Are you flirting with me?"

"Is it working?"

Definitely not brother and sister, thought Eric.

She lifted her blade and fingered the edge, adopting a philosophical tone. "Some consider it a bad omen when they unsheathe a sword and don't draw blood with it. Perhaps this is a problem you are willing to solve for me."

Unconcerned by the implication that she was going to cut him, Dari replied, "Some would consider that a threat to a Prince of Andor."

Taryn put her weapon away as Eric continued listening. "Pity. I thought you might be honored to have your blood on my blade."

"What now?" Prince Dari asked, nodding at Eric, who had stopped listening for a moment on hearing the word "Andor."

He knew the name. Ryan, lying beside him, was pretending to be Lord Korrin, a Prince of Andor. If Dari was also a Prince of Andor, he was a relative, maybe even Korrin's younger brother. While Eric didn't know what the real Champions looked like, he knew that he and his friends bore enough resemblance to fool those who hadn't met them. Dari had black hair and dark eyes, but Ryan, and therefore Korrin, had blond hair and blue eyes. He pursed his lips, wishing he knew what Korrin looked like so he could judge whether Dari seemed that closely related.

Regardless, that at least two relatives of the Ellorian Champions had tried to summon them was no coincidence. Were the rest of the families involved? Were they here? They were going to want answers and would be understandably hostile if they thought the impersonators were somehow responsible for the real Champions being missing for three years now. Eric and the others had taken their place by accident and played along, trying to figure out how to be heroes and somehow break the cycle of unwanted quests for which they were now summoned.

He perked up. Almost no one knew that the real Champions hadn't been voluntarily doing the quests. They were magically summoned into a Quest Ring that bound them to do it before they could return home. And now that was the fate of Eric and his friends. Did the Champions' families know? If so, they were almost certainly sympathetic—and that sympathy might extend to Eric and the others if he could convince them they were victims, too, not perpetrators. Maybe they would help despite Taryn's attack just now. He understood her doing that. Precautionary, at the least. The real Champions were formidable. Eric and his friends had succeeded at several quests, and caused word to spread that the Ellorian Champions had supposedly returned. Others could assume they were fearsome. He admired Taryn's quick thinking.

She broke his thoughts on saying to Dari, "Every last person here must be sworn to secrecy. They already were, that we were attempting the summoning, but it is even more important that no one knows what has happened. See to it that your men obey."

So she wasn't in charge? This surprised Eric. She certainly acted like she was.

Dari asked, "General precaution or is there more?"

She shook her head. "We need to bring them back to Andor and interrogate them to find out what has happened."

We're on Elloria, Eric thought, not surprised.

"Why wait?"

"Not here. I don't want more secrets spilled and spreading."

"Fair enough, but let's send the unconscious ones and the guards down to the dragons to get ready for the flight. We can ask that one a few questions."

Taryn ordered some to remove Korrin's golden armor from Ryan, the Corethian Amulet from Anna's neck, and to wrap Soliander's staff in a cloak. Eric nodded to himself. The items were famous across worlds. Seeing them together left little doubt as to their supposed identities. They were to be brought to Andor as four bound prisoners of no importance. He stifled any outward display of emotion as the order was carried out, the sight of his unmoving friends being disturbed upsetting him. At least he was awake to witness their treatment, and he vowed to do nothing to inspire their captors to render him unconscious, too. Only Matt stirred, a moan escaping him as men lifted him and the others, carrying them down the path and away. Finally, only Taryn and Dari stood on the hilltop, inside the Quest Ring, looking down at Eric as he sat.

"You may rise, or do you need help?" Taryn smirked at Eric, who sat cross-legged, arms behind his back. He rose smoothly anyway, years of martial arts mastery making this no challenge. She seemed somewhat impressed, which told him she admired skill.

Eric said, "Taryn of Aranor, I assume? And Prince Dari of Andor."

"And you are not Andier of Roir," she replied, unfazed by his realizations. She was a hard one to impress. "Who are you?"

Time to at least appear cooperative. "Eric of Maryland. I doubt you've heard of it."

"Planet?"

"Earth. Are you Korrin's brother?" Eric asked Dari, who cocked an eyebrow.

"How did—" The prince stopped himself, but Eric had his answer. "We're asking the questions."

Taryn asked, "Do you, like your wizard friend, somehow have memories of the Champions?"

Eric wasn't sure how much to tell them, especially if they weren't going to share intel themselves, but the answer to her question should have been obvious and he wondered if condescension would make her slip. "If I did, I would have recognized both of you and wouldn't have asked that, now would I?"

The briefest of frowns touched her lips and he knew she had pride in her intelligence. They silently regarded each other. "The names of your friends, and who is who."

"We're all from Maryland. Matt is the one you punched in the face for not being your brother. Ryan is Korrin. That leaves Anna as Eriana."

"How did you come to be here instead of the Champions?"

Eric admitted, "We don't know."

Dari snorted. "You are clearly pretending to *be* them."

Eric frowned at him on purpose, hoping that showing the same contempt for him that Taryn did might help form a bond with her. "That doesn't mean we know how we've been substituted."

Taryn eyed him shrewdly for several seconds. "Where were you when the substitution first took place?"

Eric realized she knew this wasn't the first time. The Champions had supposedly done several quests after being missing for years, with word of each quest spreading rapidly. Their families had undoubtedly heard. She had figured out that the real Champions did not complete the recent quests and wasn't bothering to ask him to confirm it.

He replied, "Earth. A place called Stonehenge. It's a monument. Looks like a Quest Ring, though we didn't know that at the time. There are no Quest Rings on Earth."

"Then why were you at this Stonehenge?"

"Vacation. It's a famous landmark. It suddenly lit up and brought us to another world, where we first learned about all of this."

"To Honyn," she surmised.

"I assume you've heard of the quest and its outcome."

She nodded. "And the others. That is how we knew they had returned after being missing, or so we thought. Why pretend to be them instead of confess?"

He shrugged. "It seemed safer. Better we wonder who people expect us to be, than everyone else wonder who we are."

She eyed him quietly again. "You must have known someone would realize the truth eventually."

"Yes. But we didn't anticipate the Champions' families summoning us. We hoped to have more answers first so we could better deal with the fallout. Why did you try to summon them?"

Dari appeared ready to tell him not to ask questions again, but Taryn put a restraining hand on his arm, calculating eyes on Eric. "What did they usually do after a quest?"

He considered, realizing she wanted to see if he could figure it out. "Go home. But they haven't because it isn't them."

"You are returned to Earth afterwards."

"Yes. So you have been wondering why, after they were missing for three years and then resumed quests, they have not come home. You want answers. And now that we're here, you want more of them. Well, so do we."

"Then I assume you'll cooperate." Taryn indicated that he should walk toward the path leading to the dragons. "Oh, before I forget," she began, following him, "you've been summoned for a quest to recover a stolen blue dragon egg and return it to the Kingdom of Novell, where we stand." Eric frowned and she laughed. "Yes, I know we must tell you the quest within an hour of your arrival or you are not bound to do it and can send yourselves home."

She didn't elaborate, and Eric knew why. Now he and his friends had no choice but to cooperate with an interrogation—because all Taryn and Dari had to do, to imprison them on Elloria forever, was never tell them how to achieve this quest. Trying to escape was pointless. That she had outmaneuvered him explained the spark of humor in her eyes. She was fearsome.

They descended the dirt path as he looked around, wondering why this place had been chosen for a Quest Ring. The rings were sometimes in a central location in a castle—but given that one was likely to be used only once, if ever, that was a waste of space. He had chatted with a few of their previous summoners and learned that the rings were like tourist attractions (not that that expression had been used). They were seen as a status symbol and conversation starter, nobles from one land expressing admiration and thinly disguised jealousy that they didn't have one. Not everyone could. It had taken Soliander and then his apprentice Everon many months to create them in various places. No one really knew how many existed except Everon.

The now familiar sight of dragons caught his attention. Having ridden a few, battled another, and even seen an undead dragon hadn't muted his awe. Most of the dragons present were red, a few gleamed silver in the sun, and one was black except for a gold streak on its chest and head. All but the latter wore a saddle and reins. Each dragon was large enough to swallow him whole. All but the black one ignored him; that one watched as he approached, a familiar intelligence and cunning in its enormous golden eyes. He wondered what sort of breath weapon it had—fire, lightning, ice?—while also hoping he didn't learn the hard way.

He had already noticed that the guards wore two different insignias on their armor. Most had a blue dragon head facing forward on the white sail of a ship. He surmised that this meant Kingdom Novell. Only a handful of warriors wore the symbol matching Prince Dari's—two gold daggers pointing downward to form a V, on a red background. Taryn wore no symbol that he saw, which made him wonder whether she worked in the official capacity of her kingdom Aranor. As he waited, guards began loading his unconscious friends onto one dragon or another, strapping them in place. Prince Dari walked away and climbed onto the larger silver one, seldom taking his eyes off Eric for long. From behind him, Taryn removed his bindings and, to his surprise, returned his sword, though she kept the knives.

"I'll be clear this time," she began, holding his gaze. "If you run, you'll get an arrow in the back. If you attack, one of the wizards will stun you. If you try to jump off your dragon into the ocean, you'll find the dragon's magic is holding you on. The dragons will not obey you. If you upset me, I'll get the information I want the hard way."

Eric appreciated both subtlety and directness when used at the right time. Sensing this might sound like he was flirting and wanting to avoid that, he said, "Only a fool would upset you."

"Most men are fools."

"I am not."

"I know. Mount the remaining red."

Eric approached the dragon, who lowered his wing for him to climb. Not until seating himself in the saddle did he notice Taryn climbing the black dragon's wing. Somehow, it didn't surprise him that this was her steed, nor that she didn't use a saddle. He had gone without a saddle once before out of necessity but still preferred the seat, mostly for its emotional and psychological comfort. He needed to get over that, he now knew, because it would toughen him up like her... but what happened if the dragon fell unconscious and couldn't keep him on anymore? He smirked. He would crash into the ground and die anyway, so maybe it didn't matter.

Prince Dari's silver dragon was the first to lift off. They circled above, clearly waiting for the others, but it wasn't until Taryn rose into the sky that anyone else did so, too. Eric permitted himself a grin, certain that Dari held little authority. If needed, maybe he could drive a wedge between the prince and anyone else. He didn't want to make enemies of anyone, but if Dari was already that, then weakening him in any way he could was wise.

Eric watched as the island and its Quest Ring, the way home, disappeared behind them. That wasn't the only way back, as another such ring could do it, but this was likely the closest one to Andor. He surmised that the kingdom didn't need one. After all, Korrin was from there. If a quest was needed, all the king had to do was ask his son to do it, not summon him and the others. He assumed the island kingdom was an ally of Andor, which was both a city and a kingdom. Getting back to the Quest Ring would be harder with both of them as enemies. He had to convince them of their innocence but sensed that Taryn, at least, was amenable to that. He would find out soon enough if the rest of the families were more like her or Dari, who seemed to have assumed the worst. Now more than ever, Eric might have to live up to the reputation of Andier, the Silver-Tongued Rogue, and talk their way into an alliance.

Without one, they were never going home.

CHAPTER TWO

THE INTERROGATION

Ryan heard the familiar, low voices of his friends as he awoke. He didn't feel like he had been sleeping. He lay on his back. A two-story ceiling of limestone was overhead, a lantern hanging from a chain to one side. To his immediate right stood a wall. Turning his head, he saw Eric, Anna, and Matt sitting on a low bench that was part of the room's opposite wall.

Sitting up, he swung his feet to the stone floor. His armor was gone, leaving only the white cloth gambeson underneath. This buttoned down the front. It had long sleeves, and a collar, and overhung his waist to mid-thigh. Somehow, it was always clean at the start of a quest, as if was just washed, or new and unstained by sweat or the chainmail to which his plates were attached.

"Hey," said Anna, coming to his side. "How do you feel?"

"Where are we?" Ryan asked, noting that the room was empty, a lone wooden door leading out.

"We'll get to that," she said. "They said you'd wake up in a few minutes and left."

"I feel fine. Who are you talking about?"

Eric answered, "The wizard who knocked you out. He reversed the spell or something and left. I only have a few minutes to bring all of you up to speed before we have to answer a lot of questions. We don't need to get a story straight, because I think we're going to need to be honest. I'm pretty sure they don't mean us any harm."

"Speak for yourself," said Matt, frowning.

Ryan noticed that Matt wore a new silver headband and didn't have a black eye. "What's on your head?"

"Something to prevent me from casting spells."

That didn't bode well, but he wasn't the only one capable of the supernatural. At first, Anna had only healed people by calling on the gods to channel their power through her, but their group had later learned that she could also do offensive spells.

"What about you?" Ryan asked.

Anna shook her head. "They took the amulet, so I'm back to having a hard time reaching the gods here. I could do it if I knew their names, but I don't."

Only now did Ryan notice that she wasn't wearing the usual white robe of Eriana, but a simple golden dress. Matt's black robe was gone, too, a red one replacing it. A tunic and leggings had replaced Eric's leather armor. He nodded at them.

"Did you put those on yourselves?" he asked.

"Yeah," said Eric. "They know we aren't the Champions and don't want anyone else to know that, so they have disguised us as regular people. They confiscated any distinctive clothes or items."

"You think we can get them back?"

"If we handle this right, yeah."

Then Eric told them all that he knew, had surmised, or had been told—including that both Anna and Matt had been healed so that neither had a head wound. They had been here an hour in a palace in the city of Andor. It lay on a plain along the western coast of the continent Veskyn. Further west across the Madura Ocean stood Onder Isle, where the Quest Ring lay inside the Kingdom of Novell. This quest was supposedly an easy one—it had only been conceived to make the Quest Ring summon them, since that wouldn't happen without a valid quest. For once, they would not be sent into considerable danger.

"And yet there may be plenty of danger from the families," Ryan observed.

Eric admitted, "There could be. We don't know who will be there or their attitude, so we need to pay attention. Read the room and the people in it. Are they hostile or disbelieving? Be honest but don't volunteer too much. No speeches or monologues about anything. Make them ask us questions. I think we have a real opportunity here."

"How so?" Anna asked.

"They know more about the people we're impersonating than anyone. If they agree to help us, think about how valuable they could be."

"There is a lot we don't know," Matt admitted.

"They may agree to help us," continued Eric, "if they understand that we did nothing to hurt the real Champions, and we're innocent victims doing what we can in this. We know the real champs weren't voluntarily doing this. That means their families probably know, too, even though other people don't. The families could realize that we need their help. We may even be their best chance of getting back Eriana, at least, since we know exactly where she is."

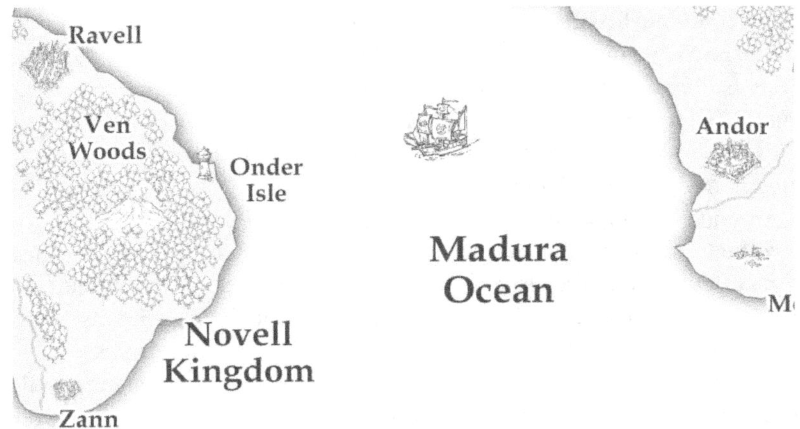

Map of Kingdom Novell

Ryan appreciated Eric's ability to think through these issues. And he was right, as always. The priestess Eriana, the Light Bringer, was back on Earth helping them set up a home base with the few people who knew the truth about what was going on and why they kept disappearing from Earth. This was a card they had to play, being able to trade information about Eriana for help. But they had to be careful. Volunteering that would go down better than only coughing up the info for something in return. But it would relieve their hosts to learn that one of the Champions still lived. That she was helping them strongly suggested their hosts do the same. The problem was proving it.

A knock on the door ended further talk before a guard shoved it open and gestured for them to follow. From habit of being their apparent leader, Ryan went first, striding down a long, narrow hall and past its doors. Soon, they entered a tall oval room, bright with sunlight from tall windows, tapestries of battle scenes flying from the walls. Ryan stepped through between an area of raised benches, most of them empty. More lay along the far wall. In the room's center awaited four high-backed chairs with red and gold cushions, all facing his right, where two empty thrones stood. Other, less ornate chairs sat on either side of the twin thrones, Ryan's impression being that the other seats were temporary. Were these for the family members of the Ellorian Champions?

He flushed a bit, feeling guilty for pretending to be Lord Korrin. For the first time, no one on a quest looked at him and believed he was the dragon-slaying knight. He was just an imposter with no stature. A prisoner. The change was almost comic. It was time to be Ryan LaRue, a rich kid who hadn't done much with his life because he'd been atoning for accidentally paralyzing his younger brother in a childhood accident. It wasn't until these quests had started that he'd finally accepted that Daniel didn't really need him. He felt it important to show their hosts that he and the others had done well on their quests, that they weren't some sort of embarrassment to the reputation of the true Champions.

A middle-aged man in a fine tunic of gold and red, and whom Ryan took to be the Court Marshal, banged the steal-shod butt of a wooden staff on the parquet floor. The din reverberated around the hall, and the chatter quieted.

"We shall introduce the families and friends of the Champions, should any be present. Andier of Roir, as expected, has none in attendance."

That's interesting, thought Ryan. They had learned little about Andier, and all of them suspected that this was by design—not because no one would tell them, but because Andier kept everyone from knowing anything to tell them. But that was conjecture. Maybe this quest was a chance to learn more about all of them.

"Solun of Coreth, brother to the Lady Eriana of Coreth."

Ryan's eyebrows rose. They had all met Eriana on Earth and learned much about the quests, but only now did he realize how little he knew of her personally—including that she had a brother. An attractive, blond-haired and brown-eyed young man entered from one side, his left hand missing at the wrist. He wore a plain tunic with no symbol on it, suggesting that he was not nobility.

"Her Highness, Princess Alia of Coreth." In strode a regal woman in her forties, a purple gown flowing behind her as she moved to sit beside Solun.

"Commander of the Dark Blades, Taryn of Aranor, sister to Soliander of Aranor."

Ryan hadn't seen Taryn since she initiated the attack on them. Now she strode in wearing a black gambeson and trousers like his, her black boots sounding as commanding as she looked. One hand gripped the hilt of a black dagger at her waist. He didn't want to cross swords with her. She walked an air of authority and yet somehow still seemed feminine.

"Prince Dari and Princess Cariss of Andor, brother and sister to Lord Korrin, Prince of Andor and Heir-Apparent to the throne."

That surprised Ryan. They hadn't known that Korrin was heir to the throne. The prince and princess took seats to either side of where their parents would sit, Dari frowning, his sister curiously looking at Ryan and his friends without malice. She was pretty, long blonde hair braided, her blue eyes bright.

"His Majesty, King Sarov of Andor, and Her Royal Highness, Queen Lina, father and mother to Lord Korrin."

Ryan felt curious to meet the only parents of a champion who were present. It begged the question of where the other parents were. Such thoughts ceased when a tall, big-boned man entered, gray eyes sorrowful as if something weighed on him, though his bearing was erect and proud. He appeared to have once been a physically powerful man and retained some vigor into his fifties. Beneath a simple crown of gold, with inset rubies, his long blond hair was streaked with gray. He wore a tastefully embroidered gold tunic and red leggings that gave the impression he wasn't overly impressed with himself while still making a good showing of his status.

Beside him, one hand linked with his arm, walked the queen. She was slender and regal in a gown of light gray, the color somber as if she were caught between hope and mourning. With rich parents, Ryan could at least relate to the idea that an heir was missing; to his parents, he fit that description even now. It might give him a way to bond with Korrin's parents. A crown lay atop the queen's golden hair. Her blue eyes were alert and kind.

Once the king and queen were seated, Prince Dari rose and strode forward—still dressed in his fine tunic, polished black shoes having replaced his boots. He took a position halfway between the thrones and the four Earth friends, on whom he turned his back to address the court. Nearly twenty in all, some present hadn't been introduced and sat on either side of the room.

"Lords and ladies," he began, "our first matter is the most important. What is revealed here today cannot leave this room under any circumstances. To do so could jeopardize the reputations and lives of the Ellorian Champions. They remain missing despite our attempt to summon them on Onder Isle earlier today. The spell did work, but in place of those we love and admire, these four arrived."

This caused a murmur, but neither the king nor queen seemed surprised. King Sarov asked in a booming tenor, "They arrived via the summoning spell? You are certain it was no other way?"

"Yes, father. The stones of the Quest Ring lit as expected and faded after. And in talking with them, we know that they have somehow been substituted for the Champions. They are the ones who have completed each of the recent quests."

A groan followed this revelation, and the queen asked, "Does this mean there is no sign of them?"

"We do not yet know. We only discussed the situation briefly with one of them, and thought it prudent to have this interrogation with all interested parties present."

"I can answer your question, Your Highness," Ryan said, "if I may." The queen's eyebrows rose, but then she nodded. He stood up slowly to show that he was no threat. "We have seen both Eriana and Soliander, but have not seen or heard any word of Korrin or Andier. Two of them live, at least." Another murmur spread through the room. "We have been impersonating the real Ellorian Champions, but I can assure you that we want no part of doing so and have only done it to save our own lives. Just as the Champions were summoned and bound to a quest against their will, so are we. We believed that admitting our real identities would make it more likely that we would be killed. I am grateful to hear Prince Dari caution everyone to keep this secret until we can all determine how best to proceed."

He paused for a moment and chanced a look at Eric, who nodded in approval. Ryan turned back to the nobles. "We are all from a planet called Earth, and a country called the United States—in a state, or what you might call a province, called Maryland. My name is Ryan LaRue. I have pretended to be your son, the knight Korrin. The woman with me is Anna, in the role of the priestess Lady Eriana, of course. The slender man is Matt, and he has acted as the wizard Soliander, while the shorter man is Eric, in the role of Andier, the rogue."

Taryn rose and came closer. "You have seen my brother. Where?"

"On the planet Honyn. He attacked Matt in Castle Darlonon while we were there to close the Dragon Gate. We had no opportunity to discuss anything with him. I'm afraid we don't know much more, or what he is doing and why. Or where he is now."

"Why did he attack Matt?"

"We aren't sure, but as you noticed when we arrived here, the summoning spell changes us into their clothes and gives us their items. From what Matt told us, there are now two copies of Soliander's staff, because Soliander had one during the attack and so did Matt. He may just have been trying to retrieve it, though our impression was that the encounter surprised him and he did not expect to see Matt at all... not to mention with his possessions, or copies of them."

Taryn turned a cold eye on Matt. "Did you harm my brother?"

The wizard looked a little wide-eyed at first, then assumed a relaxed confidence that surprised Ryan, especially since Taryn had slugged him the last time they met. "It was self-defense. He had cast the *Mind Trust* spell on me and was, well, going through my memories. I had to get away."

Taryn shook her head. "The spell is forbidden. Soli would not have done that."

"He did, and my impression was that it wasn't the first time he used it on someone."

"No."

A bit snidely, Matt said, "I'm sorry if it bothers you to hear, but he has done worse. He is the only one who could have opened the Dragon Gate on Honyn, and he is the one who did. You know of that quest and that I am not lying about this. He put the lives of everyone on that planet at risk just to lure someone into a trap."

"What trap?" Dari asked.

Matt replied, "Someone had stolen a scroll, which he had written, from the rulers of Honyn. The scroll reveals the location of soclarin ore, a precious metal Soliander uses for fashioning powerful items, which includes the keystones in the Quest Rings. Soliander didn't know who had stolen the scroll and wanted to find out. He suspected it was Everon, the man who had trapped the Champions in the unwanted cycle of quests. He would be able to get revenge on Everon if true, and if Everon sprung the trap, but it was someone else who did so. The Dragon Gate kept the dragons banished from Honyn to the only planet where soclarin ore could be found. Letting the dragons loose to destroy Honyn was a risk Soliander was willing to take in his desire for revenge on Everon. Many people died for that, and *we* nearly died. It would have been worse if we could not close the gate and complete the quest, because he left it open. You understand? He left it open and we're the only reason it's closed and the dragon horde has not obliterated Honyn." He paused and looked at Taryn. "I don't know who your brother used to be, but he isn't doing things that heroes do anymore."

Taryn stood silently glaring at him. "What were you trying to hide from him that you needed to attack him?"

Now it was Matt's turn to glare. "Have you ever had that spell cast on you? No? Maybe I'll learn it and cast it on you, then go through every private memory of yours."

"Matt," cautioned Eric.

"I can laugh at every mistake you've made. Every embarrassing moment. Remember things you've told no one."

"Matt!"

"I can learn everything and make you feel my amusement about it all."

"Matt!"

He finally stopped, nostrils flaring, eyes bright with energy. No one said anything for a moment before he quietly added, "Don't stand there disapproving of me for putting a stop to it. Your brother deserved me setting him on fire. If I cast that spell on you, you would split me down the middle and enjoy it."

Ryan looked at Taryn and saw a troubled gaze that had softened, if only a little. Matt had made an impression on her, at least. The sincerity may have held value.

Taryn observed, "You claimed to have Soliander's memories." This caused a stir.

"Only some of them," said Matt.

"How? How did this happen?"

"I had a copy of his staff when he immobilized me, then cast the spell. He had somehow made my staff unable to function, but I could control his and made fire erupt from it. His pain ended the spell chaotically instead of in a controlled way. Something about this caused a transfer of his scattered memories into me."

"He was injured?" Taryn asked Ryan had the impression that this answer might be dangerous.

Matt shrugged as if not worried. "I didn't stay to find out, but he later attacked Lorian, so he lived."

"Lorian?" Prince Dari asked. "I know that name. An elf of Arundell."

"Yes," said Ryan, trying to wrest the conversation away from Matt, in case the wizard started giving attitude again. Enough of that. He wondered what was going on with him. "Lorian has been a great friend to us. He is the one who told us what we knew, until recently, about the Champions. Without his help, we would never have survived."

"And what *do* you know?" Dari asked, turning to him.

"Wait," said Taryn, looking at Matt. "What memories of my brother do you have? Do you know where he has been these past three years?"

Matt shook his head. "The problem is that whatever memories of his I have are scattered. I can't recall anything on purpose. For example, when you summoned us, I didn't recognize you—not until you said something about me impersonating your brother. Then I recognized you from Soliander's memories. When you were kids, I know that he used to call you—"

"Stop," she said, looking flustered.

Ryan glanced at Eric, who seemed to smile slightly. Matt had unnerved her. But he was playing with fire—Taryn didn't seem to be the sort who tolerated being screwed with. Not by a long shot.

Dari began, "We could use the same spell on him to learn what—"

Taryn snapped, "It is forbidden."

After a long silence, Ryan said, "We are happy to tell you what we know. Such a spell is not needed. We are hoping you can help us, just as we may be able to help you."

Dari frowned. "And what could you possibly help us with?"

"We know where Eriana is." Amid the stir that followed, Ryan added, "She is on Earth and contacted us in the last week. She is safe and in good spirits. She very much wants to come home, but there are no wizards on Earth powerful enough to send her. But you may have wizards who can get to Earth and bring her back."

Nodding at Matt, Dari asked, "What about him? He has bested Soliander. Surely he has the power to do it."

Ryan shook his head. "That was luck. He is not that strong yet." He saw Matt shoot him an irritated look. "This is complicated, but on Earth, magic hasn't worked in a long time. There are no wizards. Matt hasn't even been able to practice what he's learned when we go back. He can't take a spell-book with him. Or Soliander's staff. None of us can take anything."

"That makes little sense," said Dari. "You're lying."

"No. Something has happened to change how everything works, and we think we know what, but it's a long story. We pieced it together with help from Eriana."

He explained how someone on Earth had summoned the Champions from Elloria to Earth's past, a thousand years ago. Magic was about to stop working. Their quest was to prevent that. But Soliander saw an opportunity. Knowing they were somehow magically bound to the Quest Rings and una- ble to refuse being summoned, he tried to let the magic on Earth die and send them all back at the same time. This would free them from the sum- monings. But disaster struck. Only Soliander appeared to have returned home. Eriana remained trapped on Earth and was thrown forward in time to twenty years ago. There was still no sign of Korrin or Andier.

"She has aged twenty years?" someone asked. It took a moment for Ryan to realize it had been Eriana's brother, Solun.

"She has lived twenty years on Earth, so the aging is natural. We can let her tell you the details of the life she has lived, but I will say that until we met with her and told her only a few years had passed, she thought that a thousand years had gone by. And that all of you were dead. She was under- standably emotional to discover that this was not the case."

"If I may speak, Your Majesty?" asked Princess Ali of Coreth. The king nodded and she continued. "You may be unaware, but Lady Eriana once saved the king and several others in my family, being granted land and title for the honor. She is a dear friend of the crown. We are grateful to hear that she lives. We pledge our full support to any efforts to return her home and will aid you as needed."

Ryan tried to not let on how relieved he felt. "We would be grateful for any help."

"You say magic did not work there... or does not?" asked Dari, frowning at him. "Which is it? You can't seem to get your story worked out."

"It didn't work until we unknowingly returned a magic pendant to a place called Stonehenge. It wasn't designed as a Quest Ring, but the person who summoned the Champions to the past turned it into one. When we returned the pendant, not knowing its true nature, magic was unleashed once again. It appears to be slowly awakening."

"But no one knows how to use it?" Taryn asked. "What of the elves?"

"There are none, and no dwarves or other creatures, like dragons. The spell that stopped magic also banished them."

That caused a murmur. Ryan knew that what he thought of as fantasy creatures had been on every world they had visited so far, though he and the others had only seen a handful each time. It no longer surprised him, now that he knew the truth, but seeing an elf or ogre still took getting used to. And their return to Earth was only likely to accelerate. How was the world going to react to that? Not well.

Dari asked, "So we know the wizard has limited skill, and yet you have survived several quests. What of the rest of you? Are you a real knight?"

"No," Ryan admitted. He was going to say more when the prince interrupted.

"So, you know nothing of honor."

Ryan deadpanned, "You're the ones who summoned us without our permission, then attacked us."

After a moment, Taryn laughed, then looked at a red-faced Dari. "Well, assuming you're telling the truth, we can certainly help train any of you. What of the others? Can you heal people?" she asked of Anna.

"I have learned to. Eriana just taught me how to use her amulet, as well."

"You were doing it without it before?" Taryn seemed impressed.

"Yes. It is now easier to reach gods I do not know. That is what the amulet is for."

Taryn turned to Eric. "And you? You fight well enough with hands and feet. What of the sword?"

"Still learning."

Dari snorted and addressed the room. "Here we are, worried about the Champions' reputations being ruined if people know these are imposters. But it seems apparent that we should tell everyone before these buffoons destroy their reputation by continuing to pretend—and embarrassing them, and us, with whatever disastrous quest they ruin next!"

Matt bristled. "If I could substitute you for us, I still wouldn't. You'd probably only do half as well as your brother." He stopped, then added, "You seem half the man."

"Matt!" Anna whispered, aghast.

Dari turned crimson and whirled toward the wizard, drawing the dagger at his waist. But Taryn cut in front of him with a look of cold menace that stopped him.

"You would protect them?" he snapped.

"The wizard is the key to finding my brother," she began, "and you won't touch him until I say."

"Enough!" said the king, sounding weary. "Dari, put that thing away and sit down. Has anyone examined the items they arrived with?" He gestured to one front corner of the room. There stood a table on which lay Soliander's staff, Eriana's amulet, Korrin's lance, and Andier's many knives. Behind it were armor stands—one bearing Korrin's full suit and sword, another with Andier's leather and sword, and the remaining two with Soliander's and Eriana's robes draped over them.

Taryn walked over and hefted her brother's staff. "Yes, Your Majesty. Each has been examined by those most familiar with them. They appear to be authentic."

His tone calmer, Dari asked, "How do we know they didn't just *steal* them?"

Taryn snorted. "No one is getting the staff from my brother unless he's dead. Your Majesty, we have no reason to think these aren't real. But I do think we need to confirm the imposters' story."

"Agreed," he said. "We will privately discuss how to do so."

"There is another matter," Dari said, before pointing at Ryan. "This one is impersonating royalty in our kingdom. That is a crime punishable by death. Surely we will not overlook it?"

Ryan quickly scanned those present to judge their reaction, which seemed contemplative but not enthusiastic. Then Eric spoke.

"Technically, we were pretending in Kingdom Novell, not in Andor, and that is outside your jurisdiction. There has been no crime of that sort committed here."

To his surprise, Taryn laughed, a reaction shared less strongly by others. Ryan flashed a smile at Eric, hoping that there wasn't the equivalent of an international agreement to honor the laws of another country if they were similar, like the United Nations on Earth.

"The prisoner has a sound argument," began the king, amused, "if only on a technicality. Still, we cannot overlook the impersonations, however well-intentioned or self-preserving they may have been. Until we decide how next to proceed, they will remain under guard as special guests. Confine them to the royal guest suites. They are to be treated well in the meantime."

This last part seemed directed at his son, who looked at Ryan with an expression he wasn't sure how to read. Maybe Eric had seen it. He was better at that sort of thing. It almost seemed like Dari was angry with him, or resentful. Even jealous? Maybe it didn't matter, but Eric was always keen to know exactly what someone felt, because it could matter if things came to a head. Better to be prepared than not. But Dari was just one of many here, and he seemed to have less stature. How much trouble could he cause? He almost laughed at the sentiment, knowing underestimation when he thought it. He would monitor Korrin's brother and see if he could befriend him, if only to keep closer tabs on Dari. But he would have to be sincere, not because he thought Dari was wily, but because Ryan was not. He could approach it as just trying to understand Korrin better. But then maybe he should ask the princess. What was her name? Cariss? Yes, she seemed excited and more receptive. He'd get more out of Korrin's sister, he was sure. But then maybe each could tell him different things.

As they were escorted from the room, he cast a look back at the table with the real Champions' possessions. He didn't quite feel naked without the armor, because he'd gone without it before when safe in a castle prior to a quest, but they were literally defenseless. Of all the reasons to feel vulnerable away from Earth, this was one he hadn't seen coming.

CHAPTER THREE

MANDRELLAN

Princess Cariss loved a delightful surprise. The one she left behind her as she strode from the great hall had certainly been unforeseen. Four imposters pretending to be the Champions... her brother Korrin still missing! The story nearly burst from her lips with every step on the parquet floors, and yet she could tell no one. A secret of this magnitude wouldn't last. She knew at least one person she simply had to tell. The wizard Mandrellan could be trusted. He had saved her life once and proven his good counsel countless times since. Her parents might even now be contemplating informing him. The thought added urgency to her steps. She had to be the first, for if she couldn't tell Mandrellan, no one else offered an ear.

He had kept secrets before. Only a few people knew that the Champions—the real ones—hadn't been voluntarily questing. The families had all agreed to keep that secret closely held for the same reasons they didn't want this new revelation spreading. The truth would harm the Champions' reputations, inspire people to stop summoning them, and thereby deprive countless worlds of hope. She had always admired the Champions' willingness to sacrifice themselves in this way. Admitting that they didn't want to do it was the obvious way to stop it all, and yet they had kept quiet. The toll of the unwanted quests had been apparent to those closest to them—though Korrin tried to pretend, even to them, that he had no issue with it. Soliander had been the most vocal and angry. Eriana tried to soothe him, Andier watched with those appraising eyes, and Korrin stifled his disapproval of Soliander's fury. Cariss had witnessed one of these exchanges, and something about it told her that it hadn't been the first.

Her older brother had always been noble to a fault. Long before the quests or her learning that they had ceased to be voluntary, she had admired Korrin even as her younger brother Dari resented him. Her sympathy for

Dari's ego had been limited. She hadn't appreciated his lack of remorse when Korrin went missing. Dari had seemed almost happy about it, and had once claimed prematurely that he should be named heir-apparent to the throne in Korrin's ongoing absence. Sometimes he tried to downplay all those snide remarks he'd previously made, not only about Korrin, but also about the other Champions, whom he had refused to refer to that way. Any similar words like "heroes" also made him frown. And until the Champions disappeared, he had reacted that way to anyone people admired, finding amusement in those who died while trying to help others.

Dari didn't reveal such sentiments anymore, of course. He hadn't been dumb enough to outwardly gloat that his famed brother had vanished, but she knew he didn't miss Korrin. Not once had he expressed concern, so she wasn't sure what to make of his performance in the great hall just now. Had it been a show? And for whom? Likely their parents. He had seemed more confident and somehow invigorated by Korrin's absence, as if the sun could never shine on him until Korrin was gone. And once word had reached them the Champions had resumed their quests, the cloud that once hung over Dari had reappeared in his brown eyes.

Korrin was a threat to him, she now understood. A threat to his claim to the throne, surely, but that had never been real anyway. Then again, that wouldn't stop a man from fancying it his, she knew. Korrin had personally cut down one such pretender on a quest. But surely it wouldn't come to that here in Andor! No, Korrin was a threat to the esteem in which everyone held Dari, or even the attention he received. Part of her didn't blame Dari for thinking this way, but she thought he needed to grow up.

She sighed as she rounded another corner, nodding absentmindedly to others passing by. That they had told no one of the attempt at summoning her brother and the others was just as well now that it had resulted in this surprise. Dari had insisted on being at the Quest Ring, ostensibly to welcome Korrin back and represent the family, but she had wondered if that was all. Taryn was more than capable of overseeing the whole affair. Cariss wished she could have been present see Dari's reaction when the four imposters had appeared. Had he been thrilled? Relieved? Disappointed and surprised? She would never know. One thing was certain—he was genuinely curious where Korrin was now that two of the four had been seen alive, and perhaps equally fascinated to know that his brother was free of that cycle of unwanted quests. He had once laughed about the involuntary part, saying it was ironic punishment for Korrin's pride, that he could save so many people. What did he think now?

As she arrived at her suite of rooms, the door stood open, and a guard advised her that he had let Mandrellan into her sitting room beyond the antechamber. Her heart lifted. The wizard could once again offer her helpful counsel. He was quite astute, and knew that a gathering of nobles had taken place without him being invited this time. He had probably assumed she had news, but he would never guess what it was.

Thoughts of Dari had dampened her excitement, but now she tried to relax. She pulled a long pin from her blonde hair to let it fall past her slender waist, which a lavender belt held her flowing, green dress against. She loosened it slightly and kicked off her shoes to walk barefoot on the cool stones here, as was her habit since childhood.

She swept into the room to find Mandrellan already standing, arms folded so that each hand clasped the other forearm inside the sleeves of his plain blue robe. Dark, penetrating brown eyes smiled warmly at her. Cariss had always found his gaze mesmerizing. His black stubble beard framed his jaw from below, matching the short hair atop his head. His eyes stood out from the pale face, their deep brown making even a smile seem intense. He was only a few years older than her in his late twenties, but his command of situations suggested he was much older and wiser, that mind of his seeing things hers seldom did. She hadn't known another person from the planet Artimon and could never tell what, if anything, about him was the influence of home or just him.

"Are you alone, my lady?" Mandrellan asked, his voice smooth and strong.

For an answer, she turned back to the guard. "You may close the doors." She turned to the wizard and smiled, noticing as she neared him that he seemed relieved. "I have the most interesting news, but you must promise to tell no one of it."

"Of course." He bowed. "Your trust is as sacred to me as your life."

Cariss moved to sit on a velvet divan, gesturing for him to join her. "This time, it is especially important that no one knows what I am going to tell you."

That playful smile she so often admired appeared. "You have my full attention."

She casually remarked, "My family just tried to summon the Champions." Cariss watched in anticipation of his reaction, which she had imagined countless times over the past week as plans unfolded, but the expression of alarm wasn't what she had expected. It vanished almost as quickly as it came, a look of quiet urgency replacing it. Maybe it hadn't been fear after all. But then she realized the reason it might have been and gushed, "I'm sorry for not telling you sooner! My family made me swear to secrecy! I still trust you. You must believe me."

His eyes widened, and he gripped one hand with his, smiling. "Of course, my dear. I did not doubt this for a moment. You merely startled me. I trust the summoning was not successful?"

She smiled anew. "Oh, it worked."

Mandrellan's gaze intensified, and his eyes darted to the door and back to hers. "You must not joke with me about something so important."

Cariss laughed. "You are taking this much too seriously! I can see this matters as much to you as to myself."

"Yes. I have offered my counsel and aid in finding them many times precisely because I want to see you happy that Lord Korrin is safe and home. Given this, I am disappointed that I was not among those chosen to assist."

"I am so sorry, Mandrellan." The last thing she wanted was for the bond between them to suffer. "I lobbied on your behalf but—"

"You should have tried harder." He rose and turned away from her, stepping toward the exit.

She felt a stab of pain at his rebuke and, for a moment, was at a loss for a response. Would she lose her trusted advisor over this? He had literally turned his back... "It's not my fault. I—"

"I fear you do not trust me at all, even after all that I have done for you." He took more steps to leave.

Cariss rose and quickly caught up with him. "Please don't leave, Mandrellan! I could not bear it. I need you here. Please tell me what I can do to make it right."

He stopped and turned to her, frowning, his eyes hurt. "I don't see what you can do. It is clear I am not to be told what is happening. My counsel cannot be of use to you in my ignorance."

That gave her an idea and she took one of his hands with both of hers. "I came to tell you what happened!"

"You did not even know I was here."

"Yes, but I was going to come find you if you weren't here. I knew you would be here because you hear so much, even that which is not meant for your ears. You would hear of a gathering of nobles and wait for me to find out why. And you did! I know you trust me to tell you what happened, or you would not be here even now!"

"And yet you are teasing me instead of being forthcoming."

Again, she wasn't sure how to respond. "Well, I, I only wanted to have some fun revealing the extraordinary news. Please forgive me. I'm just a silly girl. You say so yourself all the time. Please. I will tell you everything."

He sighed in apparent resignation. Then he smiled and relief consumed her. "Well, perhaps if this silly girl can stop being silly long enough, I may still be able to counsel her."

"Yes!" She tugged him back toward the divan, nearly dancing with excitement. "Come, come. I will tell you everything." His smile broadened, and she lost any sense of hesitancy. He could have every last secret she had. "What do you want to know first?"

"Where is Lord Korrin now? And the others?"

"We still don't know. He didn't show up. Neither did the others." He shot her a penetrating look that made her tremble. "Four imposters appeared! It's the most amazing thing! My brother and the others are still missing. I'm not *happy* about this, but these four friends from a place called Earth are the ones who have done these recent quests. And when we summoned the real Champions, these four appeared instead."

Brow furrowed and eyes dark, the wizard asked, "How can there be substitutes? It's not possible."

"No, I wouldn't have thought so."

"It's not."

She smiled. "How can you be so sure? It's almost like you know how the Quest Rings really work." When he looked startled, she laughed. "I'm only teasing."

"Yes, of course. I have read about them. That is all. I have no firsthand knowledge. But the spell could not..." He trailed off.

"Replace them? Yes, I know, and yet it has happened. How could this be?" She wasn't really expecting an answer. He didn't know how the spells worked any more than anyone else—except that awful wizard Everon, who had trapped her brother and the others in the cycle of quests. But it appeared that cycle had come to an end.

The wizard rose and began pacing. "You are certain that it is not them, but do these imposters know the whereabouts of Korrin and the others?"

"Nothing about Andier or Korrin, I'm sad to say. But they met Eriana on Earth."

His eyes bored into hers so intently that for a moment she felt afraid. "They are sure? How can we know they speak the truth?"

She rose and put one hand on his arm to calm him. "If you had been there, the details they gave, they could not have been lying. The story is fantastic, beyond anything but the true story of the Champions. Eriana has helped them. You know what this means? The quest cycle is broken, and at least two of them live!"

Mandrellan's eyes sparkled with intensity as he looked away, thinking. "The cycle... Yes, it must be... And others have taken their place. Eriana is free to..." Suddenly his eyes swung to hers and he gripped both of her arms forcibly. "You said two? The other is Soliander?"

"Ow, Mandrellan. Please!"

He frowned before he suddenly let go and retreated. "I beg your forgiveness, my lady. I am overexcited."

Cariss crossed her arms, feeling flustered. "Alright," she said, hearing herself sounding pouty about it, so she collected herself. "Well, anyhow, the news on Soliander is quite disturbing."

Mandrellan arched an eyebrow. "How so?"

"It seems that he attacked these four imposters on Honyn, where he opened the Dragon Gate as some sort of trap."

The wizard pulled back. "A trap for whom?"

"Someone on that world. He had stolen a scroll that detailed the whereabouts of soclarin ore. Soliander didn't want anyone to have that. You remember that the keystone inside each Quest Ring is made from it, and so are many of Soliander's most powerful items, like Korrin's sword."

"Yes. I recall. Where is this scroll now?"

"Back with the rulers of Honyn."

Mandrellan looked away, clearly thinking. "And if the scroll is stolen, what happens? Or what happened then?"

"Apparently, with the scroll stolen, Soliander assumed its possessor might want to go through the Dragon Gate to the world where the ore is and get it. So he opened the gate to lure him there and killed him! We think he had hoped it would be Everon, but it was not. I should like to kill that wizard myself, if I ever meet him."

The wizard nodded, eyes alight. "Perhaps you will get the chance. I admire your devotion. One could assume that stealing the scroll again might cause the same result, Soliander trying to trap the perpetrator. That would make it easy to know where Soliander would arrive to catch that person, assuming anyone knows what we just discussed."

"Only those in the throne room just now, and these imposters, or perhaps a few on Honyn. Are you thinking that if someone stole the scroll on purpose, we could meet Soliander when he arrives?".

He smiled. "Something like that, yes."

"You are clever! I should suggest that to my father."

"No, no. Please don't. I think there is too much going on now that is unknown. It is an opportunity we can discuss with him later."

Her excitement turned to disappointment, but she trusted his judgement. "Sure. We may have another way to find Soliander. The wizard, the one pretending to be Soliander, said that he has some of Soliander's memories. Those might include his location." Cariss saw Mandrellan's eyes grow intense again, then dart to the door and back.

"How? What does he know? Where is he now?"

She related Matt's story about how the mind reading spell had given him some of Soliander's memories, but the thoughts were scattered and he couldn't recall anything on purpose. She included how he recognized Taryn despite never having met her. "The imposters are under guard for now until we can confirm some of their story."

Mandrellan rose to his feet and grabbed his staff. "And Taryn? Where is she?"

Cariss shrugged. "Still in the great hall. They were making some arrangements. Where are you going?"

He had taken several steps toward the door, but now stopped and turned back. "You must trust me. I have an idea of my own that I dare not share with you now. The secrets you have entrusted to me, I will keep. I ask only that you do me the same courtesy and tell no one that we have spoken of these matters, even after they say the truth can be known."

That confused her. Why would he want that? But she still felt the need to smooth over their relationship and agreed, watching in dismay and concern as he left. The talk had not gone the way she'd anticipated. Something about it still bothered her, but when dwelling on such things, he was the one she normally spoke to. Well, lately anyway. They had met several months after the Champions disappeared, and since then, he had come and gone for weeks at a time, often updating her on inquiries he had made about their whereabouts. It was as if he were scouring the worlds himself for some sign of them. This filled her with gratitude, that he was such a great friend he would do this when he had no other reason beyond wanting the heroes found, on principle. Maybe that was the reason for his hasty departure.

It had been months since she'd seen him, but when word first spread of the Ellorian Champions doing the Honyn quest for the Dragon Gate, their first quest since going missing, he had arrived within days to ask for details. Now that she thought about it, he had seemed similarly intense and concerned, then confused like the rest of them that Korrin had not come home following the quest. He hadn't left since then, vowing to remain close by to assist if needed. Where he went when not here was no secret; his home and own affairs on Artimon beckoned. She wondered if that was where he was going now, as he sometimes did not tell her before disappearing again. She would ask the guards at the World Gate to tell her if he left. There had been enough worrisome surprises lately.

It wasn't until her thoughts drifted to these imposters and how little she knew of them that she realized the same was true of Mandrellan, despite all the time they had spent together.

OIL AND LILAC

For the umpteenth time, Matt fingered the thing on his head that stopped him from accessing magic. He suspected magic was keeping it there and badly wanted to know how to take it off. Or put it on, for that matter. Being off Earth normally excited him because he could do magic, because otherwise he was the same old Matt Sorenson—weak and uninteresting. With the power of magic available on quests, that had all changed, even when he was back home, because he achieved things on quests that made him feel powerful, invigorated, and just awesome. It was like he finally had some sort of purpose. And he knew he enjoyed these quests more than his friends.

Instead of being sent back to the room they were in before, they had walked through the high halls of a palace; he had expected a castle. Tall windows provided a view of manicured gardens with sculptures and fountains below their position on the second floor. They were on a hill overlooking the port in the distance. Tall wooden ships lay at anchor in the harbor, their sails furled, except on the two that were sailing away. Such a sight often filled him with wonder that they got to visit places like this. And he so often wished they could do more than immediately set off on a quest. Might it not be wonderful to learn about one of these kingdoms in a way that didn't involve monsters, dragon hordes, or some other threat to all life?

Their escort of a dozen King's Guards, all in golden uniforms, had led them past curious onlookers. They no longer looked important except for their treatment. Whispers were bound to start. This was something they really needed to discuss with the families—how best to handle revealing the truth to those who didn't know, whenever that happened.

After several minutes of walking through gilded halls, past ornate paintings, and mostly human gawkers, they were shown into the large Blue Suite, which had two bedrooms and a sitting area between them. Windows provided views in several directions, inspiring Matt to gaze out to snow-capped mountains in the distance. Now he wanted a map.

Breaking his thoughts from behind him, Anna asked, "How do we think that went?"

Matt turned back and watched while Eric inspected the room, as if searching for surprises.

"I thought it went pretty well," began Ryan as he sniffed at a decanter or of what appeared to be orange juice, "but then I was doing the talking. How do you guys think I handled it?"

"Better than Matt," remarked Eric, who looked at the wizard, "but I think you got lucky with the reaction you received."

"Thanks," Matt said dryly.

Anna took a proffered OJ from Ryan and sat down on a couch. "Let's not wait for their decision on what happens next. What do we want out of our next talk with them?"

"The quest," Eric started at once. "We'll still need to get details on that. There's some small chance we can escape and do it and go home, so let's at least find out what we have to do."

"Yeah," said Matt, "but it's gonna be a lot harder if I can't get this damn thing off my head. I doubt anyone's going to tell us, but we need to figure out how to remove it. For all I know, I might not even be able to use the Quest Ring to send us home!"

Anna frowned. "I hadn't thought of that, but I think all of us can do it. We would need Soliander's staff. If they don't let us go or cooperate, we could be in trouble here."

"Well," began Eric, sitting down near Anna, "I think we need to figure out who seems like a soft target for getting information out of. I mean, Dari isn't likely to tell us anything unless we trick him into it. He's got an ego and some sort of chip on his shoulder. I'm probably the best to trick something out of him, but Ryan, since you're pretending to be his brother, he's probably more interested in you."

Ryan agreed. "Yeah. I'll see what I can do. Maybe challenge his pride in some way."

"Right," said Eric, "but first you'll have to see if that's what's driving him."

Matt smirked. "He's transparent. Maybe I'd have better luck goading him."

"I'd really like to talk to Eriana's brother," began Anna, "and that princess from Coreth. If I update on her in more detail, they could be allies."

Eric nodded. "I want to talk to Taryn. I'm not sure the rest of you can handle her. No offense. She's just very clever. Talking to her is like playing chess."

Matt said, "She's like the female version of you."

Eric laughed. "Exactly. Another big factor here, one we'll need their co-operation for, is to see Korrin's Home Ring. I'm dying to know what one looks like."

An image of one appeared in Matt's head, not for the first time, from Soliander's memories. "I could draw one, but yeah, let's see his. Part of me is wondering if it still functions, or if there's any sign of something being wrong. In fact, it would be good to compare his to the others'. What if Eriana's and Soliander's are fine, and we know they're alive, but Andier's and Korrin's are damaged? It could suggest something."

"Interesting," said Eric. "Let's ask about the Home Rings. If they agree to help us, I'd also like to know if they can send people or things to Earth."

"Yes, like spellbooks," Matt suggested, "and any materials I need to cast spells. With magic starting to work on Earth, I really need to be able to practice."

"What would be even better is training," said Ryan. "Magic, sword fighting, archery. We can only do archery at home, but the modern bows we have are too different. We haven't had any training since the first quest. They mentioned it back there, too."

Eric said, "You know, that brings up another point. Taryn told me the quest we're summoned for is an easy one and not urgent. What if they agree to cooperate and help us? We could stay here indefinitely and get trained up before doing the quest and going home. There's nothing urgent back there."

Matt was about to express his enthusiasm when a knock on the door preceded the arrival of Taryn, who strode in with several of the King's Guard a step behind and to each side. She flicked an indifferent glance at the others but came straight toward him and stopped within arm's reach. She smelled slightly of oil and lilac.

"Matt, I'd like you to come with me."

"Why?"

"There are things you may know about my brother's whereabouts, or at least his activities, and I would like to learn what they are."

He couldn't blame her, but he wanted something, too. "Maybe if you remove this thing from my head, I'll answer your questions."

Taryn pursed her lips. "I understand your reluctance. I was hoping this wouldn't be viewed as a trade, but as potential allies helping each other. But if you have questions about my brother, or anything else, I would be happy to answer them."

He arched an eyebrow. "Why would you?"

"The way I see it, if you are in the situation you say you are and you need our help, we'll be allies. If not, you'll be imprisoned here a long time and unable to pass along what I tell you to anyone. In either case, there is no reason not to give you some information."

Matt held her gaze for a moment. "I can't argue with that."

His glance at Eric received a nod of approval and he followed Taryn from the room. While several guards stood outside, none accompanied them on their walk. She apparently didn't consider him a threat without magic. He frowned on thinking that this was true. As if reading his thoughts, she interrupted them.

"I wanted to apologize for striking you at the Quest Ring. You were potentially very dangerous, and I had to act quickly."

Matt looked at her wryly. "I still am."

Taryn smiled. "Not with that Crown of Voids on your head."

"When are you going to remove it?"

"Once we confirm enough of your story to believe you."

He shook his head. "You already believe me."

She nodded. "I do, yes, but it is the king's decision." She looked up at the Crown as they walked, for he was taller than her. "You are not the first wizard I have put this on."

Images flashed in Matt's head, of a young and terrified Soliander, waking from a nightmare of undead climbing up through the floors of their home to consume both of them. He was about to lash out with magic to stop a threat that wasn't there when Taryn slid the device onto his head. Then she pinned him to the crude cot, talking gently to calm him. As with Matt's own memories, he didn't feel them so much as recall the images and random phrases, but he did sense the gratitude and admiration Soliander felt for his older sister. He loved her.

Matt stayed silent until she led him into an unguarded suite that he realized was her quarters. Several swords lay on a table, a pointed shield leaning against a chair. The dark blue décor suited her boldness. This was not a woman who would live somewhere pink. She went over to a bar in this sitting room while he glanced into the bedroom, seeing the sheets thrown back and rumpled. Tidying up wasn't her thing either. He wondered if a maid service had been told to stay out because she didn't like things too neat. Watching her shapely backside and thinking about the bed made him wonder what sort of man would attract her attention—and survive it. Probably Eric, but certainly not himself! Still, she was sexy.

"Let's forget about your brother for a minute," he began, as she began pouring red wine into silver steel goblets with dragons carved on them. Somehow that seemed more appropriate for her than glass. "You're obviously just visiting."

"I live where I am," she said, coming toward him with the drinks. He took the one she offered and watched her sit on the edge of the couch. He remained standing, sipping the bitter drink. It tasted like Merlot. He failed not to make a face. She smirked and asked, "Should I get you milk instead?"

He returned the expression and asked, "Do you have any?"

She laughed. "Good. I like some banter. It's a warrior thing."

"I think you liked it before you became one."

"We understand each other already."

"And what do you think you understand about me?"

"That you're in over your head. That you're a nice guy. That your life has been upended and you should be rattled, desperate for help, needy and scared. And yet you're not. You stand at your full height instead of cowering. You show defiance. You're quick-witted and aware of nuances that some people twice your age cannot grasp when they're explained to them. You challenged Dari in front of the king. You defeated the dragon horde of Honyn. You even beat the Lords of Fear. There is steel in you. And power. You are strong, more so than even you may realize. To be honest, you remind me of my brother."

That startled him out of wondering if she was flirting with him. "Right now, I'm more curious about *you*."

She swallowed a mouthful of wine. "I have a place in Aranor. But you could've guessed that. Don't see it much."

"I was about to ask if you don't stray far from home, but you do."

"I go where my blade is needed and I like the work. I may not be the hero my brother is, but I don't let the evil shits of this world destroy the lives of their betters."

"Good." Matt could admire that, as someone long bullied growing up. "What's this about you being Commander of the Dark Blades?"

Taryn lounged on the couch. "We're a thousand strong, mostly warriors. Those who need us can hire us. There are places that are too small to have their own knighthood or army. They can hire mine. Sometimes we briefly add to one that already exists. We're often the ones with the most dangerous or important job, like protecting a royal family. We're the most elite."

Matt noticed that she said this with pride but not braggadocio. She seemed comfortable with who she was, authority exuding from her. "You're its leader."

Taryn nodded. "From the start. It was my idea."

A formidable woman. And out of his league. No wonder she didn't feel threatened. "All humans? Any women besides you?"

"Mostly men, but we have elves and dwarves among us."

"So then you must act nobly or no elves, at least, would be with you."

"Did you doubt that?"

"Not really. Are your Dark Blades here?"

"Only a few. I've been here often since the Champions supposedly returned. It was my idea to summon them when they weren't returning after quests. It seems I am responsible for you being pulled away from your world this time."

He felt glad for the information. "You could not have known."

Her eyes narrowed. "You said you are not a wizard on Earth, but I cannot tell what it is you do. I seldom meet a man I cannot understand."

He smirked. "Do you like a mystery? Spoiling it by telling you might have you lose interest in me."

She looked him directly in the eye. "Nothing is going to make me lose interest in you."

Matt flushed a little and tried not to show it. She was too alert to, well, everything, and he knew what Eric meant about how talking with her was like playing chess. He would lose. He returned her direct look, not bothering to hide his attraction; she could think what she liked of it. Pursuing her wasn't something he felt would work anyway—for any number of reasons, including her being out of his league, him being awful at flirting, and there being far more important things on his mind. If she wanted him by some miracle, she knew how to find him and likely exactly what to do with him. And he felt certain she would take what she desired if that came to pass. It wasn't like Matt was going to say no. The thought brought some humor to his eyes and, to his surprise, she seemed to flush a little.

"I am not a wizard on Earth," he admitted. "Life is very different there." He paused, not sure how to explain something like computers. Saying he was a software developer wasn't going to make any sense. He spent a while trying to describe modern life, using objects like a wagon to say how they had become machines called cars—and that these didn't need horses, but something dug up from the earth to run. His description of gasoline, as poor as it was, had her wondering if it was a magic potion, and he struggled not to overexplain anything. He avoided mentioning airplanes in case they sounded too unplausible. He didn't want her to think he was lying. Through it all, Taryn was fascinated. He'd never had someone hang on his every word like this. At times she seemed to doubt him anyway, but he always had an answer to her questions, and those led to more so that he spoke in depth about Earth.

Finally, she said, "Well, you are either the most fantastic liar I've ever known, or you speak the truth."

By now, he had taken a place near her on the couch. She got off the arm of it to sit beside him, turning so that one calf was on it as she faced him. Sensing her conclusion, he asked, "Which do you think?"

"You're no liar. So, I was right that you were not a wizard before this began. You work with these devices, computers you called them. I am all the more impressed that you have succeeded on your quests."

"I learn quickly. Lorian trained me on the first quest. He knew we were imposters and helped us." Matt briefly recounted their experience with the elf Lorian, who had known the real Champions and learned the truth about him and the others and their situation. "I've done okay since then, but I really need more training. There is no time on a quest, and none between quests. There is no one to teach me on Earth and I do not have access to anything I would need."

She leaned forward, scrutinizing him before nodding. "I will see to it that something is done about this."

"I would be very grateful for that."

"I am impressed that you have survived this long."

He confessed, "I am able to control your brother's staff very well. I rely on it to draw power, to control it, and even to help me decide what magic to do. I may not be able to cast a fireball spell, but I can summon fire from the staff."

She appeared to think for a moment before patting his leg and rising for the decanter, refilling both goblets before sitting again. "Well, I certainly want to know more about you, but I really brought you here to see what you know about my brother. You have concerned me."

"I'm afraid that anything else I tell you will only worsen your concerns."

"Tell me."

He wasn't sure where to begin, but said, "He had a dark elf working for him on Honyn. The elf was spying on us and we caught him. Soliander killed him through a communication orb so that the elf couldn't talk to us." He saw that all of this took her aback.

"You are certain?"

"Yes. He also killed the wizard who had stolen the scroll, the one that revealed the location of soclarin ore. It was a trap. I assume actions like these are out of character for him?"

Eyes troubled, she nodded. "Do you have any sense of what would make him do these things?"

"He is searching for Everon. That much I know."

"Aren't we all," she muttered, frowning. "You know who he is?"

"Yes. Eriana told us and I began to remember from Soliander's memories. He was Soliander's apprentice. He is the one who trapped the Champions in the cycle of unwanted quests, which were originally voluntary. My sense is that Soliander wants revenge. He also believes that Andier, Korrin, and Eriana are dead, and that Everon is ultimately responsible."

"That would explain it," she said. "He was never very forgiving. And he has a volcanic temper. But to kill others who get in his way is not like him."

Matt asked, "What can you tell me about him? I'm not sure if it would help, and he's your brother, so I understand not wanting to, uh, betray his confidence to me. He sees us as enemies, I think. Well, I'm not really sure what he sees us as, but given that he attacked us…"

She waved him off. "No, it's okay. I don't know what would help you."

There was something he'd been wanting to know for two months. "How would he view the four of us impersonating the Champions?"

"Good question. He would understand that you are trapped, too, like they were. He should be sympathetic, not upset with you. Honestly, he was the most upset about the whole thing. I know he felt responsible for it because Everon was his apprentice and betrayed him, and did this to them. I don't understand why he would attack the four of you or be after you in any way."

"Maybe he just wants information?"

"Yes, that could be it. He is keen on knowing as much as he can. He may be wondering what you know of him. Oh. I know a reason. He knows you have a copy of his staff now, and he'd be wanting that back." She chuckled.

Matt watched her, unsure what to make of that. "Was that an understatement? Is that why you laughed?"

"Yes. I'm sorry, Matt. But I'm afraid you are a big target for him."

"Great. That's just what I need."

"Maybe I should stay with you, to protect you."

Matt smirked. "I got away from him the first time."

She shook her head. "You won't a second. Trust me. You caught him by surprise. He'll be prepared for you next time. If he catches sight of you…"

"You think you would be able to stop him? Reason with him?"

She nodded. "Yes. He would never harm me and has always listened to me."

He sensed that that was true from the memories, but still asked, "You are certain? My sense is that he has changed."

"It's a chance I would be willing to take. If he has committed himself to evil, he knows that I more than anyone else would come after him. I would spank him senseless."

A memory of her spanking her younger brother's bare red butt as a boy popped into his head. His eyes widened. Then he laughed. Nothing took the intimidation out of Soliander like that memory.

Seeming amazed and amused, Taryn asked, "Did you just remember a spanking I gave him?" Matt nodded. "What other memories of me do you have in there?"

He shrugged as, a montage of her and Soliander as children drifted through his mind. The one that stood out was of Soli walking in on a nude, teenage Taryn, who didn't bother to cover herself before she made him leave. Matt blushed furiously, eyes darting to her breasts and away. She arched an eyebrow, then smiled.

"Well, now you're making me curious," she teased.

"Let's change the subject. Do you have any idea why he wouldn't come home?"

Taryn pursed her lips. "I really don't. I haven't had a chance to think about it. It could be guilt if he thinks the others were dead. Maybe he doesn't want to answer questions; he was never interested in explaining himself much. He likely didn't want to face the families. Some of it is trying to get revenge on Everon, I'm sure. Keeping everyone from knowing he's back makes that easier. Everon may come out of hiding if he thinks Soliander is dead. There could be a lot of reasons."

Matt nodded. "Yeah, it makes sense."

"Can you tell why he hasn't come home?"

"No. I have memories, but not the thoughts that led to them. While I can sometimes see what happened, I can't understand why unless the reason is part of the memory. I also can't tell the order of memories. It makes it harder to make sense of them."

"Maybe it's not as useful as I was thinking."

"Yeah. But it has its moments." He pictured her nude again without meaning to and flushed.

She smirked knowingly. "I always wondered if Soli remembered that. Now I know."

He began to laugh. She was way too astute, but he liked it. Trying to change the subject, he asked, "Since Soliander went missing, have you tried to go to his home?"

"Yes. Couldn't get in." She eyed him curiously. "Can you tell why?"

Knowing that this was a test, he thought for a moment. "I'm not remembering anything, if that's what you're asking. But I assume he has magical protections there." As he said it, something occurred to him. "I have the staff. It got me past spells of his before on Honyn. I think... yes, it can get me by some of them. I remember them now."

She leaned forward. "You're certain?"

"Yes. I would remember more if we were there. Seeing things can trigger a memory."

She appeared to consider that. "Then maybe we should go. But I'm not sure what point there is, since we know he isn't there. I had wanted to go before to find some sign of him."

"There might still be things to see, though he isn't there anymore. He doesn't live there. We want to see all the Home Rings to see if there's anything different about them now, but we would need... well, no, the memories just came back. I can remember what they looked like before they disappeared."

"You wanted someone who already knew what they had looked like before. You think they have changed?"

He shrugged. "We don't know. We're just trying to figure out where Korrin and Andier might be, if they need help, or if they would be able to help us. We have some idea what happened with the quest on Earth to break them out of the cycle."

She rose to refill her goblet. "Tell me about that. You only touched on it before." Bringing the decanter, she filled their cups.

Matt saw no reason not to tell her, so he explained about the quest that brought the Ellorian Champions to Earth. The part they had left out before was Morgana's threat to all life—and that the only way Merlin could stop her was to stop magic from working, which was why he cast the spell to drain magic from Earth and into the fae world. The last of the magic lay in a pendant that, if returned to Stonehenge, would undo his spell. Magic would return.

Morgana had a vision of the Champions. She modified Stonehenge to act like a Quest Ring and summoned them to her time frame, a thousand years ago. Their quest was to undo Merlin's spell before it finished draining the magic, by returning the pendant to Stonehenge, but they refused once they learned the danger she posed. When Soliander realized that they could break free of the quest cycle by letting Merlin's spell finish, they decided to let it happen but use the last of Earth's magic to send themselves home at the last moment. The resulting explosion sent him back as expected, but there had been no sign of Korrin or Andier—and Eriana did not arrive in the present in Coreth, but twenty years ago on Earth.

In the thousand years since, the pendant somehow made its way to Anna—who unwittingly brought it to Stonehenge with Matt, Ryan, and Eric while on vacation in Europe—and Merlin's spell was undone. Moments later, a wizard on Honyn tried to summon the Ellorian Champions, and somehow they appeared in the Champions' place. They'd been stuck in the same unwanted cycle of quests ever since.

"That sounds too extraordinary to be invented," Taryn admitted.

Matt nodded. "We only know these things from Eriana. That reminds me. I have a favor to ask."

"Name it."

"Anna would like to talk to Eriana's brother and the princess from Coreth, to tell them more about the life Eriana has lived on Earth these past two decades."

"I'll arrange it."

"Thank you."

She watched him. "I appreciate your honesty. I can tell that you are telling me the truth. There are those who say honest people are weaker because they can be known and therefore manipulated. There is a wisdom to this—but honesty is still a quality I admire and respect. You would do well to learn more duplicity, as much as I hate to suggest that. It will just help you protect yourself. But in lieu of that, you have my sword at your disposal, should you need it. I am confident that you will soon be free here in Andor and I will have the pleasure of removing that device from your head."

Matt held her gaze and lifted his goblet as if to toast, feeling a little tipsy. "To those having the strength to do what's right."

Taryn smiled and raised hers. "To those having the strength to do what's right."

Then they drank.

CHAPTER FIVE

NEW FRIENDS, OLD FRIENDS

When Matt returned later that afternoon, he filled in Anna, Eric, and Ryan, who thought he'd done a good job with Taryn. Ryan had removed his gambeson in favor of a gold tunic and tights they had brought him. Before long, they were served dinner in their suite, which they weren't allowed to leave for the rest of the day. It was just as well. Since the quests began, they'd become used to having too much excitement at once—but it was still fatiguing. They talked over their situation for a bit.

First came a frank talk about whether Anna could trust one of the boys in bed with her. She was the one to casually raise the subject, for while two of the guys could fit into the other bed, one would need to sleep on the floor unless he joined her. She didn't want someone getting sore or a poor night's rest. She trusted them all they all decided to act like adults. She chose for Matt to join her without explanation.

In the morning, Taryn made good on her promise to get Anna an audience with Eriana's brother and the Princess of Coreth, whom Anna told everything she knew about the priestess. The hardest part was explaining that Eriana had lived for twenty years on Earth because the quest had taken her a thousand years into the past, and when Soliander broke the quest, she was hurled almost to the right timeline, just two decades short. Anna told them that Eriana hadn't known about the time issue. She'd thought the quest to Earth was in the present, that it had hurled her forward nearly a thousand years, and that therefore everyone she knew was dead. Her brother and princess took this hard, empathizing with Eriana's apparent loss and how relieved she must have been to learn the truth from the new Champions. From this reaction, Anna knew that they were good people, and they were grateful to her for giving Eriana this peace of mind. She came away from the meeting certain they had become allies.

She returned to their suites to find Matt burying his nose in a spellbook. Taryn had tried to get Soliander's for him but been denied, so she'd obtained another one. The others were reading scrolls or other books about the world. Ryan was learning about the kingdoms of the Champions—Andor, Roir, and Aranor—and Novell, the one with the Quest Ring. His studies included histories and heraldry. Eric was looking into street-smart information like the cost of goods, which organizations were respected or feared, and local customs.

Shortly after lunch in their rooms, Ryan sent word to Prince Dari that he would like to meet. He provided a reason at Eric's suggestion. The true motive was to learn more about Dari's bad attitude toward them and whether it could be mitigated, but that wasn't the kind of thing he could admit. One story they discussed—claiming to want help in understanding Korrin's role. That would allow them to bring honor to the family by behaving as expected. But they wondered if this would backfire. Afterall, it meant continuing to impersonate Korrin instead of admitting the truth, and Dari already seemed angry about the ruse.

"Maybe I should just challenge him to a duel," Ryan joked in frustration. "*That* he would accept."

Eric laughed. "He might. But seriously, saying you want to apologize won't work. I'm not sure insulting his ego in some way would either. Maybe you could ask his opinion on what would happen when, not if, we admit to not being the Champions—and how we can minimize the problems this causes for his family. I think we need to seem like friends who want to help, not like a threat. He views us as enemies now, I'm sure."

They all agreed and sent a messenger, who returned so quickly with a refusal that they felt the strength of Dari's scorn. Undeterred, they asked Korrin's sister, Princess Cariss, the same question and received an equally quick invitation for Ryan to join her in her rooms, with two of the King's Guard present at all times. She brimmed with curiosity while greeting him, and accepted his suggestion to walk around the palace as they spoke. This gave him the chance to know more about their location, and possibly into life in Andor.

At first, he had little opportunity to ask anything because her questions came so quickly. Like Matt, he steered clear of subjects that might invite disbelief—but he told her about being from a wealthy family like her, hoping to create a bond. He sensed that Cariss was kindhearted and sympathetic, so he even confessed to the once deeply-held secret that he had accidentally paralyzed his younger brother Daniel in childhood.

"And healers could do *nothing*?" she asked, seeming wounded by the idea. He'd already noticed that she wore her heart on her sleeve. That he liked her apparent innocence made it easy to connect with her. Her presence was as warming as the morning sun streaming in through floor-to-ceiling windows in the galleries where they walked. Outside, he saw the bustling city streets and badly wanted to go there for a stroll instead of here, but it would have to wait. And likely never happen. One of these days they would get to do a quest that involved spending time in a big settlement, instead of in the wilderness fighting monsters or worse.

"Nothing to make him walk again. He is bound to a wheelchair," Ryan added, explaining what that meant.

"I can see why you devote yourself to him. This speaks very well of you. I would do the same, giving up my life to make amends. Well, more to ease the suffering I had caused."

"Are you close with your brothers?" Ryan asked, fishing for details of family dynamics. They rounded a corner and ascended wide steps toward a room full of portraits.

"Yes, both of them. They are not close with each other, however. Dari has always resented Korrin, and it is easy to see why. Everyone admires Korrin, who became a knight like our father, exceeding him in every way. Dari refused even to train as a knight because he rightly knew he wouldn't match Korrin's prowess."

"Korrin is older?" They had stopped at a painting of the family, which he only knew from recognizing everyone except the man he impersonated. They did look alike, except that Korrin's portrait bore a confidence Ryan had never felt. Now he at least knew what the man looked like. He would get the others here before long to see him. A world without photographs made it hard to know who anyone was unless you met them personally. Maybe there was a portrait of the Champions around here somewhere. He hadn't personally seen Soliander, so only Matt knew what he looked like. And no one had any idea about Andier. They could bump into him and not know it.

"Yes," Cariss answered. "I am second. Dari is third. He is so sensitive to comparisons that I cannot even call him my little brother without vexing him. I am not surprised that he refused to see you, much to his shame. That is the trouble with him. He acts in ways others cannot admire, then resents their disapproval—and so he continues to act that way out of spite, or resentment."

Ryan had heard of such cyclical behavior. "A feedback loop. That's what we call it on Earth. I wanted to ask you something. Your brother seems very upset with us, and I understand that we have been impersonating Korrin and the others and that this could upset everyone, but I felt like there was more there. By contrast, Soliander's sister has been open to the idea that we are not simply villains."

Princess Cariss nodded. She described how Dari had been overshadowed by their brother, then freed of that with Korrin's disappearance, and finally felt apprehensive about his return. But she said she didn't know how to interpret his reaction to Ryan and the others.

"I don't think he is disappointed that Korrin didn't appear," she admitted. "I suspect he's not sure how to react to you. You have, through no fault of yours, introduced uncertainty to all of us—but his fortunes, or what he believes to be his fortunes, are more affected."

"In what way? Does he feel that Korrin's return would be bad for him?" By now they had moved toward a balcony they stepped onto for a view of the port.

"I am certain he does. He felt invisible before. Then he didn't, until today. Even the idea of Korrin returning has sent him into turmoil. He is not sure what to wish for, I think."

Ryan observed, "So then maybe he would be interested in helping us understand Korrin's whereabouts? At the least, it would remove his uncertainty."

She beamed at him and laid a hand on his arm. "Yes!"

"The best way for him to do that is to help us understand what might've happened to Korrin."

"How could he do that?"

"We know Soliander purposely didn't come home. Eriana was trapped. Is there any reason to believe Korrin would not have come home if he could?"

"No. None at all. He would be here. Of that I am certain."

"I am hoping to see his Home Ring in case that gives us any ideas. We understand that the return spell was bound to the Home Rings and that something clearly went wrong."

She perked up. "Yes! You must see it. Something has happened to it, and we have long feared what that could mean."

Princess Cariss took his hand and led him back toward Korrin's suite, not far from hers, as the guards followed. Her touch was gentle, her hands smooth, and they reinforced the impression that she was quite the opposite of Taryn. He wondered if she had ever set foot outside the palace at all, not to mention by herself. She seemed to live in a protected environment—not on account of the guards, who were there because of him, but because she seemed oddly unworldly. Was her life all courtly gossip and unimportant issues? It didn't matter much, but he kept thinking the real world would eat her alive. Rather than finding that contemptible, he thought that she was charming in a naïve sort of way. He felt a little protective of her and wondered if that was how her brothers saw her. Were they overly protective? Was that the reason for her seemingly untarnished innocence?

They soon arrived at a pair of double doors bearing the carving of a knight on horseback charging a dragon. A lone guard stood there and let them into a large suite.

"Is the room always guarded?" Ryan asked, unsurprised that their escort continued to follow them. Only now did he realize they were protecting the princess from him more than preventing him from going anywhere. He frowned and wondered what he needed to do to convince them he wasn't the sort to attack a woman.

Princess Cariss answered, "Yes, on account of the Home Ring. Sometimes people are curious. You might think that anyone admitted to the royal palace would be on their best behavior, but the number of boors among the aristocracy is rather high. Even without a drink in them, some take a fancy to seeing Korrin himself, or his armor, or the ring."

"It was guarded before he disappeared."

"Yes. Come. Let me show you."

She explained that they had turned an adjacent room into Korrin's Quest Room, where he kept armor, weapons, and other items he might need for a quest. And, of course, his Home Ring was in there. She led him to the wide doors and pushed them open. Beyond lay a knight's armory—rows of lances and spears on one wall, various swords, maces, hammers, flails, and other weapons hanging from another. On armor racks stood several suits of armor, seemingly one of every kind: plate armor, plate mail, chain mail, leather armor, studded armor, and more. A wall of shields hung behind them. Bows, arrows, and accessories filled cases around the room, and in the center stood the Home Ring.

The circle spanned eight feet in diameter and bore similar rune carvings to each Quest Ring Ryan had seen, magic words presumably lighting when used. He wondered whether they glowed blue like Quest Rings or another color. While parquet formed the palace floor here, they had fashioned the ring of white marble with gold markings. A matching wall two feet high surrounded it and had to be stepped over to get inside. Altogether, the circle seemed simple enough in construction. What caught his eye was the long, jagged crack across the floor of it and up the wall, then around from the inside, over the top, and partway around the outside. Marble dust was visible on the floor outside the ring, and black scorch marks followed the crack. A chunk of stone had broken off and fallen inside the circle.

"I assume it wasn't always damaged like this."

She shook her head. "At first, when Korrin disappeared as he always did, we thought nothing unusual of it, but sometime later the guard out front heard a cracking sound and came inside to find this."

"It hasn't been touched since?"

"No. This was our first sign that something was wrong. Before long, when he still didn't return, we asked Princess Alia about Eriana and learned she hadn't been seen in Coreth either. Inquiries were made about Andier and Soliander, though they were more difficult to learn about. But it soon became apparent they were also gone. We have left Korrin's Home Ring untouched. What do you think it means?"

"I don't know. We were hoping to see each of the Home Rings and compare them. Maybe that will suggest something."

"Like what?"

Ryan pursed his lips. He didn't want to admit the logical conclusion—that if Korrin's and Andier's Home Rings were damaged and they were missing, and if Soliander's and Eriana's were intact and they lived, that might imply something he didn't want to say.

"We honestly don't know. Do you know the condition of the others?"

"Not Soliander's. No one can reach his. But Eriana's is damaged as well, split in two I believe. Andier's is blackened as if burnt, but not cracked. That's just one more reason we've been concerned these past years—but we've also wondered whether they were unable to return home because of the damage. We had hoped that this was the explanation, but it seemed unlikely."

"Why?"

"Soliander is powerful enough to send all of them home even without using the Quest Rings. We had wondered if he was hurt or killed. Now we know it is not true. I wish I understood why he has not returned."

"So do we." Ryan walked around the Home Ring to see it from all angles. "I have wondered what these things looks like."

She arched her eyebrows. "You don't have... Oh, I hadn't thought of that." Something seemed to occur to her. "How do you get home? The Quest Ring returns you, but to where?"

"To wherever we were before being summoned."

"Oh. That makes sense. I think." She did seem to be mulling that over, and he waited quietly. "But what if you were on a quest just completed, and another quest summoned you? You would be sent back to the last quest, would you not? You could be sent somewhere unfavorable."

He hadn't thought of that. "We don't know. We haven't had two quests back-to-back, but we *have* been sent back in circumstances that were a problem."

She frowned. "How so?"

He took a deep breath and explained about how they'd been stranded at Stonehenge after the first quest, as three weeks had passed and their transportation had been taken in the meantime. When she seemed sympathetic, he decided to tell her what happened to Anna—being returned in the middle of a highway and being struck by a car and paralyzed—all while skipping over details about what a car really was. With no healers available, Anna had remained in that condition until the next summoning spell healed her. Princess Cariss got the point anyway and was horrified, tears in her blue eyes.

"Will this happen when you leave *here*?" she asked, taking his hand in both of hers.

Feeling a pang at her distress, he shook his head. "No. No, we were asleep in a friend's home. We will be safe this time."

Barely relieved, she asked, "But what of the next time?"

He shrugged. "It could happen again. It's one reason we'd really like to know how to create our own Home Rings, as long as we're substituted for the real Champions."

She dropped his hand to take both his cheeks in hers. "You poor man! All of you! I will speak to my father about this." Then suddenly she gave him a hug that he couldn't have returned even if he thought that was wise, both his arms pinned to his sides by hers.

"Step away from her!" a voice shouted.

Ryan turned to see a glaring Prince Dari striding toward him with several more guards behind, hands on their sword hilts. He frowned and didn't move as Cariss pulled back and turned to her brother.

"Hands weren't *on* her," remarked Ryan, irritated. He didn't like this guy. Besides, he had another source of information and help. Who needed this assclown?

"Dari!" protested Cariss. "Do not speak this way to our guest."

Ignoring that, the prince scowled at Ryan. "You do not have the king's permission to be in this room, or anywhere but confined to your quarters."

"The princess invited me. Perhaps if you had not turned down my invitation to talk, you would not be so quick to find fault."

Dari frowned. But before he could speak, his sister put both hands on his chest and loudly announced, "You are embarrassing me with your boorish behavior. Step out of these rooms at once, and take your guards with you.

We were having a fine time getting acquainted until you decided to play the hero."

Ouch, thought Ryan in amusement, wondering what she was talking about. Maybe she was made of sterner stuff than he had realized. Dari looked startled, then embarrassed, and finally angry. He turned a hate-filled gaze on Ryan, who wasn't sure how to react. Part of him wanted to goad the guy, but he also suspected that wouldn't be wise. He silently stood his ground.

"You've shown him enough," the prince said. "Until we verify his story—and even after that—they are not to be treated as guests, but prisoners. Rectify this at once." Without waiting for a rebuttal, he turned and left.

Princess Cariss waited until the footsteps faded away, then turned to Ryan. She pursed her lips. "I'm afraid you have made an enemy of him, though I agreed with your response in its entirety." She smiled. "We will worry about him later. Don't concern yourself. I will talk directly with our parents to make sure he doesn't lie about what happened here today. He is known to be subjective and is unlikely to be believed if his details differ from mine."

Ryan bowed his head. "Thank you. I sincerely appreciate that. I regret what just happened and wish there was some way to be friends with him."

She smirked. "Sadly, he is not known for having friends. I suspect you can see why." Ryan decided not to reply, and she added, "Would you be so kind as to join me for dinner? I would love to learn more about you and your friends. In fact, they are invited as well. I will make some arrangements."

Ryan smiled at her. "Yes, we would love that."

She beamed at him again. "Wonderful! I look forward to it." She turned to the guards. "Please escort him back and inquire as to whether they need anything. I expect their needs to be met as if they were my own."

The guards nodded and turned to go but paused at the door to wait for Ryan. He bowed to Princess Cariss from the waist, wearing a big grin. "My lady."

"Sir Ryan," she replied, smiling fondly.

He walked away feeling lighter on his feet. She was certainly pleasant company, but the important part was that he felt certain they had at least one friend in the court. Seeing Korrin's Home Ring had also resolved a mystery, and he suddenly realized how much he disliked the ignorance that came with their situation. Information reassured him like never before. His only worry now was that the certainty that he, if not the rest of them, had an enemy in Prince Dari.

But at least Dari's enmity wouldn't come as a surprise.

Not for the first time, Anna wondered how things were going back on Earth. Their friend Jack was supposed to be working with Eriana, Ryan's brother, and Ryan's family lawyer to find and purchase an estate for them to stay in. The media and authorities were always trying to track them down, compromising their privacy. But they needed somewhere to live—and seldom, if ever, leave—so that they no longer had to worry about being returned to a highway like she had been. The real Champions had Home Rings that they were sent back to after a quest, but she and the boys did not. Staying at the estate all the time, they would never be traveling when summoned. It would be a kind of prison, but better safe than dead. It would also allow them to practice swordsmanship, archery, or even magic when Matt could tap into Earth's awakening energies.

She wondered what could free them from their current predicament. No one, including the lovely Princess Cariss, could tell them what was happening. People seemed eager to verify their story, but there was no word on how that was being done. She knew that word spread of each quest, so it seemed plausible that inquiries had been made on each of the three worlds they had visited before. But how long did this take? Whose word would their hosts accept as proof that they were innocent victims and not perpetrators who had done something to the real Ellorian Champions?

And then, just after lunch, the answer strode right into their suite. An elf with long, blond hair soundlessly appeared, his brown leather embossed with forest designs. A bearded dwarf tromped beside him in boots, clanking with each step as his armor and a hammer at his waist made a racket. Behind them waited Taryn, Princess Cariss, and the King's Guard.

Anna jumped to her feet as her friends rose. "Lorian! Rognir!"

"Aye, lass!" said the dwarf, his voice gruff but friendly. "It's good to see you still in one piece!"

The elf Lorian smiled and looked ready to bow in greeting, but Anna ran to him and gave him a big hug, noticing he still smelled like the wilderness. She disengaged to see Rognir approach Ryan and look up at the big guy.

"You didn't come to hug my knees, did you?" Ryan asked with a grin, resuming an old joke about the difference in their heights.

The dwarf bellowed, "A quick blow to the back of those wobbly knees and you'd be down where I can give you a proper greeting!"

Anna noticed that both Eric and Matt were grinning, too. If there was anyone they trusted when away from Earth, it was these two, who had shepherded them along their first quest to the Dragon Gate and taught them so much that their gratitude could never be properly expressed. And now here they were, saving them again, which became apparent with their next words.

Lorian began, "The King of Andor sent word to my king that you were here. Of course, only a few of us on Honyn know you are not the Ellorian Champions. We were asked for an account of your identities, your character, and the story you had told us. Rognir happened to be visiting, so instead of simply replying, the king sent us. We have just finished meeting with King Sarov and a few others and have shared what we know."

Taryn interrupted, "We also received messages—not about your identities, but about your handling of quests—from the other worlds you have helped. You are heroes regardless of your situation, even in spite of it."

A beaming Princess Cariss came forward. "On behalf of our families, please accept our apologies for your confinement. You are no longer to be under guard and have the free run of the palace grounds as our honored guests. We also recognize that you have not pretended to be the Ellorian Champions out of malice. You are innocent victims of the villain Everon as much as they were, maybe even more so. To this end, we are united in our desire to help you in any way we can."

An audible sigh of relief filled the room, and a celebratory mood took hold. They soon decided to spend several days on Elloria. They had no pressing business back on Earth, and this was the safest they had felt since the whole questing business began. Within an hour, each was given their own rooms for additional privacy. They were adjacent to each other and in a less-used wing of the palace. Lorian and Rognir received nearby quarters, and they cleared out a hall to use as a weapons training area and meeting room, far enough away from others not to be overheard.

Lorian and Rognir intended to stay until the Earth friends returned home, mostly to lend a hand with training. The dwarf was a priest and spent time chatting with Anna, giving her more ideas about how gods could help her when channeling power through her. She had learned on a recent quest that she could not only heal people, but also hurt and even destroy the undead. Being a weapon wasn't something she really wanted—but if it turned the tide of battle in their favor, so be it. It seemed like a long time ago that she didn't believe in gods, the atheist in her quieting as proof of divinity mounted. Her new occupation was humbling but inspiring and she still felt great curiosity about interacting with the god of Earth, whom she had finally reached right before this quest. She still had more work to do there, she knew. Eriana would help once they were reunited.

Lorian once again assisted Matt with magic training. Since no one now thought Matt was Soliander, the Majestic Magus and one of the most powerful wizards anywhere, this could be more openly pursued. Taryn was able to retrieve her brother's spellbooks and staff for him, but as a matter of secrecy, everyone agreed not to publicly use anything belonging to the real Champions. They were to admit only to their real names and origin. This meant Matt could not use Soliander's recognizable staff, nor could Ryan or Eric wear Korrin's or Andier's armor or weapons. Taryn took it upon herself to secure new items, and, for the first time, Ryan and Eric felt they had their own equipment.

That reminded that that they couldn't bring anything back to Earth with them. No one understood why this was, but it may have had something to do with not having Home Rings, and their substitution being some sort of seemingly permanent accident. So they started talking about someone traveling to Earth, which held multiple advantages. Spellbooks and needed materials could be brought for Matt. Training could take place at home. Help could also be there if Soliander or anyone else showed up to cause trouble—in fact, Taryn even suggested that her force of Dark Blades make the journey and guard this new estate. Of course, they weren't aware that men and women with guns were needed, not swords. But that raised the subject that several of them—Taryn, Lorian, and Rognir—were deeply curious about Earth and wanted to visit. But first, someone had to know how to find Earth to travel there.

"There is a spell," said Lorian, as they gathered in their new meeting space—just the four Earth friends, elf, and dwarf. "It can be used to locate worlds, but we need something from them, usually."

"Like what?" Anna asked, worried that this doomed their chances. "We can't bring anything with us on a quest, any more than we can take something back."

The elf smiled. "A drop of blood from one of you could do it."

Matt frowned. "That makes sense."

Anna remembered how squeamish Matt was about blood. The same had been needed for the magic affinity test Lorian had conducted on him back on Honyn.

The elf said, "We should first try to locate the world that way. If it works, we can try to connect a magic portal to the world. We could then travel there without the locator spell."

Eric pursed his lips. "I certainly trust you, Lorian, to come to Earth. But I do wonder about setting a precedent by opening the planet to visitors from other worlds. Would others be able to locate Earth once that happened?"

"There are other spells that would allow one to locate a planet. It is just difficult to do so without something from that planet. Someone may have already located Earth."

Matt said, "Earth was locked for a thousand years so that magic wouldn't work, but that ended when we took the Champions' place. We know that Soliander might have an interest in finding us, and he knows we're from Earth. I hadn't considered an inability to find the planet, but what if he got our DNA from something on the Honyn quest?"

"DNA?" Rognir asked, puffing on a pipe, the sweet-smelling smoke pleasant. No one seemed to know about secondhand smoke or the dangers of smoking at all.

Anna began, "Each of us has DNA in our hair, blood, and more. It can be used to identify someone because DNA is unique to each person. If Soliander had blood or hair from one of us, he could theoretically locate Earth and go there."

The elf nodded. "I think we need to try ourselves. It is all the more reason to have friends there, ones who understand your situation. I would like to research the spell and gather what we need. It shouldn't take long."

In agreement, the others watched him and Rognir go. Left alone, they discussed Eric's point. Did they have the right to bring people from other planets to Earth? What if Lorian brought a pathogen that infected people and caused widespread sickness? In fact, why hadn't they caused such sickness on the worlds they visited? But Matt had the answer from Soliander's memories. All spells that traversed worlds inoculated those using them. It was like getting a flu shot so that, even if you carried the virus, you weren't contagious. Skilled healers had helped to invent or modify world-crossing spells, and even spells for magical travel between any two points on the same planet. There had been mayhem before that.

All the same, they agreed to limit the number of people visiting Earth. Rognir could pass for a short person, but Lorian would have to hide his ears. Neither were going to fit in at first, and they would likely gawk at everything for a time. This resulted in some tension-breaking jokes about elves in space, or both of them getting addicted to afternoon soap operas. Or coffee. But the seriousness returned when the elf did.

"I have everything we need," he said, laying a spellbook on a table, then flipping it to a spread, where elven script flowed across two pages. Pictures of worlds spinning, solar systems, and shooting comets lay among the words. The elf had once cast a permanent spell on all of them to let them read, write, and speak various common languages—so Matt and Anna, the only two who looked, were able to read the words. These were in either elvish or Nu'Eiro, the language of magic.

The spell indicated that it would only show the planet in its solar system, meaning it only proved a planet could be found. Since Matt was still squeamish about blood, Eric offered his finger, giving a drop of blood to the small mirror Lorian lay on the table. Then the elf cast the spell.

In the air before them, a kaleidoscope of galaxies flashed by while the spell searched for its target. Spiral, elliptical, and irregular, they spun in different colors like a computer animation from NASA. Finally, the familiar-looking Milky Way galaxy appeared as the searching slowed to focus on one of the swirling bands—into which it dove before soaring past the outer solar system, passing recognizable planets like Neptune, Saturn, and Jupiter. Soon, the spell stopped zooming as a blue planet rotated slowly before them.

"That's Earth!" Matt said, looking fascinated.

"You are sure?" Lorian asked.

"Of course. I'd recognize it anywhere. I don't suppose we can zoom in?"

Lorian arched an eyebrow and Anna explained, "He means getting a closer look."

"No. This is only for locating the world among the planets."

She asked, "What does it take to arrive in a particular spot, if you're casting yourself there?"

"Visualizing it is the best way. If you know what a place looks like, it is easy enough to arrive there."

Matt said, "Good. That's something we can do."

"Yes, but I cannot."

Matt asked, "Well, is there a way to give you memories without, you know, using that *Mind Trust* spell on me?"

The elf nodded. "There are spells that will allow you to show someone your memories."

Ryan asked, "Is this a current view of Earth?"

"Yes. Why?"

"I was just curious. We have devices back home that can store images, and I just wondered if the spell would work in a similar way, with an old image, but probably not."

Eric asked, "Now that we've located it this way, is it also possible to communicate with someone there? Every time we leave, no one knows where we went or what's going on. We don't have Home Rings, and if we could talk to someone there, we could tell them exactly when we would be arriving so they could be there to help. Maybe Matt could learn such a spell."

"That's brilliant," said Anna. Eric always had the best ideas and thought farthest ahead.

Lorian said, "It is possible to magically communicate across worlds. Is there anyone you would like to contact? We could arrange it."

"Jack."

Matt asked, "What is needed to contact a particular person?"

The elf said, "Without a communication orb, it is helpful to have something of theirs, but not necessary if you are certain where they will be."

Matt sighed. "We know where he lives but can't be sure when he'd be there. That would matter, I assume?" The elf nodded.

"Not true," said Eric. "We know we were asleep when summoned, though we don't know what time that was. Still, we can figure out the time of day there based on the time of day here."

They agreed to try reaching Jack. But first, Matt would learn the spell and try it the next morning when they knew Jack would be in the apartment asleep. Anna looked it over with Matt and saw that the only materials needed were those easy to find in a city or town, like glass to aid seeing to another world, water to aid a connection, and a bit of someone's blood to locate the planet. The rest would depend on his visualization and concentration. He spent some time picturing Jack's apartment in as much detail as he remembered, but since he had seldom been in the bedroom, Anna drew some pictures. She had been sleeping there the night of their summoning and had a fresher memory.

With this settled—and now that they felt the palace was safe—they went their separate ways until meeting back in their wing just before dinner. Anna asked Rognir for more time to study together and he agreed. Ryan sought out Princess Cariss, who introduced him to some knights. They believed him to be an aspiring one, so they agreed to teach him about not only weapons and armor, but chivalry and expectations. Matt worked with Lorian on magic. No one had any ideas for the Silver-Tongued Rogue, so Eric found himself alone and decided to see about getting into trouble.

CHAPTER SIX

PRINCES AND TROLLS

The trick to no one knowing what you were intending was to act like you were intending something else altogether. A bit of misdirection could do wonders. To that end, Eric strolled the palace halls and inquired about everywhere other than where he intended to go, as if he was just familiarizing himself with palace life. There was some truth to this, as his curiosity coupled nicely with a sense that such knowledge might benefit him and his friends. And so he learned where the kitchens and dining halls were, and whether jails were here (they weren't). He found out where the guests' quarters were and which parts of the palace were used and how often. Galleries of artwork were scattered throughout the palace, with servants answering questions about the people in each and their importance. He saw a portrait of the Ellorian Champions, and now knew what his counterpart looked like. They could have been brothers. Statues of one hero or another helped him learn about important figures from Andor's past. He noticed that one of the largest statues was one of the Dragon Slayer, Lord Korrin. What did his brother, Prince Dari, think of this? There was no statue of *him*.

Most people in the palace were human, but he now encountered several elves, dwarves, and even halflings in his wanderings. The latter seemed the friendliest and provided a wealth of information on recent happenings, from trade issues to gossip... including the rumor that the families of the Ellorian Champions had gathered for an unknown reason. Many people were chattering about it, and the consensus was that they were trying to understand why the heroes weren't returning home. Some people believed there had been a falling-out of some kind. Others thought the Champions were too busy with quests. One rumor even suggested that Eriana had married Korrin. Or Andier. Or Soliander. And started a family. That this didn't explain anything didn't seem to matter to anyone.

After two hours of walking around, Eric finally stepped from inside the palace onto the grounds. He had been told not to leave, but he didn't consider this a departure, as the U-shaped building enclosed this garden. Here he found a few lords and ladies but more servants than anyone, as they tended the grounds. The four-story building cast much of the garden into shadow, a few small towers extending higher into the sky from the golden roof.

He sat on a bench and observed those in attendance occasionally glancing up behind him at the path to his destination. It wouldn't be a difficult climb. The challenge was timing it so that no one shot him in the back with an arrow, but he saw no archers. Still, a private word with the person he sought would last longer if no guards appeared. It was time to make an impression on someone, an impression designed to create doubts as to whether screwing with him or his friends was wise.

His bench provided cover behind some of the taller manicured hedges and, after he'd sat there for some time, it appeared that others nearby had largely forgotten him. They were also moving away on their business, whether that was gardening or exchanging gossip. The time had come, so he turned around, rose, and strode to the wall.

Clearly, the architect hadn't considered how easy it was to climb the exterior by placing various decorative stonework designs for Eric's use. Skirting the windows, it took less than thirty seconds to climb onto the fourth-floor balcony. He cast a quick glance at the garden below and felt satisfied that no one there had noticed, though someone looking through one of the many windows might have. With little to do about that, he cautiously stepped inside Prince Dari's rooms.

No one was there. This didn't surprise him—and it gave him a chance to look around, though there wasn't much to see except some maps spread on a table. He had long wondered about this planet, Elloria, since they were pretending to be people from here. The Kingdom of Andor lay on the western coast and seemed to be mostly grasslands except to the forested north, where a town called Elfton hinted at the origin of the elves he'd seen in town. Due east were several mountain ranges—the Hills of Andor, the Towering Peaks, and farther east, the Peaks of Aranor, beyond which lay the Kingdom of Aranor, on the eastern coast. Even on the map, the deserts there made it seem harsh, just like Soliander, the most famous person from Aranor.

South of the mountains lay the town of Coreth, Eriana's home. Only now did Eric fully realize that it wasn't a kingdom in its own right, just another place inside the Kingdom of Roir, whose capital lay farther south. This meant Andier and Eriana were from the same sovereign power. Knowing this would prevent him from making a mistake in conversation. He needed to hit the books again, having focused on the kingdoms of Andor and Roir so far.

He studied the map and then decided to fold up it up and take it. He likely could've gotten a copy, but stealing something trivial from the prince amused him. It would anger Dari without being important enough to throw him into prison. Besides, they were honored guests. While they weren't invulnerable to getting in trouble, such petty irritations warranted nothing, and Dari complaining would only make him seem more unreasonable and subjective. That was part of Eric's plan—to reduce the esteem in which the prince was held so that if he had planned to cause trouble for them, he wouldn't be taken seriously. But what he really wanted was to goad the prince into being an ally. And from what he'd seen and heard of the man, goading was what it would take.

Map of the Kingdoms Andor, Roir, and Aranor

He moved about the suite, seeing a desk full of letters. Some were scented in perfume and written in flowing script. He scanned a few, seeing that most were from fawning admirers, but a few were less flattering, even rebuffing him. Among the authors was a princess of Novell, the island kingdom they had arrived on. He wondered what sort of arranged marriages took place here or if they even mattered for Dari. Maybe such things were on hold until Korrin's fate was known. With Korrin alive, his wife would become queen, but with him dead, Dari's wife would be. Other letters were from other lords, whether princes, dukes, or lesser ranks. Some were nearly as fawning, others bawdy, and several quite formal in tone. They revealed Dari's habits—card games, hunting, and the opera.

The rest of the suite held little interest—there were only a few swords that appeared ceremonial and showed no signs of wear on the hilts. Only one differed in that regard, but not by much. A closet full of shoes, tunics, hose, and even a few robes made him wonder which occasions called for what attire. He didn't see a suit of armor anywhere but suspected one existed and must have been elsewhere. A brief check for hidden doors or compartments yielded nothing. Dari seemed the sort to sneak around, especially in light of those letters. How many bastards had he fathered?

After half an hour, Eric grabbed a book on trade that appeared to be well-used and settled in at the map table with a decanter of wine. He poured a glass from it, not because he intended to drink, but to put on a show of making himself comfortable. To that end, he also put his feet up on the arm of another chair and did his best to look overly familiar. Nearly an hour passed before the doors to the suite opened, heeled footsteps echoing on the stone floor. Eric hefted the wine glass to his lips and tried to act like he was being interrupted as the steps neared and Prince Dari appeared, a smirk disappearing at the sight of him.

"How did you get in here?" the prince demanded, eyes darting around the room as if looking for trouble.

Eric gestured to the window. "No guards on the balcony. You might want to fix that. It appears anyone can get to you at any time, and you'd be defenseless."

The prince frowned and came closer so that only a few steps separated them. "I'm hardly defenseless. You're the one without a weapon." He put one hand on the dagger at his waist, an embroidered tunic of blue and white above his white hose and black shoes.

Eric slid one of the prince's own daggers out from under one of the maps. "You shouldn't leave weapons lying around, either. I took the liberty of rescuing this from the floor."

Dari frowned. "I should have the guards throw you off the balcony."

"If you were man enough, you'd do it yourself. But let's stop flirting with each other and get down to business. I surmised you wouldn't agree to meet with me, so I took matters into my own hands."

Not disputing that, the prince asked, "What do you want?"

Eric decided to get to the point. Chitchatting with the prince wasn't going to get him anywhere. "I want to know if we can count on your help while we're here on Andor, or when we return to Earth."

The prince snorted. "You've managed to get this far without it."

"Yes, you aren't necessary. You might even be useless. But what concerns me is that you might be a problem—yet another thing we must overcome to succeed at a quest, to escape from this cycle of them, or even to find your brother and Andier."

Dari's eyes had registered increasing outrage. "Watch your words, imposter."

"Is that the issue? You don't like us impersonating them?"

"Of course not. It is a crime, regardless of how you escaped punishment for it. It is also wrong."

Eric didn't disagree, but wasn't going to admit it. He and the others had discussed admitting they weren't the Champions on every quest more than once, and always arrived at the same conclusion—that it was safer to pretend they were such formidable people as a way to ward off additional trouble. It didn't always work. "Do you think it wiser to admit the truth? Most who know agree that we are safer with the ruse."

"I couldn't care less if you are safe or not."

"A charming sentiment. So I am right that you do not have our best interests at heart."

"My only interest is in the whereabouts of Korrin. You would—"

Eric purposely interrupted him. "Then our interests are shared. Your best way of finding him is to help us. No one thinks *you* have the ability to locate him."

Dari frowned. "You have no idea what I am capable of."

"Enlighten me." He had long been good at seeing through an empty boast, and when the prince looked startled and changed the subject, he smirked to show he knew it.

The prince asked, "What is it that you think you can do to locate Korrin? Eriana found *you*, as did Soliander."

"And you'll notice they both sought us, not you. Your brother would do the same. We are of greater interest to him than you, for obvious reasons." He purposely tried to imply that this was personal. Dari glowered, and Eric got the impression he'd struck a nerve.

"Nothing is more important to my brother than family—especially not *you*. He likely doesn't even know you exist."

"Maybe he's forgotten that *you* exist." Eric sipped some wine and made a face as if it wasn't good enough. That wasn't hard, given that he was more of a beer drinker.

Dari's face turned purple, and he snapped, "I am a Prince of Andor! Next in line to the throne!"

Eric had wondered about whether his older sister, Princess Cariss, was next in line, but one thing he'd learned was that such things changed with every kingdom. He said, "You're not next in line as long as Korrin lives. Is that the problem? Does he stand in your way, even while missing?"

Dari glowered. "You dare say such things?"

"Only with the confirmation of his death do you become heir-apparent, is that right? As long as he's missing, you don't know. If he's dead, you face one future you can prepare for. If he shows up, you can go back to living whatever life you had before his disappearance called your future into question. I would think you, of all people, would want to help us learn what has happened to him. What is Korrin's fate? What is yours? And yet you claim not to care what comes next. Explain that to me."

"I owe you *nothing*."

"You don't. But you owe yourself some certainty. Aren't you tired of wondering? We can do everything without you. And maybe that's what you want—to stay comfortable here in your fine hose and tunic, drinking wine, dancing with ladies, playing cards, and watching the opera, while we go off into danger. And sooner or later, we'll hand you the answer to the question of your fate if we find Korrin. That's kind of weak, though, isn't it? To let us do it? How good a leader would you be as king if you can't be proactive and rise to a challenge? With that attitude, all of Andor must be praying for Korrin to be found safe. They'll still have a strong leader in him when your father is gone."

Eric decided to stop there, thinking he'd overdone it. But it had to be said. The prince's face had turned various colors, from white to red and back again.

"Listen to me," Dari began quietly, full of suppressed menace, one hand on his dagger, "do not ever call into question my desire to find my brother again. You dare spread rumors like this, and I will personally cut you in half."

More politely, Eric lied, "This is what people are already wondering. I only came to tell you so that you can prove them wrong. You can lose their faith, or you can renew it with a show of interest in finding your brother."

Dari sneered triumphantly. "No one knows who you supposedly are, so they won't care if I help you or not."

"They'll eventually know. We'll be famous once the truth gets out. And they'll find out you did nothing to help us, or even that you stood in our way. Whether Korrin is alive or not, your honor, integrity, and devotion to family will be questioned. Is that what you want?"

The prince's eyes hardened and he pursed his lips. Eric felt certain he had successfully cornered the man and it was time to go. He slowly rose, mindful of the prince's white knuckles on the dagger as he skirted him toward the door, where he stopped and looked back. The prince hadn't turned.

"I know what it is not to want this," he began, trying to sound like he commiserated. Part of him actually did—and he had long ago learned to sincerely embrace sentiments like this to get the reaction he wanted from his listeners. "I would rather stay home and live my life, but my choice has been taken from me. Yours has not. I know you can be a great asset to everyone, most of all yourself. I believe this is in you, even if no one else does. This may be the opportunity you have been waiting for—to show everyone you are a match for Korrin in bravery, honor, integrity, and more. You will face the consequences of your decision about helping us either way. The smarter play is to take command of your reputation and future rather than letting it command you. Should we need your help, I look forward to seeing you step up and do so as if it was your idea and not mine. Our little secret."

He opened the paneled doors and stepped out between two guards, who looked surprised to see him emerge instead of the prince. He nodded at them and was several steps away when the muffled sound of glass shattering came through the door amid cursing. He surmised that the decanter now lay in ruins. It was unfortunate. The wine wasn't half bad.

The next morning, Matt sat leafing through one of Soliander's two spellbooks, the one with gold lettering on its black leather surface. He had skimmed through the entire book more than once so that he knew most of what was in it, just not how to cast them. Practice was the only way to memorize them all—unless there was a spell for that, but he hadn't seen one. He seldom had time to study on the quests and could never bring the books back to Earth. The others liked to tease him that he was just being a geek, burying his nose in this book or the other all the time, but they all knew he needed to do it.

A messenger soon arrived to tell them that the Champions' siblings had invited them to breakfast, and that afterwards they would complete at least part of the quest. The dinner Princess Cariss had intended to arrange the night before hadn't happened. They escorted the four friends to a nearby private dining room used only by the royal family and their more personal guests. Soliander's sister Taryn, Eriana's brother Solun, and Korrin's brother and sister, Dari and Cariss, were the only ones present. Prince Dari glowered and his smiling sister excused his surliness, saying she had forced him to be there as a princely duty.

Dari frowned. "There are many duties of our station, dear sister, but this is not one of them."

Matt cleared his throat. "Don't take this the wrong way, but if you'd rather not join us, I see no reason you need to. With respect to Princess Cariss."

"He'll be fine," she replied, and Matt got the impression that she was forcing a smile out of awkwardness about her brother's behavior. "I almost wish Mandrellan were here to cast some sort of spell to improve your manners."

"Mandrellan?" Anna asked. "Who is he?"

"Her pet wizard," replied the prince. He recounted how Mandrellan had saved her life once, before snidely remarking, "Everyone is a hero around here."

Matt sensed that they were going to continue bickering and decided to change the subject. He looked to Taryn as he asked, "So we're only doing part of the quest today?"

Taryn nodded. "Yes. We will retrieve the dragon egg that is currently east of here and bring it to Andor for safekeeping. When you are ready to return home, we will go to the Novell Kingdom, where the Quest Ring stands, to complete the quest—giving them back the egg. You can then go home from there."

Matt had wanted to try contacting Jack now with the spell, but it would have to wait. It wasn't urgent anyway. "What happened before summoning us for this quest?"

"This is not to leave this room," Taryn began, "for reasons that will become obvious. The blue dragons of Novell are sacred to that kingdom. Dragons don't lay eggs that often, but as a group there are always some every year. The dragons allow the people of Novell to know about new eggs due to the celebrations this causes, so word always spreads. Well, someone stole one of the eggs and they want it back."

"Do we know who?"

Taryn smiled. "Yeah. It was us." She let them absorb that before continuing. "We had to think of a quest in order to summon the Champions, but we didn't really have one, so we invented one."

Eric frowned. "How does that work? It has to be a valid quest."

"There is a way to fool the Quest Rings, and this isn't something you should go around telling people."

Matt nodded. The last thing they wanted was someone summoning them for quests they couldn't even achieve. From what they knew, each Quest Ring had an oracle-like property that determined whether a quest could be done and was worth their time. A quest to open a can of peanut butter would not be deemed important enough for the Ellorian Champions. A quest to create world peace was too vague and unlikely to be successful. It had to be realistic but challenging, and to that end, those using the Quest Ring to summon them had to try resolving the situation themselves at least twice. Those attempts had to be mentioned when casting the spell that activated a Quest Ring.

"How does it work," Eric asked, "when a wizard stands at the Quest Ring and casts the summoning spell? I know you must answer some questions, but who is asking them? I know it's the Quest Ring, but is it just a voice, or is there an illusion of some kind?"

Taryn replied, "The wizard casts the spell, which awakens the oracle in the keystone. The oracle appears as an illusion of a man that looks like my brother. It asks a set of questions that must be answered. They include not only what the quest is, but also what has already been done to resolve the situation. The oracle evaluates the replies—and it can sense whether people are lying, or have bad intentions, and even whether the account they have given is true. It's quite a good oracle."

Matt noticed that she seemed proud of her brother's work inventing it. "How were you able to fool it?"

"Careful planning by King Sarov. What I'm about to tell you was his idea. He hired someone to steal the dragon egg and take it somewhere, while spreading misinformation about its location. The people of Novell tried to retrieve it but failed. So did the dragons. King Sarov then asked me and some of my men to do it, but we were unable to as well. I didn't know it then, but while I was tracking it, King Sarov knew my plan and told those who had the egg how to evade me. Until I returned, I also didn't know that he had invited Eriana's brother and Princess Alia of Coreth here."

Eric observed, "He was orchestrating something."

"Yes. He had told Kingdom Novell of my attempt, and this led Novell to suggest that we use the Quest Ring in their lands to summon the Ellorian Champions. It seemed to be their idea but, once again, King Sarov had instigated it. This meant that none of us who were present to summon you had any idea what was really going on and so we could fool the oracle into agreeing to summon you."

"Clever," remarked Matt.

"And troubling," said Eric. "I hope no others think of such a ploy."

Taryn said, "We have a better understanding of how everything works."

"So now you know where the dragon egg is," said Anna.

"Yes. It's a few hours away on dragonback, in the mountains to the east. We can be there by noon, get it from those who have been ordered to hand it over, and return."

"An easy quest," observed Ryan. "I'm almost disappointed, but not really."

"Who is coming along?"

Taryn replied, "Just the four of you, me, and three of my men."

"When do we leave?"

"The dragons will be saddled as we speak."

Talk turned to their destination, which lay with the borders of the Kingdom of Andor. The dragon egg was being held in a small village in the foothills of the Hills of Andor, which were technically mountains. The king had sent word to expect Taryn and others soon. They expected a peaceful handover.

Matt noticed that Eriana's brother Solun, who was younger than her, seldom said much, though he often looked at Anna as if he wanted to talk to her. She noticed his gaze and finally engaged him in conversation—more about his sisters more than himself, by his preference. They had known little about Eriana's life before the quests except the hints Lorian had dropped months earlier—that her rough childhood led to a spiritual awakening of tremendous power. Solun was light on details, but he said all three of them were kidnapped as children and used for slave labor. Matt got the impression that sexual abuse was involved but felt uncomfortable asking.

After years of this, Solun said, he and Eriana tried to escape, with their youngest sister Diara. But Diara was afraid of punishment and resisted. Solun sacrificed himself by fighting their pursuers so that Eriana could escape alone and return for help. His captors cut off his hand for it. Years passed before Eriana, now a powerful priestess, found Solun with help from knights. But Diara and Solun had been separated and it took longer to find and free her.

"Were the people who did this to you ever punished?" Anna asked.

Solun looked away and down, then nodded. "Yes. Soliander found them years later, after Eriana told him about it."

Matt cocked an eyebrow, wondering what the powerful wizard might have done. This time, no memories popped into his head. He was no stranger to bullying, though he'd experienced nothing of this magnitude. "What did he do to them?"

Solun glanced at him, and then smiled in satisfaction. "He never told anyone."

Matt's eyes narrowed and he tried to look encouraging. "But he told you, didn't he?"

A twinkle lit Solun's eyes. "Yes. I wanted to know. Eriana didn't. Diara did, but he wouldn't tell her. Only me."

Matt couldn't help wondering why that was. Did Solun look up to the wizard? Did they have a bond? "What was it?"

Solun pursed his smiling lips. "Just don't hurt anyone Soliander is loyal to."

Anna asked in concern, "Are they still alive?"

Solun paused. "In a manner of speaking."

Matt watched him closely, seeing a young man who enjoyed the vengeance Soliander had taken on his tormentors. What did that say about Solun? He wasn't forgiving, certainly. Could Matt blame him? Not really, not without more details. The missing hand had to be a permanent reminder of trauma, making it harder to leave behind. Had Soliander earned Solun's loyalty? It seemed like it. He glanced at Taryn, who watched Solun with an unreadable expression.

He asked Solun, "Do you think Soliander is still loyal to his old friends?"

"Absolutely. Nothing could ever change that." He paused and shook his head in admiration. "You should've seen his face when he told me what he did to them. You'd think they had hurt him instead of us."

Note to self, thought Matt. *Don't piss off Soliander.*

Eric observed, "It sounds like there is precedent for him doing, uh, wicked things."

Taryn spoke up. "My brother has always hated those who hurt others. He is a good man, which is why he's so offended by awful behavior. He is very idealistic and, in a way, unrealistic about what people are really like."

"You seem pragmatic," Eric observed.

She nodded. "I am, as are you. But Soli wants the world to be different from how it really is. He struggles to accept that it is not. I'm certain that drove him into the quests, the desire to make wrongs right again. I think it's partly why he's so infuriated by Everon betraying him. It wasn't just the physical problem of unwanted quests, but the philosophical betrayal. For all the good he had done, he was punished. I spoke with him about it a number of times, and I've never seen him so angry."

Matt could understand that, and almost wished he could just talk to Soliander without fear of being attacked by him. Taryn's words had raised a question. "We haven't actually done anything to hurt him, so this is all making me wonder whether we really need to be concerned about him coming after us."

Taryn sighed. "He has no reason to, except for information. I don't think he would actually hurt you."

Ryan smirked. "Tell that to Lorian. Soliander cast a lightning bolt at him."

Taryn smiled. "He doesn't miss unless it's on purpose."

"Really?" Anna asked in surprise. "That would be encouraging."

"And nice to know." Matt laughed. He imagined throwing his hands up in surrender if something similar happened to him. He felt like their next meeting with Soliander was destined to be violent. Maybe he should worry less. He shook his head. The guy was too intimidating. Matt doubted he would ever stop being afraid of him.

They got ready after breakfast, bearing the weapons of the Ellorian Champions, but wearing different clothes so that they wouldn't be recognized. Anna hid Eriana's Corethien Amulet under a cloak. Matt wore a tunic and trousers. He brought Soliander's spellbooks and the staff, wrapped in a blanket so they wouldn't be identified. Ryan left behind his lance, since they weren't expecting to fight dragons. He wore the silver plate mail loaned to him, and sheathed Korrin's sword in a different scabbard. Eric had done the same with Andier's short sword—but his new brown leather didn't have nearly as many places to hide throwing knives, forcing him to leave half of them behind. Still, they didn't expect to need them.

At the palace stables, they met Taryn and stowed their gear on horses. Mounting quickly, they trotted behind her on cobblestones that led into the streets of Andor. Matt smelled the chilly spring air, the horses they rode upon, the sea at the docks, and a mixture of baking bread and the acrid stenches of medieval sanitation. He was now accustomed to horseback riding. The gait of the black gelding beneath him felt natural, his hands absently controlling the reins. The clacking of hooves mixed with the sound of a hammer rhythmically hitting metal on an anvil. It echoed between buildings, wagon wheels rumbled nearby, and the voices of men, women, and a baby crying were all heard. It still seemed quiet compared to Earth cities.

While the palace lay at Andor's heart, the castle stood on a hill at the north end. Rainwater stained the light limestone, and pennants flew from its towers. The streets narrowed, their pace slowing. Matt read off the red and gold street signs nailed to houses of light stone and dark wood—Fountain Road, Blade Street, Wicker Way, and Castle Road. Elves, dwarves, and halflings in simple clothing mixed with the mostly-human population, but the market square just outside the castle walls was mostly empty when they arrived. Stalls of familiar-looking fish, fruits, meats, and breads stood on the loose straw strewn over the dirt to either side of the road.

Three of Taryn's Dark Blade warriors awaited them at the open castle gates. One was a business-like elf, more muscular than slender, black plate mail over his light skin. Matt saw dragons in the courtyard—one black, one red, and two silver. Their size never failed to intimidate. They were taller than a two-story building and wider than a dump truck, with heads bigger than a car. Their huge mouths and teeth drew Matt's eyes before their massive, taloned feet. Their tails could knock someone over with ease. Wings blotted out the sky when extended. That Matt and his friends had killed two on the Dragon Gate quest still amazed him. He knew dragons differed across worlds and even on the same one, but most dragons on Elloria could shapeshift and do magic. Two people would ride each.

"You're with me," Taryn said to Matt, to his surprise. He followed her to the black dragon, the biggest of all, and avoided taking Taryn's proffered hand to steady him. Gingerly trying not to hurt the huge beast made it more difficult. Once he started walking like it was just another thing to step on—the thought making him chuckle—he found it easier. He soon sat behind Taryn, hesitantly following her instruction to put one arm around her. She somehow seemed soft despite the black chainmail. Unlike the other dragons, this one had no saddle. Matt held onto his staff, which lay across his lap. A glance revealed Ryan and Anna together, and Eric with the elf on the red dragon. The remaining dragon carried the other two Dark Blades warriors.

They took to the sky, leathery wings snapping at the cool morning air. The sun streamed across the mountains in the distance, casting beams of gold into the valleys. He saw frost on the shadowed hillsides to the north and east and south, the blue of the ocean becoming very dark just a hundred yards from shore. He'd watched just enough nature shows to know that this meant the continental shelf dropped away quickly to deep water.

Andor was a large city of red-roofed homes, most of them two to three stories high. Towers throughout the city soared into the crisp air. Some had high bridges between, which swung in the gusty sea breeze. You would have to be crazy to walk on those spans, and yet he saw a few people doing so, clinging to the railings. He spied the streets they had ridden on before gazing out over the port where ships came and went, smaller fishing boats heading out.

As the dragon gained altitude, they flew away from the ocean and into the blinding sun. Matt wished he had sunglasses. He settled for gazing down at the cobblestone roads, which gave way to dirt farther from Andor. They followed the river northeast, nearing a lake that sparkled with reflected sunlight, the sprawling, unwalled town of Godsted on its southeastern shore.

From the map, he knew that the Hills of Andor, a low mountain range, were due east. Beyond them rose the Towering Peaks. Somewhere to his right, to the south, lay the Kingdom of Roir, Andier's home, and Eriana's hometown, Coreth.

An hour after passing Godsted, the dragons descended west of the mountains. Aside from a dirt road, Matt saw no sign of a village. The ground rushed up and their black dragon thrust out its wings to slow them. They touched down gracefully, dust and loose grass kicking up.

As the other dragons landed beside them, Matt and his friends looked around warily. He only relaxed on seeing Taryn and her men calm. He got down to the ground, where he unwrapped Soliander's staff and shoved the wrapping into his spellbook bag.

"Where's the village?" he asked.

Taryn pointed toward the foothills. "Allowyn is that way. They have a lot of livestock that the dragons would terrify, so they'll stay here. It's a half-hour walk. Bring anything you think you'll need."

She indicated that it was safe out this way because all danger lay on the other side of the village, deeper into the mountains. The mountain trolls around here had scared away everything else, but they knew better than to attack Allowyn because of the response from Andor. The result was a veritable truce, though skirmishes happened when villagers went too close to the troll caves. Taryn intended to spend a little time here and told the dragons to be back in two hours if they decided to leave.

They began the hike up a slight incline, a mix of deciduous trees and evergreens dotting the light forest. The dragons disappeared behind them as the way turned frequently around boulders and hills no wagon could get over. Grooves and gullies in the path from wagon tracks gave way to a cobblestone road in disrepair, random stones missing and sometimes a hole big enough to trap a wagon. A stone pillar had the town's name carved on it, and Matt spied an old, dilapidated low stone wall in the trees.

"Taryn," said the Dark Blade elf, holding up one hand. Everyone stopped, listened, and looked around. Matt didn't hear anything, but Taryn and Eric both pulled out their swords. The elf unslung a bow from his back and the other two Dark Blade warriors did the same.

Ryan put his hand on his hilt. "What is it?"

"Something's wrong," said Taryn, eyes up the trail. The elf took the lead, Taryn and Eric moving behind warily. Ryan, Matt, and Anna were in the middle as the two remaining Dark Blade warriors brought up the rear. They took another two dozen steps before Matt heard faint voices in the distance, in the direction of Allowyn. The voices were shouting, but the tone didn't sound panicked.

They broke into a jog, stopping from time to time to listen, but something about Taryn's demeanor suggested her wariness was dropping. At last, they finally rounded a curve in the road to see the village's oak walls and wide doors, which were open but guarded. Three men and a woman in chainmail turned at the sight of them, hands going to sword hilts and a crossbow until Taryn held up one hand and put away her sword. The others followed suit and approached the guards, who mostly relaxed.

"Ho there," said one. "What business have you here?"

"Taryn of Aranor, Commander of the Dark Blades. King Sarov sent word I would be coming."

They lowered their weapons. "He did. Too bad you didn't arrive sooner."

The group reached the gate and peered past. They didn't see much happening but heard a commotion further in. Outside the walls to one side, Matt saw numerous pens of cows, pigs, and what he thought were elk. They were restless, sometimes moving as a pack to one side of a fence and back again as a man there sought to calm them.

"What happened?" Taryn asked, scowling.

"Trolls. At the far gate. We fought them off, but not before they did a lot of damage. Killed a few people. They attacked the men King Sarov had here and made off with some case they had. It was almost like they were looking for it."

"Shit!" Taryn jogged onto the main street through town, the rest of them following behind. The buildings were one or two stories high and close together, with wooden beams for walls and thatched roofs. Except on the main road, straw-covered dirt was all that lay underfoot, a few puddles from rainstorms still drying out.

"Do we care about this case?" Eric asked, loping along beside her.

She snorted. "Yeah, unless it was empty. The dragon egg was in it."

"God da—" Eric stopped himself.

The village wasn't large and they soon passed into the market square, which looked like a triage center, people in bloody clothes here and there. Matt saw a middle-aged man crouch beside another wounded man and put one hand on his forehead, lips moving as if praying. But nothing happened to the groaning man and the apparent priest apologized. Anna saw this and went to help. By silent agreement, Matt and the others waited nearby as Taryn got the attention of a guard and had a tense conversation Matt didn't overhear. When he next looked at the man Anna was helping, he was sitting calmly and not moaning in pain.

"So glad you're here," said the priest wearily, rising as Anna did. "I'm afraid my strength is spent."

"Sure," she replied. "Who else can I help?"

"This way." He led Anna around the wounded and Taryn returned.

"We're going to need to go after them," she said.

"Who?" Ryan asked. "The trolls?"

"Yes, and the king's men. One of them was killed here. So were a few guards. The king's men took off in pursuit of the trolls and we need to follow, and quickly."

"What about the dragons?" Matt asked. "Should we go back to get their help?"

"No time. I'll send a guard to tell them. Maybe they will reach us in time. It depends on whether they stayed there or not."

"What's the rush?" Matt asked. Taking four dragons into a fight seemed quite comforting, though he didn't know how bad these trolls were.

"Trolls think dragon eggs are a delicacy and aphrodisiac. That egg isn't going to last long."

Eric and Matt exchanged a look. If they didn't return the intact egg to Novell, they were trapped on Elloria. "Right. Then let's move. Anna!"

The priestess finished healing a man and joined them and got filled in as they walked. They soon reached the western gate, which the trolls had demolished along with several nearby buildings. Matt was used to seeing dead bodies covered by sheets from on TV and in movies, but here they either lay where they had fallen or had been dragged into a row. He counted seven altogether. Three trolls lay unmoving—one at the gate, one farther inside in the ruins of a building it had crashed into as it fell, and another outside the walls with arrows in its back. They were twice as tall as Matt, with gray, mottled skin covered in sparse, black, coarse hair. Their arms seemed disproportionately long, their heads bulbous and hideous, with two tusks jutting up from fat lower lip. They wore ill-fitting shirts, vests, and trousers, all stained, ripped, and not big enough. Their bare feet were filthier than the rest of them, and Matt could smell one from ten paces.

"This is what we have to pursue?" he asked, wrinkling his nose. "How smart are they?"

"Not very," answered the elf with them. "They will be easy to track. The guards said they left two hours ago, though. They likely have entered their caves by now."

"Great," muttered Eric. "This isn't going to be so easy after all."

"Well," Taryn began to Ryan, "you said you were almost disappointed not to have a real quest. It looks like you've got one."

CHAPTER SEVEN

THE DRAGON EGG

Ryan adjusted his armor as they looked over at the entrance to the troll cave. This plate mail wasn't as nice, or quiet, as Korrin's, and he now realized he had become spoiled. It didn't fit as well, either, with some of it chafing enough to distract him despite the sight before him. He and the others stood behind trees and a boulder, the worn dirt path to the caves to one side. The large footprints were unmistakable and had been easy to follow. The trolls had done little to hide their trail. He wondered whether that was down to stupidity, confidence, or acceptance that tracking them wouldn't be hard regardless of what they did.

Three trolls stood outside the entrance, tossing rocks at pieces of wood floating down a stream of rushing water, which emerged from the mountain to the right. The wood looked like it had been part of a crate or barrel, suggesting that someone was destroying these inside the mountain. Ryan remembered hearing that the trolls had stolen a few items along with the dragon egg case. It seemed they were smashing them open inside, taking the contents, and throwing the destroyed containers in the river. The trolls outside had made a game of hitting the pieces with stones, sometimes groaning or laughing deeply at each other's performance.

The black cave beckoned behind them. It was set into a mountain face of dark stone that looked like it had once seen a landslide. Piles of rock had been moved aside and the cliff face was mostly smooth except for cracks. The path split, one fork entering the cave, the other fork continuing left into the trees and foothills surrounding them.

The dragon egg was almost certainly inside the cave network. So were any men from the village. They had found no bodies, just blood and a few pieces of torn armor or broken arrows. The evidence suggested that the men had caught up with the trolls and been defeated, then carried, dead or alive, into the troll cave. This had potentially become a rescue mission for both them and the egg, though Ryan knew where his priorities lay. When asked, Taryn admitted that trolls were not above eating people. No one knew how many men had pursued the dozen trolls, so they decided to rescue who they saw but not search the caves or they'd never make it out.

"So what do we do?" Ryan asked. "Maybe Matt can cast a spell. Don't trolls turn to stone in sunlight? I'm surprised they attacked the village during the day."

The elf responded, "That may explain the morning raid. The sun's rays were not upon the village or the path there."

Ryan looked up and then back the way they'd come. The sun was getting higher, the shadows in which they stood likely gone in an hour, and those trolls were going inside to escape it. But they didn't have an hour to wait.

As if reading his mind, Eric asked, "Can we lure them into the sun?

"Doubt it," said Taryn. "They aren't smart, but not that stupid either. Luring them down the other path might work because it'll stay in shade a lot longer. But then what? Fighting them will make noise that brings others from inside."

Anna said, "I was able to make weeds come out of the ground and pull down undead. But I'm not sure if it would work. The god I contacted then was offended by the undead existing and agreed to help."

"Are there any gods who care about dragons?" Eric asked.

"Yes!" said Taryn. "Anna, if you can reach the goddess Drakonon, there's a good chance of her intervening."

"Okay. I will try, but it might take a bit." She placed a hand on the amulet, which would help her connect with the gods of this world, especially now that she had a name.

Ryan turned to Matt, who appeared to be thinking. "Got anything? Something quiet, so we don't cause attention? Put them to sleep? Open a pit that swallows them and then closes?"

"There's always fire from the staff, but it would make them scream."

"Sudden death is better," said the elf, surprising Ryan. Elves revered life like he did. But he had to admit that a quick death was probably best if they could not be subdued.

He said, "I'd prefer a way to immobilize and silence them for however long this takes."

They soon agreed on a plan to set in motion. Ryan and Eric walked onto the path and into full view of the trolls, acting as though they were caught up in conversation and didn't realize what lay ahead until too late. The three trolls looked at them in surprise that turned to amusement. One troll could easily handle two men. They began approaching and Ryan and Eric turned away, sprinting along the path parallel to the mountain and into the trees, the mountain's shadow on them. Ryan didn't have to look back to know that the trolls were following at an awkward run, their heavy footsteps making loud thuds, tree branches cracking.

Ahead, the dirt path twisted and turned around trees and hills, the foliage thin enough to see through.

After several minutes of this, he and Eric saw behind the trolls, where the elf and Taryn flanked Matt, who ran between them. Now seemed far enough, and they turned to face their pursuers.

Ryan held up two weaponless hands as if for mercy. "Please. We don't want any trouble."

"Trouble?" one troll asked in a deep, raspy voice, leering. Or maybe it was trying to smile. Ryan couldn't tell. "We have fun now."

Ryan risked a glance past them and saw Matt standing still and concentrating. "This fun wouldn't involve eating us, would it?"

"Yes!"

Eric asked, "Did your friends carry a dragon egg into the cave? That sounds like it would taste better than us."

"Yes!" one bellowed, scowling. "No sharing! Only for the king."

"How many trolls inside get to eat dragon egg?"

"Good question," said Ryan. Eric was always wily. "Is it a hundred? A thousand?" Could the trolls even count that high? They looked confused, especially when a cloud of green gas appeared around their heads. Their eyes bulged as they grabbed at their throats, coughing as they struggled to breathe. Ryan backed up, sensing that the brutes were going to collapse—which they did moments later, the ground shaking with the thuds. Everyone waited a minute in case they moved again. Beyond Matt, Taryn, and the elf, Ryan saw Anna and the other two warriors, who joined them.

"No one should find their bodies any time soon," said Taryn, heading back.

They pulled out swords and reached the dark cave entrance, which was ten feet wide and twice as tall. They listened carefully before entering. Only dim torches lit the way. Stepping around loose or jutting rocks required constant vigilance. The last thing Ryan wanted was to fall with a loud, echoing clatter. The cave floor rose around a few corners before ending in a larger cave. Ahead of them lay a gorge twenty feet across and forty feet down to the stream Ryan had seen. A drawbridge of thick tree trunks lashed together spanned the distance but was raised, and the mechanism to lower it was on the far side, where a troll sat napping. Beyond it, a tunnel awaited.

Ryan turned to Eric. "Think you can get over there somehow? You're the rock climbing, parkour guy. We should knock the troll into the water so no one finds it."

Eric examined the rough, jagged walls while the elf prepared his bow and Matt got a spell ready as backups. Eric found a viable path and descended toward a stone outcropping that extended over the water. Then he unwound the rope from around his waist, making a wide loop. Across the water, at the top of the other side, was a stalagmite. It took three tries, but he got the loop around it, tightened the slack, and wrapped the rope around one arm. Then he gently swung over the river to strike the far side feet first, but he had rotated slightly, his side striking the wall, too. This made an audible sound and he bounced out a few feet. The troll stirred but didn't awake as Eric reached the wall again, steadying himself. He got a secure position and nodded up at them with a grimace. Using the rope, he climbed to the top, peeked over the edge at the nearby troll, and clambered up.

Ryan let out a breath. "Now what? It seems unsportsmanlike to kill a sleeping troll."

Matt replied, "You should've thought of that before. Better than a woken troll killing Eric."

"I guess I can't argue with that."

As they watched, Eric slowly drew his sword and approached the troll. He hesitated, then examined its rickety chair next to the drop-off. He seemed to be considering how to knock the troll down the gorge instead of killing it. He began doing sign language to Matt, whose mother was deaf. At Eric's request long ago, Matt had taught him the skill, which sometimes came in handy. Ryan and Anna were supposed to be learning it but hadn't gotten far.

"Eric wants us to be ready in case this doesn't work," said Matt.

Taryn frowned. "It's just a troll. He should kill it and be done with it."

Matt shrugged and didn't relay that to Eric, who had found a loose rock he could easily swing. He practiced a few times before finally slamming it into the front chair leg, the one closest to the gorge. It cracked but didn't snap until a second blow hit just as the troll stirred awake groggily. The chair wobbled. Eric ran away from the edge, turned, and charged the troll, who was struggling not to fall as the chair began to collapse in the desired direction. Eric jumped and kicked forward with both feet, striking the troll in the waist. It lunged for him even as it began to go over the edge, one giant hand catching his foot. Anna gasped, but then a bowstring snap split the air and an arrow pierced the troll's forearm so that it let go. With a cry of surprise and anger, it tumbled over the side with the chair, striking the wall once before plunging into the stream with a loud splash.

Ryan wondered how deep the water was and got his answer when an unconscious troll floated to the top, blood on its head, one arm twisted at an odd angle. But the stream was deep enough to carry it away. He thought it might have been dead anyway, but he saw it move just before it disappeared around a bend.

With a look of relief, Eric grabbed the winch and began lowering the six-foot-wide drawbridge, which squeaked uncomfortably and struck the other side with a hard thud. Everyone held still, listening for footsteps or voices, but they heard nothing. Then they crossed the bridge and joined Eric. Only one troll could cross this bridge at a time, but two careful humans—or those fleeing for their lives—might do it together.

"Just kill it next time," said Taryn to Eric. "There are likely hundreds in this place, so being nice could mean your death. And maybe mine."

Eric sighed. "Fair enough."

Ryan had always been the one who didn't want to hurt anyone or take a life, after accidentally paralyzing his brother. It had taken their entire first quest and several brushes with death or serious injury to snap him out of it. Eric had always been the one with the almost ruthless attitude. Had something changed? Or had it been killing a sleeping troll that gave him pause?

They crept farther into the cave and the next tunnel, going only twenty steps before they reached a crossing route in a widened area. This time they heard a commotion of loud voices—perhaps cheering?—in the distance straight ahead. With no sounds right or left, they continued on to a similar but larger intersection, with the noises once again louder before them. To the right and left were stairs. This time Ryan wanted to check one side out— so he and one warrior went to the left, while Eric and another went right. All returned within a minute.

"What did you find?" Eric asked.

Ryan replied, "Just a bathing pool with that stream running past it to a little waterfall. No one there. You?"

"Dining area, kind of big, mostly empty. Four trolls, stuffing their faces. There were other tunnels. I wonder if the egg is in a kitchen in that direction."

Taryn was looking the way they had been going, deeper into the mountain. "My gut tells me the commotion we're hearing has something to do with the egg, and the men who were captured. We may find both there."

"And a lot of trolls," said Ryan.

Taryn looked at Matt. "You're sure you don't know spells that can hide us in some way?"

Matt made a face. "I know a fog spell, but it won't make sense in here. I assume they would get suspicious."

She nodded. "Yeah, but if it's thick enough it could help us anyway. Maybe get it ready? And anything we can use to slow them down, get them disorganized and confused."

Matt nodded and got out a spellbook, flipping through it.

Eric suggested, "What if you cast the fog spell and the poison gas one? The gas can only kill a few, I'm guessing, but the fog spell you did once before spread really far. What if they think the fog is what killed some of them? They would try to stay away from it, not realizing it wouldn't hurt them. It could cause a panic."

Taryn said what Ryan was thinking. "That's genius. But also dangerous. Panicking trolls could crush us in a stampede."

"And they might destroy the egg by accident," observed Anna.

"And I can't cast two spells at once," said Matt.

Eric nodded. "Right, but when you cast the fog spell before, you got it started and then gave the vial to someone else. They kept blowing over the top of it to spread the fog. Do it first, give it to someone else, and then do the gas spell."

Matt said, "Yeah that could work, but we still need to know where the egg is first, and it would be better to make the panicking trolls go away from it."

"Drakonon, the dragon goddess I've reached, might be able to help me spread the spell," said Anna.

Eric said, "Time for me to sneak up there and see what I see. All agreed?"

They exchanged looks without dissent. Taryn accompanied him into the tunnel, which soon turned so they were out of sight. Ryan felt nervous. All it would take was for one troll to see them, but maybe they were distracted by whatever celebration was going on. Quiet footsteps announced Eric and Taryn's return sooner than he expected.

"What did you see?" he asked.

"A big cave," said Eric, "with at least a hundred trolls. Most have their backs to us, facing the troll king. He's on a platform with a few others. They've got several men from the village tied up or hanging from a pole. Some looked dead already. Others were being beaten, and the trolls were cheering. Four trolls ripped apart one guy as we watched."

Ryan swore, feeling sick at the thought. "The egg? Did you see it? We have to get the hell out of here before they catch us."

"No way they catch us," Matt said, and Ryan saw his knuckles white around the staff, his face uncharacteristically cold, eyes hard. "I'll fry them all if they try."

"We did see the egg," said Taryn. "It's on the platform with the king. It's still in its case, which is open. If the case was closed, we could risk the fog and poison gas idea."

Eric said, "Yeah, but did you see the other tunnels? Two of them were near him. I'm wondering if that dining area we saw has a tunnel that connects to one. We could get up there and do the spell near the front. The panic would go in the other direction, away from the egg and toward where we are right now."

"Yeah," said Ryan, "but how do we get the hell out of here after we have it?"

"The water," Eric answered. "If they panic and run down this way, we could follow, then make it to that pool you saw. I think if we jump in there, it will carry us all the way out. We might have to fight our way to the pool some, and Matt could do some other spells, or get fire out of that staff. I think we can make it."

"First I need a vial of water from that pool to do the fog spell," said Matt, searching for it in his possessions. "I have the vial. Just need to fill it."

"I'll do it," said Eric. "I want to see the pool and the waterfall."

Matt gave him the vial and together, Eric and Ryan went to check it out. The pool cave had filthy discarded clothes in various places, many wet. Giant goblets and empty plates lay haphazardly about. The remnants of food, most of it still on a bone, were also here. One thing was certain—the trolls were slobs. A barrel had been smashed, and Ryan had the impression that this was the source of some of the wood he'd seen floating in the stream outside. The pool seemed natural, and to one side of it all lay the rushing stream and then a waterfall. Having a surer step, Eric went closer, peering down to assess the likelihood of being hurt when going over it.

"I think we'd be okay."

"You *think*?"

Eric smiled and put away his sword. "I'm more worried about you sinking in that armor."

Ryan hadn't thought of that. "Yeah, some of us might need a buddy to help us stay afloat. It doesn't look that deep."

"We'll figure it out."

Eric filled and stoppered the vial before they rejoined the others. Then they crept toward the dining area Ryan had seen earlier. It was fifty feet wide and had several tunnels leading away. The trolls only seemed to have one construction style—logs or branches lashed together with vines or rope. Each of the tables and benches were made this way, with abandoned plates and goblets suggesting that something had interrupted the trolls. Maybe they had been called to the celebration, which could be heard from two different tunnels. No pattern existed for the placement of furniture. Of the trolls Ryan had seen here before, only two were left, their backs turned as they loudly talked of their resentment that the king and his favorites would get to eat the dragon egg.

"What do we do?" Ryan whispered.

Taryn looked at the elf, who got another arrow ready. So did her other two Dark Blade warriors. Eric pulled a couple of throwing knives from beneath his clothes.

To Ryan, Taryn said, "Let's try to sneak up behind them. If they hear us, we move aside and the arrows fly. Then we close in. Quickly."

Ryan nodded and they stepped from the tunnel into the room. Korrin's armor would have been quieter, but the trolls were making enough noise not to hear them. The real danger was that one would turn its head and see an approaching threat from the corner of its eye. He couldn't tell if the haphazard layout helped or hindered their attempt to stay directly behind their target. They had to move left around one table, and which put them too close to the peripheral vision of one troll—so they went right around the next, but had the same problem with the other. Ryan glanced back and saw that the archers had entered the room and moved to one side a bit for a clearer shot around him and Taryn. Eric had crouched below the top of tables and was using them as cover to get nearer from another side. Another fifteen feet to go.

Suddenly one of the trolls turned its head too much and caught sight of Ryan, its eyes widening. They grew wider still at the sound of bowstrings. Two arrows struck its head, another thudded into its throat. It reached up with one arm as if to pull at them, but Eric's knife hit it in the neck and it fell forward onto the table.

The other troll was already turning to rise, but Ryan and Taryn were on it before it could do anything but raise its arms defensively. Sword blows sliced into it several times before first Taryn and then Ryan plunged their swords into its chest. It opened its mouth, blood spewing out, and Ryan thought it would yell to draw attention. Taryn was faster than he was, yanking her blade out and slicing across its throat to kill it. The troll fell back on the bench and then rolled to the floor, knocking the table aside with a clatter. She stabbed the other one to be certain and everyone regrouped at the bodies, listening intently.

"Nice work," said Eric, getting his knife back and wiping it on the dead troll's shirt. "I can hear the celebration through this other tunnel, so let's check it out."

The group quickly surveyed the other tunnels to make sure no one would come up behind them. It appeared that either the egg, or more likely the torturing of the prisoners, had practically cleared out the place. Eric and Taryn set off in the lead again. They followed the tunnel a short way around several turns. This revealed one fork they didn't take before a last turn just yards from where it ended, the voices very loud.

Ryan got his first look at their destination, but he mostly saw a natural pillar eight feet wide standing two steps into the cavern. The few trolls he could see were facing to his right, but he barely saw any at all due to the obstruction, which hid them from view as well. Not until they stepped out would they be seen. He wanted to get past Taryn and Eric to see better but sensed they wouldn't let him out of caution. Both were carefully peering out for longer than Ryan wanted. What if someone saw the bodies they'd left behind?

He heard a deep voice speaking a language he didn't understand. Lorian had once cast a spell on them so they could understand elven, dwarven, magic, and a few other languages, but troll hadn't been one of them. The tone was celebratory, boasting, and cajoling, sometimes causing laughter, a jeer, or a cheer. Then a human shout and a scream of pain split the air. A roar of approval followed.

Finally, Taryn and Eric came back.

"Get ready," said Eric to everyone. He fingered two of his throwing knives. "Matt, time to start that fog spell."

"What's the layout?" asked Ryan.

"We're near the front, but not all the way. When we do the spells, most of the trolls will go left toward where we were before."

"And the rest?"

"Probably toward the egg to the right, where the Troll King and the prisoners are. I think we might have to fight our way to it. Anna, see if you can help spread the fog back toward the tunnel we were in before, even down it. We want the trolls to stay away from the room with the waterfall, or we'll be fighting our way to that, too. If the fog is thick enough, maybe we can sneak through it."

"I'm not sure about this plan," Anna admitted, looking nervous, "but I think I can do that."

With the risk of being caught rising by the minute, Matt held the vial of cold water to his mouth and whispered the magic words.

"Obscure all sound and light,
A haze that blinds like night."

Then he blew across the top of it. Fog began to form and pour over his hand to the floor. He gestured outward with the other arm, and it began to flow toward the trolls. Ryan took the vial from him and continued blowing over it and gesturing—this time upward to create a wall of fog, rather than a creeping carpet. He didn't anyone to see them when they looked over at it. A glance at Anna showed her concentrating, one hand on the golden amulet around her neck. How would he know when and if she succeeded in gaining godly help? But it soon became clear, for the fog thickened at once and began to push away from them at the speed of a foot a second.

"Matt," said Eric, who had stepped into the fog, "Do the poison spell when I give the cue. Come up here."

Ryan could no longer see what was happening beyond the tunnel exit, because his friends blocked the way. But even they were barely visible through the fog despite being five feet from him. This might actually work.

A muted commotion sounded from the trolls, but it sounded like surprise, not fear. Ryan didn't hear Matt cast the poison gas spell, but he could tell when it happened. The voices turned concerned. Then bellows began, so many that even with the fog dampening the sound, the panic impossible to miss. A rumble of many footsteps lasted only a few seconds before shouting replaced it. A bellow sounded from some distance behind them, and Ryan turned in alarm.

"The bodies," said the elf.

"Right. I think we're about to have company," replied Matt. It seemed like Anna was capably handling the fog spell in one direction—so Ryan turned around and blew across the vial, sending fog back toward the dining area, gesturing wildly to speed it up. At the least, any approaching trolls wouldn't immediately see them.

Taryn said, "Let's move."

Ryan wondered what to do with the vial. Then one of the Dark Blade warriors took it and jogged back into the tunnel, returning without it moments later.

The fog toward the dragon egg was so thick that Ryan took Anna's hand and led her forward, coming up behind Taryn and Eric. They were moving past the pillar with Matt, to the right. In that direction, the fog was thinner and revealed a handful of trolls. One wore a big, fur-lined cloak and carried a jeweled mace—the Troll King. He saw them and hollered, pointing.

"Down!" shouted the elf behind him. Everyone ducked—until arrows whistled overhead and Taryn yelled to attack. Chaos erupted.

Eric threw two knives before yanking his sword out as Ryan passed him. Taryn had taken the first troll. As a fist swung at her, she stepped back and cut into it with her sword. Ryan went past her for the Troll King, who swung a mace prematurely. It whooshed by. There would be no blocking that, and a blow would incapacitate him. He stabbed the king in the thigh and yanked the sword back out. Then a roar of heat over his head made him duck, a spout of flames from Matt's staff catching the king's cloak and setting it on fire. The flames otherwise missed him on their way to the trolls beyond him. They screamed, the smell of burning flesh making Ryan gag. The king yanked at the burning cloak as Ryan sliced across his leg again. Suddenly the elf was next to him, the Troll King's mace swinging at them. They stepped back and it missed. Then the Troll King yelled something.

The elf cursed. "He's telling them the fog isn't deadly or we wouldn't be in it."

"Shit," Ryan said, not sure the others heard that. "Guys, we're getting company!"

He heard a sickening crunch behind him. And then a body land hard in the fog, flung by contact with something. He risked a glance and saw Eric and Taryn still fighting. It must have been one of the Dark Blades. A human voice he didn't recognize screamed in pain from within the fog before suddenly being cut off. The footsteps and voices were getting nearer. But Matt turned to face them and spoke a word.

"Kunia!"

The sound of bodies falling made Ryan wonder what Matt had done.

The king nearly hit Ryan but missed. He stood on wobbly legs covered in bloody gashes. Beyond him, the fog had cleared from the burning trolls, who had fallen dead. The captured men were spread on three racks, grievous wounds on their naked bodies. One man had his head caved in. Another had been torn in half. The remaining one had a mangled arm and wasn't moving. Beneath them on the platform were two other crumpled bodies.

The Troll King lunged and hit Ryan in the chest with the mace, knocking him to his back, his chest in agony, his breathing painful. But the motion made the king lose balance and stumble on his weak legs. He was going to land right on top of Ryan, crushing him.

"Kunia!" Matt yelled, thrusting with one hand, and the Troll King's body flew five feet away to land with a thud. The elf was instantly on him, stabbing him through the chest and neck until his body stopped moving.

"Ryan!" said Anna, appearing above him as he lay on his back. She laid both hands on him. "Please, heal this man so we may save this dragon egg."

A soft glow spread over her hands and suddenly Ryan could breathe. He rose as Taryn finished off the other troll, who had been down on one knee. Eric was already moving onto the platform with everyone else following. The sounds of cautious footsteps grew louder in the fog, which had begun to thin, hulking shapes lurking and nearing.

"Where's the egg?" Ryan asked, not turning his back on the fog to look.

"Got it," said Eric. Ryan heard a case closing and buckles snapping.

"Can you heal him?" Taryn asked, voice strained. Ryan didn't turn to see who she meant.

"You're hurt," answered Anna.

"I'll live. He's nearly dead. Are you strong enough?"

"Let me try."

Ryan backed up with Matt, glancing over to see Anna healing the remaining hostage, whose wounds closed quite a bit, though he still didn't look good. "How do we get out of here now?" he asked.

Matt looked at the tunnel. "Back the way we came. Quickly. It's the only way."

He was right. Ryan helped Anna, who seemed fatigued, as Taryn and the elf quickly cut down the prisoner and dragged him along. Eric and the remaining Dark Blade warrior held the black dragon egg case between them. The box was two feet long and a foot wide, eighteen inches high, but one person could handle it if needed. Ryan frowned. No one was able to fight, because their hands were full.

They entered the tunnel, where the fog from the discarded vial was only two feet high. To his surprise, the trolls from the dining weren't here. Hadn't they heard all the commotion? But maybe they had gone the other way to see what the panic was about. He and Matt were in the lead and went past the fork in the tunnel, around two corners. The trolls were coming and saw them, shouting. Even if Matt burned them, getting over the corpses would be difficult. They weren't making it to that stream again, so they took the only option—the other fork.

The group hurried into the other tunnel, ascending, the climb steeper and more arduous but only a minute long. They reached another cave, where two female trolls in tattered clothes were chatting—one topless, with misshapen breasts that he wished he'd never seen. Their features were more delicate than those of the males, but they were still hideous. Ryan tried to look menacing but saw from their startled, wary faces that they weren't going to try anything. There were two ways out of this tunnel. The sound of trolls getting nearer below added urgency.

"We need to find the stream if we can," said Eric.

Matt shook his head. "It might've worked before, but there's a good chance there's no way into it now."

Taryn eyed the female trolls and observed, "We have two hostages if we want."

Ryan turned to the elf. "You speak troll. Ask them how to get out of here or we kill them." The elf cocked an eyebrow but did it, got an answer that was obviously defiant from its tone, and turned back, frowning.

"It's that one," Ryan said, pointing at a tunnel. "She glanced at it when you asked."

"Good enough," said Eric, and he made the other guy carry the chest so he could take the lead.

This tunnel opened into a large cavern, where light shone in from an opening far above them. Hundreds of trolls were here. Some stood around a fire roasting an animal. Others sat on a giant rock drinking and laughing. Children who were as tall as Ryan ran around after each other. More tunnels branched off in different directions, with no way to tell which led outside. The group stood frozen, shouts behind meaning they were trapped. A troll in the cavern shrieked at them and scores came at a run, most brandishing weapons.

Eric pointed to one side, where the cavern wall jutted out twenty feet and would protect them from some directions. They took up position and put down the dragon egg case and wounded prisoner, Anna staying near him and the archers getting bows ready.

"Fire at will," said Taryn, and the archers let fly at a target the elf called out. Better for them all to hit the same one and possibly kill it than just to wound three of them.

"What do we do?" Ryan asked. There were too many.

"My shield," said Matt, and he gripped the staff with both hands. Moments later, a white light shone from the crystal atop his staff. A translucent barrier with a soft white glow to it cascaded down around them with a radius of twenty feet.

Taryn observed, "That'll buy us some time."

A running troll threw a rock that bounced off the barrier and Matt winced. "Not much. Remember, every blow weakens me. Time to say a prayer."

"That gives me an idea," said Anna, and Ryan turned to see her touching the Corethian Amulet around her neck and closing her eyes. He exchanged a look with Eric, wondering if his friend had any ideas, but saw only an uncommon look of worry in place of calculating intelligence. They were going to die in this troll cave. And judging by what had been done to the prisoners, it was going to be horrific.

Was it okay to kill themselves to avoid it? The God of Earth forbade it. Would Ryan even get to heaven from this planet? Did it matter where he died? He hadn't thought of that before. Watching the hostile trolls reaching the barrier and beginning to swing at it, he questioned the mercy of killing each of his friends rather than letting them be tortured and killed. He had gotten past his fear of hurting anyone, but this was "next level" moral agony.

The trolls from the tunnel they'd exited arrived, looking furious. One bellowed at the others, pointing fingers and clearly announcing something. Ryan looked at the elf for translation, but the archer was busy aiming an arrow he let fly, striking the speaker in the head and killing him. Then he turned to the others.

"He was telling them we killed the king, but I stopped him."

CHAPTER EIGHT

A Lady of Fear

Eric looked around in desperation and saw movement by the ceiling opening. Something big was outside. It had two wings that flapped once before being pulled close. It plunged toward the hole and passed through. The wings snapped outward, and Eric recognized a descending black dragon. A red dragon came through, then a silver and another red. The trolls scattered for the tunnels, trampling each other. One of the red dragons sprayed a spout of fire at them but missed. Taryn's black dragon landed and morphed into a tall man with dark skin and blue eyes, clad in black leather. The others remained in dragon form as he strode over to them. The trolls continued running.

"How'd you find us?" Taryn asked, as Matt dropped the shield.

"I told them," said Anna, dropping her hand from the amulet. "Well, I told the goddess where we were. I asked her to guide them here."

"I could kiss you right now," Ryan said, laughing. "You just saved all of us. I'm surprised we didn't take more damage."

"I healed myself once with the Trinity Ring," revealed Eric, putting his sword away and grabbing the egg case. "Let's get out of here. I see you aren't wearing saddles."

The dragon nodded. "We did not have time to retrieve them, but our magic can hold you on until then."

"Then let's go," said Eric.

Everyone mounted up. The black dragon, still in human form, lifted the wounded, naked prisoner with ease and laid him atop one of the other dragons before climbing down. Eric was no stranger to male nudity but felt relieved when the remaining Dark Blade warrior, rather than himself, had to sit with the guy. With a jump, one by one, each dragon lifted off and flew straight up with powerful thrusts. Eric's dragon used the cavern ceiling to grab onto and pull itself through the opening, which was small enough to make flying out more difficult than dropping down and in.

Then they were up in the sky, cloudiness having overtaken the sun. This wasn't Eric's first time Eric on a dragon without a saddle, and he once again found that his legs were held firmly in place by the dragon's magic. A glance at the others showed that they looked worried. He laughed a little, letting the tension fade. They had narrowly escaped alive. He tried to ignore the likelihood of their luck or ingenuity running out eventually. But he felt that they were getting better at this.

Hours later—after retrieving the saddles—the group landed in Andor, changed clothes, and ate a late lunch. This was the safest Eric had felt on a quest. It was almost too bad that they had to go home soon, probably the next day, with no chance to practice the skills they needed. He hadn't done badly with his sword this time, but then he hadn't been facing someone with a similar weapon, just two giant fists. He'd only needed to dodge those, then thrust into the troll's thighs and calves. The Dark Blade warrior who was flung back into the fog and killed could have easily been himself. His martial arts skills had once again helped him to survive a sword fight.

They had secured the dragon egg in a vault under the king's protection. Eric and his friends had looked at it. It was hard, leathery, and uniformly oblong, unlike bird eggs back home. A slight blue hue to it was the only indication of the color of the dragon inside. No one was certain how old it was, but it was not expected to hatch. That was almost too bad. They'd never seen a baby dragon.

The others seemed more fatigued than he, and they retired to their rooms one by one, leaving him alone with Taryn. He liked Soliander's sister for her pragmatic attitude, command, and take-no-shit demeanor. She handled herself well and was a welcome addition to any mission, not that they would have another with her. He knew Matt was attracted to her and tried to put in a good word for his buddy, who needed to get laid. Then again, so did Eric. Their situation made dating impossible, though being a conquering hero who got the girl was still a possibility. But while Taryn had his attention, he wasn't one to fool around with a girl who a friend of his might have been interested in. This was true even if Matt had less than a day to make a move, which he wasn't good at doing, partly from lack of trying. But Eric felt there was a decent chance of seeing Taryn again, just like Lorian. With that in mind, Eric cut short the drinking he was doing with her because he got the impression that she was getting frisky.

As Eric reached his wing of the palace, he stepped past the two guards at the double doors and went in. He looked forward to some time to unwind alone. On every quest, they were almost always together. Even when separate, they spent time with other people, never truly being alone. He didn't mind, really. With the danger so often around them, being alone meant more danger. For once, he felt at peace with their setting. He reached his rooms and pushed open the double doors, shoving them closed without looking around.

Someone grabbed him from behind and put a knife to his throat, so close to his jugular that he didn't dare move. A sweet perfume seemed familiar and told him it was a woman, the body that pressed into his back soft despite what felt like leather up against him. Whoever it was didn't stand as tall as him.

A sultry alto voice said, "It's nice to see you again, Andier of Roir."

He tried not to react to the name, since no one here thought that was his identity. Did this person know his real name, too? The voice sounded familiar. "Who are you?"

"I'm sad you don't remember. We fought so passionately together, and then sweetly held hands as we walked."

Ignoring the sarcasm, he thought hard, realizing that the only person he'd held hands with anytime in the past few months was... *Oh shit.* "Kori of Nysuun."

Mockingly, she said, "You *do* remember me!"

This was bad. She was a ruthless assassin who had ably fought him by hand and foot, which reminded him of something. "I remember that you had one less hand the last time I saw you with the other Lords of Fear. You seem to have grown it back."

"Aeron was nice enough to heal me. I'm sure Eriana would do the same for you. Now, enough chatter. I want you to move toward the bed and face me. You know what I put on my blades, so you need to cooperate."

"A fighter of your skill doesn't need poison."

"And the best part is that I know you mean it." She nudged him and he moved to where she indicated, halfway between her and the bed, three strides separating them. When he turned to face her, he saw her in the familiar black leather, sensual and yet poised for violence. The last time he'd seen her, she'd sported red hair, but now it was golden blonde with a streak of red, like the colors of Andor. And her hand had indeed grown back. All he could think was that the other lords might be here capturing his friends.

"Are your friends with you?"

"Do you see them?"

"Don't be coy."

"Will you relax if I tell you no?"

He paused. "Yes."

She smirked, her dimples making her lovelier. "You're a poor liar. Your friends are safer than you."

"Very reassuring."

She looked at him almost fondly. "I enjoyed our little fight on Rovell, except it was too brief."

Did she really come here for banter? He wondered whether she was stalling while something else happened to his friends. He knew better than to try something with her. They would have to be on their own for now.

Eric asked, "Why are you here? What do you want?"

"Information. But first I need to make sure you won't try to hurt me." She smiled.

"You're the one with a poison knife in your hand."

"And you usually have knives all over you. And you're fast with them. You may not be wearing the leather, but I assume you're still armed. So take off your clothes."

Eric cocked an eyebrow. "This isn't a ploy to get me nude?"

A mischievous twinkle appeared in her eyes. "I didn't say that. Now strip before I cut your clothes from you. Don't be modest. You don't seem the type."

Eric sighed and began removing his shoes, then tunic, and then undershirt. He met her gaze and she nodded, so he stripped off his leggings to stand nude.

"Satisfied?" he asked with a smirk.

She eyed him. "Very. It's nice to see a nude man who is still well-armed."

"Maybe you should undress as well. That way I won't have to worry about your knives or anything else you have. We can be equals, like when we last fought."

She smiled mischievously. "Interesting idea. I heard another one—that you and your friends are not the real Ellorian Champions. Perhaps that explains your poor swordplay."

Great. So much for keeping that a secret. Who else knows? "I don't suppose we can trouble you not to tell anyone."

She put away the dagger and unbuttoned her leather top. "Maybe if you tell me what I want to know, I'll keep your secrets."

"And what do you want to know?"

Kori opened her top to expose her torso, dropped the leather behind her, and then started on her pants. Eric felt himself stirring and didn't bother to hide it. It had been a while, regretfully. He wasn't sure having sex with this assassin was a good idea, but stripping her of poisoned knives couldn't hurt.

Her boots came off, and then she slipped out of the pants to stand as bare as him. She quietly padded across the floor to him, stopping within inches, eyes playful. He saw that his body wasn't the only one reacting to this.

Kori said, "Now we can have a proper interrogation."

Voice husky, he replied, "I'm kind of not in the mood to answer questions."

"Good, because I'm not in the mood to ask them."

She took both his hands in hers and slowly lifted them to her breasts, then reached down for his manhood, biting her lip. He leaned forward as if to kiss her, then hesitated, still unsure about this. Were her lips poisoned for a kiss of death? Slowly, she put her hands on his chest and shoved him backward onto the bed, then gently climbed on top of him to straddle his waist. He touched her breast and felt her shudder. Her lips went to his neck. He finally decided this was the best way he was likely to die on one of these quests and let himself do what he wanted...

Several hours and trysts later, he leaned on one elbow as she lay beside him on her back, arms above her head. He traced a scar on her side, getting a better look at the dragon tattoo she bore.

Eric asked, "So, did you come all this way for this?"

She held his gaze. "Yes." He flushed but didn't look away. "I don't have to tell you it was worth it."

"No, you don't," he admitted, leaning down to kiss her shoulder. "What now? Was this part of torturing me for information?"

"No. It was part of enjoying you."

The suspicious part of him wondered if she was flattering him to make him think she liked him, but he didn't really think so. Their lovemaking had been especially surprising in one particular way—the constant staring into each other's eyes, even when passion brought them to their most unguarded moments. Either she was a good actress—and he had no doubt she was—or some sort of honest connection had been formed. She did like him, was even fond of him, and had smiled shyly more than once, her body flushing. And for that reason he flushed, too, at her words. Now the question was what, if anything, had changed between them. Where did they go from here? But to get that answer, he wanted to know where she came from before now.

"Tell me about yourself," he suggested, lying close. "Where did you learn to fight?"

She stretched luxuriously. "I'll tell you one thing for each thing you tell me."

"I asked you first."

"Okay. Eric." She smiled at his visible surprise that she knew his real name—but then maybe he should have expected it, given that everyone here used it. "The Blackened Brotherhood taught me to fight. Hands, feet, knives, the sword."

He wondered what that organization did, but instead asked, "Did they teach you to poison, too?"

"Yes. Now, where did you learn to fight?"

The answer wasn't as interesting as hers. "There are schools that teach different kinds of fighting with hands and feet. Nothing fancy, and nothing about knives and swords."

"You seem like a beginner with a sword, but your knife throwing, where did you learn it?"

"Where I grew up, we have something called a Renaissance Festival, where people put on a show of skills with contests like knife throwing. My talent was noticed when I attended, so someone invited me to be a performer and helped me improve."

"You did not learn it to kill."

"No, but you did?"

"Killing was the goal." She said this matter-of-factly.

"Anyone in particular?" He hoped for a good reason and that she wasn't just interested in murdering people for amusement.

"Yes, everyone who destroyed my life. They murdered the woman I loved." She looked him in the eye. "And now they're all dead."

He watched her, sensing that she had told the truth. Her bisexuality came with no hint of embarrassment like it might have back home, and he accepted it without judgment. Showing no disapproval, he remarked, "That is fierce justice and loyalty."

She ran her hand through his hair. "I am loyal to those who deserve it. Maybe one day that will include you. Are you loyal to your friends, Anna, Matt, and Ryan?"

"Very. How do you know our names?" She could have heard them from the conversations here at the palace, but he hadn't seen her here and wanted to be sure.

"My master has spies in many places, including now on Earth. A fascinating world, from what I've heard. I am eager to visit and learn more."

He tried not to react to this. How did her master get to Earth? And who was he? The man had clearly been of evil intent before, and the last thing he wanted was the Lords of Fear showing up back home. "Maybe I can tell you what you need to know and spare you a trip."

She pressed against him. "You don't want the pleasure of me in your own bed?"

He smirked. "I didn't say that. Who was this woman you loved? Why was she murdered?"

She pursed her lips. "Love between women, or between men, is forbidden in Nysuun—even for a princess like her."

"And were you a princess?" He really needed to study how kingdoms and titles worked to understand who had what sort of power in the places they visited. A crash course was in order once they got home.

"I was a countess. We were young, and never touched each other, but our love was plain, and they condemned us to death. On two pyres facing each other, so we could watch the other die, they tied us naked and standing. Then they lit the fires."

"But you escaped."

She nodded. "A boy who loved me was among those who tied my bonds. He had purposely done so poorly so that they were loose, and I escaped through the flames. A guard nearly stopped me before the boy struck him and I got away. But they threw him onto the pyre in my place and he died for my freedom."

Eric watched her carefully and saw the look of someone remembering, her eyes not on him. Such barbarism rarely happened in the United States, and was never sanctioned by the state; even the death sentence was carried out humanely. It was the sort of evil story heard about third-world countries. He noticed she seemed angry about the boy's death. That spoke well of her.

"How did you go from fugitive countess to assassin through this brotherhood?"

"I stole what I could to survive and made my way to my family's estate. They gave me what they could. They were good people, and would not punish me for my love, but others were not so kind. I fled as the king's guards were arriving. I learned later that a stable boy told the guards of my family's aid to me. They burned our home to the ground with my family inside, as a warning to others about my forbidden love and about aiding enemies of the king, who had burned his own teenage daughter to death."

Eric had felt her body stiffen and move restlessly with anger and turmoil, as if she could not lay still while revealing what he again sensed was the truth. "Why are you willing to tell me these things?"

She looked him in the eye again. "My history is no secret, and I would rather you hear it from me. And because you asked."

Was it really that simple? She seemed more complicated than that. But then maybe she just missed a human connection. Or everyone was too afraid to talk to her. She was certainly intimidating, but there was a vulnerability to her that made her exciting. He wondered how lonely her life was now, serving some master who sent her and the other Lords of Fear to destroy people. Did no one show interest in her like he was doing? Or were they only men she didn't consider worthy for whatever reason? A foolish guard. A court dandy. A man who couldn't keep up with her mind or physical skills like he could. Had he truly attracted her attention? But maybe he was kidding himself and she was just using him as a means to some end he didn't know. He had to admit, he liked her. And only a fool wouldn't respect her.

"You found this brotherhood, or they found you?"

"Both. They learned that I was looking for them and who I was. They claimed they also wanted the King of Nysuun killed for their own reasons, and didn't much care who else I eliminated. Like all in their service, I had to be magically bound—so that I could not leave them—before they would accept and train me. I foolishly let them bind me, having lost everything already. I was willing to lose my freedom for the chance at vengeance."

Thinking that was savage and desperate, he asked, "How long before you got it?"

"Years. Years of training, years of denials, years of lying. They never wanted the king killed. I learned that they had tricked others into the brotherhood with false promises, those who had nothing left but hate. We were powerless due to the binding."

"And yet you escaped this, too. How?"

She smiled without humor. "The one I work for now. He found me and revealed that he could undo the spell binding me to the brotherhood. He asked only that I sometimes work for him, but promised that I would otherwise be free."

"And so you had your revenge at last."

"Yes, and on the brotherhood, too. I killed them first—all but the others bound like me, and who my master also freed. I then returned to Nysuun and killed that stable boy who betrayed my family, and the guard who threw the boy who loved me on the fire, and finally my king and all his evil brood."

He watched her quietly, noting the spark of excitement that had appeared while she talked of revenge. She was fierce, passionate, and deadly. And he admired her.

"What does your master have you do?"

She shrugged and ran a finger down his cheek. "That I cannot tell, but it is only the evil who have something to fear."

He doubted that but stayed silent about it. "So you have a life without love and friends now?"

"A woman in my position makes few connections that matter. You interested me, especially after I learned you were only pretending to be Andier, and so I came. I will enjoy what's left of my humanity in these brief moments, between all the things I must do." She caressed his cheek with what seemed like genuine fondness.

"You seem to have plenty of humanity left."

"Maybe. But what good is it? For forming connections? All those who love me die."

Is that what she really thought? "It doesn't have to be that way. You can live a less dangerous life."

"Perhaps I prefer not to create the opportunity again. I lost years of my life to love and hate and almost lost it all."

"Aren't you still losing years of your life to it, in service to some wizard?"

"I do not serve him out of love or hate."

"Loyalty?"

She considered. "Yes."

"And now you have no life at all but in service to another."

"I did not say that. I come when he calls. I am otherwise free to do as I please. Now, enough about me, Eric of Gaithersburg."

He stiffened again. They had not told anyone on Andor the city where they lived, only the state. And her master was on Earth. Were people back home in danger? They needed to attempt contacting Jack now. He tried to still the alarm she had awoken.

She pushed him onto his back and climbed atop him, playfully pinning his arms above his head with hers and kissing him. "I know who is out here," she said, touching his cheek, "but I want to know who is in here." She placed her hand on his heart, and then his temple. "Who are you?" She sat up and pulled his hands atop her thighs, her hands over them.

He took a deep breath. "I appreciate how forthcoming you've been."

"But you're not going to do the same?"

"I have concerns that you and your, uh, friends, and your master, are a real threat to me and mine."

"I already know you are Eric Foster of Gaithersburg. And Anna Sumner, Matt Sorenson, and Ryan LaRue all live there. Or nearby. There is nothing you can say about where you live that we don't already know."

There was no question that they were all moving the minute they got back. Concern for their families had him wondering what to say to get them to leave town and never return. It was something to think about later.

When he said nothing, she said, "I'm sorry if that bothers you. I did not mean it to. We are not trying to kill you. It's true that my master isn't exactly pleased with what you did to the Orb of Dominion, but it's better anyway."

He cocked an eyebrow. "You don't care that we broke it?"

"Oh, I care. I am not a fan of enslavement. My master has his reasons, which he did not share, but that just makes it harder to agree with him. The orbs are evil for what they can do. Part of me is glad that you broke one and that I was still able to fulfill my oath to do what he wants."

He decided not to admit that it could be put back together and that only he, Matt, and the dragon Jolian knew where the pieces of the slave orb were. The wizard Kori worked for had the master orb, which allowed him to perpetually control anyone who looked into the slave orb, until the sphere broke and released everyone's minds. "And your friends? Lord Voth wants Matt dead. I think Garian does, too."

"Yes, both of them would be happy to kill Matt—or worse—for the injuries he caused. They have no sense of humor."

He smiled, then began to laugh. Matt had burned the undead knight Lord Voth to a crisp, melting away whatever flesh was still on him so that only a skeleton remained. He turned serious. "Do the others know where we live?"

"No. My master doesn't tell them as much as me. In this case, it is because he knows they want revenge—and my master has ordered us not to harm you. But angry men do dumb things."

He smirked. "*Now* you tell me you are ordered not to harm me. What does he want with us?"

"He seeks the real Champions. I don't know why, so don't ask me, but he knows you aren't them. I'm assuming he knows what they look like and was surprised at the sight of you in Ortham through the orbs."

"You didn't know before then?"

"I did not."

"Do the other lords know, too?"

"I don't believe so." Kori shifted atop him. "Now, I've answered more of your questions. Time to answer mine. How did you come to replace the Ellorian Champions?"

He wasn't sure what to admit and who wanted to know this—her, her master, or both, which seemed likely. Maybe if they found out, they would leave them alone. "We don't know. It wasn't on purpose. We don't have a choice."

Kori's eyebrows rose. "What do you mean? You do not choose to come on quests? Or you did not choose to replace them?"

"Both. One day we were summoned to another world and welcomed as them. We had no idea what was going on, or who they were. We don't know how it happened and there's nothing we can do about it. We get summoned without warning and we have to finish the quest or we can never return to our world. We've been pretending to be the Champions because everyone thinks we are. Except here, of course."

Kori gazed at him intently—judging, he knew—and long moments passed before she spoke. "Did they do this to you? Make you take their place?"

He shook his head. "It seems to be an accident of some kind. And our impression is that things don't work quite like they did for them."

"What do you mean? Give me an example."

He wondered what to say that wouldn't cause a problem. "We can't take anything back with us. The real Champions could, but not us."

She looked intrigued. "So if you tried to take the Orb of Dominion to Earth, you wouldn't have had it anymore when you arrived."

"Right." From the thoughtful expression she wore, he could tell she believed him.

"What happens to the item? Does it stay where you were before you returned to Earth?"

"We don't know. We've never been back to a world that summoned us to ask if anything was left behind when we disappeared. For all we know, the item comes with us but..." He shrugged, not sure what would make sense to her. "Maybe it's stuck between worlds or something."

"That would be one way of hiding something so no one could get it."

He hadn't thought of that. "Including us. So don't give me a gift you might value, or you'll never see it again after I go home."

She smiled and scrutinized him again, pursing her lips. "You are trapped as I once was. And yet you don't seem angry."

He nodded slowly, considering how he felt about all of this. He seldom had time to think about it. "I think our circumstances are not at all similar aside from that, so maybe that's why. Mine is an accident, not someone trying to kill me because of who I love. I understand why you wanted revenge. Are you still angry?"

She sighed. "No."

And yet there was something. "Bitter?"

She looked down. "Empty."

Eric squeezed her thighs with both hands. He had the impression she was lonely and far more vulnerable than he would have guessed, though that could just make her more dangerous. "Do you trust anyone?"

"No," she said at once.

"Not even the other Lords of Fear?" Was the necromancer, Aeron, summoning undead in the palace even now? Was the wizard Garian after Soliander's items or Matt? The undead knight Lord Voth could be after Matt right now, too.

Kori frowned. "Especially not them. They have a bond."

"How so?"

"Aeron freed Voth, with my master's help. And Aeron and Garian enjoy the dark side of wizardry together. And they are all boys, of course."

"And their master favors you."

Her startled gaze suggested she hadn't thought of that. Rather than deny it, she squeezed his hands and sighed. "I would like to see you freed one day. Until then, you have my sympathies."

"And after?"

"Maybe I'll come visit for a tryst." She shook her hips and he felt himself stirring again.

Holding her gaze, he said, "You won't leave again if you do."

To his surprise, she blushed but didn't look away, showing a boldness he found sexy. "I knew there was something about you I had to investigate. You haven't disappointed."

"Your master didn't send you?"

"I didn't say that." She leaned over, giving him a long, deep kiss before pulling away and climbing off. He suddenly felt cold and sat up as she slid off the bed, sighing on the way to get her clothes. "Unfortunately, I must be going. But I do have a few last questions."

"Am I going to see you again?"

She slipped her pants on. "Maybe. What about the Champions? Do you know where they are? Soliander is the most important."

"We don't know where he is, but we think he attacked us on our first quest." He didn't see any reason not to admit they didn't know much about the real Champions. He reluctantly got up and walked to the foot of the bed beside his pile of clothes.

She cocked an eyebrow. "So he *is* alive. Why did he attack you?"

"We don't know. It happened fast and then he left. Wasn't feeling chatty."

"He wasn't known for conversation. What about Andier?"

"No sign of him."

"Korrin?"

"Same."

She finished dressing silently—and somehow looked sexier in the outfit now that he'd seen her without it. She turned and headed for the exit, pulling a knife into one hand. Kori looked at him and smiled, then tossed him the weapon, which he let hit the floor just in case the blade nicked him. "I know you can't take it with you, but something to remember me by."

He leaned over and picked it up. "I couldn't possibly need something for a reminder."

She appraised him. "You are a worthy replacement for the Silver-Tongued Rogue."

He noticed that she hadn't asked about one of the Champions. "You haven't asked about Eriana."

She paused at the door, eyeing him one last time. "I know she was with you on Earth, but when you return to Jack Riley's apartment, you won't find her there."

The comment startled him. No one had mentioned Jack to anyone, not even to their hosts. "Why is that?"

"My master took her."

CHAPTER NINE

OTHER WORLDS

Having finished using it to commune with more gods on Elloria, Anna once again wrapped Eriana's Corethian Amulet in a soft cloth. She was in the guarded meeting hall where the boys also practiced combat. They could only use the Champions' items here or in a closed room.

Everyone but Eric had now emerged from a brief rest. Earlier, she and Rognir had talked about how to contact aloof gods, or those who didn't agree with her personal outlook. He knew less than Eriana, whom Anna vowed to speak with once back on Earth.

She turned away from the Amulet's cabinet to see Matt still at a table. His nosed was buried in two different spellbooks as he sat beside Lorian, who was looking through one of Soliander's. Matt still memorized as much as he was able to. All of them had memorized a few spells for him, too, writing them down on Earth. They also needed to do more to gather materials back home, but it had been less of a priority with magic only starting to awaken. Hopefully, Matt would be able to cast something at home soon.

She went to sit near them and watched Ryan swing a hammer at Rognir's direction. The dwarf was more of an expert at this than the elf. Ryan had already finished swordsmanship practice with Lorian earlier. He was getting better. The training he had for playing a knight at the Renaissance Festival helped, but those mock battles didn't compare to the real fights against warriors with years of training and experience. Sometimes it was a wonder the four of them were still alive. Since swords were less useful against undead, Ryan was learning some basics with the hammer, mace, and flail. He was athletic and seemed to make good progress, though she saw that he looked frustrated. He was pushing himself all the time with good reason, but maybe he needed to cut himself some slack.

They had filled in both Lorian and Rognir on the details they had learned about the Champions and Eriana—including that Soliander's apprentice, Everon, had betrayed them and made the quests involuntary. And that Eriana was on Earth and doing fine. Both the elf and the dwarf could be trusted to keep secrets. They had proven their loyalty and friendship.

She'd been wondering where Eric was, but now he strode into the room, adjusting his tunic as if putting it back on. His hair looked mussed, and he seemed either agitated or excited. Anna wasn't sure which until Eric called Ryan over to the table as he paced beside it.

"What's wrong?" she asked, sitting up straighter.

"We have a problem," he announced under his breath, coming close enough that Anna caught the scent of perfume. She leaned closer and inhaled, then pulled back, asking a question she felt certain she knew the answer to.

"Why do you smell like a woman?"

He flushed and that confirmed it. "You don't want to know."

A sweaty Ryan reached the table with a non-sweaty Rognir and poured himself a goblet of water. "What's up?" he asked, breathing hard.

Eric said, "Listen! Kori of Nysuun, one of the Lords of Fear, is here."

Anna's eyes widened. "What? Wait a minute. Is *that* who you just had sex with?"

He looked at her in annoyance. "Is that really the part you want to hear about?"

"Yes," said an enthusiastic Matt. "Well, mostly. Was, uh, the Garian guy there? Not in the mood to fight him again. Or Lord Voth."

"She said none of the others are here—but that's not something to just believe."

"Did you really have sex with her?" Ryan asked, with less judgement than Anna. When Eric looked unsure how to answer, he joked, "Asking for a friend."

"Enough kidding," said Anna, thinking they weren't taking this seriously. "What happened?"

Eric sighed. "She came to get information about me. Us. She knows we aren't the Champions, what our real names are, and what city we live in on Earth. So does the wizard she works for—and he's looking for not only us but the Champions."

Amid the looks of alarm, Matt asked, "I don't suppose she admitted who he is?"

"No. But there's something more important. She said the guy kidnapped Eriana from Jack's apartment after we came here."

Suddenly they were all talking at once until Anna finally quieted them. "We need to contact Jack now. Matt, are you ready to do that spell?"

He nodded. "Yes. But let's work this through first. Why would Kori just tell us that? Seems odd."

Eric shook his head. "I don't know."

"You didn't ask?"

"She left right after."

Anna frowned at him. "Why didn't you go after her? You should have captured her." *And not had sex with her*, she irritably thought.

He opened his mouth, then shut it.

"What?"

He pursed his lips. "I wasn't wearing anything."

Anna huffed in irritation. "Well, with the way you never cover yourself, running around the palace buck naked after Kori shouldn't have deterred you."

Rognir gave a short laugh and slapped Eric's back.

"Do you think it's a trap?" Ryan asked, refilling his goblet. "Maybe she wants us to try rescuing Eriana."

Eric admitted, "Yeah, it could be. But we don't know who she works for, so I don't see how we could even attempt to get to Eriana. We have no idea where she could be. It doesn't seem like a trap to me."

Lorian asked, "Why else would she admit it? What were you talking about before she said it?"

Eric gave them a brief recap and added, "I think she was just telling me the truth. It didn't seem planned."

"Maybe she's wilier than you think," suggested Anna, frustrated. What Eric was doing having sex with one of their enemies, who'd once tried to kill them, was beyond her. He'd always been the smart one, but here he was acting like the dumbest. She was trying hard not to scold him; she wasn't the sort to do it normally, but these were unusual times. Their lives depended on good judgment, and his had been the best before now. Maybe that was why she suddenly felt so threatened and vulnerable. She counted on him. How was she supposed to trust him after this?

Ryan said, "I think we need to gather as much info on them as we can. We heard that there are rumors about who they work for. That could give us an idea where Eriana is."

Eric appeared to be thinking hard as he said, "The other question is who could possibly know about Eriana being on Earth, or about Jack's apartment, well enough to do this—or even get there from another world? The only people who knew about that are in this room."

Matt shook his head, face serious. "Only one person comes to mind—Soliander. He could've learned about Jack from the spell he did on me. We didn't know about Eriana then, but we thought he might come after us. What if he did—and he found out he could look for us in Jack's apartment—and then he found Eriana there?"

Ryan looked puzzled. "But that would mean that... oh shit. The Lords of Fear work for Soliander."

There were groans of realization. Then Eric observed, "That would mean Soliander has the master Orb of Dominion. His voice was the one we heard through it in Ortham."

Matt's eyes were wide, but Ryan spoke first. "Do you remember when Garian reached for Matt's copy of Soliander's staff, and the voice snapped at him not to touch it?"

"It's him," said Matt, eyes far away. "I remember now. I can see all these images. I remember him talking with Kori when she was still with that brotherhood, and after he freed her from it. I see Aranor, the throne room, and Lord Voth as the king encased in ice until Aeron and Soliander freed him. Voth is King of Aranor, but his allegiance is to Soliander, who is really in charge of the kingdom. I can see Soliander teaching Garian wizardry. Garian is his apprentice. They are all afraid of him but respect him and are loyal."

Lorian swore in elven, startling Anna. "We must keep this a secret, but we need to tell those who must know."

Rognir said, "We should prove it first. The lad's memories may not be enough to convince anyone outside this room."

Ryan looked at Matt in annoyance. "I wish you would remember stuff sooner."

"I can't, man. It's just like when someone reminds you of something and you go, 'Oh shit! I remember!' There's nothing I can do. But I can see it. Now that I have these memories, I can think about them to uncover more."

Anna said, "So if Soliander is the guy controlling the Lords of Fear, that might be why he wanted us captured instead of killed. He wanted information from us."

"Right," said Eric, "and Kori admitted that the Lords of Fear didn't know we weren't the real Champions at the time. They acted like they didn't know—and Kori claimed that she's the only one of the four who knows now. Also, she doesn't seem to know her master is Soliander, from the way she talked about it. She said they're looking for Soliander, too."

Lorian observed, "That might be useful, knowing something about her master that she does not."

Anna asked, "Why is Kori the only one of the four Lords of Fear who knows?"

Eric replied, "She appears to be Soliander's favorite."

Matt nodded, then blushed. "Yes. He cares about her, but he's not in love with her. They are having sex." After a moment, he asked Eric ruefully, "Did you get a good look at the tattoo?"

Eric's eyes widened, and then he looked embarrassed.

Ryan smirked at him, "Soooo, you're sharing a lover with Soliander."

"Let's change the subject."

"Okay. We'll talk about that later."

"No, we won't."

Anna felt slightly amused despite the situation—but like many women, she refused to show anything but disapproval. "If we hadn't defeated the Lords, he would've enslaved our minds and been able to learn everything he wanted... if the slave Orb of Dominion had actually worked on us."

"Why did it not?" Lorian asked.

Matt said, "I had cast the *Mind Shield* spell to prevent it. Then we captured the slave orb, chased the lords through the gate to another world, and destroyed the orb. We hid the pieces so it can't reform itself."

Anna said, "I think we need to talk to our hosts immediately."

Eric shook his head. "Let's confirm it first, then figure out what to say. We don't want then to overreact."

"Agreed."

"We need to think about the timing of our spell to contact Jack," said Matt, flipping through the spellbook before him. "We don't know exactly what time it was on Earth when we were summoned to Elloria, but it seemed like maybe 9 AM here. Does anyone recall the last hour they saw a clock?"

They thought for a moment and Ryan said, "Before midnight."

The others nodded.

"Okay," Eric began, "so a nine-hour difference, I think. We forgot to ask how many minutes and hours there are in a day here, but it seems pretty close to Earth. And now it's around 6 PM here, I think, so that means it would be around 3 PM on Earth. I'm not sure how likely it is that Jack would be home."

"He doesn't have a job anymore," said Ryan, "since I'm now paying him to work for us full-time, so he might be."

Eric said, "Right, but it's the middle of the day and he will not be sitting around waiting for us. He's probably doing things out of his apartment."

"Is it worth a shot?" Anna asked. "How hard is the spell, Matt? Lorian?"

The elf considered. "It is not difficult to cast, but it does take significant energy from the user. If we try now and fail, Matt may not be recovered in a few hours to try again. I could do it instead, however."

"I think it's worth a try," said Matt. "Give me a few minutes of quiet and we'll do it and see what happens."

The others agreed and moved away to talk amongst themselves. Anna bit her lip, wanting to say something to Eric, but he saw her frown and looked chagrined, an uncommon sight. Maybe she didn't need to say anything at all. He likely knew what she was thinking. Had Kori seduced him in some way? Was that a goal? Had Eric been compromised? That was almost more suspicious than her deciding to reveal her master had Eriana. There had to be some ploy going on here. Anna normally wasn't suspicious, but these were uncommon times.

Matt indicated that he was ready and they stayed back as he cast the spell, Lorian looking on. The wizard reluctantly nicked himself with a knife to get a drop of blood, which he squeezed onto a small piece of glass. He then dropped it into a goblet of water, speaking magic words they all understood.

"Hear my words across the stars,
Our minds are one, near or far."

A shimmering curtain of air hung before them, about the size of a large TV but square. Jack's apartment could easily be identified from the vantage point of the front door. The couch stood to one side, an end table next to it, another in front, and a TV hung on the wall across the room. Horizontal beams of sunlight slanted through the blinds across the tan carpet, suggesting that it was late afternoon. They couldn't see a clock or any sign of movement. An open laptop sat on one table, but the screen was dark and a pad and pencil lay beside it. There didn't seem to be anyone there, even after Eric yelled Jack's name a few times.

"He would be able to hear us, I assume?"

"As if you were standing there," confirmed Lorian.

"He could see us, too?"

"Yes."

Eric yelled a few more times before Anna asked, "Can we make this view move at all?"

The elf cocked an eyebrow. "You mean as if we stood there and turned our head, or walked further into the room? No. Interesting concept, however."

"How long can the spell last?" Ryan asked.

Lorian shrugged. "It depends on the strength of the caster. This sort of spell can be draining, given the distances involved. I would suggest we stop after a few minutes and try again later, or else we run the risk of being too fatigued to do it again."

Anna sighed, disappointed. But he was right. They gave it another five minutes before ending the spell. They would try again in the morning here, when it was night there. They would use Jack's bedroom next time. Despite not seeing Jack, she felt encouraged that Matt had succeeded with this spell. He was getting stronger, more confident and more controlled. Now, anytime they were on a quest, they could still communicate with people back home. It took a moment for that to sink in, the others sharing her growing enthusiasm and discussing how they might benefit, such as contacting Lorian when they needed him. They remembered his estate from their visit, so they briefly discussed a room Matt could always use as a place to contact someone. Lorian pledged to always have a servant within hearing range of it. For the first time, Anna felt like they were getting more control over their situation.

That night, they resolved to stay together until bedtime, which would be early so they could wake in time to reach Jack in the morning. They decided to tell their hosts what they had learned regardless of how that went, agreeing to let Eric decide what to reveal. Anna was no longer so trusting of his judgment. He hadn't lied to them, at least, telling them straightaway—well, after he finished having sex with her—about Kori. The revelation that Soliander controlled the lords, and had even created them as a team, raised concerns about Kori's motives. Maybe this was a trap after all. It hadn't taken them long to realize he was her master.

But this raised an important question—did Soliander know that Matt had some of his memories? Because that was how they had figured out Soliander controlled the lords. If he didn't know Matt had his memories, it was less likely this was a trap. If he did, it was almost certainly a trap to get them to rescue Eriana. Regardless, they would assume the worst. Anna sighed, tired of the uncertainty.

In the morning, the four Earth friends, elf, and dwarf once again convened in the meeting room, the doors closed. After consulting with Lorian, Matt said he felt ready to do the spell again—and did so. This time, the window across galaxies showed blackness, but the glow of a white digital clock read 2 AM and cast soft light over Jack's bedroom. Under the sheets lay a lone figure, one bare leg sticking out.

"Hopefully, he's not naked," said Ryan, breaking the suspense.

Matt said, "Yeah, there should be a kind of etiquette to this. It's like a Peeping Tom spell."

Anna frowned. "Just what the world needs."

"Jack!" yelled Eric. But the figure in bed didn't move. He yelled again and it gave a groan of displeasure. "Come on, Jack. Wake up. It's Eric and the others. You aren't dreaming. We need your help."

Clearly groggy, the familiar but hard-to-see figure of Jack sat up and looked around, the sheets falling to his bare waist. His head whipped in their direction. "What the hell?"

"Hey," said Eric, "try not to freak out. Matt learned a new spell so we can talk to you from where we are."

"Damn. Wow. Okay. Um, shit, what time is it?"

Eric said, "Sorry, but because of the way the spell works, we had to do this when we were pretty sure you'd be there. We can see you, so don't get up if you're not decent."

The shirtless Jack pulled the sheets around his waist more. "Yeah. Yeah, I can see you guys, too. You look like you're at RenFest or something. No armor and all?"

"We don't have time to explain right now."

"Sure, but who is that with you? Is that a dwarf?"

"Yeah, and the elf, Lorian. Listen—"

"Wait. Are you guys back on Honyn?"

"No. Look, I know you have questions—but the spell only lasts so long, and it makes Matt weaker."

"Yeah, sorry. What do you need?"

"Is Eriana still there? Not at the apartment, but—"

Jack sat up more, then flipped a light on the nightstand, his lean torso and facial features more defined. His short brown hair was sticking up. "No, man. You're not gonna believe this. Soliander showed up here and took her." This prompted several groans of resignation, and Jack cocked his head. "Did you guys already know that?"

Anna said, "Sort of. One of the Lords of Fear, Kori, told us—but she didn't say who'd done it, and she can't be trusted anyway. That's actually why we're contacting you. What exactly happened?"

Jack answered, "They talked for like five minutes before he grabbed her, muttered some magic word, and they both vanished. It was definitely him."

"Shit," said Ryan. "We thought he might show up."

"When was this?" Eric asked.

"The morning after you were gone."

"We would've been there if it wasn't for this quest," said Ryan.

"Are you okay?" Anna asked.

"Oh yeah, I'm fine. He didn't know I was here or listening until the end, and he clearly didn't care as he left with her."

Anna asked, "Did Soliander know she was there?"

"No. He was looking for you guys. I can't figure out how he knew to come here. Freaked me out a little. Haven't seen any sign of him since. They were both surprised to see each other. She hugged him. He saw that she'd aged twenty years and learned why. He felt bad about it. Guys, he feels guilty about the betrayal by Everon, his apprentice, the guy you said trapped all four of them in the cycle of quests."

"Yeah," Matt said. "Everon altered the summoning spell inside the Quest Ring keystones, which he made without Soliander being aware of it. That's what made the quests involuntary and binding. He also created a ton of Quest Rings on a lot of planets. We don't even know how many."

"To be fair," started Eric, "I don't blame Soliander for wanting revenge."

"There's something else," said Jack. "When he was here, he admitted to living under a new name—Zoran the Devastator. Does that mean anything to you guys?"

Lorian breathed sharply through his nose. He stood up and began pacing. "No. No, this can't be. How can he be Zoran? The things that man has done." He closed his eyes, shaking his head.

"What is it?" Anna asked.

"It makes sense. Awful sense."

Rognir puffed at his pipe. "It does explain a few things. I think we will have to talk about this after we're done with Jack here, but if this is true, then we all have reason to fear Soliander. He is wicked."

Eric said, "Okay, let's table that. But Lorian, do you know where Zoran lives? What planet? Continent? City maybe? Where might he have taken Eriana?"

The elf started to answer, but Anna noticed Matt's eyes widen despite his gaze being far away. She motioned for Lorian to be quiet and they all watched Matt in silence. Finally, he turned to them and smiled, a gleam in his eye.

"I know where he would take her. Oh, and he's got her sister, Diara, imprisoned there."

Eric's eyes narrowed. "Didn't she betray Eriana with Everon somehow?"

Matt nodded. "Yes. She helped Everon trap them in the quest cycle by getting hair and other stuff from each of them for Everon to use in the altered spells. Soliander kidnapped Diara for information about Everon. And bait. Everon is thought to love her." He grunted. "Huh, they have three children."

Anna arched an eyebrow. "Are the children with Soliander, too?"

"No."

Anna asked, "Why do you think he took her? Jack, did he say anything? Did she go with him or did he actually force her?"

"Oh, he forced her," said Jack. "She was struggling. He apologized but said he couldn't leave her behind again, not after years of trying to find her. Also, guys, I really got the impression that they were in love with each other. That reminds me. He said he thought he had killed her and the others. So I think he's been a pretty angry guy, guilt-ridden, and ruthless."

Matt was nodding, eyes faraway as if remembering. "Yes. All true. He doesn't have much to live for, in his view. Or he didn't. I wonder how the discovery that she is alive will change him."

"Couldn't have changed him much," said Ryan, "since he kidnapped her."

"Shit," said Eric. "Eriana was supposed to be handling the funding of the estate, too. Minor problem, but we have to do something about this."

Anna touched his arm. "Like what? What are we going to do?"

Eric looked at her. "Rescue Eriana."

CHAPTER TEN

BRIARDALE

S econd guessing himself wasn't one of Jack's habits, but life wasn't normal anymore. He was in over his head. Knowing his friends were in far deeper tempered any desire to complain—but figuring out how to buy an estate for them wasn't going well. With Eriana gone, there was no one else to do it. He couldn't even get a real estate agent to show him one. The first time he'd walked into an agent's office, the man had laughed and asked how he would afford it. He still flushed at the memory. The guy had been a dick to scorn a customer, but he'd known Jack didn't have the means to buy it, so it wasn't like doing so would cost him a client.

Except it would.

After Soliander kidnapped Eriana in front of him, Jack got a hotel room, afraid the wizard would show up again or kill him from a distance. Was that even possible? Everything he supposedly knew about wizardry came from games, books, and movies. He'd been back to his apartment since the incident and had finally became comfortable enough to spend the night. And wouldn't you know, a magic window had opened up while he was sleeping— the exact sort of scenario he'd been most afraid of. Eric had at least been smart enough to immediately say who it was, or Jack might've shit himself and run naked out the door. The thought made him laugh. Maybe he needed to start wearing clothes in bed. These days, you never knew what the hell was going to happen. Better not to get caught with your pants down—or off.

Ryan's brother Daniel had not been pleased about the real estate agent's attitude because he would've gotten the same treatment despite being rich. This was partly due to being in their twenties and trying to buy a multimillion dollar estate. They were the same age and didn't dress that different. Jack was relatively normal, with his close-cropped brown hair and penchant for khakis and a polo shirt when doing formal stuff, like the job he'd quit as a

Starbucks manager to work full-time trying to arrange life on Earth for Eric, Ryan, Matt, and Anna now. The pay was good. Officially, he worked for Ryan, but he really worked for all of them, even Daniel, who had tattoos on his arm, long black hair, and a penchant for t-shirts of heavy metal bands. Being in a wheelchair hadn't curbed his life much.

They grabbed Quincy, the LaRue family attorney—or one of them—to help. He was a big, distinguished-looking black man in his 30s and got them appointments at several estates. Jack drove Daniel's wheelchair-equipped van to each location.

They had decided to leave Susan out of everything. She was the live-in nurse Daniel's parents kept on staff for him, even though he didn't need it, and the time to insist that stop was approaching. She was already asking too many questions after being with Daniel when he found the stash of arrows, armor, swords, and more at the family guest house, where Ryan and Eric had been setting up a practice space. And, like the rest of the planet, Susan knew they kept disappearing. She didn't need to know Daniel was now shopping for an estate. They kept dropping her somewhere to shop for him, or for herself, saying they were having some guy time without her. She knew they did not really need her and was actually pretty cool, so she didn't question it much.

Now Jack and Daniel wandered around an estate north of Darnestown, the last major suburb of Gaithersburg, before rural areas took over. The estates here were used for farming or horse boarding—or just for rich people wanting land. Aside from the 3,000-foot-tall Sugarloaf Mountain in the distance, the land was long rolling hills or mostly flat. Wide swaths of open land alternated with patches of trees and the occasional forest. White fencing and a wall of evergreen shrubs lined many estates to prevent people seeing more than a large house far back from the winding Route 28. All the estates had a long driveway through wide lawns. Some had stonework around a steel entrance gate. Most had a guest house, a barn of some kind, and a pond. The trick was finding one where his friends could live together but also take a break from each other.

Then there was security. If the authorities found the property, they would need a justification to enter. But it already seemed like they were trying to manufacture an excuse to interrogate the Stonehenge Four, so keeping the place hidden was preferred. And ignorance was the only way to stop Soliander or someone similar showing up. He could bypass any defenses. Then there were the media. The threat of lawsuits would keep them out, but news trucks out front would reveal the group's location to the curious. White picket fencing wouldn't keep anyone out. Guard dogs, armed guards, and better fencing were all under consideration. But any personnel would realize supernatural forces were at work if Matt practiced wizardry outside.

From the news, Jack knew that some people with newly acquired magic abilities wanted to reach Matt for training. How would he handle such a person showing up? Who knew what they could do to him or anyone else in their way? He wished Eriana had brought her stash of magic items from Florida before Soliander kidnapped her. One or more might protect Jack and the estate, which he felt responsible for. He had kept an eye out for a property that seemed easier to secure and felt that he was now walking on the best option.

"What do you think?" he asked Daniel, eyes still on the big, forested hill behind the property and to one side of it. The underbrush was thick, and getting through it would deter most trespassers. On the other side of it was the Potomac River. It was unlikely that anyone curious about them would trespass from that direction.

"This is the one," said Daniel, sitting beside him in the motorized wheelchair. "We can put fencing up back there, inside the trees so it's barbed wire and no one sees it from here. I'd like to get my drone from the van and fly it around to check it out."

Jack agreed, having helped with that on one other property. "We'll need cameras everywhere else. Some should be in obvious places, like the front gate, to deter people, but too many visible ones would make people think there's something to hide."

"Right. Didn't Eriana say something about having a private detective? Maybe he's good at that."

"Don't know how to reach him. Maybe we should ask about security firms. You mentioned drones and now I'm worried about someone flying one onto the property. The bigger issue is moving forward on this."

"I think it's time to tell my parents what's going on. That video you have of Soliander taking her from your place will convince them I'm not fucking with them."

Jack didn't really know them, but had a feeling he was about to. He looked over his shoulder at the real estate agent, who was hovering twenty yards away to give them space. "What do we tell her?"

Daniel started in her direction across the asphalt driveway. "I have a few questions first."

Jack followed him, admiring the place, which was called Briardale. An older, two-story guest house with three bedrooms stood across the pavement from the much bigger, two-story house with six bedrooms and a full basement. This newer building was twenty-five years old, with a big kitchen, sunroom, and covered porch running around it. Owned by horse breeders, the state-of-the-art stables had enough room for twenty horses. An apartment over the separate barn could house a barn manager, or one of them. The barn had an indoor ring they could also use for weapons practice. There were two more outdoor rings and a plenty of open ground. Even if they bought it this week, they'd still have a tremendous amount of work left to get it ready. Daniel could help buy things, but Jack would be setting it all up.

They reached the smiling real estate agent, who wore the hopeful expression of salespeople. Her tan business suit, long bob, and elegant glasses made her seem professional and trustworthy. She took them seriously thanks to the paperwork Quincy had done to prove that Daniel, or at least his parents, had the funds to buy such a place in cash.

Stopping in front of her, Daniel said, "I know this place has been on the market for two years, so I assume they want to sell fast."

She nodded. "Yes. It is priced to sell."

"But why hasn't it sold?"

"It's not unusual for big estates to take longer. Only so many people can afford one or have the need or desire. It will pass any new inspection, if that's your concern."

"Sort of. We're not concerned about having any issues fixed, just about delays moving in."

"Well, I can tell you they are very reasonable, so if there's anything you'd like, please let me know. But I will say they've had everything repaired or upgraded already, so there shouldn't be anything of real concern."

Daniel nodded and indicated they were done. They made the 25-minute drive back to Potomac, where mansions lined River Road and the side streets. Some of the lots weren't more expensive than Briardale, but they had gorgeous houses and hardly any land. Briardale had the land and more ordinary housing, except the newer house's size.

The media presence had died down in the last couple of days, another advantage of vanishing from Earth without being caught on camera. But Jack sighed in frustration as he slowly drove the van past the few news trucks still loitering, two police cars keeping everyone at bay. He'd heard that a similar presence existed outside the homes of Matt's and Anna's parents; Matt lived with his folks, but Anna had a condo that was always being watched. Hopefully Daniel could convince his parents to buy the estate and all of this would be behind them.

It was time to tell his parents the truth, but Daniel wasn't looking forward to it. How do you explain that your brother is being teleported to other planets as a knight who must go on fantastical quests? Weeks earlier, they would have assumed he was joking. That was his personality. But he felt all too sober about it. And the tension with his parents had to end. They knew something was going on with Ryan and the other three. The whole world knew about the Stonehenge Four. After that first disappearance, Ryan managed to dodge a lot of questions, but the subsequent vanishing acts had left their parents wondering.

And they sensed that Ryan had confided in Daniel, who could tell they knew it even before they demanded he tell them what was going on. With Ryan often missing—even if he was still on Earth—the arguments with their parents had become Daniel's problem. He didn't mind covering for his older brother. They had been through a lot together, and now Ryan was the one who needed his help instead of the other way around. It seemed like a different lifetime from when Ryan was always doting on him to make up for having accidentally paralyzed him as kids. Daniel had resented all of that well-meaning attention.

But now that was in the past. Ryan needed him. And one problem Daniel could solve for him was their parents. He had been over this in his head many times, just how to convince them he wasn't kidding with the story he was about to tell. They had seen Matt disappear on live TV. They had seen footage of Anna vanishing from behind the wheel of her car, the three friends still inside in a terrible accident that paralyzed one, maimed another, and killed the third. They knew that Anna had reappeared in the middle of the street, a car's dashcam having caught the scene right before another vehicle struck her. She had been paralyzed for days in the hospital before disappearing again. And some time later, security footage had shown her walking out of the hospital on her own two legs with an unknown woman in her forties—Eriana. The media had broadcasted it all, because the Stonehenge Four were famous and highly sought after for interviews and interrogations—by the police, FBI, CIA, and God knew who else.

Quincy was now handling legal matters for all of them, himself, and even Jack, who was helping to keep their lives and secrets safe on Earth. Daniel's wealthy parents knew about the attorney's involvement because the money to pay him ultimately came from their accounts. At Ryan's insistence, Quincy was handling the legal problems Anna's accidents had caused for her. That meant Anna's parents knowing Ryan was paying for it. And since Anna's parents lived next door to Matt's parents, they *also* knew. The time to tell all of them the truth was now. And Daniel's parents deserved to be first.

He reluctantly used the joystick to guide his wheelchair out of his bedroom at the LaRue family estate in Potomac, Maryland. The main house wasn't big enough to get lost in, but still qualified as a mansion. Using it as a home base wasn't a good option because everyone already knew that Ryan, at least, lived here. Security problems already abounded. The media were omnipresent. Curious troublemakers sometimes scaled the walls. They had hired a new security firm. They had installed more cameras. The police were out front all the time. Leaving meant being followed. And Daniel's parents didn't really know why, just that their oldest son and three friends were vanishing as if by magic, legal troubles were mounting, and secrets were being kept from them.

Daniel sighed as he rolled into the kitchen, where his parents were talking over drinks before dinner. The granite counter tops and stainless-steel appliances were as pristine as ever thanks to the maids. His mother sat at the island, blonde hair around her shoulders, blue eyes clouded until she saw him. Then they turned disappointed and disapproving, a look he had become accustomed to lately and wanted to end. She wore a white blouse and matching, tight skirt to just above her knees, and looked no less lovely at 50 than she ever had.

His father held a bottle of red wine in one slender hand, a gold watch at his wrist, button-up shirt neat and tucked into khakis, a black belt around his waist. Clean-shaven with salt-and-pepper hair, he always looked distinguished and respectable—his blue eyes strong, clear, and direct. That intimidated some people, but had never bothered Daniel before now. The steel in them was a new look that had replaced the kindness he usually showed his children.

They had argued about all of this just this morning, so Daniel didn't bother working his way up to it. "Are you ready to hear the truth?"

His father met his gaze, unimpressed with the suggestion. "We've been ready. Are you?"

Daniel pursed his lips. "I'm sorry for not telling you sooner. None of us thought you would believe us."

"Who's us?" his mother asked before sighing. "You and Ryan? Or the others?"

Daniel decided to start slow and not list everyone who knew at first. That would just piss them off, that they were the last to know. "Me and Ryan, Anna, Matt, and Eric. I don't really have their permission to tell you, but they do trust me to handle things while they're gone, and I'm making the call on this."

She asked, "Why are you telling us now?"

"We need your help. You may want another glass of that wine."

Instead of pouring one, his father took a stool. "Out with it."

Daniel took a deep breath. "I don't want to rehash things, but you know they've been disappearing, whether anyone sees it happen or not."

"Have you?" his father asked.

"No. Not in person."

Looking pained at his own question, his father asked, "Is this wizardry or something? Things are happening all over the world. Some are doing magic by accident, and killing people. Others are doing healing without meaning to, then trying on purpose."

Daniel knew of his father's disdain for fantasy books, movies, and games. Magic happening for real had to irritate him. "I know, and yes, it is magic. They just aren't causing it. They have no choice."

His mother grabbed the wine bottle, her expression equally unimpressed so that he knew she didn't believe him yet. She asked, "What does that mean, they have no choice?"

This was the part they would struggle with, and he had thought long and hard about how not to sound outlandish. Not at first. "They're being magically summoned somewhere. It is different each time, a different place. They have to do something before they can be sent back, and what they have to do also changes each time."

Scowling, his father asked, "Summoned to where? Who is doing this? And how?"

"What do they have to do?" his mother asked, and Daniel wondered if they were peppering him with questions to see if he actually had answers. They were going to be surprised if they thought they could catch him unprepared.

"Slow down. It's never the same twice, except that they disappear without warning and they can't stop it from happening. They always go together, even though they're often apart when they are summoned. And when it's over and they can go home, they go right back to where they were when they're summoned."

His father's calculating eyes were on him. "That's why Anna reappeared on the highway."

"Right. And it's a problem."

His father snorted. "Yeah. How are they supposed to go anywhere when this can happen?"

"That's one of the reasons we need your help. They need to stay in one place while they're on Earth, so that when they're sent back here, they arrive somewhere safe and not on a highway."

His mother fingered her wine glass. "Did you say 'on Earth'?"

Daniel hesitated, not having realized he'd admitted it. Then he wondered whether his accidental revelation and the "oops" expression he wore might convince them he wasn't kidding. "Yes. I know that may be hard to believe—"

"Yeah," his father interrupted, "I was starting to take you seriously."

"Dad, look, I *am* being serious."

"So there are aliens summoning them?" his father snidely asked. "Why don't they come in a spaceship and get them?" His mother laughed and Daniel sighed.

"They're usually humans, for one, and so far they've always been from worlds less sophisticated than ours."

His father asked, "Well, if that's true, then how would people from another planet know who they are to summon them? Multiple other planets? You're going to need a good explanation for that one. And why them?"

"I have a good answer for that. Just hear me out. I swear this will all make sense and explain everything that is happening in the world. Ryan and the others are the cause of it all."

That seemed to get their attention from the way his parents exchanged a look, his father pouring both of them a glass and settling in.

"No bullshit, Daniel. I'm serious."

"So am I."

And so Daniel explained who the Ellorian Champions were, and that someone had once summoned them to Earth's past for another quest.

His father asked. "Time travel now? Who summoned them?"

Daniel didn't want to admit it, but his father's frown told him the omission might cost him. "Look, now you accept that magic is real because you've seen it, on camera anyway. Supernatural healing is also being reported. Well, lots of things we thought were myths are real, but they disappeared or stopped working a thousand years ago. The Ellorian Champions and their quest are why."

"Who summoned them?" his father repeated.

"Morgana. And yes, I mean the one you are thinking of. She was real. So was Merlin." He paused, gauging their reaction. No one said anything. His father just stared at him. Finally, he spoke.

"Go on."

"It's a long story, but Morgana was doing bad things with magic. Merlin wanted to stop her. The only way he could was to drain the magic from Earth back into the faerie world, so he cast a spell to do that. It took time to complete, and before it did, Morgana summoned the Ellorians to stop it. But they talked with Merlin and learned it had to be done, so they refused the quest."

Smirking as if she'd caught him, his mother said, "I thought they had to do it to go home."

"Yeah, and that's the issue. They were magically bound to do the quests against their will. But if they were still here when the magic stopped working, it might free them from the unwanted quests. But it would trap them here. It worked. Sort of. Magic stopped working here. All the faerie creatures were pulled into the faerie world. That world and Earth had been separated ever since—until Ryan, Anna, Matt and Eric went to Stonehenge."

This time his father looked intrigued, no doubt because he already accepted that Ryan had been missing from Stonehenge for three weeks. "Why? Is Stonehenge one of these Quest Rings?"

"Sort of. Not really. Morgana turned it into a makeshift one. It's really a portal between the faerie world and Earth. It's the most powerful doorway. From what they told me, Merlin had a failsafe for the spell, which could be undone if a pendant he created was brought back to Stonehenge. We still don't know how it happened, but that pendant somehow ended up with Anna. You've seen it before. She's been wearing it since I've known her."

He stopped again, sensing from their expressions that they were now invested, things clicking into place for them. Stonehenge was the key to making them believe him. He saw that now.

His father asked, "So they went to Stonehenge on vacation and brought this pendant there without knowing it would, what, unleash magic? This is why magic is working? And healing?"

"Yes. They had no idea what the pendant was at the time."

His mother's brow was furrowed. "Is this how Anna went from paralyzed to walking again? You said those Quest Rings heal them."

"Yeah. The summoning spell does it. So does the one sending them back. It took her right out of the bed at the hospital and healed her before she and the others arrived for their quest."

"Wait," his father said intently. "Are they on... they're on a quest right now? Is that why he's not around?"

"Yes."

"A quest to do what?"

"We won't know until they get back and tell us." Daniel knew the answer this time but wasn't going to say it. The trip to Elloria was too complicated to explain.

His mother asked again, "Us?"

Daniel nodded sheepishly. "Me, Jack, and Quincy. We're the only ones who know."

"*Quincy* knows about this?" his mother asked.

"Yeah. Look, Jack already knew because they told him after they returned from Stonehenge. Then they disappeared right in front of him at Anna's apartment Long story. He's been helping them."

"Helping them how?"

"Just trying to cover for them, or look after their things while they're gone. Look, he's literally working for them now. Jack quit his job at Starbucks and is full-time trying to take care of any problems for them here while they're gone. Quincy and I are, too."

His father continued scowling, but Daniel noticed his parents had stopped being snide. "How did Quincy get involved?"

"When Anna reappeared in the highway and was hit by the car, they'd known it might happen. Ryan raced off to get there, but it was too late. A car had already struck her. He was upset and pushed through the police barriers, and they arrested him."

"I remember."

"Quincy got him out, of course—and Ryan and the others, and Jack, decided to tell me and Quincy the truth. I had found the stash of weapons at the quest house here. Susan was with me."

His father put up both palms toward him. "Wait. Wait. Does Susan know?"

"No."

"What stash of weapons?" he asked.

Daniel sighed. "We're getting ahead of ourselves. Listen, when they get summoned, they have to go on quests just like the Ellorian Champions—but they don't have the skills, so they've been trying to practice while they're back on Earth. They bought a bunch of swords, longbows, and other shit. Ryan had them at the guest house and was unloading them from his car when they were summoned. I was playing with my drone later and saw his car there, so Susan and I went to check it out and found of the stuff in there. That's how I started to learn what was going on."

His father said, "So wait, why are they doing these quests instead of the Ellorians?"

"That's the interesting part. We don't really know how it happened, but they've been substituted for them. You asked why people from other worlds would know who they are and summon them. The answer is that they don't. People think they're summoning the Ellorian Champions and they're actually showing up, but it's Ryan, Anna, Matt, and Eric. They've been playing along because they think the reputation of the real Champions prevents people from realizing how vulnerable they are."

His mother asked, "Doesn't anyone realize they aren't these Champions?"

Daniel knew the elf Lorian had but didn't admit it. "No. Few inhabitants of places that summoned them ever saw the real Champions, and Ryan and the others bear enough resemblance in hair color, size, and all of that. Remember, these worlds don't have cameras, so it's not like you can compare photos to them and realize it isn't them."

She said, "Yeah, but the clothes give them away, don't they? The style would be all wrong."

"The summoning spell changes their clothes. Ryan arrives in golden armor and is expected to be the knight Korrin. Matt is the wizard Soliander. Eric is the rogue Andier. And Anna is the priestess Eriana."

His father chuckled. "I bet Anna loves that."

Daniel pursed his lips and admitted, "Yeah, she was really against it, but seeing healing and magic working got through to her and she believed it the more she saw it. From what I understand, she's healed people with the power of a god on these other worlds." He stopped and let them process that. It seemed like every answer had the ability to make them believe him or grow skeptical again, an ebb and flow of taking him seriously.

"So if they're on a quest right now," his mother observed, "they're in danger?"

"Probably." He explained how the elf Lorian had trained Matt in some wizardry, and helped Ryan and Eric with swordsmanship. A dwarf had helped Anna get over her atheism, at least a little. Then he added, "Yes, they are always in danger while they're gone. They've done pretty well despite not being the real Champions."

His father asked, "Well, what about these Ellorians? Where are they?"

Daniel took a deep breath. "That's another interesting bit, and leads up to why we need you now. The Ellorians have been missing for years. But we've found out about two of them. We don't know where Korrin or Andier are, but Ryan and the others ran into Soliander on the first quest. He attacked them."

"Wait," his father interrupted, scowling. "I thought he was a good guy."

"He was. We don't know what happened to him yet, but he's a threat, and one we need to worry about. And this time by 'we' I mean all of us in this room, too, which is one of the reasons I'm telling you all of this. Soliander knows about all of us—where we live. He has been here."

"To our house?" his mother asked, looking around nervously.

"To Earth. He's been to Jack's apartment, looking for Ryan and the others. We don't understand how he knew to look there. It's possible that he'd come here to our house at some point, or even to the Sorenson's house, or Anna's parents', and found out about Jack and tried going there. Remember how after Anna's accident, the one that put her in the hospital, Ryan wasn't here? None of them were at home. They were all hiding in a hotel, hiding from the police and the media. But also hiding from Soliander. He must have found out about Jack somehow and tracked him to the apartment."

His father asked, "Is Jack okay?"

"Yeah, he's fine. Soliander didn't realize he was there."

"Why is he after them?"

"We don't really know—but Matt has a copy of his staff, and he likely wants that back. And it seems like he's searching for the other Champions and hasn't found them. Or, well, he hadn't. Listen, we also know where Eriana is. Or we did. She has been on Earth for the last twenty years." He explained how, when Merlin's spell was completed, an explosion hurled Soliander back to the right world and time... but it trapped Eriana on Earth and threw her *almost* back to the present. She had been living under an assumed name in Florida, married to a banker, and collecting supposed magic items in case they ever worked and were needed.

He concluded, "When Eriana saw the broadcast of Ryan and the others being found near Stonehenge, she recognized the pendant Anna wore and knew they had caused magic to start working again. She sought them out and arrived in Maryland not long ago. She introduced herself and befriended them. She told us a lot of history and has promised to help. And this is where I'm going with all of this. Days ago, she was at Jack's apartment with him. Ryan and the others had been there overnight but were missing in the morning and we assumed someone had summoned them again. While Jack was in the kitchen, Soliander knocked on the door. Eriana opened it and they were face-to-face for the first time in a long time, both shocked to see each other. She let him in, and Jack overheard and recorded their conversation on the security camera he has inside."

Daniel picked up his phone and started the video and audio that Jack had shared with him. It showed the wizard and priestess reuniting, and her expressing concerns about his behavior. The video ended with Soliander grabbing her wrist and speaking a word as Jack ran into the room. He dove for them, but the pair vanished. Both of Daniel's parents reacted out loud with shock and amazement.

His father ran a hand over one cheek. "My God, you really aren't kidding about all of this."

"No."

He asked, "What's to stop this Soliander from doing this to anyone else?"

"Honestly, nothing. It's one reason why you need to know what's happening. So do Matt and Anna's parents. We could all be targets. Maybe Eriana can talk some sense into Soliander, but I don't know. I mean, he just kidnapped her. Anyway, we need to make certain things happen here while Ryan and the others are gone."

"Like what?" his mother asked.

This was it. The big ask. But he now knew they were on board. That video had been the final key. "They need a home base set up, one no one knows about. Not the media, not the authorities, and not someone like Soliander. We were going to buy an estate up near Darnestown. Eriana was going to pay for it, since she's wealthy and she feels some responsibility for all this. But now she's gone. You guys have the money and, well, I'll just say it—you need to buy the estate Daniel and I agreed on, and do it in such a way that it's hard to track who actually owns it. Quincy was working on something for that, like a shell corporation or some shit. I don't know how that really works."

His father waved that off. "I do. Okay, listen, this is a lot to digest. But we get it. That video... Well, if that wasn't convincing, nothing is. I can see now why you didn't tell us sooner."

His mother suddenly grew tearful and came over to him, throwing her arms around him. "I'm sorry we've been hard on you lately. This is a lot. I don't know how you guys are managing it."

"It's okay, Mom," Daniel said, as she pulled away. "You know, you guys have doted on me most of my life. It's Ryan's turn. He's the one who needs you. Magic is starting to work again, and healing, and somehow he and the others are the focal point of the whole thing."

His father nodded slowly, eyes calculating, his jaw clenching with resolve. "Call a meeting tomorrow morning with Quincy. Get Jack here. We'll get this going and then bring in Anna's and Matt's parents." He walked over to a cabinet, opening it to reveal a steel safe, which he unlocked before pulling out a handgun.

"It's time for us to get serious."

CHAPTER ELEVEN

THE PRISONERS

Eriana wasn't sure how long she had been asleep. That was the side-effect of magically induced slumber; it could last minutes to years, though only skilled wizards could do the latter. The one who'd done it to her was among the most skilled to ever live. But she suspected it couldn't have been more than a day, if that. There was no reason for more, unless Soliander needed to think. To figure out what to do with her. She had no doubt he had acted impulsively when kidnapping her, that he'd had no plan. It almost didn't surprise her that, at the very moment they'd arrived wherever they were, Soliander had put her to sleep.

Eriana felt alert, refreshed, and unharmed as she leaned up on one elbow. She was on a soft bed with a plush mattress. Her eyes quickly scanned the room for company, finding no one. Then she examined it more carefully as she tossed the thick blanket off herself and sat up. She still wore a t-shirt, jeans, and short socks from Earth, but her shoes were gone. Beside the bed on a table stood a pitcher of water and a tray of what she presumed was food under a steel cover. It smelled like ham and seasoned potatoes and she sighed. He had prepared, or made someone else prepare, one of her favorite foods. Should she be that pleased he remembered after all this time? Then she realized it had only been a few years for him, not the two decades she'd experienced. Her other thought was unusually suspicious for her, that it was a bribe or peace offering, its sincerity in doubt.

Her stomach rumbled... and she didn't think for one second that Soli would poison her. She had always trusted him with her life and still did, despite knowing he had changed. That was what she most needed to know—who he had become. He had refused to tell her what he'd really been up to these past few years while apparently living under an assumed name. She had no way to compel the truth from him.

But she knew that he had hardened himself, partly from the thought he had inadvertently killed her. Now he knew better. It seemed obvious that a crack in that hard shell must have formed from his discovery that she still lived. She almost wasn't concerned that he'd kidnapped and imprisoned her—not really. He'd said it himself that, having found her after all this time, he couldn't very well just leave her behind on Earth. And so instead of kidnapping Matt, Anna, Ryan, and Eric, he'd kidnapped her.

That made her wonder—was the room designed for one or more of them? Looking around, she doubted it. The accommodations were pleasant, if seemingly not much used. An elegant dresser stood along one wall. A swivel mirror sat upon a stand. A marble bathtub peeked out from behind a foldable privacy screen. There were no paintings on the walls, just lanterns, a crystal chandelier on the ceiling, and windows on each wall. She rose to peer out of one, discovering that she was in a tower.

Snow-capped mountains loomed just outside the window, and she knew they were on the other three sides without having to look. Soliander had always been dramatic, something of a romantic. She had so often caught him staring off at a mountain range as if he was curious what wonders lay within. He found the deep shadows, the surprises around every corner, and the ruggedness appealing. She preferred being able to see danger from a long way off, like she could on a grassy plain.

From one of the windows, she saw more of the castle her tower was a part of. The dark structure seemed unguarded, and below her lay a parapet. Nearby, stairs led down to the rocky ground, a trail winding away among the peaks to who-knows-where.

"Too bad my hair isn't longer," she quipped, thinking of Rapunzel. She spied her shoes casually discarded on the stone floor but left them there. With little else to do, she helped herself to the food and waited for her old friend to appear.

An hour passed before she heard footsteps approaching on the stone floors. Somehow, after all this time, she still recognized Soliander's footfall. He padded quietly like a cat, the leather soles of his boots scraping the stairs just enough for her to hear as she sat still. In bare feet, he could sneak up on anyone. A key clicked in the lock of a dark wooden door, the black metal handle turning. Then the door slid open to reveal Soliander in a black tunic and trousers, tucked into matching boots. He had never explained his preference for the color. She had long ago thought it accentuated a goodness in him that he seemed to want no one to notice, though she knew better. Now, the somber color made her wonder whether it had been a harbinger of the darkness that consumed him.

Soliander entered alone, the heavy door swinging shut. His wavy brown hair hadn't changed, though it had grown longer past his shoulders. But his eyes looked different. She had seen many things in them before. Guilt. Turmoil. Anger. Intelligence. Those were all present, but what struck her was what was missing. Kindness. Humor. Warmth. Nobility. And their absence made his intelligence seem cunning, cruel, remorseless. He was frightening. He'd always had enough power to worry any rational person, but his finer qualities meant only the wicked had something to fear. Now she wondered if everyone did.

Except her.

"First, I must apologize," he said.

Eriana frowned, trying to ignore the rush of pleasure she felt on hearing his voice again. "Do you expect me to take it seriously?"

He looked startled, then seemed to accept that. "No, but I will say it anyway."

"Good." Showing remorse was a good sign, but she hid her relief.

"I meant what I said before bringing you here. I could not leave you again after thinking you dead for three years and suddenly finding you alive, albeit aged twenty years. A long conversation in that place was not the best option."

"And this was?" she interrupted.

Ignoring that, he said, "You wouldn't come. I felt I had no choice but to bring you anyway."

"You could have respected my choice." Something about his demeanor made her remark, "I get the impression you no longer respect what others want for themselves."

He shrugged. "When did anyone respect what I wanted for myself?"

Knowing he meant being summoned against his will, she said, "That doesn't make this right." When he didn't respond, she asked, "What did you gain by putting me to sleep?"

He sighed. "Time to think. I will take you back to Earth, or to Elloria, if you prefer that to being with me. I would like your help first."

Eriana relaxed a bit. He sounded reasonable, at least. "What I *want* is to go to Coreth to see my family. I *need* to go to Earth to help Anna and the others. I also want to stay with you to learn what you know about what has happened, and what you have been doing. But the need outweighs the wants and is urgent."

"Then we both want information from each other. The sooner we exchange it, the sooner you can meet your needs."

She leaned against the bed to make this less confrontational than standing squared off with him. Genuinely curious, she asked, "What help do you need?"

"I need to know who these imposters are and how they came to be impersonating us. What have you learned that you can tell me?"

She certainly had that information to barter with, and there was another advantage to telling him the truth. Hoping to extract a promise, she asked, "If I tell you, will you avoid using that *Mind Trust* spell on them?"

He appeared to consider this, but without much regret on his face. "I can't promise anything, but I trust you, even if you do not trust me. I am not judging you for that. I would not trust me either."

"Very reassuring."

"You know that my reason for seeking them was to learn how they were substituted and whether they knew anything about you, Korrin, and Andier. Tell me what they have told you and I won't need to hear it from them. That would mean not capturing them, which you seem to oppose."

She watched him for a moment, thinking that he had always been both logical and practical. And so she related what she knew, focusing on details that she thought posed no danger. Unfortunately, he fixated on one issue for which no one had an answer. When Merlin cast the spell on Earth to drain magic into the fae world, stripping it from the Earth, he created the magical pendant that, when returned to Stonehenge, would undo the spell and allow magic to return. The fairy creatures—elves, dwarves, dragons and more— would also return.

"No one knows the history of this pendant?" he asked again. "It survives for a thousand years and somehow makes it into the hands of a girl who goes to Stonehenge on holiday."

"I know. I am an expert in antiquities there, and I can tell you no one has ever seen it. I have been looking for it for two decades, and there's no mention of it in any books."

"If I can get my hands on it, I can cast a spell to retrace where it has been. I've traced something for more than a few years, but a thousand?" He then asked, "You have been studying this?"

Eriana nodded. She related how she had married a wealthy man with the means to acquire every potentially magical item—and so she had been collecting them, even though none of them worked. She was partly just searching for the pendant, but she also wanted them in case magic ever started working again, though she had eventually given up hope and only continued out of habit, curiosity, and wishful thinking.

Soliander asked no questions as she spoke for several minutes, and his first question almost didn't surprise her, mostly because his face had tightened as if under strain.

"You have a husband?"

She nodded. "He is a good man who treats me well. That is all you need to know." The last thing she needed was a jealous Soliander imagining any details about her husband or personal life.

He held her gaze, and then changed the subject back to the imposters. "I know their names and more from the spell I did on Matt, but you have talked with them. What do you think of them?"

"They are good people, Soli. And they are not a threat to you, or me. They are victims of this just like we were, only it's worse. They aren't qualified. You don't need to go after them."

"I need the copy of my staff back from Matt."

Eriana shook her head. "No, he needs it. They would be dead already without it."

"What is that to me?"

"You never used that to be so callous," she observed, hoping he wasn't now either and was just being rude. "Everyone thinks they are us. Do you want everyone thinking we are dead when they get killed, because you took the staff?"

"I already thought everyone was dead. People accepted that we were missing or presumed dead. What does it matter if they get confirmation this time?"

"Because it's a lie, one that I won't go along with. And we all have families. That would be a cruel thing to do to them. Look how you felt when you thought *I* was dead."

The way he pursed his lips told her he didn't have a counter for that. "Maybe I'll keep you here after all, and then no one will know."

"Some people already know. This secret isn't going to last. More people will try to summon them, and succeed, and it's just a matter of time before people who knew us see them instead. Besides, are you really going to keep me a prisoner for the rest of my life? You may have changed, but Everon trapped us together for years in the quest cycle. You aren't going to trap me any longer than necessary."

"I've changed."

Eriana knew he was bluffing. "Not in that way. You said it yourself, that everything you've done since breaking free was to ensure you weren't a prisoner again. You will not imprison one of us for your own freedom, especially when setting me free would not harm your freedom in the least."

"You seem awfully certain of that. Is that why you're so calm about this?"

"Who said I was calm? I'm furious that you took me away. I am needed back there. Urgently."

He frowned. "For what? They have done well on their quests."

She shook her head. "They all need training—and I'm the only one on that planet who can help the girl, Anna." She wasn't going to mention buying the estate for them as a new hideout. Soli knew where to find them now. She wouldn't help him understand that they were going somewhere he wouldn't know about. But she had another point.

"Magic has begun to awaken there. That means healing, too. I've lived there for two decades, Soli. They aren't ready for it. People are already freaking out about the Stonehenge Four, as they're known, disappearing on camera like they have. And random people with magic talent can suddenly make things happen. Those people are scared, and people fear them. And then the healers are just gaining their powers, which sounds good, but that world is more desperate for faith and hope than any we ever visited. I don't know how much technology you saw, but it's going to get ugly there soon."

"What does any of that have to do with me? Or you?"

"I can help people. I'm not sure how, but I'm the only skilled person who knows that world."

"Maybe so, but it will presumably be a while before the planet falls apart."

He was right that the Earth itself didn't need her help just yet, but the four friends did. "The new Champions need me back on Earth. The missing Home Rings are a huge problem because of what happens when they return. I am one of the few who can help, partly because only I can heal them if they get as badly injured as before when they go back. They could have returned already. They could be hurt even now."

He sighed. "Yes, I know. I am not completely unsympathetic."

Then maybe some good part of him remained. After hesitating, she added, "You could really help them. Give them the spell to create the Home Rings, at least. Some soclarin ore. Or even create the rings for them. Give them a chance to live their lives when they aren't on some damn quest they don't want. They're just trying to survive, Soli, and they are a lot more like kids than we were. They are in over their heads. This is not their fault—and the last thing they need is not to be able to safely return home, or to be a prisoner there for fear of leaving and being summoned and sent back into the middle of a highway. And they certainly don't need you attacking them."

He said nothing for a minute. She watched his troubled eyes, feeling some relief at the concern they revealed. He was still in there—her Soli, not this cold, calculating man who he wore like a bad suit. Except it somehow seemed to fit him, as if giving in to all the anger he'd felt for so long suited him in an awful way. Was he misdirecting it at everyone? Because going after Everon was one thing. Attacking Anna and the others was going too far and she felt renewed hope that he saw that, however much he might have changed. And his next words comforted her.

"You're making me feel guilty."

"Good. If you won't create the Home Rings for them, then you can at least tell them how to do it for themselves. Or tell me."

He shook his head. "They can't create them."

"Why not?"

"They need soclarin ore to create the keystones for the rings, but they don't have any. And no, I'm not giving them some. Besides, the only place to create the keystones is my old home, because the forge there is enchanted for it, and I'm not letting them in there."

Memories of his home saddened her, for she had spent considerable time there and it was one of the many things lost. She had known at once that they weren't there now, from the construction if not the atmosphere. "Why? What are you hiding there?"

He pursed his lips. "Bad memories."

She eyed him. "Funny. I only had good ones." Then she realized what he meant. "But you mean it's where Everon betrayed you, making the keystones for all the Quest Rings he created without telling you. Us."

"I never should have taught him. I didn't know who he really was. If only I'd been using the *Mind Trust* spell on people back then, none of this would have happened."

"You knew better then."

He shook his head. "I was a fool then. You can't tell me that not doing it was the right thing when someone did the wrong thing to us as a result and we have suffered ever since, our lives destroyed. And for what? To protect the privacy of someone who was there to deceive and then betray me?"

Eriana sighed. "So what now? You become ruthless?"

"Absolutely."

"For what it's worth, I understand what you're saying. I just don't like what you're doing."

Looking grim, he asked, "Have you ever wondered how many other people we've angered on our quests? For every kingdom we save, we destroy the plans and sometimes lives of the so-called villains we defeat. And they have families, people like Everon, who can come for revenge. We may have more enemies than anyone."

"Yes, I have wondered. Is that the reason why you live under another name now?"

"No."

He wasn't one to live in fear, she knew. And now that he was ruthless, anyone would have to be a fool to go after the Majestic Magus, Soliander of Aranor. He was revered and respected—and dreaded by those up to no good. But was he also now feared by those living good lives? Maybe he still cared enough about his reputation to do everything under another name. What would their families think of him now?

Eriana began, "I have been away from my family for two decades. I want to see them, Soli. What do you know about them?"

He seemed relieved by the change of subject. "Your brother is managing your estate and doing well. You needn't worry about him. I have kept watch from afar."

Startled, she smiled at him, relief flooding her. "You are still a good man. I knew it. *Thank you*, Soli. That means so much to me, I hardly know how to tell you."

He poorly hid a blush as he waved this off. "You would've done the same, except Taryn needs no help."

"How is she?" Eriana asked, curious about the no-nonsense warrior she had always liked. She knew Soliander loved and respected her even if he'd never say so. "You haven't seen her?"

"I keep tabs on her as well. She is fine. Commander of a force of men, of course. You know her. No one tells her what to do—it's the other way around."

"She doesn't know you're alive?"

"No."

"Why? You know she adores you."

He shrugged and then smirked halfheartedly. "Maybe I don't want to break her heart."

Eriana sighed, suspecting she wouldn't get anything about that out of him any time soon. But she wanted to ask about her own sister, a subject likely to upset him. But she had to know. "And my sister? What of Diara?"

His expression turned distant. "You don't want to know."

Eriana shook her head. "Is she still with Everon?"

The thought didn't pain her. Not anymore. Without Diara's cooperation, Everon's could not have betrayed them. It was she who had secured a piece of hair or something else with DNA—though only people from Earth thought of it that way—from her, Korrin, Andier, and Soli. Using these, Everon altered the summoning spells he imbued the keystones with, and this was what had made the quests involuntary.

"She still loves him, if that's what you're asking."

"Soli!" she said, tired of him dodging questions.

He looked startled, then frowned. "She is not with him, no. I have separated them for some time."

When he didn't elaborate, she asked, "How can you be sure? You haven't found him. You have found her?"

He held her gaze for a long time. "Yes. I know where she is." He didn't elaborate and she hardened her expression, knowing he was withholding the answer. She wasn't going to ask again, settling for glaring. He looked uncomfortable and she felt suspicious.

"What did you do with her?"

He went to the window and looked toward one of the other towers. "She is here," he admitted.

That was the one answer she hadn't expected. But maybe she should not have been surprised. Vengeance had been such a frequent desire of his. That he would turn that on her sister wasn't unexpected, even if she might find out. Had he truly given up hope that Eriana was alive? Because learning what he'd done to Diara might've ended any chance of her forgiving him for whatever awful behavior he'd engaged in during the last three years. Her sister's condition would therefore tell her more than just Diara's fate.

"What have you done to her?"

"She is fine. I would not hurt her, on account of you."

A good answer. "Why not?"

He shrugged. "You would not approve, whether you still lived or not."

"I want to see her." She joined him at the window and followed his gaze. "Is that where you keep her?"

"I'm not sure it's a good idea for you to see her."

"Why not? You said she was fine."

He nodded. "Physically, yes. But she is ever more in the grip of Everon. Your sister is lost, Eriana. No good that can come from you interacting with her."

"I would see this for myself."

Soliander shook his head. "This is a decision I am making for you."

She gripped his arm and turned him toward her. "No. You don't get to do that. Do you understand me? You will not disrespect me that way. Ever."

He frowned. "Eriana. You must trust me. There is no good that can come from this."

Anger welled up in her, but she hid it well. The man she admired was still in there, but enough of this new guy remained to warp his judgement about what was appropriate. Maybe he needed a reminder that wielding power over others without their permission was exactly what had gotten them into this mess. She put one hand on his heart and spoke a word. From the sudden alarm on his face, he recognized it. But then his eyes rolled back, and he slumped to the floor, audibly snoring.

"You're not the only one with power, old friend."

Eriana leaned down over the wizard and examined his face. The coldness, anger, and contempt had gone and left him more like she remembered— noble, goodhearted, and sensitive. He had never let his power or strength go to his head, but that seemed long over. She felt confident the man she had loved was still in there—she just had to get him out. She sighed in resignation, unsure where to go from here But she finally straightened, walked to the pitcher of water, and returned, dumping it over his head.

He sputtered and came awake with a look of shock, surprise, and outrage. But he quickly recognized the situation and looked up at her smirking face. He relaxed despite his muted glare.

"Was that really necessary?"

Her humorless smile broadened. "No."

Soliander rose, shook the arms of his soaked tunic, then spoke a few words and became instantly dry. He eyed her for several seconds, as if trying to downplay being caught off guard. "Why didn't you leave?"

"For starters, I need your help to get back to Earth or even Elloria. But I already told you. I want to know what you have been doing, so are you going to tell me or not?"

"I haven't decided."

That was better than a no. "Why don't you start with immediately after I last saw you on Earth. Surely you didn't go evil immediately, and you can tell me what you experienced."

With the way he pursed his lips, she knew she had cornered him. He confirmed it by gesturing for her to sit—but he remained standing, slowly pacing as they talked. He let out a deep breath and she feared he would stall, so she took control of the conversation.

"Did you arrive on Elloria?"

"Yes, a few miles from home, in the mountains. I was injured."

"But you used your Trinity Ring?" she asked. With his help, she had designed them for exactly that sort of scenario—when either Andier, Korrin, or Soli, who all had one, were hurt and she wasn't there to heal them. Just as the Quest Rings restored them to health on summoning them or sending them home, they replenished the three healing spells of different strengths in each ring's gemstones.

Soliander shook his head. "No. The stones in it were shattered."

That surprised her, but maybe it shouldn't have. She only remembered a little about the moment he'd attempted to send them back with magic just as magic stopped working on Earth. His look of alarm had told her something was wrong, but she saw nothing like an explosion—just a flash of blinding light at Stonehenge before she found herself standing in a New Zealand field, instead of at home in Coreth.

"What injuries did you have?"

"Broken leg and a few ribs. A concussion."

Frowning in concern, she asked, "How did you get home?"

"I crawled." He seemed a little indignant about that. Changing the subject, he asked, "Were you injured after the spell?"

"No. Nothing. I'm sorry that happened to you. I am curious now, and concerned, what might have happened to the others."

He nodded. "Now you know why I thought you were all dead and I'd killed you, especially when you remained missing. I searched for your bodies." He looked pained, and she knew that must have been awful. No wonder he was angry. She wondered whether survivor's guilt was part of what had driven him since.

She ventured, "You were closer to the spell, since you were casting it. That may have had something to do with your injuries."

"Possibly. It doesn't matter."

"So you made it back, got healed with a potion I assume... and then what?"

"I cast myself to Coreth and your Home Ring. It was damaged and there was no sign of you. I asked around. Your brother hadn't seen you. I went to Korrin's ring, and Andier's. Both were damaged, and only then did I check mine. Neither of them had been seen and that remained true in the weeks after."

"You saw my brother?" Eriana asked in surprise. Then something occurred to her. "Wait. Everyone thinks we all went missing and never returned. How is it that you..." She trailed off, a suspicion forming.

He flashed a rueful smile. "Yes, I made everyone who had seen me forget they had done so."

She stared for a moment. "Why?"

"Lots of reasons. I didn't want people asking what had happened, wanting explanations I couldn't give them. I didn't want people giving up hope on all of you, like I soon did. And I didn't want people asking why I was the only survivor, as if I had done something to all of you. I felt like I had. But having anyone else look at me like I had was too much. Some of them already did, like Korrin's brother, so I used a spell and wiped his memory of my return. He was the first. Then came the others."

Eriana watched him closely, seeing grief, shame, and other signs that the good man she had known was still in there. "What then? You assumed a new identity, moved here?"

He flashed a smile. "Something like that. It's a longer story."

"I have time."

"I do not."

"Is something more important than me?"

He looked startled, smiled, then sighed. "No, but I am important and there are things I must do. Not everything can be delegated."

"Who is Zoran the Devastator?" she asked. "You referred to yourself that way back on Earth. If you're going to walk out of this room to go devastate someone or something, I'd just as soon you stay here and talk to me."

"Why? So you can talk me out of it?"

"Something like that."

"Some people deserve to be devastated."

"Like you?" she asked, hoping to get him to recognize that his upset of the past three years could lift. "Are you a little less devastated to know I'm alive and well?"

He looked at her and slowly smiled like the man he used to be. The expression transformed his face entirely. "I am more thrilled than I know how to tell you."

"Well, why don't you think about how to express it and come back later. I would like to hear it. For my part, I am far beyond thrilled to see you again, Soli. It has been three years for you, twenty for me. Based on the math, I should be more upset about the time apart than you, but I am not. Maybe it's time to start letting it go."

He pursed his lips. "You were always the best of us." They stood in silence for several moments before he went to the door, opened it, and turned back. "I need to decide what to do after what you've told me. It might be a while, as I have matters to attend to. I'm sorry for all of this. It is not what I would have wanted, if I'd foreseen finding you. I will return you to wherever you want, and soon. In the meantime, you will come to no harm here. You must know that."

Meeting his eye without humor, she admitted, "I don't know what to trust about you. But even if you let me go now, I would not leave. I want to know what you have been doing, Soli. Don't come back in here until you're prepared to tell me."

He sighed again. Then he left.

When the door next opened that night, Eriana half-expected Soliander despite not recognizing the footsteps as his. Instead, a dark elf entered, his skin and hair black, red eyes unfriendly. It had been a long time since she'd seen one. No dwarves, dragons, or anything else for twenty years on Earth, and the first non-human she sees is a sinister dark elf. She had nearly forgotten their existence—and the haughtiness in their expressions and body language. This one seemed deferential, and even bowed his head slightly. Soliander must have intimidated him, and the reality of the unsavory dark elves working for him did nothing to put her at ease about his activities.

"What do you want?" she asked, remembering that bluntness worked best.

"I am Darron, my lady," he answered smoothly, waiting by the open door. His eyes lingered on her clothing a moment, but he didn't seem intrigued by her Earth clothes. She wondered if he had been there. "I am to escort you to another guest."

She cocked an eyebrow. There could only be one other guest she cared about. "My sister?"

"Yes."

Eriana rose at once and donned her shoes, gesturing for the dark elf to proceed. She had considered what to say to Diara since Soliander had left hours earlier, but she really wasn't sure where to begin. The tension between them had dominated their relationship, but she held out hope that it was gone. It had been twenty years for her. Being negative wasn't her focus. But it had only been three years since her disappearance for Diara, who always seemed to dwell on negative thoughts. Had anything changed since then? Had she come to her senses and regretted what she had done? Or had she gotten worse, as Soli suggested? Eriana was well aware that the one wound she could never heal was the hate in her sister's heart. Had time done anything to soften it?

She eyed the slender dark elf before her, a torch in his hand, as they descended stone steps that curled along the inside wall of the tower. She had spent half her life in castles, towers, and homes without much convenience— the other half spent in the luxury of modern plumbing, toilet paper, soap and shampoo, and convenient ways of dealing with feminine problems. Smooth cars with air conditioning, radio, and comfortable seats had replaced bumpy wagons on hard wood with nothing but the elements around her. She had become used to glancing at a clock instead of the sun or night sky for the time. And information came at the touch of a finger, whereas now she didn't even know what planet she was on, not to mention what was going on in the world. For the first time, she realized that going back to her old life might be something she just couldn't do. And she felt renewed appreciation for how the replacement Champions were coping.

She and Darron passed several landings they passed before arriving at what she assumed to be one of the main levels of the castle. She confirmed this as they walked down several halls, peeking into doorways to sense that they were on an upper floor. She saw few other people, and wasn't surprised because Soliander had never been one for much company. Those people she did see were either humans or more dark elves.

They soon ascended another tower, once again climbing in winding circles. She knew from experience that imprisoning someone in a tower had advantages—there was only one way down, unless jumping to your death counted as a second. The keep seemed well-kept given how few people she'd seen, but then Soli wasn't above using magic for even mundane tasks. She wondered what the dark elf did for the wizard.

"How is it that a dark elf works for… Zoran?" No sense in revealing Soliander's true identity without understanding the consequences.

"The master offers unparalleled opportunities."

"For what? Power?"

"Yes. Everything else follows."

"And yet you seem afraid of him."

"He is demanding. And he does not tolerate failure."

"What does he do to those who fail?"

The elf cast a haunted look at her. "Something you don't want to experience. I had done it to others before he did it to me."

"Well, you survived, so it couldn't have been that bad."

Darron shook his head. "I did not."

"Then how… ? You…" She wasn't sure she wanted to finish the sentence. It was too ghastly.

"It is as you surmise. He turned me to a pile of hot ash, but the necromancer Aeron restored me at his behest. I have been given a second chance to please the master and in this I will not fail."

Eriana followed in aghast silence. This matter-of-fact story of murder and rebirth at Soliander's hands was her first true hint of the crimes he had committed. She didn't want to hear any more right now, feeling fatigued after a long day that was probably going to get worse.

Unused to the climbing, she felt her legs protesting as they reached a wooden door some hundred steps up. Dim light shone under it, but no sounds came from the other side—even as Darron unlocked it with a dark key and thrust it open without knocking. He gestured for her to enter.

"I will await you at the bottom." He turned and descended, soft steps fading with the disappearing torchlight.

The room before Eriana was similar in size and furnishings to the one she had just left, two dim lanterns casting light on the cold stone floor and the bed against the far wall. The only sign of life was a lump there under the sheets and comforter. It didn't stir, and she wondered if her sister had been told she was coming. She hoped for ignorance. Diara's initial reaction could tell her much for its honesty.

She stepped into the room and swung the door closed behind her with a mild bang that caused no movement. For a moment, she considered how best to continue before walking to the foot of the bed, grabbing a firm handful, and yanking down the comforter all at once. As expected, the figure, which had been laying on one side, lurched upright. Long, disheveled brown hair hid much of her angry face, though several thick scars were still visible through the strands. But the hair couldn't hide her furious brown eyes.

"Stop your games, dark—" She stopped. Her eyes widened, then rapidly scanned Eriana up and down, narrowing in suspicion, and finally glaring anew.

"It's nice to see you, Diara," Eriana said, relieved and concerned at once.

At the sound of her voice, her sister recoiled as if struck. Then called out to the room. "Is this another trick, Soliander? Darron? You got the voice right but she's as old as my dead mother, you fools."

Eriana absorbed that for a moment, wondering what the wizard had been doing to her, before saying, "It's not a trick. It's really me, Diara—and yes, I am twenty years older than when I disappeared with the others."

Diara snorted. "I don't believe that for a second. If it's really you, prove it."

Eriana knew no illusion could do what she was about to do. "Come closer."

Her sister smirked and crawled across the bed, closer than they had been in years even before the Earth quest. The strain of their relationship had kept them apart long before Diara's betrayal, and in fact had led to it. But Eriana gripped Diara's jaw from below, thumb on one side, fingers curling around the other, just like their mother used to do to them. This near, she could smell sweat and see that her sister hadn't washed in some time, although there was a tub in one corner. Was she refusing to use it or had Soli lied about taking care of her? She'd learn soon enough.

She spoke a few words and a soft glow spread over Diara, her hair straightening as if freshly washed, dirt vanishing from her face and fingernails. A healthier color was restored to her face, now clearly visible. Only now could Eriana see that she had gained weight, her face and breasts fuller, neck thicker, and hips tugging at the waist of a sleeping gown that had seen better days. Eriana recognized the sight of a woman who had given birth at least once. It startled her. Diara kneeled back on her heels and regarded her as if trying to make sense of her.

"That grip," she began almost fondly, "mother used to do that." Then something seemed to occur to her and she sneered. "You could have gotten that memory from the spell you did on me."

"The spell?" Eriana stopped herself and clenched her fists. "He cast the *Mind Trust* spell on you? Damn it, Soli." Then she realized it was obvious. Of course, he would have done that. Diara could know where Everon was. He wouldn't have left this up to an interrogation.

"Don't you ever get tired of these games?" Diara asked. "What's the point? You already know everything."

Eriana wondered that, too. Was Soli trying to break her? "I guess the first thing I need to do is get you to accept that it's really me."

Diara laughed. "Can't wait to see how—"

Eriana spoke again and felt her sister's eyes lock onto hers, Diara's sight in a magical grip that let her see the truth of what was before her so that it couldn't be denied. It was a spell used to bring brief sanity to the insane, peace to the delirious, or clarity to the deceived. After a few seconds, it ended. Her sister blinked a few times as if clearing her eyes from a bright light. And now would come the expression that told Eriana where they stood.

But Eriana couldn't read it. Diara's eyes held too many questions—too much surprise. No hatred, at least—but no happiness. A kind of neutrality lay there, disguised by lack of understanding.

"I have been on another world for twenty years," she explained, "because a spell took me back in time. And I was trapped there until Soliander found me and brought me here, yesterday, I believe."

Her sister arched an eyebrow, the first sign of old contempt returning. "You *believe*?"

Eriana pursed her lips. "He put me to sleep. I did not yet ask for how long."

Diara's eyes narrowed. "Why would he do that? He adores you." She sneered. "You mean to tell me you are enemies now? How wonderful!"

Sighing, Eriana said, "We are not anything. We have lived different lives and hardly know each other."

"You're like an old hag now. He wouldn't want you anyway. Who would? You can't even have children!"

Eriana's heart clenched at the confirmation that her sister was just as hateful as ever. "But you did. How many nieces and nephews do I have?"

Briefly startled, Diara responded, "It won't matter. You will never meet them."

"Where are they? Surely Everon isn't raising them while running for his life from Soliander?" She hadn't meant to goad her, but it slipped out.

Diara glared. "You know a lot about running, don't you? You ran from Jorad so fast you forgot to bring me and Solun with you, and look what that bastard did to us. Maybe I should be happy just to have scars on my face instead of a hand chopped off. Our brother didn't deserve that for trying to help you escape. You did. You're the one Jorad should have chopped a piece from, but you got away clean."

Eriana had heard some of this before, but that last part was too much. She snapped, "Really? You think him stabbing me in the stomach so I wouldn't have his bastard child was getting away clean? Never being able to have kids because of that?"

"Oh, but you have kids, remember? You baby me and Solun like you think you're our dead mom. And look at you now! You even *look* like her!"

"That's enough, Diara."

"It'll never be enough! No amount of pain and suffering is too much for you."

"Is that why you betrayed me to Everon?"

"Yes! You deserved it. Jorad just wanted you. Beautiful, lovely Eriana. He kidnapped all of us just to get *you*. And then you betrayed us by running away without us. And then you had the nerve to come back a healer, of all things, to save us! A renowned priestess! The Lady Hope, they call you. If only they knew, knew how you crushed the hope out of your dear brother and sister to save yourself. They all think you're so noble, going around saving everyone, everywhere on your damn quests. It makes me sick. Just looking at you makes me want to vomit. So yes. Yes, I made sure you could never say no again. Forced you to have to save everyone whether or not you wanted to. You can never run away again. You'll never escape being a hero now, dear sister! I hope you choke to death on your false heroism!"

Eriana flushed at the awful, vengeful logic, which struck home precisely because it made sense. But that just gave rise to her own upset.

"You are the betrayer in this family, Diara. And I haven't seen you since you stabbed me in the back to tell you how *sickening* it is. We were Jorad's prisoners *together*. You more than *anyone* should know just how horrific it is to be a prisoner, and you imprisoned me again. How dare you? Who do you think you are to do that to me? *I'm* the one who *freed* all of us from it. Not you. You didn't do a thing to help us escape. Your brother and I tried to get you out of there *with* us. If you hadn't been such a fool when we were running, we might all have made it. Instead, he sacrificed his hand for you just so I could get away and come back to get you both, and you're nothing but resentful about what we gave up. I forgave you for your cowardice that night because you were eleven years old."

"Well, you *should* have! Don't act like your *forgiveness* was so noble. I was a child!"

Fury tore through Eriana. "So was I! And you're still a child now. You might have the body of a woman, but that's the only part of you that's grown up. I'm sorry I didn't save you sooner, Diara. I got men killed trying to help me find you. I had to leave the priesthood to come get you. I gave up everything to rescue you. I didn't want or expect a thank you, but I sure as hell didn't expect you to repay me by *imprisoning me all over again!*"

"Well, you should have. It just shows how big a fool you are not to see it coming. And now I'm a prisoner again!" She jabbed an accusing finger at Eriana. "And it's all your fault!"

"How is this my fault? You know what? I don't want to hear it. Just shut up."

"What's the matter? Afraid of an argument you can't win?"

With an angry thrust of her hand, Eriana spoke a word and Diara collapsed on the bed, unconscious. Eriana was shaking, years of wondering about the logic behind this betrayal having an answer more terrible than any she could have anticipated. She knew Diara had hated her. It wasn't like she'd tried to hide it. But this was a stab in the heart like she had never known. Tears filled her eyes as she strode from the room. They had dried by the time she swept past Darron at the bottom and climbed to her own "prison," where she slammed the door shut and stalked back and forth.

However much this logic of Diara's was her own, she was certain Everon had contributed to it. For the first time, Eriana thought she might not stop Soliander from killing Everon if she found herself there when he tried.

CHAPTER TWELVE

THE SONS OF THE MAGI

Luna Rose Williams stared at the smoking screen of her laptop in shocked disbelief, then at her hands. The energy had come from her fingertips. She was certain, though there was no evidence—no scorch marks or anything. No, that was just the computer—a small fire still crackling in the cracked screen. It was already unplugged, and she knew the battery hadn't exploded. She had seen the fiery darts fly into the laptop.

Andy was going to be upset, even though the computer wasn't his. She needed a good story. She hadn't expected to be the first person they knew who'd cast a spell, however accidentally.

She got up and started pacing around her London flat, bare feet nearly soundless on the hardwood floor. The kettle began whistling that her hot water was ready, but she needed something stronger than tea now. She just turned it off before grabbing red wine from the rack beside the stainless-steel fridge. Andy would help her decide whether to tell the others. She wasn't sure she wanted the attention. Bloody hell, she was so scared right now and didn't even want to tell her boyfriend.

The front doorhandle rattled and she poured herself a big glass, noticing that her hand shook. What if it happened again? She didn't even know what caused it, so how could she prevent it?

Wearing just his running shoes, socks, and grey jogging shorts, Andy Rion opened the door. His sinewy torso gleamed with sweat, his chest not heaving even though he'd probably run here up four flights of stairs like usual. He met her gaze, his face immediately falling, dark eyes going to her shaking hand. He always noticed everything. Always.

"What happened?" he said, his accent a familiar but odd mix of British and American English.

Luna gulped her wine and was about to answer when he sniffed the air and turned toward the laptop, his face registering surprise that swiftly passed. He was always so quick to mask his expressions, but she still thought, maybe wrongly, that she was the only person for whom he dropped his guard.

"I, uh, the battery, I think it did something."

He arched an eyebrow, and she knew he didn't believe her. The man was impossible to lie to, but she actually liked that he could see right through her. Just not right now. He was kind enough to let the fibs go without comment and did so now.

He came over and leaned up to kiss her, since she was two inches taller than his five-and-a-half feet. She cupped his smooth cheek, then ran a hand through his black hair. It was a couple of inches long and perpetually disheveled. She'd made a game to try messing it up so that it looked bad, but it never worked. It somehow symbolized his perpetually unfazed demeanor, down-to-earth attitude, and internal strength. Maybe it was the black belts he held in multiple disciplines, but he always came across as being able to handle anything thrown at him.

Except maybe some fiery darts she hadn't meant to throw.

"Well," he began, pouring himself a glass of wine, "as long as the hard drive is fine, we can get stuff off it. I'll try in a bit."

"Can I borrow yours?"

He smirked and walked over to it. "Not sure I should let you."

When he placed it on the counter, she opened it and he typed in a passcode. With the screen unlocked, she saw what she thought of as a camera gallery. A dozen video feeds were running, but most were off. Some cameras—especially the one at Stonehenge—were only on at night, and were carefully hidden.

"What if you're wrong," she began, "and some faeries come through during the day?"

"We'll find out about it on the news when they scare the shit out of everyone. It's only the remote doorways between worlds where I think they might show up in daytime, but I still think the first fae to arrive will be from the Unseelie Court."

She sipped more wine. The Unseelie Court preferred nighttime shenanigans, but something worse than that was probably coming. A decapitated dwarf had already been found, minus the head, near Stonehenge but not been identified. Andy suspected it hadn't been one of Earth's little people, but an actual dwarf from Elfhame, the land of fae.

"I hope you're wrong," she said. "They're going to be angry that humans made magic, and them, disappear from Earth for a thousand years. Even the good fae from the Seelie Court might be furious."

"I suspect a war is coming. Speaking of, Oliver wants a meeting tonight. Something about a big announcement."

Luna chuckled. "I like how a war coming reminded you of Oliver."

"Knew you would. I'm hitting the shower." Andy began walking away, as silent as ever even with his shoes on. He could've been a cat burglar.

"Maybe I'll join you." Luna pulled the tie from her long brown hair and tried to relax. The last person she felt like dealing with tonight was Oliver, their fearless Grand Master. He'd been calling more frequent meetings of the Sons of the Magi ever since the Stonehenge Four appeared on the world's stage. But this was the third time in a week even though they only used to meet once a month. She couldn't blame him. After a thousand years of the society waiting for magic to return, it had actually happened. Part of her had never really believed any of it. If anything, Andy had always been more serious about it, even though she was the one who'd introduced him to the Sons of the Magi and got him accepted.

The stash of supposed magic items he'd acquired had gotten him in more than Luna being second in command. Luna had seen him at multiple auctions where they had sometimes competed for the same item and before meeting. While her parents were wealthy and gave her the means to pursue her hobby, Andy had always been coy about where he got the money, as some items went for over a million. Between that, his quiet footsteps, and his jokingly evasive remarks about an innocent past, she sometimes wondered if he really was some sort of jewel thief. But then he'd likely just steal the magic items, wouldn't he? Why purchase them? Maybe he was a computer criminal. He certainly knew more about computers than anyone else she'd known, and she sometimes wondered if he knew how to hack.

Then there was the way he could scale a wall, or jump over things, skills he said parkour had given him. She didn't doubt it, having seen him in action. For a man in his thirties, he was in superb physical condition. He even seemed to know his way around swords, knives, and other medieval weapons in a way that suggested he'd used them for real, but he always shrugged off her questioning looks. One of these days he'd tell her more about his life, especially if they were going to spend the rest of theirs together, as often seemed the case. The story about him making his own way since he was a boy in America before moving to Britain seemed plausible, but sometimes that made her wonder if he was just a good liar.

Despite all of that, she trusted him and didn't wonder anymore why he'd stayed with her all these years. For all his evasiveness about his past, he was remarkably direct with her about what he thought and felt about her. No one had ever said the things he did, not to mention looking her in the eyes like she was the only person who existed. She bit her lip and decided to join him in the shower. A little fooling around was just the thing to take her mind off the rest of the day.

Hours later, the couple entered an old, three-story library in Knightsbridge, the posh west side of London, the noisy streets silenced when the doors closed behind them. A few patrons were spread out among the ancient books in which the Gilded Library specialized, but none looked up. The redheaded librarian, one of their society's members, smiled as they walked along the front wall's bookcases to one end. A quick look around and a nod from the librarian, and Luna briefly pulled *The Necronomicon*, *Tobin's Spirit Guide*, and *The Occido Lumen* to trigger the secret door in the corner to swivel open. She and Andy stepped inside, and it closed behind them. Dimly lit stairs curled downward, past the first basement level to the second, hidden one, reachable only this way or by another secret passage.

Her family had owned the building for generations, but few of them were members of the Sons of the Magi—a name she had once suggested this be changed to "Children of the Magi" only to get a snicker. Apparently ancient sexism wasn't to be removed from the society. Her mother had believed in all of it before her death, but her father didn't and hadn't been told about any of it. He had suggested selling the library more than once until Luna just bought it from him to put an end to that. Now the place was considered a cultural site. If only people knew what was in the hidden basement, and that generations of collected magic memorabilia were suddenly relevant and housed here.

Luna reached the hidden basement behind Andy, who took her hand. They came around the corner to hear the low voices of a dozen members, who had a tendency to speak quietly here even though the place had been soundproofed. There were no windows down here, and so the lighting was bright enough to reveal the ancient cracks in the grey stone walls—some repaired, others newer. The problem with a secret location was that you couldn't bring just anyone down here, so society members of varying skill levels did any maintenance. Andy was surprisingly handy with tools and had fixed a thing or two for her.

Their peers said hello as people began filing into the Sanctum, a room with an old, mahogany table long enough for twenty people on each side. At its head sat Oliver, his receding hairline cutting into his close-cropped brown hair as he leaned over a book while facing them. He had taken this business a little too seriously even before magic started happening, always dressing in black jeans and a black shirt, his round spectacles making him look like a scholar. And she supposed he was, for he had read every book in this place more than once, she was sure. Not the books upstairs for Londoners to peruse, but the spellbooks and scrolls collected in antiquity and ever since, all sitting one room over across the hall. Beside that was the treasure room, the walls filled with supposedly magic items. Other rooms had seen little use until recently. Now people were trying to get spells to work in one of the three labs: one for potion work and the like, another for summonings, and a third for everything else. But none of them had worked so far.

Luna and Andy sat in two of the high-backed chairs closest to Oliver, who scrutinized a spellbook, his dragon-embossed goblet of red wine beside it. He always insisted the room be lit with only candles or torches, for effect, though that just made it harder to read anything. The walls weren't tall enough for tapestries, so they had settled for paintings of fantastic scenes depicting dragons, knights, fairies, and more. A few swords, maces, and suits of armor graced the walls or stood in corners. Everything had had the air of being pretend until recently—and it had all become very real for Luna this afternoon. As she mused, other members took positions at the table or along the walls. They had room for fifty and numbered twenty-eight, all but three in attendance. These were the heady days of the Sons of the Magi, and some had canceled vacations to get back to England for these meetings.

A young man they called the herald stood up once everyone was seated, and started the meeting. "This gathering of the Sons of the Magi is called to order, presided over by your Grand Master, Oliver Leiber."

He sat down as Oliver rose.

"Wizards," he began in a commanding voice, "we have called each other thus for a millennium, though none of us had the power flowing through us. None of us could wield the might of the gods. None of us could rule over others as wizards should. Until today. Today is a day we and our ancestors have long sought, for today, one of us has finally cast a spell."

Luna started, as a murmur went through the room. How did Oliver know she had cast one? She wouldn't put it past the bastard to have cameras in her place, but Andy was too observant not to notice even something carefully hidden. Sometimes he checked their flat for cameras or listening devices out of an abundance of caution, as he put it. Perhaps he hadn't been diligent enough. But Oliver's next word made her growing upset quiet.

"Rebecca Stinson, please come to me so we can show our brothers and sisters you are the chosen one, the first to lead us into this new world for which we have waited."

Luna frowned as a petite blonde rose to her feet and came to the head of the table across from them, a tight tan skirt and blouse combination revealing her ample curves. Why did it have to be her, of all people? That she and Oliver were having sex was no secret, though they acted like no one knew. It wasn't like they went on dates, but their amorous looks weren't fooling anyone. The looks Rebecca had sent Luna over the last year had suggested Rebecca thought she was the new #2 in the society just because she was screwing Oliver. Now Luna felt some jealousy about what spell she was going to do.

She didn't have long to wait. The lovers made a few more remarks about the importance of what everyone was going to see. Then Rebecca appeared to concentrate, holding out one hand as if cupping something invisible. For several moments, nothing happened. Then a ball of light the size of a tennis ball appeared, hovering over her hand, which she dropped, leaving the ball hanging in space. No one made a sound. With a slow flicking motion, Rebecca sent the light gliding down the table to the far end, then brought it back, though it sputtered and faded out before returning to her. Then the questions started.

"When did you first cast this spell?" someone asked.

"This morning," Rebecca replied.

"How many times?"

"This is now the third. It is easier each time, and I am able to control the ball more."

"Were you intentionally trying to do it? Or was it an accident, like so many of the stories we hear?"

"A little of both."

Luna stopped paying much attention to the chatter, as it was clear this wasn't as momentous as Oliver made it seem. Rebecca was nothing special, just another random person who had magic talent. She just happened to be one of them, and Luna agreed with Andy not to give in to a frequent idea of Oliver's—to recruit people who had shown magic talent from around the world. Oliver seemed to want to do it as if to gain control over all of them, promising them training or help in exchange for some sort of allegiance to the Sons of the Magi. But that wasn't what the group was for.

Their ancestors had formed the society after magic mysteriously stopped working a thousand years ago. They had wanted to preserve spells and magic items for the day when magic returned. Most had thought that wouldn't take long. The earliest books in their secret library included the diaries of those who had lost their powers, and their fading memories of how to cast anything as they neared old age and died. Like everywhere else in the world, magic had become a myth even to some of their descendants, who had never seen a spell done. Or a faerie, goblin, troll... the list went on.

How odd it was that today was the first time Luna had seen magic. And she'd seen it twice. Who among them might be next?

Oliver interrupted her thoughts with a veiled question. "Unless one of you is holding back, Rebecca is the first among us to perform magic."

Luna opened her mouth—and then a sharp pain struck her shin. "Ow! Andy!"

"Sorry," he said, looking sheepish before turning to Rebecca. "This is all great news. I think we need to come up with some sort of plan for your advancement."

Luna sat frowning as the others talked of ways to help Rebecca, even though none of them knew the first thing about wizard training. Somewhere in the middle of it, Andy took her hand and turned to her, giving a quick wink no one else saw. When he squeezed her hand, she squeezed back. He had stopped her from admitting she had cast a spell. Did he know? Of course he did. He could be so infuriating. He kept secrets so well, and somehow knew one of hers. She would've pulled her hand away in annoyance, but she wanted him to know she was cooperating and understood his message not to say anything. She just didn't understand why he wanted that. Or how the bloody hell he knew!

As she watched Rebecca bask in the glow of being the first to do magic, Luna was kind of glad she had said nothing. If she had wanted to be the center of attention like that, she would've accepted her rightful place as Grand Master. Oliver only had it because he was a man, for one thing, but also because he had pushed for it and Luna didn't care much. She owned the place, after all, and that brought its own power. Since magic had started working, she had wondered whether her decision was a mistake—but it was too late now.

Oliver rose at the head of the table. "In light of Rebecca's achievement," he said, "we must once again consider contacting the Stonehenge Four. You know my thoughts on this—that they seem to be central to the reawakening of magic on Earth—and therefore, we might be able to get answers about what is happening. Perhaps they know why. Perhaps they can help us regain the power of our ancestors. Perhaps they can help us gain control over what is happening in the world.

"But now it is even more important. We don't know how much control they have over their own abilities, and we've already discussed how Matt Sorenson looked surprised when he vanished in front of the TV cameras. But it is possible that he and the others have more control than we think—so they can teach Rebecca, and then others among us. And they may be very interested to hear about our treasure trove of items, and that we are descendants of wizards from long ago. We can position ourselves as partners with them, maybe ones even able to train them as much as they can help us. This is an alliance we should pursue—and, as Grand Master, I am making the decision to contact them."

"Hold on," said Luna, irritated. "You don't have that authority. Might I remind you this is a secret society and no one, not even a Grand Master, has the authority to just reveal us to the world?"

Oliver sneered at her. "You revealed us to the man sitting beside you and we welcomed him. He's not the only one who was brought into the Sons of the Magi instead of born into it. And we are not revealing ourselves to the world, as you put it, but to four people worthy of being included in our aspirations."

"You mean *your* aspirations?" she asked. "You've always talked of wizards resuming their rightful place as masters of the world, as if they ever were before. Just because some people have power like that doesn't mean they should have power over other people's lives."

He smirked. "Of course, it does. But I am not talking about bringing the world to its knees." He adopted a friendlier tone. "Listen, Luna, we've all heard reports of people being killed for their new powers. The healer in India who couldn't heal people on demand, so they decided she was holding back and tore her to pieces. The shaman in Africa who people decided was possessed by evil spirits, so they stabbed him to death. The wizard in the southern United States, who got burned alive when people decided he had made a pact with Satan. And we know that the police, the FBI, or whoever are hunting the Stonehenge Four. Will they hunt us if they know about us? Will they hunt Rebecca? Will they hunt you if you prove to have the talent and anyone finds out?"

Luna said nothing, frustrated that he was making sense. She didn't want him to. Something told her he could not be trusted with power of any kind. With any luck, he would have no talent for wizardry. They should've been thankful that it was Rebecca and not him that showed signs. It was just as well she hadn't revealed her own magic.

Andy said, "The problem with contacting the Stonehenge Four is that they have the most media attention on them. They seem to be in hiding, with good reasons, as you just mentioned. It might not be so easy to gain access to them."

Oliver looked down his nose at him. "This, coming from you? The man who has found so many magic items? Surely you can find a way—or do you not want to?"

Andy replied, "As you made clear to Luna before I was accepted here, we need to know more about new recruits before making them some sort of offer or arrangement."

"Then I suggest you get busy reaching out to them before I take matters into my own hands."

Andy frowned at him. "You haven't already?"

"No. I recognize your talents and delegate, so this is something you need to do before I delegate to someone less capable—someone more likely to screw it up and ruin our chances of forging a mutually beneficial arrangement."

Luna stifled a groan on hearing Oliver outmaneuver Andy. She'd never heard that before. Her boyfriend always seemed a step ahead of everyone. But he was also wilier than anyone had a right to be, and she half expected he would turn this to his advantage in some way. After all, Oliver had just ceded control to him.

"Fine," said Andy, and Luna knew he was thinking the same thing from the slightly forced sound of annoyance in his voice. She knew what he sounded like when genuinely annoyed, and this wasn't it.

"There is something else we should discuss," began Oliver. "Samhain is just days from now. As all of you know, Halloween is the night when the barriers between this world and Elfhame are thinnest. We have a better chance of seeing faeries now than ever before—perhaps even of greeting and welcoming them to Earth. This is the first Halloween since magic returned. There have been scattered reports around the globe of elves, pixies, and even a goblin appearing in the wilderness. Many people don't believe the tales, but I do, and so do some of you.

"I predict that at this year's All Hallows' Eve, there will be a great awakening and we will see many creatures, great and small. We should collectively go to some of the most prominent places rumored to be doorways between worlds, and there we should wait for their arrival. We can communicate with each other throughout the night, videotaping what happens and ensuring that mankind's reborn relationship with fae is beneficial to us and the world.

"This All Hallows' Eve will also be special for another reason, and I believe it is foreordained that the night will be magical in every sense of the word. The harvest moon, a full moon, fell on October 1st. When there is a second full moon in a month, it is called a Blue Moon, and we will be having one on All Hallows' Eve for the first time in seventy-six years. The first full moon after the harvest moon is also known as the hunter's moon. So we will have at once a hunter's moon, a full moon, and a Blue Moon, all on All Hallows' Eve, the very first Halloween to occur after the reawakening of magic."

Luna had known some of that, because the Sons of the Magi were aware of many legends of old—but she hadn't realized this conjunction of moons would occur. "What sort of opportunity do you think this provides? You think the fairies will truly walk among us?"

Having resumed her seat, Rebecca answered coolly, "Yes. We've been monitoring this for some time. And we know that there are many—in England and Ireland especially—who are preparing to ward off the evil spirits, the faeries, like people did in the days of old."

"If that's true," said Andy, "then people will protect themselves."

"Yes," said Oliver, "but many will not, and there will be nothing we can do for them. There will be too many people. I do anticipate many shocked people that night. It is possible that it will forever change the world."

Luna thought that that had already happened, and it wasn't for the better. Was there to be some sudden explosion of changes now? The world could hardly handle what was already happening. She asked, "But what does this have to do with *us*?"

Oliver turned to her. "I would like the Sons of the Magi to be more proactive—to be at some sites where fairies are believed to cross into this world."

"What for?" Andy asked, scowling. "I'm very familiar with these myths—and most of them say that the faeries are nothing like Disney movies make them out to be, but very sinister. If you're right, then we just set ourselves up to be attacked, or kidnapped to Elfhame, or something worse."

Oliver said, "You know there are ways to protect ourselves. Like iron. This is known to hurt the faeries so they won't touch us. And we can dress in—"

"Yes," interrupted Luna, "but they might think we mean to harm them with it. They could see iron as provocation. And we don't know if it's gonna work anyway. All of this is myth. What if real faeries aren't even fazed by iron? Is that really something you want to take a chance on?"

Oliver smiled and looked around them. "Perhaps we should take a vote and see who wants to be present and who does not. No one is forcing anyone to go, and no one will make people stay behind. I, for one, will be at Stonehenge that night. Rebecca, too. And I would like others to be at other locations we think are the most likely to have visitors. What does everyone say?"

Luna watched as some people nodded and others cocked their eyebrows. None of them knew what they might be getting themselves into, and those without caution were likely to come away from Halloween changed forever, and not in a good way. She had no intention of going anywhere near these supposed doorways and increasingly thought Halloween was an especially good night to stay indoors—maybe with the blood of a slaughtered animal over the threshold, like people used to use, to keep fairies out. She caught Andy's eye and felt certain he agreed.

As the meeting turned into a long planning discussion, Andy led her out and to the treasure room. That was the informal name for the place where all the supposedly magic items were kept. All four walls were lined with mismatched bookcases, floor to ceiling. Cabinets with glass doors formed two hallways between them, and there were a number of items atop cabinets on stands or in small cases. In the room's center stood a pedestal with a small skull reputed to belong to a faerie, and to let the holder control the fae. Security cameras were in two corners.

No one else was here, and Andy said, "I think we need to do something about security in here now. We never did it before, because none of the expensive stuff is here. But now we have to worry about inexpensive stuff having actual power."

"Yes, I know you like to call it the trinket room instead. I think there's a chance some of this stuff is real."

He looked about to say more when Oliver walked in. "Let's talk about it at home."

"There you are, Luna," said Oliver, sauntering over. He seemed even cockier now than usual. "What do you think about having Rebecca try her hand at some items in here? Maybe she can figure out which ones are real."

Andy responded before she could. "The only problem with that is that she might set something off. I think we should wait a bit and have a plan. And I'm not sure testing anything while we're in here is a good idea. One item could set off others, blow the building up, you never know."

Oliver chuckled without humor. "Well, you do make good points, as always. Let's think about this and get started with at least a few this week. I want to make progress. You never know when we might need to use something, if only we can find out how it works or what it really does." He looked around at the hundreds of items. "This could take a while, but yes, let's not blow ourselves up."

"Okay, Oliver," replied Luna. "We'll think of something."

The Grand Master left, and Andy turned to her. "Him using these is exactly what concerns me. No one is ready for any of this. There are things here that, if the description we have is right, could set in motion events we can't stop. This might be the most dangerous room on the planet."

Luna bit her lip. He was right. Suddenly it all seemed so foolish, this society of theirs. More security was needed, but not just something to know who came and went. This room needed to be locked up—and almost no one should have the key.

She trusted Andy, and a quarter of the items were his. But Oliver, as Grand Master, would insist on having a key. Did they care what he wanted? Luna owned the building and could just lock it all up. Andy could take his items back. She could remove hers. But what precedent would that set? Both of them probably had useless, non-magic items, very powerful ones, and more that were in between. That same mix could exist among the few items Oliver or the others had brought. Most of what lay here belonged to the society, and had been here hundreds of years. No one could lay claim to it. Somehow, Andy had the biggest trove. One day he really had to tell her how he was so good at acquiring supposedly magic items.

They spent an hour socializing with their peers before walking home. She had to wait until they got inside her flat before asking Andy how he knew she'd done a spell. The door had hardly shut when she asked, "So how did you know?"

"Know what?"

She smacked his arm. "Don't be coy. I know why you kicked me under the table. Tell me, or you'll sleep in the rain tonight."

He smiled as if not taking her seriously. "I didn't know you could be so draconian! But I saw the laptop and that was no battery issue. I don't know what you did, but it looked like some sort of energy struck the screen in several places, smashing it and burning holes. There were at least four impacts that I could see."

Luna turned away, hands on her forehead, heading for the kitchen and stopping to kick off her shoes. When she didn't respond, he followed.

"You didn't do it on purpose. And you don't know how it happened or how to repeat it."

"One of these days you're going to tell me how you figure everything out all the time."

"It wasn't that hard, partly because I know you. You haven't said one word about trying to do anything magical. What actually happened?"

She sighed. "I was mad at the computer because it was giving me this error I couldn't get past. I yelled at it and made an angry motion with both hands. Suddenly these fiery darts shot out of my hands and into the screen."

He thought about that and said, "That sounds like a spell in one of the books. I think we should get it and have you try it on purpose. Or maybe a cantrip, like what Rebecca did. The important thing here is that you have magic talent."

Luna let out a breath. "I'm not sure I want it. It's dangerous. I mean, look what I did."

"That's exactly why we need you to learn control. I'll help in any way I can." He opened his laptop and began looking through the folders, searching for a file. "I've taken photos or scanned so many of the spellbook pages over the years, and saved them with names the spells on them. We don't even need to grab a book from the library."

Suspecting that he knew the answer, she asked, "Why exactly didn't you want me to tell Oliver? Or the others?"

"I don't trust him. Neither do you. He's always talked about wizards being the rightful dominant force on Earth—and now that magic's working, I don't want him thinking he's going to get his hands on you and turn you into some sort of tool to help him in whatever stupid fantasies he has."

She agreed and wondered if Oliver was no longer all talk now that this fantasy was technically possible. "Do you think he'll do that with Rebecca?"

"Of course." He opened an image and she leaned over his shoulder to look at it, seeing a picture of a hand with multiple blazing darts emerging from it.

"What do you think he's going to do?" Luna asked.

"I don't know, and that's what bothers me. We need to secure that treasure room even if he gets upset about it, and we need to make sure no one can find the magic items we have elsewhere."

"Have you sensed any power in yourself?"

"No."

She noticed that he didn't think about that long, and seemed certain. But then she would've felt the same way up until this afternoon.

They spent a while looking at the spell, but she didn't want to try it. Not here, anyway. Maybe they needed to find a field somewhere. That led them to start talking about places like Stonehenge, other henges, stone circles, and long barrows in the countryside. Each was distinctive in design or purpose, but Andy was certain that all but the barrows were doorways to the fae world—though he couldn't explain why he thought this. There was nothing in legend about it, but that was why he had set up cameras at dozens of them. It had taken a while, given that most of them were at least ninety minutes from London, and he had to do it at night when no one would stop him. That he was that good at sneaking around, or that comfortable in the dark coun-tryside at night, didn't really surprise her.

They finally stopped for the night and settled onto the couch for a little quiet time—or so she thought. Then he opened his mouth and surprised her.

"I have a confession of my own," Andy began, one arm around her shoul-ders as she leaned into his chest. "Do you remember how I've been looking for Merlin's pendant for so long? Well, I finally found it."

"You did? That's great."

"Not really."

Luna chuckled. "Why?"

"The woman from the Stonehenge Four was wearing it, on that news broadcast about their reappearance at Stonehenge two months ago."

Luna remembered the blonde woman from that broadcast and others since, but not the necklace. And this was a long time ago for him to just be saying something now—but she let that slide. "That seems like an amazing coincidence, for one of them to have it. You've never told me what the pen-dant supposedly does. Are you going to confess that, too?"

"That's because I wasn't sure it was true and, given the story about it, Ol-iver finding out might be trouble. The story goes back a long way, and I've never seen it written down in all the books we've collected here over the years. It's the whole reason I got into searching for magic items to begin with. Supposedly, Merlin's pendant made all the magic on Earth disappear into Elfhame—and all the creatures, too, because if they stayed here when the magic went away, they would die. That's because they were all partly magical in nature. Even Merlin was half-fae."

She turned to him. "Yeah, I remember that bit. But you're saying this is why magic disappeared? That's new to me. And why is it dangerous for Oli-ver to hear this?"

"There's more to it. The story says that if the pendant is ever returned to Stonehenge, it would reopen the doorways between this word and Elfhame. Magic would flow from the fae world back into Earth, and the creatures would be able to return, too."

Luna's mouth fell open. "What? Wait. That would explain pretty much everything that's happening now, except we haven't heard much about things like faeries appearing."

"I think it's just a matter of time. It's why I put the cameras up—and if Ol-iver and the others are serious about going to some doorways in person, watching from the safety of a video feed is a lot smarter."

She almost laughed at the understatement. "Yeah, you said they were doorways before. I just didn't understand why you thought they were open now. I mean, I thought it was just a general thing about the world changing." Something occurred to her. "So you think the Stonehenge Four have Merlin's pendant and took it there?"

"Yes. I doubt they knew what it was, but I think they did."

"Does that explain their disappearance? Did they go into Elfhame?"

He cocked an eyebrow. "Maybe, but I don't think so. It's supposedly hard to get from here to there, but easy for fae to come here. I don't think they could've gone by accident—and it wouldn't explain their other disappearances. But do you see why it's dangerous for Oliver to know this?"

She considered. "Actually, no."

"If he knew about this and it's true, he would be doing what I'm doing, except more aggressively. I have those cameras set up at the doorways between worlds for a reason, Luna. I am positive creatures are coming through. If Oliver knew, he would be trying to meet them and get help amassing power for himself. Maybe he'd offer to be their guide in this world. I think it would be dangerous for everyone else for Oliver to gain some any prominence among the fae folk that return, like he's some sort of chosen human ambassador for the rest of us. I'm sure he'd put himself in that position if he knew. This is what I've been thinking for a while, and he just proved me right tonight. I'm certain it's why he wants to be at Stonehenge."

Luna stifled a groan. "Bloody hell, you're right. So what do we do?"

"I want to make sure Oliver doesn't get ahead of himself. I think there are forces at work here that none of us really understand. His ambitions might lead him to do something before anyone is ready."

"Like playing with magic items."

"Yes. The spell Rebecca did wasn't much, but you know he's going to push her. We just need to keep an eye on that. And you need to push yourself to see what you can do, safely. But my big worry is that treasure room."

"What do you want to do?"

"Steal every last magic item in it."

CHAPTER THIRTEEN

THE DEVASTATOR

Matt looked around the room at his friends and asked, "So what are we going to tell our hosts?"

Along with Lorian and Rognir, they had been in their meeting room discussing several things—the conversation with Jack that morning, the revelations about Eriana and Soliander, and Kori's appearance within the Palace of Andor. But so far, they had only agreed that the news would upset everyone.

Eric said, "I think it depends on what we decide about this rescue attempt. We need to be proactive. I don't want to walk in there and say Zoran the Devastator has her and we don't know where he is or what to do. We need to hash out what we know about Soliander's alter ego."

Matt nodded. "Let's have a solution, even if they disagree or suggest changes. I think this is our mission, not theirs."

Eric nodded and turned to Rognir and Lorian. "So what can you tell us about Zoran the Devastator?"

Lorian said, "Not much is known before two years ago—which makes sense, now that we know he is Soliander. He conquered the Kingdom of Esson on the planet Delonin. Esson is a military junta, run by warlords. They believe power comes to those who take it. Perhaps it is fitting that Zoran used wizardry to summon monsters, dragons, ogres, trolls, and dark elves into the halls of power and subdue those in charge. They were outmatched and unsuspecting."

"I remember!" said Matt, images having flashed through his head. "He let them live as they had before, except they could only make major attacks at his direction. If they obeyed, he would make their strength rise with his. Most of them agreed. He killed those who didn't. Any resistance ended when he used them to invade the nearby Kingdom of Marduna from Esson, and they grew rich on the spoils."

The elf said, "Can you tell why he invaded Esson, or Marduna?"

Matt's eyes widened and he stood up. "Yes! For Everon."

Eric scowled in confusion. "What's the connection?"

Matt pieced it together while they waited for him. "Long ago in Marduna, a wizard killed a dragon and cast a spell on its blood. Anyone drinking the blood daily gained the ability to control the dragons. Naturally, the wizard only let his family drink it. Together, they controlled enough dragons that they soon conquered Marduna, and the wizard became king.

"The royal family ruled for generations, but the wizard king died without writing down the spell he'd cast on the dragon blood. It would not last forever, so they killed a new dragon annually, draining its blood into the Dragon Pool, which was a specially designed and heavily guarded place. The new blood, mixing with the enchanted blood there, would gain the same enchantment. This is how they stayed in power, using their control of the dragons to inspire obedience within Marduna and cooperation elsewhere.

"The Ellorian Champions were summoned to destroy the Dragon Pool and succeeded. The result was that the royal family lost their source of power. The inevitable happened. Most were killed, either by the dragons or the unhappy population. But one member of the royal family, the heir-apparent, wasn't there at the time and survived."

"Everon?" Eric guessed.

"Yes. Real name, Prince Alinor of Marduna."

Anna said, "So now we know why Everon hated the Champions. We can assume that he became Soliander's apprentice for revenge, which ended up meaning he altered the Quest Rings. Eventually, Soliander broke the Champions free of the quest cycle. And within a year, he conquered Esson as Zoran, then Marduna."

Rognir asked, "But why Marduna?"

Matt said, "Revenge by proxy."

Ryan frowned. "What do you mean?"

"He can't find Everon, but he knows who Everon really is. He doesn't think Everon really cares for his own people, because the royal family had a brutal regime, but he's conquered them anyway. He's destroyed cultural places. He's stolen most of the kingdom's riches—not because he cares, but just to take it. He's enslaved people. And he's let the warriors of Essos have their fun, doing what we would call war crimes on Earth. He did this to Marduna while becoming their new king. That's what first earned him the nickname of Zoran the Devastator."

Ryan asked, "He rules more than two kingdoms, so he is an emperor. Has he declared himself one?"

Matt said, "Yes. Emperor Zoran of Essos. He considers that Zoran's home base."

"That was two years ago?" Eric asked. "What's he been doing since?"

Lorian answered, "He has attacked other kingdoms on other worlds. Some he leveled to ruins, reducing them to a state of lawless barbarism. In those kingdoms, he razed major cities and towns. In other kingdoms, he destroyed defenses, leaving people to suffer the consequences of being attacked by ogres and the like. In one island nation, he destroyed all the ships, leaving them defenseless against seafaring enemies and destroying their ability to work the sea for food. These campaigns have also lived up to his nickname. Sometimes he makes himself ruler, other times not."

Eric asked, "Matt, do you sense why he has done this?"

Matt found himself nodding slowly even before being asked. "Wow. Yes. His anger is titanic. This is revenge. The kingdoms he has obliterated all have one thing in common, as far as I can tell." He looked at them with a gleam in his eye. "The Champions did a quest there and interfered with whoever was in power. Ended their conquest—or their possession of land, or an item used for evil purposes. Sometimes the Champions ended up killing the existing ruler. At other times, they killed beasts that had allowed the ruler to maintain power by threatening others, like the dragons of Marduna. Many of these places had ruling families or others who the Champions made enemies of. And that's where it gets interesting."

"How so?"

"Soliander suspected that some of these enemies later worked with Everon to trap the Champions—that Everon sought their aid in creating the network of Quest Rings. Soliander thinks there's no way that Everon could have traveled alone to so many worlds and created so many of the rings unless he had help. Soliander investigated some of these enemies—and in several cases, he learned that he was right. This is why he leveled the kingdoms."

Anna asked, "What are you saying?"

"I'm saying that if Soliander confirmed that a kingdom had worked with Everon to imprison them in the quest cycle, he obliterated that kingdom as Zoran the Devastator. Essos was the exception. He just used them to destroy Marduna and other places."

"Holy shit," said Ryan. "That is messed up. I mean, that's an awful lot of revenge."

Matt nodded. "Remember, Soliander thinks Everon—and anyone who helped him—not only destroyed Soliander's life, but also Korrin's, Eriana's, and Andier's. Like us, they couldn't just live their lives when they could be summoned at any moment. But then Soliander still feels guilty for apparently killing the others when he broke them free of the quests. He also feels guilty that it was his apprentice who betrayed them. He is mad as hell and he wants people to suffer. He also loved Eriana, likely still does, and felt like he got her killed. Of course, this week, he learned that she's alive."

"Wait a minute," said Ryan, looking alarmed. "These places he destroyed still exist. Even if a kingdom or whatever fell, the land's still there. The people still exist. Destroying a kingdom just means destroying a government, unless he did as you say and actually leveled major buildings. But what if the Quest Rings are also still there? People who loathe the Champions could summon us."

"Yes," said Lorian, "but the quest must be a valid one—not one designed to trap you, for example. So you probably don't need to worry about someone trying to get revenge on you and thinking you're the real Champions."

Eric said, "There's something else that suggests we shouldn't worry about it much. No one knows that Zoran is Soliander. They won't know that one of the Champions has destroyed their country. They won't try to summon us in revenge."

"Unless he told whoever he was destroying," observed Anna.

Eric conceded, "True. But he clearly hasn't. Maybe the reason he doesn't tell anyone he's still alive is so no one knows what he's done. An Ellorian Champion is destroying kingdoms. He doesn't know where the others are. He may think they're dead, but he probably hopes they're alive. What if they are and someone knows their location? And goes after them because of what Soliander is doing as Zoran? He could want to stop people taking more revenge on himself or them. I mean, Everon's revenge is what got them into this mess."

"And us," observed Anna.

Rognir remarked, "Revenge can be taken on families, too. By living as Zoran, Soliander may be protecting the family here with us. It allows him to do what he's doing with fewer repercussions."

Anna nodded. "So maybe there's a small chance he's not as bad a guy as his recent behavior suggests."

Matt shook his head, knowing Anna tried to find a bright spot in someone's awful behavior. "No. He's killed a lot of people, directly—or by letting it happen. He's changed. I've seen memories from throughout his life. The ones from the last few years, as far as I can tell anyway, are pretty dark. He's in a bad place. Has been since the Merlin quest."

Anna asked, "Do you think finding that Eriana's alive has changed him? It's only been days, but still. Maybe there's hope."

"No way to know, but I would assume so."

Rognir suggested, "Then perhaps he can be redeemed."

"To be honest," began Eric, "as long as he doesn't come after us or anyone we care about, it doesn't concern me now."

For the next hour, they discussed a plan to rescue Eriana. Matt revealed that Castle Oste was Soliander's true home base. It could only be reached by magic or flying—and, even then, it was invisible from the outside. No one but the Lords of Fear ever came and went, unless Soliander brought a prisoner. The staff were just enough to keep the place running, and they never left. Soliander wouldn't suspect a rescue, because he didn't know Matt had some of his memories of Castle Oste or its magic defenses. With the place mostly unmanned, they hoped for an easy mission because they could cast themselves right inside.

But they planned for Soliander and all four Lords of Fear to be there, even if that was unlikely. The lords were rarely present, and Soliander had many things to attend to. But they reasoned he had ditched any plans, if possible, to be with Eriana.

Partly for that reason, they agreed Taryn should come. Her presence might stop Soliander from attacking them, or at least compromise his aim. Matt knew the arch-wizard wouldn't hurt her. No one thought Taryn would side with her brother against them, especially after learning of his actions as Zoran, but they also felt certain she wouldn't attack Soliander either. She was compromised, as Eric put it, but they wouldn't be able to talk her out of going.

The plan was for the four Champions, Taryn, Lorian, and Rognir to go. But they needed help. Lorian was primarily a swordsman and archer who happened to have magic skills, making him a fair wizard. But he wasn't strong enough to cast *himself* anywhere, never mind eight people. The magic affinity test he'd once administered to Matt suggested Matt was more than strong enough—but between his inexperience, nerves, and pressure, Matt didn't want to do it for himself, not to mention so many others. He imagined arriving a thousand feet above the ground, or halfway inside a wall. No, someone else had to do it.

This was among the issues they discussed with their hosts, in another meeting with tightly controlled attendance. Only the king and queen, Prince Dari and Princess Cariss, Taryn, Eriana's brother, and the princess from Coreth were present. As expected, Taryn insisted on coming and met no objections. To their surprise, Dari insisted on joining the rescue party. Visibly startled, the king seemed pleased by his show of courage—while the queen only looked worried and tried to talk him out of it, to no avail.

Eric had confided in Matt about his talk with the prince, but he hadn't discussed it with the others. Eric and Matt were arguably closer, even though Matt had grown up next door to Anna. Eric had wanted someone else to know about the conversation. Anna sometimes disapproved of things like goading someone, even if they worked. They hadn't told Ryan either; Eric said he didn't want Ryan to think he was sneaking around too much and hiding things, even though he had! Matt was more understanding and didn't object. He also shared Eric's wariness of the prince.

Discussions revealed that Andor's wizards could open a temporary magic portal to Castle Oste, allowing everyone to step through. This was safer for the travelers than being cast there, but it brought the risk that someone on the other side could step through to Andor, unless the wizards ended the spell. That meant doing it again for the return trip. Cariss suggested that her wizard friend Mandrellan help with this, but she admitted she hadn't seen him since their arrival and didn't know where he had gone. Eric said he didn't like it anyway, because they'd need to get back to the portal location with Eriana and that might not be possible. After looking over the spell with Lorian, Matt felt confident that the two of them could do it. This would allow them to leave from wherever they found Eriana.

Later that day, they tested it and successfully created a portal to Lorian's home on Honyn. The portal looked like a doorway—an inch off the floor and surrounded with golden light. It gave a view of Lorian's empty bedroom, which they had chosen so they wouldn't startle anyone and find themselves attacked. Matt saw elegantly carved furniture and bedding with a tree embroidered on it.

The elf stepped through to the other side—but when Matt tried to join him, he found he couldn't! He bounced off the portal like he'd walked into a closed glass door. It even hurt his head where he'd bumped it. He tried sticking his hand through but couldn't. A perplexed Lorian stepped back into Andor without trouble. First Eric, then Ryan, and finally Anna all tried to stick their hands through and couldn't, but Rognir could.

"Jesus," said Eric, shaking his head. "We're idiots. The quest has bound us, and we've always heard we can't leave. We forgot about it, maybe because we never tried before."

"Language, please," said Ryan. He was never one for taking the name of the Lord in vain, as religious as he was.

Anna looked dejected. "Great. What now?"

Matt was frowning. Something wasn't right. "But we've left a planet before. We left Honyn to go to Soclarin on that quest, so why can't we do it now?"

Eric observed, "Going to Soclarin wasn't really part of the quest, either. Maybe it was considered relevant. We left Honyn through the Dragon Gate to Soclarin. We were there to close the gate, which we could have done from the Soclarin side, not the Honyn side. Maybe that's why we were able to go through."

Matt conceded, "That makes sense."

"Doesn't help us here," said Ryan.

Matt saw that Eric was thinking hard. So was Lorian. He tried to work out a way around their problem, privately admitting Eriana's rescue might not include him and his friends. But his knowledge of Castle Oste was invaluable. He really needed to go.

Eric's head snapped up. "I have an idea. Wait here. Can you keep the portal open? I need ten minutes."

Matt looked at Lorian, who nodded, and Eric ran out of the room. Some spells drained his energy while they were active, but this one didn't. The portal would last only five minutes, but it could be shut off with a few words and extended with a few more. Lorian indicated that extending it was far less taxing than casting it again—so they waited, wondering what Eric was up to.

Fifteen minutes later, they heard Taryn's authoritative voice commanding someone to get out of the way. Not too many people were allowed in this wing, to minimize the number of witnesses to anything they said or did. She opened the doors wide and stepped aside as Eric came in carrying the dragon egg case. He stopped in front of the portal as Taryn closed the doors.

Matt arched an eyebrow. "What are you planning to do with *that*?"

Eric smiled. "Send it to Honyn." He didn't elaborate and the others exchanged glances. Sometimes he could be cryptic.

"What's the thought here?" Ryan asked.

"The egg goes through, and since it's on Honyn and we're supposed to get it, we can also go through."

Matt's eyes widened before he laughed. "That's brilliant."

Grinning, Eric said, "I thought so. Here goes."

He stepped up to the still-open portal and gently tried to push the case through before any part of his body. The end of the case did indeed pass through, but then it stopped. He tried again to no avail, then turned the case around, but the same thing happened at roughly the same point. Watching it, Matt knew why.

"The moment the egg itself touches the threshold, even inside the case, it stops."

"Shit," said Eric, stepping back. "I thought that would work."

Rognir stepped forward with one hand out for the case. "May I?"

Eric shrugged and handed it to him. The dwarf repeated the same test, but this time the case kept going. He stepped all the way through the portal with it to stand on Honyn. He turned back and gestured for someone to join him. Standing nearest, Matt extended his hand, expecting it to stop again, but it went through. Surprised, he then passed into the portal and out the other side to stand beside the dwarf. On a hunch, he suggested Rognir stick the case partly back through, and it worked. Matt then took it and tried, able to pass back to Andor with it. Rognir followed.

"So what just happened?" Ryan asked.

Matt answered. "We're not supposed to take the egg off the planet, so we can't. Rognir can. And then I could pursue him. I was able to bring it back because we're supposed to."

"Interesting," said Lorian. "The case is quite a large thing to take on the mission with us, but I know of a magic Bag of Desires that will reduce it to almost nothing inside. I used one for the soclarin ore."

"I remember," said Matt. "Maybe you should go get it now while the portal is open?"

The elf smiled and spoke a few magic words to extend the portal's life. Then he stepped through and into his bedroom and out of view.

Anna asked, "So we're going to take a delicate dragon egg on a potentially violent mission? If something happens to that egg and we never return it, the quest fails and we never go home."

"We can protect it," said Eric.

"How?"

He opened his mouth, then shut it. From the doorway, Taryn said. "The easy way would be to enter my brother's castle, then hand the egg back to someone here and continue without it."

Matt smiled at her. "Simple and obvious. Thank you."

"That I can live with," said Anna.

Lorian came back moments later, and they closed the portal. Their hosts had already agreed that they would be allowed to wear and use the Ellorian Champions' equipment, provided that no one let it be seen until they left. King Sarov wanted them to capture Soliander if possible. While they assured him they would try, they didn't think they had much of a chance—until the king gave them the Crown of Voids Taryn had used on Matt. If they could get it around Soliander's head, he'd be far easier to deal with, though no one believed they'd get near enough. They hoped to see no sign of him at all.

With the plan settled, they rested for two hours and then reconvened in their meeting room, the doors sealed. Behind a changing curtain, the four of them put on their respective outfits. Taryn, Lorian, Rognir, and Prince Dari were all present. So were a dozen of Taryn's Dark Blade warriors, whom she had sent for after the dragon egg quest trouble. A handful would come with them, just in case more trouble than expected broke out. The remaining Dark Blades would stay behind in this room in case trouble followed them back or reinforcements were needed. Eric had also suggested that two wizards remain to open the portal in case Matt or Lorian couldn't make one themselves. This would allow them to send the Dark Blades through if needed—and, if the group at Soliander's made it back to the portal location, it would mean they could also return that way.

After a final check to ensure everyone was prepared, Matt and Lorian cast the spell and the portal to a lower room in Soliander's hidden Oste Castle opened. They saw only darkness until one of the Dark Blades threw a burning torch through. It landed just a few feet inside on dark stone and cast dancing light around the storage room, filled with crates and barrels. It seemed obvious to Matt that no one was there—he'd chosen it for that reason—and so the warrior stepped through, picked up the torch, and made room for the others. Rognir went through with the dragon egg case, and the Earth friends all stepped through without issue. The dwarf then handed it back to someone on Elloria and the remaining party joined them.

Matt looked around, experiencing a kind of déjà vu from having been here as Soliander. The small room was damp, musty, and cold. Only one stairway ascended, and he noticed that Soliander's staff did not send a pulse up his arm, as it usually did when it detected magic, other than the portal. When he was the one casting a spell, it didn't pulse, presumably by design so that didn't distract him.

"Let's leave the portal open a minute," said Eric. "I want to check up these stairs first."

"No," Dari disagreed. "It leaves Andor exposed to a threat, and I cannot allow that."

Eric sighed. "There's no one here but us. It'll just be a minute."

"There won't be anything there," said Matt, "just a larger storeroom with stairs descending to rooms like this one. Whoever goes first, leave the light behind in case anyone's there."

"Right," Eric said. "I'll go first, Taryn and you behind. You're our guide, Matt, so I need you up front all the time."

"Yeah, I know. Let's go."

The three of them went up the stairs, being careful not to trip or scuff their feet and cause noise. They could see a dim light, and Matt knew that a single torch lit the big room above. He was right. No one was there. They could see an assortment of supplies, a table and chairs, and a lone torch burning next to an ascending stairway. They listened, then crept over. For a moment, it seemed like all was quiet, but then they heard two voices speaking elven. That surprised Matt until he remembered that Soliander had dark elves working for him.

The voices came nearer. He, Taryn, and Eric hid behind a crate once they realized the elves were coming down. The elves reached the bottom of the stairway, one carrying a torch, and remained unaware of the intruders until Eric and Taryn approached from behind. The pair nearly reached the elves when the elves sensed them and turned. Eric punched one elf in the face, knocking him and the torch he held to the floor, while Taryn put a choke hold on the other. Then Eric jumped on the fallen one and put a hand over his mouth.

"Don't make a sound," he said in elven. "You're going to tell us where Eriana is. Do you understand?"

Matt was standing beside them by now, and saw only defiance in the dark elf's eyes. "They're not going to cooperate. They fear Zoran more than anything we can do to them. Just tie them up."

By now, the rest of the group had come up the stairs with Prince Dari in the lead. The dark elves were soon bound, gagged, and put into two different storage rooms so they couldn't help each other.

"What's up these stairs?" Dari asked, peering up.

"We're below a courtyard. This stair leads to a hall within the exterior walls of the castle. We're getting close to the tower where he does his work."

By now, they were all familiar with such buildings and terms. While 'the castle' meant the entire structure, it could also mean only the fortifications—like the walls, towers, courtyard, and a drawbridge if one existed. Then there was the keep, the building inside the castle.

Ryan asked, "Why is there a courtyard if no one can get here by foot?"

"Dragons need somewhere to land."

"Good answer."

A frowning Dari observed, "I thought we were trying to be under one of the other two towers, where we're likely to find Eriana."

Matt knew where Soliander's rooms were, and which tower Diara was in unless she had been moved. That meant Eriana was likely to be in one of the other two towers. She could still be anywhere, but he knew those towers had the best rooms and Soliander wasn't going to put her somewhere repugnant.

"We are, but this was a better place to arrive—and the upper rooms have magical wards on them, ones that would've interfered with the portal. Besides, I want to get into his rooms. There are very useful things in there."

Eric shook his head. "Stealing from Soliander wasn't part of the plan."

"This is an opportunity we can't miss. And there's a chance Eriana is there."

"There's an even better chance my brother is," Taryn said, "and I would very much like a reunion, even though that isn't smart."

"The king wants us to capture him," Matt reminded them. He glanced at the Crown of Voids attached to Taryn's belt. He hated that thing, but wouldn't think twice about putting it on Soliander.

Dari added, "I agree with the wizard."

Matt looked at Eric. "We could get some very helpful things, like the scroll on how to create the keystones for a Home Ring."

Seeing Eric's grudging acceptance, he flashed an apologetic smile. He hadn't been sure about mentioning it earlier, afraid they would disagree. Now he asked to borrow Lorian's magic Bag of Desires, which reduced items to such small sizes that the bag still looked empty. The elf handed it to him.

After discussing a plan, they crept up the stairway, finding a corridor straight ahead. To their left side stood the exterior castle wall. The other side was open to a courtyard. No one was there. The sun cast long shadows, suggesting that it was late afternoon. The main building, or keep, loomed overhead. Behind them to one side stood the wooden door to Soliander's hundred-foot-tall tower.

They made it inside without trouble, closed the door, and began to climb. They passed a handful of potentially occupied rooms, one on each story. Always quiet, Eric went first, with Taryn and Matt following. The others waited, to minimize noise.

As they ascended, Matt saw that the first- and third-floor doors were already open, with no one inside. The topmost room was for magic experiments. One floor down was Soliander's study, where Matt expected him to be. And one floor down from that was the Scribe Room, full of less important scrolls and books. It was from this floor that Eric came back down to him and Taryn quietly.

"There's an elf in there," he whispered, firelight from a wall sconce dancing over his intense features. "He's copying scrolls. From the way he's sitting, he'll see us."

"I don't leave enemies at my back anyway," said Taryn, fingering her sword.

"I think I will have to take care of it," said Matt. "Gotta be quiet in case Soliander's up one level."

"I might get him with a knife," Eric suggested.

"What if you miss? Anyone in there is likely to be a wizard. He might have magical protection, too, even if he doesn't expect anything here."

Matt had learned quite a few other spells—but he'd rarely had no chance to practice casting them on people, because it would hurt or they wouldn't like it. Now he could have no such scruples. He reached into one of his robe's pockets to get a piece of valerian root. Pulling the hood up and over his face, he left Soliander's staff with Taryn and confidently strode into the Scribe Room like he was Zoran the Devastator.

The dark elf looked up in surprise. "Master, I didn't realize you were—"

"Sleep," Matt commanded, and the elf's eyes closed, his head landing on the table before him with a thud. He started to slide off, but Eric came forward and caught him, then gently lowered him to the floor. "Darron," whispered Matt in recognition. "An apprentice."

As Taryn entered and gave Matt the staff, Eric asked, "Anything in here you want to take?"

Matt thought for a second, looking around the room, getting a sense of what was where, and what Soliander was unlikely to miss any time soon. The last thing he wanted was that guy coming after him. As a result, he didn't take many tempting items, but he did grab several spellbooks of rarer magic, and books on demonology, witchcraft, and necromancy. To cover the theft, he moved the books a little to disguise a gap.

"Okay," he began, "let's go."

They reached the next level together, seeing the closed mahogany door and its scenes of wizards, dragons, and knights battling. Soliander's staff sent a pulse up his arm. If the door had been open, that would've meant the arch-wizard was there. But the door being closed didn't tell them anything because it formed a perfect seal that let no light—or anything else—out. Eric held two knives as Taryn took the Crown of Voids in one hand and Matt thought over the word to magically unlock the door. Only Soliander and he knew it.

With a final nod, he whispered the word and threw open the door, eyes darting to the empty chair behind the huge black desk, and then around the room. He strode in, Taryn right behind. But Soliander wasn't here.

Eric entered. "Think he's above us?"

Matt listened for a few moments. "No. The stuff he does up there makes lots of noise. Let's check after I look around."

Eric turned to Taryn, "Why don't *we* check? He doesn't need us in here."

"Right."

They stepped out and disappeared up the stairs. Matt tried to sense from Soliander's memories where certain things were. The square room was familiar and yet new. A hulking fireplace to one side sat cold and dark, with no burning embers. Bookcases lined with jars, vials, and jugs filled two walls.

Papers, books, and an assortment of loose items like quill pens lay on the desk.

In the corner stood a rosewood cabinet, the sight thrilling him. This was where Soliander kept the staff and robe he wore as an Ellorian Champion. Matt stepped toward the cabinet but stopped on feeling the strongest pulse he'd ever received from the staff. He couldn't remember what the spell was or how to get rid of it. Maybe it was just as well. Stealing those would be tempting but foolish. He imagined opening the cabinet and leaving a sarcastic note about not stealing them and suggesting the arch-wizard return the favor and let Matt keep the copies.

His eyes fell on a bookcase full of rings, headbands, wands, and more. He saw one orb under a black velvet cloth, then pulled that off to see a dark sphere. He had seen one like it before, right before smashing it into three pieces. With a quick glance at the door, he took it, the stand it was on, and the cloth, which was a bag for it. These disappeared into the magic bag, and he re-spaced the items on the shelf to disguise their absence. Right as he finished, Eric and Taryn returned.

"He's not here," revealed Taryn, sounding relieved and disappointed. "Are you done?"

"Almost." Matt moved behind the desk, trying to sense where the scrolls about creating keystones, Quest Rings, and Home Rings were. Then suddenly he knew. They were in the dreaded rosewood cabinet that he didn't...

...the spell came into his head, along with the knowledge of what guarded it. His eyes went to it immediately and Eric stepped toward it.

"Don't!" Matt cautioned.

Eric winced and clutched his stomach, doubling over and backing away as his breathing grew hard. But once he had backed up, the pained expression left and he straightened, questioning eyes on Matt.

"One spell will make you sick if you get close."

"And the second one?" Taryn asked.

"Nasty demon shows up to take you somewhere you don't want to be."

She arched an eyebrow at him. "And you're getting in there?"

"Will the staff let you get to it?" Eric asked.

"No, because his copy of the staff is in there, so he can't use it to open it from the outside. There's a counter-spell."

The others moved away as Matt walked close to the cabinet but not near enough to trigger a reaction. He closed his eyes, focusing on the words Soliander used. This cabinet wasn't opened often, but the memory was vivid due to its importance. He began gathering energy and felt the familiar surge of power.

"From other worlds where you abide,
Do not come here and to my side,
A moment's rest to let me by,
After me, all others die."

The magic flowed into the space before the cabinet. Nothing had visibly changed, but he felt the sense of menace lift.

"The demon spell is suspended. I can eliminate the other one, but I can't put it back, and that would let him know we'd been in here sooner. Leaving a pile of vomit wouldn't help."

"I have an idea," said Eric, turning to Taryn. "Can you get Anna?" She left and Eric said, "I'm wondering if she can either heal one of us as we get closer or suppress the effect on us."

"We each have a Trinity Ring, too. One of its healing spells might help."

Eric looked at the silver ring. "Yeah. I already used one."

"There's another problem. The actual lock. Think you can pick it?"

"While I'm puking? Soliander is clever—I'll give him that."

Taryn returned with Anna and explained the situation. They knew by now that Anna tried to reach out to a god every time they arrived on another planet, so it came as no surprise when she said she had already made contact. Eriana and Soliander had created the Corethian Amulet to help with that, because they had often arrived somewhere with no knowledge of the gods, not to mention a relationship with one.

They let Anna commune with the god. Matt grew impatient to leave. Soliander could cast himself into the room at any moment. If Matt learned more control, he might be able to create portals on his own, but casting himself somewhere still unnerved him. Maybe he'd try it in a field sometime.

Anna soon surrounded them with a shield that muted the spell's effects. Eric pulled his lockpicking tools from a pocket and stepped toward the cabinet, feeling only a slight twinge of nausea. He knelt before the gold lock and fiddled with it until it clicked.

"Wait," said Matt, stepping closer. He pressed a secret handle on one side and the cabinet doors opened. "If you pull the actual handles, a poison needle pricks you. Puts you in a coma until he revives you for interrogation. I must admit, he knows how to protect something."

"No shit."

"Stand back. *Enumisar.*" The word of power switched on the light atop Soliander's staff. An identical light, on the staff leaning against one corner inside the cabinet, also came on. Hanging beside it was the robe. Matt bit his lip, tempted. But he reached for the drawers to one side, finding the scrolls he wanted. It made sense that Soliander hid hidden them here. These were the original instructions, which someone else could alter—like Everon had—to imprison them in quests. He picked up the scrolls and stepped back.

Then he had an idea. "Try to find two scrolls just like these for decoys. If he sees them, he may never look inside to realize they've been replaced."

Eric and Taryn scoured the room, but saw nothing, so they went down one level and returned with two scrolls. Matt put them in the drawer, dropped the real ones in his Bag of Desires, and cast a final glance at Soliander's staff, still glowing. He switched off the lights on both staffs, closed the cabinet—the lock clicked shut—and stepped away. The demon spell would resume in minutes. They tried to make sure the room didn't look disturbed before leaving, Matt remembering that the spell on the door would reactivate by itself.

They descended the stairs to find Ryan waiting by the room on the first floor. He nodded at the doorway beside him.

"We caught two more servants. They wouldn't tell us where Eriana is. They're tied up."

They continued to the bottom and regrouped. They were standing in the front corner of the rectangular castle, beside the courtyard. Each corner had a tower. Matt knew that Diara was in the tower diagonal to their position, at the back of the castle. They would only get her if Eriana wanted them to. There were two other towers, which gave them a 50-50 chance of guessing which one Eriana was in. He opted for the nearest one at the front, across the courtyard. They skirted the outside wall. The walkway on the second level would hide them from above if anyone was in the keep, which was several stories high.

Matt said the tower was the same as the one they'd just been in, and since they weren't expecting magic trouble, he did not go up with Taryn and Eric. The others waited impatiently, Matt feeling good about how things had gone so far. Sneaking around Soliander's home took some of the intimidation out of the arch-wizard.

Then he saw movement through the tower door, which they had neglected to close. Across the courtyard, a figure in dark leather sauntered toward Soliander's tower, but looked their way and stopped. She could almost certainly see Matt and probably Ryan.

Kori of Nysuun turned and sprinted toward the keep, screaming for Lord Voth.

CHAPTER FOURTEEN

A LADY OF HOPE

Anna heard the shouting and saw her friends' alarmed faces. Lorian sprinted up the tower. They had two options. If Eriana was above them, they could all just get her, cast the spell to open a portal, and disappear back to Andor. If she wasn't, they'd be fighting Kori, Lord Voth, and whoever else to reach her. Kori hadn't screamed Soliander's name, at least, suggesting that he wasn't there. Their third option was leaving without Eriana, but there was no way. Anna wasn't abandoning her. They only had one shot and it had just gone to hell.

Lorian reappeared, with Eric and Taryn right behind. No Eriana.

"Which way did Kori go?" Eric asked, eyes intense.

Ryan pointed at the tower diagonal to them. Was it the one with Diara? Matt hadn't said. Anna was about to ask when Eric said they had to run to evade an attack. They started into the courtyard toward the main building. Soliander's tower stood to the left, a rear tower rose to the right, and the other rear tower was across the courtyard and beyond the keep straight ahead. Halfway to the keep, dozens of undead raced from a door in it and from the left and right toward the rear towers. Some were skeletons with maces and hammers in their gloved hands, but most seemed like wights, with mummified flesh, soiled clothes, white hair and eyes, and long nails like claws, their hands empty except for a few that wielded swords or a flail. Since many gods saw undead as an abomination, Anna felt this battle was hers more than anyone else's, and she reached for the Corethian Amulet.

Ryan took center position while Taryn and Eric flanked him. Lorian stood beside Eric, and the Dark Blade warriors completed the line on either side as the battle began. Prince Dari hung back with Anna, Matt, and Rognir. Was it cowardice, or did he mean to protect them from the swarm?

Behind the attackers stood Kori and Aeron, a short black man with a shaved head, curving welts covering his face and hands. Anna didn't understand where the necromancer had summoned the undead from. Was there a graveyard nearby? Lord Voth, the undead knight, strode through the keep's door and into the fray, wielding a black sword rimmed with frost. He turned toward Ryan, baleful eyes settling on Matt behind him. Lord Voth had a score to settle. Matt had burned away his flesh so that he wore gloves to control his sword. He seemed eager to cut his way through Ryan to reach him.

Anna urgently reached out to a god. She instantly felt the deity seeing through her eyes, then an indignation not her own. When she swung her arm, it felt like someone else controlled it. Four of the wights flew back. Three crashed hard into the stone keep, their bones audibly shattering. The fourth tumbled across the courtyard, landing on an area of broken cobblestones where bare earth could be seen. Weeds sprang up to entwine around its limbs, repeated tugs downward cracking its body as the weeds pulled it under to disappear.

"The name of the goddess, lass," said Rognir, "so I may help?"

Anna gripped the dwarf's shoulder, giving him an immediate connection. His hammer glowed white. He ran into the melee beside a Dark Blade warrior, whose sword had had little effect. One hit of Rognir's hammer shattered the wight's leg so that it fell, and another blow caved its head in. The dwarf then enchanted the warrior's sword.

Those with magic weapons were faring better. In Ryan's hands, Korrin's sword gouged huge chunks of mummified flesh from wights, but he barely kept pace with the onslaught of slashing hands, his armor deflecting blows that made it past his sword. Eric had bloody cuts to his hands, all of them turning black. Anna warned him she was behind him and healed him before stepping back.

She heard Matt yell, *"Kunia!"*

Anna looked over in alarm, knowing that anyone in the spell's path—friend or foe—would go flying. A half dozen undead flew backward, two striking Lord Voth, who stayed upright and went for Ryan. Anna focused her thoughts on everyone's weapons and made a rising gesture with her hands. Their swords began to glow, slicing through body parts more easily, severed limbs dropping but still crawling toward them on the ground.

Someone screamed, and Anna turned to see a Dark Blade warrior pulled into the wight throng by his sword arm. Two of the wights tore at him, then threw his body to Aeron's feet. With his palm over the corpse, the necromancer made circling motions. The body struggled to its feet, turned back to the fight, and only took two steps before the enchanted sword in its hand burst into flames that quickly consumed it.

A second wave of undead surged around Aeron and Kori and through the keep door. Anna thought they needed to flee to the right and other tower there, but then more undead ran from it around the line of defense toward Matt. He conjured a huge fountain of flames to set them ablaze, but they kept coming.

Eric yelled, "Matt, which tower is Eriana in?"

But the wizard fell under the swarm. His screams were high-pitched, wild, and incoherent until he roared *"Enumisar!"* and a fireball rose upward, throwing burning undead into the air forty feet and shocking Anna with the heat. The still-burning undead landed with a snapping of limbs that didn't stop them from rising.

Anna went to heal the numerous gashes on Matt's hands and face but heard him say *"Minurarki"*, activating the least powerful healing spell in his Trinity Ring. She turned away and saw Kori looking back over her shoulder at the tower behind her, then at Eric. Kori nodded. Was she telling him which tower Eriana was in? It seemed improbable. It had to be a trick. They would need to cut through the undead to reach it. Eric seemed to agree. He turned toward the remaining tower on their right.

"That way!"

Anna watched Kori's face register alarm and disappointment. Then she flung aside more undead to clear a path as Prince Dari led them. She followed him, her eyes darting around to see who else she could help. Taryn and her men were retreating while fighting, but it seemed that Lord Voth would be the biggest challenge, because any spell to thrust him back wasn't working. Dari bashed open a door to the keep and they began retreating inside. Then Anna realized how to slow Lord Voth.

She yelled, "Everyone but Ryan and Eric, into the room right now! Trust me!" As they ran in, the undead surged forward and she again called out, "Ryan and Eric, now you!"

They obeyed and ran for the door, but Lord Voth slashed Eric across the back. He screamed in pain, but kept moving. The undead surged forward, Lord Voth right behind. In grim satisfaction at her plan's success, Anna swung her arm again and the undead flew back and into Lord Voth, toppling him. With the way clear, they slammed shut the door and barricaded it. Anna rushed to Eric and healed him, sudden fatigue making her weak. Rognir began healing others as needed. The barricade would not hold, and the doors leading outward beckoned. Two of the Dark Blade warriors tried to hold the barrier as repeated thumps against it came near to knocking it off its hinges.

Dari said, "We need to escape to Andor before the elf and wizard get too badly injured and cannot open a portal. You saw what just happened to Matt."

"No," said Taryn, her face gashed in two places. "We are not defeated yet."

Breathing hard, Eric said, "We have to keep moving and reach the other tower, the one behind Kori."

"No!" said Anna. "I saw the look she gave you. It's a trap."

"It's the right tower," said Matt. "Diara is in the one nearer to us."

Anna didn't know what to believe now. Why would Kori help them? A tryst with Eric couldn't end years of service to Soliander, or Zoran. Then she had no time to ponder it as a big crash at the door sent both Dark Blades tumbling. One stayed on his feet and backed away but the other fell and was immediately set upon by undead tearing at him. Fear and anger tore through Anna, and she once again made a throwing motion that hurled the undead from him. But she was too late. They had ripped his throat out. She nearly stumbled from fatigue.

Someone yanked her by the arm into a shambling run, and she turned to find Taryn pulling her away. Matt brought up the rear, stopping to engulf the undead in flames and set the room ablaze before he joined them. Allies standing in the way had constrained Matt before, but now he did horrible damage to what pursued them. Flames were engulfing the keep.

She stumbled into another room with a wide table, with maps, goblets, and plates of food spread on it. Dari, Ryan, and Lorian thrust it against the door and followed the rest of them into another room. They seemed to be going in the right direction, but once half their group had made it past a door on their left, it burst open. Undead flooded the room and separated the group. Rognir slammed his hammer through leg after leg as Anna hurled the undead up against the wall one more time. Everyone heard Matt yell *"Kunia!"* and ducked as he threw this onslaught back, too. Dari grabbed her arm and pulled Anna onward, stumbling. She was so tired. They couldn't keep this going.

By now they had reached a hallway leading to the tower, and they hurried to catch the others. Anna heard the clanging of swords ahead and came around the corner to see her friends battling Lord Voth, wights, and a half dozen spectral knights. The new and terrifying additions looked like ghosts in white, their silvery swords cleaving an arc of light through the torchlit darkness. Only those with enchanted blades could ward off the blows, and she saw with dismay her earlier enchantment had had worn off. She didn't have the strength to do it again—and so she watched as men's swords turned to frost, then shatter on the next parry. Several Dark Blade warriors went down screaming.

Matt yelled, "Down! *Kunia!*"

Everyone ahead of him had dropped to one knee, and now the wights flew backward, narrowly missing Kori and Aeron. Ryan rose with his sword up to block Lord Voth's blade, which had wounded his other arm, chest, and leg. He was being beaten backward and taking more damage. Fear surging, Anna focused her will and squeezed with one outstretched hand. Lord Voth was in mid-swing when his sword arm stopped. He seemed confused until his eyes blazed with hatred for Anna. Ryan stabbed him through the heart and pulled out the bloody sword, but the undead knight cocked his head as if amused—until Ryan chopped it off. The head didn't move, because Anna still held him, but then she pushed and the body and head tumbled away. She fell to one knee and Prince Dari helped her up.

Only now did she really see and hear the spectral knights howling in pain from a bright light consuming them. She saw the cause—Rognir chanting and swinging his hammer in a circle by its handle, the light fanning out from the whirling weapon. Taryn bashed open the tower door and they began filing through it, Rognir coming last and ending his assault. There was nothing to barricade the door with and they began climbing as fast as they dared, Dari and Lorian helping Anna until Ryan hoisted her over one shoulder despite having to climb so far. Using a spell, Matt blew open every door as they climbed. The one far below burst open, and she heard the scrambling of many feet. Whether or not Eriana was at the top, it was time to go.

"Eriana!" Taryn was shouting as they ascended. "It's Taryn of Aranor and the new Ellorian Champions! Are you here?"

Anna thought she heard a faint woman's voice answer, then hard banging on a wooden door. Ryan carried her over a landing, through a doorway, and into a room, where he set her down and she straightened, feeling woozy. The group slammed the door shut and tried barricading it as she turned and came face to face with the Lady Hope, Eriana of Coreth.

"My god," said Eriana, putting hands on her, "you're pale." She spoke a few words and sudden strength and energy filled Anna, who blinked in surprise. Then she laughed in relief at seeing the priestess, whose power they sorely needed. Despite the situation, she still noticed that Eriana wore a yellow robe, which struck her because she'd only seen her in Earth clothing before. She looked well.

"We're here to rescue you," said Anna.

"Time to get the fuck out of here," said Eric. Loud bangs rocked the door. "Matt! Lorian!"

"On it," said Matt. "Clear a space."

With so many people in the small room, they had nowhere to create the portal without being bumped into. They grabbed the bed and shoved it up against the other furniture now by the door. Lorian and Matt moved to the place where it had been. Then glass shattered to one side. Anna saw a wight climbing in through the window, having scaled the tower's exterior. Another wight followed as Rognir clubbed the first one. A second window shattered, then a third, wights entering to separate the rescuers into small groups. The door finally splintered, more wights pushing in. Anna backed away, seeing them about to be overrun.

Suddenly, a concussive blast hit the room and smashed all of the wights to dust against the walls. It also shattered the mirror and any remaining glass. Anna turned in surprise to Eriana, seeing grim satisfaction.

"Wow," she said, "you *are* strong."

"You'll get there," said the priestess.

Anna doubted that, but wasn't going to argue. She saw that Matt and Lorian had the portal open. Through the shimmering doorway, she saw the meeting room in Andor and Taryn's Dark Blade warriors watching intently as if debating whether to come through.

"Time to go!" shouted Ryan.

Then suddenly everything was happening at once and Anna couldn't keep track. A spectral knight glided through the door. Another followed, more thuds knocking back the furniture before a huge bang shoved it away and Lord Voth, head reattached, stepped into the room. One of the Dark Blades struck at him and was cut down. Dari was nearest and traded blows as he retreated. A wight clambered through the window behind him only to have Rognir bash it to pieces, but more of them were swarming in the other windows. A roar of flames from Matt's staff set three wights afire, one hitting the bed and setting it ablaze as smoke filled the room.

Lorian called out, "Eriana! Anna!" and they stepped toward the portal, the priestess hesitating.

"I have to help," Eriana said, thrusting her hand forward at the spectral knights. A blast of wind halted their attack. Lord Voth paused his swings at Dari long enough to pull out a knife, which he tossed at Eriana.

"No!" shouted Anna, jumping in front of it. The blade cut into her chest, a searing cold chilling her. She fell into Eriana, who pulled her back. And now the spectral knights pressed onward, more sliding through the walls and one rising through the floor.

"Into the portal!" Lorian shouted. He grabbed Anna and hauled her backward. Suddenly she passed through to Andor with him, her wide eyes watching the unfolding scene. Then a robed man was beside her, removing the knife, the pain causing her to look away from the portal until he healed her. By the time she looked again, another Dark Blade warrior had gone down and more wights were surging through the windows. They surrounded Dari as Rognir clubbed one down, trying to reach the prince. They were being overrun. Eric grabbed Ryan and pulled him back, eyes on Matt, who blasted more undead backward. Her three friends stood by the portal with Eriana.

Rognir, Dari, Taryn, and a few Dark Blades were struggling to retreat. And then one warrior was cut down. Rognir bashed the offending wight, trying to reach Dari, but one of the spectral knights traded two blows with the prince, shattering his sword. Then Lord Voth grabbed Dari by his wrist, which turned white. He screamed and tried to jerk free to no avail. Eriana made a gripping motion, and from across the room, seemed to snap off Voth's hand at the wrist.

"Go!" said Eric, shoving Ryan toward the portal. He clambered through reluctantly.

"I have to help my men!" Taryn shouted, moving forward.

"No!" Eric yelled. "It's too late. Look at him!"

Anna looked around Ryan's shoulder at the action, seeing Rognir dragging a grimacing Dari toward freedom. One of the remaining Dark Blades had hideous wounds to his torso and was already stumbling to one knee, about to be killed. Only a few of Taryn's men were left as more wights came through a window. Eric pulled a reluctant Taryn toward the portal and into it with him. Anna had to get out of their way and couldn't see anything more as Matt arrived, too.

She heard another scream of pain, a shout from Rognir and a kind of battle cry that sounded like Dari. Then Rognir stumbled through the portal dragging a protesting Eriana behind him. Two of the Dark Blades came through, one falling to the floor and being dragged away by the other. Over Eric's shoulder, Eriana saw two wights holding the prince by the arms and bearing him to the ground. Lord Voth and the spectral knights approached the portal. Behind them stood an impassive Aeron, his undead wreaking havoc. Eyes intense, Kori watched beside him.

"Close it!" Eric shouted to Matt and Lorian. "We can't save him. Close it or they'll come through!"

With a few frantic words from Lorian, the portal shut off, sudden silence filling the room. Anna turned Eric around by the shoulder.

"What happened?"

Eric shook his head, eyes clouded. "He saved Eriana. The wights came in and were charging her. She was looking elsewhere, so Dari charged them and knocked them all down." He looked at the priestess. "He saved her."

Anna opened her mouth, then closed it. "And then we left him."

"I know," Eric said, eyes troubled. "I know. We couldn't get to him."

Eriana put a hand on Anna. "He's right. There was no way to reach him without more of us getting hurt or killed. What he did was extremely brave."

Anna sighed, wondering how they were going to explain this to the king and queen. First Korrin had gone missing for three years, and now Dari had been captured by Soliander's Lords of Fear. That reminded her of the missing Lord.

"It's good Garian wasn't there. Or Soliander. Just one of them and we wouldn't have made it. Barely did as is. Is everyone okay?"

Virtually all of them had the black, festering injuries, while a few had frosty handprints on their armor or bodies. Those who could help began healing them. They had lost Dari and most of Taryn's warriors. But they had gained Eriana. Was her life worth theirs? Probably, as much as Anna might have once thought all lives were worth the same. That kind of thinking went out the window in circumstances like these.

Standing beside Matt, Taryn put her sword away and regretfully said, "I don't like leaving men behind, though they knew the risks." She reached up to wipe sweat from Matt's face, an act that surprised Anna. "You were impressive back there."

Eric asked him, "Any sense of whether Soliander will kill Dari?"

Matt pursed his lips. "I don't think he would. He's still loyal to the Champions. The real question is whether the Lords of Fear will know who Dari is and avoid killing him, or even whether they'll know Soliander wouldn't want it."

"Kori would know who he is, I'm sure," Eric said. "I doubt we can rescue him. They'd be expecting us now. Not sure how to frame this to his parents."

"They'll understand," said Taryn. "It's something Korrin would do. Honestly, the king might be happy to know Dari sacrificed himself like that. We'll just be honest."

No one said anything for a moment as they began to disperse, put away weapons, and decompress. In watching Eriana, Anna saw a look of resigned acceptance about the loss of life incurred to rescue her. It presumably muted her relief. Anna knew from her own experiences that death was part of the job, something they all had to get used to. It was harder for some, like her and Ryan, than others. Then Anna realized the priestess had no idea of where they were or everything that had just happened.

"It's okay," she began, smiling. "We're on Elloria, in Andor, at the castle. The king and queen agreed to let us rescue you when we found out Soliander had taken you from Jack's apartment. You are safe here and they know the truth about the rest of us, that we aren't the real Champions. Almost no one outside this room knows, though, which is why we need to change out of these outfits before we leave. You're fine in yours."

As Eriana absorbed that, a slow smile spread across her face. "You brought me home? This is really Elloria?" She strode to the nearest window. Would she recognize the city? Eriana threw open a partially closed curtain, sunlight streaming over her as she pushed the windowpane out. Warm air wafted in. A view of the port and ocean lay beyond the flags of Andor flying from various buildings and on the sails of ships.

Anna couldn't imagine being away from Earth and everything she'd known for twenty years and then suddenly getting back. It felt good, having done this. Their goal had been to rescue Eriana from Soliander, mostly because Jack had said she hadn't gone voluntarily. Until now, she hadn't really considered that a side effect would be getting Eriana home. Coreth was technically many miles to the southeast, but it wasn't worlds away anymore. When Eriana turned around, tears on her cheeks, Anna felt her own tears gathering.

Eriana walked up to her and wiped one from her face. "You look great in my robe. It suits you." She turned to the others. "It's the first time I've seen you in action. Very impressive—all of you. And I cannot thank you enough. Gratitude hardly begins to describe it."

"Many worlds owe you a debt," began a smiling Lorian as he approached, "so thanks are not needed, my lady."

"Lorian!" Eriana gave him a hug, which he awkwardly returned. While she had undoubtedly noticed the elf in the fighting, there had been no time for greetings. "Not elven custom, I know. I never thought I'd be so happy to see an elf! Or a dwarf!" She turned to the usually-taciturn Rognir.

"There must be some dust in my eye," said Rognir, wiping at it to muted laughter.

"Your brother is here," Anna revealed. "And Princess Alia of Coreth. We can take you to them."

Eriana put one hand to her mouth and fresh tears spilled down her cheeks as she nodded.

First, they changed out of the Champions' clothes once more. Anna offered her copy of Eriana's robe and Corethian Amulet to the priestess, who demurred, saying that they belonged to her now. Anna had never felt that was true, but the blessing changed that. She thought it would be nice for other people to see the Lady Hope, Eriana of Coreth, striding down the halls of Andor once again after having been missing for three years. But then maybe this had to be kept a secret a little longer. Questions would swirl, especially about her aging.

Taryn left to arrange a meeting with the king, queen, and others who had known about the mission. Anna sensed that the warrior and Matt were developing an interest in each other, however subtle. And then there was Kori and Eric. The assassin had told him with a look which tower Eriana was in. Anna didn't understand it.

As the group escorted Eriana to meet their hosts, she wore a cloak with the hood up to hide her face, but this couldn't last. It wasn't fair to her. She was finally home home after twenty years and had to pretend she was still missing.

Once the door to the secured throne room closed behind them, she pulled back the hood to a cry from her brother. He ran to her, Princess Alia following. With their laughing and crying, Anna gave into the tears. Ryan put an arm around her and smiled. To her surprise, his eyes were moist. Was this the first time he had felt like a hero, too?

The grinning king, queen, and Princess Cariss broke whatever protocol might have been in place and approached Eriana, the queen giving her a hug and chatting privately for a few minutes while Anna and her friends pretended not to listen. With the initial reunion over, talk turned to the mission with all of the survivors present.

"What of Dari?" Princess Cariss asked, worry dampening her smile. "Why is my brother not here?"

Eriana put one hand on her arm, her face sorrowful, and described what had happened. The king stood taller as if proud, the queen put one hand over her mouth but didn't cry, and Princess Cariss openly wept.

"He has finally earned the statue he so long desired," King Sarov remarked, "though he may never see it."

Anna tried not to look shocked at what struck her as a cold remark. Was that all he could think of, that it was a good death?

Ryan cleared his throat. "Your Majesty, there is still some chance we may be able to recover him."

But the king shook his head. "Soliander will not fall victim to this ploy a second time."

Anna knew that he was right. They had gotten lucky, too.

"I think we need to address Eriana's presence, Your Majesty," said Eric. "While she may be older, some people will recognize her anyway, and it's not fair to ask her to pretend she's not who she is. But we need to work out the repercussions of acknowledging she has been found. Questions will be asked about where she's been, and where the others are. And we might have to address the fact that we are not them."

The king turned to Eriana. "We may need you to pretend a while longer, my lady, for the sake of your replacements."

"I agree," said the priestess.

Feeling relieved, Anna said, "We might need the help of Eriana and the others, when we find them, to say that we've impersonated them with their blessing."

The king nodded. "We will also say that Andor approved of the charade, and that you rescued Eriana. I will formally declare you friends of the Empire of Andor." He turned to Princess Alia of Coreth. "While I cannot speak for your king, please encourage the same from him."

The princess smiled at them. "You will be friends of Coreth, certainly, and I will speak to His Majesty about an official declaration of friendship from the Kingdom of Roir."

For the first time, Anna felt excited about the truth becoming known. Coming to Andor was the best thing that had happened to them so far. The king announced a private celebration that evening.

But first they split up, Eriana going with her brother and Princess Alia to get reacquainted. The royal family left to deal with their grief over Prince Dari. And the four Earth friends freshened up before meeting with Lorian and Rognir, who would soon return to Honyn.

From their meeting room, they decided to send Lorian to Jack's apartment with a note about developments. Jack wasn't there, but had left a note beside his laptop for them. The elf seemed fascinated by the décor and a glimpse of cars moving past the windows. They almost had to yell at him to get him back.

With the portal closed, Ryan read Jack's note aloud:

Eric, Anna, Ryan, and Matt—

I'm leaving notes about what's happening in case you come back when I'm not here. More details are in the computer. Login information on the fridge. We found a suitable estate and are buying it. Daniel told his parents the truth about what's happening. The video of Soliander kidnapping Eriana convinced them it's all true. They are onboard, funding the estate. We'll tell Matt's and Anna's parents next. Your phones are here and charged up. Frozen food in the fridge.

—Jack

"Well," said Eric, sitting back in relief, "it sounds like he's got things under control."

Ryan sighed. "I'm not sure how I feel about my parents knowing."

"They were going to find out sooner or later," said Eric. "Maybe he did you a favor."

"I must admit," began Anna, "I love being able to communicate with someone back home."

"Hey," said Matt, looking excited, "I just realized we can send other stuff to Earth. We can't bring anything back ourselves, but why wait until we're returning? Open a portal and send things through."

They talked it over and agreed to send spellbooks and materials to Jack's apartment before completing the dragon egg quest and going home. Matt could finally practice magic and worry less about memorizing spells to bring back. Lorian could send more supplies from Honyn with help from friends. Matt could even go to the elf's home for training. If a quest happened, he would just be summoned from there.

Anna felt so much better about their situation. They could communicate with Earth. They could send someone else through. They could even go back, provided they carried something like that dragon egg first. They were also getting much-needed training. They had allies—and many more answers than before. This was nowhere near being over, but their situation had improved a lot. And then another possibility walked through the door when Eriana joined them, having freshened up.

They got each other caught up. The priestess admitted that she'd believed Soliander could be redeemed, but her faith took a hit on learning of his activities as Zoran the Devastator. And yet she understood that his actions were born of grief and revenge.

And she had a big revelation.

"It should be possible for you to create your own Home Rings," she began, "based on what he told me. I tried to get him to help with creating the keystones, but he's not there yet. You have the scrolls telling you how. Now you just need soclarin ore to do it."

Matt arched an eyebrow. "We gave a bunch to Lorian on the Dragon Gate quest."

The elf nodded. "I still have it."

"I haven't looked at the scrolls yet."

Eriana said, "You should before you do the quest here. There is one last thing you need. The keystones can only be created at Soli's old home in Aranor. I know where it is and can lead you there."

Matt perked up. "Yes, I see the room we need in my head now. It is guarded with spells." His eyes narrowed as he thought hard. "My copy of his staff will get me past most of them at his place. He's cleaned it out, though. There shouldn't be much there."

Eric observed, "I'm worried he's altered the spells since you interacted with him. He knows the staff can get you past them."

"Yes," said Ryan, "but he doesn't know we have soclarin, or the scrolls, and maybe he won't realize Eriana's told us this. He wouldn't expect us to go there."

"Maybe," said Eric. "We need caution, and we should hurry before he figures anything out."

Anna sighed. He was right, but it had been a long day. "First thing in the morning? Matt needs to study the scrolls. Maybe Lorian, too, and we need the ore."

Eriana said, "Yes, tomorrow at the earliest. I need to look at the scrolls as well. My help was needed to add the healing to the original keystones, and I think I'll need to do it again. No offense, but I'm not sure you're strong enough."

"What about me?" Matt asked. "Do you think I'm strong enough to create these keystones?"

Erianna nodded. "I think so, yes. From what Soliander told me, Everon wasn't that strong a wizard and yet was able to create them. The reason more healing strength is needed is that it takes great energy to heal even one person, not to mention four at once—and unlike the wizard, I can't just use a spell. He has to use multiple spells, like the one to change our clothes, or to actually summon us, and the one to create the oracle that asks summoners questions. These are all different and must be done one at a time. If it was all one spell, I'm not sure even Soliander could cast something that complex."

That made sense to Anna. She hadn't considered that the magic came in pieces, like parts of a puzzle or machine. It did raise the question of what happened when one part of it failed. What if they arrived somewhere and hadn't been changed into their outfits? Or showed up nude? Or they stayed home but were suddenly in the Champions' attire? Was there a failsafe that would leave them all at home if one part of the magic failed? Everon could have tampered with all of this. But Soliander presumably had the original spells in the scrolls, not Everon's tampered versions. Anna wondered whether and how the keystones for a Quest Ring and for a Home Ring were different, but Matt wouldn't know until he looked at the scrolls. Now she wanted to see them, too.

That night, they had a private and muted celebration with their hosts—absent Princess Cariss, who was still grief-stricken over the loss of her brother. The queen was similarly muted, and Anna made a point of not seeming too jovial. She whispered to the others to be sensitive. Ryan took it a step further and approached the queen for a few private words that Anna didn't overhear, though she saw the queen take his hand and put her own hand on his shoulder. In all their adventures, Anna had almost forgotten how thoughtful Ryan could be. Shortly after the exchange, the queen left early.

The king seemed more jubilant and even gave a toast in Prince Dari's honor, beaming like a proud father. Had he waited until his wife and daughter weren't present? Did he consider being captured and possibly killed honorably better than staying behind, safe here at the castle while others went into danger? She suspected that this was so. She would never understand people who thought that way. The pride that Dari had done something noble and selfless she understood, but not the rest.

After dinner, they gathered once more as Matt, Eriana, and then Lorian went over the spells in Soliander's scrolls. The elf would cast some of them for Matt, who would do those requiring the most power. Everyone else departed to let them study in peace. Anna was the last to go, her eyes on Taryn sitting with Matt and offering encouragement she only heard some of. She wondered how many times Taryn had done the same thing with her brother. Had she helped Soliander become so strong? Had she guided his character? According to her, she was the big sister who had kept him in line. Sometimes Anna felt the same way about all the boys, but especially Matt, since they'd grown up next door to each other.

Anna didn't doubt Taryn had guided Soliander's development as a person. The woman was capable, commanding, rough, and able to physically take on men. Anna could only do the latter with words and logic. Taryn seemed like she could do that, too. Maybe she would be good for Matt, however brief their relationship was likely to be. He could use a strong woman—someone who understood his position. Taryn knew better than them the struggles Matt faced, maybe even the fear he felt on wielding such power. Matt hadn't said much about it to them, but Anna had seen him muted when doing some spells. In battle, he showed no sign of it. Was he somehow in his element there—not confused, not overthinking, just doing what he was capable of?

But now he faced his biggest challenge, with a lot riding on it. If they could create these keystones for their own Home Rings, it would significantly impact their fortunes and feelings of safety on being sent home. He had to know that. With that in mind, she walked over to him, interrupted his talk with Taryn, and gave him a kiss on the forehead, smiling at the questioning look he gave her.

"For luck," she said. "I know you can do it. But we're all here to help."

He flashed the sweet smile she had so often seen when growing up together but had not seen much of lately. They had come a long way and she wanted him to know she was proud of him, so she told him so and then left them alone.

CHAPTER FIFTEEN

KIRA MORI

Special Agent Kira Mori preferred to work alone, but she couldn't say being assigned a partner had surprised her. The investigation into the disappearance of Erin Jennings had taken some unexpected turn—and the world seemed full of those lately. What started as a missing person's report had led her straight to the Stonehenge Four, FBI leadership praising her for the lead of the century, as they called it. She had to admit, it was big, and too important for just one agent to handle. It seemed like she had half the D.C. field office working on what she had uncovered in the hottest case in the country. She stood before them now, ready to brief the teams executing search warrants on a handful of properties as a result of her work.

Someone at the upper levels of government had decided these four friends from Maryland were able to magically disappear and reappear wherever they wanted. What was to stop any or all of them from dropping into the White House and killing the President? Nothing that she could see. But her investigation led her to believe they weren't that kind of a problem, if they were one at all. Logic suggested that the woman, Anna, had not purposely disappeared from her moving car on I-270 while driving it, hurting or killing her three friends. Or that she had intentionally reappeared in the middle of the same road and gotten herself struck by a car.

Kira sighed. Logic had little to do with any thinking in politics anymore, but that and the truth were her job. There was no room for bullshit. While she couldn't deny that there was a problem with the Stonehenge Four, and that they were somehow involved with the missing Erin Jennings, her impression was that they were caught up in something beyond their control—just like so many people involved in reports of sudden magic abilities hurting or killing people. She'd already investigated one of those and knew that everyone was, in effect, a victim of things they didn't understand. While she needed to find out what was going on, she wasn't of a mind to cause problems for people who already had them.

But she wasn't going to tell Jack Riley that when she arrested him.

First, she had to bring her new partner, Special Agent Wade Carter, up to speed—along with the rest of the agents. She brushed her long, black hair bob out of her face and stepped in front of the podium, rows of agents before her and a slideshow at the ready. Most were white, a few were Asians like her, a handful were black, and only three were women. After a quick introduction, she got started.

"This began as a missing person's report for Erin Jennings of Florida. Her husband indicated that she flew to Maryland to meet an unnamed person in Gaithersburg. She is a collector of antiquities that are rumored to have magical properties, and she has been doing this for over a decade. As we all know, reports are coming in around the world of magic happening, so in light of more recent discoveries in her case, we have confiscated all the items found in her home.

"One person of interest is a private investigator, Karl Parsons, also of Florida. She kept him on retainer to find these antiquities and arrange meetings with buyers, but he claims he had no knowledge of this particular transaction, and Mrs. Jennings had arranged it on her own.

"We were able to track the rental car she obtained near BWI airport in Baltimore, and we found it near an apartment complex in Gaithersburg. Witnesses said it had been there for several days without being moved. We impounded the car but found nothing of significance, including no signs of a struggle or blood.

"And now we get to the more interesting part.

"We found that Mrs. Jennings stayed at the Hilton hotel in Gaithersburg and then, without checking out, she got a room for a single night in a nearby Marriott. We checked the security footage and found nothing of interest at the Hilton, but the Marriott turned up something unexpected. Mrs. Jennings was seen in the company of Eric Foster, Ryan LaRue, and Matt Sorenson, three of the Stonehenge Four. At that time, the remaining one of them— Anna Sumner—was in Shady Grove hospital in Gaithersburg.

"In the video footage, it appeared that Mrs. Jennings acquired the room at the Marriott after walking across the street from another hotel, the Spring Hill Suites, which she exited with them. Further investigation revealed that none of them had a room at Spring Hill Suites. However, Quincy King, the LaRue family attorney, did have a room there—and yet he was not seen to enter or leave the property. It is believed that Mr. King acquired the room on behalf of Ryan LaRue and the other two men. This may have been to help them evade the considerable media attention on them, or for some other purpose. It also appears that the Stonehenge Four were the people that Mrs. Jennings had come to meet, but we don't know that for sure. Why they exited the Spring Hill Suites with her, and why she acquired another room at the Marriott across the street, is also unknown.

"There was another man with them at these hotels. He was seen using a car at the Spring Hill Suites, which is how we acquired his license plate and identity. His name is Jack Riley. He recently quit his job as a manager at Starbucks for unknown reasons, but possibly in anticipation of a ransom for Mrs. Jennings, who is wealthy. He has an apartment in Gaithersburg near where Mrs. Jennings' car was found. So near, in fact, that we believe she was last with Jack Riley before her disappearance.

"Despite all of this, Mr. Riley has remained in the area, and we have been monitoring his activities. He does not appear to be using his own credit cards for transactions, but rather cards associated with Mr. King, the attorney. Furthermore, he has been seen in the company of Daniel LaRue, the younger brother of Ryan, one of the Stonehenge Four. Mr. Riley and Mr. LaRue have been visiting estates for sale in Darnestown Maryland, with the intent to purchase one.

"I should also mention that Mr. King, the LaRue family attorney, is representing Anna Sumner in her legal troubles stemming from both car accidents in which she was involved on I-270. This strengthens the connections among the Stonehenge Four.

"We investigated footage of Ms. Sumner at Shady Grove Hospital. It was known that she was paralyzed and in a coma. And yet she vanished without a trace some days ago. There is no footage of her exiting the hospital, leading to speculation that, as has already been documented, she left by supernatural means. A thorough search of the hospital did not find her. Despite this, days later, she was not seen reentering the hospital, but she *was* seen leaving in the company of Mrs. Jennings. She was walking and appeared to be in perfect health. The pair got into Mrs. Jennings' rental car.

"At present, all of the Stonehenge Four are unaccounted for, as is Mrs. Jennings, who disappeared sometime after this after a final communication with her husband in Florida. He subsequently filed the missing person's report that opened this investigation. There is an arrest warrant out for each of the Stonehenge Four, and for Jack Riley, for potential involvement in the disappearance of Mrs. Jennings. There are also arrest warrants for Ms. Sumner and Mrs. Jennings, for assaulting a guard at Shady Grove Hospital during Ms. Sumner's escape. And we also have search warrants for the homes of the Stonehenge Four, their families, and Jack Riley.

"This is still primarily a missing person's case, and potentially a kidnapping one. However, due to the national security concerns regarding the Stonehenge Four, we will face a lot of scrutiny. For those of you unfamiliar with this, some people believe that they can appear where they want without warning, bypassing all traditional security measures. This means they are a potential threat to elected officials like the President. However, we have examined their social media and see no signs of domestic terrorism or interest in it. Out of an abundance of caution, we have sought them for questioning—but now that they are involved in a missing person's case, we have the justification for warrants that some agencies and individuals in government had previously sought and been denied by the courts.

"I do want to observe that none of the suspects has a history of violence, except Eric Foster, a trained martial artist and instructor. However, he has not used a weapon before. He was a juvenile delinquent in and out of the foster system. It seems he lived on the streets for a number of years, using petty theft and burglaries to sustain himself. We do not consider the suspects to be armed, or at least not with traditional weapons. Due to their apparent ability to use magic, they are still considered to be dangerous. It is imperative that we capture them alive due to the extraordinary nature of their apparent abilities and their potential role in magic events throughout the world."

Her partner, Special Agent Carter, spoke up. "Why do we think they have something to do with magic?"

Kira replied, "No one witnessed their original disappearance at Stonehenge, or their reappearance. However, it was around this time that magic seemingly began, based on the earliest reports of incidents around the world. They did not have a believable explanation for their absence of three weeks. It was only later when they disappeared again, this time on camera, that we realized that this might have been what happened at Stonehenge, minus the camera. We therefore suspect that the Stonehenge incidents were the first instances of magic happening on Earth. But this is conjecture. It is one of the many reasons why we must get answers from them."

She fielded a few more questions before the teams began to disperse. A number of simultaneous but hopefully peaceful raids were to be carried out in the next two hours. She and Special Agent Carter were soon knocking on the door of Jack's apartment, a dozen other agents and field technicians standing by to collect evidence. No one answered after repeated knocks and announcements that the FBI had a warrant, so she used the apartment manager's key to open the door. But no one was inside. It didn't take long to find Mrs. Jennings' purse on the kitchen counter—and that was all she needed to know that Jack was involved. No woman leaves her purse behind. She turned and saw login information on a note attached to the fridge, wondering whether it went with the laptop in the other room.

Kira was about to grab it when she heard a strained voice ask, "Hey, what's going on?"

She stepped out of the kitchen into the living room to see a tall, slender young man with short brown hair and a friendly demeanor. He wore jeans and a grey t-shirt under a light jacket for the fall weather. He held a bag of groceries in one hand, his keys in the other. His concerned eyes moved among the people helping themselves to his possessions, no doubt noticing the "FBI" emblazoned on their jackets.

"Good afternoon, Mr. Riley," Kira began, approaching him and pulling out her handcuffs. "I'm Special Agent Mori with the FBI. You are under arrest for the kidnapping of Erin Jennings."

Jack wasn't having a good day. The surprise of arriving at his apartment and seeing the FBI agents going through his things wasn't one he'd forget. He'd known at once that it related to his friends—or he'd thought so, anyway. The female agent telling him he was under arrest for kidnapping Eriana, aka Erin Jennings, was the new shock of his life—perhaps even more startling than the moment Eric and the others had reappeared in front of him months back. He'd known enough to keep his mouth shut. Now, it seemed especially smart that he and the others had already signed paperwork to retain Quincy as their attorneys.

Now he and the lawyer sat alone beside each other in a holding cell somewhere in Rockville, Maryland. In a few minutes, his questioning would begin, and aside from saying nothing at all, he didn't know what to do.

"Did they tell you anything?" he asked.

"They found Eriana's purse in your apartment and her car nearby. And they have footage of you with her at a hotel. Her husband reported her missing. That's something we didn't see coming. That set all this in motion."

"Shit. So what do we do? Can you get me out of here?"

Quincy sighed. "Honestly, I'm not sure. She's gone and you're the prime suspect. They have reason to hold you and even have you arraigned. That will take a few days, and I can't get you out until then."

Jack went cold. "So I'm spending a few days in jail?"

"Listen, we both know what really happened, and you didn't kidnap Eriana."

"Yeah, but what am I supposed to tell them? That a wizard from another planet did it?" Then he realized something. "Well, I do actually have the footage of Soliander taking her. Not sure it's a good idea to let them see it."

Quincy's eyebrows had risen. "They've already got it. It's on your phone?"

"Yeah. And laptop. I didn't think of that. So if they've seen it, why not let me go?"

"They might not have seen it yet. But they probably will. I know they've got your stuff. The question is whether we want to tell them about it to get you out."

"They'll have a ton of questions. Do I have to tell them anything?"

"No. It's proof you didn't do anything to Eriana, and that's enough. You don't have to explain how you know her, or why she was at your place. Normally they would want your help in locating her, but that doesn't really apply here, given that a wizard took her, presumably off the planet."

"They're going to hear a bunch of things on that video that maybe Eric and the others don't want them to."

"No stopping that now. We'll just have to deal with it. This might be an opportunity, to be honest."

"How so?"

"The FBI have been wanting to talk to them about a lot of things, assuming them to be a problem or dangerous in some way, but they haven't had much to go on. The legal case against Anna for the accidents is the closest, but that didn't open itself up to FBI involvement. Eriana's disappearance did even though it had nothing to do with them. It led right to them and you. But that footage makes it clear someone was after them and they had good reason to be evasive."

"Are you thinking that instead of the FBI being a problem, they could help protect all of us?"

"Something like that. I don't think we can get far with it yet, but that tape is the first sign that they're victims and not perpetrators. I think we need to approach this from the standpoint of wanting to tell them more but thinking they won't believe us, and they can't make you say anything or hold you after they see that tape. Today we set the stage for them becoming allies, I think."

"Okay. So let's tell them about the video. Part of me feels like it's not my place to tell them what's going on with Eric and the others after they see it, so I don't want to say—"

"You're in jail for it," Quincy interrupted. "It just became your place to tell. You're a part of this if you weren't before. Time to act like it."

He got up and left the room to tell the agents they were ready to talk. When he returned shortly afterwards, Special Agent Mori was with him, her black, button-up collared shirt tucked into black pants. She cut an athletic figure and seemed sharp-eyed, like someone he'd rather have as an ally than after him and his friends. He sat up straighter, trying to look less intimidated. The agent slid a picture of Eriana across the table to him.

"Mr. Riley," she began, not wasting time, "do you know Erin Jennings?"

Jack felt better handling this now that he and Quincy knew the FBI would see the video. No sense in lying about certain things. "Yes."

She slid another photo over, showing him with Eriana. It looked like a picture from a hotel security camera. "What was she doing at your apartment?"

"Visiting."

"Can you be more specific?"

"Do I need to be?"

"Were you having an affair with her?"

Jack's eyebrows shot up. He hadn't expected that. "No."

"We found her purse inside and her car nearby. Why would she have left without either?"

"The better question is, why would I be dumb enough to leave evidence like that if I *had* done something to her?"

Her gaze hardened but her tone remained neutral and cold. "Your intelligence is still being assessed, Mr. Riley, as is your honesty and forthrightness, all of which may affect what happens to you. You appear to be the last person to see her. When was the last time?"

He thought back. "Five days ago, in the morning."

"Have you had any contact with her since?"

"None."

"Don't you think that's odd that she would leave her purse and rental car behind, and not go to her hotel room for five days? Aren't you concerned?"

Jack knew how to answer that one. "Yes, I'm very worried about her, and you would be, too, if—"

Quincy waved him off.

Agent Mori asked, "If what, Mr. Riley?"

Jack frowned, and wondered how long they would play games here for. "What else did you want to know?"

Special Agent Mori placed a velvet cloth on the table, something hidden under it, between them. She pulled it back to reveal a golden amulet, which showed one figure kneeling beside another that was rising from a supine position. He recognized Eriana's Corethian Amulet, which Anna supposedly had a copy of while on her quests. This was the only known magic item on Earth, though he suspected there were others. That the FBI had it meant Eriana wasn't getting it back anytime soon, not unless Eriana returned to claim it. Even then, would the FBI hold onto it? Could they? If they knew it was magical, they might try, so he wasn't admitting shit.

"Do you know what this is?" she asked—and he realized from her eyes that she'd seen his look of recognition.

"An amulet," he said.

"We found it in Erin's hotel room. It doesn't seem like normal jewelry, does it?"

He shrugged. "I'm not familiar with women's fashions. Looks bulky."

"Did she get this from you?"

He failed to hide his surprise. "No. Why would you think that?"

"She came up here to meet someone to acquire antiquities she thinks are magic items. We were wondering if that someone was you."

Listening to Special Agent Mori piecing this together was interesting and disturbing at the same time. "No."

"Why don't you just tell me what you were doing with her? And, better yet, where she is now."

Jack looked at Quincy, thinking that there wasn't much left to do here.

The attorney spoke up. "You've confiscated his phone and laptop. There's a video on there that you might want to see."

She didn't look intrigued. "And what's on it?"

"We think it's better that you just watch it and come back to us."

Agent Mori leaned back. "Since you seem to be repping a lot of them, you probably know that we executed search warrants on the LaRue estate, Anna Sumner's condo, Eric Foster's apartment, and Matt Sorenson's home—so we have a lot of evidence to go through. I'm sure we'll get to yours eventually."

Quincy frowned. "Cut the crap. You didn't find anything at those locations because there's nothing to find, including any sign of Erin Jennings."

She leaned forward. "You seem awfully confident she's not at any of them. It's almost like you know where she is."

Quincy leaned forward, too. "I know where she's not, and so do you—because if you'd found her, we wouldn't still be sitting here having this conversation with the questions you asked about her whereabouts."

Jack watched the agent sit back, her expression suggesting Quincy had her on that one. Then she reached into a bag and pulled out four red iPhones, several wallets, some keychains, and Anna's purse. Jack's face fell. Since Eric, Ryan, Matt, and Anna had all been asleep in his apartment when summoned, all of this had been left behind instead of going with them. From what they had told him, if they had the stuff in their pockets, it went with them—but it stayed in some sort of buffer, to use Matt's computer analogy, while they were on a quest. When they returned to Earth, the spell gave back everything. This last time, that hadn't included the items on the table now because they'd been asleep, and who sleeps with a wallet, keys, or phone on them? Jack had put the items away, but now the FBI had them.

"So tell me," Special Agent Mori began, "why do you have the phones, keys, wallets, and purses of Anna Sumner, Eric Foster, Matt Sorenson, and Ryan LaRue? Did you kidnap them, too?"

"Of course n—"

Quincy held up a hand to quiet him. "Is that a crime?"

"Kidnapping? Of—"

"No, having the possessions of his friends."

"Who are all missing?"

"Who said they were missing?"

Jack tried to keep his face neutral. It was true that they had been gone almost a week, but no one knew that. More importantly, Daniel having told his parents the truth suddenly seemed like a stroke of genius. They hadn't reported Ryan missing. Since then, Jack, Quincy, Daniel, and Daniel's parents had talked with Matt's and Anna's parents. As a result, Matt and Anna had not been reported missing. They had so far left Eric's former foster parents out of it. While he kept in touch with them, they didn't talk that frequently, especially since all of this had started. Jack doubted someone had reported Eric missing either. He tried not to smile.

Special Agent Mori looked startled by the question, and Quincy asked, "Has a missing person's report been filed on any of them? Because I'm their attorney and I haven't seen one."

She hesitated. "No, there hasn't been."

"Then this is irrelevant. And you had no business taking these things. I'll be taking them with me when I leave here."

"It's evidence."

"Of what?

"They were found in the same place as Erin Jennings' items, and she *has* been reported missing."

"That doesn't mean they are related to her supposed disappearance."

Agent Mori rose to her feet, wrapping up the amulet to take it with her. "Until we find her, we're adding the Stonehenge Four to the suspect list. Since you don't seem to be in a cooperating mood, Mr. Riley, I'll give you time to think over your situation. We have a nice cell picked out for your overnight stay."

CHAPTER SIXTEEN

A DEAL WITH A WIZARD

The one place Soliander felt the safest had been violated. He wasn't a man given to fear. Wielding as much power as he did, that wasn't the issue. His name inspired reverence, awe, and terror. No one defied him and lived to boast about it—not anymore. Everon and others had done it once, and look what had happened. Years of his pain, suffering, and forced servitude. Most of them he had tracked down and killed—or worse. Many were lying in the crypt below for Aeron to summon when needed. In the bowels of this castle suffered the worst offender, the priest who had lent his healing powers to Everon during the creation of the altered keystones. His torment would never end—not until Soliander's did, and he felt certain his never would.

Or he *had* felt certain until finding Eriana. He wasn't given to disbelief. That paralyzing reaction could get a man of his power killed—or worse, ensnared again. So no matter how fantastical something appeared, he could quickly accept its reality and counter any threat it posed. But Eriana was no threat, though she had briefly spelled him. He might have seen that coming but he hadn't expected it, his guard down. She had never spelled him before, but then he had never spelled her either. Was this to be the new normal or an aberration? He had lost her again now, but it wasn't the same. He would find her but not kidnap her like that. He had meant what he'd told her that he couldn't bear to leave Earth without her.

He still grappled with the implications of her being alive, of all that had happened since those imposters first appeared, and of what he had learned. They had changed much, and it was too early to tell where all of this was headed. That Eriana lived mattered more than anything. He was curious about Andier and Korrin, but that was all. That planet Earth would be fascinating one to visit again. These imposters were intriguing, repeatedly proving themselves far more capable than he had expected. They certainly didn't seem to fear him or his Lords of Fear. Perhaps they were worthy replacements for the Ellorian Champions, but he couldn't let them keep using his name indefinitely. Regardless, their lack of fear seemingly matched his own, or appeared to. The fact that they had violated his home had made him uncomfortable, but not because of fear.

This was about power. For so many years, all control had been wrested from him—and he'd sworn it never would be again. He'd laid waste to kingdoms or conquered them, partly in the name of control. He'd seized the Orbs of Dominion, again for control. And he'd built an impregnable castle that no one was allowed to enter or leave except for him and those he brought. All for control. No one was to enter the castle without him personally making it happen. No one knew this place existed unless he wanted them to, and he now realized that this had made him lax in his preventative measures. His control here was absolute.

Or had been. How the imposters had known to enter Castle Oste, then subdue some of his servants, fight off the Lords of Fear and a host of undead, and rescue Eriana before leaving with her was a mystery Soliander would solve by any means necessary. On his initial examination, he had noticed two minor scrolls missing, but nothing else important—and of course they hadn't gotten into the rosewood case. He would double-check his tower later. But the fire had destroyed the keep and he wasn't sure it was worth rebuilding. As bold as they were, he doubted they had been looking for him and they must have been there for something more important than a few spells that weren't worth the trouble.

But first, he would deal with the prisoner.

Prince Dari of Andor sat before him, bound to a chair—not with ropes, but with magic, and unable to move anything but his head. His sword lay on the floor beside him, his own blood dripping to the floor beside it, several festering black wounds on his skin. One hand was still white and painful from the touch of Lord Voth. A look of strain marred what handsomeness he had, but somehow the sullen expression Soliander was used to remained.

It had been a long time since he had seen Korrin's brother, but nothing had changed. He was still a boy in a man's body—all insecurity, resentment, and fear. Soliander knew why, though not because Korrin had discussed it. The knight seemed a little oblivious to his younger brother's jealousy. No, he knew from rumors, observations, and Dari's own words, but this knowledge was no achievement. Dari lacked many things, and subtlety was among them. He would make a poor king, unable to hide his thoughts, and yet he considered himself worthy. He was alone in that regard, and that only seemed to make him whinier about being denied, by birth, a role he wasn't suited for anyway. Could he have been suited for it had Korrin never been born? Such questions weren't worth pondering. What mattered now was just what to do with the prisoner.

In a silence broken only by Dari's pained panting, Soliander watched him from behind his black desk and admitted, "I have no use for you."

Dari's tortured eyes met his and looked away, dancing between shelves of spellbooks, scrolls, glass vials, and other magic items. The prince asked, "What does that mean?"

"Maybe you can help me decide. If Korrin lives, he would not be pleased if I killed you. If he's dead, it doesn't matter."

"Then I hope he's alive."

An unsurprising answer. Or was it? "Do you? You've often seemed to wish he'd never been born. Wishing him dead was only a small step from that."

After hesitating, the prince said, "All men want to be king, but few are as close as I am and yet doomed to never be one. You are a king now and should understa—"

Soliander's gaze intensified and silenced the prince. Nearly everyone thought Soliander was missing and had never been a king. Zoran the Devastator, on the other hand, was. Several times over. But how did Prince Dari know this?

Coldly, he asked, "What makes you think I am king?" Dari looked unsure how to answer and Soliander said, *"Soranumirae."* The prince's eyes widened as he struggled to breath, eyes bulging and imploring the wizard to stop. Soliander let his victim's face start turning blue before releasing him. *"Earimunaros."*

The prince sucked in a huge breath and sat gasping for several seconds, starting to babble. "Jack. On Earth. He heard you tell Eriana you are Zoran the Devastator. When you took her."

Interesting, he thought. "But the imposters were already on Elloria when I did that, and have not returned to speak with Jack."

Dari shook his head. "They cast a spell and spoke with him. That's how we knew that you had taken her and who you are. There were also rumors that the Lords of Fear work for Zoran."

Soliander had made no secret of that. He hadn't known that Jack was there when he'd spoken to Eriana, or that he was going to kidnap her, or that the imposters would learn of it so soon. He frowned. This was exactly the kind of mistake that had him keen to plan things carefully. It was also why he had incinerated people like his apprentice Darron. Maybe he should be more forgiving. He hadn't done anything to Darron this time; the elf could hardly be blamed for not being prepared for the raid, given that Soliander hadn't been either. If only he had been here, instead of training Garian before their own next raid...

Dari seemed to have recovered and said, "You know what it is to have this power, this esteem."

"I had both before I became king. You have neither, and would likely remain that way even if you *became* king."

Petulantly, with defiance, Dari said, "You don't know that. Power changes a man."

"Usually for the worse."

"Not in my case. You know, I can tell, that I resent being overshadowed by my brother, that nothing I do is considered enough. With him and my parents gone, this changes. I will be free to be viewed on my own merits instead of as a lesser version of my damned brother or father."

"If you were man enough to take command of a kingdom, you would be man enough to take command of yourself."

"I have. That is what I am doing here. I did not wait for anyone else to rescue Eriana. I did not sit back. I am here."

"And you are captured."

"I let it happen so they could get away. You know that."

He had a point. The Lords of Fear had confirmed it. For once, Prince Dari had surprised him—not only by joining this mission, or fighting in it instead of cowering in a corner, but by giving himself up to the Lords of Fear of all people, so that those whose power Dari resented could escape to safety. Maybe Soliander had misjudged him. But he didn't think so. Dari had always had the potential, just not the will. He wondered what had changed.

"Why did you do it?" Soliander asked.

Dari breathed hard through his nose twice as if working up the nerve to say it. "I've had a taste of life without Korrin around for three years now. And it has been good." He paused as if to gather his thoughts. "I don't need everyone to respect me. I know I am not the Pride of Andor like Korrin. I just need them to stop making comparisons and acting like everything I do is shit. I can be my own man if they let me, but they wouldn't until he was gone. I had done things even before then, despite what you say—and no one cared. Just like you, they pretended I'd done nothing. That attitude is the problem, not mine. I didn't need anyone's praise, but to do good things and be sneered at for them? Just because they weren't as grand as Korrin's? Of course I resent that. You would feel the same."

Soliander agreed with that, but wasn't going to admit it. "What changed?"

"He was gone. That was it. That was all it took. It's almost laughable. I wasn't what changed, just the judgments thrown my way. No longer harsh, not even praise, just recognition. Simple. In time it was almost like Korrin had never existed. But as I became used to not having his shadow over me, not being denigrated, yes, I changed. I lost all the attitude I had about my damn brother."

"And now he might be back."

Dari snorted. "Yeah, now he might be back."

Soliander didn't have to think through the threat this likely posed to Dari's inner life. Korrin's return would be the worst thing that had ever happened to the prince. It made him wonder. "Have you become reckless now? Did you throw yourself into danger to prove your courage, or something else? Do you even care what becomes of you if Korrin is found alive?"

Dari laughed bitterly. "I have nothing left to lose."

"But you have lost nothing yet. Does the mere possibility of Korrin's return threaten you so much?"

"Yes. And I have already lost something. The chatter, the rumors about the famed Ellorian Champions returning, they have turned all eyes to Korrin already—and he hasn't even been found! Oh, I understand the fascination, you've all been missing all this time. I see it. The whispers had disappeared along with you, but now they are a roar of interest. If anything, the Ellorian Champions returning after three years will make you even more fascinating."

"Yes, it will." Soliander wasn't really interested in it, but he understood the fame nonetheless. Imagine how it would be if everyone knew what he'd been doing? He almost laughed at the tongue-wagging that would ensue.

"And I will become more invisible than ever. I've already heard some people joke that they wish I was the one who had disappeared."

Soliander saw the anger and defiance in the prince's eyes. Now he had some understanding of why the prince was here. "You seek glory."

"I seek respect."

Those could almost be the same thing. Almost. "Whose respect do you truly want?"

"First? Yours."

"And how do you plan to get it? You have nothing to offer me to earn this respect."

Dari shook his head. "You don't want the imposters meddling in your affairs any more than I want them meddling in mine, but we both interfere with them. In that sense, we are already allies."

Soliander had no allies and liked it that way. He preferred people who were beholden to him in some way—and very afraid of him. His ruthlessness, often demonstrated to witnesses very much on purpose, was a means to an end. A life without trust was a lonely one, but being at peace was more important to him than anything else. No one needed to know the extent of his plans or aspirations. His Lords of Fear knew some of the things he was doing; other subordinates knew different things. But no one knew everything. He carefully chose what to reveal, always anticipating betrayal and making it impossible. People could fail and disappoint him, but they could not betray effectively if they didn't even understand what they were being made to do. It was the closest he could come to feeling secure in his new life. And it was one of the reasons why the intrusion into his home unsettled him.

And Dari had helped make it happen.

The wizard said, "I don't see you meddling, but helping."

Dari nodded. "This time, yes, to gain their trust. But I have already caused problems for them." He lifted his head as if with pride. "You know of the quest to return the dragon egg, I assume? It was my father's doing. When I learned, about the egg and his plan, I made a plan of my own. I sent word to the trolls nearby and they attacked and stole the egg. If they hadn't been so slow to destroy and use it, these imposters would be trapped on Elloria even now, never going home. They would be out of your way."

Soliander watched him carefully. Dari was more dangerous than he had realized. The depths of his resentment came as no surprise, but he had thought better of the prince. Such feelings could turn many towards wickedness; he just hadn't thought Dari was one of them. How unlike Korrin he truly was. A darkness lay inside the prince, and Soliander knew what to do with such men. They were perhaps the easiest to manipulate, to bend to his will. However much Dari might've tried to hide what he felt—and he didn't try hard—it was plain to see. He would have to do better at that to be truly useful. Openly wearing one's heart on one's sleeve makes it easier for someone else to rip it out.

That Dari had wanted to trap the imposters on Elloria also surprised him. He and the real Champions had been acutely aware that failing to complete a quest meant they would remain in that world for good. The pressure had been intense, always lurking at the back of their minds—if not the front. Somehow, they had never failed. And neither had these imposters. He had to admit to intense curiosity about them and how they were managing to get by. Eriana said the presence of his staff in Matt's hands had much to do with it, and he'd considered taking it from Matt to see how they would fare without.

But it only occurred to him now that he might want these imposters not to fail. Or at least, only to fail when—and where—he wanted them to. Should he choose the land in which they became trapped? He normally only found out where they'd been summoned to once they were done, it difficult to interfere with them—or even help. Maybe he should take a cue from King Sarov and devise a quest for them on his own terms. The idea had merits, and Dari had given it to him. Perhaps the prince was useful after all.

Soliander asked, "What did you hope to gain from trapping them on Elloria? Surely you don't want them around in Andor forever? As places to be trapped go, it is ideal for them, and our families are sympathetic."

"You would have chosen somewhere else? I cannot disagree, but this was my only option at the time. Perhaps another chance will arise, if you let me rejoin them."

"But what is your reason? They have done nothing to you."

Dari sneered. "Haven't they? They're the ones doing these quests, creating renewed interest in the famed Ellorian Champions. Even when they are unmasked before the worlds as imposters, that will only cause *more* interest."

Soliander almost smiled. Truly, there was no winning for the prince. "And you can either rise with them by helping as you did today, or destroy them." He felt grudging admiration for the prince's maneuvering.

"I would do both, with them none the wiser. If they do not know I work for you, then I will be a spy in their midst and learn many things I can pass—"

"I already have spies in Andor."

Dari smirked through his pain. "Then why didn't you know we were coming?"

Soliander arched an eyebrow. He couldn't very well argue with that. "Go on."

"They are keeping things a secret, and have done well with that—but it will not last. On other quests, they'll be discovered as imposters. Sooner or later, someone who knew you and the others will summon them and recognize the situation, even they don't understand it. The elf, Lorian, from Honyn, already knew. Now dozens in Andor know. Eriana has been found and is back on Elloria walking around, where she will be recognized. And we know you are alive. It is only a matter of time."

This was a problem Soliander would need to address. Only in the last few days, on since learning that the imposters were in Andor, had he begun to consider it. Eriana and the others also knew he was Zoran the Devastator. She wasn't bound to keep that a secret, and likely wouldn't, nor would others much longer, if at all. He felt no need to explain himself to anyone, but it might be better if he controlled the narrative. He ruled with ease as Zoran partly because his behavior was consistent and therefore not a mystery. But everyone would question why Soliander had pretended to be gone and lived under the name Zoran—and they'd be disturbed by the contrast between Zoran's destructive actions and Soliander's heroic quest work. That mystery could undermine faith in him as Zoran, people questioning whether he'd still be the ruthless Zoran or the noble Soliander.

The truth was a threat, and he cursed himself for not having seen it coming. He had assumed his friends were gone forever, and so he'd no contingency plan for their reappearance. He certainly hadn't foreseen these imposters. Something would have to be done. And he might have to decide who he wanted to be going forward—Zoran the Devastator, or Soliander the Majestic Magus? Maybe the best idea was to let everyone know the truth about the Ellorian Champions and what Everon had done to them. Sure, it would make people realize they hadn't wanted to do all those quests, but he no longer cared about their old reputation. Not really. People might even realize he wasn't as noble as he'd seemed and be less surprised by his behavior as Zoran. Would people blame him for his actions if they knew he was hunting down everyone and every kingdom involved in Everon's betrayal and destroying or conquering them? People might even sympathize—especially if they learned how he had broken free and thought the other three Champions, his friends, were dead, and that it was his fault.

Yes, it was sympathetic. Maybe he should just admit it all, his dirty secret, the one he'd worked hard to keep hidden, and begin to live openly. He would still be feared, maybe even more so. No one crossed Zoran—but to go against Soliander? And after what he had done to those who'd betrayed him? Maybe the truth was not a threat, but the greatest asset he had. The idea almost made him laugh.

Prince Dari interrupted his thoughts. "I am among those who know everything they are planning and doing right now."

"Only while they remain on Andor. Once they finish the quest, that will not be the case anymore."

"Not if I win their trust. They've discussed having some people go to Earth to help them set up there. I can be among them."

Soliander had to admit that he was learning much from the prince, and without even casting the *Mind Trust* spell on him. Sometimes an old-fashioned interrogation was more entertaining, if not so revealing. "And how do you plan to earn their trust?"

"This mission was one way. My sacrifice at the end was another. I can change their hearts about me and likely already have. I can show that I have changed, that I will risk my life for theirs."

Soliander nodded. The prince was more resourceful than he'd expected. "And after all of this? What happens when they have no more need of you?" The prince hesitated and Soliander frowned, then raised one hand, bluffing that he would suffocate Dari again.

"I want to be King of Andor," the prince quickly admitted.

That was not exactly unforeseen. "Your father is."

"He must die, of course."

This was getting interesting. "And you plan to let that happen naturally? Or were you hoping to accelerate it?"

"It won't matter to me if I am not to be king."

"And if you *are* to be king?"

"Do you need me to be king sooner or later?"

Soliander replied, "I don't *need* you to be king at all."

"Of course, but once you have time to think how I can be of use, with the forces of Andor at your disposal, you may realize I can help you sooner as king."

He had a point, but making him king based on some vague possibility of future usefulness was a lame offer that seemed in perfect keeping with Dari's lack of esteem. Soliander stifled a smile. What Prince Dari failed to realize was just how much betrayal upset him, though the prince was wisely dancing around killing his parents or asking Soliander to do it. If Dari thought Soliander would hand him the throne of Andor later for some cooperation now, but Soliander ultimately failed to live up to his part of the bargain... well, that would be the perfect fate for him. It was almost too easy. Certainly, if Korrin showed up and claimed the throne, Soliander would not back Dari over his old friend. But neither could he help Korrin's brother to murder their parents. The prince would have to do it on his own, but he would worry about that later.

"Your brother is heir-apparent," he said. "Have you given up hope that he still lives?"

"That doesn't matter. My parents have not given up hope and will not name me heir-apparent."

"And what if they do and die? What if you are king and Korrin still lives and returns to claim what is his?"

"It will be too late."

"By the laws of Andor, he would still be the rightful heir."

Dari shook his head. "Not if I change those laws once made king, before his return. And I will rule in allegiance to you. I understand you have a similar arrangement with Lord Voth in Aranor."

"King Voth has shown his allegiance. But you have not."

The prince held his gaze. "I can give you something to show you I can be of use to you as King of Andor. Aren't you wondering how we knew where this place was?"

Soliander's gaze intensified. "Tell me."

"The news is worthy of a kingdom."

"If you are correct, I will make you King of Andor, in servitude to me."

Dari's eyes blazed triumphantly. "The wizard, Matt. You attacked him with the *Mind Trust* spell. When he broke free, some of your memories—many of them it seems—became his. They are scattered... and it is hard for him to recall anything on purpose, or sometimes to understand what they mean. But that is how we knew about this place."

A feeling of vulnerability swept over Soliander like never before. No one had ever cast that spell on him—and he had long ago vowed that no one would survive doing so for long. But now his own use of the forbidden spell had backfired. Worst of all was that he hadn't realized for what, two months now? What did Matt know? It could be anything from his entire lifetime. Secrets he had never shared. Embarrassments carefully hidden. Plans yet to come to fruition. The reason why the spell was forbidden had never been so clear to him before, his every thought and feeling potentially laid bare.

But he couldn't stop using it, even if he resented the intrusion into his own privacy. No, he would have to persist. There was only one way to find out what Matt knew—to repeat the spell on him, this time with better precautions.

Soliander eyed Dari. If he had known this sooner, things would not have stood as they now did. The prince could indeed be very useful, and he was right. This one piece of information was of extraordinary value, surely worthy of a kingdom—for it might allow Soliander to evade many problems and set many traps, provided no one found out Dari had told him. He decided to make use of the prince for now and let things play out. A spy this close to the imposters could gather even better intelligence. Now it was time to see if Dari could think of his own solutions to problems. Soliander had already made up his mind what to do next, but decided to test his captive.

"How do you propose to return to Andor?" he asked. "You are no wizard, so you can't send yourself. They will not try to retrieve you—either because they do not value you, or because they know we would be expecting them."

The prince appeared to consider this. "You would have to send me."

"But they will wonder why I would do so."

"You said it yourself. You have no use for me. Why not just return me as a sign of good faith?"

"But I could just kill you. Will they not wonder why I have not? And why would I show good faith?"

Dari shook his head. "They don't know whether you're good or evil, and they're not sure what you're capable of. Letting me go would confuse them; surely that would be beneficial. Besides, killing Korrin's brother would send a clear message about what to expect from you, and that would not be tactically sound. Keeping them guessing is better."

Soliander nodded. It wasn't a bad answer, but it wasn't quite good enough. He hadn't expected Dari to suggest the rest that he had in mind—but few men would, even Korrin. "I should also demonstrate that I am still someone to fear, should I not?"

"Absolutely."

"I'm so glad you agree." Soliander rose and walked over the prince. "Are you right-handed or left-handed?"

"Why?"

Soliander picked up Dari's sword.

CHAPTER SEVENTEEN

THE KEYSTONES

The one thing Ryan would never get tired of was riding a dragon. He rode a glistening silver dragon with Anna strapped in behind him. Eric and Eriana rode a red one, while Matt sat behind Taryn on her black dragon. Lorian and Rognir followed on another while four of Taryn's Dark Blade warriors rode two more. They weren't expecting much of a fight because Matt was certain the place was abandoned and only magical traps awaited them.

They had flown instead of using another magic portal, to save both his strength and Lorian's for what was to come. Creating one keystone would take a lot of energy, even from Eriana. Making four had inspired Matt to ask Anna if she could heal or rejuvenate them in some way, and she was fairly certain she could. It would take much of the day, but they were hoping to fly back before nightfall and had left before dawn. Taryn warned that the skies near the Towering Peaks were more apt to fill with unsavory creatures at night, though she refused to describe them when Ryan asked. She didn't say no when he said 'griffon' or 'wyvern'. Now part of him wanted to see them. Surely, they wouldn't take on this many dragons, would they?

Though their destination had been due east of Andor, they had flown northeast past Allowyn and over the low mountain range, the Hills of Andor. The aptly named Towering Peaks farther west caused this detour. At nearly thirty-thousand feet tall, they posed a challenge for their mounts. He had always though dragons were incredibly powerful—and there was no denying it while riding upon one's back—but the thinner air coupled with swirling winds made it harder for them to fly over the mountains. The dragons that called the tallest areas of the Towering Peaks their home were often much smaller, their habitat inhibiting their growth.

Since their rides weren't from those mountains, they skirted them east toward Ogreton before swinging south into Aranor. The mountains formed the western edge of the kingdom, foothills stretching eastward into a desert Ryan saw in the distance. Only from maps did he know that the Dorman Ocean lay farther off. The only signs of water he saw were lakes and one river rushing out of the Towering Peaks.

But now they were descending in tightening circles that were still a safe distance from Soliander's rectangular, four-story keep of grey stone and a taller, lone tower. A two-story wall and moat surrounded them until it ended in the sheer cliff mountain face behind the keep. As they descended, the dragons veered off toward the structure's front, scouting for any trouble on the ground.

Ryan's eyes skimmed over the tall grassy areas. He saw a trampled path indicating recent passage. At least something was down there, he knew. Enough groups of trees were present to hide a few people, but there was clearly no significant force here—not that he expected one. He just wasn't sure what people would do on learning that the most powerful wizard anyone had heard of had been missing for three years. Taryn had told him all about rumors of Soliander having fantastic magic items or creatures here. Long before he vanished, foolish people had tried to steal things from him and regretted it. But with the wizard gone, had they become emboldened?

The dragons landed on a grass-covered hilltop and settled low so the riders could disembark. They would be coming inside for added protection, which made Ryan feel significantly safer. No one in their right mind would fight a dragon, and yet he was supposed to be Lord Korrin, the Dragon Slayer. Part of him wondered if the real Korrin was nuts. Sure, Ryan had killed one on Honyn, and helped Matt kill another, but that had been out of necessity. Korrin had apparently sought out problematic dragons to stop them. The man had to be crazy. He couldn't really blame Prince Dari for not following in his older brother's footsteps, could he?

The dragons morphed into their human form. The black and red dragons had dark skin, but the others were light-skinned yet tanned. Their hair color revealed which was which. Their huge saddles would be left unattended because no one could steal one easily, but they would bring any valuable contents.

Eric interrupted his thoughts by saying, "Matt, Taryn, I think you're up. We'll stay right behind."

The group set off, one of the dragons trailing farther behind after listening intently in one direction and apparently being satisfied. They stepped onto the dirt road winding through the trees and foothills. It sometimes blocked sight of the keep and its tower, which didn't look like they had been damaged in a siege or attack. If anyone had come here for the contents of the castle, it hadn't been an army. He saw no footprints or even horseshoe tracks, and wondered if people kept to the path or just didn't come at all.

"Is this road safe or booby-trapped?" he asked Matt.

"Pretty sure it's safe for now. But that will change as we get closer."

Taryn said, "You cannot rely on the scattered memories of my brother. You may not understand them as much as you think. But in this case, I am familiar with Soli's approach to safeguarding what it is. A wizard once captured me to gain that knowledge."

Ryan noticed she didn't say what had happened. "Something tells me you took care of him with a sword."

"Dagger, technically," she replied, smiling. "I know some of what may lie before us."

Eriana said, "I am also familiar with this place, but mostly the inside. He preferred just leaving the spells outside alone and casting others directly inside."

They stepped around a final group of trees to see a cleared area a hundred square yards to the moat. But it wasn't empty. Two figures appeared to be standing on the path not far from the drawbridge, but neither were moving. Ryan stepped to one side to get a better look. The skeletons of several horses lay together not far from them, with more piled closer to the raised drawbridge. There seemed to be other piles of something Ryan couldn't identify, but he saw a shield against one pile and a sword sticking up from another.

"The staff just warned me something is here," said Matt.

"No surprise," muttered Eric. "Can you tell—"

A roar from beyond the wall interrupted him and a blue dragon climbed from within the courtyard and over the wall to stand before their destination. It roared again and bolts of lightning crackled from its mouth to strike the ground near them.

"It's an illusion," said Matt, watching it.

Ryan snorted. "Could've fooled me."

"Not me," said the black dragon with them. "Very good spell, but no dragon would believe that."

"So we just ignore it?" Ryan asked. That wasn't going to be easy.

"Basically, yeah," said Matt.

"What about those two men standing out there?" Anna asked. The fake dragon roared again.

After a moment, Matt said, "Pretty sure that's a time delay spell. I've seen it in his books. Anyone who steps within its radius will move about one inch a day but have no idea that it's happening."

Ryan looked over at the men again. "I don't suppose we can tell how long they've been in it?"

"When we get closer," said Matt. "The staff can help me tell where it starts. Based on that, do the math. They might have actually been caught in it long before the Champions disappeared."

"They're on the path," Ryan observed, "so I assume we don't want to be."

They waited as Matt surveyed the area, the dragon roaring again. He finally sighed. "The only things I know for certain are that it's like a minefield, with different spells set to do different things in different places. And the staff will warn me when I get close to one."

Rognir smacked him on the back. "Lead the way, my friend!"

Even some of the dragons smiled at this. The group set off, letting Matt go first, with Taryn, Eriana, and two of the dragons next. One dragon said they would be prepared with a magic shield if something dangerous started. And it did, more than once. A cloud of poisonous green gas surrounded them at one point until dissipating. A volley of energy darts struck at them just after they continued; Ryan wondered whether Soliander had planned for the gas to make someone run forward only to be struck by the darts. It might have worked, too. They soon came across the first skeleton, its armor full of round holes, each charred and with no sign of a projectile remaining. As they neared the dragon illusion, one of the real dragons flicked a wrist at it and the spell vanished. Matt detected any other spells and guided them safely around until they stood at the moat.

"How do we get the drawbridge down?" Ryan asked, eyeing two stone pillars that would flank the bridge once lowered.

"Here," Taryn said, stepping forward. She rubbed her black boot across the dirt to reveal a square metal plate. In the center was a hole with several notches in it.

"Made of soclarin," Ryan said.

Matt flipped Soliander's staff upside down and inserted the crystal at the top into the hole, where it clicked. The stone drawbridge creaked as it lowered. Ryan looked down into the dark moat, unable to see if anything lived in it. They walked across without incident. Matt explained that because the staff had opened it, any spells that might have been there were deactivated.

"I assume any spell we undo remains that way, so he'd have to come back and re-cast it?"

"Yes. So if he ever comes here, he'll know someone was inside."

Taryn observed, "He'll know it was you, but that's his problem. Honestly, I believe he should be helping you create these keystones for your Home Rings and if he has a problem with us doing this, he can talk to me about it."

Ryan smiled. "We can be nice and close the drawbridge before we leave."

"Yeah," started Eric, "let's not piss him off any more than necessary. We broke into two of his homes in two days."

Matt made them wait. A spell to detect someone's presence was active until one dragon dispelled it to save his strength. Ryan wondered if they could help Matt and Lorian with the magic needed for the keystones, so he asked.

The black dragon replied, "We need to see the spells. Let us get there first."

They crossed the courtyard to the keep, where the room they sought lay in the basement. When they reached the iron door before them, Taryn stopped them.

"I know this one."

"So do I," said Eriana. "It's a physical trap."

Eric asked, "How do you get—"

Taryn ignored the door handle and shoved inward three times, the door swinging freely on the third push. "It's not actually locked, but if you grab the handle, you'll get a surprise. Never told me what it was."

"Poison," said Eriana, frowning, and Ryan sensed she disapproved. "It's part of the door handle and kills in seconds. He said the poison will never run out."

Ryan remarked, "Then no one has made it this far. No body."

They stepped inside a dark entryway, Matt lighting his staff to reveal cobwebs in one archway and a stone stairway rising into the dark. To either side were passages leading away. They followed one of these passages around corners and through doors to the back of the keep, disarming a few traps both physical and magical. Taryn knew about some of them, Eriana about others, and Matt about the rest. They soon found a stairwell curling down into blackness.

Taryn flipped up a lever on the wall twice. "Don't go down the stairs without doing that. There's another at the bottom, but you pull down twice."

"I'm starting to think he doesn't want anyone to come in here," joked Eric.

On reaching the bottom, they found three doors. Taryn indicated the right one. Matt stopped at the door to Soliander's laboratory, and hesitated.

"Everything okay?" Eric asked.

The wizard didn't answer at first. Then he did so slowly, pausing between sentences, and Ryan could tell he was trying to recall things from Soliander's memories. "There's more to this than having the staff. There are spells. Physical traps. We have to disarm them all to get in. He made them to stop

Everon from ever using this room again, from ever creating more keystones and Quest Rings. Now it's our problem. This might be the single most secure place of Soliander's. He doesn't come here anymore. I may not be able to disarm it all, and even if I can, I might not have the strength afterward to create the keystones."

Ryan sighed. "Great. I bet that was part of his plan."

The black dragon offered, "We should be able to help."

Everyone but the dragons and Matt stepped back. After a few minutes, they cleared one spell, then another. Matt guided Eric on how to disarm a physical trap. With that done, a panel in the wall opened for Matt to insert Soliander's staff, a seemingly failsafe way to protect the room. Two more magic traps and one physical one remained, but then the door finally opened, the dragons having done most of the dispelling.

As Ryan stepped through with the others, he saw a large room with empty shelving, bookcases, racks, and tables, some askew as if ransacked. At the room's rear, a furnace made of soclarin ore waited for Rognir and the soclarin ore he dumped from Lorian's Bag of Desires. The dwarf suggested breaking shelves to start the fire, but a dragon breathed flames to start it instead. Ryan hadn't known they could do that while in human form.

Ryan watched as Rognir, Matt, and the dragons set about creating the physical component of the keystones. First, Rognir bashed the ore with his hammer until it became a fine sand, into which he mixed charcoal Matt found in a nearby bin. Rognir added the soclarin ore and charcoal mixture to the furnace. Molten soclarin soon fell from the bottom, where the dwarf collected it for the dragons to reheat, and then he hammered it into a long, flat bar on an anvil. The dragons melted it until it oozed into four keystone molds, each with a center hole into which Soliander's staff would fit. The four new Champions each added a piece of their hair to their own six-by-six inch keystone.

With this done, a tired Rognir flopped onto a stool. During the hours needed for the molten keystones to cool, the supernatural component had to be added. Matt and the dragons had been studying the scroll, and they began their work with Eriana. Eric suggested that the rest of them leave. Ryan knew it was a good idea, though he'd wanted to watch. Everyone was afraid to wander around Soliander's home, so they just sat outside the door and on the stairs for hours, chatting. Finally, the door opened.

Rognir said, "It is done."

Ryan got to his feet. "It worked?"

"Yes. You have four keystones. And an exhausted wizard."

They filed back inside to see Matt slumped in a chair. Anna knelt beside him and put her hands on his chest, where a soft glow preceded the wizard sitting up a little more. But it seemed that no amount of healing would take the fatigue away. Eriana seemed exhausted, too.

Ryan walked with Eric over to the keystones. They were wet and steaming from having been dipped into an old vat of water. Each was of a bluish metal. They didn't seem as important as he knew them to be, but then magic items seldom gave off signs of what they could do. He hefted one in excitement, seeing Lorian turn to him with the magic Bag of Desires, into which Ryan placed them one by one.

"We should get out of here now," Ryan said. He realized they were fortunate to be able to create keystones on a planet other than Earth, where the supernatural was only just awakening. Maybe Eriana and Matt would not have been able to harness enough power there.

"Wait," said Anna, her white robe stained by the charcoal, ore, and dirty room. "I know we've seen Korrin's Home Ring and what happened to it. This might be our only chance to see Soliander's."

Ryan frowned, "You're right, but I think it's too dangerous here."

Matt spoke up, his voice weak. "It's a little melted. I remember now. There's really nothing to see. The top and bottom are melted, but the keystone is intact. Not sure it would work, but it doesn't matter."

"Good enough for me," said Eric.

Ryan couldn't disagree. Seeing Lorian lend his support to Eriana, who leaned on him, he went to Matt and put an arm around him, half carrying him from Soliander's laboratory. They wasted no time climbing the stairs, going across the courtyard, and passing over the drawbridge. Eric placed Soliander's staff into the hole to close the bridge, and they carefully picked their way back through the field to where they had landed before. It didn't seem like anyone or anything had disturbed their saddles. Before long, the group had mounted and took to the sky with just enough sunlight to avoid worrying much about skirting the dangerous areas of the Towering Peaks. Night had fallen by the time they reached Andor, Matt sleeping most of the way.

The wizard recovered some energy by the time they changed and ate a late dinner with their hosts, who surprised them. Prince Dari had returned, but he wasn't present. Soliander had let him go with a message—that he was not coming after Eriana or the imposters, as he called them. The arch-wizard understood that he would have done the same thing to rescue Eriana, had their positions been reversed. But he warned them not to get in his way again. He also claimed that if he encountered any sign of Korrin or Andier, he might take them away for a time to talk with them, too, though he would ultimately let them go. As a sign of his good faith, he had returned the prince—but as a sign that he would still be a menace should they confront him again, he had removed one of Dari's hands at the wrist.

"What do we think of this?" Ryan asked as the four friends sat alone in Anna's room that night.

Eric shook his head as he sat beside her. "I don't trust Soliander."

"What about Dari?" Matt asked. "Not sure what to make of him since the mission."

"Me either," said Eric, "but we may have misjudged him. We'll be going home tomorrow, and probably won't see him again anytime soon."

"Part of me wishes we could stay longer," said Anna. "We're safe. No one can summon us. And I could use the rest. We all could."

Eric squeezed her hand. "Yeah, it's a nice thought, but we have to protect Jack and our families by setting up the estate."

"You know what I'd like?" Matt began, yawning. "Lorian wants to visit Earth. He can stay and help Jack. Hide his ears and he's set. Maybe someone else from here, like Taryn, can come. That way, we aren't the only ones able to deal with a Soliander."

Ryan laughed. "I'm not sure we can deal with him, but point taken. Taryn is an especially good idea in case he shows up."

Eric nodded. "I'm not sure we can ask her. She has a life here."

"I'll do it," said Matt. "I think she'll say yes."

Eric smirked at him. "I think she has a soft spot for you."

"It's strictly professional," Matt deadpanned.

As Matt left the others behind, he sought out Taryn because he felt like it was his last chance to see her alone. He didn't really know what he wanted to say, just that he hoped she would come to Earth and see them. Well, no—to see *him*. Should he make it personal? Or make it sound like it was just business? He frowned.

He had often acted like a chicken shit, as he thought of it, doing things like making an excuse to stop by and see a woman. He knew that that was driven by insecurity. It was as if he somehow felt his company wasn't enough reason for someone to talk to him and he needed another justification. He had been dimly aware of this for a long time and tried to make himself stop it, but he hadn't quite gotten the hang of it.

But he felt certain Taryn would respect him more if he just admitted that he wanted to talk with her. No explanations—no excuses. He would enjoy her company and offer only his. If she turned him away, that would suck, but at least he'd have tried. With the mortal danger he faced seemingly every day, this wishy-washy thing didn't suit him—not that it ever had. But he had grown into himself, escaping Soliander, killing a dragon in midair, and facing down undead. Surely women couldn't still strike fear into him, could they? He laughed and felt renewed confidence. Maybe he would even kiss her when she opened the door. If she looked at his lips even once, he was doing it.

As he had often done in Andor, he had taken a less crowded route to his destination, not that many people were around once after dark. It wasn't like on Earth, where it could be so bright at night that many people didn't care the sun had gone down. This particular hall looked empty until he rounded a corner and found a tall man in a blue robe approaching him. The hood was pulled up and partially hid his face. Matt glanced at him, lost in thought, his mind drifting to Soliander and his days working with soclarin ore to fashion the keystones.

By now he had come within paces of the hall's other occupant, and he looked at him to nod a greeting. The man lifted his head, dark eyes unfriendly and staring at him. Suddenly another image flashed into Matt's head, one familiar but not his own. He recoiled, a defensive spell struggling to form in his panic.

"*Kunia!*" the man snarled. Matt slammed into the wall, cracked his head, and fell unconscious to the floor.

CHAPTER EIGHTEEN

THE CRIME SCENE

Eric was looking forward to going home. However much they got used to living in a medieval or Renaissance era—and he wasn't sure of the difference, but he missed taking a shower. And coffee. And watching videos, whether YouTube, TV, or cable. But he had to admit that things were quieter without those modern amenities. Last night he'd fallen asleep reading a book.

As he thought about it while dressing in the morning, he wondered if the Home Rings should be built for mobility. What if someone like Soliander or the FBI showed up at the estate and they couldn't return? Putting the rings on wheeled platforms would mean they could roll them into a truck, if the measurements were done right. He didn't know if the Home Rings had to be a set size. The Quest Rings were pretty much never the same as each other, being built from local material. The one element common to all was a keystone.

He soon knocked on Matt's door, but got no answer and decided to let him sleep in. There was still no sign of the wizard as Eric enjoyed a quiet breakfast of boiled eggs, omelets, pastries, fresh bread, and fruits with Ryan and Anna. He finished eating first and finally went to wake Matt again but got no answer, no matter how much he banged on the door. Anna and Ryan joined him, looking amused. Two of the guards heard the banging and approached, unlocking the door at his request. He threw open the doors to see a made bed. It was obvious that he hadn't slept here.

Turning to the others, he asked, "You don't think he spent the night with Taryn, do you?"

Anna nodded. "He might have."

"Good for him," said Ryan.

"Good for who?" asked a female voice, and Eric turned to find Taryn walking up to them, dressed in her leather armor to escort them.

"Uh, nothing. Matt's not with you?"

"No. I came to bring all of you to the king. He'd like a final farewell."

Eric exchanged a look with the others, growing concerned. "Matt's not here, and he didn't spend the night in his room."

Taryn scowled and strode into Matt's room, quickly assessing it before addressing Eric as she turned to question the guards. "Check for the staff and robe."

"Right." He didn't see why Matt would take Soliander's items, but their presence or absence might tell him something. On opening the cabinet in the meeting room, he found everything there, so he closed it again and they caught up with Taryn.

"Who was on duty last night?" she asked a guard, getting a name before turning to the three friends. "He didn't leave this morning. Not this way. We need to check with last night's guards."

Eric agreed and they set off in search of Matt. None of them had ever gone missing. Maybe there was an innocent explanation, but he doubted it. When the previous night's guards revealed that they hadn't seen Matt, the grim determination on Taryn's face matched what Eric felt—and the worry from Ryan and Anna.

While Taryn didn't have official authority, she derived influence from her commanding presence, being Soliander's sister, and having the ear of the king. She made the captain of the King's Guard start a room-by-room search of the palace and lock it down. Word went out for others to meet in the great hall, where the king and queen, Eriana, Lorian, Rognir, Solun, Princess Alia, Prince Dari and Princess Cariss all straggled in. A tense hour passed before they learned that they had found the body of a nobleman in an unused room.

"How did he die?" Eric asked, wanting to confirm if this was murder.

The guard replied, "A spell that burned holes in his flesh. Each wound had a black mark around it, like fired caused it."

"I know that spell," said Lorian, scowling. "A simple attack one."

Eric turned to Eriana. "Do you think it was Soliander? He's the most likely suspect after the raid we did."

She nodded. "He would do whatever got the job done. But you said his staff and robe are still here?"

"Yes. So it wasn't him?"

Ryan asked, "Do we think he'd want Matt more than his stuff? Wouldn't he get it all?"

Eriana shook her head. "No, Matt's not more important to him. Not unless he knows Matt has some of his memories, but he doesn't. And I don't know what he *would* do on finding out. It's not like he can remove the memories without..."

Eric grew cold. "Killing him."

"Or messing up Matt's mind in some way," she said. "In my talks with him, I told him how important the staff is to your continued success. He wouldn't agree to let Matt keep it, but I don't see him taking Matt and not the staff at least."

"Who else would take Matt?" Anna asked. "Almost no one knows we're here and who we really are."

Eric saw that Prince Cariss seemed lost in thought, her brow furrowed. He asked, "How many wizards are in the castle?"

The guard looked unsure, and the king ordered all of them politely rounded up, so someone went to do it.

"Can you tell exactly when he died?" Anna asked.

"Last night, my lady."

Taryn asked, "Where was the body found?"

The guard answered and Eric swore. "Matt tended toward less crowded ways to get around. Can we see this location? The body?"

Before these quests started, he had never seen a dead body. Now it sometimes felt like hardly a day passed without a corpse. That it could one day be him or his friends had never felt more real. He wouldn't tolerate any chatter about this being a coincidence. The world so often seemed to revolve around them once they were summoned, and it pretty much did. This had everything to do with them. He was certain.

The king agreed to let them see the scene, Prince Dari and Princess Cariss joining them. Eric hadn't seen the prince since his return, and had been eyeing him for how he seemed to fare. Losing a hand wasn't the change that concerned him. Rather, Dari had been moody and upset with them right up to the raid on Soliander's Castle Oste. He had fought well there, as if he'd grown up during the fight. But what about now? The missing hand had to bother him. He had asked Eriana about it because Aeron, the necromancer, had grown back Kori's hand, so why not Dari's? The answer was that Lord Voth's grip on Dari's wrist had damaged it in such a way as to prevent that.

The change concerning Eric was the prince's inner life. Dari seemed somehow more sure of himself. King Sarov was certainly proud of him. Was that it? Had he finally earned the esteem he craved? Was the missing hand even a sign of his valor? It kind of was—but no one except their small group knew why it had happened. This suggested that Dari might want to tell people the truth.

When they reached the small room with the body, Eric stepped inside with Taryn, Eriana, and Lorian. The thin, middle-aged, balding man still had his eyes open and looking in different directions until Eriana closed them. The elf and priestess examined the body, confirming that the wounds were from spells. What caught Eric's attention was the body's position.

"Look at the way he's lying," he said. "It's like he was thrown in here. Unceremonious. Whoever did this was in a hurry."

"Yes," said Lorian. He straightened to examine the walls. "Either that person has excellent aim, or this is not where he died. I do not see any damage to the walls from a stray missile."

Eric exchanged a look with Taryn. They stepped into the hall to examine the walls. Eric saw it first—a hole about the size of a quarter had burned the wall next to the lantern. The hole was above his head, and yet the victim's wounds had been at chest level. As Taryn stopped beside him, he delivered his conclusion.

"The wizard was down on the floor when he cast the spell upward. It's the only thing that makes sense."

"I agree," she said. Taryn pointed to a red smudge a few feet away. "This is blood with a bit of brown hair in it, but that man is bald. So he was attacked with magic in one place—but someone with brown hair like Matt was attacked here, and left the blood mark."

Lorian stepped out of the room with a blue cloth and a blood-covered dagger. "I did not see blood on the victim. The energy wounds don't bleed but they were in places that would take a minute or two for him to die from. This means he was alive when he was put in this room. I turned the body over and found a dagger with blood on it and a piece of torn cloth on the blade. Neither the blood nor the cloth is from him. I believe he stabbed the wizard who killed him."

Eric mulled that over and finally said, "I'm speculating, but what if something the wizard did to Matt made him strike the wall with his head and leave that blood mark? Then maybe the wizard was bent over him when the other guy came around the corner and caught him, so he did the spell that killed him. But maybe he wasn't quite dead when the wizard put him in the room there, and the guy managed to get out a dagger and stab him."

They considered that and Taryn said, "Plausible. Right now, I think we have to assume someone has Matt. We need to round up the wizards and their clothing. Whoever it was would have changed and maybe healed themselves with a potion or device, or with someone else's help, in which case there's a witness."

Standing a bit removed from the group, Princess Cariss had put one hand to her mouth and stood scowling, lost in thought, her eyes troubled. Eric remembered that she had a wizard friend she'd mentioned a few times. He approached her.

"My lady, do you know of anyone?"

She looked up, startled, then met his eyes and looked away before nodding. "Mandrellan."

Eric remembered the name. "You said you hadn't seen him in a while, is that right? Since our arrival? Is it still true? Was he here recently?"

Her eyes widened. "Yes. Yesterday. But, I, uh—"

Dari stepped forward and gripped her arm. "You are always gossiping with him! I saw how excited you looked when you left the throne room the day these four arrived. You didn't tell Mandrellan who they are, did you?"

She looked guilty and unsure how to respond. "I, I did, yes. I'm sorry. I didn't think... he's always been so loyal. He has tried to find our brother so many times."

Dari frowned at the others. "He wears blue robes most days. We may have found our man."

Eric asked, "Would he have a reason to want Matt? What does he know, Your Highness? Can you remember what you told him?"

"Yes. Yes, I first teased him that we had successfully summoned the Champions, and—"

Eric interrupted. "I'm sorry, how did he react to that?"

"Well, with concern, really. But I think it was because I hadn't told him we were trying it and he felt I didn't trust him enough to tell him."

Eric wasn't sure what to make of that and asked, "Was he relieved to learn it wasn't true?"

"No. It excited him to learn that we had seen Eriana and Soliander."

"Happy excited?" Eric turned to Eriana. "Ever hear of Mandrellan?"

"No," she said. "I do not know him. He could've been excited for many reasons."

"It wasn't that kind of excitement," said Princess Cariss. "He seemed concerned, especially about Soliander. Oh, and when I said Matt had some of Soliander's memories, he grew quite agitated and left shortly after."

Eric's eyes narrowed. "I've heard enough. Taryn, I—"

"Let's go," she said, and they began walking. "Princess, where would he be?"

Princess Cariss explained that Mandrellan had a house a few blocks from the palace. It didn't take long for them to settle on a plan of action—the palace guards and King's Guard would be questioned to learn if Mandrellan had been seen leaving. No one could say that he had, and so their search of the palace intensified in case he was on the grounds. The princess wasn't sure how strong a wizard Mandrellan was, or whether he would be able to open a portal or cast himself from the palace to the house.

As the palace search continued, Taryn led Eric, Anna, Ryan, Lorian, and Eriana to Mandrellan's two-story house, but he wasn't home. The servants claimed that Mandrellan had come and gone several times during the week without saying where he was going, often not returning for a day or two. In their opinion, this meant he had gone to his home planet, as that was the usual reason he gave for overnight absences. He had last been there the day before. They assumed that he had left Elloria once more.

Eric cursed. The last thing they needed was to have to chase the wizard to another planet, assuming he had gone. Taryn said that the World Gate was the most likely way he would have left if so. It was in the Hall of Worlds, a name in frequent use among planets that had such gates, which the kingdom operated for its citizens or those who could pay to travel between planets. The heavily-guarded building lay on the opposite side of town from the castle. Before long they were mounted and cantering or trotting through town as fast as they dared, a horseman ahead blowing a trumpet to signal people to clear the road. To Eric's surprise, that actually worked, and they reached the plaza before the Hall of Worlds in a few minutes. The building stood three stories tall in white marble, with wide double doors and a row of statues out front—including those of the Ellorian Champions. Eric glanced at Eriana, who smiled sheepishly.

Once inside, Taryn led them left toward the departure gate, which was on the opposite side to the arrival gate. Scores of people were here, but it was nothing like an airport terminal back home. Most of those able to travel between worlds were wealthy or on state business. Eric hoped this meant it would be easy for someone to remember seeing Mandrellan come through here—but they might once again have to round up everyone who worked here, just like in the palace. It could get time-consuming.

The chainmail and tunic-wearing guards who were present saw them approaching with a handful of the King's Guards and snapped to attention. Taryn ordered that the area be cleared of witnesses to their conversation, so Eric waited impatiently with the others. He saw the concern on Anna's face, and the grimness on Ryan's. They could not let Matt down. The thought heightened his determination and he turned to one of the guards at the gate.

"Do you know a wizard named Mandrellan?" he asked. "Have you seen him pass this way and through the gate in the last day?"

The balding guard perked up. "Yes. He said he would be back tomorrow. Just going home for some rest."

The first part of that calmed Eric. Now they knew something, at least. "Was he alone?"

"Yes. Just a small bag with him, nothing more."

Eric turned to Lorian. "That magic Bag of Desires you guys use. You can't put someone in it, can you?"

The elf said, "Actually you can, but they'll die."

"How quickly?"

"Seconds. They suffocate because their lungs collapse."

Taryn said, "We'll need to go after Mandrellan, but we should get a better idea of where he went after stepping through the gate."

The guard perked up again. "He said he would be back tomorrow. Just going home for some rest."

Eric cocked an eyebrow. Those were almost the same words, and his demeanor had been the same, too. He looked sideways at Taryn, who met his gaze and turned to the man.

"Did Mandrellan go through the gate?" she asked.

The guard perked up. "Yes. He said he would be back tomorrow. Just going home for some rest."

Taryn swore and banged a fist on her leather-clad thigh. "He's been spelled. Lorian? Eriana?"

"Got it," said the priestess, stepping forward. She put her hands on the man's temple and spoke a few words, upon which he blinked rapidly and seemed surprised to see her standing so close.

"Have you seen Mandrellan pass this way?" she asked.

"Yes, my lady, several hours ago."

She asked, "Was he with anyone else?"

"No."

That Mandrellan had put a spell on the guard spoke volumes about his evil intent to Eric, who asked, "Did he have anything with him?"

"A large chest."

"Large enough for a body?"

The guard's eyebrows shot up. "Uh, well yes, technically. But he couldn't get it through the gate. It wasn't for lack of trying. I mean, it was small enough to fit, but every time he tried, the end of it would go through and then stop when he pushed it more. I helped him, but we couldn't get it to budge. Then he seemed to realize something and cursed."

So did Eric on realizing what this meant. "That motherfucker has him. I'm gonna kill him."

"I don't understand," said Eriana, scowling. "How do you know that?"

Eric felt surprised he had to explain to her of all people standing there. "We can't leave this planet because the quest bound us here. He tried to take Matt through and couldn't."

Eriana nodded, then scowled again. "How did you get me from Soliander's?"

"Someone stepped through with the dragon egg, and then we could follow. Then we put it back and continued the quest while it was still here, safe. Presumably, Mandrellan doesn't have the egg." He looked alarmed and turned to Taryn, who wheeled away and barked orders at the guards. Several took off toward their horses at a run, sent to ride back to the palace and protect the dragon egg.

"Okay," said Eriana, "I get it. It's been a long time since a quest bound me. And I hadn't stopped to think about how you achieved that before. Very clever, by the way. We never tried that."

Ryan asked the guard, "Where did Mandrellan go when he realized he couldn't get the chest through? Did he still go through without it? Or is he still on Elloria?"

"He walked away with it and went through there." The guard pointed at a doorway to one side.

"Answers that question," said Rognir, hefting his hammer. "Let's go get him."

Matt was dreaming about Soliander again. First came images of the wizard issuing orders to a dark elf in a room with black walls. Then came memories of his staff, the one Matt had a copy of, in a cabinet along with the robes he had always worn as one of the Ellorian Champions. The same robes Matt had. The room had jars along shelves, and rows of spellbooks and scrolls. Matt had been there, but these didn't seem like his memories. He saw an image of a dark castle among mountain peaks. It was on the planet Cygnus.

The dark elf appeared in another scene, speaking of someone he had succeeded in locating at Soliander's behest. Names of a planet and city flashed through his mind before images of Soliander leveling a city block in pursuit of someone. The devastation was horrifying, though Matt experienced it as rage, satisfaction, and pleasure. But it turned to disappointment when the one he sought was not among the many bodies found in the rubble.

Someone cursed and Matt stirred. A pain in the back of his head made him moan. For a moment he straddled two worlds, both being asleep and awake, before he left one for the other. But something was wrong. He felt groggy, certainly, but not from sleep or fatigue, just a haze of confusion. And yet his mind still raced through dreams. No, memories. These were Soliander's memories, in his mind. Someone held his forehead gently. A cloth was over his mouth. A gag. He tried to pull away but couldn't, his eyes slowly opening as the visions continued so that he saw one thing in his mind and another in front of him. A man in a blue robe stood before him in a room so dark Matt could see nothing else.

And suddenly Matt knew what was happening. He had experienced it once before, when another wizard had violated his mind this way. Like Soliander before him, the man had cast the forbidden *Mind Trust* spell on Matt and was sifting through his memories. Like a sedative, the spell made him feel compliant, but he knew it didn't always work. He reached out to feel magic power and gather it within him to unleash on this wizard, but he felt nothing. Just like on Earth, there seemed to be no magic to touch and control. The only other time he'd experienced that was...

"Yes," said the man, his voice commanding, "you're wearing the Crown of Voids. I keep one on hand. Terrible device. As a wizard, I object to it on moral grounds if for no other reason—but that's solely when someone intends to use it on me, of course. They're really quite useful. I offer yourself as a case in point. You'll cast no more magic, Matt Sorenson of Earth. Because when I am through with you, you will die."

Matt tried to talk but couldn't, not that he needed to. The man could read his every thought. As he'd done with Soliander, Matt resisted the sifting through his mind. Instantly, the images shifted away from Soliander's memories to his own—personal memories of him nude in the mirror, or lying on his bed touching himself. He felt heat in his face, a sheen of sweat soaking his clothes.

"That won't be very impressive to the ladies," the man said, laughing. Humiliation tore through Matt. "The spell works whether you're conscious or not. You just can't be dead. I can see whatever I want. Should I keep going until you succumb and stop fighting me? Maybe then I'll leave your most embarrassing memories alone."

Anger filled Matt like never before. He tried to pull his hands forward but found them bound behind him as he sat on a chair, to which his ankles were also tied. At his resistance, the man dove straight into detailed memories of sexual encounters, thoughts, and fantasies, porn Matt had viewed, bathroom troubles, encounters with girls he had poorly flirted with, and more. And all the while he kept up a commentary on what he saw—laughing, mocking, disapproving. Matt flushed with a shame that grew deeper by the moment, sweat dripping down his back, his heart pounding. He fought again only to have the invasion of privacy worsen. Matt moaned at the complete command the man had over him, his helplessness making him cry out for him to stop. But the man dove deeper still and Matt trembled.

Finally, the invasion stopped. Matt blinked in confusion—relief, even gratitude overwhelming him. But that caused a new shame, to feel thankfulness toward someone humiliating him. He sobbed on realizing he just wanted to cooperate, to let the man see what he wanted so that he would be satisfied and maybe not see it all, leaving Matt at least something private.

The man accepted his surrender, then asked Matt to voluntarily show him something embarrassing as proof of compliance. He felt a tear roll down his face and did as he was told, more tears falling once it was done. Then the man helped himself to whatever he wanted to know, which was everything. About Soliander. Eriana. The quest to Earth. The Earth itself. The quests they had done. When his attention turned to Matt's families and friends, their homes and personalities, Matt realized he posed a threat to everyone he knew and loved. What if this man captured them and did this to them? He begged the man to stop, to leave them out of it. But he kept going. With a scream, Matt fought back again.

A bolt of lightning lit the room as it struck him, causing a shock of pain beyond anything he'd ever felt. It knocked the breath from him. And then he couldn't breathe, another spell stopping all air from filling or leaving his lungs. His body convulsed as he suffocated for what seemed like forever. When it finally stopped, his lungs heaved for air that was suddenly burning as a fire engulfed his legs. He screamed uncontrollably and didn't even notice when it stopped.

"Shall I keep going?" the man asked, before grabbing his jaw and pouring a liquid down his throat over the gag. Too senseless to resist, Matt swallowed. The physical pain faded and was soon gone altogether so that he sat dazed, grateful, and bizarrely calm. Had he been drugged? He no longer cared. Avoiding pain of any kind was all that mattered. He knew that the man was training him to submit and that doing so was shameful, but he didn't care anymore. Tremors came and went through his body—as if a cold deep inside him, one that no fire could ever warm, had taken hold. The man gripped his forehead and began the *Mind Trust* spell again. Matt stared up at him blankly, compliant, terrified, and unresisting. Two words filled his mind over and over, first directed at his friends, and then at his master before him.

"I'm sorry."

Anna let Eric and Ryan lead the way, Taryn right behind them. Lorian and Rognir brought up the rear, though the elf was their only wizard right now and perhaps he should've been up front. Only now did she realize how much she had come to rely on Matt. He was a novice but a powerful one, and he always got the job done. Lorian was more swordsman and archer with a dose of magic. Would it be enough to counter whoever this wizard was? Maybe she would have to do something personally. She needed to spend more time talking with Rognir about defense options, like putting up a shield as Matt had done. As she walked, she put one hand to her amulet and began communing with a god to get a sense of what help she could hope for.

They had stopped at the door leading from the Hall of Worlds into whatever lay beyond, Eric turning to Taryn. "Do you know where this leads to?"

"Let's find out," she said, pushing past him.

The rest of them followed her into a stairwell that went up and down. They descended, Anna wondering why they'd chosen that direction, but there was no time to ask. They exited into a long hallway on the first level down, servants moving supplies of one kind or another. This floor seemed to act like a warehouse, and they searched rooms one by one without finding Matt. They descended from a staircase in the middle to the final floor, which had only two lanterns on the wall.

Eric and Taryn motioned for everyone to be quiet as they started toward one side, listening and trying the door handles. Some were locked. Eric suggested they return to those. Then a door farther away opened, and a blue-robed man stepped into the hall. He turned in apparent surprise, and then ran for the stairs at the end as everyone chased after him. Eric was fastest, Lorian right behind, but Taryn stopped at the door the man had exited and tried the handle. It was locked. She bashed at it with her shoulder until Eriana put a hand to the door and spoke a few words. It glowed briefly, but a spell kept it closed.

They dashed after the others, hearing the commotion up the stairs as a boom of thunder sounded and someone screamed. On reaching the main level, Anna heard a huge rumble as the ground shook, an awful cracking sound following through the door to the World Gate room where her friends had gone. Stones loudly thudded on stones. More screams and yells split the air, and a cloud of dust washed over her. Fearing that the building had collapsed, Anna waved her hand in a futile effort to clear the dust and stepped through the door.

At first, it was hard to tell what had happened with the dust kicked up, but the stream of sunlight through the broken ceiling left no doubt about a cave-in. Eriana brushed past her to a man with a bloody gash on his head, healing him before moving on to another person. Men were shouting for help, either for themselves or others, and as Anna moved farther into the room, she could see why. Huge stone blocks had crushed several people, either killing them or smashing their limbs. People were trying to lift the blocks off, but got nowhere until wizards magically lifted them away. Eriana moved between the wounded, her healing touch bringing quick relief. Anna wanted to do the same—but first she frantically looked for her friends. She finally saw Eric crouched beside Ryan, who had a smaller slab pinning one leg. Just as she arrived, Eric and another man managed to move it, Ryan gritting his teeth. His leg was broken.

Anna knelt beside him and put a hand on the leg, reaching out to the goddess Drakonon and finding the healing touch easy due to their repeated connections. The power flowed through her and into Ryan, who stopped gasping as his leg mended.

"What about you?" Anna asked Eric.

"I got out of the way faster."

That didn't surprise her, as agile as the martial artist was. As she moved to help another victim, she asked "Where is the wizard?"

"He made it through the gate after pulling the ceiling down on us."

Anna stifled a curse, thinking that they needed to head back to that closed room immediately. But first she and Eriana finished healing the wounded. She peeked at the priestess to see if there was anything noticeable about her technique to pick up on, but it didn't seem so. When she straightened, she saw Taryn forcibly arguing with an intimidated-looking wizard, whom she grabbed by the wrist and began dragging toward the stairs.

She followed ahead of her friends, catching up with Taryn and the wizard just as he broke the spell on the door the blue-robed man had exited. Then Taryn bashed it with her shoulder twice and it splintered enough to stick an arm through and unlock from the inside. Taryn and Anna entered, taking different paths around a chest-high wall of crates before them. More crates lined the walls of the twenty-square-foot room, a lone torch burning by the door. Once they'd navigated the crates in the way, Anna saw Matt tied to a chair in the room's center, his head hanging down as if unconscious. Relief washed over her as she and Taryn reached him together.

Anna got down on one knee before Matt. "Are you alright?" She pulled the gag from his mouth, but he still didn't respond except to move his head a little. She wondered if he was only partially conscious and gently lifted his chin to see his face, which bore a haunted expression, jaw slack and eyes half-open. He didn't seem to recognize her.

"Matt, it's Anna. We're all here. You're safe now."

At that, a lewd smile ran across his features and he began to laugh, the sound turning a little wild. She checked him for physical wounds but saw none. Taryn began untying him as the others gathered around.

"What did he do to you, that wizard?" Anna asked. "He's gone now, okay? He's not even on this planet anymore."

Matt began to rock against the chair like a toddler trying to comfort himself. With the ropes no longer holding him to it, he almost fell off into her and would have if Taryn had not grasped him by the shoulders. Anna finally breathed a prayer to grant Matt peace and watched hopefully as he stopped rocking and slumped more, leaning back in the chair. He blinked several times as if clearing his sight or mind. Some clarity appeared in his eyes, which turned to look at her. This time recognition appeared—but no other reaction. Not relief. Not happiness. Not anything. He just stared blankly at her.

Anna asked, "Who did this to you?"

When he didn't answer after several seconds, Taryn came around to his front and knelt, one hand taking his. "Was it my brother?"

Matt's head turned toward her. Then he smiled broadly, beginning to laugh silently as he shook his head, like a schoolboy with a funny secret he wouldn't tell.

"Who?"

"He knows *everything*," Matt finally said, his voice cracking.

"Who? Who did this to you?" Taryn asked. "Mandrellan?"

He leaned toward her, unsteady, and whispered the answer. "Everon."

It had been a long day and Eric lay down on his bed, tired and unsure of what to do. He was sick of talking, guesswork, and machinations. His life had been full of those since that fateful day at Stonehenge, when they were first substituted for the Ellorian Champions. At least on Elloria, they didn't have to pretend, but everything felt different now. They had been physically wounded before, supernatural healing sparing them weeks or months of recovery. But now Matt had wounds of the mind and spirit. And no spell was going to fix that. Anna had done something to calm him, but it wasn't enough. When Taryn helped Matt to his feet, he had wobbled as if mental imbalance had led to a physical one. Even once he was on a horse, with Taryn behind him and controlling it at a walk to the palace, Matt's face had been oddly blank—like a mask, his eyes down. And he wouldn't meet anyone's gaze.

Hours had passed since then, with Matt in his room and only Taryn beside him. Eric wasn't sure what to make of that. He had noticed Taryn's determination to find Matt and concern at his condition. Was she taking care of Matt like she'd taken care if Soliander when they were kids? Was that a reason why she seemed drawn to him? Matt hadn't said much beyond admitting to Everon's use of the *Mind Trust* spell.

"He's afraid," Matt had said. "Soliander is hunting him. He's very afraid."

And he had better be, because now Eric wanted Everon dead and would happily turn him over to Soliander in a bargain for peace.

They let Matt rest but didn't want to leave him alone, and the wizard chose Taryn to keep him company. Eric didn't disagree, but found trust harder to come by. Still, of all the people they had met on Elloria, Taryn was the most trustworthy—and so he, Anna, and Ryan regrouped with Lorian, Rognir, Eriana and their hosts.

Talk turned to raiding the places belonging to Everon as Mandrellan, on Elloria or any other planet. But Matt was in no condition for it. Lorian stepped up, taking Rognir and a force of men, including some Dark Blade warriors with Taryn's approval. Eriana went with the expedition, which returned hours later. They hadn't found Everon, just Mandrellan's house. After investigating, Lorian surmised that Everon had killed the real Mandrellan years earlier and taken his place, moving to a new city and giving himself a plausible origin story. Then he'd come to Elloria and introduced himself to Princess Cariss by saving her life in a scene they believed he had concocted to gain her trust. The princess was furious, guilt-ridden, and embarrassed that the man who had betrayed her brother had been here all along. They surmised that Everon had placed himself where he would be among the first to hear if the Champions returned.

They knew he'd kidnapped Matt because Matt had some of Soliander's memories, which could include how close to catching Everon Soliander was. Now he knew of Soliander's hideouts and where Diara was. Would he be foolish enough to attack Castle Oste to recover Diara? Soliander wouldn't be expecting him, but had undoubtedly fortified the place. Everon wasn't a fool, and maybe a bigger threat to them, but Matt had likely been a means to an end. Maybe they didn't have to worry about Everon, another enemy.

They decided to stay another night for Matt's sake—and theirs. Once home, they could be summoned once more. Matt needed a break even more than the rest of them, but one day wouldn't be enough. In the meantime, Eriana and Rognir decided to visit Earth with the keystones. The dwarf could fashion the Home Rings, while Eriana could keep Rognir out of trouble on the unfamiliar planet. He wasn't an elf and could pass for a little person, but he didn't know the world and might be too much for Jack to handle. It would likely take them days to create the rings, and speed mattered.

Eriana expressed mixed feelings about returning to the place that had been her home for half her life. She had only just been reunited with her brother. But the king and queen pledged to bring her to Elloria whenever she wanted. They granted Solun a permanent room in the palace beside one set aside for Eriana, not the guest quarters they had been using. Eriana would split her time between worlds as needed and eventually make it to Coreth. She admitted that she felt obligated to help the four Earth friends, find Andier and Korrin, and discover how to convince Soliander either to help or to stay out of their way. Eric gave her a bigger hug than he meant to before she disappeared through a portal with Rognir to Jack's apartment.

Thinking of Matt with Taryn still in his rooms, Eric lay on his bed, remembering his own time alone with a woman. Part of him wanted Kori to show up now, partly so he could tell her about Everon being here so she could tell Soliander. The information wouldn't just be a peace offering, but a fresh lead for the arch-wizard to get revenge. It could solve two problems at once—keeping both Soliander and Everon busy.

One in pursuit. The other fleeing.

CHAPTER NINETEEN

SHARDS

Taryn asked minutes after his friends left, "What do you want to do?"

Matt wasn't sure how to answer and lay staring up for a long time on the bed, still fully dressed. She lay next to him, facing him, one hand on his chest. The feeling of being exposed would not leave him, he felt, until the person to whom he had been so exposed was dead. And now he knew the answer to her question. "I want to kill Everon."

"I will help you," she said at once.

He turned his head to her, their noses nearly touching. He saw clear-eyed resolution, and a strength he had admired since laying eyes on her. This admiration had grown. He felt drawn to her in a different way now—beyond attraction to her beauty, to her sharp mind, to her personal power and command. Now she offered a kind of safety, like a rock to steady him. Something about that steel gaze calmed him. He wanted more. Needed....

Matt kissed her and met no resistance. Instead, a firm, confident response drew him in. He gladly lost himself in it, feeling like he found himself in doing so. Always awkward with a woman, he somehow felt sure now when nothing else seemed certain. She made love to him the first time, and he to her the second. And, through it all, there were no thoughts of anything outside their shared bed.

When it was over, they napped—and he wondered if a nightmare would tear him from sleep, but it never came. He fancied nightmares to be afraid of Taryn, if not himself. When they finally woke, her growling stomach brought attention to his own hunger. She called a servant for some food and hot water for a bath. They spent more hours just being quiet together. Somewhere in all of it, Matt felt remarkably restored, wondering if it was an illusion. He wasn't dealing with what had happened, he knew, just escaping it. Perhaps that was all he needed today, but he also had some thinking to do.

Taryn sat sharpening her sword as he read through his spellbooks, not saying what he was looking into for. Something about making preparations while she sat there tending to her weapons pleased him. They could be fearsome together, and likely would be. But first he had something to do without her. There would be no going after Everon today or anytime soon. Matt wanted to be stronger, but he also wanted to feel safer. Taryn couldn't be with him all the time. She had already said she wanted to come to Earth, but even so, Matt would just get summoned, and she wouldn't be there on the next quest.

She could still come with him on the one he was about to attempt—but he wasn't sure if she would approve, and he felt too vulnerable ever to truly be at peace unless he did what he was planning. He could protect himself, all of his friends, and the woman he was falling in love with. Everon would never do to them what he had done to Matt. The idea threatened his self-control, only just restored, and so he pushed it from his mind.

He looked into the spells he needed, sometimes sending for a guard to get him the ingredients. Taryn eyed him curiously but without judgement, and he knew what she was thinking. If his next act was to return to Earth, and he couldn't take anything with him, why was he gathering spell materials? The fact she didn't ask was a sign of respect, maybe even trust, which made him feel guilty that one of the spells he was going to cast would be on her. He thought about it every few minutes, part of him wondering if he was repeating the explanation to himself to silence the doubts in his head. He told himself it was a simple spell, a small one, and it would only accentuate what was about to happen anyway. And that excuse would have to suffice.

He also looked into a spell to make people forget that he had passed by. The invisibility spell would've been better, but it seemed a little advanced. He really needed to practice these things, and he reminded Taryn to send spellbooks to Earth for him when she got a chance. That was a good explanation for his gathering of materials, but he didn't say it. She was easily smart enough to conclude that that was what he was doing, even though it wasn't. Another pang struck him. But at least he wasn't telling her a lie.

By late afternoon, Matt decided to put on a show of feeling better, so they left his rooms and met up with Eric, Anna, and Ryan. His friends seemed both concerned and relieved that he appeared to be feeling better. And he was, partly from Taryn, and partly from resolve. He learned that Eriana and Rognir had left for Earth, and agreed that this was sound. They ate dinner together and resolved that they would return to Earth the next day, arriving in the middle of the night. Jack should've been expecting them soon. Eriana had been told of the time differences to remind Jack that the friends would be appearing in the middle of the night. He should probably sleep on the floor of his bedroom unless he wanted to find Anna beside him. Ryan joked about wanting a woman to magically appear in his bed, prompting laughter Matt imitated but didn't really feel. Maybe he could be okay again after all of this was over—but he wasn't sure whether he meant this quest or all of them. Or murdering Everon. He had changed and left parts of himself behind. He wasn't sure he was ever going to feel whole again.

He and Taryn retired to bed early for another round of intimacy. It once again filled him with peace that surprised him after the day's events. He waited for her to drift off, then slipped from bed to review the sleeping spell, casting it on her moments later. He couldn't risk her waking and wondering where he had disappeared to again.

Matt took some gold from her coin pouch, wondering how to make it up to her. He put on undergarments and a robe, but carried his boots as he snuck out. He wasn't supposed to use Soliander's attire or staff, but he would need it all where he was going.

Taking a cloak with him, he padded quietly in long socks to the meeting room, knowing Eric was a light sleeper and just a door down. He probably wasn't even asleep yet. The meeting room had not been guarded so much as their wing of the palace, and he slipped inside. It didn't take long to outfit himself, a feeling of comfort filling him once he had Soliander's staff in one hand. He needed to stop thinking of it that way. This was Matt Sorenson's staff. Fuck Soliander.

He threw the cloak over himself and left. On reaching the doors of their wing, he opened them to find the two guards turning to him. One began to ask if he needed anything, but Matt wasn't in the mood for a conversation the men would never remember anyway. He immediately cast the spell to make them forget having seen him, and walked away.

Knowing where the dragon egg was kept, he wasted no time in getting there, again casting a spell on the guards. On reaching the case, he deposited it into the Bag of Desires and headed for a palace exit. Then he left the grounds and entered the city streets, making every guard he passed forget his passage. It was fortunate that the spell wasn't taxing because he had to cast it so much.

Walking the dark streets of Andor alone would have given him pause just a day earlier, but not now. Something had taken all the fear from him. He felt aggressive and dangerous. Just let anyone try to stop him and he would in-cinerate them if needed. That might get him in trouble with their hosts—and they seemed like good people, so he wasn't interested in doing that to any-one—but he still didn't feel concerned for his safety. He didn't feel safe so much as like he had nothing left to lose. It gave him a kind of abandon, a willingness to take risks. He felt free, as awful as the source of that freedom was. Something about Everon violating him so utterly had made him cease to give a damn about his physical safety. There were worse things that could be taken from a man.

He had previously seen beggars on the street. Now he offered one a gold coin to assist him, so the young man eagerly followed. No one molested him on his walk to the Hall of Worlds, where lanterns and torches lit the exterior, the gusts of ocean air making them cast dancing shadows. He had been here before, apparently, while unconscious in a box, the thought of which hardened his glare.

Entering the large main room with his beggar in tow, Matt wasn't surprised to see few people present. The gate would likely have been turned off if all planets were on the same time frame. He approached a guard, explaining his need to visit the planet Rovell and offering more than enough gold coins. The guard agreed to change the gate's location via the wizards who were controlling it. With that done, Matt cast the *Forget* spell, which would work for another two minutes. He made sure to capture everyone in its radius, including his beggar. Then he pulled the Bag of Desires from a pocket, gave it to the beggar, and unceremoniously shoved him through the World Gate.

Matt followed, seeing the Hall of Worlds in Ortham once again. Nothing had changed in the weeks since he'd been here except the presence of more guards, many of whom recognized him as Soliander. He waved them off, gave the beggar another coin, took the Bag of Desires with the blue dragon egg in it, and shoved him back through to Elloria. World Gates were technically bidirectional like most portals, but to control traffic, many places would not allow them to be. Matt didn't care, since he was going to make everyone in Ortham forget him anyway. He cast the spell and left. So far, so good.

Putting the cloak and its hood back on to evade recognition, he left the Hall of Worlds. It was mid-morning here, and this suited him. Part of him didn't care who saw the dragon, but he wanted no question and no trouble. He asked for the nearest stables and bought a horse, food and drink, and left Ortham to go north. He ignored anyone he passed on the road.

An hour later, he left the road for the wilderness, unafraid of wild animals or even worse dangers. But nothing came, and he got off the horse and set about summoning an old dragon friend. Another hour passed before the huge red dragon flew toward him and he removed his cloak. Jolian soon landed and morphed into a human in red, form-fitting leather. She looked as sleek and powerful as ever as she sauntered over, wavy crimson hair to her mid-back.

"It is good to see you, Soliander," she said, smiling.

"And you as well. I'm afraid I have an urgent need, or I would not have asked you to come."

"Whatever I can do for you, I will. What of the other Ellorians?"

"There was no time to get them. I need you to take me to the dwarves of Morcanon Kingdom immediately. Can you do that?"

"Of course. Is this about the Orb of Dominion shard you left with them?"

He wasn't sure whether he should admit it, but said, "Yes. I have reason to believe someone knows where each of the pieces are and has the means to get them. We must prevent that."

Her eyes intensified. She knew just how dangerous the shards were because Soliander had used the master Orb of Dominion to enslave her brother through the slave Orb—she just didn't know it was the real Soliander who'd done it. Matt had the master now, so there was no danger to someone having the slave, but he wanted both in his control. It was only by good fortune that he had stored the Bag of Desires with Soliander's items. If he'd had it with him when Everon captured him, the bastard would have the master orb even now. There was nothing stopping him from getting the slave shards, now that he knew where they were. Matt had to get there first.

Jolian morphed back into dragon form and Matt climbed up her wing to sit upon her back, where she would hold him on using magic. He knew a spell to do that himself, but hadn't learned it. He needed to not be dependent on anyone anymore. As she lifted into the sky, he realized he felt comfortable without a saddle now, his bravery seeming both familiar and new at once.

They soared away from Matt's horse, which he had tied to a tree branch. Hopefully it would be there when he returned, but if not, so be it. They flew past Ortham, its towers and castle far below, then south over the green treetops of the Artem Woods. To the east rose the snow-capped Galla Mountains, which they flew parallel to for many miles. They finally turned toward them into the morning sun, arcing between the peaks, the streaming rays of sun casting shadows they flew in and out of as they descended.

The dwarves had seen dragons before, including this one—but, even so, the sight of one unexpectantly trying to land in the cleared space outside their mountain fortress at Hamarven caused a brief panic. Jolian settled onto the stony ground, and kept still and unthreatening as Matt climbed down. Then she morphed into human form beside him. Only now did the dwarves calm, some of them recognizing him as Soliander. He used that name to good effect, asserting that an emergency required him to see the Queen of Morcanon at once. He chafed at their delay in arranging a meeting but knew that this delay would be the longest.

It didn't take long to convince her that he needed the slave orb shard he had left with them. It wasn't theirs anyway. With apologies for his haste, he had it tucked into his Bag of Desires beside the master orb and was airborne on Jolian within twenty minutes. They flew halfway back before veering east into the mountains again, past the town of Valegis to the nearby Kirii Cave. The almost man-sized, batlike kirii were likely to attack them inside, but the injured leviathan that Jolian had almost killed in the underground lake within was potentially worse. This was another task that Matt would previously have avoided—but he felt no fear as they descended through a tunnel with Jolian striding beside him, his staff lighting the way.

On reaching the dark shores of the lake, he didn't bother hiding their presence, instead blasting the cavern roof with fire and setting enough kirii ablaze that they would likely avoid him. They screeched and screamed, scattering to other areas farther away. The waters surged as the leviathan moved, but at Matt's suggestion, Jolian morphed back into a dragon and spat fire at the surface. The speed with which the leviathan moved away told Matt that Jolian would keep it at bay.

Matt stripped naked, no longer shy. Then he cast a water-breathing spell and another spell to help him see. He waded into the icy lake, not complaining like he would have before, and dove in headfirst. The water appeared bright to his magicked eyes, schools of various fish spread throughout. He looked in the direction of the leviathan and saw huge eyes watching him in the distance, tentacles swirling, a mouth of teeth as big as him opening and closing. The sight gave him pause, but he turned away and swam into the depths.

Spires of rock rose from the bottom. It was a hundred feet below him in deeper areas, but less so between here and the small islands before him. That was where they had thrown the shard. Ryan had done it, and Matt was glad he'd seen where the splash was. He had never been skinny-dipping and now felt freer than ever as he continued down, occasionally glancing at the leviathan, which hadn't moved. Soon he was between the spires and other formations at the bottom, forty feet deep, fish moving out of his way. He didn't know much about them but had attack spells at the ready, and the Trinity Ring on one finger to heal himself if something hurt him. He spent ten minutes searching in vain, wishing he knew a locator spell. Then he saw the shard, further right than expected, the curved part of it facing up. His fingers closed around it and he began ascending.

Halfway up, he looked toward the leviathan and saw that it was gone. Head whipping around, he saw nothing and struck out for the surface. There were still another ten feet left when he saw it coming like a torpedo, ghastly burn marks and wounds from Jolian's claws on across its head and body. Jolian's huge feet splashed into the water, too far away to help. Matt stopped swimming and faced the beast, ready with the force blast spell he so often used. With a simple change, he could use it on himself rather than a target, but he wasn't sure that would work. Failure meant death. He turned his back to the surface, and just before the gaping jaws reached him, invoked the spell.

"Kunia!"

Matt felt himself hurled backward, up and out of the water and into the air, flailing wildly as he turned to see his trajectory. He heard thrashing water where the leviathan swarmed below him. The stalactites above were nearing fast, kirii clinging to the ceiling. Jolian moved toward him—but so did the leviathan, even as he began to fall. The dragon and leviathan were converging on his apparent landing spot in the water. Jolian spat another torrent of fire into the lake below Matt, the heat washing over him. He splashed into the water and could see nothing for the bubbles.

Suddenly, a huge mouth closed over him and he panicked as it pulled him through the water. He broke the surface, water gushing from the mouth and over him—a huge, rough tongue against his bare backside and enormous teeth all around him like a cage, except behind him where the blackness of a throat waited. A spell on his lips, he suddenly noticed that the teeth were shaped differently from the leviathan's. And they weren't closing to crush him. Water dripped from his hair into his eyes until he wiped it away to see past the teeth and out into the cavern, its walls rushing by until the stone floor hurtled toward him—and then stopped. The jaws slowly opened. He climbed down, past the teeth, and out of Jolian's huge mouth to turn back to her, a mix of fear and gratitude rising up in him. His heart had never pounded so hard. And he had never felt so alive.

"You are unhurt?" she asked, still in dragon form, her voice booming off the cavern. Matt turned and saw the leviathan lurking—not too far away, but keeping its distance.

"I think so," he said, still amazed. He held up the shard, a little surprised he hadn't dropped it in the madness. He glanced around again. They were on the shore near where they'd entered, his robes piled to one side. He walked over and put them on, stuffing the shard into the Bag of Desires. Then he came to the surface again.

"Get that fucking thing out of here," he said, referring to the leviathan. Jolian roared another spout of flames and the beast disappeared under the waves.

But it wasn't yet time to go. He had to acquire a second item, one that was almost as important for protecting his mind from ever being intruded upon again. The *Mind Shield* spell countered the *Mind Trust* spell and required the eyes of blind fish to cast. He pulled out a vial with oil in it and spilled two drops into the waters, then spoke the spell.

Into the waters, seek and find
All the creatures, make them mine
Bring them here, all of one mind,
Caught like a fish on hook and line

The water trembled as sea life from within it sprang toward him. He only cared about the blind, silver sparis fish among the smaller red ones and the larger black fish. He began scooping them into a second bag, aware that putting anything living in the magic one would kill it. He was going to kill them anyway for their eyes, but he needed to avoid damaging them.

He had brought multiple jars to fill because they'd be less conspicuous to carry back than a big, heavy bag of wiggling fish. Matt had always been squeamish about anything slimy or slippery—but after filling the bag with as much as he could, and throwing a bunch of other fish ashore, he sat down and started cutting eyes from heads quickly and efficiently. Jolian offered to help, and they quickly had the jars full and stowed. He rinsed his hands of the smell as best he could for now, and soon they were on their way.

This time, they flew northeast toward the ruin of Ashing on the plains beyond the Galla Mountains. Matt had been here with Jolian (and Eric) once before, and she knew where to land on the yellow grass outside the shattered town walls. She morphed into human form again and walked beside him as he led the way to the empty square. They had probably been the last people here, but he and Eric had made her stay away from where they'd hidden the piece. One less person to know. Now it didn't matter, but he asked her to wait as they reached the empty square, a low, broken wall surrounding it. In the center stood a broken statue that seemed like the obvious place to hide something, which was why Eric had suggested using the wall instead. Matt knew the piece was still there before he even saw it, because the two pieces he already had begun to vibrate from the bag. This was why he had left Jolian behind—to prevent her from knowing what he was about to do.

He placed the first two pieces on the ground where she couldn't see. Then he pulled the final piece from inside the broken wall, placing it next to the others. They moved toward each other before lifting up and reassembling into a dark sphere. As the cracked pieces merged, a soft white light emanated from them and then vanished. The slave Orb of Dominion had recreated itself. He took one last look at it, dark and silent, wondering how soon he would cross a line that, once crossed, offered no hope of redemption. He felt dimly aware that this was an early step into evil, and that awful men had likely justified their actions the same way he was justifying his.

For a moment he almost gave in to tears, his desperation was so strong, his conscience still intact. Would any goodness in him end when he used the orbs? Was it immediate, or a slow descent into evil? He never thought he would stand on the precipice of moral wrongs, but here he was. Would he look back on this one day and regret it, or be glad of the protections he had wrought despite the consequences to others? Better them than him. He sighed. His decision had been made and he would question it no further. He could get what he wanted by more honorable means, but that required trust, and he wasn't feeling trusting. He wasn't sure he would trust anything ever again.

For a moment, he pulled out the master Orb of Dominion to compare them, seeing that it was also dormant, dark and silent, as expected. One could almost be forgiven for not realizing the awful power it held, to control the minds of others forever once they had looked into the slave orb. But as a wizard, he felt it calling to him, compelling him to use it. The two spheres were otherwise identical when turned off. With an effort, he ignored it.

His mission accomplished, Matt put them away, rejoined Jolian, and flew back toward Ortham and his horse. By now, it was mid-afternoon and he needed to finish this. He let Jolian leave after giving his thanks and a farewell, and galloped back to Ortham. He encountered no problems, gave the horse away, and reentered the Hall of Worlds. Using his identity as Soliander, he convinced the gate operators to change the destination to Elloria. Then he cast the *Forget* spell and stepped through.

Upon arriving in Andor, he spelled the guards there, too, feeling fatigued from all that he'd performed. This was the most magic he'd ever done in a row—and now he had pulled an all-nighter, too. He knew that he and his friends would be sent home within a few hours, the Quest Ring rejuvenating him. He just had to last until then. He'd run out of what he needed for that spell, too, so he'd have to do his best to look like he'd just gone for a walk when he returned to the palace. He left the Hall of Worlds behind and stepped outside, seeing the dark sky beginning to lighten. Then a smooth elven voice spoke to him from behind.

"Matt?"

He turned to see Lorian coming out of the hall as well, brow furrowed. *Shit. What is he doing here?* He decided to ask.

Always polite, the elf answered, "I just returned from Honyn. I was asking my queen permission to join you on Earth for a time, perhaps in the company of other elves. I would need assistance with that level of travel, as you do not have a World Gate there for me to step through."

"Of course."

"Where are you from? I thought I saw you walking away from a gate. Aren't the others with you?"

Matt continued toward the palace with him, wondering what answer to give. "No. There was something I needed to take care of."

"Where?" When Matt didn't answer at once, Lorian mused, "I assume not to Honyn? There are only so many World Gates, and you weren't at the one I used. I would have seen you. Did you go to Rovell?"

Matt stifled a frown, aware that Lorian knew of the Orbs of Dominion quest. "Yes. I went to ask the dragons if they would come to Earth to help us."

The elf said, "Did you check on the shards from the orb? You said Everon knew everything, and I assume that he'd learned their location."

While Matt normally loved smart people, this one was becoming a problem. "I did retrieve the shards, yes. That was my other reason for going."

"Why didn't you bring the others?"

"I only realized late last night, and felt I needed to go immediately." Matt sensed from the troubled look in Lorian's eyes that he wasn't convinced. Worse, he was going to say something to the others.

"Is it reassembled?"

Thinking fast, Matt answered, "No. If we go to your room, I can show you." He suddenly felt nervous about what he was thinking. There was an obvious way to prevent Lorian from saying anything, but the idea sickened him. Did the moral precipice have to loom so soon after falling over it became possible?

The elf said, "Maybe I should hold onto a piece, or take it to Honyn."

"Let's talk about it in your room."

Lorian nodded, and they walked to the elf's suite in silence, passing the palace guards without issue. They soon stopped by a room near Matt's wing of the palace, Lorian leading him inside and pouring himself a drink. Matt discreetly put his hand into the Bag of Desires and rearranged the two orbs.

The master was inside a velvet bag designed for it; the slave was not. He could only tell because the slave orb felt slightly repulsive to his hand while the master seemed comforting, as if willing him to hold and use it. He reversed them and then pulled out the velvet bag, now holding the slave orb, and placed it on a table.

"Will you be able to bring other people with you to Earth?" Matt asked. He felt nervous. A little sick to his stomach. But he had to do it.

"Yes. And I am looking forward to learning more about your world and how I may help you there, especially when you are gone."

"Thank you. You have always been a good friend to us." Matt walked toward the bedroom as if just stretching his legs, the knot in his stomach growing. "I guess you haven't seen the orb before, have you?" he asked, turning back to see the elf gazing at the bag. "It's off, so I don't think it's dangerous now. Not much to see, really."

He slipped his hand into the magic bag and grasped the master Orb of Dominion as Lorian stepped over to the bag, fingers gently touching the velvet as if unsure whether he should open it. The elf glanced at him and Matt smiled as if to mock Lorian's concern, even as he drew magic power to himself and felt the master orb in his hand grow warmer from turning on. Lorian looked at the Bag of Desires, then tentatively pulled it open for a quick peek. Matt yanked out the master orb and saw with grim satisfaction that Lorian's visage appeared in it via the slave orb. "Obey and serve," he said into the master, which now had a golden sheen to it. "My will be yours."

Lorian's face grew relaxed. "My will is yours."

Matt looked at the elf, who hadn't moved. The knot in Matt's stomach had gone. He felt calm. Regretful, but safer. He wouldn't make Lorian do anything unsavory, certainly. He just needed help right now, and Lorian was the one who could provide it. In time, he would use the orbs as needed to protect himself and those he loved. And a task he had for Lorian would set this protection in motion.

First, he had to test the bond.

"Come to me, my friend," he said, and the elf walked toward him obediently, stopping before him. Their eyes met. Matt searched them for reproach, or fear. Hatred. But he saw nothing like that. Just calmness, a kind of trust and willingness that caused embarrassment to fill him. He had betrayed that trust, and yet Lorian only trusted him more! Was he just as evil as Everon now? He wouldn't do the same *things* with the power, just protect himself—but then was that all Everon felt he was doing? He frowned. Soliander had cast that *Mind Trust* spell on Matt, too. He wasn't sure whether he was going down the right or wrong path now, but it didn't matter. Protecting himself mattered. What good was all this power if he couldn't even do that? He sighed.

"I'm sorry, Lorian, but I must do this. I want you to act normally toward me in all ways, except that when I tell you to do something, you do it. Do you understand?"

The look of obedience disappeared from the elf's face, and yet he answered, "Yes."

"I want you to come to Earth like you were planning to do. But you will bring these orbs with you, and you will give them to me when we are alone. No one can know that you have them. Do you understand?"

"I understand what you want, just not why."

"I am not going to tell you."

"This does not surprise me."

Matt scrutinized him. He had to know how much of the elf was still there. How he felt. How he judged what Matt had done. He wanted the elf's respect and felt certain he would never have it again if he undid this spell, and the thought filled him with remorse. "Do you know what I have done to you?"

"You have used the Orbs of Dominion to make me obey you."

Hearing Lorian admit it made a pang of guilt strike him. "How do you feel about that?"

Lorian seemed to consider before answering. "I want to help you. I do not mind this. I do sense that my desire to help you has risen considerably."

"Are you offended?"

Lorian raised an eyebrow, then smiled. "If you undid the spell, I sense I would be greatly offended and never forgive you without a great explanation. As it is, I am content. And I trust you."

Matt sighed and turned away. "I still want you to think for yourself. Can you do that?"

"Yes. I have not become a thoughtless servant, if that is what you are thinking."

"I kind of was, yeah. It's not what I want. I just need you to sometimes do something for me without arguing, and while keeping it a secret."

"I am otherwise free to act as before?"

"Yes. Please believe me that I don't want any more control over you than necessary."

"Thank you." The elf looked at the master orb. "I will need a way to carry these to Earth. The Bag of Desires?"

"Yes."

"Say no more. I will take care of it." He turned to go as Matt watched in resignation. He suddenly realized he had to make sure Ryan never cracked the slave orb—which had a silver sheen to it now that it was on—like he'd once done, to make it stop working. Lorian would be one potentially angry person confronting him. He didn't know how many more there would be, but he intended only to use it on enemies. And yet he had just established precedent.

Matt had another task for Lorian. Now that he no longer had the materials for the *Forget* spell, he couldn't take the dragon egg back to where it belonged without arousing suspicion. At his direction, Lorian left with the dragon egg case in the magic bag and the slave orb in the other, inside the velvet pouch. Every time Lorian encountered resistance from guards, he pulled out the orb, which the men looked into. And Matt ensnared their minds from the safety of Lorian's room. He didn't have to make the guards forget. He just had to stop them saying anything about it. The elf put the egg case back and then repeated this stunt with the guards standing outside Matt's wing of the palace before returning to Matt. The wizard left both orbs with the elf in the magic Bag of Desires before returning to his rooms. The guards let him by without comment, and he ordered them not to speak of it. They agreed, having no choice.

With all the evidence of his actions elsewhere, Matt crept down the hall to the meeting room, where he changed out of Soliander's clothes and put the staff back. Then he returned to his own room. Taryn was still asleep. He gently climbed in beside her, exhaustion and relief filling him. Wondering if the Trinity Ring would restore some energy to him, he still let himself drift off. But his dreams offered no comfort, alternating between visions of Everon probing his mind at will and Matt doing the same thing to Lorian, or Taryn, or his friends. He wasn't really the same, was he? He vowed not to become a monster, but he had an awful feeling it was already too late.

Ryan had mixed feelings about going home, but it was too late for them to change their minds. Hours earlier, they had returned the dragon egg to the blue dragons of Novell. Unlike when they first recovered it, the delivery was as uneventful as they had hoped. The dragons were suitably appreciative— which made Ryan feel guilty, even though King Sarov was the one who had arranged for the theft, not them. That secret was closely-guarded so as not to make enemies of the blue dragons or the Kingdom of Novell that worshipped them. He had felt chagrined during the celebratory banquet thrown in their honor in the island kingdom, but at least it had been quick and that kept the size down.

Earlier that day, they had made their farewells to their hosts in Andor. With Prince Dari returned, minus a hand, the king and queen had been in better spirits. Dari himself seemed a changed man, no longer hostile towards them, but Ryan wasn't sure why. Had he accepted that they were victims in this whole situation and hadn't done something to his brother? The mission to Soliander's current castle had seemingly cured his attitude problem, which was fine with Ryan. The last thing they needed was more crap to deal with.

Princess Cariss was now the one who seemed haunted, but Ryan knew it was because she'd befriended the man responsible for betraying Korrin and the others. Her guilt had been plain to see, and several people—Anna, Eriana, and himself—had tried to convince her no harm had come of it. But she wasn't ready to let it go. To make amends, she had pledged to help them, though she admitted she didn't know how she could. She saw Everon's treatment of Matt as her fault and couldn't meet Matt's eyes. Ryan wished he could do something more to ease her mind, but had run out of time to think of anything.

Taryn and some of her Dark Blade warriors had flown with them on dragon-back from Andor to Novell, she and Matt sharing a ride. She seemed to be a good influence on him and Ryan resisted the urge to tease his friend. It didn't seem right—not because of what Matt had been through, whatever it was, but because Matt suddenly seemed like a man instead of an awkward boy in a man's body. That was another thing he didn't really understand. But if Taryn made him feel that way, then Ryan considered her a friend. She seemed trustworthy, and their relationship was certainly better than what-ever had happened between Eric and Kori. *That* was something to tease someone about.

Now they stood inside the Quest Ring on the hill where they had first ar-rived. So much had changed since then. This had been their most consequen-tial quest yet—he doubted that another would rival it. They now had friends, help, and keystones, plus a way to communicate with Jack or anyone else back home while they were gone. He felt so much better about their situa-tion—and once they had created the Home Rings, a major problem would be resolved. Now that they had turned in the dragon egg, they could be sum-moned at any moment, but he was hoping to get home first.

Matt was still outside the Quest Ring, getting a last kiss from Taryn and not being shy about it. His friends shared an amused glance.

"Why don't *we* get a kiss?" Ryan joked, holding his lance and glad he hadn't needed it.

Eric smirked at him. "Come here, big fella."

"I didn't mean from you!"

Anna laughed. "I don't think I need to see this."

They were still laughing when Matt joined them, cocking his eyebrow at their amusement. In the past, the wizard would've looked like he assumed he was being made fun of, but now he seemed indifferent. Once again, Ryan thought he seemed more confident and that the change suited him.

One of Andor's wizards cast the spell to turn on the Quest Ring. Ryan watched as the words of blue fire swirled up the pillars around them and Elloria vanished. The familiar roaring sound and buffeting wind struck him as he faced Matt, whose black robes had vanished to leave him nude. Ryan knew the same thing had just happened to him, and covered his crotch with one hand. Eric never bothered—and, to Ryan's surprise, Matt didn't either this time. He always kept his eyes straight ahead at Matt, unless he glanced at Eric—which he'd done enough times to know that Eric was always staring straight ahead at a point above Anna's head as she stood across from him.

Then each of them were dressed in their Earth clothes, but since they'd all been sleeping, this wasn't much. Ryan and Eric only wore shorts, while Matt also had a t-shirt on and Anna stood in a shirt and pink panties. Jack's apartment materialized around them, Matt lying on the couch, both Ryan and Eric on the floor. Ryan quickly got up and stuck his head into Jack's bedroom, where Anna had been, and saw her sitting up in bed. It was early afternoon and Jack wasn't there.

But there was a note from him on the table next to the laptop, urging caution.

CHAPTER TWENTY

THE DRAGON LORD KING

Vianden, the Dragon Lord King of Elfhame, felt certain he could smell Earth all the way from his throne of human skulls. That was how much he longed for it. A thousand years had passed without that scent, and while it was familiar, something was off. There was a mustiness, a dirtiness, a toxicity, all sapping some of his enjoyment of the otherwise nostalgic aroma. The Land of Fae had its own delights, but he wanted to go home.

Dragons were of the Earth, not Elfhame. He didn't belong here any more than the rogue humans who had sometimes wandered in. But unlike them, he remained uncorrupted—a dragon is not so easy to pervert. And yet it had happened in a good way long ago. As the magic of the fae world first crept into the Earth, the oldest of its creatures, the dragons, had merged with it so that it became part of their nature. As such, they could not survive without it.

And so they were here—many of them, anyway. That wretched human, Merlin, had drained all the magic from the Earth, leaving the dragons with a choice to flee into Elfhame or die. Some had chosen to remain, though he never found out what happened to them. They had refused to believe, flying above the forested fields even as Merlin's spell ended. But he'd heard that others intended to bury themselves deep within the earth, below the mountains, slumbering until such time as magic returned and they awoke. He hadn't been among those who believed they would survive, and he was curious to find out if they had. The dragons of Elfhame numbered in the hundreds, and that was enough for the revenge he sought. Humanity was to pay for what Merlin had done, because saving them was the reason he had done it.

The doorway stood open. They all did, but then the smaller ones had always cracked ajar at times, as if they hadn't quite been sealed all the way.

This let the magic flow for a few yards, and sometimes a faerie or two stepped onto the Earth for just a minute. Some had died that way, like fish flopping on land and unable to breathe unless yanked back to safety in time. And occasionally a human had come through and been seized upon. Since no one had watched the doorways for hundreds of years, these wayward adventurers sometimes traveled quite far into Elfhame before being discovered. And they told such interesting tales of the world beyond! But Vianden hadn't believed any of that nonsense, thinking them mad.

Now, though—with all the doors, big and small, wide open—he wondered at the truth of it. It was the stench that gave it away, that Earth had changed in the last thousand years. And something told him he wouldn't like what he saw any more than he enjoyed what he smelled. What had they done to Earth to make it stink like that? His long pent-up desire for revenge had fostered in the weeks since the open doorways had first been noticed.

And it was partly his force of will keeping the fae from rushing into Earth en masse. But they also knew that the magic had to flow through the gates and far enough, and that this would take time. He could feel the potency of it falling in Elfhame, his own strength fading from what he had become accustomed to. A millennium ago, when first arriving here, he had been stunned by the burst of power in him—all that magic concentrated here and filling him. It had helped him conquer this land into which he was never supposed to come. Other dragons and even the fae had been slower to adapt to the surging magic, unsure what it meant, unable to accept what had happened. Their indecisiveness had kept them passive and led to his rule over them. Fortune favored the aggressive. And he would retain his power here when he left for Earth. Why rule one land when he could rule two?

He had sent a dwarf through to Earth, but it hadn't returned—and when he'd sent others after it, its decapitated body had been found and brought back. This seemed like a declaration of war to Vianden, who already had an appetite for destruction. If the Earth had been poisoned in some way, as a creature of nature, he was not going to be pleased. Nor would the other fae. There was already chatter among them that something was amiss, concern muting their pleasure at finally returning. This played right into his hands, for he intended to conquer the Earth and needed his fae army to do it. The humans might have sealed their fate.

What they called Stonehenge, a shrine to their relationship with the fae, was the most powerful of the doorways—but so many more existed all over the planet. Perhaps it had been a mistake to send the dwarf through the Stonehenge one. Was it under watch? Could the humans even tell that magic had returned and that the fae were not far behind? Were people expecting them? He had heard of damage to the monument, another rumor that sowed discontent among the fae. Were the humans so disrespectful as to not honor this relationship, long severed, in hopes that they would return? The fae had always been capricious. Moody. Vengeful. And while they blamed Merlin for their banishment to Elfhame, they weren't above blaming humans. Their wave of anger was growing into a tsunami.

He suspected Earth would be easy to conquer. The fae had had the last thousand years to continue practicing magic; the humans had nothing. Had they forgotten it altogether? They didn't live long enough for anyone who'd used it before to still be alive. His advantage seemed so clear that he felt no particular rush to visit, given the risk that magic had not spread far enough. Step farther into Earth than the magic had gone, and fae would fall over dead. But he felt confident that the time had come. Samhain was coming, the night when the barrier between worlds was thinnest, the magic ready to surge forth and complete its rebalancing between Elfhame and Earth.

Merlin had long since died when his spell was finished—whether he had remained on Earth and perished, or that awful explosion of magical energy had killed him. It had destroyed a wide swath of Elfhame before it regrew, the fields burnt, the ponds poisoned, the air burning with toxic fumes. And many had died. So many that even those in the Seelie Court were angry and pliable with thoughts of revenge, like Vianden had been putting into their heads for centuries. His own heart burned with hatred—for the blast had kicked up faerie dust in a storm of nearly molten, liquid debris that had seared itself into his chest, a silver crest on his otherwise black scales. The scar was a permanent reminder. But with Merlin gone, there was no one specific to take revenge upon.

The Ellorian Champions were long gone, too, since humans don't live a thousand years—though some people who had been brought here had been made to suffer nearly that long, the effects of Elfhame on humans the stuff of legend. He knew the Ellorians' names and faces as surely as they would have remembered his. He had stood beside Morgana when she summoned them to Earth. He had heard them promise to stop Merlin's spell. He had learned that they intended to betray Morgana and work with Merlin. There had been nothing he could do to stop it, having spent all his magical strength to help Morgana summon them. And so he had left Earth for Elfhame—and now he would leave Elfhame for Earth.

He rose from his throne of skulls and strode down the steps in the obsidian hall of the Unseelie Court he had conquered, the glistening glass reflecting all who walked upon it or between its shining walls. A few elves and dwarves watched in silence, as did another dragon in human form. A satyr shifted on its hooved feet, its bare-chested torso the closest thing to a human form Vianden regularly saw. Each of those in attendance commanded a host of others and would lead his forces to Earth. But it would take time to conquer all that he desired. Only days remained before their invasion began. The fae would return en masse to Earth and take back a world they were meant to rule all along. The humans had had a thousand years. The fae would take forever as punishment.

And Vianden, the Dragon Lord King of Elfhame, would rule over it all.

"This gathering of the Sons of the Magi is called to order," Luna announced, standing at the head of the table in the Gilded Library's secret basement, twenty of their nearly thirty members sitting at the high-backed chairs. She hadn't waited for the usual guy to say it or for their Grand Master, Oliver, to arrive, because she really didn't care and would've preferred this talk to happen without him. But no sooner did she say the words than the man himself strode in with his pet, Rebecca, following. Both wore tight-fitting black clothes, as if they were signaling their alliance with attire.

"You have no authority to call this meeting, Luna," said Oliver, coming toward her.

"And yet you showed up. You had no authority to remove magic items from the treasure room, especially ones that didn't belong to you, and yet you did it, anyway." A murmur of disapproval spread through the room.

She and Andy had discussed his idea of stealing every magic item from the treasury but concluded that this would've been overkill. They were justified in taking back the ones they owned until further notice. Storing the inexpensive ones here hadn't mattered before magic worked, and now that it did, they could be dangerous. Most were supposedly not that powerful or important. And so they had decided to take all of theirs and install a dual locking mechanism whereby Luna and Andy would have one key, and Oliver could have the other, both being needed to get into the room. It seemed the only fair way to prevent Oliver, or themselves, from taking anything without the other party knowing.

But when they had arrived the night before to collect their share, they had discovered dozens of items missing. This included all the ones they considered important, and several that belonged to either Andy or Luna. They knew Oliver had done it—though when they checked the security footage the found that the cameras had gone dark and remained that way, leaving them only able to see the last time the items had been there.

Before leaving, they had helped themselves to their own items. They didn't install the new lock. Andy thought he knew where Oliver would've put the pilfered pieces, admitting that he had followed their Grand Master more than once due to distrust. The result was them driving to an office Oliver rented and Andy breaking in.

But they hadn't found the items. They next tried Rebecca's place, and on seeing that she wasn't home, Andy again succeeded in breaking in with skills Luna found surprising. Once more, they found nothing. Where they were hiding them, they couldn't tell, but Andy suspected Oliver kept them close at hand—either at home, in a locker somewhere, or maybe in his car. He ducked all of Luna's questions about how he knew different ways of breaking into places. The ones with only physical security were one thing, but he seemed able to bypass computer measures and PINs easily, sometimes pulling out a little computer to help. Her suspicions that he was a hacker seemed too real, and she stopped herself from asking for fear of the answer. Maybe later.

They weren't sure what might happen if they told the society of Oliver's theft. But putting pressure on him to reveal the items or the reason why he'd taken them was what Andy called a "discovery" ploy, getting him to reveal information that might help to recover them. And so here they were.

Oliver asked, "What makes you think I was the one who re—"

Seated beside Luna's empty chair—as she still stood at the table's head beside Oliver—Andy interrupted. "Because you and Rebecca are the only ones who didn't act surprised just now."

Smirking unconvincingly, Oliver asked, "Did you check the security cameras?"

"They were disabled."

Another murmur of disapproval and, from the looks of those in the room, they seemed to sense that Oliver already knew all of this and was being coy. And that Andy's and Luna's accusation was correct. His next words revealed that he sensed the mood, as he dropped the act.

"As Grand Master, I have the authority to protect them, to ensure their safekeeping."

Frowning, Luna said, "That's not your job. And to protect them from whom? This is a secret society, remember? No one but us knows they're here."

"Perhaps not everyone here can be trusted."

Andy replied, "Says the man who stole property from just about every person in this room. You need to return all of it immediately."

"I need to do no such thing. What are you going to do, call the police? MI6? They are confiscating all items believed to be magical, so even if they found the items for you, you'd never see them again."

Not wanting to be so close to him, Luna took her seat and said, "Better with them than in your hands."

Oliver stood alone at the table's head, his eyes boldly moving from one member to the next as if to scare them out of questioning him with Andy and Luna. "That's ridiculous. I have shown no signs of magic talent, and might be unable to use *any* of the devices for all you know."

"Then you won't mind returning them."

"I'm not going to do that. And you can't compel me."

Andy rose, dark eyes glittering. "How about if I bash your head in?"

Luna put a hand on his belly to restrain him and stifled a smile. Everyone knew he was a trained martial artist and had an element of danger to him, so it came as no surprise when the smirk fell from Oliver's face. But Oliver looked at Rebecca in such a way that Luna wondered if she'd learned an offensive spell instead of just that ball of light trick.

She said, "I would like the Sons of the Magi to vote on whether it is appropriate for the Grand Master to take these items that belong to individuals here, and yet are on loan to the society, and hoard them for his own purposes."

"I second the motion," said Andy.

And soon others agreed to the vote. It didn't go in Oliver's favor, though several people known to be his friends sided with him. Luna wasn't surprised but felt satisfied, especially with Andy's next words.

"I further propose that Oliver has by sundown tomorrow to return the items or be removed as Grand Master, with Luna taking his place."

This caused another murmur that quickly turned into agreement. Some wanted Oliver removed immediately, and Luna saw the tide turning in her favor. If Oliver kept acting as he had, he would soon be out. She wondered if that would make him more of a problem and not less.

"The next order of business," Luna began, "is tomorrow night, Samhain. Some of you have decided to be present at places we believe to be magical doorways between Elfhame and Earth. In the event fae *do* come through, I want to remind you to be cautious. The fae can be dangerous. If you have any charms or offerings to prepare, I suggest doing so. And remember that iron hurts them, so having it may be viewed as an act of aggression instead of self-defense. There is no telling how they will react. I think it is best if none of you go."

"Yes," Oliver sneered, "we already know of your fears. No reason to repeat them."

"Then you and Rebecca are still going to Stonehenge?"

"Of course."

"Perhaps we will see you there."

Rebecca said, "Not if we see you first."

Very mature, thought Luna, refusing to show irritation. The meeting didn't last much longer, but they did bring up the dual lock mechanism and it met with near-unanimous agreement—so Andy installed it and kept one key, Oliver taking the other.

The next day, October 31, saw Luna and Andy making plans for that night. Some of it was the ordinary stuff, like turning off all the lights so no one thought they would answer the door for trick-or-treating. The rest related to their impending visit to Stonehenge. Andy insisted they not bring any supposedly magic items because they didn't know what they did and couldn't control them, whereas a faerie *might* know and turn the items on the humans. They had confirmed that Oliver hadn't returned the items by the deadline, meaning Luna was now Grand Master. This was a less important result than the return of the items, but they would go after Oliver soon enough. They spent time reading about the monument again, and about legends of the fae and Samhain. They didn't know what time the fae might arrive but suspected midnight, so they packed a cooler of drinks and snacks and got dressed.

Luna wasn't wearing anything special. Thinking it better to not draw attention to herself, she had on jeans, jogging shoes, and a sweater over a t-shirt. To her surprise, Andy emerged from the bedroom wearing what could only be described as tight-fitting black leather armor, a sword at one hip. He wore a belt that seemed to be made of black rope. She had seen him in the outfit once or twice on previous Halloweens but never with the sword—and what he had previously said were knife holders had always been empty, but were now filled with blades. He also sported well-worn, matching boots and wore a silver ring she'd seen on one hand. A different unfamiliar ring was on the other hand.

"Where did you get that?" she asked, eyeing the weapon.

Smiling, he did a slow turn as if to give her a good look at the outfit, which seemed more like real armor to her than a costume. "I've had it for a long time, but never took it before. Police frown on real weapons being worn for Halloween."

"Can't imagine why," she deadpanned, coming closer and putting one hand on the hilt. "Do you think we'll need that?"

"Yes," he said, and she met his gaze, seeing he was serious.

"Is it magical? Is there anything about fae only being hurt by magical weapons?"

"I guess we'll see. You have everything else? Then let's go." Andy led her out of the flat and down the elevator to the basement parking garage, where they headed for his black Jeep.

"Why don't we take my car?" Luna asked. "It's more comfortable." It was also far nicer. She had never understood why he kept the fifteen-year-old Jeep, though he maintained it well. He could afford better and had a second vehicle, a BMW, too.

Andy shook his head. "We may need to turn off the daytime running lights to approach Stonehenge the way I intend to, without anyone seeing us."

"Can't we do that in mine?" she asked as she opened the door.

"No. All newer cars in the UK have the lights. You've always asked me why I keep this old Jeep. Now you know."

As she got in the passenger side, she said, "Just how long have you been riding around in the countryside without any lights on?"

He flashed a smile as he started the vehicle. "A long time. I told you that I've always thought Stonehenge was a portal between worlds and I might one day see something there. I used to go out there all the time without the lights running."

"You don't go anymore?"

"You would've noticed if I went, since it's a three-hour round trip. I'd given up seeing anything by then, anyway. Or at least, up until the Stonehenge Four arrived."

"I wish you'd had a camera there then."

"So do I."

The traffic diminished as they drove further west into the countryside, away from London. Using Andy's phone camera feed, Luna repeatedly checked the various cameras. Most locations were considerably less famous than Stonehenge; there, either no one had gathered, or there were just a few people who she sometimes identified as Sons of the Magi. The night vision cameras gave a good view of people who had no idea they were being watched.

Soon, though, things began to happen.

"Hey," she said, "there's something going on at one of them. It looks like a ball of light, maybe two. Yeah, it's definitely two of them, circling around the three people gathered there."

"A Will-o'-the-wisp?" Andy asked as he drove.

"Maybe. It doesn't seem like it's fake in any way."

"How are people reacting?"

"They're just watching them. They don't seem afraid."

Andy sighed. "You know a Will-o'-the-wisp is supposed to lead people away to harm. Let me know if they follow it."

"Okay. I want to check the other cameras." Most of them didn't show much, if anything, and she finally turned to Stonehenge. "We're going to have company there."

"More than Oliver and Rebecca?"

"Yeah. A lot more. I don't see them, but there are maybe two dozen people right now."

"Anything happening?"

"Doesn't seem like it."

"I have a bad feeling about this."

Luna didn't disagree and wasn't sure what to say. Nothing else changed on the cameras as they neared Stonehenge, which stood in the middle of open fields with no bushes or trees to hide behind. Andy had set up the hidden camera in a ditch where the landscapers allowed grass to grow long for wildflowers. The distance wouldn't provide much detail, but he hoped faeries would give off light and be easily visible. The full moon shone brightly across the dark sky. Only a few clouds cast deep shadows on the ground. The Jeep would be visible even after Andy turned off the lights.

As they approached on the A303 road, the monument appeared in the distance. It looked creepy in the moonlight, like something out of a painting. They saw no lights on or near it, except flashing blue police lights that gave them pause. They drove past it on the right, then bypassed a narrow access road they could've used if they were unconcerned with being seen. Instead, they continued to a traffic circle and then north. Seeing no other cars on the road now, Andy turned off the vehicle lights, but it was still easy to see where they were going. A minute later, they reached another circle and turned right again, going past the visitor center, its lights off. The access road was the main route to Stonehenge.

"How close do we go?" Luna asked. "I'm wondering where others parked."

"They're probably at the bus drop-off point, really close, and less concerned with being seen. There's a stand of trees up there, halfway to it, with a little dirt road inside—and a gate, but the lock is easy to pick. It's a bit of a hike from there but I want to keep out of sight, including from the police."

He slowed the Jeep and rolled down the windows, cool air coming in. Luna reported that the camera showed no changes—nothing supernatural. Yet. Andy inched the car along before turning left into the trees toward a steel gate. He got out and picked the lock with a speed that surprised her before returning to drive further in and park. They exited, taking a final swig of water, Andy strapping the sword to his waist.

"Are you sure that's a good idea?" Luna asked. "I mean, if the police see it, they might object."

"They'll assume it's part of a costume and not real. If what I think is about to happen *does*, the cops are the least of our problems."

Luna eyed him. "You're starting to worry me."

Andy held her gaze. "I'm sorry, but I think a host of faeries are about to come through Stonehenge to this world, and the results are going to be awful. I'm leaving the car unlocked, the keys inside. If something happens and I can't stay with you, I want you to run for the car, get in, and drive away. Even if you have to go without me. Do you understand? Can you do that?"

Luna felt a coldness creeping over her with every word. "I...I think so."

"You will be fine. I'm not trying to scare you."

"Okay. Okay. Let's just go and see what's happening."

Andy led her away from the Jeep and they jogged on the paved road—passing the crossing street they had ignored earlier, then the visitor drop-off point, which buses from the visitor center used. Most of the vehicles, including the police cars, were well past that toward the road's end, where they shouldn't be. Stonehenge lay farther still across the mostly flat, low cut green grass, away from the pollution of the roads. Reaching the first of several parked cars, they recognized Oliver's black BMW and slowed to a walk. Now Luna realized that the one van she'd seen belonged to a TV station. No one else was here, just at the monument, where the police didn't seem to be bothering anyone—making Luna wonder if they'd just arrived.

At the street's end, a walkway veered right to pass near Stonehenge. Straight ahead, another path went toward the Heel Stone, a fifteen-foot-high rock over two hundred feet outside the stone circle. She and Andy had visited before to stand in the center of Stonehenge and gaze at the Heel Stone, which marked the place where sunrise appeared on the horizon at the summer solstice. But people could also stand at the Heel Stone at sundown and watch the sun fall through and behind Stonehenge. Two people stood at the Heel Stone now as midnight approached.

Luna couldn't yet identify a reporter or cameraman within the monument. They definitely didn't want to be on camera. She saw that someone had brought a goat. People in the past had sometimes sacrificed animals on Samhain. Surely they wouldn't, would they? Andy led her toward a point between the Heel Stone and Stonehenge, but they hadn't quite made it there when a commotion started at the monument.

"Down!" whispered Andy, and they dropped to their bellies on the cold grass inside the actual henge, or ditch, surrounding the place.

Luna watched as a soft light began to glow within the monuments. The outer circle of stones had once held stone slabs atop them, running all the way around. But many had collapsed or gone missing since, except around the area that was considered the entrance—the side facing the Heel Stone. Inside the circle should have been five trilithons arranged in a horseshoe shape. Each trilithon was made up of two pillars with a slab across the top. The two on one side were intact, but only one on the other side was, because one trilithon had fallen, the top slab and one supporting stone toppled. The same thing had happened to the lone trilithon at the top of the horseshoe; its stone had fallen inward to lie next to an altar stone that had been knocked out of position. The bottom of the horseshoe shape lay open in the direction of the mostly intact entrance and the Heel Stone in the distance.

Now, across the bottom of the horseshoe, a shimmering wall of blue and golden light began to glow, starting from the ground and rising to the height of the stones. It grew in brightness as if becoming more substantial, the onlookers nearby backing away in all directions. The new light made it easier to see that most attendees were in costumes with masks depicting skeletons and undead, though one seven-year-old girl was dressed as a fairy.

Andy admitted, "I've seen things on the video feed before and haven't told you, because I wasn't entirely sure they weren't human."

Luna looked at him in annoyance, trying to let that go. "Seen what?"

"A few floating balls of light, short figures moving, and once a man in a black robe walking around, not necessarily in that order. But I haven't seen a portal like that open."

Luna wasn't sure what to say about that—but if there was any doubt that a portal to another world had opened now, it ended when a small ball of white light emerged to fly above the onlookers, who gasped and murmured. A second ball joined it, then a third. All three whizzed around the stones, weaving in and out and above in widening circles.

"Will-o'-the-wisps?" Luna asked, trying to piece together fairy stories she had heard. She could make out the cameraman now, and the reporter near him. The police were standing around dumbfounded.

"I think so, yes. They are supposed to be bad luck and to lead people to their deaths."

Luna pointed at the Heel Stone. "Look!"

Andy followed her gaze. Two people stood by the stone, one of them with a ball of light before her. "Rebecca," he said. "She cast that cantrip again."

"And Oliver beside her." The ball of light made the pair easier to see, but it quickly moved away from them and toward Stonehenge, passing very near to where Luna and Andy lay in the ditch. It flew over the entrance and near the Will-o'-the-wisps that it resembled. They began to swirl around and follow the ball, which started moving back toward the Heel Stone. Intent on their pursuit, they didn't seem to notice Andy and Luna as they passed by.

"I hope she knows what she's doing," Luna whispered.

"They are fools."

Another commotion came from the portal. Something larger passed through this time, a bare-chested man with curled horns amid his long brown hair. He carried a quiver of arrows around his shoulders and a bow in one hand. From the waist down, he was a goat.

"A satyr!" whispered Luna in disbelief, as people began backing away again in fear.

"Two more coming through."

But there were more than that, some of them jumping onto the fallen sarsen stones and looking around, sniffing at the air. One began playing a merry tune on a pan flute and gesturing at the humans around them, as if to encourage them to dance and relax. At first, no one moved, but then the girl in the fairy costume broke away from her parents. She was the first to start dancing with a satyr. After a minute, the mood shifted. The girl's mother reached into a bag she held and pulled out a cupcake. They couldn't hear her words, but she clearly offered it to a satyr, who bowed and took it, eating it in one bite. Other satyrs then crowded around seeking more, which she gave, a celebratory mood evident as the satyrs hooted and howled with pleasure, causing laughter. The officers had their hands on their Tasers but hadn't drawn them, and the reporter was making the cameraman film it all after backing away for a wider shot.

A satyr pulled a treat from a pouch and offered it to one of the men. He sniffed at it and then took a small bite, as if to be polite. Seeing that nothing happened to him, a woman accepted an offered treat and ate it all in two quick bites, to the delight of the satyrs, like they were breaking bread together. Luna had heard stories of such food making all Earth fare taste like ash so that people could only consume the faerie food or die. But those present were unwary and soon half a dozen had shared the treats. Even some of the police took part.

Now the men and women began dancing in greater numbers—some by themselves, others with each other or with the satyrs, who moved everyone away from the portal and toward the altar. The reporter joined in as her cameraman backed away even further to frame the shot. More figures emerged from the doorway—short figures, with long beards and hammers on their waists or in their hands. The dwarves ignored the merrymaking and instead began to lament the state of Stonehenge, with its missing pieces and fallen stones, their gestures and body language revealing their upset. Nearly twenty came through, all inspecting the damage and gesturing like they were wondering how to fix it.

More figures arrived, this time people who looked like humans but taller, slenderer, and carrying bows and long swords. Their skin was dark, and they moved with a lithe grace that made Luna wonder if they were elves. But she was too far away to see any pointed ears or slanted eyes. She assumed that they were dark elves because nothing else matched the stories she'd read. They took up positions leaning against the stones, watching but not participating in the dancing, which was becoming increasingly frenzied.

A woman cried out that she needed to rest, but somehow she couldn't. And as Luna watched, the woman began to transform—her shoes falling off, horns appearing on her head, and a satyr ripping off her blouse and bra from her to bare her upper body to the night sky. The woman laughed, but it was the sound of madness as she helplessly danced while turning into a satyr, the faerie food she had consumed transforming her. Others began to transform as well, sometimes ripping their own shirts off, their pants and shoes splitting to accommodate the goat legs and hooves. The little girl broke free of the dancing and hid behind a standing sarsen stone, but her smile showed that she seemed to think this was a game.

"We should help," Luna said, though she had no idea how and felt too afraid to go over there.

Andy shook his head. "I don't think there's anything we can do, and I'm certain worse is going to come through. It's better to see what that is first before exposing ourselves. I don't want you doing anything but leaving anyway."

Over at the Heel Stone, Rebecca had ended her spell. The three Will-o'-the-wisps were hovering around her and Oliver without much movement.

Andy said, "I'm dying to know what's going on over there."

Luna saw the phone in Andy's hand light up, so she covered it with one hand. Then she looked at it, seeing a notification from one of the cameras.

Andy unlocked it and kept an eye on their surroundings as Luna pulled up the camera feed. And there she saw at Silbury Hill that a black, yellow-eyed horse had someone on its back as it bucked, trotted, and jumped around the mound, another portal open atop the hill. The rider was a terrified-looking man who appeared to be trying to jump off but was unable, his arms flailing wildly instead of hanging on. Then the horse turned toward the hill, charged up it, and leapt back through the portal, carrying the man to Elfhame.

"My God," said Luna, watching the other people on the camera feed running away, "it took him."

"Damn Oliver," said Andy, scowling. "I knew this kind of shit might happen."

Watching the camera feed, Luna gasped again as the horse reappeared on Earth without the man and cantered down after one of the fleeing attendees. Andy turned off the phone.

"They're all dead already. And we have our own problems."

Luna shivered. These weren't Disney fairies—they were more like the those from the old stories. She kept her eyes on Stonehenge, where two satyrs suddenly leapt upon the goat someone had brought and tore into it with their teeth. The animal bleated in terror right up until they ripped its throat out. Other satyrs, including some of the transformed humans, set upon it and gorged themselves before lifting blood-covered mouths to the sky and singing. One offered something to the little girl, and Luna had the horrible impression it was the goat's heart. The girl came forward timidly, but, on seeing it, screamed.

And the scream changed everything. Several faeries flew through the portal into Stonehenge and immediately turned to the little girl in her fairy costume. She continued screaming as they whirled around her so fast that blurs of light were all that could be seen. Suddenly the girl began to lift into the air from the force of the wind they'd whipped up. Above the monument she rose, kicking and shrieking as the faeries carried her away. The spell of merriment broken, her mother yelled at them to stop and a satyr grabbed her, viciously kissing her. One of the officers pulled out a Taser and could be heard shouting orders. Others shouted back at him, likely not to fire for fear of hitting the girl. Up, up and away she rose, hundreds of feet—and then the whirling faeries around her separated and flew away. Luna gasped as the faint sight of a bundle fell from the sky, shrieking all the way down until it struck the ground with a sickening crack. The screaming ended abruptly.

One of the officers who was still human opened fire at the faeries—but missed the fleeting targets, who encircled him as he fired his Taser at them. It struck one of the elves, who fell back against a stone. As the officer began to rise into the air, another policeman pulled out a Taser and an elf leapt at him, sword swinging. It chopped off his hand as he screamed. Luna couldn't watch as the faeries dropped the other officer from a great height. He crashed onto the altar stone and didn't move again.

The cameraman began scampering toward the cars, but an elf fired an arrow that struck him through the neck. He fell twitching to the ground, his camera bouncing across the grass to lie facing the monument. Four of the dwarves ran over to him and hefted their axes high in the moonlit sky, chopping him to pieces and brandishing his limbs and head in the sky as they returned to Stonehenge.

The commotion had stopped Luna from noticing another new arrival. This one stood tall in dark leather that matched his skin, a silver crest on his chest. Short, spikey black hair topped an angular face and a jaw that seemed harsh. Several of those present snapped to attention on seeing him, creating the impression of authority.

"Oh my God," said Andy, eyes wide. "I know him."

That startled Luna. "You do? From where? I mean, what legend or drawing?"

He shook his head. "No. No, we've met before."

She didn't quite believe him. Magic had only awakened a few months earlier. "Where? When?"

Andy didn't answer at first, his face mostly blank save for a mild scowl as he stared. "A long time ago, right here."

"You're not making any sense. How is that possible?"

He looked at her sideways, then pursed his lips as if resigning himself to something. "I'm afraid I'm not who you think I am."

Her heart lurched. All those times she had wondered if she really knew him, and if he was hiding something, roared to the surface. She opened her mouth to say something when the new arrival spoke in a voice so loud they heard him clearly, even though they had been unable to make out anyone else's words.

"Greetings, one and all," he said, the voice commanding and smooth—and the elves dropped to one knee, the dwarves bowing. The satyrs grabbed everyone else and made them lie face down. "I am Vianden, Dragon Lord King of Faeburn in Elfhame, Lord of the Fae. I am pleased to see you gathered here to welcome us, for we have waited a thousand years to be reunited. But I must say that I am already disappointed. You have let this shrine to the doorway between our worlds suffer so mightily that I could easily think you never wished to see us return. And so few of you have come. Do you not respect us? Do you not love us? Do you not fear us? Perhaps I should sum-

mon my friends to rectify all this." He turned to the portal behind him and
spoke words that sent a chill down Luna's spine.

"As darkness falls, so may you rise,
To see this world with burning eyes.
Hooves of flame and breath of fire,
Ride again through fen and mire.
Innocent or evil be,
Spy the chosen as you please!
Come forth my friends and be set free;
Hunt for souls to fill our need."

The sound of horses galloping thundered into being as Vianden stepped
aside. A giant black horse jumped from within the portal, bearing a huge man
with a helmet made of a deer skull, enormous antlers wicked in the bright
moonlight. The horse's flaming yellow eyes glowed in the night—and, as it
jumped over the fallen altar, flaming footprints were left behind. The rider
carried a huge club with metal spikes on the end. He stopped at the top of
the broken trilithon horseshoe and pulled out a great horn of bone and gold.

As he blew a tremendous blast of sound that shook the ground, nightmare horse after hideous steed leaped from within the portal to tread upon
the Earth—each bearing a rider with translucent wings, or a ghostly appari-
tion, or a humanoid creature shifting every moment from monster to human
and back. Hundreds of them jumped and galloped past the leader of the pack
and into the fields, leaving a trail of burning hoofprints as they wheeled in
two different directions. They began to encircle the monument from a distance as if waiting for something. And then it came through the doorway—
scores of huge black dogs with flaming eyes. They charged in the directions
of the four compass, and the horses broke ranks to follow.

"The Wild Hunt," said Andy.

Luna nodded. Sure, she had heard of the legend, but seeing the actual
creatures in the flesh was an entirely different thing. She was about to ask
him about getting out of there when the reporter screamed, slugged the satyr
holding her down, and started to run. But she didn't get far. As she headed
for the vehicles, a rider broke from the pack and chased after her. For a moment, Luna thought the horse would trample her—but the rider never
slowed as he neared and leaned over, grabbing the woman by the hair and
hauling her before him, stomach down on the horse, as if she weighed nothing. The horse wheeled back toward the portal, leaping over a fallen sarsen

stone before disappearing from the Earth, the reporter's shrieking ending abruptly. They were gone.

As Luna watched Vianden, the three Will-o'-the-wisps from the Heel Stone flew past her position on the ground to encircle Vianden's head, where they slowed to a hover. Luna looked back at the Heel Stone to see Oliver and Rebecca still there. Vianden looked toward the Heel Stone and began marching that way after the Will-o'-the-wisps. One of the elves followed as the others returned to lounging idly. The satyrs struck up their tune again, making people dance, and the dwarves resumed inspecting the broken monument.

But Luna no longer had eyes for them as the dragon lord came nearer, the Will-o'-the-wisps ahead of it, an elf trailing. She slunk down further in the ditch beside Andy and held her breath as the procession passed not twenty feet from them on its way to the Heel Stone. They stepped over a raised walkway and then off it to reach their destination. Rebecca curtsied, and Oliver bowed before straightening and holding aloft a small item.

Andy cursed. "I think that's the Faerie Skull from the treasure room."

Luna turned to him in alarm. "You mean the one that's supposed to control fae?"

"Stay here," whispered Andy, starting to rise.

"What?" she asked in disbelief.

"I can't let him use that."

"But Andy..."

He had already risen and started across the ground, not trying to hide his presence as he strode with one hand on his sword. Luna watched him go, unable to decide whether to stay or follow. What Andy thought he was going to do she didn't know. He was no match for the forces at work. She finally decided she had to see and hear what was happening, if nothing else. She began moving across the cold grass in a low crouch, keeping a distance from Andy and trying to move off to one side so that when anyone saw him, she might remain unseen if she stayed low enough.

"Lord Vianden," Oliver said loudly enough for her to hear, "welcome to Earth. I have here an item rumored to control your kind. In a show of good faith, I am returning it to you for destruction."

Andy stopped on hearing these words, but Rebecca saw him and pointed. "Look!"

Luna dropped to her belly. Vianden and the elf turned as the Will-o'-the-wisps suddenly swarmed Andy, who pulled out his short sword as if to threaten them. They began to shriek in pain and fly back and away, toward Luna.

"It burns. It burns!"

The elf put a hand on its sword hilt and advanced on Andy, who stood twenty feet away. That was when Vianden ordered him to stop. He himself approached Andy with growing intensity on his moonlit features, as if delighted.

"How can it be?" Vianden asked rhetorically. "How can you be here, Andier of Roir? It has been a thousand years, and yet you have hardly aged ten."

Luna gaped at the comment, especially when Andy didn't dispute it.

"Why don't you go back where you came from?" Andy replied. "This world is no place for you."

The dragon lord smiled. "But I *am* where I came from, Andier. In fact, it is you who do not belong here, Ellorian Champion. Where are you companions? All I see is a terrified girl on the grass."

Luna started as the dragon lord looked at her. The Will-o'-the-wisps descended on her as she rose to run away, but they began to swirl around her and she felt her feet leave the ground. She screamed, knowing they would drop her to her death. When she next looked at Andy, she saw him make a throwing motion. Something silver flew toward her left side, where a shriek of pain hurt her ear and she fell a few feet to the ground, the other Will-o'-the-wisps moving away from her. She landed hard and twisted one ankle, falling to her side. Not a yard away lay the Will-o'-the-wisp, which she now saw was a faerie like the ones of Disney fame—a three-inch female in a tight green outfit, large wings spread out on the ground, with one broken. The light shining from her midsection was dimming because Andy's throwing knife had pierced her through. Moments later, the faerie died. A puff of green smoke rose from her and headed for the portal, into which it disappeared.

"So you care for this one," Vianden said, amused. "She won't get far. Why don't you come join us? I believe two of your kind were about to pledge their loyalty."

Andy said, "Oliver speaks for no one on this world."

Vianden turned and began approaching the Heel Stone again. "Perhaps I shall change that."

Andy glanced over at Luna and seemed to mouth a question as to whether she was alright. She nodded despite the ankle. Part of her wanted to crawl away after the implied threat against her. Instead, she took the nearby knife. Iron could hurt fairies, the legends said. If that was true—and it seemed to be, from the way they had reacted a couple of times—she needed to get to the car. She had no idea how much iron was in a car, but there had to be enough in the frame to keep a faerie out. She'd never manage to crawl so far, but at least she was armed.

While the dragon lord returned to Oliver and Rebecca at the Heel Stone, the elf did not, blocking the way so that Andy could not bypass him. Luna wondered why Andy just didn't go around him, but he apparently intended to go through him.

"Step aside, dark elf," said Andy.

In response, the elf drew a sword. Vianden turned at the sound and said with humor in his voice, "Kill him."

So quickly she hardly saw it, Andy threw a knife underhanded with his left hand—and was drawing his sword and charging before the blade struck the elf's shoulder. The elf grunted and pulled it out, inexpertly flinging it back. Andy caught it on his own blade and knocked it aside. Then their swords clanged in the night air. At the sound, the satyrs, elves, and dwarves began to close in. They would soon be upon her, but there was no escaping them now. She turned back to see Andy expertly parrying aside the elf's blows. She only knew his own strikes were landing because the elf grunted at each one. Then Andy plunged his sword through the elf's belly. Luna lay gaping at his display of sword-mastery as he pushed back the dead elf. It fell to the ground and lay unmoving. Only then did Andy fall, too, and Luna realized he was wounded.

"Somehow I knew you would triumph, Andier," said the dragon lord, amused. He turned back to Oliver and Rebecca. "You I shall make King of England if you swear fealty to me. And she will be your queen."

Oliver bowed his head. "Thank you, Your Majesty."

"But you must earn it first. We have much to discuss, but tonight is for celebration. Give me your arm."

Oliver hesitated but then extended his right hand. Vianden grabbed his bicep and spoke words Luna didn't hear. A burst of light appeared, and Oliver gasped in pain. Vianden let go of him and turned to Rebecca, who timidly extended her own arm. While this was happening, Luna saw a soft glow briefly appear around Andy, who began to rise.

"You will bear the Mark of the Dragon Lord," said Vianden, casting the spell on Rebecca, too. "No fae will hurt you."

Rebecca nervously asked, "Are you really a dragon?"

Luna didn't hear his answer because the approaching elves, dwarves, and satyrs had reached her. Holding what looked like a cupcake in one hand, a satyr painfully grabbed her arm and yanked her to her feet. She tried to keep weight off her injured ankle as she swung the knife in her other hand. There was no way this beast would force her to eat that food and turn her into one of them. The knife struck home, buried in its bare chest, blood already dripping from the wound. A sound somewhere between a human moan and a goat's bleat came from the satyr before it let go of her and fell dead, taking the knife with it. Luna fell to one knee and heard another grunt of pain above her. Then an elf dropped dead beside her, a knife sticking from its chest. Luna looked over to Andy and saw him throwing another even as an elf closer to her also collapsed. The blade Andy had just thrown struck a satyr in the leg and it stumbled away.

Suddenly a huge figure appeared behind Andy... and Luna realized Vianden had transformed into an enormous black dragon with a silver crest, wings outstretched to cast shadows on the Heel Stone, Oliver, and Rebecca. She stared in awe, wondering if he was going to breathe fire all over them or devour Andy—who turned and threw a knife, not at the dragon, but at Oliver. The blade hit his hand, which he yanked back with a yell, dropping something.

The Fairie Skull, Luna realized. If Andy could get it and it worked, he could control the fae.

"Take them to Elfhame." The dragon's booming voice startled Luna. Vianden launched himself into the air with powerful thrusts that made Luna shield her eyes until someone yanked her to her feet again and began pulling her toward the portal.

"No!" yelled Andy, starting toward her—but then he whirled around and ran toward Oliver, his bloody sword in one hand. For all his cockiness, Oliver was no match for this onslaught and swiftly backed away with Rebecca, nearly falling over in his haste. Luna struggled to see what was happening as an elf pulled at her. She purposely went limp so they'd have to drag her—but then someone picked up her legs as she kicked at them, trying to slow this down, her ankle badly hurting from the motion. She heard Andy's voice ring out.

"Fae of Elfhame," he yelled, holding something aloft, "I command you to stop."

But the ones carrying Luna didn't obey. Those closer to Andy, mostly elves and dwarves, had stopped. He ordered them to stop the others and began sprinting closer, likely hoping the Faerie Skull would get close enough to control the fae carrying Luna. But then a gunshot rang out. Two more, and Andy fell to the ground as Luna screamed. She heard a soft humming sound as the gold and blue light grew brighter. She looked up in horror as the portal to Elfhame loomed before her.

"Welcome home," sneered one of the elves. Then they passed through it and left the Earth behind.

At the same moment he saw Luna disappear through the portal, Andier felt the power of the Trinity Ring wash over him, the bullet wound in his leg healing completely. He had avoided using the ring for the past ten years he'd been trapped on Earth without magic, because Eriana wasn't around to replenish the healing spells in it. Now two of the three spells were gone. To one side stood Oliver, brandishing the gun that had shot him and advancing. He apparently wasn't that good a shot, having taken three bullets to hit Andier only once, and in the leg. The Faerie Skull lay on the ground several strides away, having bounced across the low grass when Andier had dropped it. Could he still control the fae nearby if he wasn't holding it?

"Stop him," he commanded, pointing toward Oliver.

The elves, dwarves, and two satyrs obeyed, striding toward a startled Oliver, who pointed the gun at them.

"You are not to harm me!" Oliver shouted, raising up his sleeve to show the Mark of the Dragon Lord. But the fae didn't stop. Andier knew that stopping his advancement and hurting him weren't the same thing. And Oliver didn't have enough bullets to kill them all. And would Vianden be pleased?

Andier rose and stepped toward the Faerie Skull. Then an arrow whizzed past his head, and two more struck the earth near the skull. He looked toward Stonehenge and saw a dozen satyrs and a few elves advancing on him. More arrows flew and he barely dodged them. The skull was so close, but they knew what he wanted and were already aiming at it. Cursing, Andier backed away, scanning the scene. Without the skull, he stood no chance. In the distance, in the opposite direction to his Jeep, he saw Vianden's huge body in the bright, moonlit sky, flying away. Below him, the Wild Hunt was returning, their fiery eyes and burning hoof prints lighting up the night. Andier had already decided to run for his Jeep when two more arrows flew at him and he rolled to the ground and onto his feet again. More gunshots rang out, and he took off at a sprint. He would have to rescue Luna another day.

He had a head start on those fae he didn't control. And he knew they'd been commanded to capture him alive, which would give him an advantage if he had to fight, since he could kill and they wouldn't. But the moment they caught him, more would surround him and it would be over. The Jeep was his only chance, especially if the iron in it kept them at bay.

He regretfully sprinted past police cars and the TV truck, since he didn't have the keys. Hotwiring a car was one of the many skills he'd picked up since arriving in the English countryside a decade earlier, but many newer vehicles were impossible to hotwire if they had a key fob and he wasn't prepared with an RFID booster. The one safe bet was his Jeep, if he could reach it. The way seemed impossibly long, but everyone was on foot and he was a fast runner who kept himself in excellent shape.

He ran past the cars belonging to Oliver and the other civilians, seldom looking back because it would only slow him down. But the dwarves were easily left behind—and the satyrs were struggling, too, their gait as unnatural as their bodies and inhibiting their speed. Only the dark elves kept up with him, but they weren't gaining.

Andier reached the tree grove and leapt over the steel gate he hadn't locked before. Another arrow whizzed past him, and then he was safe beyond the trees. He leaped into the driver's side, tossed the sword on the passenger side, and slammed his hand on the lock. He pressed a button and the Jeep revved. Something banged the back of the car and then he heard screams behind him.

"It burns!" the elves shrieked. "What evil wagon is this?"

Andier smiled in grim satisfaction. Then he put the car in reverse. They probably bad no idea what he was about to do as he stomped on the gas.

"Welcome to modern Earth, motherfuckers," he yelled as he ran over them. The Jeep bounced over their bodies as they screamed, either from being crushed or the iron underside—he didn't care which. The fae were quick studies—others jumped out of the way until he swerved to hit more of them and bashed open the steel gate onto the road. He threw the car in gear and stomped on the gas, peeling out onto the asphalt and charging toward Stonehenge. The stragglers hadn't seen him run over the others and he plowed through a couple of satyrs, windshield smashing from the impact as he purposely left the road to hit more of them. Then he was clear, careening across the grass toward the stone circle. More fae fired arrows at the Jeep, and he finally decided to turn on the headlights and roof's light bar to blind them. They put up their hands to shield their eyes, and he plowed through the elves and dwarves he had previously controlled with the Faerie Skull.

He heard more gunshots as Oliver fired at him, and decided it was time to go. The thought of driving through the portal flashed into his mind, but he'd never get the Jeep through and around the remaining stones to do it, and there was no telling what lay on the other side other than a bunch of fae.

Andier drove back onto the road to London, still scanning the area. And that's how he saw the leader of the Wild Hunt coming after him as the rest of the pack returned to Stonehenge. They began leaping back through the portal, each rider with one or more humans thrown across the saddle before them. Then Andier went over a hill and lost sight of them. In his rearview mirror, the leader charged after him, keeping pace on its supernatural hooves even as Andier reached higher and higher speeds.

A chaos of other cars filled the roads. Whether due to the passage of the Wild Hunt or the sight of Vianden, who was now breathing fire on whole streets of homes and setting them ablaze in the moonlight, the light traffic was in disarray. Some cars had stopped on the highway in haphazard positions. One had turned over on the grass. Two had crashed headfirst, with one of them still burning. Some cars were intact and had pulled over. Arrivals that Andier figured were more recent were pointing at Vianden and taking cellphone videos. Other people were running across the fields in panic. Andier expertly weaved his Jeep through the obstacles, narrowly missing vehicles as he swerved around them into oncoming traffic and then back into his lane. All the while, the Wild Hunt leader came on behind him.

Andier put his sword on his lap as the obstacles cleared. No cars would come from behind, and he'd been gaining on the taillights of those ahead in his lane. Now he slowed, giving himself room and knowing he would not outrun the beast coming for him. It gained rapidly now, coming up the left side—the wrong side, the side where he wasn't. He was about to slam the side of the car into it when it had the same idea, the horse colliding with him and whinnying as if in pain. The car jolted right and he struggled to bring it back in line, purposely slamming it into the horse again as he did so. It ran into the field and then returned, its rider swinging a huge, spiked club that smashed into the roof and crushed it down.

To do what he was thinking, he'd have to get them on the other side of the Jeep. He pressed the button to roll down the windows before the car took too much damage for them to work. The left one only went down halfway, but it was enough. He pulled a knife from within his armor as the rider smashed the other side of the windshield. Andier threw the knife out the window and struck the horse, which moved away, bucking wildly as if trying to dislodge it before the rider regained control.

Now they were behind the car and approaching the driver's side. Andier lifted his sword with his right hand, putting the blade on top of the door. The back window smashed in a shower of glass as the galloping horse came nearer, its rider swinging again at the roof and plunging downward. Andier knew that the same blow over his head would have connected with his skull. Then the horse's chest was right beside the window and Andier rammed the sword outward as hard as he could. The blade sliced cleanly into the horse's chest and it squealed in pain. Then the sword was torn from Andier's hand as the beast plunged headfirst into the ground, throwing the rider through the air, where he tumbled, the antlers on his skull helmet breaking as he rolled. Andier slammed on the breaks and skidded to a stop, then threw the Jeep into reverse and roared up beside the rider, hardly stopping the car before leaping out.

With a knife in each hand, he ran up to the fallen horseman and stopped. One of the broken antlers had punctured his chest and he lay panting, blood gushing out of his nose and mouth. He wasn't long for this world, a world in which he didn't belong. Andier felt no sympathy. He had battled too many monsters, stopped too many evil men, and fended off too many that wanted him dead or worse. Death came with the territory. When someone innocent, like that little girl back at Stonehenge, was killed, then he felt sorrow. But even then, he felt it later, not in the heat of battle, where sentiments got men killed. Whatever this rider was, the hate-filled glare in his dying eyes told Andier what he needed to know—that the world was better off without him. He wasn't one to leave a soon-to-be-dead enemy behind. Something could always heal them. The closest thing to mercy he had was cutting the rider's throat to end his suffering, and watching him bleed out.

Then Andier took the helmet of deer antlers and gathered some broken bits, tossing them in the Jeep. He also took the great horn of bone and gold. The rider himself didn't seem special, but he took the huge club, too. Then he returned to the dead horse and pulled the sword from its chest, finding the knife still lodged in its side. With Soliander's magical sword of soclarin ore, he hacked at each hoof until it came off. He carried the hooves back to the Jeep and threw them inside, then grabbed a plastic bag and returned to gouge out the horse's eyes. He also cut the heart from the beast and dropped it in the cooler with the eyes. He didn't know if any of these things might be useful as magic items or for spells, but being prepared had its advantages.

Satisfied with his handiwork, Andier went back to his Jeep. He'd need another vehicle to avoid suspicion, so he turned around and drove back to the area where all the damaged cars were. People were still milling around, so he kept going until he found an intact one that was abandoned and un-damaged. A quick look inside showed that the key fob was there. He unload-ed everything from his Jeep, then removed the license plates. There wasn't much he could do about the VIN number, but he would be disappearing an-yway. He had no friends except from the Sons of the Magi, and no family. Only Luna, and she was gone. No one would be filing a missing person's re-port or looking for him except Oliver.

Andier of Roir drove off into the night for London, intending to break in-to the treasure room and clean it out in its entirety.

And the time to contact the Stonehenge Four had come.

CHAPTER TWENTY-ONE

A New Home

Special Agent Kira Mori stared at the video as it played for the fifth time, her partner Special Agent Wade Carter beside her. This was the kind of footage that took a while to digest because it showed so much of great importance. And all of it was beyond the ordinary. It wasn't the actions, though the scene did end with an overt spell. Still, she had seen those recently. Everyone had. No, the conversation was the stunner.

At Jack's apartment, she had seen the laptop and the login info on the fridge, but she'd left it to the techs because Jack had walked in. And now the techs had seen the contents Jack and his lawyer had told her about. There was a log of Jack's activities and what had happened at the apartment, when "Soliander" kidnapped "Eriana" while Jack was there. Security footage showed the man take her wrist, speak a word, and begin to vanish as Jack ran into the room and dived at them, yelling for them to stop. The video ended shortly afterward. It also revealed that Eriana and Erin Jennings were the same person.

"Well," Kira began, mystified, "we know Jack isn't the one who kidnapped her."

"Yeah, no shit. Need to get this Soliander's face on every news channel. This guy sounds dangerous, probably a lunatic. He was talking about laying waste to kingdoms and cities. He mentioned Merlin."

That was definitely odd. The name Merlin had come up often lately, only because he was the only supposed wizard from Earth's past. And with magic turning up, people talked about new Merlins appearing any day. Apparently, one already had. But in the video, they talked of Merlin like he was real.

Kira said, "And the Ellorian Champions were mentioned, and something about imposters. My impression is that the Stonehenge Four are the imposters, whatever that means."

"I wrote down those other names. Korrin and Andier. Lorian, Zoran. Everon. She said something about this guy Soliander attacking Lorian and Matt before. And something about a Dragon Gate in Honyn."

Kira shook her head. "No, *on* Honyn, not in. He said something about a thousand worlds, and leaving this planet without her a second time—that he can't do it, so he took her with him in this video. Honyn is another planet. This is bizarre."

"Yeah, but these days anything seems possible. Certainly, we won't find her if she's not on Earth." He shook his head. "I can't believe that sentence just came out of my mouth."

"The other big thing is that this Soliander guy was after the Stonehenge Four. Jennings asked whether he would have killed or immobilized them if he'd found them here. And it makes you wonder how he was able to track them. Jack doesn't seem to be one of the people he was after, but it's hard to tell."

Carter said, "That would explain why we can't find them. They might be hiding from this guy. Here we thought they were perpetrators of something—but it's starting to look like they're victims, or intended victims. Kill or immobilize. There's a choice you don't hear every day. She obviously knew this guy."

Kira nodded, having recognized that the two in the video appeared to love each other. Or had. "Maybe all of this is why Jack quit his job, to be harder to find."

"It could also explain why they've been looking at real estate. Do you think they're trying to find somewhere to hide? Somewhere that isn't a hotel room?"

"Yes. To hide from the media. Maybe us. From this Soliander. And it's also probably why he's not telling us anything." She looked at her partner soberly. "I think they might need our help."

A knock on the door interrupted them, and she turned to see her superior wearing an expression she couldn't read. "You're not gonna believe this. Erin Jennings just walked in the front door."

When the portal to Jack's apartment disappeared, leaving Eriana standing beside Rognir, she couldn't help thinking Soliander had kidnapped her the last time she'd been here. But she brushed that aside and went looking for Jack, eager to see him. She'd last seen him charging into the room and diving at Soliander. That was brave. Foolish, but brave. The least she could do was reassure him that she was alright. But he wasn't there.

In fact, the place seemed "off" somehow. She had been here several times, and her memory tipped her off. A lamp had been moved a few inches, another turned a different way. The couch pillows were uncharacteristically organized. iPhone cables had been neatly coiled. They had put two similar pictures of the Washington Nationals back on the walls, but each in the other's place. It was as if the place had been disturbed and then someone other than Jack had attempted to restore order. Either that, or he'd changed his mind about a bunch of little things.

"What do you think that means?" Rognir asked, when she said something about it.

Opening more and more cabinets, she said, "I don't know. My purse was here and I'm not seeing it. Help me look."

They searched the kitchen, living room, hall bath, Jack's bathroom, and the master bath. There was no sign of it. The dwarf kept stopping to gawk out the window, prompting her to explain things like cars and phones, but she avoided turning on a TV, despite his curiosity. Her missing purse meant no car keys, no money or credit cards, and no smartphone. Jack's laptop also appeared to be gone. She had no way to contact him and belatedly realized she needed to memorize his phone number.

"So what do we do?" Rognir asked, sitting on the couch. "This furniture is wonderful."

Eriana smiled as he examined it. "I'm thinking. If we leave the apartment, we should lock it, but then we can't get back in. Your clothes are more conspicuous than my robe, which I can pass off as a dress if I can borrow a belt from Jack. Take off the tunic. The undershirt is not the style here, but it'll do. Your leather pants and boots might pass. No carrying around the sack of armor or weapons. And we need to protect those keystones, after all the trouble we went through to create them."

"Agree. But not even a knife?"

"Not even a knife. No one here is armed that way, and you'll just get shot by overzealous police."

"Crossbows or longbows?"

She opened her mouth, then shut it. Explaining guns could come later. "I need to call Quincy, Ryan's attorney, but I'll have to find a phone and a computer to look him up. Can you stay here? Then I can leave but not lock up. If I'm unsuccessful, we can stay the night and have food. I know you probably want to play around with stuff." She looked at the TV and sighed. "Okay, look, I'm going to turn this on and put on a news channel so you can see what's going on in the world. Just let it play, absorb what you can, but otherwise don't touch it."

"Sure, lass."

She set him up with something to watch and got herself ready, then stepped outside. It took an hour to walk to the nearest library after asking multiple people where it was. She didn't have a library card or PIN to access a computer, but she asked a teenage girl to look up Quincy's number for her. Then she found a phone and called him, learning that Jack was in jail for kidnapping her. She sighed, not blaming her husband for reporting her missing. If she'd thought of that, she might've had Jack email or text him from her phone. After talking it over with Quincy, they agreed on a plan.

An hour later, after updating Rognir and leaving him glued to the TV, the two of them walked into the building where Jack was being held. Eriana had already called her husband to put him at ease during a tough conversation for all the dancing around the truth she'd had to do. She would have to be honest with him soon, but first she had other issues to deal with. Something about her old life intruding on her new had pushed thoughts of him from her mind. Now she felt a clash of worlds and felt certain that relationship might not survive the truth.

After talking to her husband, she'd called her private investigator, asking him to catch a flight to Maryland immediately because she needed him. Telling him the truth was another conversation she wasn't looking forward to having, but he would adapt better than her husband, she thought. She wasn't really prepared for either conversation, having long since stopped thinking it would ever be needed. Even now, she didn't have time to worry about it.

Now it was time to free Jack, but Quincy had warned her about the video of Soliander taking her and that they might need to answer some hard questions. If she had learned anything from Andier, it was to play a situation by ear—so they soon met Special Agent Mori and her partner Carter in a meeting room with Quincy beside her in a suit. The mahogany table was bare except for two sealed water bottles for her and the lawyer, and a notepad for each agent. A TV hung on one wall.

As she sat, Special Agent Mori said in greeting, "Mrs. Jennings. Or should I call you Eriana?"

Not reacting to the revelation, she replied, "Erin, please."

"Has your attorney told you we have a warrant for your arrest?"

Eriana was expecting this and was prepared. "Yes, but for what? You claimed a security guard said I did something to him."

"He says you knocked him unconscious by touching his arm."

Smiling, Eriana asked, "Sounds hard to believe, doesn't it?"

"Lots of things don't sound that hard to believe any more, Mrs. Jennings."

"Is there proof? A witness? Any history of me doing this?"

Special Agent Mori frowned, and when she dodged the questions, Eriana knew this wouldn't go far. "You were seen walking out with Anna Sumner, who was under arrest."

"How was I supposed to know that? She wasn't wearing handcuffs or anything that would've tipped me off."

"Her arrest was all over the news."

Quincy spoke up. "You can't prove she knew that."

Folding her arms, Special Agent Mori added, "Maybe you weren't aware because you were spending all your time at the hospital. Footage shows you waiting around day after day. You knew she would go back there after disappearing days earlier."

"Everybody knew that from the news she'd disappeared and reappeared on the highway before that."

Special Agent Mori changed subjects and Eriana knew another angle had closed. "What is your relationship with her?"

"Personal."

Arching an eyebrow, Special Agent Mori asked, "Care to be more specific?"

"No."

"Okay. Okay. Let's try something else. When you arrived today, you said Mr. Riley had nothing to do with your recent disappearance. I just want to be clear. Are you claiming no one kidnapped you or held you against your will?"

"Jack didn't."

Special Agent Mori sighed. "Why don't we both cut the crap?" She turned on a TV and played the entire video of Soliander abducting her. "Who is this abducting you?"

Seeing the video again saddened Eriana, and she hoped the authorities weren't planning to release it. They would probably *do* it in order to find Soliander, but it would make her famous. Or infamous. "An old friend of mine. And as you can see, I am free."

"But you didn't want to go with him."

"You cannot tell that from the video. I said nothing about refusing."

"Where is this Soliander now?"

"I don't know."

"Where did he take you?"

Although they had talked about other planets on the video, Eriana wasn't going to admit it and gave a half-truth. "I'm not entirely sure."

"How did you get back?"

"The same way I left, a spell."

Special Agent Mori held her gaze. "Are you a wizard? A witch?"

"I am not."

"How do I know you didn't just cast yourself back from wherever you were?"

"If I could do that, I would have appeared in Jack's cell, then disappeared with him. Instead, I'm sitting here talking to you. I would've done the same with Anna at the hospital, and yet I walked out the door. As that video shows, Jack was not involved. He is a friend, and I would like to see him released immediately."

Quincy added, "You have no case, and you know that you don't."

Special Agent Mori said, "Oh, don't worry, Jack will be free to go. We're processing him now. But there are bigger concerns here, so I'm hoping you'll cooperate. We are not your enemy, Mrs. Jennings, or Mr. Riley's. If anything, based on the conversation on that video, the Stonehenge Four—and I assume you know who I mean—have an enemy in this friend of yours, Soliander. And it seems that you and they might be in need of our assistance."

That surprised Eriana. But she wasn't interested in training the FBI anytime soon. There were things far bigger than them going on, and they wouldn't understand or accept any of those anytime soon. Keeping them from snooping might stop things getting out of hand more than they already were. But the idea of them not bothering the new Champions held great appeal, so maybe there was a path forward.

Eriana said, "Well, if you're offering help, you can start by getting the media off their backs."

"Freedom of the Press. There's nothing we can do about that."

"Fair enough, but bullets aren't going to stop a wizard like Soliander—so, while I appreciate the offer, I don't see how there's anything you can do. Actually, no. You can return all the items you seized from my home in Florida. You know the ones I mean."

Special Agent Mori shook her head. "We have a mandate to confiscate all magical items."

Then it was good she didn't know about the keystones Rognir had with him at Jack's. "You know they are magical? Just because I collect items rumored to be magical doesn't mean any of them *are*."

The agent smiled. "After what I saw on that video, we're assuming they are. You know a wizard and apparently have for some time. That's enough for us to hold onto them. That goes for the amulet we found in your room, too."

Eriana frowned. "You have no reason to believe that is magical. I have other jewelry, a purse, a phone. Are you claiming every last thing I own is magical?"

"No, but that one was in a special case and wrapped the same way the artifacts of yours are, and so we assume it is the same."

Eriana stifled annoyance. That was a good point she couldn't counter. But she wouldn't really need the Corethian Amulet anytime soon. She'd already reached the god of Earth.

"Well, then I don't think we have anything more to discuss. Quincy."

They rose to go, and Special Agent Mori said, "Okay for now. But we'll be in touch. We have a lot of questions for you, Mrs. Jennings. You're planning to stay in the area?"

"You can reach me through my attorney."

It took a few minutes to get her things, minus the amulet, which Eriana wondered how to get back from the FBI. Some of her powers had returned—enough to knock out a handful of people—but that approach would just heighten scrutiny on her and the others. She would have to find another way. Maybe when Matt returned, or if Lorian arrived, they could use magic to reacquire the amulet or the magic items the FBI had confiscated. She wasn't sure what to make of Special Agent Mori except that having a friend in the FBI was better than an enemy. They would discuss what to tell the FBI once they were all together. Certainly, the new Champions needed fewer problems. Now it was time to assume her role as a matriarch to them, keeping both herself and everyone else out of trouble, even if she had to use her fast-returning powers to do it.

Jack felt uneasy as he drove Eric, Anna, Ryan, and Matt from his apartment to the new Briardale estate. If someone summoned them on a quest, all four of them would return to this stretch of Route 28. The trip was only fifteen minutes long, and once they were there, this danger would end. Rognir would soon make progress on the Home Rings, so maybe they would even be free to travel soon.

Less than a day had passed since Eriana and Quincy had freed him from the FBI. Being fingerprinted was one of many experiences he never expected, the black ink hard to remove with this weird, sandy-feeling cleaner goo they'd given him. His cell had at least been clean and empty of others. For the first time, he had questioned his role in everything, his life upended and in peril in various ways. He still wanted to help but now questioned the cost. Once they got the estate set up with the Home Rings, would he really still be needed? Their parents now knew, and so did Quincy, Daniel, and Eriana.

But he could never walk away. Not after what he'd seen. Curiosity about what was going on next would drive him crazy, though yet hanging around to find out might cost him dearly. He stifled his misgivings and continued bringing them up to speed on what had happened with the FBI and the estate, which the LaRue family had now purchased. The main house had five bedrooms, with another three in the guest house, and there was a room above the stables. Some furniture had been ordered, with a few temporary furnishings already set up. Except for Eric, their parents had packed up a lot of their belongings for them and would come to the house for a kind of reunion. Jack had done the same for Eric. There was a lot to do, but things were moving forward.

"What about the Home Rings?" Eric asked. "How are they coming along?"

Jack slowed down and turned off the road into a wide driveway, two black steel gates barring the entrance. As he rolled down the window and punched in the security code, he said, "We're trying to get the stone Rognir wants for it—but, like a lot of things, we can't just go get it the same day. We've ordered it, though. I forget the delivery date, but it's coming. We were thinking of putting them in the stables, each one inside a stall. They can be on platforms like you wanted, so we can easily roll them out and up into a truck. We can also store your gear in the stalls."

Ryan said, "Gotta keep the Rings away from the horses though, so we don't scare them when we return."

"The barn is L-shaped, so we can reserve one area at the end for that."

"I'm excited," said Anna, looking out the front window.

"We paid more money to get the estate immediately. Technically it will take another week or two, but the previous owners moved out long ago and they've agreed to let us rent it for a month while we finalize the paperwork."

Jack gave a running commentary as they drove down the driveway between two wide fields sparsely dotted with trees. One field, to the right, had a pond with a nearby gazebo and a walkway to the main house—which was two stories high and painted yellow with white trim. A covered porch ran around it, a flower garden with manicured bushes hugging it. To the left stood the blue and white house, which Jack called a guest house—but it was the original home, nearly a hundred years old, built long before the newer one two decades ago. It stood a bit closer to the road and had a two garage spaces to the main house's three. The driveway ran between the houses to and around the stables, which had a handful of parking spots.

The stables were a red, two-story building with a silver roof. They had left most of the upper floor empty for storage, and just to air it out. To the left of them stood a matching indoor riding ring, a covered archway running between the buildings for protection from bad weather. Further to the left were the outdoor riding rings, one of which already had several jumps set up. Typical horse enclosures could be seen in the numerous fields.

Aside from catching up with Eriana and Rognir, the new Champions made plans, including arguing over who was taking which room. They offered Anna and then Eriana the master suite, but the two women decided to take the guest house together. Eriana insisted on giving her protégé its master bedroom. With Jack as the estate's caretaker, everyone agreed he should take the main house's master suite, which flattered him. Eric and Ryan took two bedrooms on the upper floor, but Matt wanted to use a basement room because it was next to a room he would use for studying. While Eriana and Rognir had brought a few supplies to Earth with them, the fun for Matt began in earnest when new arrivals appeared in Jack's apartment and he drove them over.

Everyone expected Lorian and Taryn, who had changed into the Earth clothes bought for them. But neither Prince Dari nor the dragon Jolian, in human form, had been anticipated. Borrowed jackets had hidden their conspicuous attire long enough to get them from the apartment to the van. Once they reached the house, the sight of an elf in jeans and a t-shirt was almost as odd to everyone as that of a dwarf in shorts and flip-flops, Rognir having made himself at home. Now it was Lorian's turn to start gawking at items like the TV or microwave when someone warmed up water for his tea. Taryn did little more than cock an eyebrow, while Jolian frowned as if she disapproved. Sensing that no one was in the mood for serious talk, they enjoyed a night of just hanging out together.

Jack wouldn't accept that Jolian was really a dragon until darkness had fallen and they'd all stepped outside. They'd talked about the dangers of Jolian flying around during the day and ruled it out unless absolutely necessary. Even at night, she might be seen or, worse yet, have an encounter with planes, helicopters, or even drones—all items she needed to understand before flying. With that in mind, she morphed into a dragon now behind the stables. They hadn't brought a saddle, so when she suggested taking Jack for a quick look around the area, he declined, not ready for that. Instead, she took Ryan, and they were gone long enough that everyone went back inside.

Despite being present, Prince Dari did not join in the camaraderie, choosing to spend his time watching the TV beside Lorian. His offered explanation for coming was that the Kingdom of Andor was prepared to lend considerable aid if needed and he would act as liaison. Jack had heard only a little about the man and sensed tension between him and everyone else, like Dari was the odd one out. Jack tried to befriend him by helping the one-handed man do things like open a bottle of beer, and he seemed to lighten up a little.

To Jack's surprise, Matt looked uncomfortable, his eyes on Jolian after she returned with Ryan. He didn't know what to make of it as Matt followed Lorian into the kitchen, then excused himself downstairs. Minutes later, Lorian whispered something to Jolian, who went after Matt. Curious, Jack was tempted to sneak down to see what the wizard and dragon were up to, but he decided that being the newly appointed caretaker of Briardale still didn't entitle him to know *everything* going on. He settled back into his chair and waited for them to return.

—— ◆ · ◆ ——

Matt waited nervously for Jolian. Doing this to Lorian had been one thing, but a powerful red dragon, with her own magic, was far more formidable. He knew it would work on her because Soliander had enslaved her brother before—an enslavement that only ended when Ryan smashed his sword, made of soclarin ore, over the slave orb and broke it into three pieces. Those were the same three pieces Matt had just retrieved with Jolian's help. She would know at once what this was, so he had thought hard about how to get her to look into the slave orb. He wasn't sure what failure would mean. It wasn't like she would kill him, but he'd have a lot of explaining to do.

When asked why she was on Earth, Lorian explained that it was his idea. A dragon might be very beneficial on Earth, and with all the Honyn dragons banished and unfriendly anyway, the obvious choice had been one with whom they were on good terms. So he had gone to Rovell to ask Jolian, who was the first of potentially quite a few who would come if needed. He hadn't asked the dragons of Elloria because he didn't really know them and Taryn, who did, had been here. Lorian had learned about Matt's recent mission with her right before Matt used the Orbs of Dominion on him.

But Matt worried that Jolian would accidentally reveal their mission to get the slave orb shards. Almost as bad was her ignorance that they weren't the real Ellorian Champions. Since Jolian had been used to hearing them use their real names, she'd hadn't reacted to that here on Earth, but he had seen her questioning looks grow in frequency and intensity as the group talked in such as a way that made it clear what their identities really were. Her friends seemed to have forgotten that she didn't know. So he had decided to kill two birds with one stone. He would tell her the truth about that to put her at ease. And he would make her keep quiet about their mission. If handled right, she wouldn't be an issue.

Now he stood in his bare study, a built-in, oak bookcase with doors on the bottom the only furnishing. Reaching into the Bag of Desires Lorian had given him, he felt the cold slave orb first. Retrieving it, he placed it on its stand inside one cabinet. Next, he took out the warmer master orb in its velvet bag and laid it on the bookshelf in plain sight, still inside the bag. He put his hand in long enough to turn it on, the dark glass glowing with a golden sheen before he covered it with the bag again. He looked at the slave orb to confirm that it was also on, a slight silver sheen on it. Then he closed the cabinet to hide it.

He heard soft footsteps descending the carpet runner atop the wooden stairs, so he stepped out of the lit room to see Jolian reaching the bottom. Her eyes glanced at the shields, bows, and other items in the otherwise empty rec room. Then she saw him and came over.

He smiled. "Jolian, I am glad to see you here on Earth, though I was not expecting it."

"This world is fascinating."

"It will take some getting used to." Matt turned back into the office, and she followed. "I wanted to remind you of your promise not to tell the others of our mission to collect the Orb of Dominion shards. I haven't had a chance to tell them and would rather they hear it from me."

"I remember. Lorian reminded me as well. Is this it?" She indicated the velvet bag.

"Yes. I'm afraid that it reformed while in Lorian's possession. I will have to ask him how, as the pieces should have remained wrapped and separate."

Jolian nodded, eyes on the bag. "So, this is what enslaved my brother."

"Yes. I need to put it away, still in the bag. There's a stand in that cabinet, to one side of you, behind the doors. Would you grab it for me?"

She turned without a word and as she knelt, her hands reaching for the knobs, Matt discreetly slipped the velvet bag back from the master Orb of Dominion beside him. When she opened the cabinet, he looked into the master, seeing her face reflected in it, now that her eyes were on the slave orb.

"Obey and serve," he said. "My will be yours."

Jolian's alarmed expression relaxed. "My will is yours."

Matt breathed a sigh of relief, but noticed that he felt depressed and hollow, his victory feeling like defeat. He tried to shake it off but knew that wouldn't work. He still felt guilt every time he looked at Lorian; the dragon would be no better.

"Please close the door," he said, "and stand up. I'm sorry for doing this but, I need to be sure you won't say anything. You are free to act as you normally will, but if I want you to do something, you will agree to, though I still want you to voice any objections."

Jolian was looking at him with a sadness in her eyes. "I understand and will do as you ask." After hesitating, she remarked in disappointment, "I had thought better of you, Matt Sorenson."

He flushed and looked down. "So had I. If anyone asks what we were talking about, it was your help training me in magic."

"And is this something you want?"

"If you're able to."

"I am."

"Thank you. Please go upstairs. I'll be right there."

After she left, Matt quickly put the items back in the magic bag because it was the easiest way to hide them. He just had to keep Taryn from going through his clothes. A little tired of this new life of his and wanting her comfort, he called her to come down to him. They were soon together on the inflatable queen mattress in his new bedroom. It wasn't the sturdiest thing to have sex on, so they just held each other, Matt's growing guilt making him sleep restlessly. At least everyone thought he had an excuse for disturbed sleep after what Everon had done. No one asked him anymore how he was doing, though he sometimes still saw concern in their eyes. But it was fading, like he wanted. He didn't enjoy being hovered over, though he appreciated that it meant they cared.

The next several days were a flurry of activities as they made significant progress at Briardale. Furniture was delivered, more was ordered, and the estate started taking shape. They set the archery targets up outside and both Lorian and Taryn began instructing for all four Champions in both the longbow and crossbow. Both trainers thought the swords they had needed improvement, but they resumed training with those as well. Prince Dari offered to return to Andor and bring back a supply of suitable weapons.

Ryan and Eric worked with Lorian on building rolling platforms for the Home Rings, while Rognir chiseled away at the marble stone that had finally arrived. The dwarf had already carved a symbol into each Home Ring—a glowing hand for Anna, a shield for Ryan, a staff for Matt, and a dagger for Eric. Working tirelessly, he was able to complete one a day, starting with

Anna's. Matt used a cantrip to identify which keystone had which DNA. Each time the dwarf placed a keystone into the slot he'd reserved for it, Matt cast a spell on it so it would merge with the marble and complete the ring. This was one of the first spells he'd been able to do on Earth, and he noticed that the magic came somewhat easily now. A pulse of light would indicate that the keystone was ready, but the only way to test the Rings would be to be summoned on their next quest and returned home. Even without that confirmation of success, they relaxed.

The first horse, the one Ryan already owned, was soon in the stables, which they began stocking with things for the horses and with their personal arsenal. Ryan's mother was a skilled rider and took the lead on finding more horses for the others. Jack had been looking after Anna's cats, and now relocated them as he cleaned out her condo. They also acquired two trained guard dogs, mostly to alert them to trespassers. Matt had wondered what their reaction to Jolian might be even in human form. The cats clearly loved her, climbing into her lap—but the dogs were intimidated and meek, keeping their distance, as if recognizing a predator who far outclassed them. She had to make overtures of friendliness to get them to relax, and then they seemed to view her as the dominant one whose approval they sought.

Since it took both Matt and Lorian to open a portal to another world, and Matt could vanish at any time, they agreed that Lorian and Prince Dari would return to their respective planets to make various arrangements. They would procure supplies unavailable on Earth, like appropriate weapons or wizarding items. Once a week, someone from either Honyn or Elloria would communicate with Jack at the least and, if necessary, open a portal to Briardale to help. Since Matt could cast the spell to communicate across worlds himself, he would always be able to tell Jack where they had gone, and the others might be able to come and help. But once those arrangements were made, Dari and Lorian returned to Earth, partly out of fascination with life there.

Just when everything seemed to be going well, the FBI paid a visit. They had no search warrant, and Special Agent Mori and her partner Carter professed just to be checking up on their wellbeing. The group agreed to humor them and let them in while restricting them to the main house. Anyone from another planet was discreetly asked to sequester themselves in the stables out of sight. Each had an accent that would prompt questions about their origins, and they belatedly realized they needed some hats to cover Lorian's ears.

The four Champions, Eriana, and Jack entertained them for an hour, mostly dodging questions about their disappearances unless the honest answer might get them left alone. And so they admitted that they didn't vanish on purpose, having no control over it—and could not appear somewhere at will either. The agents accurately figured out that they returned to the same place, so they didn't bother denying it—or that this was one reason they now had the estate and were not planning to leave.

Where his friends saw potential trouble and interference in the conversation, Matt saw opportunity. The agents seemed to believe he and the others were victims of something beyond their control, and were even sympathetic, but he wanted more power over the threat they posed. And he had the means to achieve it. Being in danger on a quest was something they couldn't do much about, though his quickly-growing skill now that he could practice on Earth was helping. But being in danger while at home was unnecessary. With this home established, and hopefully with the Home Rings working, they could have so much less to fear. And now these two agents were right here in their oasis from danger.

Matt repeatedly caught the eye of Special Agent Mori, trying to suggest with a look that he wanted to tell her things alone. He finally excused himself and went to his study downstairs, where he retrieved both Orbs of Dominion from the Bag of Desires and laid them on the counter. Footsteps began to sound on the steps, and he double-checked it was her and not someone else before relaxing. She gazed around at the room, but there was little to see here now except martial arts materials like gym mats. All of the weapons, like swords and bows, had been moved to the indoor riding ring.

"Well, Mr. Sorenson, I got the impression you wanted to talk to me about something."

"You are astute," he replied, stepping into his trap. She followed, her eyes quickly going to the only items on the bookcases, two Orbs of Dominion side-by-side. "They may be my friends, but we don't always agree on things."

"You've been through a lot together—more than you're telling me, I'm sure."

"What you don't know is that I will soon tell you everything so you can best help us, but all in good time. I understand that you are interested in acquiring magic items, so I wanted to give you one without them knowing. I feel that it's dangerous."

He touched the master orb and both orbs turned on. She kept some distance, but continued looking at the slave orb Matt had put closer to her on purpose. That was all he needed. She asked, "What does it do?"

"Obey and serve," he said. "My will be yours."

A look of peace came over Special Agent Mori's face. "My will is yours."

This time, Matt felt no guilt about it. He could control someone threatening him. And this was exactly why he'd acquired the orbs. Feeling excited about what came next, he remarked, "I understand that you have a trove of magic items taken from Erin Jennings' home."

"Yes, they are being examined."

"You will find a way to bring all of them to us here. This is not to be done in secret. You will convince the FBI to let them go because it has been determined that none of them are magical, even though quite a few likely are."

"I do not understand how I will do that."

"I do. You will also get Eriana's Corethian Amulet and return it."

"I understand."

Matt pointed at the slave orb. "I would like you to take this with you to the FBI field office, the one that arranged for the raids on all our properties. Do whatever you have to, but make sure you call a meeting with as many agents and superiors as possible. Make sure that no one can see in and that the door is closed. You will tell me when this is done, leaving me on speakerphone. You will then unveil the slave orb and I will do the rest."

"I understand."

"I knew that you would. Now, would you send for your partner?"

Each of the new Champions, except Eric, had been reunited with their parents at the estate. They could finally reveal what was going on, and so it was another burden gone. Some of their parents had still found it difficult to believe—but after witnessing Anna's healing power, a cantrip from Matt, and Jolian briefly morphing into a dragon at night, there were no more doubts. All of this took place at a big dinner on Halloween night with Anna, Matt, Ryan, and their parents, Eric, Daniel, Jack, Eriana and her investigator, Lorian, Rognir, Taryn, Prince Dari, Jolian, and Quincy.

With the house not nearly big enough, they filled the indoor riding ring with tables for twenty and had a pizza party. There was continued amusement about the reactions to foods, drink, and everything else by the "outlanders," as Jack collectively thought of those not from Earth. Most had complained about the air quality, especially the elf Lorian, and Rognir had already commented that the food was making him fat. Some of it didn't agree with them either, and they were increasingly taking to eating salads. They also craved unprocessed meat. This prompted serious discussion of turning the estate into more than a horse farm, with its own garden and livestock devoid of the chemicals people in the United States were used to.

They had gathered at around 6 PM, and as dinner continued, the new Champions told stories of their quests, trying to focus on the lighter moments by silent agreement. No one needed to hear how much danger they were really in so often, but it came up anyway. They needed to warn their parents about Soliander in case he or someone acting on his behalf appeared. It served as a reminder that however much control they had gained over their situation, uncertainty still abounded. All of it prompted their parents' heartfelt thanks to the outlanders who had befriended their children and would continue to support them.

But when the clock hit 7 PM, Eric suddenly got up and turned on the big, wall-mounted TV the previous owners had left installed on one side of the indoor ring.

"I think there's something we need to see," he said, turning the channel to BBC News. "I have a Google alert set up on my phone for Stonehenge and there's supposedly a live camera crew capturing something there, something about fairies."

The television came on and immediately showed a big, shimmering wall of blue and white light across part of the monument, figures emerging from it. The satyrs caught their attention because they were so different from the elves and dwarves that came next. No one watching the TV spoke as the scene unfolded, though Eriana groaned, "No, don't eat it," when the fae presented the humans with treats.

The watchers gasped as people turned into satyrs. And someone screamed when the little girl was dropped to her death, and an elf swung a sword at an officer and cut off his gun-wielding hand. Then the camera began bouncing wildly as the cameraman fled toward the flashing lights of a police car in the distance. The view became chaotic for several moments until it went still, the camera still filming on its side—and showing the cameraman in the foreground, an arrow through his neck. Dwarves came running and chopped him to pieces as some of the parents watching reacted out loud. The camera was close enough to capture a figure in black leather appearing through the portal and announcing himself as the Dragon Lord King of Elfhame.

Eriana rose. "Vianden! I know him. He's a dragon. He was with Morgana."

No one said anything more as they listened to the spell to call forth the Wild Hunt. After this, the scene became calmer, with less to hear. But with the camera angled just enough to show the Heel Stone, they saw what happened next. A man in black leather rose from the grass. Then white lights surrounded a woman near him and lifted her into the sky, before he threw something toward her and she fell to the ground. A sword fight between him and another figure was hard to follow, the camera tilted as it was, but it ended swiftly with him victorious until he collapsed. Then a white glow surrounded him, and he rose to confront those who had left Stonehenge to approach him and the woman. Moments later, Vianden turned into a black dragon and spoke so loudly that the camera picked it up.

"Take them to Elfhame."

The woman began screaming and fighting off those grabbing her, the man in leather throwing several knives that felled them one by one. But others picked up the woman and carried her toward Stonehenge. As this was happening, Eriana walked up to the TV.

"Those clothes," she said. "The movements. Can it be?"

"What?" asked Eric, stepping up beside her, but she just shook her head. It wasn't until the man in black leather ran closer to the camera that she gasped.

"Andier! He's alive!"

A murmur of surprise went through the room. They watched as gunshots rang out and Andier fell as if struck. Then he used an apparent Trinity Ring to heal himself and rise. The woman he was chasing disappeared through the portal to Elfhame, arrows flew at him, and he turned and ran out of view with fae chasing after him. For several minutes, not much else happened. Then a Jeep careened into view, running over a few people before more gunshots rang out and the Jeep disappeared. Moments later, a dwarf with a hammer approached and the camera feed suddenly cut off. Eric muted the TV as it went back to showing a news anchor, who looked horrified.

"I recognize the outfit," he admitted, looking at Eriana. "You're certain?"

She nodded, eyes looking excited but worried. "Yes, it's him. We've found him. No one throws a knife like he does, or moves so efficiently. I must get to him."

"What the hell is happening?" asked Matt's deaf mother, her words intelligible but with that different clarity the deaf often speak with. Her son began doing sign language for her.

"You'll have to go without us," said Eric. "We can't travel yet, not until we know these Home Rings work."

They began making plans but didn't get far. If anyone had lingering doubts about it all, they were soon dispelled. Eric was still standing, but Matt, Anna, and Ryan were sitting in different places at the table when a soft glow began to surround each of them, their alarmed parents leaning back. The Champions' faces registered surprise, then resignation. Anna had time to say she'd be back soon. Eric laid his phone on the table, then nodded farewell.

Ryan tossed back the rest of his beer, and Matt turned to Taryn, planting a kiss on her lips. Most of those present looked resigned as they watched the four friends until they no longer could.

They were gone.

Continue the adventure in *The Dragon Slayer* via the QR code:

About the Author

Having written fantasy fiction since his teens, Randy Ellefson is an avid world builder whose work the Writer's of the Future contest has recognized three times. In addition to his popular world building books, he's the founder and lead instructor at World Building University, and hosts a related, popular podcast.

He has a Bachelor of Music in classical guitar but has always been more of a rocker, having released several albums and earned endorsements from music companies. A multi-instrumentalist who builds his own guitars, he's also band leader/manager, guitarist, and primary composer/lyricist for the metal band Black Halo.

A software development manager, he ran a successful consulting company for a decade.

Rand lives in Maryland with his son, daughter, and two cats.

Connect with him online

http://www.RandyEllefson.com
http://facebook.com/RandyEllefsonAuthor
https://linktr.ee/randyellefson

Buy books, music, and merch online at my store or others:
https://www.randyellefson.com/mywork

Randy Ellefson Books

Talon Stormbringer

Talon is a sword-wielding adventurer who has been a thief, pirate, knight, king, and more in his far-ranging life.

The Ever Fiend
The Screaming Moragul

www.fiction.randyellefson.com/talonstormbringer

The Dragon Gate Series

Four unqualified Earth friends are magically summoned to complete quests on other worlds, unless they break the cycle – or die trying.

Volume 1: *The Dragon Gate*
Volume 2: *The Light Bringer*
Volume 3: *The Silver-Tongued Rogue*
Volume 4: *The Dragon Slayer*
Volume 5: *The Majestic Magus*

www.fiction.randyellefson.com/dragon-gate-series

Ascension Quest

When Max awakens in a world unknown, he doesn't know how he got there or why he can't leave. And a mysterious Life Counter that no one else has is steadily descending to zero.

Death Singer

www.fiction.randyellefson.com/ascension-quest-litrpg-series

The Art of World Building

This is a multi-volume guide for authors, screenwriters, gamers, and hobbyists to build more immersive, believable worlds fans will love.

Creating Life
Creating Places
Cultures and Beyond
185 Tips on World Building
3000 World Building Prompts
The Complete Art of World Building
The Art of the World Building Workbook: Fantasy Edition
The Art of the World Building Workbook: Sci-Fi Edition
Creating Life: The Podcast Transcripts
Creating Places: The Podcast Transcripts
Cultures and Beyond: The Podcast Transcripts
The Art of World Building Podcast Transcripts Omnibus

Visit www.artofworldbuilding.com for details.

Randy Ellefson Music

Instrumental Guitar

Randy has released three albums of hard rock/metal instrumentals, one classical guitar album, and an all-acoustic album. Visit http://www.music.randyellefson.com for more information, streaming media, videos, and free mp3s.

2004: The Firebard
2007: Some Things Are Better Left Unsaid
2010: Serenade of Strings
2010: The Lost Art
2013: Now Weaponized!
2014: The Firebard (re-release)

Black Halo

Where classic Iron Maiden meets Metallica stands Black Halo, Randy's traditional metal band, where he is guitarist, primary songwriter, and band leader. For more, visit https://blackhalo.randyellefson.com

2025: Utopia